STENDHAL was one of the 171 pen names used by French author Marie-Henri Beyle. Born in Grenoble, France, on January 23, 1783, he was the son of a well-to-do landowner and lawyer with whom he never got along. His mother, whom he idolized, died when he was seven, and it was his maternal grandfather whom Stendhal called his "real father." At sixteen, he left for Paris; at seventeen, he joined Napoleon's dragoons and formed his lifelong admiration for both Italy and the general. In 1814 Stendhal retired from military life and settled in Milan, his favorite city, where he began to write. When he returned to Paris in 1821, he was thirty-eight years old. During the next nine years, he published six books, including *The Red and the Black*, which was to become his most famous novel. Always in search of an elusive happiness and love, he never had a lasting residence or love affair. He claimed to write for the "happy few," those not bound by convention who live by their own instincts. His other famous work, *The Charterhouse of Parma*, was written in the space of fifty-three days during a visit to Paris in 1839. Stendhal was never recognized during his lifetime, and when he died of a stroke at the age of fifty-nine, only three people followed his coffin to its grave. He is now widely considered one of the great French writers of the nineteenth century, along with Honoré de Balzac and Gustave Flaubert.

The Red and the Black by Stendhal (Marie-Henri Beyle)

A new and complete translation
by Lowell Bair

With an introduction by
Clifton Fadiman

BANTAM BOOKS
NEW YORK · TORONTO · LONDON · SYDNEY · AUCKLAND

THE RED AND THE BLACK

A Bantam Book / published March 1958
2nd printing . . . . . May 1958
Bantam Classic edition published August 1959
13 printings through 1988
14th printing September 1989

Cover painting of F.M. Granet
by Jean-Dominque Ingres,
courtesy of the Museé Granet, France

ISBN 0-553-21357-1

Published simultaneously in the United States and Canada

Bantam Books are published by Bantam Books, a division of Bantam
Doubleday Dell Publishing Group, Inc. Its trademark, consisting of the
words "Bantam Books" and the portrayal of a rooster, is Registered in
U.S. Patent and Trademark Office and in other countries. Marca
Registrada. Bantam Books, 666 Fifth Avenue, New York, New York
10103.

PRINTED IN THE UNITED STATES OF AMERICA

O   23   22   21   20   19   18   17   16   15   14

Introduction
by Clifton Fadiman

I. The Mind of Stendhal

TO BEGIN WITH, that was not his name, Stendhal being merely the most publicly acknowledged of the 171 pseudonyms he used for purposes of largely unnecessary deception.

This odd creature—he was christened Marie-Henri Beyle—led two simultaneous lives: one chronological, one posthumous. The seeming paradox is characteristic of him in general.

Stendhal's chronological existence extended from 1783, when he was born in Grenoble, to 1842, when he died in Paris. We know a great deal about him, for he set down his thoughts and actions in exhaustive detail, scribbling on his fingernails when paper was unavailable. The record is interesting but hardly spectacular: Hollywood will never base a film on his life.

His outward career may be described as a succession of almosts. A fairly good mathematician, he almost entered the Ecole Polytechnique but found the preparations for the entrance examinations too troublesome. Through his influential cousin Pierre Daru (whose wife he seduced, almost) he obtained a commission in Napoleon's army. During the second Italian campaign he almost saw combat. Back in Paris, living on money from his hated father, he almost wrote several plays. In Marseilles he almost became a businessman. During the Russian campaign, serving as a non-combatant officer, he almost succeeded in mildly distinguishing himself.

From 1814 to 1821 he lived in his beloved Italy but did not quite manage to succeed even as an expatriate. Suspected of liberal tendencies by the Austrian police, he decamped to Paris. In 1830 he was appointed French consul at Civitavecchia. This minor post he almost contrived to fill adequately, except during his many periods of leave. (Stendhal was a great success at wangling vacations.) In 1841 he returned to Paris on legitimate sick leave and on March 22, 1842, died of a stroke.

During his lifetime he almost gained a high reputation as wit, lover, and writer. But not quite. His writing career was managed with almost infallible negligence. He never published anything under his own name; much of his work remained in manuscript at his death; some of it is still unpublished. His many books, articles, and compilations netted him hardly a pittance. Today his fame rests largely on his novels, but his first one, *Armance,* did not appear until he was forty-four; *The Red and the Black* until he was forty-seven; and *The Charterhouse of Parma* (written in fifty-three days, and it shows it) until three years before his death.

Stendhal was a smallish, fattish man, fond of dandiacal costume, conversation, ladies, and almost-ladies. He pursued his many love affairs as if never quite certain whether he were Casanova making conquests or a psychologist making notes. As Casanova he was not always successful. His diaries record his fiascos with the same detail that others devote to an account of their triumphs. He admired and visited England and in the course of several decades of assiduous study almost succeeded in mastering the language to the degree that a second-year American high school student masters French.

At first glance, then, a rather undistinguished figure, a rather undistinguished life.

But this figure was merely the one presented to the world. This life was merely his chronological life. His real life was posthumous, and a complete triumph. By posthumous I do not mean merely that since his death his reputation has steadily grown, so that today his is one of the half-dozen greatest names in the development of the European novel. I mean that in a real sense he himself lived posthumously, that is, in the future. The greater part of his imaginative life was enacted in front of an audience he was never to encounter, those "happy few" of the coming generations for whom he wrote and thought.

The life for which he was unfitted—that of a would-be popular playwright, soldier, businessman, civil servant—he lived unsuccessfully. The life for which he was fitted—that spent grasping the history of his time in terms of the perspective of the future—he lived successfully. Thus Stendhal is something of an oddity. Perhaps part of his fascination for us springs from the fact that he was odd without being minor.

We usually think of a contemplative as one who spends his life in a meditation upon God. Stendhal spent his life, an active and worldly one, in a meditation upon men. He was that rare bird, a lay contemplative. In a period during which all men seemed to be scrabbling for "careers"—that is, money—Stendhal too went through the motions of scrabbling, though he never sought a job if a sinecure was available. Essentially, however, he remained that oddity, an unfixed man, attached only to his own thought. "I am but a passenger on this boat," he loved to say; and, as his epitaph, suggested *Visse, amo, scrisse*.

As a young man of twenty-eight he chose *nosce te ipsum* as his device; and to know himself was his profession. His whole life resembled one of those Grand Tours taken by the young English milords to acquaint them with human nature. To be "an observer of the human heart" and to portray it was his overarching ambition. One way of portraying it, he thought, was through "egotism provided it be sincere." This is one of the basic principles of Beylist philosophy, if we understand by egotism what is today called introspection. The medium of his egotism was his books. In a sense all of them, even the novels, are part of an interminable, formless diary. Everything he wrote contributed to his self-analysis; he remained throughout his life, as someone has remarked about Henry James, on very good terms with himself. Had he had any religion, his work might have been entitled *Spiritual Exercises*.

Contemplation plus self-contemplation sum up Stendhal's real life. Emerson put it this way: "Living is what a man thinks about all day." Stendhal neither worked nor idled. He thought all day.

He thought almost for thought's sake. It was for him a metaphysical necessity: "If I am not clear, my whole universe crumbles into nothingness." He believed that the mind could be formed and developed by study and will-power. At times he sounds almost like Dale Carnegie with genius: "The Abbé Hélie has swift and complete transitions. That's very good and should be imitated." As one would expect, he thought there was a "logic of happiness," and tried all his life to refine his formulas.

But this was only one side of Stendhal, the part he called "*logique*," a word he was fond of intoning with a kind of ecclesiastical preciseness. Stendhal was bipolar: part of him went back to Descartes and the rationality of the eighteenth century; part of him had an affinity with the romanticism of the early part of his own century. The interplay of forces between these poles created the tension that made Stendhal an artist as well as an observer; and it is this same interplay that he transfers to the hero of *The Red and the Black,* who is both an icy intellectual and a furious romantic. In Stendhal the bipolarity extended into almost every field. For example, he thought of himself as a champion of the democratic age to come; yet the whole bias of his temperament is aristocratic: He championed the spontaneity of Shakespeare against the frigidity of Racine; but his psychology, when it is not dazzlingly modern, is far more Racinian than Shakespearean. He combined a passion for exact analysis with a delight in the unexpected—*l'imprévu* is one of his favorite words.

Volumes have been written about the contradictions in Stendhal's personality, contradictions which, instead of tearing him apart, generated his whole intellectual life and career. What I here stress is the essential, underlying contradiction, that between what was present-minded in Stendhal, his unusual capacity to enjoy, analyze, and enjoy through analysis his day-to-day experience; and what was future-minded, his equally unusual capacity to think of himself constantly as a citizen of a culture still in time's womb.

The interesting thing about Stendhal is not that he has been re-discovered by every generation since his death, but that he foresaw that discovery with absolute clairvoyance. He seems to have felt, and not out of the simple vanity that afflicts many unsuccessful scribblers, that he was a writer with a brilliant future. In the 1830's he was already a great novelist, but there were few to recognize the fact. "I shall be understood about 1880," he remarked casually, and that turned out to be true. Again he said, "I have drawn a lottery ticket whose winning number is to be read in 1935"; and that has also turned out to be true. This prescience derived not from his *espagnolisme,* his passionate temperament, but from his *logique.* He based his claim to the attention of the future not on his sense of the *absolute* value of his work (as Shakespeare does, or Horace), but on his clear insight into the form that future was to take, a form for which he knew his special genius had a lively affinity.

Again and again, notably in his diaries, he makes statements about society which he prophesies will be commonplaces "in the days to come when my babblings may perhaps be heard." His sense of the future was sharpened by his effortless ability to see through his own time. In a way his "century in which everything can be bought" bored him, so that almost in self-defense his active intelligence went to work on the less transparent problems of the future. Like Julien Sorel, he felt deeply at odds with his period. As early as 1803 we find him saying, "In the present order of society lofty souls must nearly always be unhappy.'' As a very young man he had already marked out for himself his non-contemporary role: "I must go entirely out of my century and consider myself to be beneath the eyes of the great men of the century of Louis XIV. I must always work for the twentieth century.''

One must however distinguish his outsiderism from the *Weltschmerz* of Werther and other romantic heroes. It sprang not from a deficiency but from an excess of mind. There is no self-pity in Stendhal. Though he rejected most of the dominant moral and political doctrines of his time, he did not feel aggrieved, much less revengeful. "I do not believe that society owes me anything in the least." Stendhal would be as scornful of our Welfare State as he was of the bourgeois monarchy of Louis-Philippe. All he really wanted from his time was the leisure and opportunity to study it, and these were granted him.

This study was unsystematic, for Stendhal's scholarship was slipshod, and though he possessed high energy his organizing abilities were limited. But he had a certain power of divination, difficult to explain; and, by actually rubbing elbows with a great variety of men and women, he derived insights often denied to the most profound student of history. Thus in 1826 he was able quite casually to set a date for the Italian struggle for unification. He chose 1845, which is near enough. His clairvoyance extended even to relatively trivial matters: "What," he once speculated, "will become of the capital invested in the railroads if a carriage is invented that can run on ordinary roads?" He doesn't hedge on his prophecies: in 1813, when Chateaubriand was as much the rage as Faulkner is today, he remarked bluntly, "In 1913 people will no longer be concerned with his writings." Like most of his predictions, that one came true right on time.

Like Tocqueville, he is a Great Ancestor; that is, we are continually tracing back to him the origin, or at least the first energetic formulation, of many of our commonly received ideas and art forms. The psychological novel, for example, can claim a number of rather misty grandfathers, Diderot and Sterne and Richardson among them; but its father, as we shall see when we discuss *The Red and the Black*, would appear to be Stendhal.

Stendhal's heroes anticipate Nietzsche's superman. They anticipate Dostoevsky's too, even though their struggle is with men, whereas the Myshkins and Raskolnikovs engage God.

The idea of therapy by confession is as old as recorded history, but it is developed *consciously* in Stendhal's half-absurd, half-brilliant *On Love*.

In his novels Stendhal lays down the main lines of at least a dozen motifs which have engrossed novelists since his day: the revolt from the village, the struggle against the father, the sense of social inferiority, the position of the intellectual, the declassed man, the realistic description of war, emotional ambivalence, the non-party revolutionary.

His formula—"A novel is a mirror carried along a road" —contains the seed of Zola and the naturalistic school. It would be difficult to believe that Flaubert and Proust did not learn from him. Just because he constantly wrote against the grain of the novels of his time, he engendered a thousand novels of a future time. Novels of physical description, costume fiction, the triumphant romances of Scott—these dominated his era. He was bored with them, not necessarily because they were bad (some were first-rate of their kind) but because he felt in his bones that they had no future. And so it was not until he was forty-four that he started his first novel, *Armance,* anticipating by thirty years the victory (Flaubert's *Madame Bovary)* of psychological realism.

A whole book could easily be written about any one of a dozen aspects of Stendhal's mind, so rich is it, so various, so free. For three reasons I have chosen to stress mainly its future-ranging character. First, it happens to interest me. Second, it is what gives Stendhal his extraordinary contemporaneity: he is not merely a live classic but, if one ignores the trivial fact that he is dead, a classic of our own day. Third, it is singled out again and again by Stendhal's peers, by men with minds proportioned to Stendhal's own mind. It was Nietzsche who called him "that remarkable anticipatory and forerunning man who with Napoleonic tempo traversed his Europe, in fact several centuries of the European soul, as a . . . discoverer thereof." His own contemporary Balzac was one of the few who understood at once what Stendhal was up to and distinguished him from his rivals as "one of the most eminent masters of the literature of ideas." And it was Paul Valéry who summed it up: "We should never be finished with Stendhal. I can think of no greater praise than that."

II. *The Red and the Black*

All this praise may be quite justifiable, but it does not alter the fact that to the American reader living in the second half of the twentieth century *The Red and the Black* interposes certain seemingly solid obstacles.

There are some novels *(War and Peace,* for example) that give much, but not all, on the very first reading. There are some novels *(Look Homeward, Angel,* for example) that give all on the first reading, and nothing on the second. And there are some novels that give little—or even nothing—on the first reading but reveal more and more of themselves with each successive attempt.

The Red and the Black falls, I think, into the third category. The great French critic Hippolyte Taine declared that he had read it more than eighty-four times. While such assiduity suggests a repetition compulsion rather than pure enthusiasm, the reader who is unwilling to give *The Red and the Black* at least a second reading and preferably a third may never quite see what all the shouting is about. Stendhal is an acquired taste.

Before a relish for *The Red and the Black* can be formed several obstacles must be faced.

First, there is the title itself. The Red refers to the color of the uniform of Napoleon's soldiers. The Black refers to the cassock of the clergy. The hero Julien Sorel wears this cassock but in his heart belongs to the Napoleonic period of glory immediately preceding him. It is too late in the day for great actions. Now the road to power, for one born poor and obscure, lies through the Church. Julien therefore adopts hypocrisy as his mode of being; and the consequent war in his breast between what he professes and what he is partly precipitates his ruin.

Now this particular conflict of social forces can interest us only mildly today. We are no longer taken in by Napoleon's supposed "liberalism" and, unless we are Frenchmen, can hardly be moved by the myth of *la gloire.* Nor can we share Stendhal's hatred of clerical reaction, or fear, as he does, the sinister power of the "Congregation," an arm of the Jesuits. These are old, unhappy, far-off things, and battles long ago. The very title of the book, then, connotes something dusty and remote.

Second, there is the plot. At first reading the book smacks of opera rather than literature. The ingredients are a bit ridiculous: the poor boy who seduces the wife of his rich employer; anonymous letters; midnight assignations, followed by jumps out of windows; the aristocratic heiress who falls in love with the poor seminarist, and is willing to sacrifice all for her passion; more midnight assignations and narrow escapes; and a denouement involving an attempt at murder, a series of highly melodramatic prison scenes, and a lurid final tableau that recalls Salome and the severed head of John the Baptist.

Third, there is the dialogue. The translation you are about to read is the first complete, modern American translation in about fifty years. It is an excellent one, rapid, plain, clear. It is faithful to the original, yet manages to avoid almost completely any suggestion of Gallicism. Nevertheless it cannot (nor should it) make of Stendhal's dialogue anything other than what it is. And what it is seems to us formal, marmoreal, unreal. There are interchanges, particularly between Julien and Mathilde, that sound almost like Racine—a master Stendhal disowned but whose influence he never shook off. There are soliloquies that recall Shakespeare. The beginning reader may well ask, If Stendhal is as modern as you say he is, why doesn't he write like a modern.

These are merely three obstacles, selected from many. They are real; they cannot be waved aside.

I suggest that we do not wave them aside, then, but accept them, and seek for other qualities that more than compensate for them.

Stendhal of course, for all his future-mindedness, was a man of his time: he wrote of what surrounded him. And what surrounded him in the 1830's was, among other things, the Napoleonic legend and the power of the Jesuits. *The Red and the Black* must be read in part as an historical novel. But only in part, and that the least part.

We must also accept the fact that Stendhal was not a master of plot; he was a master of ideas and feelings.

And we must accept the fact that people in the 1830's *did* talk rather more like books than we do today, and furthermore that the phonographic rendition of actual conversation is a recent development in the novel.

On a second or third reading these obstacles, and others akin to them, diminish in importance; and the virtues of *The Red and the Black* correspondingly move into the forefront of our consciousness.

Of these virtues the most salient is the one already noted in connection with Stendhal's temperament in general. *The Red and the Black* (far more remarkably than Stendhal's other major novel *The Charterhouse of Parma*) is a precursor. It sets the tone, the angle of attack, and much of the actual content for a hundred post-Stendhalian writers of fiction. It is possible to argue that it is not one of the world's greatest novels. It lacks Tolstoy's broad humanity, Fielding's humor, Dickens's power of characterization, Dostoevsky's tragic penetration. But it is impossible to deny that if any single work deserves to be called the father of the modern novel, that work is the anticipatory compendium known as *The Red and the Black*. This is a kind of greatness in itself.

Almost a century before *Main Street* Stendhal, speaking of Julien's birthplace, writes: "The tyranny of public opinion—and what public opinion!—is as stupid in the small towns of France as it is in the United States of America." In this sentence he not only announces one of the book's major themes, but one of the major themes of the realistic novel of our century—and as a kind of extra throws in a judgment of our country that perhaps only a handful of Europeans of his time would have had sufficient intuition to make.

In Lionel Trilling's brilliant essay on Henry James's *The Princess Casamassima* the reader will find a commentary on the kind of novel that turns on the fortunes of what Mr. Trilling calls The Young Man from the Provinces. Our publishers' lists are rich in such novels; apparently there is still pay-dirt in this well-worked mine. More recent examples are perhaps the post-*Look Homeward, Angel* series of Thomas Wolfe. Back of these is Fitzgerald's *The Great Gatsby*. Mr. Trilling lists the entire genealogy, involving *The Princess Casamassima*, Flaubert's *Sentimental Education*, Dickens's *Great Expectations*, Balzac's *Lost Illusions* and *Père Goriot*. But back of all these stands *The Red and the Black,* just as back of that stand two real-life Young Men from the Provinces, Napoleon and Rousseau. *The Red and the Black* is not only the first novel to announce the theme explicitly; it is also the first to give it classic formulation. "For Julien, achieving success meant first of all leaving Verrières." That does not seem a particularly exciting sentence, until you reflect on the number and wide distribution of its progeny.

The Red and the Black, with its pitiless portrait of an empty society, bored because, as Count Altamira says, "there are no true passions left in the nineteenth century," anticipates another school of novelists, from the early Aldous Huxley to the latest duodecimo existentialist. Mathilde de la Mole, yearning for the cruelties and valors of the Wars of the League, heralds a thousand dissatisfied heroines, of whom Emma Bovary and Carol Kennicott are merely the most renowned.

In Julien's development of the theme, "Was Danton right to steal?" lies the germ of all the novels that have since debated the problem of ends and means. In Julien himself we have the first classic portrait of the Hero as Intellectual, a portrait to be eclipsed in power and clarity almost a century later by Joyce's Stephen Dedalus.

The one point upon which virtually all critics agree is that Stendhal was the first to suffuse the novel with a systematic psychology. There were great psychologists before him—Cervantes preeminently, Richardson, Sterne—but they do not watch the movements of their characters' minds with Stendhal's hawklike intentness. There is nothing unconscious about the variety and pattern of his insights. He knows precisely what he is up to. Though he wrote long before the term had passed into the vulgar tongue, he was quite aware that Julien is a study of an Oedipus complex. When we first see him, Julien is sitting astride a rafter in the paternal sawmill, symbolically high above his father—until his father brutally knocks him down. And the affair with Madame de Rênal is almost too clearly tinged with the morbid coloring of unconscious mother-incest.

D.H. Lawrence and a dozen other modern writers have accustomed us to recognize as true the fact that men are not so much ruled by a single passion as by the oscillation from one passion to its opposite. Stendhal assumes this seemingly modern viewpoint as if it were to be taken for granted. "Sure that he loved her, Mathilde utterly despised him"—and yet a little later on there is nothing she more desires than to be Julien's slave. This is not carelessness on Stendhal's part, but one of the root doctrines of his psychological system.

The most saliently modern trait of Julien's complex mind is his self-consciousness. Not only does Stendhal watch Julien; Julien watches himself. When Madame de Rênal, the first of his two great loves, withdraws her hand from his accidental contact, Julien "decided it was his *duty* to make Madame de Rênal leave it in place when he touched it." But this very consciousness of duty "immediately removed all pleasure from his heart." Before Stendhal, who ever described a love scene in terms of such cold, almost mathematical introspection?

But, in order first to be struck by, then to delight in, finally to marvel at *The Red and the Black*, one need not be a literary historian, curious about origins and connections. Had it been as infertile as a mule, it would still remain a remarkable work.

Stendhal based his plot (perhaps that is why it sounds so improbable) on a real crime of his day, a newspaper account of a French peasant who was convicted of shooting his mistress, and executed. Into this tabloid melodrama Stendhal injected virtually an entire literature of ideas.

He has no grace, little charm, less humor. His wit is so dry that it evaporates on the mind as a dry sherry does on the palate. He is not really a good story-teller. He does not know much about plausibility. He introduces people, drops them, picks them up two hundred pages later. He repeats himself. His exposition is often bald. At times his characters sound as if they belong in the libretto of a second-rate Italian opera. (It is hard to keep a straight face when Mathilde cries out "The voice of honor speaks . . . I must obey at once.")

As a matter of fact a good case could be made for the proposition that Stendhal is not really a first-rate novelist at all. But he is something just as interesting and in some respects better—a first-rate intelligence who happens to be using the novel as a medium. Unless the reader keeps this simple fact in mind he may be bored or baffled. If he does keep it in mind he will be neither.

Julien Sorel is for many reasons a lost soul. He is lost because no man can live by hypocrisy. He is lost because the tension between his passions and his rationality tears him to pieces. He is lost because he does not know how to love, but only how to observe the process of love-making. Because he attaches his passion for Mathilde to the chariot of his ambition, it has no power to enlarge him; it becomes merely a tactical move in a war against society. He is lost because his enjoyment of the fashionable world is continually vitiated by an uncontrollable clairvoyance that forces him to see through its shams and corruptions. He is lost because no one can really become his friend: "Other people could not help Julien; he was too different." He is lost because he has the intelligence to overcome his peasant background, but not the humor to place it in proper perspective. He is lost because he has an image of himself as a Napoleonic hero born out of his due time: "In those days a man like me was either killed or became a general by the age of thirty-six." He is lost because he does not have the gift, as necessary in his day as in ours, of equably enduring boredom.

But it all boils down to this: he is lost because in a society that has no place for the theoretical intelligence, he is a man of brains. This does not mean he is wise; the close reader will note that Stendhal, something of a fool himself, knows that his hero is on occasion a fool also. But a man may be foolish, and yet live by ideas, and die by them; and this is Julien's case.

The Red and the Black, then, a partly autobiographical novel, is a study of the intellectual forced to act in a society which has not yet developed any proper standards by which to judge the intellect. Mental agility is respected; mental adaptability (known in our day as conformity) is respected; success is respected. But thought is not respected.

Poor Julien is cursed with a mind so active that he cannot accept any experience without analyzing it to a point where it loses what gives it its value. Stendhal had the same kind of mind himself, but he saved himself from ruin by embracing a life of observation and reflection. If Julien had limited himself to confiding the content of his mind to a diary, he would have avoided trouble, as his creator did, and we would have had no novel.

The Red and the Black is the classic study of the outsider. Julien is an outsider because he is basely born into a class society; because he is bookish in an elegant but philistine world; because he is spiritually an orphan, feeling himself hated by his whole family; because his mind is admired for its more trivial qualities—agility, power of memory, poll-parrot scholarship. But all this bitter sense of exclusion is brought to a head by his intellectual pride. It is this intellectual pride that wins him the love of the equally arrogant Mathilde, whose pride springs from aristocracy rather than brains: "He despises others, and that's why I don't despise him."

Stendhal sees through Julien, but he respects him too. Above all he selects Julien as his hero-villain because only through a mind like Julien's can Stendhal filter his own spate of ideas about society and the human heart. A simpler-minded character, a more virtuous character, a more charming character would have been valueless to him. He needed Julien to express his own view of a world which, like ours, had not evolved sufficiently to make proper use of a mind like Julien's. He needed Julien to project his idea, for which we are now just beginning to have some sympathy, of the classless man, of the man who, by virtue of his intellect, should be relieved of the obligations of class-affiliation and class-loyalty. And finally he needed Julien because Julien was at bottom not a lover, not a Napoleon *manqué,* not an ambitious cleric, but what Stendhal himself was—a psychologist.

The difference between them is that Julien, though he succeeded as a psychologist, failed as a man; whereas Stendhal succeeded both as man and psychologist. And, should you ask in what Stendhal's success lies, I would reply—in the creation of Julien Sorel.

BOOK I

Truth, bitter truth.
—Danton

CHAPTER 1

A Small Town

Put thousands together
Less bad,
But the cage less gay.
—Hobbes

THE LITTLE TOWN of Verrières may be regarded as one of the most attractive in Franche-Comté. Its white houses, with their steep red tile roofs, are spread over the slope of a hill whose slightest irregularities are marked by clumps of sturdy chestnut trees. The Doubs flows past several hundred feet below its fortifications, built long ago by the Spaniards and now in ruins.

Verrières is sheltered on the north by a chain of high mountains, a spur of the Jura range. The jagged peaks of the Verras become covered with snow during the first cold days of October. A torrent, rushing down the mountainside, passes through Verrières before plunging into the Doubs and provides the motive power for a large number of sawmills. It is an extremely simple industry, but it gives a certain affluence to most of the inhabitants, who are more closely allied to the peasantry than to the bourgeoisie. However, it is not the sawmills that have made the little town rich. The manufacture of the printed cotton cloth known as Mulhouse calico is responsible for the general prosperity which, since the fall of Napoleon, has given a new façade to nearly every house in Verrières.

As soon as one enters the town, one is deafened by the uproar of a noisy machine of terrifying appearance. Twenty massive hammers, which make the pavement quiver when they come crashing down, are raised by a wheel turned by the water of the torrent. Each one of them makes I know not how many nails daily. Fresh, pretty girls place under these enormous hammers the little pieces of iron that are quickly transformed into nails. This work, apparently so arduous, is one of the things which most astonish the traveler making his first visit to the mountains that separate France from Switzerland. If, on entering Verrières, he asks who owns the fine nail factory which deafens everyone passing along the main street, he will be told in a drawling accent, "Oh, it belongs to the mayor."

3

If the traveler stops for a few moments in that main street of Verrières, which slopes upward from the bank of the Doubs toward the top of the hill, the odds are a hundred to one that he will witness the appearance of a tall man with a busy, important air.

All hats are quickly raised at the sight of him. His hair is turning gray, and he is dressed in gray. He wears a number of decorations, he has a high forehead and an aquiline nose and, on the whole, his face does not lack a certain regularity; at first sight, in fact, it seems to combine the dignity of a village mayor with that kind of attractiveness which may still be found in a man of forty-eight or fifty. But soon the Parisian traveler is displeased by a certain air of self-satisfaction and smugness mingled with an impression of narrow-mindedness and lack of imagination. Finally one feels that this man's ability is limited to making sure that others pay their debts to him promptly and in full, and to postponing the payment of his own debts as long as possible.

Such is the Mayor of Verrières, Monsieur de Rênal. After crossing the street with a solemn tread, he enters the town hall and disappears from the traveler's sight. If the latter continues his stroll, a hundred yards up the street he will notice a rather impressive-looking house and, through the iron bars of a gate next to this house, he will see some magnificent gardens. Farther on, there is a horizon, formed by the hills of Burgundy, which seems to have been created expressly to delight the eye. This view makes the traveler forget the foul atmosphere of petty financial interests which was beginning to stifle him.

He is told that this house belongs to Monsieur de Rênal. The profits from his great nail factory have enabled the Mayor of Verrières to build his fine freestone residence, whose construction is just being completed. He is said to be from an old Spanish family which supposedly settled in the region long before it was conquered by Louis XIV.

Since 1815 he has been embarrassed by the fact that he is in business: it was in 1815 that he became Mayor of Verrières. The retaining walls supporting the various parts of that magnificent garden which descends to the Doubs in a series of terraces are also a reward of his skill in the iron business.

Do not expect to find in France those picturesque gardens which surround the manufacturing towns of Germany, such as Leipzig, Frankfurt and Nuremberg. In Franche-Comté, the more walls a man builds, the more he makes his property bristle with stones piled on top of each other, the more he becomes entitled to the respect of his neighbors. Monsieur de Rênal's gardens, filled with walls, are also admired because of the high price he paid for some of the small plots of land they occupy. For example, that sawmill whose singular position on the bank of the Doubs struck you when you entered Verrières, and on which you noticed the name "Sorel" painted in gigantic letters on a sign towering above the roof—six years ago it occupied the ground on which the wall of the fourth terrace of Monsieur de Rênal's gardens is now being built.

In spite of his pride, the mayor was forced to carry on long negotiations with old Sorel, a stern, obstinate peasant; and he had to pay him good gold louis to make him move his sawmill elsewhere. As for the "public" stream which supplied power to the mill, Monsieur de Rênal obtained permission to have its course diverted, thanks to his influence in Paris. He was granted this favor after the elections of 182—.

He gave Sorel four acres in exchange for one. And, even though this new location, five hundred yards farther down on the bank of the Doubs, was much more advantageous for his trade in fir planks, Père Sorel, as he has been known since he became rich, managed to squeeze six thousand francs out of the impatience and "property madness" of his neighbor.

It is true that this transaction was criticized by the local wiseacres. One Sunday, four years ago, as Monsieur de Rênal was coming back from church in his mayor's attire, he saw old Sorel look at him with a smile as he stood some distance away with his three sons around him. This smile cast a painful flash of light into the mayor's mind; since then he has thought that he could have made the exchange on better terms.

In order to win public esteem in Verrières, it is essential, while building many walls, not to adopt some plan imported from Italy by one of those masons who, in spring, come through the passes of the Jura range on their way to Paris. Such an innovation would give the rash builder an undying reputation as a nonconformist, and he would be damned forever in the eyes of the wise and sober people who dole out public esteem in Franche-Comté.

The fact is that these wise people exercise the most irritating kind of *despotism;* it is because of this ugly word that those who

have lived in the great republic known as Paris find it intolerable
to live in small towns. The tyranny of public opinion—and what
public opinion!—is as stupid in the small towns of France as it is
in the United States of America.

CHAPTER 2

A Mayor

> Social importance! Is it nothing, sir? It earns the respect of
> fools, the wonderment of children, the envy of the rich and the
> contempt of the wise.
>
> —Barnave

FORTUNATELY FOR Monsieur de Rênal's reputation as an administrator, an enormous retaining wall was required for the public
promenade which skirts the hillside a hundred feet above the
waters of the Doubs. This admirable location gives it one of the
most beautiful views in France. But, every spring, torrents of
rainwater flowed across the promenade, washing out deep ruts in
it and making it nearly impassable. This disadvantage, which
affected everyone, placed Monsieur de Rênal under the fortunate
obligation to immortalize his administration by erecting a wall
twenty feet high and seventy or eighty yards long.

The parapet of this wall—for which Monsieur de Rênal had to
make three trips to Paris, because the Minister of the Interior had
declared himself a mortal enemy of the Verrières promenade—
now rises four feet above the ground. And, as though to defy all
ministers, past and present, it is now being finished off with
slabs of polished stone.

How often, thinking of the Paris ballrooms I had forsaken the
night before, have I stood with my chest pressed against those
huge blocks of bluish-gray stone and gazed down into the valley
of the Doubs! Beyond the river, on the left bank, there are five
or six winding valleys at the bottom of which one can clearly see
little streams emptying into the Doubs after tumbling down one
waterfall after another.

The sun is extremely hot in these mountains; when it is
shining directly overhead, the traveler's reverie is sheltered by
magnificent plane trees. Their rapid growth and their beautiful
bluish-green foliage are due to the rich soil which the mayor
ordered to be put behind his enormous retaining wall; for, despite the opposition of the town council, he widened the prome-

nade by more than six feet (although he is a fervent Royalist and I am a Liberal, I praise him for it), which is why, in his opinion and that of Monsieur Valenod, the prosperous superintendent of the Verrières workhouse, this terrace is worthy of comparison with that of Saint-Germain-en-Laye.

For my part, I have only one fault to find with the Cours de la Fidélité (this is the official name of the promenade, which appears in twenty or thirty different places, on marble plaques which have earned one more decoration for Monsieur de Rênal); what I object to in the Cours de la Fidélité is the barbarous manner in which the authorities keep those sturdy plane trees trimmed and clipped short. Instead of looking, with their low, rounded, flattened heads, like the commonest of vegetables, they would like nothing better than to take on the magnificent form they develop in England. But the mayor's will is despotic, and twice a year the branches of all trees belonging to the commune are mercilessly amputated. The local Liberals claim, although they exaggerate, that the hand of the official gardener has become much more rigorous ever since Father Maslon began to appropriate the clippings. This young clergyman was sent from Besançon a few years ago to keep an eye on Father Chélan and several other parish priests of the district.

An old army surgeon, a veteran of the Italian campaign who had settled in Verrières after his retirement and who, according to the mayor, had been simultaneously a Jacobin and a Bonapartist during his lifetime, ventured to complain to him one day about the periodical mutilation of those beautiful trees.

"I like shade," replied Monsieur de Rênal in the slightly haughty tone that is appropriate when addressing a surgeon who is a member of the Legion of Honor. "I have *my* trees trimmed to make them give more shade, and I can't imagine what else a tree is made for if, unlike the useful walnut tree, it doesn't bring in money."

Here we have the magic phrase that determines everything in Verrières: *bringing in money*; it alone represents the habitual thought of three quarters of the population.

Bringing in money is the consideration which determines everything in that little town which at first seemed so attractive to you. The stranger who comes to it, beguiled by the beauty of the cool, deep valleys surrounding it, imagines at first that its inhabitants are sensitive to beauty: they speak all too often of the beauty of their region. No one can deny that they attach great importance to it, but this is because it attracts a few visitors

whose money enriches the innkeepers, thus, through the operation of the municipal toll, *bringing in money* to the town.

One fine day in autumn, Monsieur de Rênal was strolling along
the Cours de la Fidélité with his wife on his arm. As she listened
to her husband speaking with a solemn expression on his face,
Madame de Rênal's eyes were anxiously following the movements of
three little boys. The eldest, who appeared to be about eleven, kept
running up to the parapet and acting as though he were going to climb
on top of it. A gentle voice would then call out "Adolphe!" and the
child would abandon his ambitious enterprise. Madame de Rênal
was apparently about thirty years old, but she was still quite pretty.

"He may live to regret it, that fine gentleman from Paris,"
Monsieur de Rênal was saying resentfully, his cheeks even paler
than usual. "I have a few friends at court . . ."

But, although I intend to speak to you of provincial life for two
hundred pages, I will not be so barbarous as to subject you to all the
monotony and "clever circumspection" of a provincial conversation.

The fine gentleman from Paris, so odious to the Mayor of
Verrières, was none other than Monsieur Appert, who, two days
earlier, had contrived to make his way not only into the prison and the
workhouse of Verrières, but also into the hospital, which was ad-
ministered gratuitously by the mayor and the leading landowners
of the district.

"But," said Madame de Rênal timidly, "how could the gentleman from Paris do you any harm, since you're so scrupulously
honest in the way you handle the funds allotted to the poor?"

"He's come only to find fault, and then he'll have articles
printed in the Liberal papers."

"You never read them, my dear."

"But people talk to us about those Jacobin articles; that kind
of thing distracts us and keeps us from doing good. For my part,
I'll never forgive Father Chélan."

CHAPTER 3
Funds for the Poor

> A virtuous and undesigning priest in a village is a gift of
> Providence.
>
> —Fleury

IT MUST BE explained that the parish priest of Verrières, an old
man of eighty, but, thanks to the keen air of the mountains,

endowed with iron strength and character, had the right to visit the prison, the hospital and even the workhouse at any hour of the day or night. Monsieur Appert, coming from Paris with a letter of introduction to Father Chélan, had gone straight to his house after wisely arriving in the inquisitive little town at six o'clock in the morning.

As he read the letter addressed to him by the Marquis de La Mole, a peer of France and the wealthiest landowner in the province, Father Chélan sat lost in thought. "I'm an old man and the people here love me," he murmured to himself at length. "They wouldn't dare!" Then he turned to the gentleman from Paris and looked at him with eyes which, despite his advanced age, were aglow with that sacred fire which reveals the pleasure of doing a noble and somewhat dangerous deed. "Come with me, monsieur," he said, "but when the jailer is present, please don't express any opinion of the things we'll see, and be especially careful in front of the workhouse attendants."

Monsieur Appert realized that he was dealing with a man of feeling; he followed the venerable priest, inspected the prison, the hospital and the workhouse, asked many questions and, despite the strange answers he received, did not allow himself to show the slightest sign of reproach.

The inspection lasted for several hours. Father Chélan invited Monsieur Appert to dinner, but the latter told him he had some letters to write; he did not want to compromise his courageous companion any further. Toward three o'clock, they went to complete their inspection of the workhouse and then returned to the prison. There, standing in the doorway, they found the jailer, a bow-legged giant six feet tall; terror had made his ignoble face hideous.

"Oh, monsieur!" he said to the priest as soon as he saw him. "That gentleman with you is Monsieur Appert, isn't he?"

"What if he is?"

"The reason I ask is that yesterday the prefect gave me strict orders—he sent them by a gendarme who had to gallop all night long—not to let Monsieur Appert into the prison."

"It's true, Monsieur Noiroud," said the priest, "that this visitor with me is Monsieur Appert. Do you acknowledge that I have the right to enter the prison at any time, and accompanied by anyone I choose?"

"Yes, Father," replied the jailer softly, lowering his head like a bulldog forced into reluctant obedience by fear of the stick. "But I have a wife and children, Father, and I'll be dismissed if anyone reports me. I have only my salary to live on."

"I'd be very sorry to lose my position, too," said the kindly priest in a voice that became increasingly charged with emotion.

"What a difference!" retorted the jailer. "You, Father, everyone knows you have an income of eight hundred francs, a fine estate . . ."

Such are the events which, commented on and exaggerated in twenty different ways, had been stirring up all sorts of malevolent passions in the little town of Verrières for the past two days. Just now they were being used as the text of the little discussion Monsieur de Rênal was having with his wife. That morning he and Monsieur Valenod, the superintendent of the workhouse, had gone to the parish priest's house to inform him of their extreme dissatisfaction. Father Chélan was under no one's protection; he felt the full force of what they said to him.

"Well, gentlemen," he said, "I'll be the third eighty-year-old parish priest to be dismissed in this district. I've been here for fifty-six years; I've christened nearly everyone who lives in this town, which was only a village when I came. Every day I marry young couples whose grandparents I married long ago. Verrières is my family, but the fear of leaving it will never make me compromise my conscience or accept any other guide for my conduct. When I saw the visitor I said to myself, 'This man who's come from Paris may well be a Liberal, there are all too many of them; but what harm can he do to our poor people and our prisoners?' "

Monsieur de Rênal's reproaches, and especially those of Monsieur Valenod, became increasingly vehement. "All right, gentlemen, have me dismissed!" the old priest finally cried out in a quavering voice. "I'll still go on living in the district. Forty-eight years ago, as everyone knows, I inherited a piece of land that brings in eight hundred francs a year. I'll live on that income. I don't make any dishonest profit from my position, gentlemen, and that may be why I'm not so frightened when people talk about taking it away from me."

Monsieur de Rênal usually got along very well with his wife, but, not knowing what reply to make to the question she timidly repeated to him—"How could the gentleman from Paris do the prisoners any harm?"—he was about to lose his temper altogether when she suddenly uttered a cry of alarm. Her second eldest son had just climbed up on the parapet of the retaining wall and was running along it. This wall rose more than twenty feet above the vineyard on the other side; the fear of startling him and making him fall restrained her from calling out to him.

Finally, laughing at his prowess, the child looked at his mother, saw her pallor, jumped down to the promenade and ran over to her. He was soundly scolded.

This little incident changed the course of the conversation.

"I've definitely made up my mind," said Monsieur de Rênal, "to take young Sorel, the sawyer's son, into my house. He'll look after the children—they're beginning to be too much for us to handle. He's a young priest, or practically a priest, he knows Latin well and he'll make the children work hard, because Father Chélan says he has a strong character. I'll give him three hundred francs a year, plus board and lodging. I had some doubt about his morals, because he was the favorite of that old surgeon, the member of the Legion of Honor, who claimed he was a cousin of the Sorels and came to live with them. The man may very well have been a secret agent of the Liberals; he used to say the air of our mountains was good for his asthma, but that's never been proved. He served in all of *Buonaparte's* Italian campaigns, and they say he even voted against the Empire in his day. That Liberal taught young Sorel Latin and left him the pile of books he brought here with him. Because of that, I'd never have dreamed of letting the sawyer's son take care of our children if Father Chélan hadn't told me, just the day before the incident that put an end to our friendship forever, that the boy has been studying theology for the last three years with the idea of entering a seminary. So he's not a Liberal, and he knows Latin well."

"The arrangement suits me in more ways than one," continued Monsieur de Rênal, giving his wife a knowing look. "Valenod is all puffed up with pride over the two fine Norman horses he just bought for his carriage. But he doesn't have a tutor for his children."

"He might take this one away from us."

"Then you approve of my plans?" said Monsieur de Rênal, thanking his wife with a smile for the excellent idea that had just occurred to her. "All right, then, it's settled."

"Good heavens, dear, how quickly you make up your mind!"

"That's because I have a strong character—Father Chélan knows that now. Let's not deceive ourselves: we're surrounded by Liberals here. All those textile manufacturers are jealous of me, I'm sure of it. Two or three of them are becoming rich; I'll be glad to have them see Monsieur de Rênal's children going for a stroll in the care of *their tutor*. That will impress them. My grandfather often used to tell us he had a tutor in his youth. It may cost me three hundred francs, but we'll have to count it as a necessary expense for maintaining our position."

This sudden decision made Madame de Rênal thoughtful. She was a tall woman with a shapely figure; she had once been the beauty of the district, as they say in those mountains. She had a certain air of simplicity and there was a youthful quality in her bearing; to a Parisian, her artless grace, full of innocence and vivacity, would even have suggested ideas of sweet voluptuous pleasure. If she had been aware of her success in this direction, she would have been deeply ashamed. There had never been the slightest trace of coquettishness or affectation in her heart. It was rumored that Monsieur Valenod, the rich superintendent of the workhouse, had once made an unsuccessful attempt to seduce her; this had given great distinction to her virtue, for Monsieur Valenod, a tall, husky young man with a ruddy complexion and bushy side whiskers, was one of those coarse, brazen, and loud-mouthed creatures who are known in the provinces as attractive men.

Madame de Rênal, extremely shy and apparently given to sudden changes of mood, was especially offended by Monsieur Valenod's constant movement and loud voice. Her distaste for what is called gaiety in Verrières had given her the reputation of being extremely proud of her noble birth. She actually gave no thought to it, but she had been glad to see the inhabitants of the town come to her house less frequently. We shall not conceal the fact that the ladies regarded her as a fool, for she never tried to outwit her husband, and she let slip the best opportunities to make him buy her fine hats from Paris or Besançon. As long as she was left alone to stroll in her beautiful garden, she never complained.

She had such a guileless soul that she had never even gone so far as to judge her husband and admit to herself that he bored her. She assumed, without thinking about it explicitly, that more affectionate relations were not possible between husband and wife. She was particularly fond of Monsieur de Rênal when he spoke to her of his plans for their children; he intended to place one of them in the army, one in the magistracy and one in the Church. On the whole, she found him much less boring than any of the other men she knew.

This wifely opinion was well grounded. The Mayor of Verrières enjoyed a reputation for wit and refinement which he owed to half a dozen pleasantries he had inherited from one of his uncles. Old Captain Rênal had served in the infantry regiment of the Duke of Orléans before the Revolution, and whenever he went to Paris he was admitted into the prince's drawing rooms, where he had seen Madame de Montesson, the famous Madame de Genlis and Monsieur Ducrest, the man responsible for the alterations in the Palais-Royal. At first these people appeared all too often in Monsieur de Rênal's stories, but gradually it became laborious for him to recall things which required so much delicacy to relate, and for some time now it had been only on great occasions that he repeated his anecdotes concerning the House of Orléans. Furthermore he was very polite, except when speaking of money, so he was rightly regarded as the most aristocratic personage in Verrières.

CHAPTER 4
Father and Son

E sarà mia colpa, se cosi è?
—Machiavelli

"MY WIFE certainly has a good head on her shoulders!" the Mayor of Verrières remarked to himself at six o'clock the following morning as he walked down to old Sorel's sawmill. "In spite of what I said to her to maintain my superiority, it hadn't occurred to me that if I don't engage that little priest Sorel, who, they say, knows his Latin like an angel, the superintendent of the workhouse, that envious busybody, may very well have the same idea and snatch him away from me. How smugly he'd talk about his children's tutor! . . . Will that tutor wear a cassock after I've hired him?"

Monsieur de Rênal was absorbed in this question when, in the distance, he saw a peasant, a man nearly six feet tall, who had apparently been busy since dawn measuring pieces of timber lying on the towpath beside the Doubs. The peasant did not seem too happy to see the mayor coming toward him, because his timber was blocking the path and had been piled in violation of the law.

Old Sorel, for it was he, was greatly surprised and still more pleased by Monsieur de Rênal's extraordinary offer concerning his son Julien. He nevertheless listened to him with that air of dissatisfied sadness and lack of interest with which the inhabitants of those mountains so skillfully disguise their shrewdness. Slaves in the days of Spanish rule, they have retained this facial characteristic of the Egyptian fellah.

Sorel's reply was at first nothing but a long recital of all the stock expressions of respect which he knew by heart. As he

repeated these empty words with an awkward smile that intensified the hypocritical, almost treacherous expression that was
natural to his face, the old peasant's active mind was trying to
discover what reason such an important man could have for
wanting to take his good-for-nothing son into his service. He was
extremely dissatisfied with Julien, and yet it was for him that
Monsieur de Rênal was offering the amazing salary of three
hundred francs a year, with board, lodging and even clothing.
This last condition, which old Sorel had been quick-witted enough
to put forward on the spur of the moment, was granted with
equal promptness by Monsieur de Rênal.

The mayor was struck by this demand. "Since Sorel isn't
delighted and overwhelmed by my proposition, as he naturally
ought to be," he said to himself, "it's clear that someone else
has already made him an offer; and who else could it be except
Valenod?" It was in vain that he urged Sorel to conclude the
bargain on the spot: the crafty old peasant stubbornly refused; he
said he wanted to consult his son first, as though, in the provinces, a rich father ever consulted a penniless son, except for the
sake of form.

A sawmill consists of a shed by the side of a stream. The roof
is supported by rafters which rest on four thick wooden pillars.
In the middle of the shed, nine or ten feet above the ground,
there is a saw which moves up and down while an extremely
simple mechanism pushes a log against it. A wheel turned by the
water of the stream drives both parts of the machinery: the saw
which moves up and down and the device which gently pushes
the log against the saw, which cuts it into planks.

As he walked toward his mill, old Sorel called Julien in his
stentorian voice; there was no answer. He saw only his two elder
sons, young giants who, armed with heavy axes, were squaring
the fir logs which they would later carry to the saw. They were
completely engrossed in following exactly the black lines drawn
on the logs, and enormous chips flew off each time they swung
their axes. They did not hear their father's voice. He walked
toward the shed; when he entered it he vainly looked for Julien
in the place where he ought to have been standing, beside the
saw. Then he saw him five or six feet above it, sitting astride
one of the rafters. Instead of carefully watching over the operation of the machinery, Julien was reading. Nothing could have
been more displeasing to old Sorel; he might have forgiven
Julien for his slender build, unfit for hard work and so different

from that of his elder brothers, but he detested his mania for reading: he himself did not know how to read.

He called Julien two or three times in vain. The attention with which the young man was reading his book, much more than the noise of the saw, prevented him from hearing his father's terrifying voice. Finally, despite his age, the latter nimbly jumped up on the log that was being cut by the saw, and from there to the rafter. A violent blow sent Julien's book flying into the water; a second blow, equally violent, aimed at the head in the guise of a box on the ear, made him lose his balance. He was about to fall twelve or fifteen feet into the moving machinery, which would have mangled him, when his father caught him with his left hand as he began to fall.

"So, you lazy rascal, you're still reading your worthless books when you're supposed to be watching the saw! You can read them at night, when you go to waste your time with Father Chélan."

Although bleeding and still stunned by the force of the blow, Julien took up his assigned position beside the saw. There were tears in his eyes, due less to his physical pain than to the loss of a book he had adored.

"Come down from there, you scoundrel, I want to talk to you!"

Once again the noise of the machinery prevented Julien from hearing this order. His father, who had stepped down and did not wish to take the trouble to climb back up on the machine, went to get a long pole used for knocking down walnuts and struck him on the shoulder with it. As soon as Julien's feet touched the ground, old Sorel began to drive him toward the house, pushing him brutally from behind. "God only knows what he's going to do to me!" thought Julien. As he passed by, he looked sadly at the stream into which his book had fallen; it was the one he had cherished above all others: the *Mémorial de Saint-Hélène*.

His cheeks were flushed and his eyes were downcast. He was a small young man of eighteen or nineteen, weak in appearance, with irregular but delicate features and an aquiline nose. His large black eyes, which in calmer moments revealed a reflective and passionate nature, were now glowing with savage hatred. His dark brown hair, growing very low, gave him a small forehead and, when he was angry, an air of viciousness. Among the countless varieties of human countenance, there is perhaps none which is distinguished by a more striking characteristic. His slender, well-built body suggested more agility than strength.

Ever since his early childhood his thoughtful expression and his extreme pallor had made his father think that he would not live long, or that he would live only to be a burden on his family. An object of contempt for everyone else in the household, he hated his brothers and his father. He was invariably beaten in the Sunday games in the public square.

It was only during the past year that his handsome face had begun to win him a few supporters among the girls. Despised by everyone as a weakling, he had worshiped the old army surgeon who had once dared to speak to the mayor about the plane trees.

This surgeon had occasionally paid old Sorel for a day of his son's time and taught him Latin and history, or at least all he knew of history, which was limited to the Italian campaign of 1796. When he died he left Julien his cross of the Legion of Honor, the arrears of his pension and thirty or forty books, the most precious of which had just plunged into the "public stream" whose course had been diverted by the mayor's influence.

As soon as he was inside the house, Julien felt his father's powerful hand seize his shoulder and bring him to a standstill; he trembled, expecting a few blows.

"Answer me without lying," the old peasant shouted harshly in his ear while he spun him around as a child turns a lead soldier. Julien's large black eyes, filled with tears, found themselves staring into the malicious little gray eyes of the old sawyer, who seemed to be trying to penetrate into the depths of his soul.

CHAPTER 5
Coming to Terms

Cunctando restituit rem.
        —Ennius

"ANSWER ME without lying, if you can, you miserable book-worm! How did you get to know Madame de Rênal? When did you talk to her?"

"I've never spoken to her," replied Julien. "I've never seen that lady anywhere except in church."

"But you must have looked at her, you shameless rascal!"

"Never! . . . You know I see only God when I'm in church," added Julien with a hypocritical expression which he regarded as useful in warding off further blows.

"Just the same, there's something behind this," replied the crafty peasant. He was silent for a moment. "But I'll never find out anything from you, you underhanded little sneak! Anyway, I'll be rid of you soon, and my saw will run better without you. You've won over Father Chélan, or someone else, and he's gotten you a good position. Go pack your things and I'll take you to Monsieur de Rênal's house, where you'll be his children's tutor."

"What will I get for that?"

"Board, lodging, clothing and three hundred francs a year."

"I don't want to be a servant."

"Who said anything about being a servant, you idiot? Do you think I'd let my son be a servant?"

"But whom will I eat with?"

This question disconcerted old Sorel. He felt that if he spoke he might say something imprudent; he flew into a rage against Julien, showering him with abuse and accusing him of greediness, then he left him and went off to consult his other sons.

Julien saw them a few moments later, leaning on their axes as they deliberated. After watching them for a long time without being able to guess anything of what they were saying, he walked over to the other side of the sawmill, in order to avoid being taken by surprise. He wanted to reflect on the unexpected announcement which had just changed his fate, but he felt incapable of sober thought; his mind was completely absorbed in trying to imagine what he would see in Monsieur de Rênal's fine house.

"I must give up all that," he said to himself, "rather than let myself be reduced to eating with the servants. My father will try to force me into it; I'd rather die. I've saved fifteen francs and eight sous; I'll run away tonight, keep to the side roads where I won't have to worry about the gendarmes, and in two days I'll be in Besançon. There I'll enlist in the army and, if necessary, cross the border into Switzerland. But that will be the end of my ambitions and my chance to enter the priesthood, which is a steppingstone to everything."

This horror of eating with the servants was not natural to Julien: he would have done far more disagreeable things than that in order to make his fortune. He derived his repugnance from Rousseau's *Confessions,* the only book which had helped his imagination to form an image of society. A collection of bulletins of the Grand Army and the *Mémorial de Saint-Hélène* completed his Koran. He would have died for those three books.

He never believed in any other. In accordance with a remark the old army surgeon had once made, he regarded all other books in the world as full of lies and written by scoundrels for their own advancement.

Along with his fiery temperament, Julien had one of those astonishing memories so often found in fools. In order to win over Father Chélan, on whom he saw clearly that his future depended, he had learned the entire New Testament by heart in Latin; he also knew Monsieur de Maistre's book *Du Pape,* and had as little belief in one as in the other.

As though by mutual agreement, Sorel and his son avoided speaking to each other that day. Toward evening, Julien went to Father Chélan's house for his theology lesson, but he judged it best not to mention the strange proposition that had been made to his father. "It may be a trap," he said to himself. "I must pretend I've forgotten about it."

Early the next morning Monsieur de Rênal sent for old Sorel, who finally arrived after keeping him waiting for an hour or two; as soon as he came through the door he began making a hundred excuses, interspersed with an equal number of bows. By raising all sorts of objections, he learned that his son would have his meals with the master and mistress of the house, except on days when there were guests, when he would eat in a separate room with the children. More and more inclined to make difficulties as he noticed a genuine eagerness on the mayor's part, and, furthermore, filled with mistrust and surprise, Sorel asked to see the room in which his son would sleep. It was a large, well-furnished room, but servants were already occupied in carrying the beds of the three children into it.

This observation brought a flash of light into the old peasant's mind; he immediately asked, in a tone of self-assurance, to see the clothes his son would be given. Monsieur de Rênal opened his desk and took out a hundred francs.

"With this money, your son can go to Monsieur Durand, the clothier, and buy himself a black frock coat."

"And even if I take him back," said the peasant, who had suddenly forgotten his reverent manners, "will he keep the black coat?"

"Of course."

"Well, then," said Sorel slowly, "there's only one more thing left to settle: the amount of money you'll give him."

"What!" cried Monsieur de Rênal indignantly. "We agreed on that yesterday: I'll give him three hundred francs a year. I think that's plenty, if not too much."

"That was your offer, I don't deny it," said old Sorel, speaking still more slowly; and then, by a stroke of genius which will surprise only those who are not acquainted with the peasants of Franche-Comté, he added, looking hard at Monsieur de Rênal, *"We've been given a better offer."*

When he heard these words, the mayor's face fell. He soon regained his composure, however, and, after an adroit conversation which lasted for two full hours, during which not one word was said without a purpose, the peasant's shrewdness won out over that of the rich man, who did not need his in order to make a living. All the many conditions which would determine Julien's new life were settled; not only was his salary set at four hundred francs a year, but it was to be paid in advance on the first of each month.

"Very well, I'll give him thirty-five francs," said Monsieur de Rênal.

"To make a round figure, a rich and generous man like our mayor," said the peasant coaxingly, "will surely make it thirty-six."

"All right," said Monsieur de Rênal, "but let's not drag this out any longer."

This time, anger gave him a tone of determination. The peasant saw that he would have to stop advancing. It was then Monsieur de Rênal's turn to make progress. He flatly refused to hand over the thirty-six francs for the first month to old Sorel, who was eager to receive it on behalf of his son. It had just occurred to Monsieur de Rênal that he would have to give his wife an account of the part he had played in the course of the bargaining.

"Give me back the hundred francs I gave you," he said irritably. "Monsieur Durand owes me something. I'll go with your son to order the black cloth."

After this vigorous action, Sorel prudently resumed his respectful expressions; they took up a good quarter of an hour. Finally, seeing clearly that he had nothing more to gain, he withdrew. His last bow ended with these words: "I'll send my son to your château." It was thus that the people of Verrières spoke of their mayor's house when they wished to please him.

When he returned to his sawmill, Sorel looked for his son in vain. Apprehensive about what might lie in store for him, Julien had left the house in the middle of the night. He wanted to put his books and his cross of the Legion of Honor in a safe place.

He had taken them to the house of a young timber merchant named Fouqué, his friend, who lived on the side of the high mountain which towers over Verrières.

When he reappeared his father said to him, "God only knows, you lazy rascal, whether you'll ever be honorable enough to pay me back the cost of your food, which I've been advancing to you all these years! Take your things and go to the mayor's house."

Julien, astonished at not having been beaten, hastened to leave. But he slackened his pace as soon as he was out of his terrible father's sight. He decided it would be useful to his hypocrisy to pay a visit to the church.

The word "hypocrisy" surprises you? The young peasant's soul had had to go a long way before arriving at that horrible word.

While still a child he was filled with intense longing for a military career by the sight of some dragoons of the Sixth Regiment, in their long white cloaks and helmets adorned with crests of long black horsehair, who were on their way back from Italy and whom he saw tying their horses to the barred window of his father's house. Later he had listened enraptured to the stories of the battles of Lodi Bridge, Arcole and Rivoli that were told to him by the old army surgeon. He had noticed the way the old man's eyes flashed when he looked at his cross.

But when Julien was fourteen, construction was begun in Verrières on a church that could be called magnificent for such a small town. He was especially impressed by four marble columns; they became famous throughout the district because of the mortal hatred they aroused between the justice of the peace and the young curate, who had been sent from Besançon and was generally regarded as a spy of the *Congrégation*. The justice of the peace was about to lose his position, or at least such was the common belief. Had he not dared to have a difference of opinion with a priest who, nearly every two weeks, went to Besançon, where he was said to see the bishop?

Meanwhile the justice of the peace, the father of a large family, passed several sentences which seemed unjust; they were all given to inhabitants of the town who read the *Constitutionnel*. The Royalists were exultant. The sums involved were only four or five francs, it is true, but one of those small fines had to be paid by a nailsmith who was Julien's godfather. This man cried out in his anger, "What a change! And to think that for more than twenty years everyone thought the justice of the peace was such an honest man!'' The army surgeon, Julien's friend, was dead.

Julien suddenly ceased to speak of Napoleon. He announced his intention of becoming a priest and was constantly seen, beside his father's saw, busily engaged in learning by heart a Latin Bible which Father Chélan had lent him. This kindly old man, amazed at the progress Julien was making, spent whole evenings with him, teaching him theology. Julien never showed anything but pious sentiments in his presence. Who could have guessed that his girlish face, so pale and gentle, concealed an unshakable determination to expose himself to a thousand deaths rather than fail to achieve success!

For Julien, achieving success meant first of all leaving Verrières; he loathed his native town. Everything he saw in it chilled his imagination.

From his earliest childhood, he had had moments of exaltation. At those times he dreamed with delight of the day when he would be introduced to beautiful Parisian women; he would find a way to attract their attention by some glorious action. Why should he not be loved by one of them, just as Bonaparte, while still poor, had been loved by the distinguished Madame de Beauharnais? For a good many years, Julien had perhaps not spent a single hour of his life without telling himself that Bonaparte, an obscure and penniless lieutenant, had made himself master of the world with his sword. This thought consoled him for his misfortunes, which he considered to be great, and enhanced his joy when he felt happy.

The construction of the church and the sentences given out by the justice of the peace suddenly enlightened him; he had an idea which nearly drove him mad for several weeks and finally took possession of him with all the power of the first idea which a passionate soul believes itself to have discovered.

''When Bonaparte made a name for himself,'' he thought, ''France was in danger of being invaded; military ability was necessary and fashionable. Today there are forty-year-old priests drawing stipends of a hundred thousand francs, which is three times as much as Napoleon's famous lieutenant generals were paid. They need people to support them, and so we have the justice of the peace, an intelligent man, so honest until now, and so old, who dishonors himself for fear of displeasing a thirty-year-old curate. I must become a priest.''

Once, in the midst of his newly acquired piety, two years after he had begun his study of theology, Julien was betrayed by a sudden eruption of the flame with which his soul was consumed. It was in Father Chélan's house during a dinner given for a group of priests, to whom Julien had been introduced as a wonder of learning. At one point in the conversation he began to praise Napoleon with great fervor. He tied his right arm across his chest, claiming he had thrown it out of joint while moving a fir log, and kept it in that uncomfortable position for two months. After this corporal punishment he forgave himself. Such was the young man of nineteen, weak in appearance and giving the impression that he was seventeen at the most, who, with a small bundle under his arm, was now entering the magnificent church of Verrières.

He found it dark and deserted. In honor of some holy day, all the windows of the edifice had been covered with crimson cloth, which, as the sun's rays shone through, produced a dazzling effect of light that was extremely impressive and profoundly religious in character. Julien was startled. Alone in the church, he sat down in the pew which had the handsomest appearance. It bore Monsieur de Rênal's coat of arms.

On the praying desk, Julien noticed a piece of paper with printing on it, spread out as though it were intended to be read. He looked at it and saw: *"Details of the execution and last moments of Louis Jenrel, executed in Besançon on . . ."*

The paper was torn. On the other side he read the first words of a line: *"The first step . . ."*

"Who could have put this piece of paper here?" he wondered. "Poor man," he added with a sigh, "his name has the same ending as mine. . . ." He crumpled the paper.

As he was leaving the church, he thought he saw blood beside the holy water stoup. It was some of the water which had been spilled: the sunlight, filtered through the crimson curtains covering the windows, made it look like blood.

He finally felt ashamed of his secret terror. "Could I be a coward?" he asked himself. *"To arms!"*

This expression, which had recurred so often in the old surgeon's war stories, sounded heroic to Julien. He stood up and walked swiftly toward Monsieur de Rênal's house.

Despite his fine resolutions, as soon as he saw the house standing twenty yards away from him he was overcome with invincible shyness. The iron gate was shut. It seemed magnificent to him; he would now have to go through it.

Julien was not the only person whose heart was troubled by his arrival in that house. Madame de Rênal's extreme timidity was disconcerted by the thought of the stranger who, in carrying out his duties, would be constantly coming between her and her children. She was accustomed to having her sons sleep in her bedroom. That morning she had shed many tears when she saw their little beds being taken into the room assigned to the tutor. It was in vain that she asked her husband to have the bed of Stanislas-Xavier, her youngest son, taken back into her room.

Feminine delicacy was developed to an excessive degree in Madame de Rênal. She formed an extremely disagreeable image of a crude, unkempt creature whose function would be to scold her children merely because he knew Latin, a barbarous language for which her sons would be whipped.

CHAPTER 6
Boredom

Non so piú cosa son,
Cosa faccio.
—Mozart *(Figaro)*

WITH THE VIVACITY and grace that were natural to her when she was out of the sight of men, Madame de Rênal was walking out through the glass doors which opened from the drawing room into the garden when she saw beside the front door the face of a young peasant, almost still a boy, who was extremely pale and had just been weeping. He was wearing a spotless white shirt and holding a clean violet rateen jacket under his arm.

The young peasant's skin was so white and his eyes were so gentle that at first Madame de Rênal's somewhat romantic mind conceived the idea that he might be a girl in disguise who had come to ask some favor of the mayor. She felt sorry for the poor creature standing motionless at the front door, apparently afraid to ring the bell. She stepped forward, distracted for a moment from the bitter sorrow she felt over the tutor's arrival. Julien, his face turned toward the door, did not see her coming. He started when a gentle voice said close to his ear, "Why have you come here, my boy?"

He quickly turned around; struck by the graciousness of Madame de Rênal's expression, he forgot some of his shyness. A short time later, astonished by her beauty, he forgot everything, even why he had come. She repeated her question.

"I've come to be a tutor here, madame," he said at length, ashamed of his tears, which he wiped away as best he could.

Madame de Rênal was speechless; they stood close together, looking at each other. Julien had never heard such a well-dressed person, and certainly not a woman with such a dazzlingly beautiful complexion, speak to him gently. She looked at the large tears lingering on the young peasant's cheeks, which had at first been so pale and were now so pink. She soon began to laugh, with all the wild gaiety of a young girl; she was laughing at herself, and she was unable to realize the full extent of her good fortune. So this was the tutor she had imagined as a dirty and badly dressed priest who would come to scold and whip her children!

"Do you mean to say you know Latin, monsieur?"

The word "monsieur" was such a surprise to Julien that he seemed to reflect for a moment.

"Yes, madame," he said timidly.

Madame de Rênal was so happy that she took the liberty of saying, "You won't scold the poor children too much, will you?"

"Scold them? I?" said Julien in astonishment. "Why should I do that?"

"You will be kind to them, won't you, monsieur?" she added after a short silence and in a voice that was increasingly charged with emotion. "Will you promise me that?"

Hearing himself addressed once again as "monsieur," and quite seriously, by such a well-dressed lady, was more than Julien had ever hoped for; in all the daydreams of his boyhood, he had told himself that no elegant lady would deign to speak to him until he was wearing a handsome uniform. As for Madame de Rênal, she was thoroughly deceived by the freshness of Julien's complexion, his large black eyes and his attractive hair, which was now curlier than usual, because he had just dipped his head in the basin of the public fountain to cool himself off. To her great delight, she found an air of girlish shyness in that fateful tutor whose severity and grimness she had dreaded so much for her children's sake. For her peace-loving soul, the contrast between her fears and what she actually saw before her was a great event. She finally recovered from her astonishment. She was surprised to find herself at the door of her house with a young man practically in his shirt sleeves, and standing so close to him, too.

"Let's go inside, monsieur," she said in a rather embarrassed tone.

Never before in her life had Madame de Rênal been so deeply moved by a purely agreeable sensation, never had such a delightful apparition taken the place of more alarming fears. Her pretty children, to whom she had given so much care, would not fall into the hands of a dirty, irascible priest. As soon as she entered the hall she turned around and faced Julien, who was timidly following her. His look of amazement at the sight of such a fine house made him seem all the more charming to her. She could scarcely believe her eyes; above all, it seemed to her that the tutor ought to be dressed in black.

"But is it really true, monsieur?" she asked, stopping once again, mortally afraid she might be mistaken, so happy was she made by what she believed. "Do you really know Latin?"

These words offended Julien's pride and broke the spell under which he had been living for the past quarter of an hour.

"Yes, madame," he said, trying to give an impression of coldness. "I know Latin as well as Father Chélan does, and he's sometimes been kind enough to tell me I know it better."

Madame de Rênal found that he looked extremely malevolent; he had stopped a few feet away from her. She moved closer to him and said softly, "You won't whip my children during the first few days, even if they don't know their lessons, will you?"

This gentle, almost supplicating tone on the part of such a beautiful lady instantly made him forget what he owed to his reputation as a Latin scholar. Her face was near his and he could smell the fragrance of a woman's summer clothes, an amazing thing for a poor peasant. He blushed deeply, sighed and said in a faltering voice, "Don't worry, madame—I'll obey you in everything."

It was only then, when her anxiety over her children had been completely dissipated, that Madame de Rênal was struck by Julien's extreme handsomeness. The almost feminine cast of his features and his air of embarrassment did not seem at all ridiculous to a woman who was herself extremely shy. She would have been frightened by the manly air which is commonly considered essential to masculine good looks.

"How old are you, monsieur?" she asked.

"I'll soon be nineteen."

"My eldest son is eleven," she remarked, completely reassured. "He'll be almost a companion for you, and you can reason with him. His father struck him once and the boy was ill for a whole week, even though it was only a gentle blow.''

"How different from me!" thought Julien. "Only yesterday my father beat me. How lucky these rich people are!"

Madame de Rênal had already reached the point of noticing the slightest changes in the tutor's state of mind; she took his sudden sadness for shyness and tried to encourage him.

"What's your name, monsieur?" she asked in a gracious tone whose charm Julien felt without being aware of it.

"My name is Julien Sorel, madame. I'm trembling as I enter a strange house for the first time in my life; I need your protection, and I hope you'll excuse me for many things during my first few days here. I never went to school, I was too poor; I've never talked with any men except my cousin the army surgeon, who was a member of the Legion of Honor, and Father Chélan. He'll give you a good account of me. My brothers have always beaten me; don't listen to them if they speak badly of me. Forgive my mistakes, madame: my intentions will never be bad."

Julien's self-confidence grew stronger during this long speech; he was studying Madame de Rênal. Such is the effect of perfect graciousness when it is natural to the character, especially when the person endowed with it has no thought of being gracious. Julien, who had a highly developed appreciation of feminine beauty, would have sworn at that moment that she was no more than twenty. The bold idea of kissing her hand suddenly occurred to him. He was quickly frightened by this thought; a moment later he said to himself, "It would be cowardly of me not to carry out an act that might be useful to me and diminish the contempt this beautiful lady probably feels for a poor workman who's just been pulled away from the sawmill." Perhaps he was somewhat encouraged by the words "good-looking boy" which he had heard repeated by several girls every Sunday for the past six months. As he was debating with himself, Madame de Rênal gave him a few instructions on how to begin with her children. The violence of his inner struggle made him turn pale again; he said, with an air of constraint, "I'll never beat your children, madame; I swear it before God."

As he said these words, he took the liberty of seizing her hand and pressing it to his lips. She was amazed by this action and, after a moment of reflection, shocked. Since it was a hot day, her whole arm was bare beneath her shawl, and it became completely uncovered when Julien raised her hand to his lips. A few moments later she reprimanded herself: she felt that her indignation had not come quickly enough.

Monsieur de Rênal, having heard the sound of voices, came out of his study and said to Julien, with the same majestic and fatherly air he assumed when performing a marriage ceremony in the town hall, "It is essential that I speak to you before the children see you."

He showed Julien into a room and detained his wife, who had intended to leave them alone. When the door was closed, Monsieur de Rênal solemnly sat down.

"Father Chélan has told me you're an upright young man," he said. "Everyone will treat you with respect here and, if I'm satisfied with you, I'll help you to establish yourself later on. I don't want to see either your family or your friends; their manners wouldn't be suitable for my children. Here's thirty-six francs for your first month's salary, but I demand your word of honor that you won't give one sou of this money to your father."

Monsieur de Rênal was annoyed with the old man, who, in this affair, had shown greater shrewdness than himself.

"And now, *monsieur*, because I've given orders that everyone here is to call you monsieur, and I'm sure you realize the advantages of becoming part of a respectable household; and now, monsieur, it wouldn't be proper for the children to see you in a jacket." He turned to his wife and asked, "Have the servants seen him?"

"No, dear," she replied, with a deeply thoughtful expression.

"Good. Put this on," he said to the astonished young man, handing him one of his own frock coats. "And now let's go to see Monsieur Durand, the clothier."

More than an hour later, when Monsieur de Rênal came back with the new tutor, who was now dressed entirely in black, he found his wife still sitting in the same place. She felt soothed by Julien's presence; as she examined him she forgot all to be afraid of him. He was not thinking of her; despite all his mistrust of destiny and mankind, at that moment his heart was exactly like a child's; it seemed to him that he had lived through whole years since the moment when, three hours earlier, he had stood trembling in the church. He noticed the coldness of Madame de Rênal's attitude and realized that she was angry because he had dared to kiss her hand. But the feeling of pride given him by the contact of clothes so different from those he was accustomed to wearing filled him with such elation, and he was so eager to conceal his joy, that there was something abrupt and wild about all his movements. Madame de Rênal looked at him with amazement in her eyes.

"A little dignity, monsieur," said Monsieur de Rênal, "if you want my children and my servants to respect you."

"Monsieur," replied Julien, "I'm ill at ease in my new clothes; I'm a poor peasant and I've never worn anything except a jacket before. With your permission, I'll retire to my room."

"What do you think of our new acquisition?" Monsieur de Rênal asked his wife.

Acting almost instinctively, and certainly unaware of what she was doing, Madame de Rênal concealed the truth from her husband. "I'm not as pleased with that little peasant as you are," she said. "Your kindness will make him insolent, and we'll have to dismiss him within a month."

"All right, then, we'll dismiss him! It will have cost me a hundred francs or so, and Verrières will have become used to seeing a tutor with Monsieur de Rênal's children. That goal wouldn't have been achieved if I'd left Julien in his workman's clothes. When I dismiss him I'll naturally keep the black coat I just ordered from the clothier. He'll keep only the coat I found ready-made in the tailor's shop, the one he's wearing now."

The hour which Julien spent in his room seemed only an instant to Madame de Rênal. The children, who had been informed of the new tutor's arrival, overwhelmed their mother with questions. Finally Julien appeared. He was a completely different man. It would have been speaking loosely to say that he was grave: he was gravity personified. He was introduced to the children, and he spoke to them in a tone which surprised even Monsieur de Rênal.

"I am here, gentlemen," he told them at the end of his little speech, "to teach you Latin. You know what it means to recite a lesson. Here is the Holy Bible," he said, showing them a small 32mo volume bound in black. "It is in particular the story of Our Lord Jesus Christ, the part known as the New Testament. I shall often make you recite your lessons; you may now make me recite mine."

Adolphe, the eldest boy, had taken the book.

"Open it at random," continued Julien, "and tell me the first three words of any paragraph. I shall then repeat by heart the sacred text, the rule of conduct for us all, until you stop me."

Adolphe opened the book, read two words and Julien recited the whole page as easily as though he were speaking French.

Monsieur de Rênal looked at his wife triumphantly. The children, seeing their parents' astonishment, opened their eyes wide. A servant came to the door of the drawing room; Julien continued to speak Latin. The servant stood still for a time, then went away. A few moments later, Madame de Rênal's maid and the cook appeared in the doorway; by then Adolphe had opened the book in eight different places and Julien was still reciting with the same ease.

"Oh, what a handsome little priest!" exclaimed the cook, a good-natured and very pious girl.

Monsieur de Rênal's self-esteem was troubled; far from thinking of examining the tutor, he was busily ransacking his memory for a few words of Latin; he finally managed to quote a line of Horace. Julien knew no Latin aside from the Bible. He replied with a frown, "The sacred ministry to which I have dedicated myself forbids me to read such a profane poet."

Monsieur de Rênal recited a considerable number of alleged lines of Horace. He explained to his children what Horace was, but the children, overcome with admiration, paid little attention to what he was saying; they were looking at Julien.

Since the servants were still standing in the doorway, Julien felt obliged to prolong the test. "And now," he said to the youngest boy, "Monsieur Stanislas-Xavier must also choose a passage from the Holy Scriptures for me."

Little Stanislas, swelling with pride, read the first words of a paragraph as best he could, and Julien recited the rest of the page. To complete Monsieur de Rênal's triumph, Monsieur Valenod, the owner of the fine Norman horses, and Monsieur Charcot de Maugiron, the sub-prefect of the district, came in while Julien was reciting.

This scene earned Julien the title of "monsieur"; even the servants did not dare to refuse it to him.

That evening, everyone in Verrières flocked to Monsieur de Rênal's house to see the prodigy. Julien answered them all with a somber expression which kept them at a distance. His fame spread so swiftly throughout the town that a few days later Monsieur de Rênal, fearing he might be lured away by someone else, suggested that he sign a two-year contract.

"No, monsieur," replied Julien coldly. "If you should decide to dismiss me, I'd be forced to leave. A contract that would bind me without placing you under any obligation would be unfair; I refuse to sign it."

Julien conducted himself so skillfully that, within less than a month after his arrival in the house, even Monsieur de Rênal respected him. Since Father Chélan was no longer on speaking terms with Monsieur de Rênal and Monsieur Valenod, there was no one who could betray Julien's former passion for Napoleon, of whom he now spoke only with horror.

CHAPTER 7
Elective Affinities

They cannot touch the heart without wounding it.
—A Modern

THE CHILDREN adored him, but he did not like them; his thoughts were elsewhere. Nothing the brats could do ever made him lose his patience. Cold, just, impassive, but nonetheless loved, because his coming had to some extent driven boredom from the house, he was a good tutor. For his part, he felt only hatred and repugnance for the high society in which he had been granted a place, although his place was at the foot of the table, which may explain his hatred and repugnance. There were certain formal dinners during which he had great difficulty in concealing his hatred of everything around him. On Saint Louis' Day, for example, while Monsieur Valenod was holding forth in Monsieur de Rênal's house, Julien nearly gave himself away; he fled into the garden on the pretext of seeing the children. "What praise of honesty!" he exclaimed to himself. "You'd think it was the only virtue in the world, and yet what consideration, what servile respect for a man who's obviously doubled or tripled his fortune since he was placed in charge of the money allotted to the poor! I'm sure he even takes part of the money set aside for foundlings, whose need is even more sacred than that of other paupers! Oh, monsters! Monsters! And I'm a kind of foundling, too, hated by my father, my brothers, my whole family."

A few days earlier, reading his breviary as he walked alone in a little wood known as the Belvédère, which overlooks the Cours de la Fidélité, Julien had unsuccessfully tried to avoid meeting his two brothers, whom he saw coming toward him along a lonely path. The jealousy of those coarse workmen had been so keenly aroused by their brother's fine black coat, his air of refinement and the sincere contempt he felt for them that they had beaten him and left him lying unconscious and bleeding.

Madame de Rênal, taking a stroll with Monsieur Valenod and the sub-prefect, happened to enter the little wood; she saw Julien lying on the ground and believed him to be dead. Her agitation was so great that Monsieur Valenod became jealous.

His alarm was premature. Julien found Madame de Rênal extremely beautiful, but he hated her because of her beauty: it was the first reef on which his career had nearly foundered. He spoke to her as little as possible, in order to make her forget the outburst of emotion which had made him kiss her hand on the day he first met her.

Elisa, Madame de Rênal's maid, had not failed to fall in love with the young tutor; she often spoke of him to her mistress. Elisa's love had earned Julien the hatred of one of the footmen. One day he heard this man say to her, "Ever since that dirty tutor came into the house, you won't even speak to me." Julien did not deserve this epithet, but, with the instinct of a handsome boy, he became doubly attentive to his grooming. And this doubled Monsieur Valenod's hatred. He said publicly that it was improper for a young ecclesiastic to be so preoccupied with his appearance. Except for the cassock, Julien now wore ecclesiastical attire.

Madame de Rênal noticed that he was speaking to Elisa more often than usual; she learned that their conversations were occasioned by the smallness of his extremely limited wardrobe. He had so little linen that he was forced to send it out frequently to be washed, and it was in performing these little services that Elisa was useful to him. Madame de Rênal was touched by his extreme poverty, which she had not suspected. She wanted to give him a few gifts, but she did not dare to do so; this inner conflict was the first painful feeling Julien had caused her. Until then his name had been, for her, synonymous with a feeling of pure and wholly intellectual joy. Tormented by the thought of his poverty, she spoke to her husband about making him a present of some linen.

"What a foolish idea!" he replied. "What? Give presents to a man with whom we're perfectly satisfied, and who does his work well? It's when he begins to be negligent that we ought to stimulate his zeal."

Madame de Rênal was humiliated by this way of looking at things; she would not have noticed it before Julien came. She never observed his immaculate, though quite simple attire without saying to herself, "The poor boy, how does he do it?"

She gradually came to feel sorry for his shortcomings, rather than being shocked by them.

Madame de Rênal was one of those provincial women who may easily be taken for fools during the first two weeks one knows them. She had no experience of life and cared little for conversation. Endowed with a delicate and disdainful soul, the instinct for happiness natural to all mankind usually made her pay no attention to the activities of the coarse creatures in whose midst chance had placed her.

She would have been noted for the spontaneity and keenness of her mind if she had received the slightest education. But, as an heiress, she had been brought up by nuns who passionately worshiped the *Sacred Heart of Jesus* and were animated by violent hatred of all Frenchmen who were enemies of the Jesuits. She had enough common sense to forget promptly, as being absurd, everything she had learned in the convent; but she put nothing in its place and ended by knowing nothing. The fawning attentions which, as heiress to a large fortune, she had begun to receive at an early age, and a marked tendency toward passionate piety, had given her a completely inward attitude toward life. With an appearance of perfect humility and submissiveness which the husbands of Verrières cited as an example to their wives, and which was a source of pride to Monsieur de Rênal, her usual state of mind was actually governed by lofty disdain. Any princess who is noted for her haughtiness pays infinitely more attention to what her gentlemen-in-waiting are doing around her than Madame de Rênal, so gentle and modest in appearance, paid to anything her husband said or did. Until Julien's arrival, she had not really paid attention to anyone but her children. Their little illnesses, sorrows and joys had occupied all the sensibilities of her soul, which, in all her life, had never adored anyone but God while she was in the Convent of the Sacred Heart in Besançon.

Although she did not deign to tell anyone, each time one of her sons developed a fever she was in almost the same state as if he had died. During the first few years of her marriage, the need to open her heart had made her speak to her husband about her torments of this nature; her confessions had invariably been received with a burst of coarse laughter or a shrug of the shoulders, accompanied by some trite saying about the foolishness of women. Such witticisms, especially when they were prompted by the illness of one of her children, turned the dagger in her heart. This was what she now received in place of the obsequious, honeyed flattery of the Jesuit convent in which she had spent her girlhood. She was educated in the school of suffering. Too proud to speak of such sorrows, even to her friend Madame Derville, she assumed that all men were like her husband, Monsieur Valenod and Monsieur Charcot de Maugiron, the sub-prefect. Crudeness, the most brutal insensitivity to everything that had no connection with money, precedence or decorations, blind hatred of all reasoning opposed to their interests—these things seemed to her as natural to the male sex as wearing boots and felt hats.

After many long years, Madame de Rênal had not yet become accustomed to the money-grubbers among whom she was forced to live. Hence her attraction to the young peasant Julien. She found sweet pleasure, radiant with the charm of novelty, in the sympathetic affinity of his proud, noble spirit. She soon forgave him his extreme ignorance, which was an additional charm, and the coarseness of his manners, which she succeeded in correcting. She found that it was worth while to listen to him even when the conversation was concerned with the most common-place things, even when it was a question of a poor dog that had been run over, while crossing the street, by a peasant's cart going at a trot. The sight of this suffering made her husband laugh loudly, but she saw Julien's beautiful well-arched black eyebrows draw together. She gradually came to feel that gener-osity, nobility of soul and humanity existed only in the young ecclesiastic. She bestowed on him alone all the sympathy and even admiration which these virtues arouse in sensitive natures.

In Paris, Julien's position with regard to Madame de Rênal would have been quickly simplified; but in Paris, love is the child of novels. The young tutor and his timid mistress would have found a clarification of their situation in three or four novels, and even in the couplets of the *Gymnase*. Novels would have outlined the part they were to play, shown them the exam-ple to follow; and sooner or later, although without pleasure and perhaps with reluctance, Julien's vanity would have forced him to follow that example.

In a small town in Aveyron or the Pyrénées, the slightest incident would have been made decisive by the heat of the climate. Beneath our more somber skies, a poor young man, who is ambitious only because the refinement of his nature makes him need some of the enjoyments that money provides, is in daily contact with a sincerely virtuous woman of thirty who is absorbed in her children and never uses novels as a guide to her conduct. In the provinces, everything goes slowly, everything happens by degrees; life is more natural.

Often, as she thought of the young tutor's poverty, Madame de Rênal was moved to tears. One day he surprised her weeping openly.

"Is something wrong, madame?"

"No, my friend," she replied. "Call the children and we'll go for a walk."

She took his arm and leaned on it in a way which struck him as strange. It was the first time she had ever called him "my friend."

Toward the end of the walk, he noticed that she was blushing deeply. She slowed her pace.

"You've probably been told," she said without looking at him, "that I'm the sole heiress of a very rich aunt who lives in Besançon. She showers me with presents. . . . My sons are making such . . . astonishing progress . . . that I'd like to ask you to accept a little present as a token of my gratitude. It's only a few louis to have some linen made for yourself. But . . ." she added, blushing still more, and then she stopped speaking.

"What, madame?" asked Julien.

"It would be unnecessary," she continued, looking down at the ground, "to mention this to my husband."

"I'm humble, madame, but I'm not base," said Julien, stopping suddenly, his eyes ablaze with anger, and drawing himself up to his full height. "You've overlooked that. I'd be less than a lackey if I put myself in the position of having to hide anything concerning my money from Monsieur de Rênal."

Madame de Rênal was thunderstruck.

"The mayor," continued Julien, "has given me thirty-six francs five times since I came to live in his house, and I'm ready to show my account book to him or anyone else, even Monsieur Valenod, who hates me."

This outburst left Madame de Rênal pale and trembling, and the walk ended before either of them could find a pretext for renewing the conversation. Love for her was becoming more and more impossible in his proud heart; as for her, she respected and admired him, and now she had been reprimanded by him. On the pretext of making amends for the humiliation she had involuntarily caused him, she took the liberty of bestowing affectionate attentions on him. The novelty of this new behavior made her happy for a week. Its effect was to appease Julien's anger to some extent; he was far from seeing in it anything that might be regarded as a personal liking.

"That's how rich people are," he said to himself: "They humiliate you and then think they can make up for everything with a few trivial antics!"

In spite of her resolutions on the matter, Madame de Rênal's heart was too full, and still too innocent, for her not to tell her husband about the offer she had made to Julien and the way in which he had rejected it.

"What!" Monsieur de Rênal exclaimed angrily. "Do you mean to tell me you tolerated a refusal from a *servant?*"

When she protested his use of this word he said, "I speak, madame, as the late Prince de Condé spoke when he introduced his chamberlains to his wife: 'All these people,' he told her, 'are our servants.' I once read you that passage from Besenval's memoirs; it's essential for understanding questions of precedence. Anyone not of noble birth who lives in your house and receives a salary is your servant. I'm going to have a little talk with this Monsieur Julien and give him a hundred francs."

"Oh, please, my dear," said Madame de Rênal, trembling, "at least don't do it in front of the servants!"

"Yes, they might be jealous, and rightly so," said her husband as he walked away, pondering the magnitude of the sum.

Madame de Rênal sank into a chair, nearly fainting with anguish. "He's going to humiliate Julien, and it's my fault!" She felt sudden loathing for her husband and hid her face in her hands. She promised herself she would never confide in anyone again.

The next time she saw Julien she was trembling in every limb and her throat was so contracted that she could not say a single word. In her consternation she took his hands and squeezed them.

"Well, my friend," she said at length, "are you pleased with my husband?"

"Why shouldn't I be?" replied Julien with a bitter smile. "He gave me a hundred francs."

She gave him an uncertain look. "Give me your arm," she said finally, in a courageous tone that was new to Julien.

She dared to enter the shop of the Verrières bookseller, in spite of his horrible reputation for Liberalism. There she chose ten louis' worth of books, which she gave to her sons. But the books were those which she knew Julien wanted. She demanded that there, in the bookseller's shop, each of her children write his name in the books that were to belong to him. While she was enjoying the partial reparation she had been bold enough to make to him, Julien was astonished at the number of books he saw in the shop. He had never dared to set foot in such a profane place; his heart was pounding. Far from seeking to guess what was taking place in Madame de Rênal's heart, he was deeply absorbed in trying to imagine a way in which a young theology student could procure some of those books. Finally it occurred to him that, by proceeding adroitly, it would be possible to persuade Monsieur de Rênal that he ought to assign his sons an essay on the lives of the celebrated noblemen who had been born in the province.

After a month of careful preparation, he saw his plan succeed, and so well that, while speaking to Monsieur de Rênal some time later, he ventured to suggest an action that would be much more painful to the noble mayor: to increase the fortune of a Liberal by taking out a subscription with the bookseller. Monsieur de Rênal readily agreed that it would be wise to give his eldest son a passing acquaintance with certain books which he would hear mentioned in conversation when he entered the military academy; but Julien saw that he was stubbornly determined to go no further than that. He suspected a secret reason, but he could not guess what it was.

"I've been thinking, monsieur," he said to him one day, "that it would be highly improper for the name of an honorable gentleman like a Rênal to appear in the bookseller's dirty ledger."

Monsieur de Rênal's face brightened.

"It would also be a black mark against a poor theology student," continued Julien in a humbler tone, "if it were ever discovered that his name had been in the ledger of a bookseller who keeps a lending library. The Liberals might accuse me of taking out all sorts of infamous books; they might even go so far as to write the titles of those perverse books after my name."

But Julien was getting off the track. He saw the mayor's face resume its expression of embarrassment and irritation. He stopped speaking. "He's taken the bait!" he thought.

A few days later, the eldest child questioned him in Monsieur de Rênal's presence about a book which had been advertised in the *Quotidienne*.

"To avoid giving the Jacobins any reason to feel triumphant," said the young tutor, "while at the same time making it possible for me to answer Monsieur Adolphe's questions, a subscription with the bookseller might be taken out in the name of the lowest of your servants."

"That's not a bad idea," said Monsieur de Rênal, obviously delighted.

"However," said Julien with that grave and almost sorrowful air which is so becoming to some people when they see their most cherished plans succeeding, "it would have to be specified that the servant could take out no novels. Once inside the house, those dangerous books might corrupt Madame's maids, and also the servant himself."

"You're overlooking political pamphlets," added Monsieur de Rênal haughtily. He wished to conceal his admiration for the clever stratagem devised by the children's tutor.

Julien's life was thus composed of a series of petty negotiations; and their outcomes were much more important to him than the feeling of marked preference which he could have read in Madame de Rênal's heart if he had chosen to do so.

The emotional climate in which he had spent his whole life was continued in the household of the Mayor of Verrières. There, as in his father's sawmill, he profoundly despised the people with whom he lived, and was hated by them in return. He saw every day, from the remarks made by the sub-prefect, Monsieur Valenod and other friends of the family concerning things which had just taken place before their eyes, how little their ideas corresponded to reality. If an action impressed him as admirable, it was sure to be condemned by the people around him. His inner reply was always, "What monsters!" or "What fools!" The amusing part of it was that, with all his pride, he often understood nothing whatever about what was being discussed.

He had never spoken sincerely with anyone in his whole life except the old army surgeon; the few ideas he possessed concerned either Bonaparte's Italian campaigns or surgery. His youthful courage took delight in detailed accounts of the most painful operations; he said to himself, "I wouldn't have flinched."

The first time Madame de Rênal tried to have a conversation with him about something other than her children's education, he began to speak of surgical operations; she turned pale and asked him to stop.

Julien knew nothing else. Therefore, although he spent most of his time with Madame de Rênal, a strange silence set in between them as soon as they were alone together. In the drawing room, despite the humility of his bearing, she found in his eyes a sense of intellectual superiority over everyone who entered her house. Each time she was alone with him for an instant, she saw that he was obviously embarrassed. This troubled her, for her womanly intuition told her that his embarrassment had nothing to do with tender feelings.

As a result of some idea derived from a story about good society such as the old army surgeon had known it, as soon as conversation ceased in a place where he found himself in the company of a woman, Julien felt humiliated, as though he were personally to blame for that silence. This feeling was a hundred times more painful in a private conversation. His imagination, filled with the most extravagant, the most Spanish notions of what a man ought to say when he is alone with a woman, offered him in his agitation nothing but inadmissible ideas. His soul was in the clouds, and yet he was unable to break the humiliating silence. Thus his air of severity, during his long walks with Madame de Rênal, was intensified by the cruelest of suffering.

He despised himself terribly. If, to his misfortune, he forced himself to speak, he found himself saying utterly ridiculous things. To climax his misery, he saw and overestimated his own absurdity; but what he did not see was the expression of his eyes: they were so attractive and revealed such an ardent soul that, like good actors, they sometimes gave a charming meaning to things which actually had no meaning at all.

Madame de Rênal noticed that when he was alone with her he never managed to say anything worth while except when, distracted by some unforeseen occurrence, he lost all thought of making well-phrased compliments. Since the friends who came to her house did not spoil her by presenting new and brilliant ideas to her, she was delighted by Julien's flashes of intelligence.

Since the fall of Napoleon, all manifestations of amorous gallantry have been sternly banished from the provincial code of behavior. Everyone is afraid of losing his position. Scoundrels seek support from the *Congrégation,* and hypocrisy has made excellent progress, even among the Liberal classes. Boredom is rapidly increasing. The only pleasures left are reading and agriculture.

Madame de Rênal, the rich heiress of a pious aunt, and married at the age of sixteen to a respectable gentleman, had never in her life felt or seen anything remotely resembling love. Her confessor, the good Father Chélan, was almost the only person who had ever spoken to her of love, and then it was with regard to Monsieur Valenod's advances; he had drawn such a revolting picture that the word now meant nothing to her but the most sordid kind of sensuality. She regarded as an exception, or even as something totally removed from nature, the concept of love she had found in the very small number of novels which chance had brought her way. Thanks to this ignorance, Madame de Rênal, perfectly happy and constantly preoccupied with Julien, was far removed from the slightest feeling of self-reproach.

CHAPTER 8
Minor Events

Then there were sighs, the deeper for suppression,
And stolen glances, sweeter for the theft,
And burning blushes, though for no transgression.
—*Don Juan*, I. 74

THE ANGELIC serenity which Madame de Rênal owed to her character and her present happiness was somewhat troubled only when she happened to think of her maid Elisa. This girl had received a legacy, gone to Father Chélan to make her confession and told him of her plans to marry Julien. Father Chélan was genuinely delighted at his friend's good fortune; but his surprise was great when Julien resolutely declared that he would not accept Elisa's offer.

"Pay close attention to what's taking place in your heart, my son," said the priest, frowning. "I congratulate you on your vocation, if it's the sole cause of your disdain for a more than adequate fortune. I've been the parish priest of Verrières for more than fifty-six years, and yet, in all probability, I'm going to be dismissed. I'm terribly upset about it, even though I have an income of eight hundred francs a year. I'm telling you this detail so that you won't have any illusions about what's in store for you as a priest. If you're thinking of currying favor with the men in power, your eternal damnation is assured. You may be successful in this world, but you'll have to harm the poor, flatter the sub-prefect, the mayor and all other important men, and minister to their passions. Such conduct, which the world calls sagacity, may not be absolutely incompatible with salvation for a layman. But in our calling we have to choose: we must strive to succeed either in this world, or in the next; there is no middle way. Go, my dear friend, think it over and come back in three days to give me your final answer. It pains me to see, in the depths of your character, a smoldering ardor which doesn't seem to indicate the moderation and complete renunciation of worldly advantages necessary in a priest. I have a high opinion of your intelligence, but allow me to tell you,'' added the good priest with tears in his eyes, ''that if you enter the priesthood I'll tremble for your salvation.''

Julien was ashamed of his emotion; for the first time in his life, he saw himself loved. Weeping for joy, he went off to hide his tears in the great woods above Verrières.

''Why am I in such a state?'' he asked himself at length. ''I feel that I'd gladly lay down my life for that good priest, and yet he's just proved to me that I'm a fool. It's more important for me to deceive him than anyone else, and he sees through me. That secret ardor he mentioned is my plan to make my fortune. He thinks I'm unworthy of being a priest, and just when I thought the sacrifice of an income of fifty louis would give him an exalted idea of my piety and my vocation. In the future, I'll rely only on those parts of my character that I've already tested. Who could have known I'd find pleasure in shedding tears, that I'd love a man who proves to me that I'm a fool?''

Three days later, Julien had found the pretext with which he should have armed himself in the beginning; this pretext was a calumny, but what did that matter? He admitted to Father Chélan, with much hesitation, that a reason which he could not explain to him, because it would harm a certain person if it were known, had made him reject the proposed marriage as soon as he learned of it. This was equivalent to accusing Elisa of misconduct. Father Chélan detected in his manner a fire that was wholly mundane, and very different from that with which a young Levite should have been animated.

''My friend,'' he said to him again, ''be an honest, respectable and well-educated country gentleman, rather than a priest without a vocation.''

Julien replied to these fresh remonstrances quite well, as far as words were concerned: he found the expressions that a fervent young seminary student would have used; but Father Chélan was alarmed by the tone in which he spoke them and the ill-concealed fire that flashed from his eyes.

We must not be too dubious about Julien's future. He correctly used the language of cunning and prudent hypocrisy. This is no mean achievement at his age. As for his tone and gestures, he lived among country people, so he had been deprived of seeing the great models. Later, almost as soon as he had the opportunity to approach these gentlemen, his gestures became as admirable as his speech.

Madame de Rênal was surprised that her maid's new fortune had not made her happier; she noticed that Elisa was constantly going to see Father Chélan and coming back with tears in her eyes. Finally Elisa spoke to her about the marriage.

Madame de Rênal believed herself to be ill; a kind of fever prevented her from sleeping and she felt alive only when she had her maid or Julien before her eyes. She could think of nothing but them and the happiness they would find in their marriage. She formed an enchanting image of the poor little house in which they would live on an income of fifty louis. Julien might very well become a lawyer in Bray, the seat of the sub-prefecture, two leagues away from Verrières; in that case, she would see him occasionally.

Madame de Rênal sincerely believed she was losing her reason; she said so to her husband, and she finally became genuinely ill. That same evening, as her maid was serving her, she noticed that the girl was weeping. She now loathed Elisa and had just spoken harshly to her. She apologized to her, but Elisa's tears redoubled; she said that, with her mistress's permission, she would tell her the whole story of her misfortune.

"Go on," replied Madame de Rênal.

"Well, madame, he doesn't want me. Spiteful people must have told him bad things about me, and he believes them."

"Who doesn't want you?" asked Madame de Rênal, scarcely breathing.

"Monsieur Julien, madame, who else?" replied the maid, sobbing. "Father Chélan couldn't convince him; because Father Chélan thinks he shouldn't refuse a decent girl just because she's been a servant. After all, Monsieur Julien's father is nothing but a sawyer. And how was he making *his* living before he came to this house?"

Madame de Rênal was no longer listening; her excessive happiness had almost deprived her of the use of her reason. She made Elisa repeat to her several times the assurance that Julien had refused categorically, in a manner that would not allow him to come to a more reasonable decision later.

"I'll make one last effort," she said to her maid. "I'll speak to Monsieur Julien."

The next day after lunch, Madame de Rênal gave herself the exquisite pleasure of pleading her rival's cause and seeing Elisa's hand and fortune persistently rejected for an hour.

Julien gradually abandoned his stiff, formal manner and began to make intelligent replies to Madame de Rênal's sober arguments. She could not withstand the torrent of happiness now pouring into her heart after so many days of despair: she fainted. When she had recovered and was comfortably settled in her room, she asked to be left alone. She was in a state of profound amazement.

"Can I be in love with Julien?" she asked herself at length.

This realization, which at any other time would have plunged her into remorse and violent agitation, came to her as a strange but almost uninteresting discovery. Her heart, exhausted by everything she had just gone through, had no more sensitivity left to place in the service of her passions.

She tried to work, but fell into a deep sleep; when she awoke, she was less alarmed than she should have been. She was too happy to see the dark side of anything. Naïve and innocent, this honest provincial lady had never tormented her soul in an effort to wring a little emotion from it in response to some new shade of sentiment or unhappiness. Entirely absorbed, before Julien's arrival, in that mass of work which, outside Paris, is the lot of a good wife and mother, Madame de Rênal regarded the passions as we regard the lottery: an unfailing disappointment and a happiness sought only by fools.

The dinner bell rang; she blushed deeply when she heard Julien's voice as he brought in the children. Having acquired a little adroitness since falling in love, she complained of a severe headache to account for the color of her face.

"That's how women are," replied Monsieur de Rênal with a coarse laugh. "There's always something in their machinery that needs repairing!"

Although she was accustomed to this kind of wit, his tone of voice offended her. She sought to distract herself by looking at Julien's face; even if he had been the ugliest man in the world, he would have seemed attractive to her at that moment.

As soon as the first warm days of spring arrived, Monsieur de Rênal, always eager to copy the customs of the court, moved his family to Vergy, the village made famous by the tragic adventure of Gabrielle de Vergy. A few hundred yards from the picturesque ruins of the ancient Gothic church, he owned an old château with four towers and a garden laid out like that of the Tuileries, with numerous borders of box trees and lanes formed by chestnut trees that were trimmed twice a year. An adjoining field, planted with apple trees, served as a promenade. There were nine or ten magnificent walnut trees at the far end of the orchard; their massive foliage rose to a height of something like eighty feet.

"Each one of those cursed walnut trees," Monsieur de Rênal would say to his wife each time she admired them, "costs me half an acre of crops—grain won't grow in their shade."

The sight of this landscape seemed new to Madame de Rênal; her admiration knew no bounds. The feeling with which she was animated made her much more quick-witted and resolute. Two days after their arrival in Vergy, Monsieur de Rênal having returned to town to deal with some municipal affairs, she engaged some workmen at her own expense. Julien had given her the idea of making a little gravel path which would wind its way through the orchard beneath the walnut trees, making it possible for the children to walk there in the early morning without wetting their shoes in the dew. This idea was carried out less than twenty-four hours after its conception. Madame de Rênal gaily spent the entire day with Julien, directing the workmen.

When the Mayor of Verrières returned from town he was greatly surprised to find the path completed. His arrival also surprised Madame de Rênal: she had forgotten his existence. For the next two months he spoke with annoyance of her audacity in making such important "repairs" without consulting him, but he was consoled to some extent by the fact that she had done it at her own expense.

Her days were spent in running around the orchard with her children, and in chasing butterflies. They had made large nets of light gauze with which they caught the unfortunate *lepidoptera*. This was the barbarous name for them which Julien had taught her, for she had sent to Besançon for Monsieur Godart's fine book on the subject, and Julien told her of the poor creatures' strange habits. They mercilessly pinned them to a large sheet of cardboard which Julien had also prepared.

At last Madame de Rênal and Julien had a topic of conversation; he was no longer exposed to the frightful torture inflicted on him by their moments of silence.

They spoke to each other constantly, with extreme interest, although always of very innocent things. This busy, active and gay life pleased everyone except Elisa, who found herself overworked. "Even during the carnival," she said, "when there's a ball in Verrières, Madame has never taken so much trouble with the way she dresses; she changes clothes two or three times a day."

Since it is not our intention to flatter anyone, we shall not conceal the fact that Madame de Rênal, whose skin was superb, ordered dresses which generously revealed her arms and bosom. She had a very good figure, and this way of dressing was extremely becoming to her.

"You've never been so young, madame," her friends from Verrières told her when they came to dinner at Vergy. (This was a local expression.)

It is a curious fact, which our readers will find difficult to believe, that Madame de Rênal had no deliberate intention in taking all these pains with her appearance. She enjoyed doing so, and, without thinking about it beyond this, whenever she was not chasing butterflies with the children and Julien, she was making dresses for herself with Elisa. Her one trip into Verrières was due to her desire to buy some new summer dresses which had just been brought in from Mulhouse.

She brought a young woman, a cousin of hers, back to Vergy with her. Since her marriage, she had gradually formed an intimate friendship with Madame Derville, who had gone to school with her in the Convent of the Sacred Heart.

Madame Derville laughed a great deal at what she called her cousin's fantastic ideas: "I'd never have thought of such a thing myself," she would say. When Madame de Rênal was alone with her husband, these unexpected ideas, which in Paris would have been called witty remarks, made her feel ashamed, as though she had said something stupid; but Madame Derville's presence gave her courage. She always began by confiding her thoughts to her in a timid voice, but when the two ladies were alone together for a long time, Madame de Rênal's mind would become animated, and a long undisturbed morning would go by as though it were only an instant, leaving the two friends extremely gay. On this visit, the sensible Madame Derville found her cousin much less gay and much happier.

As for Julien, he had been living the life of a child since he came to the country, as happy to be running after butterflies as his pupils were. After so much constraint and clever maneuvering, alone, away from the eyes of men and instinctively having no fear of Madame de Rênal, he abandoned himself to the pleasure of being alive, which is so keen when one is his age and in the midst of the world's most beautiful mountains.

As soon as Madame Derville arrived, Julien felt that she was his friend. He hastened to show her the view from the end of the new path under the great walnut trees; as a matter of fact, it is equal if not superior to the most admirable scenery which Switzerland or the lakes of Italy have to offer. If one climbs the steep slope which begins a few paces farther on, one soon arrives at high precipices bordered by oak trees which extend nearly to the river. It was to the summits of those sheer rocks that Julien, happy, free and, what was more, lord of the household, led the two friends so that he could enjoy their admiration of the sublime view.

"To me it's like Mozart's music," said Madame Derville.

Julien's enjoyment of the landscape around Verrières had been spoiled by his brothers' jealousy and the presence of a despotic, ill-tempered father. At Vergy, he found none of those bitter memories; for the first time in his life he saw no enemies. Whenever Monsieur de Rênal was in town, which was rather often, Julien dared to read; soon, instead of reading at night, and even then being careful to shade his lamp with an inverted flowerpot, he could abandon himself to sleep. During the day, in the intervals between the children's lessons, he climbed up to the rocks with the book that was his only manual of conduct and the source of all his raptures. In it he found happiness, exaltation and consolation in moments of discouragement.

Some of Napoleon's remarks about women, and several of his discussions of the merits of novels that were in vogue during his reign, now gave Julien, for the first time, a number of ideas which would have occurred to any other young man his age long before.

The hot weather came. Julien and the two ladies formed the habit of spending their evenings beneath an enormous linden tree several yards from the house. The darkness was intense there. One evening he was speaking with animation, enjoying the pleasure of expressing himself well to young women; as he gesticulated, he happened to touch Madame de Rênal's hand, which was resting on the back of one of those painted wooden chairs that are placed in gardens.

The hand was instantly withdrawn, but Julien decided it was his *duty* to make Madame de Rênal leave it in place when he touched it. The idea of a duty to be performed, and the fear of making himself ridiculous, or rather of feeling inferior, if he failed to perform it, immediately removed all pleasure from his heart.

CHAPTER 9
An Evening in the Country

Monsieur Guérin's *Dido*, a charming sketch!
—Strombeck

WHEN HE SAW Madame de Rênal again the next day, there was a strange look in his eyes; he watched her as though she were an enemy with whom he would soon be engaged in combat. His expression, so different from what it had been the day before, profoundly upset her; she had been kind to him and now he seemed to be angry. She could not take her eyes from his.

Madame Derville's presence enabled Julien to speak less and devote more attention to what he had in mind. All day long, his sole concern was to fortify himself by reading the inspired book which invigorated his soul.

He drastically curtailed the children's lessons, and then, when Madame de Rênal's presence summoned him to devote himself completely to the service of his glory, he decided it was absolutely essential that she allow her hand to remain in his that evening.

As the sun began to set, bringing the decisive moment nearer, Julien's heart began to beat wildly. Night fell. He noted, with a joy that lifted an immense weight from his chest, that it would be very dark. The sky, filled with large clouds swept along by a hot wind, seemed to announce a storm. The two women continued their stroll until a late hour. Everything they did that evening seemed strange to Julien. They were enjoying that weather which, for certain sensitive natures, seems to enhance the pleasure of loving.

They finally sat down, Madame de Rênal beside Julien and Madame Derville beside her friend. Preoccupied with what he was going to attempt, Julien found nothing to say. The conversation languished.

"Will I be so trembling and unhappy the first time I fight a duel?" he thought, for he was too mistrustful, both of himself and others, not to be aware of his state of mind.

In his mortal anguish, any other danger would have seemed preferable. How often did he long to see some unexpected occurrence oblige Madame de Rênal to leave the garden and go back into the house! He had to make such violent efforts to control himself that his voice faltered; her voice soon became strained also, but he did not notice it. The ruthless struggle between his sense of duty and his timidity was so painful that he was in no condition to observe anything outside himself. The clock of the château had just struck a quarter to ten, and still he had not dared to attempt anything. Indignant at his own cowardice, he said to himself, "At exactly ten o'clock I will either do what I promised myself all day long I would do tonight, or go up to my room and shoot myself."

After a final moment of tension and anxiety during which the violence of his emotion nearly made him lose all self-control, the clock above his head struck ten. Each stroke of that fateful bell resounded in his chest, causing an almost physical upheaval in it.

Finally, while the echoes of the last stroke of ten were still hanging in the air, he put out his hand and took Madame de Rênal's; she withdrew it immediately. Julien, not too clearly aware of what he was doing, seized it again. Although he himself was deeply moved, he was struck by the icy coldness of the hand he was holding. He squeezed it with convulsive force; she made a final effort to draw it away from him, but finally it remained in his grasp.

His heart was flooded with joy, not because he was in love with Madame de Rênal, but because a terrible ordeal had just come to an end. He felt obliged to speak in order to prevent Madame Derville from noticing anything; his voice was now loud and resonant. Madame de Rênal's voice, on the other hand, betrayed so much emotion that her friend believed her to be ill and suggested that they go inside. Julien realized the danger: "If Madame de Rênal returns to the drawing room," he thought, "I'll fall back into the horrible position I was in all day. I haven't held her hand long enough to make it count as an advantage I've won."

When Madame Derville repeated her suggestion that they return to the drawing room, Julien tightly pressed the hand that lay passively in his.

Madame de Rênal began to stand up, then sat down again and said faintly, "I do feel a little ill, but the fresh air is doing me good."

These words confirmed Julien's happiness, which, at that moment, was extreme; he spoke, he forgot to dissimulate, he appeared the most charming of men to the two women listening to him. However, there was still a certain lack of courage in the eloquence that had suddenly come to him. He was mortally afraid that Madame Derville, tired of the wind that was beginning to rise as the storm approached, might decide to go inside, leaving him alone with Madame de Rênal. He had found, almost by accident, the blind courage sufficient for action, but he felt that it was beyond his power to carry on the simplest conversation with her. However mild her reproaches might be, he would be defeated, and the advantage he had just gained would be destroyed.

Fortunately for him, his emotional and grandiloquent speeches found favor with Madame Derville that evening; she very often found him as awkward as a schoolboy and rather boring. As for Madame de Rênal, whose hand was still in his, she thought of nothing; she abandoned herself to her feelings. The hours spent under that great linden tree, which, according to local tradition, had been planted by Charles the Bold, were for her a time of happiness. She listened with delight to the moaning of the wind in the thick foliage of the tree and to the sound of the first few raindrops beginning to fall through to its lowest leaves. Julien did not notice a detail which would have greatly reassured him: Madame de Rênal was obliged to withdraw her hand from his in order to help her cousin pick up a flowerpot the wind had just overturned at their feet, but as soon as she sat down again she let him resume his hold on it almost without difficulty, as though it were an accepted thing between them.

It was long past midnight; it was finally time to leave the garden: they separated. Madame de Rênal, carried away by the joy of being in love, was so ignorant that she scarcely reproached herself at all. Her happiness kept her awake. Julien sank into a leaden slumber, utterly exhausted by the battle between timidity and pride that had been raging in his heart all day.

He was awakened at five o'clock the next morning; and—it would have been a cruel blow to her if she had known of it—he scarcely gave a thought to Madame de Rênal. He had "done his duty" and it had been a "heroic duty." Filled with happiness by his awareness of this fact, he locked himself in his room and devoted himself with an entirely new pleasure to reading about the exploits of his hero.

By the time the luncheon bell rang, he had forgotten, while reading the bulletins of the Grand Army, all the advantages he had won the night before. As he went down to the drawing room he said to himself nonchalantly, "I'll have to tell that woman I love her."

Instead of the passionate glances he had expected to meet, he encountered the stern face of Monsieur de Rênal, who had arrived from Verrières two hours earlier and did not conceal his dissatisfaction with Julien for having spent the whole morning away from the children. Nothing could have been uglier than that self-important man when he was irritated and felt he had a right to show it.

Each of her husband's harsh words pierced Madame de Rênal's heart. As for Julien, he was still so enraptured, so engrossed in thoughts of the great things which had been passing before his eyes for the past few hours, that at first he was scarcely able to lower his attention to the point of listening to the stern remarks Monsieur de Rênal was addressing to him. At length he told him, rather curtly, "I was ill."

The tone of this reply would have stung a man with far less vanity than the Mayor of Verrières; he had an impulse to answer Julien with an instant dismissal. He was restrained only by a maxim he had adopted: Never be too hasty in business matters.

"This young fool," he soon told himself, "has made a kind of reputation for himself in my house; Valenod may hire him, or he may marry Elisa; in either case, he'll laugh at me up his sleeve."

Despite the wisdom of his reflections, Monsieur de Rênal's dissatisfaction burst forth in a series of coarse expressions which eventually angered Julien. Madame de Rênal was on the verge of tears. As soon as the meal was over, she asked Julien to give her his arm for their walk; she leaned on it in a friendly manner. To everything she said to him, he could only murmur under his breath in reply, "That's how rich people are!"

Monsieur de Rênal walked close beside them; his presence increased Julien's anger. Suddenly he noticed that Madame de Rênal was leaning heavily on his arm. This horrified him; he repulsed her violently and drew back his arm.

Fortunately Monsieur de Rênal did not see this new impertinence; it was noticed only by Madame Derville. Tears welled up in her friend's eyes. Just then Monsieur de Rênal began to throw stones at a little peasant girl who was trespassing by taking a short cut across one corner of the orchard.

"Monsieur Julien, please control yourself," said Madame Derville rapidly. "Remember that we all have moments of irritation."

Julien looked at her coldly with eyes in which the haughtiest contempt was visible. This look astonished her, and it would have surprised her still more if she had been aware of what it really expressed: she would have read in it a vague hope of the most terrible revenge. It is no doubt such moments of humiliation that have made men like Robespierre.

"Your Julien is very violent," Madame Derville whispered to her friend. "He frightens me."

"He has a right to be angry," replied Madame de Rênal. "After the amazing progress the children have made with him, what difference does it make if he spends a morning without speaking to them? Men are very harsh, you must agree."

For the first time in her life, Madame de Rênal felt a kind of desire for vengeance against her husband. The intense hatred of the rich with which Julien was filled was about to burst out into the open. Fortunately, Monsieur de Rênal summoned his gardener and became occupied with him in blocking off the short cut across the orchard with fagots of thorn. Julien did not utter a single word in response to the attentions that were bestowed on him during the rest of the walk. As soon as Monsieur de Rênal was gone, the two ladies, claiming to be tired, each asked to take one of his arms.

Between the two friends, whose cheeks were flushed with intense agitation and embarrassment, Julien formed a strange contrast, with his lofty pallor and his sullen, determined air. He despised those women, and all tender sentiments.

"What!" he said to himself, "not even an income of five hundred francs a year to help me finish my studies! Oh, what I wouldn't tell him then!"

Absorbed in these stern thoughts, the little he deigned to understand of the kind words the two ladies were addressing to him displeased him as meaningless, silly, weak—in a word, *feminine*.

In the course of talking for the sake of talking, trying to keep the conversation alive, Madame de Rênal happened to mention that her husband had returned from Verrières because he had just bought some corn shucks from one of his tenant farmers. (In this region, corn shucks are used for stuffing underbeds.) "He won't rejoin us," she added. "He'll be busy with the gardener and his valet, restuffing all the beds in the house. This morning they finished all the beds on the second floor, and now they're on the third."

Julien changed color and gave her a strange look. He soon quickened his pace, drawing her with him until they were a certain distance ahead of Madame Derville, who let them move away from her.

"Save my life," he said to Madame de Rênal. "You're the only one who can do it because, as you know, the valet hates me like the plague. I must confess to you, madame, that I have a portrait: I keep it hidden inside my bed."

On hearing these words, Madame de Rênal also turned pale.

"You alone, madame, can go into my room now. Put your hand into the corner of the bed nearest the window, without letting anyone see you; you'll find a little box made of smooth black cardboard."

"There's a portrait inside it?" asked Madame de Rênal, scarcely able to stand.

Julien noticed her dismay and immediately took advantage of it.

"I have a second favor to ask of you, madame; I beg you not to look at that portrait; it's my secret."

"It's a secret," she repeated feebly.

But, although she had been brought up among people proud of their wealth and interested only in money matters, love had already instilled selfless feelings in her heart. Cruelly wounded, it was nevertheless with an expression of unquestioning devotion that she asked Julien for the information she needed in order to carry out her mission successfully.

"So," she said as she left him, "a little round box, made of very smooth black cardboard."

"That's right, madame," replied Julien in that hard tone which danger gives to a man's voice.

She went up to the third floor of the château, as pale as though she were going to her death. To climax her misery, she felt that she was on the verge of fainting; but the necessity of helping Julien gave her strength.

"I must have that box," she said to herself as she quickened her pace.

She heard her husband speaking to the valet; they were already in Julien's room. Fortunately they went on into the children's room. She raised the mattress and plunged her hand into the underbed with such violence that she scratched her fingers, but, though usually quite sensitive to such small pains, she was not even conscious of this one, because almost immediately she felt the smooth surface of the cardboard box. She seized it and hurried out of the room.

Hardly was she free of the fear of being surprised by her husband when the horror which the little box aroused in her made her feel that now she was really going to faint. "Julien is in love," she thought, "and I'm holding the portrait of the woman he loves!"

Seated on a chair in the antechamber of the apartment, she fell prey to all the horrors of jealousy. Her extreme inexperience was again useful to her at that moment: her anguish was tempered by astonishment. Julien came in, snatched the box from her without a word of thanks or any comment at all, ran into his room, made a fire and burned the portrait immediately. He was pale and overcome with emotion; he exaggerated the danger he had just escaped.

"A portrait of Napoleon," he said to himself, shaking his head, "found hidden in the room of a man who professes such hatred for the usurper! Found by Monsieur de Rênal, who's such a rabid Royalist and so angry with me! And, to climax my foolhardiness, on the white cardboard in back of the portrait there were lines in my own handwriting which could leave no doubt about the fervor of my admiration! And each of those outbursts of love was dated! Some were written only two days ago. . . . My whole reputation shattered, destroyed in an instant!" he added as he watched the box burning. "And my reputation is all I have, I live by it alone . . . and what a life at that, dear God!"

An hour later, exhaustion and self-pity had softened his feelings. When he saw Madame de Rênal again he took her hand and kissed it with greater sincerity than before. She blushed with happiness and then, almost at the same instant, repulsed him with the anger of jealousy. His pride, so recently wounded, made a fool of him at that moment. He saw in her nothing but a rich woman; he scornfully let go of her hand and walked away. He went off to take a thoughtful stroll in the garden.

A bitter smile soon appeared on his lips. "Here I am, walking around as though I were my own master," he said to himself. "I'm not taking care of the children! I'm exposing myself to Monsieur de Rênal's humiliating remarks, and he'll be justified!" He hurried to the children's room.

The caresses of the youngest boy, of whom he was very fond, helped to soothe his burning pain.

"At least *he* doesn't despise me yet," thought Julien. But he soon reproached himself for this relief from his pain as though it were a new form of weakness. "These children caress me the same way they'd caress the puppy that was bought yesterday."

CHAPTER 10

A Big Heart and a Small Fortune

> But passion most dissembles, yet betrays,
> Even by its darkness; as the blackest sky
> Foretells the heaviest tempest.
> —*Don Juan*, I. 73

MONSIEUR DE RÊNAL, who was visiting every bedroom in the house, returned to the children's room with the servants when they brought back the underbeds. His sudden entrance was the last straw for Julien. Paler and more sullen than usual, he rushed up to him. Monsieur de Rênal stood still and looked at the servants.

"Monsieur," said Julien, "do you think your children would have made the same progress with any other tutor? If your answer is no," he went on, without giving Monsieur de Rênal a chance to speak, "how dare you complain that I neglect them?"

Monsieur de Rênal, scarcely recovered from his fright, concluded from the little peasant's strange tone that he had some more attractive offer in his pocket and was going to leave him.

Julien's anger mounted as he spoke. "I can live without you, monsieur," he added.

"I'm very sorry to see you so upset," replied Monsieur de Rênal, stammering a little. The servants were ten paces away, occupied in making the beds.

"That's not enough for me, monsieur," said Julien, beside himself with rage. "Think of the infamous things you said to me, and in front of the ladies, too!"

Monsieur de Rênal understood only too well what Julien was asking for, and he was torn by a painful inner conflict. It so happened that Julien, who had by now completely lost his head, cried out, "I know where to go when I leave your house, monsieur!"

At these words, Monsieur de Rênal saw him established in Monsieur Valenod's house.

"Very well," he said at length, with the sigh and the expression he would have used in summoning a surgeon for a painful operation, "I grant your request. Starting day after tomorrow, which is the first of the month, I'll pay you fifty francs a month."

Julien had an impulse to laugh and remained speechless; all his anger had vanished. "I didn't despise the man enough," he thought. "He's just made what is no doubt the greatest apology such a base nature is capable of."

The children, who had been listening to this scene open-mouthed, ran out into the garden to tell their mother that Monsieur Julien was in a great rage, but that he was going to be paid fifty francs a month.

Julien followed them out of habit, without even glancing at Monsieur de Rênal, whom he left in a state of intense irritation.

"That's a hundred and sixty-eight francs Monsieur Valenod has cost me," the mayor said to himself. "I'll have to say a few harsh words to him about his contract to supply the foundling home."

A moment later, Julien was again standing before him. "I have a matter of conscience to discuss with Father Chélan," he said. "Allow me to inform you that I shall be absent for several hours."

"Very well, my dear Julien," said Monsieur de Rênal with an utterly false laugh, "take the whole day if you like, and tomorrow too, my good friend. Take the gardener's horse for the trip into Verrières." Then he said to himself, "He's going off to give Valenod his answer. He hasn't promised me anything, but I'd better let the young hothead cool off a little."

Julien hurried away and took the road up into the forest through which one can go from Vergy to Verrières. He was not eager to see Father Chélan. Far from wishing to undergo another hypocritical scene, he needed to see clearly into his own heart and give audience to all the tumultuous feelings with which it was agitated.

"I've won a battle," he said to himself as soon as he was in the forest and out of everyone's sight, "I've really won a battle!"

This reflection painted his whole situation in glowing colors and restored a certain degree of tranquillity to his heart. "Here I am with a salary of fifty francs a month," he thought. "Monsieur de Rênal must have been trembling with fear. But of what?"

His meditation on what could have frightened the fortunate and powerful man against whom he had been seething with rage an hour earlier completely restored his serenity. For a moment he was almost sensitive to the enchanting beauty of the forest through which he was walking. Enormous fragments of bare rock had long ago fallen into the middle of it from the mountainside. Tall beech trees rose almost as high as those rocks, whose shade provided delightful coolness within a few feet of places where the heat of the sun's rays made it impossible to linger.

Julien stopped to catch his breath for a moment in the shade of the great rocks, then resumed his climb. Soon, after following a narrow and almost invisible path used only by goatherds, he found himself standing on an enormous boulder, certain that he was isolated from everyone. This physical position made him smile, for it suggested to him the moral position he was burning to attain. The pure air of the lofty mountains breathed serenity and even joy into his soul. The Mayor of Verrières still represented, in his eyes, all the rich and insolent people on earth, but he now felt that, despite the violence of the hatred which had been agitating him, there was nothing personal in it. If he should cease to see Monsieur de Rênal, he would forget him within a week, along with his house, his dogs, his children and his whole family. "I've forced him, I don't know how, to make the greatest sacrifice," he thought. "More than a hundred and fifty francs a year! And I'd escaped from a terrible danger only a few moments before! That makes two victories in one day, although I can't take credit for the second one; I must find out the reason for it. But I'll postpone that tiresome investigation till tomorrow."

Standing on his great rock, Julien looked up at the sky, which was aflame with the August sun. The cicadas were chirping in the field below the rock; whenever they ceased, everything around him was silence. Twenty leagues of countryside stretched out beneath him. Now and then he caught sight of a hawk which had taken flight from the crags above his head and was now gliding in vast, silent circles. His eyes mechanically followed the bird of prey. He was struck by its calm, powerful motion; he envied its strength, its isolation.

Such was Napoleon's destiny; would it some day be his own?

CHAPTER 11
An Evening

Yet Julia's very coldness still was kind,
　And tremulously gentle her small hand
Withdrew itself from his, but left behind
　A little pressure, thrilling, and so bland
And slight, so very slight that to the mind
　'Twas but a doubt.

—*Don Juan,* I. 71

HOWEVER, HE still had to put in an appearance in Verrières. As he was leaving Father Chélan's house, by a stroke of good fortune he happened to meet Monsieur Valenod, whom he hastened to inform of his increase in salary.

When he returned to Vergy, Julien did not go down into the garden until after nightfall. His soul was exhausted from the many powerful emotions that had shaken it in the course of the day. "What shall I say to them?" he asked himself anxiously, thinking of the ladies. It did not occur to him that his mind had now sunk precisely to the level of those trivial details which wholly occupy a woman's interest most of the time. He was often incomprehensible to Madame Derville, and even to Madame de Rênal, and he in turn only half understood the things they said to him. Such was the effect of the violence and, if I may use the word, the grandeur of the waves of passion which rocked the ambitious young man's soul. For that strange creature, nearly every day was stormy.

As he entered the garden that evening, Julien was ready to devote all his attention to the ideas of the two pretty cousins. They were waiting for him impatiently. He took his usual place beside Madame de Rênal. The darkness soon became intense. He tried to take hold of the white hand which he had seen beside him for a long time, resting on the back of a chair. There was some hesitation, but the hand was finally withdrawn in a way that showed displeasure. Julien was prepared to let the matter drop and lightheartedly continue the conversation when he heard Monsieur de Rênal approaching.

The harsh words he had heard that morning were still ringing in Julien's ears. "Wouldn't it be a good way to ridicule that man who's been so lavishly endowed with all the advantages of wealth," he said to himself, "if I took possession of his wife's hand right under his nose? Yes, I'll do it, I for whom he's shown such contempt!"

From then on the tranquillity that was so unnatural to his character rapidly vanished; he could think of nothing except his anxious desire to make Madame de Rênal consent to leave her hand in his.

Monsieur de Rênal was angrily talking politics: two or three manufacturers in Verrières were becoming decidedly richer than he was, and they were determined to thwart him in the elections. Madame Derville listened to him. Julien, annoyed by what he was saying, moved his chair closer to Madame de Rênal's. The darkness concealed all his movements. He ventured to place his hand very close to the pretty arm left bare by her dress. He was troubled and his thoughts were no longer his own; he moved his cheek toward that pretty arm and dared to press his lips to it.

Madame de Rênal started. Her husband was only four paces away; she hastened to give her hand to Julien, at the same time pushing him back a little. While Monsieur de Rênal continued to rant against the good-for-nothings and Jacobins who were making themselves rich, Julien covered the hand that had been left to him with passionate kisses, or at least so they seemed to Madame de Rênal. And yet the poor woman had had proof during that fateful day that the man she adored, without admitting it to herself, was in love with someone else! All during his absence she had been in the grip of intense unhappiness, and this had made her think seriously.

"What!" she said to herself. "Can I be in love? I, a married woman, in love? But I've never felt for my husband that dark passion which makes it impossible for me to take my mind off Julien. He's actually only a boy who's filled with respect for me! This madness will pass. What difference do my feelings for the young man make to my husband? Monsieur de Rênal would be bored by the conversations Julien and I have about things of the imagination. He thinks of nothing except his business. I'm not taking anything away from him to give to Julien."

No hypocrisy soiled the purity of her guileless soul, led astray by a passion it had never known before. She was mistaken, although she did not know it, and yet a certain instinct of virtue in her had been alarmed. Such were the inner conflicts that had been troubling her when Julien appeared in the garden. She heard him speak almost at the same moment she saw him sit down beside her. Her heart was carried away by the delightful happiness which, for the past two weeks, had astonished her more than it had beguiled her. Everything came as a surprise to her. A few moments later, however, she said to herself, "Is Julien's presence enough to wipe away all the wrong he's done?" She was alarmed; it was then that she had withdrawn her hand.

His passionate kisses, unlike any she had ever received before, suddenly made her forget that he was perhaps in love with another woman. Soon he was no longer guilty in her eyes. The cessation of her keen anguish, born of suspicion, and the presence of a happiness she had never even dreamed of, gave her intense surges of love and wild gaiety. It was a delightful evening for everyone except the Mayor of Verrières, who could not forget his increasingly wealthy manufacturers. Julien was no longer thinking of his dark ambitions or the plans he was finding so difficult to carry out. For the first time in his life, he was carried away by the power of beauty. Lost in vague, pleasant dreams that were foreign to his nature, gently pressing a hand that delighted him by its perfect loveliness, he listened half unconsciously to the rustle of the leaves of the linden tree as they were stirred by the soft night wind, and to the distant barking of dogs from the mill on the bank of the Doubs.

But this emotion was a pleasure, not a passion. When he returned to his room he thought of only one happiness: that of taking up his favorite book again. When one is twenty, thoughts of the world and the part one is to play in it prevail over everything else.

Soon, however, he put down his book. Thinking over Napoleon's victories, he had seen something new in his own. "Yes, I've won a battle," he said to himself, "but now I must press my advantage: I must crush that haughty gentleman's pride while he's still in retreat. That was the heart of Napoleon's strategy. He's accused me of neglecting the children; I'll have to ask him for a three-day leave of absence to visit my friend Fouqué. If he refuses, I'll threaten to leave again; but I'm sure he'll give in to me."

Madame de Rênal was unable to sleep a wink. It seemed to her that she had not been alive until then. She could not tear her thoughts away from the happiness of feeling Julien cover her hand with burning kisses.

Suddenly the horrible word "adultery" burst into her mind. All the disgusting overtones which vile debauchery can give to the idea of physical love arose in her imagination and strove to tarnish the tender, divine image she had formed of Julien and the joy of loving him. The future took on a frightening aspect for her. She saw herself an object of contempt.

It was a terrible moment; her soul was penetrating into unknown realms. The day before, she had enjoyed a totally new kind of happiness; now she was suddenly plunged into atrocious pain. She had never even conceived the possibility of such suffering; it began to trouble her reason. For an instant she thought of confessing to her husband that she was afraid she had fallen in love with Julien. That would have meant speaking about him. Fortunately she recalled a piece of advice her aunt had given her on the eve of her wedding: she had warned her of the danger of confiding in a husband, who is, after all, his wife's master.

She wrung her hands in anguish. She was swept along at random by conflicting and painful images. She was afraid of not being loved, then a moment later she was tormented by the terrible thought of her sin, as though the next day she were going to be exhibited in the pillory in the public square of Verrières with a sign proclaiming her adultery to the populace.

Madame de Rênal had no experience of life; even if she had been wide awake and in full possession of her reason, she would have seen no interval between becoming guilty in the eyes of God and finding herself publicly subjected to the most vehement manifestations of universal scorn.

When the horrible idea of adultery, and all the ignominy which she believed to be the necessary result of that crime, left her in peace for a few moments, and when she began to think of the sweet pleasure of living innocently with Julien as she had done in the past, she was suddenly overwhelmed by the terrible thought that he was in love with another woman. She could still see his pallor when he was afraid of losing her portrait, or of compromising her by letting it be seen. For the first time she had seen a look of fear on his usually calm and noble face. He had never shown so much emotion over her or her children. This climaxing pain was added to the most intense anguish it is possible for the human soul to endure. Without realizing it, she uttered cries which awakened her maid. She suddenly saw a gleam of light beside her bed and recognized Elisa.

"Are you the one he loves?" she cried out in her frenzy.

The maid, taken aback by the frightful state in which she found her mistress, fortunately paid no attention to this singular question. Madame de Rênal became aware of her imprudence. "I have a fever," she said to Elisa, "and I think I'm a little delirious. Stay with me.'' Brought back to her senses by the necessity of restraining herself, she felt less unhappy; her reason recovered the power that had been taken away from it by her drowsiness. In order to escape from her maid's scrutinizing gaze, she ordered her to read the newspaper aloud to her, and it was during the monotonous droning of the girl's voice as she read a long article from the *Quotidienne* that Madame de Rênal virtuously resolved to treat Julien with absolute coldness the next time she saw him.

CHAPTER 12

A Journey

> One finds elegant people in Paris; in the provinces there
> may be people with character.
>
> —Siéyès

THE NEXT morning at five o'clock, before Madame de Rênal was up and dressed, Julien had already obtained from her husband a three-day leave of absence. Contrary to his expectations, he found himself longing to see her again; he thought of her pretty hand. He went down into the garden; she kept him waiting a long time. But if he had been in love with her, he would have seen her behind the half-closed shutters on the second floor, with her forehead pressed against the window pane. She was looking at him. Finally, in spite of her resolutions, she made up her mind to go into the garden. Her usual pallor had given way to the most glowing color. That naïve woman was obviously troubled: a feeling of embarrassment and even of anger now marred the expression of profound serenity which usually made her seem far removed from all the commonplace concerns of life and gave such charm to her angelic face.

Julien hurried toward her, admiring the shapely arms that were visible beneath the shawl she had hastily thrown over her shoulders. The coolness of the morning air seemed to increase the glowing beauty of a complexion which the turbulent emotions of the night before had made still more sensitive to every impression. Her beauty, modest and appealing, yet animated by thoughts that are not found among the lower classes, seemed to reveal to Julien a faculty of his soul which he had never been aware of before. Wholly absorbed in admiring the charms his eager eyes had taken by surprise, he gave no thought to the friendly greeting he expected to receive; he was therefore all the more astonished by the icy coldness which she tried to show toward him, and beneath which he even thought he could discern an intention to put him in his place.

His smile of pleasure died on his lips; he remembered the rank he occupied in society, especially in the eyes of a noble and wealthy heiress. A moment later his face showed nothing but haughtiness and anger against himself. He was keenly annoyed that he had postponed his departure for more than an hour only to meet with such a humiliating reception.

"Only a fool," he said to himself, "loses his temper with other people; a stone falls because it's heavy. Will I always be a child? When will I form the good habit of giving these people no more than their money's worth of my soul? If I want to be respected by them and by myself, I must show them that only my poverty is concerned with their wealth, that my heart is a thousand leagues away from their insolence, in a sphere too lofty to be reached by their petty marks of favor or disdain."

While these sentiments swarmed through the young tutor's mind, his mobile features took on an expression of hostility and wounded pride which greatly upset Madame de Rênal. The virtuous coldness she had tried to impart to her greeting gave way to an expression of interest, and an interest that was quickened by all the surprise she felt at the sudden change she had just witnessed. The stream of empty words which people usually exchange in the morning—inquiries about each other's health and comments on the weather—dried up in both of them at once. Julien, whose judgment was not disturbed by any passion, soon found a way to show her how little he regarded himself as being on friendly terms with her; he told her nothing of the little journey he was about to make, bowed to her and left.

As she was watching him walk away, overwhelmed by the somber disdain she had read in his glance, which had been so friendly the night before, her eldest son ran up to her from the other end of the garden, threw his arms around her and said, "We have a holiday—Monsieur Julien is going off on a trip."

When she heard this, Madame de Rênal felt a deathly chill; her virtue had brought her unhappiness and her weakness had increased it.

This new turn of events now occupied her mind entirely; she was carried far beyond the wise resolutions that were the outcome of the terrible night she had spent. She was no longer

concerned with resisting her charming admirer, but with the fear
of losing him forever.

She had to take her place at lunch. To add to her chagrin,
Monsieur de Rênal and Madame Derville spoke of nothing except Julien's departure. The Mayor of Verrières had noticed
something unusual in the firm tone in which he had asked for a
leave of absence.

"The little peasant probably has an offer from someone else in
his pocket," he said. "But that someone else, even if it's
Monsieur Valenod, must be a little discouraged by the sum of six
hundred francs, which is what the yearly expenditure comes to
now. Yesterday, in Verrières, he no doubt asked for three days
in which to think it over; and this morning, to avoid having to
give me an answer, the little gentleman has gone off to the
mountains. Forced to bargain with a wretched workman who
treats us with insolence—that's what we've come to!"

"Since my husband, who doesn't know how deeply he's
wounded Julien, thinks he's going to leave us," Madame de
Rênal said to herself, "what am *I* to think? Oh, it's all settled!"

So that she could at least weep in freedom, and avoid answering Madame Derville's questions, she complained of a severe
headache and went to bed.

"That's how women are!" Monsieur de Rênal remarked once
again. "Something's always going wrong with their complicated
machinery!" And he walked away with a sarcastic laugh.

While Madame de Rênal was suffering the cruel torments of
the passion into which chance had led her, Julien was lighthearts-
edly pursuing his way amid the most beautiful scenery the
mountains have to offer. He had to cross the high range to the
north of Vergy. The path he followed, rising gradually through a
large beech forest, forms an endless series of zigzags on the
slope of the high mountain which marks off the northern side of
the valley of the Doubs. Soon his gaze, passing over the lower
ridges which bound the river bed on the south, extended to the
fertile plains of Burgundy and Beaujolais. Insensitive as the
ambitious young man's heart was to this type of beauty, he
could not help stopping from time to time to look at the vast and
imposing sight.

Finally he reached the top of the high mountain over which he
had to pass, following his short cut, in order to reach the isolated
valley in which his friend Fouqué, the young timber merchant,
lived. Julien was in no hurry to see him, or any other human
being. Hidden like a bird of prey among the bare rocks crowning

the high mountain, he could see from a great distance anyone who might come toward him. He discovered a small cave in the almost vertical side of one of the rocks. He went over to it and ensconced himself inside it. "Here," he said to himself, his eyes sparkling with joy, "no one can do me any harm." It occurred to him that he could now indulge in the pleasure of writing down his thoughts, something it was dangerous for him to do elsewhere. A flat stone served as his writing table. His pen flew; he was aware of nothing around him. He finally noticed that the sun was setting behind the faraway mountains of Beaujolais.

"Why couldn't I spend the night here?" he asked himself. "I have some bread, and *I'm free!*" His spirit soared at the sound of this great word; due to his hypocrisy, he was not free even when he was with Fouqué.

Leaning his head on his hands and looking out over the plain, he remained in his cave, happier than he had ever been before in his life, engrossed in his dreams and the joy of freedom. Without thinking about it, he saw the last rays of the setting sun fade away one by one. In the midst of that vast darkness, his mind was lost in contemplation of what he imagined he would some day find in Paris. First of all, there would be a woman of far greater beauty and loftier intelligence than any he had been able to see in the provinces. He would love her passionately, and she would return his love. If he left her for a few moments, it would be to go off and cover himself with glory, thereby making himself worthy of still greater love.

Even assuming him to have as much imagination as Julien, a young man brought up amid the sad realities of Parisian society would have been roused from his romantic reverie at this point by the cold touch of irony; the mighty deeds and the hope of performing them would have vanished to give place to the well-known maxim, "When a man leaves his mistress, he runs the risk of being deceived two or three times a day." The young peasant saw nothing but lack of opportunity between him and the most heroic actions.

But black night had succeeded the day, and he still had two leagues to go before reaching the hamlet in which Fouqué lived. Before leaving his little cave, he made a fire and carefully burned everything he had written.

He greatly astonished his friend by knocking on his door at one o'clock in the morning. He found Fouqué occupied in making up his accounts. He was a tall, rather badly built young man with coarse, hard features, an endless nose and a great deal of good humor concealed beneath this repellent exterior.

"You must have quarreled with your Monsieur de Rênal, to come here unexpectedly like this."

Julien related to him, but in a suitable version, the events of the day before.

"Stay with me," said Fouqué. "I see you now know Monsieur de Rênal, Monsieur Valenod, Sub-Prefect Maugiron and Father Chélan; you've seen the fine points of their characters and now you're ready to take another offer. You're better at arithmetic than I am: you can keep my accounts for me. I'm earning a lot of money from my business now. Every day I have to pass up good opportunities because I can't do everything by myself and because I'm afraid of taking a partner who might turn out to be dishonest. Less than a month ago I let Michaud de Saint-Amand make six thousand francs; I hadn't seen him for six years and I happened to meet him at the Pontarlier sale. Why shouldn't you have made that six thousand francs, or at least three thousand? If you'd been with me that day, I'd have bid for that lot of timber, and I'd have soon outbid everyone else. Be my partner."

This offer annoyed Julien: it disturbed his obsession. During supper, which the two friends prepared for themselves like Homeric heroes, for Fouqué lived alone, he showed his accounts to Julien and proved to him the many advantages of his timber business. Fouqué had the highest opinion of Julien's intelligence and character.

When Julien was at last alone in his little fir-walled bedroom, he said to himself, "It's true that I could make a few thousand francs here, and then I'd have a better chance of success when I took up the career of soldier or priest, according to what the fashion happened to be in France at the time. The money I'd saved up would eliminate all the small difficulties. Alone in these mountains, I could dispel some of my terrible ignorance of so many of the things those drawing-room gentlemen are concerned with. But Fouqué has given up the idea of getting married, and he's always telling me it makes him unhappy to live alone. It's clear that if he takes a partner who has no money to invest in the business it will be in the hope of having a companion who will never leave him.

"Could I deceive my friend?" cried Julien angrily. This young man, whose hypocrisy and total lack of sympathy were his usual means of salvation, was now unable to bear the thought of the slightest unscrupulousness toward a man who loved him.

But suddenly he felt happy: he had found a reason for refusing. "What! Why should I abjectly throw away seven or eight years of my life? I'd be twenty-eight by then, and at that age Bonaparte had already done his greatest deeds! After obscurely earning a little money by making the rounds of timber sales and winning favor with a few insignificant scoundrels, who knows whether I'd still have the sacred fire with which a man makes a name for himself?"

The next morning Julien very calmly replied to his good friend Fouqué, who regarded their partnership as settled, that his vocation for the sacred ministry would not allow him to accept his offer. Fouqué could scarcely believe his ears.

"But do you realize," he repeated, "that I'm willing to take you in as my partner, or, if you prefer, give you four thousand francs a year? And yet you want to go back to your Monsieur de Rênal, who despises you like the mud on his shoes! When you have two hundred louis in front of you, what's to stop you from going to the seminary? Furthermore, I promise to get you the best parish in the district, because," he added, lowering his voice, "I supply firewood to Monsieur le ———, Monsieur le ——— and Monsieur ———. I give them oak of the very best quality and charge them for it as though it were softwood, but no money was ever better invested."

Nothing could prevail against Julien's vocation. Fouqué finally began to believe that he was slightly mad. On the third day, early in the morning, Julien left his friend and went off to spend the day amid the rocks of the high mountain. He found his little cave again, but he no longer had the same peace of mind; it had been destroyed by Fouqué's offer. Like Hercules, he found himself torn, not between vice and virtue, but between safe, comfortable mediocrity and all the heroic dreams of youth. "So I have no real strength of character," he said to himself, and this was the doubt that pained him most. "I'm not the stuff great men are made of, because I'm afraid that eight years spent providing myself with the necessities of life would rob me of the sublime energy that makes a man do extraordinary things."

CHAPTER 13
Openwork Stockings

A novel is a mirror that is carried along a road.
—Saint-Réal

WHEN JULIEN caught sight of the picturesque ruins of the old church of Vergy, it occurred to him that he had not once thought of Madame de Rênal in the past two days. "When I was leaving the other day," he said to himself, "she reminded me of the infinite distance that separates us; she treated me as a workman's son. She no doubt wanted to let me know how much she regretted having let me hold her hand the night before. . . . It's still a very pretty hand, though. What charm, what nobility in her eyes!"

The possibility of making a fortune as Fouqué's partner gave a certain facility to Julien's reasoning; it was less often impaired by irritation and a bitter awareness of his poverty and humble position in the eyes of the world. As though standing on a lofty promontory, he was able to judge and, so to speak, tower above both extreme poverty and the moderate affluence which he still called wealth. He was far from judging his position philosophically, but he was perceptive enough to feel that he was *different* after his little journey into the mountains.

He was struck by the extreme agitation with which Madame de Rênal listened to him when he told her about his journey after she had asked him to do so.

Fouqué had made plans to marry and suffered from unhappy love affairs; the conversation of the two friends had been filled with long confidences on these matters. After finding happiness too soon, Fouqué had discovered that he was not the only man his mistress loved. These stories astonished Julien and taught him many new things. His solitary life, composed of imagination and mistrust, had kept him away from everything that might have enlightened him.

During his absence, life had been for Madame de Rênal nothing but a series of torments, all different but all unbearable; she was really ill.

"You mustn't go out into the garden tonight, in your condition," Madame Derville told her when she saw Julien arrive. "The damp air would make you worse."

Madame Derville was surprised to see that her friend, whose husband was always reproaching her for the excessive simplicity of her clothes, had just bought some openwork stockings and a pair of charming little shoes made in Paris. For the past three days Madame de Rênal's only diversion had been to cut out and have Elisa sew together in all haste a summer dress made of a light and attractive material that was very much in fashion. They had just been able to finish this dress a few moments after Julien's return; Madame de Rênal put it on immediately. Madame Derville no longer had any doubt. "She's in love, poor woman!" she thought. She now understood all the singular symptoms of her illness.

She saw her speaking to Julien. Her vivid blushes were followed by pallor. Her eyes, fixed on those of the young tutor, were filled with anxiety. She constantly expected him to explain his intentions, to announce whether he was going to leave the household or remain there. Julien had no thought of saying anything on this subject, which had never entered his mind. After terrible inner struggles, Madame de Rênal at last ventured to say to him, in a quavering voice which revealed all her passion, "Are you going to leave your pupils and take a position somewhere else?"

Julien was struck by her uncertain voice and the look in her eyes. "She loves me," he said to himself, "but after this moment of weakness, for which her pride is reproaching her, and as soon as she's no longer afraid I'll leave, she'll be just as haughty as ever." This view of their respective positions flashed through his mind with the speed of lightning. He replied hesitantly, "It would be hard for me to leave such charming and wellborn children, but I may have to. A man has certain duties to himself also."

As he uttered the word "wellborn" (it was one of the aristocratic words he had recently learned), he was filled with deep animosity. "In her eyes," he thought, "I'm not wellborn."

As she listened to him, admiring his intelligence and good looks, Madame de Rênal's heart was pierced by the possibility of his departure, which he had just suggested to her. All her friends from Verrières who had come to dinner during his absence had almost vied with one another in congratulating her on the amazing young man her husband had been fortunate enough to unearth. They had no understanding of the progress the children had made, but the fact that Julien knew the Bible by heart, and in Latin, too, had filled the inhabitants of Verrières with an admiration that may last for a century.

Julien, who spoke to no one, knew nothing of all this. If Madame de Rênal had had the slightest self-possession, she would have complimented him on the reputation he had acquired and, when his pride had been reassured, he would have been pleasant and friendly to her, especially since he found her new dress charming.

Madame de Rênal, also pleased with her pretty dress, and with what Julien said to her about it, tried to take a stroll around the garden, but she soon had to confess that she was not feeling well enough to go on walking. She took his arm, but, far from giving her new strength, the contact of that arm took away the little strength she had left.

Night had fallen. As soon as they were seated, Julien, exercising the privilege he had already acquired, took the liberty of pressing his lips to her pretty arm and taking her hand. He was thinking of the boldness Fouqué had shown with his mistress, and not of Madame de Rênal; the word "wellborn" still weighed heavily on his heart. She pressed his hand, but it gave him no pleasure. Far from being proud, or at least grateful for the feelings she betrayed that evening by signs that were all too obvious, he was almost totally insensitive to her beauty, elegance and freshness. Purity of heart and the absence of all hateful emotions no doubt prolong the duration of youth. It is the face which ages first in most pretty women.

Julien was sullen all evening. Previously his anger had been directed only against chance and society, but ever since Fouqué had offered him an ignoble means of becoming prosperous, it had been directed against himself. Absorbed in his thoughts, although he said a few words to the ladies from time to time, he finally let go of Madame de Rênal's hand without noticing it. This action upset the poor woman terribly; she saw it as a revelation of her fate.

If she had been sure of his affection, her virtue might have given her the strength to resist him. Trembling with the fear that she might lose him forever, her passion carried her to the point of taking back his hand, which he had absentmindedly left resting on the back of a chair. This action roused the ambitious young man from his reverie; he wished it had been witnessed by all those proud noblemen who, at table, as he sat at the lower end with the children, looked at him with such patronizing smiles. "She can't despise me now," he said to himself, "so I must respond to her beauty; I owe it to myself to become her lover." Such an idea would not have occurred to him before he had listened to his friend's artless confidences.

The sudden decision he had just made gave him a pleasant distraction. "I must have one of these two women," he thought. He realized that he would greatly have preferred to make advances to Madame Derville; not that she was more attractive, but she had always seen him as a tutor honored for his learning, not as a workman with a rateen jacket folded under his arm, as he had first appeared to Madame de Rênal.

It was precisely as a young workman, blushing to the whites of his eyes, standing at the door of the house and not daring to ring the bell, that Madame de Rênal took the greatest delight in picturing him to herself. This woman, whom the people of Verrières regarded as so haughty, rarely gave any thought to social position, and, in her mind, the slightest achievement far outshone the promise of character made by a man's rank. A wagon driver who had shown real courage would have seemed more courageous to her than a terrible captain of hussars, complete with mustache and pipe. She believed Julien's soul to be nobler than that of any of her cousins, all of whom were highborn gentlemen, several of them with titles.

As he continued to survey his position, Julien saw that he must not think of trying to seduce Madame Derville, who had probably become aware of Madame de Rênal's feelings for him. Forced to return to the latter, he asked himself, "What do I know about her character? Only this: before I went away, I took her hand and she pulled it back; now when I pull back my hand she seizes it and presses it. Here's a good chance to pay her back for all the contempt she's shown me! God only knows how many lovers she's had! She may have decided in my favor only because it's so easy for us to see each other."

Such, alas, is the disadvantage of being excessively civilized. By the age of twenty, a young man's heart, if he has any education, is a thousand leagues away from that natural abandon without which love is often nothing but the most tiresome of duties.

"Another reason why I owe it to myself to succeed with this woman," continued Julien's petty vanity, "is that if I ever make a name for myself and someone reproaches me for having once held the base position of tutor, I can let it be understood that love drove me to accept it."

He again let go of Madame de Rênal's hand, then took it back and pressed it. As they were returning to the drawing room, toward midnight, she said to him softly, "Are you leaving us, are you going away?"

He answered with a sigh, "I must go away, because I love you passionately. It's a sin . . . and what a sin for a young priest!"

She leaned on his arm, and with such abandon that her cheek felt the heat of his.

Each of them spent the rest of the night in a very different way. Madame de Rênal was exalted by the delights of the loftiest mental ecstasy. A coquettish young girl who falls in love early becomes accustomed to the turbulence of love; when she reaches the age of true passion, the charm of novelty is lacking. Since Madame de Rênal had never read any novels, every aspect of her happiness was new to her. No sad truth came to chill her heart, not even the specter of the future. She saw herself as happy ten years later as she was at that moment. Even the thought of virtue and the faithfulness she had sworn to her husband, which had distressed her several days earlier, presented itself in vain: she dismissed it as an unwelcome visitor. "I'll never grant him any liberties," she said to herself. "We'll go on living just as we've been living for the past month. He'll be my friend."

CHAPTER 14

The English Scissors

A girl of sixteen had a rosy complexion, and she put on rouge.

—Polidori

AS FOR JULIEN, Fouqué's offer had destroyed all his happiness; he was unable to decide on any course of action.

"Alas, I may be lacking in character," he thought. "I'd have been a bad soldier for Napoleon. But," he added, "my little intrigue with the lady of the house will at least distract me for a while."

Fortunately for him, even in this inconsequential train of thought his innermost feelings bore little relation to the flippancy of his tone. He was afraid of Madame de Rênal because of her pretty dress. That dress was, in his eyes, the advance guard of Paris. His pride was determined to leave nothing to chance or the inspiration of the moment. Using what he had learned from Fouqué's confessions and the little he had read about love in the Bible, he made highly detailed plans for his campaign. Since he was filled with anxiety, although he did not admit it to himself, he set down his plan in writing.

The next morning in the drawing room, Madame de Rênal was alone with him for a moment.

"Don't you have another name besides Julien?" she asked him.

Our hero did not know what answer to give to such a flattering question. This occurrence had not been foreseen in his plan. If he had not been so foolish as to make a plan, his quick mind would have served him well, and his surprise would only have made him more perceptive.

He behaved awkwardly, and believed himself to be more awkward than he really was. Madame de Rênal quickly forgave him for it. She saw it as the effect of a charming candor. And candor was the one thing she had found lacking in the young man whom everyone regarded as so brilliant.

"I don't trust your little tutor at all," Madame Derville had said to her several times. "It seems to me that he's always thinking and that he never does anything without a reason. He's crafty."

Julien was deeply humiliated by the misfortune of not having known what to reply to Madame de Rênal. "A man like me owes it to himself to make up for that failure," he thought, and, seizing the moment when they were going from one room to another, he felt it his duty to give her a kiss.

Nothing could have been less natural, less pleasant for both of them; and nothing could have been more imprudent. They just missed being seen. She thought he had gone mad. She was frightened and still more offended. His foolish behavior reminded her of Monsieur Valenod.

"What would happen to me," she asked herself, "if I were alone with him?" All her virtue returned, because her love was fading. She arranged to have one of her children always with her.

It was a tiresome day for Julien; he spent the whole of it clumsily carrying out his plan of seduction. Not once did he look at Madame de Rênal without a definite reason; however, he was not so foolish as to be unaware that he was not succeeding in even being pleasant, much less seductive.

Madame de Rênal could not get over her surprise at finding him so awkward and at the same time so bold. "It's the shyness of an intelligent man in love!" she finally said to herself with inexpressible joy. "Can it be possible that my rival has never loved him?"

After lunch, she went back into the drawing room to receive a

visit from Monsieur Charcot de Maugiron, the sub-prefect. She
began to work at a high little tapestry frame. Madame Derville
was seated beside her. It was in this situation, and in the full
light of day, that our hero saw fit to move his boot forward and
press the pretty foot of Madame de Rênal, whose openwork
stockings and attractive little Parisian shoes were obviously attracting
the gaze of the gallant sub-prefect.

Madame de Rênal was horrified; she dropped her scissors, her
ball of wool and her needles, and Julien's movement could have
passed for a clumsy attempt to catch the scissors when he saw
them fall. Fortunately these little scissors, made of English steel,
broke when they struck the floor, and she profusely expressed
her regret that he had not been sitting closer to her.

"You saw them falling before I did," she said, "so you could
have caught them; but instead of that, your zeal succeeded only
in giving me a violent kick."

All this deceived the sub-prefect, but not Madame Derville.
"That handsome young man has a stupid way of going about
things," she thought. The worldly wisdom of a provincial capital
does not forgive mistakes of this kind.

Madame de Rênal found an opportunity to say to Julien, "I
order you to be careful."

He realized his awkward blunder and it annoyed him. For a
long time he debated with himself as to whether or not he ought
to take offense at the words, "I order you." He was foolish
enough to think, "She could say to me, 'I order you,' if it were
a question of something to do with the children's education; but
in responding to my love she should assume equality. It's
impossible to love without equality." And he became lost in
commonplace reflections on equality. He angrily repeated to
himself the line from Corneille which Madame Derville had
taught him a few days earlier: "Love creates equalities, it does
not seek them."

Julien, stubbornly determined to play the part of a Don Juan
even though he had never had a mistress in his life, behaved like
an utter fool for the rest of the day. He had only one sensible
thought: annoyed with himself and with Madame de Rênal, he
was alarmed at the approach of evening, when he would be
seated in the garden beside her in the dark. He told Monsieur de
Rênal he was going to Verrières to see Father Chélan; he left
after dinner and did not return until late that night.

In Verrières he found Father Chélan preparing to move out of
his house; he had just been dismissed at last, and he was to be

replaced by Father Maslon. Julien helped the kindly priest, and he conceived the idea of writing Fouqué a letter telling him that, while the irresistible vocation he felt for the sacred ministry had at first prevented him from accepting his generous offer, he had just seen such an example of injustice that it might be better for his salvation if he did not take holy orders.

Julien congratulated himself on his shrewdness in taking advantage of Father Chélan's dismissal to leave a door open for his return to business if, in his mind, dreary prudence should ever prevail over heroism.

CHAPTER 15
Cockcrow

In Latin, love is *amor*, and so from love comes death [*mort*] and, leading the way, gnawing anxiety, sorrow, tears, snares, crime and remorse.

—*Blason d'Amour*

IF JULIEN had actually possessed a little of the shrewdness he so gratuitously attributed to himself, he might have congratulated himself the next day on the effect produced by his trip to Verrières. His absence had caused his blunders to be forgotten. He was again sullen all day. Toward evening a ridiculous idea came to him and, with unusual boldness, he communicated it to Madame de Rênal. They had scarcely sat down in the garden when, without waiting for adequate darkness, he put his lips to her ear and, at the risk of compromising her terribly, said to her, "Madame, tonight at two o'clock I will come to your room; there's something I must tell you."

He was trembling for fear his request might be granted; the role of a seducer was such a horrible burden for him that if he could have followed his inclination he would have withdrawn to his room for several days and never seen the two ladies again. He realized that, by his clever tactics of the preceding day, he had destroyed all the progress he had made two days before, and he was at his wits' end.

Madame de Rênal replied with genuine and by no means exaggerated indignation to the insolent declaration he had dared to make to her. He thought he could detect a note of scorn in her brief answer. He was certain that this answer, uttered in a very low tone, contained the words, "You ought to be ashamed!" On the pretext of having something to say to the children, he went off to their room. When he returned, he sat down beside Madame Derville, very far from Madame de Rênal, thus eliminating all possibility of taking her hand The conversation was serious and he acquitted himself quite well, except for a few moments of silence during which he racked his brain. "Why can't I think of some clever maneuver," he said to himself, "that will force her to show me those unmistakable signs of affection that made me think she was mine three days ago?"

He was extremely disconcerted by the almost hopeless situation in which he had placed himself. Nothing, however, would have embarrassed him as much as success.

When they separated at midnight, his pessimism convinced him that he had incurred Madame Derville's contempt and that Madame de Rênal's opinion of him was scarcely any better.

Feeling intensely irritated and deeply humiliated, he was unable to sleep. He was a thousand leagues away from any idea of giving up all pretense, all plans, and living with Madame de Rênal from day to day, contenting himself like a child with the happiness each day would bring. He exhausted his brain in devising shrewd maneuvers which he found absurd a moment later; in short, he was utterly miserable when the clock of the château struck two.

This sound aroused him as the crowing of the cock aroused Saint Peter. He knew that it was now time for him to carry out the most difficult undertaking of all. He had given no further thought to his insolent proposal from the time he had made it—it had been so badly received!

"I told her I'd come to her room at two o'clock," he said to himself as he stood up. "I may be inexperienced and crude, which is only natural for a peasant's son—Madame Derville has made that quite plain to me—but at least I won't be weak."

Julien was right to praise his own courage: he had never set himself a more painful task. When he opened his door he began to tremble so violently that his knees buckled and he was forced to lean against the wall.

He was in his stockinged feet. He went to listen at Monsieur de Rênal's door and heard him snoring. He was bitterly disappointed. He no longer had any excuse for not going to her room. But what in the name of God would he do there? He had no plan, and even if he had had one, he was so overwrought that he would have been incapable of following it.

Finally, suffering a thousand times more intensely than if he had been going to his death, he entered the little corridor leading to Madame de Rênal's room. He opened the door with a trembling hand, making a fearful noise in doing so.

There was a light in the room: a night lamp was burning below the mantelpiece; he had not expected this new mishap. When she saw him enter, Madame de Rênal quickly leapt out of bed. "Wretch!" she cried. There was a moment of disorder. Julien forgot his vain plans and became his natural self again; not to please such a charming woman appeared to him the greatest of misfortunes. His only reply to her reproaches was to throw himself at her feet and embrace her knees. As she spoke to him with extreme harshness, he burst into tears.

When he left her bedroom a few hours later, one could have said, in the language of novels, that he had nothing more to desire. He was indebted to the love he inspired, and to the unexpected effect produced on him by her seductive charms, for a victory to which all his awkward scheming would never have led him.

But, a victim of his grotesque pride even during the sweetest moments, he was still intent on playing the part of a man accustomed to subjugating women: he made incredibly concentrated efforts to destroy his natural charm. Instead of being attentive to the raptures he aroused, and to the remorse which made them more keenly felt, he constantly had the idea of *duty* before his eyes. He was afraid of terrible remorse and everlasting ridicule if he deviated from the ideal model he had set up for himself. In a word, what made Julien a superior person was precisely what prevented him from enjoying the happiness that lay at his feet. He was like a girl of sixteen who has a charming complexion and is foolish enough to put on rouge before going to a ball.

Mortally frightened by Julien's sudden appearance, Madame de Rênal was soon in the grip of cruel apprehensions. She was deeply moved by his tears and despair.

Even when she had nothing left to refuse him, she pushed him away from her with genuine indignation, then threw herself in his arms a moment later. There was no apparent purpose in this behavior. She believed herself to be damned without hope of remission, and she tried to shut out the vision of hell by showering Julien with ardent caresses. In short, nothing would have been lacking in our hero's happiness, not even the passionate responsiveness of the woman he had just seduced, if he had been capable of enjoying it. His departure ended neither her raptures,

which took possession of her against her will, nor her struggles
with the remorse that was piercing her heart.

"My God! Is this all there is to being happy, to being loved?"
Such was Julien's first thought when he returned to his room. He
was in that state of amazement and turbulent uneasiness into
which a man falls when he has just obtained something he has
desired for a long time: he has grown accustomed to desiring,
but he no longer finds anything to desire and he has not yet
acquired any memories. Like a soldier returning from a parade,
Julien was attentively engaged in reviewing all the details of his
conduct. "Did I fail in anything I owe to myself?" he thought.
"Did I play my part well?"

And what part was he playing? That of a man accustomed to
brilliant success with women.

CHAPTER 16
The Next Day

> He turn'd his lips to hers, and with his hand
> Call'd back the tangles of her wandering hair.
> —*Don Juan*, I. 170

FORTUNATELY FOR Julien's pride, Madame de Rênal had been too
deeply disturbed and astonished to notice the foolishness of the
man who in a moment had become everything in the world to
her.

As she was urging him to leave, seeing the day beginning to
dawn, she said, "Oh! If my husband has heard anything, I'm
lost!"

Julien, who had taken the time to compose a few stock
phrases, remembered this one: "Would you regret losing your
life?"

"Ah! Very much at this moment! But I wouldn't regret having
known you."

Julien felt that his dignity required him to return to his room in
broad daylight and without taking any precautions.

The constant attention he gave to his smallest actions, with the
absurd idea of appearing to be a man of experience, had only
one advantage: when he saw Madame de Rênal again, at breakfast, his conduct was a masterpiece of prudence.

As for her, she could not look at him without blushing to the
whites of her eyes, and she could not live for an instant without

looking at him; she was aware of her agitation, and her efforts to conceal it only increased it. Julien looked at her only once. At first she admired his prudence, but soon, seeing that his single glance was not repeated, she became alarmed. "Can it be that he's stopped loving me?" she wondered. "Alas, I'm very old for him: I'm ten years older than he is."

On the way from the dining room to the garden, she pressed his hand. In the surprise he felt at such an extraordinary indication of love, he gave her a passionate look, for she had seemed extremely pretty to him at breakfast and, while keeping his eyes lowered, he had spent the time making a detailed inventory of her charms. This look reassured her; it did not take away all her anxiety, but her anxiety took away nearly all her remorse with regard to her husband.

This husband had noticed nothing during breakfast; it was different with Madame Derville: she believed Madame de Rênal to be on the verge of yielding to temptation. All day long her bold, incisive friendship led her to give Madame de Rênal a series of hints designed to paint a hideous picture of the risks she was running.

Madame de Rênal was burning to be alone with Julien; she wanted to ask him if he still loved her. Despite the unfailing gentleness of her character, she was several times on the point of letting her friend know how unwelcome her presence was.

That evening in the garden, Madame Derville managed to seat herself between Madame de Rênal and Julien. Madame de Rênal, who had formed a delightful image of the pleasure of pressing his hand and raising it to her lips, was unable even to say a word to him.

This mishap increased her agitation. She was consumed with remorse over one thing: she had scolded Julien so much for his imprudence in coming to her room the night before that she was now trembling for fear he might not come that night. She left the garden early and withdrew to her room. But, unable to contain her impatience, she went to listen at Julien's door. Despite the uncertainty and passion that were devouring her, she did not dare to enter. This would have seemed to her the most degrading action possible, for there is a provincial proverb on the subject.

The servants were not all in bed. Prudence finally forced her to return to her room. Two hours of waiting were two centuries of torment.

But Julien was too faithful to what he called his duty to fail to carry out point by point the line of conduct he had laid down for himself. On the stroke of one, he slipped out of his room, made sure the master of the house was sound asleep and entered Madame de Rênal's bedroom. This time he found greater happiness with his mistress, for he was less constantly concerned with the part he had to play. He had eyes to see and ears to hear. What she told him about her age helped to give him some degree of self-assurance.

"Alas, I'm ten years older than you! How can you love me?" she repeated for no reason, simply because the idea oppressed her.

Julien did not understand her unhappiness, but he saw that it was real, and he almost forgot his fear of appearing ridiculous. His foolish idea that she regarded him as a subordinate lover, because of his humble birth, also vanished. As his raptures reassured his timid mistress, some of her happiness returned to her, and with it the ability to judge her lover. Fortunately he now had very little of that self-consciousness which had made their meeting of the night before a victory rather than a pleasure. If she had noticed his intentness on playing a part, the sad discovery would have robbed her of all happiness forever. She could have seen it only as a painful consequence of the disparity between their ages. Although she had never given any thought to the theories of love, difference of age is, after difference of fortune, one of the great commonplaces of provincial humor whenever love is mentioned.

Within a few days, Julien, having recovered all the ardor natural to a young man his age, was madly in love. "No one could deny," he said to himself, "that she has the heart of an angel, and no woman was ever prettier."

He had almost completely lost the idea of playing a part. In a moment of abandon, he even told her of all his anxieties. This confession brought her love for him to a climax. "So I have no fortunate rival!" she said to herself blissfully. She dared to question him about the portrait over which he had shown such great concern; he swore to her that it was the portrait of a man.

When she was calm enough to reflect, Madame de Rênal was overcome with astonishment that such happiness could exist and that she had never had the slightest inkling of it before. "Oh, if only I'd known him ten years ago," she thought, "when I could still pass for a pretty woman!"

Such thoughts were far from Julien's mind. His love was still a form of ambition; it was the joy of possessing a noble and beautiful woman while knowing that he was poor, unfortunate and despised. His acts of adoration, his ecstasy at the sight of her charms, finally reassured her a little about the difference between their ages. If she had possessed a little of that worldly wisdom which a woman acquires long before the age of thirty in more civilized regions, she would have trembled for the duration of a love which seemed to live only on surprise and gratified self-esteem.

At times when he forgot his ambition, Julien rapturously admired everything about Madame de Rênal, even her hats and dresses. He never tired of the pleasure of breathing in their perfume. He would open her wardrobe and spend hours admiring the beauty and order of everything inside it. His mistress would lean on him and look at him while he continued to examine the array of jewelry, ribbons and lace like those which a bridegroom gives his bride on the eve of their wedding.

"I might have married a man like him!" she sometimes thought. "What a fiery spirit! How wonderful life would be with him!"

As for Julien, he had never before been so close to those terrible weapons of feminine artillery. "It's impossible," he said to himself, "that there's anything finer in Paris!" He could then find no objection to his happiness. Often his mistress's sincere admiration and passion made him forget the vain theory which had made him so stiff and almost ridiculous at the beginning of their affair. There were times when, in spite of his habits of hypocrisy, he found extreme pleasure in confessing his ignorance of all sorts of little social usages to the noble lady who admired him. His mistress's rank seemed to raise him above himself. For her part, she found exquisite emotional satisfaction in giving instructions about countless little things to that brilliant young man whom everyone regarded as sure to go far some day. Even the sub-prefect and Monsieur Valenod could not help admiring him; this made them seem less stupid to her.

As for Madame Derville, her feelings were quite different. In despair over what she believed she could discern, and seeing that her wise advice was becoming distasteful to a woman who had completely lost her head, she left Vergy without giving an explanation and without being asked for one. Madame de Rênal shed a few tears at first, but it soon seemed to her that her happiness had doubled: her friend's departure meant that she could now be alone with her lover nearly all day long.

Julien was all the more willing to abandon himself to the pleasant company of his mistress because Fouqué's fateful offer always came back to upset him whenever he was alone too long. During the first few days of this new life, there were times when he, who had never loved or been loved before, found such sweet pleasure in being sincere that he was on the point of confessing to Madame de Rênal the ambition which until then had been the very essence of his existence. He would have liked to be able to consult her about the strange feeling of temptation which Fouqué's offer aroused in him, but a minor event made all frankness impossible.

CHAPTER 17
The Chief Deputy

> O, how this spring of love resembleth
> The uncertain glory of an April day;
> Which now shows all the beauty of the sun
> And by and by a cloud takes all away!
> —*Two Gentlemen of Verona*

ONE EVENING at sundown, sitting beside his mistress at the end of the orchard, far from all intruders, he was deep in thought. "Will such sweet moments last forever?" he wondered. His mind was absorbed in the difficulty and necessity of taking up a profession, and he lamented that period of intense unhappiness which puts an end to childhood and spoils the first few years of manhood if one is not rich.

"Ah!" he exclaimed. "Napoleon was really sent by God for the young men of France! Who will take his place? Without him, what will become of the poor wretches, even those richer than I, who have just enough money to give themselves a good education, but not enough to pay a man to take their place in the army at the age of twenty and launch themselves in a career? No matter what happens," he added with a deep sigh, "that fateful memory will forever prevent us from being happy!"

He saw Madame de Rênal frown suddenly. Her face took on a look of cold disdain; this way of thinking seemed to her worthy of a servant. Having been brought up with the idea that she was extremely rich, she unthinkingly regarded Julien as rich also. She loved him a thousand times more than her life; she would have loved him even if he had been ungrateful and faithless, and money meant nothing to her.

Julien was far from guessing her thoughts, but her frown

brought him back to earth. He had enough presence of mind to choose his words carefully and make it clear to the noble lady sitting beside him on a grassy mound that he was merely repeating some remarks he had heard during his journey to visit his friend the timber merchant. They illustrated the reasoning of the impious.

"Well, don't have anything more to do with such people," said Madame de Rênal, still keeping a trace of that frosty expression which had abruptly replaced a look of sweet and intimate affection.

Her frown, or rather the regret he felt over his own rashness, dealt the first blow to the illusion that had taken possession of him. "She's kind and gentle," he said to himself, "and her feeling for me is strong, but she was brought up in the camp of the enemy. They must be especially afraid of that class of men of spirit who, after receiving a good education, don't have enough money to take up a career. What would become of those noblemen if we were given a chance to fight them with equal weapons! For example, if I were Mayor of Verrières, and as well-meaning and honest as Monsieur de Rênal is at heart, how quickly I'd drive out Father Maslon, Monsieur Valenod and all their underhanded schemes! How justice would triumph in Verrières! Their abilities certainly wouldn't cause me any difficulty. They're constantly groping."

Julien's happiness was on the point of becoming durable that day. What our hero lacked was the courage to be sincere. He needed the courage to give battle, but on the spot; Madame de Rênal had been taken aback by his remarks, because the men in her social set often said that the return of Robespierre was possible especially because of those young men of the lower classes who had received too much education. Her cold manner persisted for a rather long time, and it seemed marked to Julien. This was because her distaste for his ill-chosen remarks was followed by the fear of having indirectly said something that was unpleasant to him. Her distress was reflected clearly in her face, which was so pure and artless when she was happy and free from boring company.

Julien no longer dared to give free rein to his daydreams. Calmer and less amorous, he decided it would be imprudent to go on seeing Madame de Rênal in her bedroom. It would be better if she came to his: if a servant should see her walking through the house, there would be a score of different reasons with which she could explain her action.

But this arrangement also had its drawbacks. Julien had received from Fouqué certain books for which he, as a theology student, could never have asked a bookseller. He dared to open them only at night. He would often have been glad not to be interrupted by a visit, and the tension of waiting for one, even before the little scene in the orchard, would have made it impossible for him to read.

He was indebted to Madame de Rênal for a new understanding of his books. He had dared to question her about all sorts of small details, ignorance of which brings to a standstill the intelligence of a young man born outside the ranks of good society, no matter how much natural genius one may attribute to him.

This loving education, given to him by a woman who had very little learning, was a stroke of good luck for him. He was directly led to see society as it is today. His mind was not confused by what it was like in the past, two thousand years ago, or only sixty years ago, in the days of Voltaire and Louis XV. To his inexpressible joy, a veil fell from before his eyes; he finally understood the things that took place in Verrières.

In the foreground appeared the very complicated web of intrigue which had been centered around the Prefect of Besançon for the past two years. It was supported by letters from Paris written by the most eminent people imaginable. The goal was to make Monsieur de Moirod—the most pious man in the district—the chief, not the second, deputy of the Mayor of Verrières. He had a rival, an extremely rich manufacturer, whom it was absolutely essential to relegate to the position of second deputy.

Julien at last understood the veiled references he had overheard when the high society of the district came to dinner at Monsieur de Rênal's house. The members of this privileged circle were deeply concerned with the choice of a chief deputy, although the rest of the town, especially the Liberals, did not even suspect the existence of such a possibility. What gave the matter importance was the fact that, as everyone knew, the east side of the main street of Verrières was to be moved back more than nine feet, for that street had become a royal highway.

Now, if Monsieur de Moirod, who owned three houses that would have to be moved back, succeeded in becoming chief deputy, and therefore mayor if Monsieur de Rênal should be made a member of the Chamber of Deputies, he would keep his eyes shut and it would be possible to make little imperceptible repairs on the houses extending into the public thoroughfare, as a result of which they would last for a hundred years. Despite

Monsieur de Moirod's recognized piety and honesty, it was taken for granted that he would be "accommodating," because he had many children. Nine of the houses that would have to be moved back belonged to some of the most distinguished people in Verrières.

In Julien's eyes, this intrigue was much more important than the battle of Fontenoy, whose name he had seen for the first time in one of the books Fouqué had sent him. There were things which had puzzled him during the five years since he had begun going to Father Chélan's house in the evenings, but, since discretion and a humble spirit were the most important qualities of a theology student, it had always been impossible for him to ask questions.

One day Madame de Rênal was giving an order to her husband's valet, Julien's enemy.

"But madame, today is the last Friday of the month," replied the man, with a strange expression.

"You may go," said Madame de Rênal.

"Well," said Julien, "he's going to that hay warehouse that used to be a church and was recently given back to the faith; but why? That's one of the mysteries I've never been able to fathom."

"It's a very beneficial but strange institution," replied Madame de Rênal. "Women aren't admitted; all I know about it is that they're all on intimate terms with each other when they go there. For example, the servant who just left will find Monsieur Valenod there, and that proud and stupid gentleman won't be at all annoyed to hear Saint-Jean speak to him with great familiarity, and he'll answer him in the same tone. If you really want to know what they do there, I'll ask Monsieur de Maugiron and Monsieur Valenod for details. We pay twenty francs for each servant, so that they won't cut our throats some day if there should ever be another reign of terror like the one in '93."

The time flew. The memory of his mistress's charms distracted Julien from his dark ambition. The necessity of avoiding all discussion of sad or serious things with her, since they were on opposite sides, added, without his being aware of it, to the happiness he owed to her and the power she was acquiring over him.

At times when the presence of keen-witted children reduced them to speaking only the language of cold reason, Julien, looking at her with eyes aglow with love, listened with perfect docility to her explanations of the world as it really was. Often, in the midst of an account of some clever machination concerning a contract or the laying out of a road, her mind would suddenly begin to wander, and he would have to rebuke her for allowing herself the same intimate gestures with him as with the children. This was because there were days when she was under the illusion that she loved him as though he were her son. Was she not constantly obliged to answer his naïve questions about a thousand simple things which a child of good family knows by the age of fifteen? A moment later, she would be admiring him as her master. His intelligence was so brilliant that it frightened her; it seemed to her that every day she could perceive more clearly the future great man in the young ecclesiastic. She saw him as the pope, or as the chief minister of France, like Richelieu.

"Will I live long enough to see you in all your glory?" she asked him. "The place is already prepared for a great man; the monarchy and the Church both need one. Every day I hear it said that if some Richelieu doesn't stem the tide of personal judgment, all is lost."

CHAPTER 18

A King in Verrières

Are you good for nothing but to be cast aside like a corpse,
a soulless people with no blood left in your veins?
—From the bishop's address, delivered
in Saint Clement's Chapel

ON THE THIRD of September, at ten o'clock in the evening, everyone in Verrières was awakened by a gendarme galloping up the main street. He brought the news that His Majesty the King of ——— was coming the following Sunday, and it was now Tuesday. The prefect authorized, i.e., requested, the formation of a guard of honor; all possible pomp had to be displayed. A courier was sent to Vergy. Monsieur de Rênal arrived during the night and found the whole town in turmoil. Everyone had his own claim to importance; those who had the least to do were renting balconies from which to see the king enter the town.

Who would command the guard of honor? Monsieur de Rênal saw at once how important it was, in the interest of the houses that would have to be moved back, that the command should be given to Monsieur de Moirod: it might be regarded as entitling him to the post of chief deputy. There was nothing to be said against Monsieur de Moirod's piety, it was beyond all comparison; but he had never ridden a horse in his life. He was a man of thirty-six, timid in every way, who was equally afraid of taking a spill and being laughed at.

The mayor sent for him at five o'clock in the morning. "As you can see, monsieur," he said, "I'm asking for your advice as though you already held the office which all respectable people want you to have. In this unfortunate town the factories are prospering and the Liberals are becoming millionaires; they aspire to power, and they'll make a weapon of anything they can. We must consider the best interests of the king, the monarchy and, above all, our holy religion. To whom do you think, monsieur, we might entrust the command of the guard of honor?"

In spite of his terrible fear of horses, Monsieur de Moirod finally accepted the honor like a martyr. "I'll maintain a dignified manner," he said to the mayor. There was scarcely time to recondition the uniforms which had been used seven years earlier when a prince of the blood passed through the town.

At seven o'clock, Madame de Rênal came in from Vergy with Julien and the children. She found her drawing room filled with Liberal ladies who preached the union of the parties and had come to beg her to persuade her husband to place theirs in the guard of honor. One of them claimed that if her husband were not chosen, his chagrin would cause him to go bankrupt. Madame de Rênal quickly dismissed them all. She appeared to be extremely busy.

Julien was surprised and still more annoyed by the fact that she made a mystery of what was agitating her. "It's just as I thought," he told himself bitterly, "her love is being eclipsed by the joy of receiving a king in her house. She's dazzled by all this commotion. She'll begin to love me again when her mind is no longer troubled by the ideas of her caste." The surprising thing was that this made him love her all the more.

Upholsterers and decorators began to fill the house; for a long time he watched in vain for an opportunity to say a few words to her. Finally he met her coming out of his room, carrying one of his coats. They were alone. He tried to speak to her, but she hurried away, refusing to listen to him. "What a fool I am to love such a woman!" he thought. "Her ambition makes her as mad as her husband."

She was even more so; one of her strongest desires, which she had never confessed to Julien for fear of offending him, was to see him discard his gloomy black coat, if only for a day. With an adroitness that was truly admirable in such a naïve woman, she persuaded first Monsieur de Moirod and then the sub-prefect, Monsieur de Maugiron, to agree to Julien's appointment as one of the guards of honor in preference to five or six other young men, sons of well-to-do manufacturers, at least two of whom were noted for their exemplary piety.

Monsieur Valenod, who had been counting on lending his carriage to the prettiest women in town, thereby exposing his fine Norman horses to the admiration of the public, agreed to let Julien, whom he hated more than anyone else in the world, ride one of them. But each member of the guard of honor either owned or had borrowed one of those handsome sky-blue coats, with a pair of colonel's epaulettes in silver, which had made such a fine show seven years earlier. Madame de Rênal wanted Julien to have a new coat, and she had only four days in which to send to Besançon for the uniform, weapons, hat and everything else that makes a guard of honor. The amusing part of it was that she thought it would be unwise to have the coat made in Verrières. She wanted to surprise Julien and everyone else in town.

When the guard of honor and public sentiment had been properly organized, the mayor had to turn his attention to arranging for a great religious ceremony: the king did not wish to pass through Verrières without seeing the famous relic of Saint Clement which is preserved at Bray-le-Haut, less than a league from the town. It was thought desirable to have a large body of clergymen present, and this was the most difficult thing to arrange. Father Maslon, the new parish priest, was determined to exclude Father Chélan at any cost. Monsieur de Rênal vainly pointed out to him the imprudence of doing so: the Marquis de La Mole, whose ancestors had been governors of the province for so long, had been chosen to accompany the king, and he had known Father Chélan for thirty years. He would be sure to ask about him when he arrived in Verrières, and if he found that he was in disgrace, he was just the kind of man who would go to seek him out in the little house to which he had retired, accompanied by as many members of the procession as he could command. What a slap in the face that would be!

"I'll be dishonored here and in Besançon if he appears among my clergy," replied Father Maslon. "Good heavens, he's a Jansenist!"

"No matter what you say, my dear Father Maslon," replied Monsieur de Rênal, "I will not expose the municipal government of Verrières to the risk of receiving an affront from Monsieur de La Mole. You don't know him; he behaves well at court, but here in the provinces he's a mocking, satirical practical joker who's always trying to embarrass people. He's quite capable of covering us with ridicule in the eyes of the Liberals, just for his own amusement.''

It was not until Saturday night, after three days of discussion, that Father Maslon's pride yielded to the mayor's fear, which was turning into courage. It was now necessary to write Father Chélan a honeyed letter asking him to attend the ceremony in honor of the relic at Bray-le-Haut, if his advanced age and his infirmities would allow him to do so. Father Chélan requested and obtained a letter of invitation for Julien, who was to accompany him as a sub-deacon.

Early Sunday morning, thousands of peasants began to pour in from the nearby mountains, flooding the streets of Verrières. It was a beautiful sunny day. Finally, toward three o'clock, a tremor ran through the whole crowd: a great fire had been sighted on a rock two leagues away from Verrières. This was the signal announcing that the king had just entered the territory of the department. Immediately the pealing of all the bells and the repeated firing of an old Spanish cannon belonging to the town proclaimed its joy at this great event. Half the population climbed up on rooftops. All the women were on balconies. The guard of honor began to move. The brilliant uniforms were admired by the onlookers, each of whom recognized a relative or a friend. Many of them were laughing at Monsieur de Moirod's fear: his cautious hand was constantly ready to clutch the pommel of his saddle.

But one observation made all others be forgotten: the first rider in the ninth file was a handsome, very slender young man whom no one recognized at first. Soon the indignant cries of some and the astonished silence of others announced a general sensation. The young man, riding one of Monsieur Valenod's Norman horses, had been recognized as young Sorel, the sawyer's son. There was a loud outcry against the mayor, especially among the Liberals. What! Just because he had hired that little workman disguised as a priest to tutor his brats, he had the audacity to place him in the guard of honor, to the detriment of Monsieur So-and-So and Monsieur So-and-So, who were rich manufacturers!

''Those gentlemen,'' said a banker's wife, ''really ought to put the little upstart in his place; he was born in the gutter!''

''He's a surly young fellow and he's wearing a saber,'' replied her companion. "He'd be treacherous enough to slash them across the face with it."

The remarks of the nobility were more dangerous. The ladies wondered whether the mayor alone was responsible for that flagrant breach of propriety. Most of them gave him credit for his contempt of humble birth.

While he was arousing so much comment, Julien was the happiest of men. Naturally intrepid, he sat his horse better than most of the young men of that mountain town. He could tell from the women's eyes that they were talking about him.

His epaulettes were shinier than the others because they were new. His horse reared every few moments; his joy could not have been greater.

His happiness knew no bounds when, as they were passing near the old rampart, the sound of the small cannon made his horse leap out of the ranks. By sheer chance, he did not fall off; from then on he felt himself a hero. He was Napoleon's aide-de-camp and he was charging a battery.

There was one person happier than he. First she had watched him pass from one of the windows of the town hall; then, getting into her carriage and swiftly making a wide detour, she arrived in time to tremble when his horse carried him out of the ranks. Finally, after ordering her coachman to gallop through one of the other gates of the town, she succeeded in reaching the road along which the king was to pass and was able to follow the guard of honor at a distance of twenty paces, in a noble cloud of dust.

Ten thousand peasants shouted "Long live the king!" when the mayor had the honor of addressing His Majesty. An hour later, when the king, having listened to all the speeches, was about to enter the town, the little cannon began to fire again at rapid intervals. But this caused an accident, not to the gunners, who had proven their worth at Leipzig and Montmirail, but to the future chief deputy, Monsieur Moirod. His horse deposited him in the only mud puddle along the highway, which caused a great commotion, for he had to be pulled out to allow the king's carriage to pass.

His Majesty alighted in front of the fine new church, which was decked out for the occasion with all its crimson hangings. He was to have dinner and then get back into his carriage immediately afterward to go to pay his respects to the famous relic of Saint Clement.

Almost as soon as the king reached the church, Julien galloped off to Monsieur de Rênal's house. There, with a sigh, he took off his handsome sky-blue coat, his saber and his epaulettes and put on his shabby little black coat again. He remounted his horse and a short time later he was at Bray-le-Haut, which stands on the summit of a beautiful hill. "Enthusiasm is multiplying these peasants," he thought. "There isn't room to move in Verrières, and yet there are more than ten thousand of them around this old abbey." Half ruined by the vandalism of the Revolution, the abbey had been magnificently rebuilt since the Restoration, and there was already some talk of miracles. Julien joined Father Chélan, who sternly reprimanded him and gave him a cassock and a surplice. He quickly put them on and followed Father Chélan when he went off to join the young Bishop of Agde, a nephew of Monsieur de La Mole who had received his bishopric only recently and had been chosen to exhibit the relic to the king. But the bishop was nowhere to be found.

The clergy were growing impatient. They were awaiting their leader in the dark Gothic cloister of the old abbey. Twenty-four parish priests had been assembled to represent the former chapter of Bray-le-Haut, which, before 1789, had been composed of twenty-four canons. After deploring the bishop's youth for three quarters of an hour, the priests decided it would be advisable for their dean to go to him and notify him that the king was about to arrive and that it was time to go to the chancel. Father Chélan's great age had made him their dean; in spite of the annoyance he had shown with Julien, he motioned him to follow. By some mysterious process of ecclesiastical grooming, Julien had made his beautiful curly hair lie flat; but, through an oversight which redoubled Father Chélan's anger, the spurs he had worn in the guard of honor were visible beneath the long folds of his cassock.

When they reached the bishop's apartment, the tall, elegantly dressed footmen scarcely deigned to inform the old priest that the bishop was not receiving visitors. They sneered when he tried to explain that, as dean of the noble chapter of Bray-le-Haut, he had a right to be admitted into the presence of the officiating bishop at any time.

Julien's proud spirit was offended by the insolence of the footmen. He began to walk through the dormitories of the old abbey, trying every door he saw. A very small one yielded to his efforts and he found himself in a cell amid the bishop's valets, who were dressed in black and wore chains around their necks. He seemed to be in such a hurry that they assumed the bishop had sent for him and let him pass. He took a few steps forward and found himself in an enormous, gloomy Gothic room, completely paneled in dark oak. With one exception, its pointed windows had been walled up with bricks; the crudeness of this masonry was disguised by nothing, and it formed a sad contrast with the antique splendor of the woodwork. The two longest sides of this room, which was famous among the antiquarians of Burgundy, and which Duke Charles the Bold had built some time around 1470 to expiate some sin, were lined with richly carved wooden stalls on which all the mysteries of the Apocalypse were represented, inlaid in wood of different colors.

Julien was moved by that melancholy splendor, degraded by the sight of bare bricks and plaster that was still white. He stopped and stood in silence. At the far end of the room, near the only window which admitted any light, he saw a portable mirror framed in mahogany. A young man, wearing a violet robe with a lace-trimmed surplice, but bareheaded, was standing three paces away from the mirror, which seemed out of place there and had no doubt been brought from town. Julien noticed that the young man appeared to be irritated; with his right hand he was gravely giving benedictions in front of the mirror.

"What does this mean?" thought Julien. "Is that young priest performing some preliminary ceremony? He may be the bishop's secretary. . . . He's probably as insolent as the footmen. . . . Well, let's try him anyway."

He began to walk rather slowly toward the other end of the room, his eyes fixed in the direction of the solitary window and watching the young man, who continued to give benedictions, slowly, but in endless number, and without resting for a moment.

The closer he came, the more clearly he saw the young man's expression of irritation. The splendor of his lace-trimmed surplice made him stop involuntarily a few paces away from the magnificent mirror.

"It's my duty to speak," he said to himself at length; but the beauty of the room overwhelmed him and he was offended in advance by the harsh words he expected to hear.

The young man saw him in the mirror, turned around and, suddenly discarding his expression of anger, said to him gently, "Well, monsieur, is it ready yet?"

Julien remained speechless. He had seen the pectoral cross on the young man's chest as he turned toward him: he was the Bishop of Agde.

"Monsignor," he replied timidly, "I've been sent by the dean of the chapter, Father Chélan."

"Oh yes, he's been warmly recommended to me," said the

bishop in a polite tone which doubled Julien's enchantment. "But I beg your pardon, monsieur: I thought you were the man who was to bring me my miter. It was carelessly packed in Paris and the silver brocade was ruined at the top. It will make a terrible impression," added the young bishop sadly, "and besides that, they're keeping me waiting!"

"With your permission, Monsignor, I'll go and find the miter for you."

Julien's expressive eyes produced their effect.

"Please do, monsieur," replied the bishop with charming politeness. "I need it immediately. I'm terribly sorry to keep the gentlemen of the chapter waiting."

When Julien reached the middle of the room he turned around to look back at the bishop and saw that he had resumed his benedictions. "What can it mean?" he wondered. "It must be some sort of religious preparation necessary for the ceremony that's about to take place." When he entered the cell where the valets were waiting, he saw the miter in their hands. These gentlemen, yielding in spite of themselves to his imperious gaze, gave it to him.

He was proud to carry it: as he crossed the room he walked slowly, holding it with respect. He found the bishop sitting in front of the mirror; but from time to time he raised his right hand, tired though it was, to make one more gesture of benediction. Julien helped him put on his miter. The bishop shook his head.

"Good, it will stay on," he said to Julien in a tone of satisfaction. "Would you please step aside a little?"

The bishop quickly went to the middle of the room, then, walking slowly toward the mirror, resumed his expression of irritation and gravely gave more benedictions.

Julien stood motionless in astonishment; he was tempted to understand, but he did not dare. The bishop stopped and, looking at him with an air which rapidly lost its gravity, said, "What do you think of my miter, monsieur? Does it look right?"

"It looks perfect, Monsignor."

"It isn't too far back? That would look a little foolish; but it shouldn't be worn down over the eyes like an officer's shako, either."

"It looks very good to me."

"The King of ——— is used to venerable clergymen who are no doubt very solemn. I don't want to look too frivolous, especially because of my age."

And again the bishop began to walk to and fro, giving benedictions with his right hand.

"It's clear," thought Julien, finally daring to understand.
"He's practicing his benedictions."

A few moments later the bishop said, "I'm ready, monsieur.
Go and tell the dean and the gentlemen of the chapter."

Soon Father Chélan, followed by the two next eldest priests,
came in through an enormous and magnificently carved door
which Julien had not noticed. But this time he remained in his
place, behind everyone else, and was able to see the bishop only
over the shoulders of the ecclesiastics crowded around the door.

The bishop walked slowly across the room; when he reached
the threshold the priests formed a procession. After a few short
moments of confusion, the procession began to move forward,
intoning a psalm. The bishop came last, between Father Chélan
and another very old priest. Julien moved in close to the bishop,
taking advantage of the fact that he was attached to Father
Chélan. They followed the long corridors of the abbey of Bray-le-
Haut, which were dark and damp in spite of the bright sunshine.
At length they reached the door of the cloister.

Julien was overcome with admiration for such an impressive
ceremony. His ambition, reawakened by the bishop's youth, con-
tended with the prelate's sensibility and exquisite politeness for
mastery of his heart. This politeness was very different from
Monsieur de Rênal's, even on his good days. "The closer you
come to the highest rank of society," thought Julien, "the more
you find those charming manners."

They entered the church by a side door. Suddenly its ancient
vaulted roof resounded with a terrifying noise; Julien thought the
building was about to collapse. It was again the little cannon,
which had just arrived, drawn by eight galloping horses. The
veterans of Leipzig had prepared it for action immediately and
were now firing five rounds a minute, as though they were
facing the Prussians.

But this admirable uproar no longer had any effect on Julien;
he had ceased thinking of Napoleon and martial glory. "Bishop
of Agde at such an early age!" he thought. "But where is Agde?
And how much is that bishopric worth? Two or three hundred
thousand francs a year, perhaps."

The bishop's servants appeared with a magnificent canopy.
Father Chélan took one of the poles, but it was actually Julien
who bore the weight. The bishop took his place beneath it. He
had really succeeded in making himself look old; our hero's

admiration was boundless. "What can't a man do if he's clever enough!" he thought.

The king entered. Julien had the good fortune to see him at close range. The bishop addressed him with unction, and without forgetting to show a slight touch of nervousness that was flattering to His Majesty.

We shall not repeat the description of the ceremonies at Bray-le-Haut, which filled the columns of all the newspapers in the department for two weeks. Julien learned, from the bishop's address, that the king was a descendant of Charles the Bold.

It was later one of Julien's duties to check the accounts of the money the ceremony had cost. Monsieur de La Mole, having secured a bishopric for his nephew, had chosen to pay him the compliment of bearing all the expenses personally. The ceremony at Bray-le-Haut alone had cost three thousand eight hundred francs.

After the bishop's address and the king's reply, His Majesty took his place beneath the canopy and then knelt piously on a cushion near the altar. The chancel was surrounded by stalls raised two steps above the floor. It was on the second of these steps that Julien was seated at Father Chélan's feet, somewhat like a train-bearer at the feet of his cardinal in the Sistine Chapel in Rome. There were clouds of incense, a *Te Deum*, and endless volleys of musket and artillery fire; the peasants were intoxicated with joy and piety. Such a day undoes the work of a hundred issues of the Jacobin newspapers.

Julien was six paces away from the king, who prayed with genuine fervor. He noticed, for the first time, a small, intelligent-looking man wearing a coat with almost no embroidery on it. But over that extremely simple coat he wore a sky-blue ribbon. He was closer to the king than many other noblemen whose coats were so thickly covered with gold embroidery that, as Julien put it, you could not see the cloth. He learned a short time later that this was Monsieur de La Mole. He found that he had a haughty, even insolent air.

"This marquis can't be as polite as my handsome bishop," he thought. "Oh, how gentle and wise an ecclesiastical career makes a man! But the king came here to pay his respects to the relic, and I don't see it. Where can Saint Clement be?"

A young cleric sitting beside him informed him that the venerable relic was in a "blazing chapel"* in the upper part of the building.

*"*Chapelle ardente*": a mortuary chapel brightly illuminated with candles.—L.B.

"What's a blazing chapel?" wondered Julien. But he did not want to ask for an explanation of the expression. He concentrated his attention.

On the occasion of a visit from a reigning monarch, etiquette requires that the canons shall not accompany the bishop. But as he set out for the mortuary chapel, the Bishop of Agde summoned Father Chélan; Julien dared to follow him.

After climbing a long flight of stairs, they came to an extremely small door whose lavishly gilded Gothic frame looked as though it had been painted the day before.

In front of the door knelt twenty-four young ladies, all belonging to the most distinguished families of Verrières. Before opening the door, the bishop knelt among these girls, who were all pretty. As he prayed aloud, it seemed that they could not sufficiently admire his fine lace, his charm and his young, gentle face. This sight made our hero lose what was left of his reason. At that moment he would have fought for the Inquisition, and in earnest.

The door suddenly opened. The little chapel seemed to be ablaze with light. On the altar could be seen more than a thousand candles divided into eight rows separated by bouquets of flowers. The sweet odor of the purest incense floated in clouds from the door of the sanctuary. The newly gilded chapel was very small, but extremely high. Julien noticed that some of the candles on the altar were more than fifteen feet high. The young ladies could not restrain a cry of admiration. No one had been admitted into the little vestibule of the chapel except the twenty-four girls, the two priests and Julien.

Presently the king arrived, followed only by Monsieur de La Mole and his head chamberlain. Even the guards remained outside, on their knees, presenting their arms.

His Majesty abruptly dropped to his knees on the prayer stool. It was only then that Julien, pressed up against the gilded door and looking over the bare arm of one of the girls, saw the charming statue of Saint Clement. It was hidden beneath the altar, in the uniform of a young Roman soldier. There was a gaping wound in the neck from which blood seemed to flow. The artist had surpassed himself. The eyes, dying but full of grace, were half closed; a budding mustache adorned the charming mouth, which, slightly opened, still seemed to be praying. At this sight, the girl beside Julien burst into tears, and one of her tears fell on his hand.

After a moment of prayer in the most profound silence, broken only by the distant sound of bells from all the villages for ten leagues around, the Bishop of Agde asked the king for permission to speak. He concluded a deeply moving little address with words that were simple, but whose very simplicity made them all the more effective:

"Never forget, young Christians, that you have seen one of the great kings of the earth on his knees before the servants of our all-powerful and awesome God. These servants, weak, persecuted and martyred in this world, as you can see from the still bleeding wound of Saint Clement, triumph in heaven. I believe you will remember this day all your lives, young Christians. You will detest the ungodly. You will be forever faithful to our God, so great, so awesome, but so good."

As he spoke these words, the bishop stood up with authority. "Will you give me your promise?" he said, extending his arm with the air of a man who is inspired.

"We promise," said the girls, bursting into tears.

"I receive your promise in the name of our awesome God!" concluded the bishop in a thunderous voice. And the ceremony was over.

The king himself was weeping. It was not until much later that Julien was calm enough to ask where the bones of the saint, which had been sent from Rome to Philip the Good, Duke of Burgundy, were kept. He was told that they were concealed inside the charming wax figure.

His Majesty graciously permitted the young ladies who had accompanied him into the chapel to wear a red ribbon on which were embroidered the words, *"Hatred of the Ungodly, Everlasting Adoration."*

Monsieur de La Mole had ten thousand bottles of wine handed out to the peasants. That evening, in Verrières, the Liberals found a reason for illuminating their houses a hundred times more brightly than the Royalists. Before leaving, the king paid a visit to Monsieur de Moirod.

CHAPTER 19
To Think Is to Suffer

> The absurdity of everyday events conceals from you the real
> suffering caused by the passions.
>
> —Barnave

AS HE WAS moving the ordinary furniture back into the room
which Monsieur de La Mole had occupied, Julien found a sheet
of very heavy paper folded into four parts. At the bottom of the
first page he read: "To His Excellency the Marquis de La Mole,
Peer of France, Knight of the Royal Orders, etc."

It was a crudely written petition which looked as though it
might have come from the hand of a cook. It read as follows:

Monsieur le Marquis:

I have held religious principles all my life. I was under
bombardment in Lyon during the siege of '93, of execrable
memory. I take communion; I go to mass in the parish
church every Sunday. I have never failed in my Easter
duties, even in '93, of execrable memory. My cook—before
the Revolution I had a whole staff of servants—never serves
meat on Friday. In Verrières I enjoy general and, I venture
to say, merited respect. I walk beneath the canopy in
processions, beside the parish priest and the mayor. On
solemn occasions I carry a large candle purchased with my
own money. There is documentary proof of this in the
Ministry of Finance in Paris. I ask Monsieur le Marquis to
have me placed in charge of the Verrières lottery office.
The position cannot fail to be vacant soon in one way or
another, because the man who now holds it is seriously ill,
and furthermore he votes for the wrong party in the elections, etc., etc.

De Cholin

On the margin of this petition there was an endorsement
signed by Monsieur de Moirod, beginning with these words:
"Yesterday [*sic*] I had the honor of mentioning the upright man
who makes this request . . ."

"And so even that imbecile Cholin shows me the path I must
follow," thought Julien.

A week after the King of ———— had passed through Verrières, the main thing that emerged from the innumerable lies, stupid interpretations, ridiculous discussions, etc. etc., to which the king, the Bishop of Agde, the Marquis de La Mole, the ten thousand bottles of wine, the poor fallen Moirod (who, in the hope of receiving a decoration, did not leave his house until a month after his fall) were in turn subjected, was the extreme impropriety of having thrust Julien Sorel, a sawyer's son, into the guard of honor. On this subject, it was edifying to hear the rich calico manufacturers who, morning and night, talked themselves hoarse preaching equality in the café. That haughty woman, Madame de Rênal, was at the bottom of the outrage. Her reason? It was obvious from young Abbé Sorel's beautiful eyes and fresh complexion.

Shortly after returning to Vergy, Stanislas-Xavier, the youngest of the children, came down with a fever. Madame de Rênal was suddenly seized with terrible remorse. For the first time, she coherently blamed herself for falling in love; she seemed to realize, as though by a miracle, the enormity of the sin she had allowed herself to be drawn into. Although deeply religious by nature, until that moment she had given no thought to the seriousness of her crime in the eyes of God.

Long ago, in the Convent of the Sacred Heart, she had fervently loved God; her fear of Him was now equally intense. The struggles that rent her heart were all the more terrible because there was nothing rational in her fear. Julien found that any attempt to reason with her, far from calming her, only increased her consternation; she regarded such arguments as the language of the devil. However, since Julien was also very fond of little Stanislas, he evoked a warmer response when he spoke to her of his illness; it soon took a turn for the worse. Then her constant remorse even deprived her of the ability to sleep. She never broke her grim silence; if she had opened her mouth, it would have been to confess her crime to God and the world.

"I beg you," Julien said to her whenever they were alone, "not to say anything to anyone: confide all your sorrow to me. If you still love me, say nothing; your words can't cure our Stanislas of his fever."

But his attempts to console her had no effect; he did not know that she had taken it into her head that, in order to appease the wrath of a jealous God, she must either hate Julien or see her son die. It was because she realized she could not hate her lover that she was so unhappy.

"Go away from me," she said to him one day, "in the name of God, leave this house: it's your presence here that's killing my son. . . . God is punishing me," she added softly, "and He is just. I worship His justice: my crime is horrible, and I was living without remorse! That was the first sign that I was abandoning God; I deserve to be doubly punished."

Julien was deeply moved. He could see neither hypocrisy nor exaggeration in what she said. "She believes she's killing her son by loving me," he thought, "and yet the poor woman loves me more than her son. There lies the remorse that's killing her, I can't doubt it; there lies the nobility of her feeling. But how could I have inspired such love, I, so poor, so ill-bred, so ignorant, and sometimes so coarse in my manners?"

One night the child's condition became critical. Toward two o'clock in the morning Monsieur de Rênal came in to see him. The child, consumed with fever, was extremely flushed and did not recognize his father. Suddenly Madame de Rênal threw herself at her husband's feet. Julien saw that she was going to tell him everything and ruin her life forever.

By a stroke of good fortune, her strange behavior annoyed Monsieur de Rênal.

"Good night, good night," he said, walking away.

"No, listen to me!" cried his wife, on her knees before him, trying to hold him back. "I want you to know the whole truth. It's I who am killing my son. I gave him life and now I'm taking it away. Heaven is punishing me; in the eyes of God, I'm guilty of murder. I must ruin my life and humiliate myself; perhaps that sacrifice will appease the Lord."

If Monsieur de Rênal had been a man of imagination, he would have guessed everything.

"Romantic nonsense!" he exclaimed, pushing her away as she tried to embrace his knees. "That's all romantic nonsense! Julien, have the doctor brought in at dawn."

And he left to go back to bed. Madame de Rênal fell to her knees, half unconscious. She convulsively pushed Julien away from her when he tried to help her.

He stood still in amazement. "So this is adultery!" he said to himself. "Is it possible that those corrupt priests . . . are right? Can it be that they, who commit so many sins, have the privilege of knowing the true theory of sin? How odd!"

For twenty minutes after Monsieur de Rênal's departure, Julien looked at the woman he loved, her head resting on the child's little bed, motionless and almost unconscious. "Here's a woman of superior intelligence who's been reduced to the depths of despair because she met me,'' he said to himself. ''Time is passing swiftly. What can I do for her? I must make up my mind. I don't matter here any longer. What do I care about men and their stupid pretenses? What can I do for her? Leave her? But I'd be leaving her to suffer terrible anguish alone. That automaton of a husband does her more harm than good. He'll say something harsh to her, just because he's naturally crude, and she may go mad or jump out a window.

''If I leave her, if I stop watching over her, she'll confess everything to him. And who knows—perhaps, in spite of the fortune he hopes to inherit through her, he'll make a public scandal. Good God! She may even tell everything to that swine Father Maslon, who uses the illness of a six-year-old child as a pretext for never leaving this house, and not without a purpose. In her grief and her fear of God, she's forgotten what she knows about the man: she sees only the priest.''

''Go away,'' said Madame de Rênal suddenly, opening her eyes.

''I'd give my life a thousand times to know the best thing to do for you,'' replied Julien. ''I've never loved you the way I do now, my angel; or rather, it's only now that I've begun to adore you as you deserve to be adored. What will become of me apart from you, knowing you're unhappy because of me? But let's not talk about my suffering. Yes, I'll leave you, my love. But if I do, if I stop watching over you and constantly placing myself between you and your husband, you'll tell him everything and ruin your whole life. Think of the ignominy in which he'll drive you from the house. Everyone in Verrières, even everyone in Besançon, will be talking about the scandal. They'll put all the blame on you; you'll never escape from your shame. . . .''

''That's what I want!'' she cried out, standing up. ''I'll suffer—so much the better!''

''But you'll ruin his life, too, with that abominable scandal!''

''But I'll humiliate myself, I'll throw myself in the mud, and perhaps in that way I'll save my son. My humiliation in the eyes of everyone may be a kind of public penance. As far as my weak mind can judge, it must be the greatest sacrifice I can make to God. Perhaps He'll deign to accept my shame and leave me my son! Tell me a more painful sacrifice and I'll hurry to carry it out.''

''Let me punish myself,'' said Julien. ''I'm guilty too. Do you want me to shut myself up in a Trappist monastery? The austerity of such a life may appease your God. . . . Oh, if only I could take Stanislas' illness on myself!''

"Oh, you love him too!'' said Madame de Rênal, standing up again and throwing herself in his arms. She immediately pushed him away in horror. "I believe you! I believe you!'' she went on, falling to her knees again. "Oh, my only friend! Oh, why aren't you Stanislas' father? Then it wouldn't be a horrible sin to love you more than your son.''

"Will you let me stay and love you only as a brother from now on? It's the only reasonable expiation; it may appease the wrath of almighty God.''

"And what about me?'' she cried. She stood up, took his head between her hands and held him at a distance. "Could I love you as though you were my brother? Is it in my power to love you that way?''

Julien burst into tears. "I'll obey you,'' he said, falling at her feet. "I'll obey you, no matter what your orders are; it's the only thing left for me to do. My mind has been struck blind: I can't see any course of action to take. If I leave you, you'll tell your husband everything, you'll ruin your life and his too. After such a scandal he'll never become a member of the Chamber of Deputies. If I stay, you'll believe me to be the cause of your son's death and you'll die of sorrow. Would you like to test the effect of my absence? If you want me to, I'll punish myself for our sin by leaving you for a week. I'll spend it in seclusion, anywhere you say—in the abbey at Bray-le-Haut, for example. But give me your word you won't confess anything to your husband while I'm away. Remember that I can never come back if you speak.''

She gave him her promise and he left; but two days later she called him back.

"It's impossible for me to keep my promise without you,'' she said. "I'll speak to my husband if you're not constantly here to order me with your eyes to keep silent. Each hour of this abominable life seems to last a day.''

Heaven finally took pity on the wretched mother: Stanislas gradually passed out of danger. But the ice had been broken; her reason had become aware of the magnitude of her sin and she was unable to recover her equilibrium. Her remorse remained, with all the intensity it was bound to have in such a sincere heart. Her life was both heaven and hell: hell when Julien was out of her sight, heaven when he was at her feet.

"I'm no longer under any illusion,'' she said to him, even at

those times when she dared to abandon herself to her love.
damned, beyond all hope of redemption. You're young, you
yielded to my seduction—God may forgive you. But I'm damned.
I know it by an infallible sign. I'm frightened—who wouldn't be
frightened by the sight of hell?—but in the depths of my heart
I'm not repentant. I'd commit my sin again if I had it to do over.
If God will only refrain from punishing me in this world, and
through my children, I'll have more than I deserve.''

At other times she cried out, ''But you, my Julien, are you at
least happy? Do you feel that I love you enough?''

Julien's mistrust and suffering pride, which needed above all a
love that made sacrifices, could not hold out against the sight of
such a great and unmistakable sacrifice that was renewed at
every moment. He worshiped Madame de Rênal. ''It doesn't
matter that she's of noble birth and I'm a workman's son—she
loves me. . . . For her I'm not merely a servant performing the
duties of a lover.'' With this fear out of his mind, he fell into all
the wild delights and terrible uncertainties of love.

''At least let me make you very happy during the few days we
have left together!'' Madame de Rênal cried out whenever she
felt that he doubted her love. ''Let's hurry—tomorrow I may no
longer be yours. If God strikes me through my children, it will
be useless for me to try to live only to love you, to try not to see
that it's my crime that's killing them. I wouldn't survive that
blow. Even if I wanted to, I couldn't; I'd go mad. Oh, if only I
could take your sin on my conscience, as you so generously
wished you could take Stanislas' burning fever on yourself!''

This great moral crisis changed the nature of the feeling that
united Julien to his mistress. His love was no longer merely
admiration for her beauty and pride in possessing her.

From then on, their happiness was of a far higher nature; the
flame that consumed them became more intense. They had moments of rapture that were full of madness. Their happiness
would have seemed greater than ever in the eyes of the world,
but they no longer found the sweet serenity, the unclouded bliss
and the spontaneous joy of the early days of their love, when
Madame de Rênal's only fear was that Julien did not love her
enough. At times their happiness now bore the aspect of a crime.

In their happiest and apparently calmest moments, Madame de
Rênal would convulsively press Julien's hand and suddenly cry
out, ''Oh, dear God! I see hell before me! What horrible torments! I fully deserve them!'' She would then hug him, clinging
to him like ivy on a wall.

He tried in vain to calm her troubled soul. She would take his hand and cover it with kisses. Then, sinking back into somber meditation, she would say, "Hell would be a blessing to me: I'd still have a few days on earth to spend with you; but hell in this world, the death of my children . . . And yet, at that price, my sin might be forgiven. . . . Oh, dear God, don't grant my pardon at such a price! Those poor children haven't offended you; the guilt is mine, mine alone: I love a man who is not my husband."

Julien would then see her go through moments of apparent calm. She would try to control herself, for she did not want to poison the life of the man she loved.

In the midst of these alternations of love, remorse and pleasure, the days passed for them with the speed of lightning. Julien lost the habit of reflection.

Elisa went to Verrières to conduct a minor lawsuit. She found Monsieur Valenod extremely annoyed with Julien. She now hated the tutor and often spoke of him to Monsieur Valenod.

"You'd ruin me, monsieur, if I told you the truth," she said to him one day. "Employers all stick together on important things. . . . They never forgive us poor servants for telling certain secrets. . . ."

After these conventional phrases, which Monsieur Valenod's impatient curiosity managed to cut short, he learned things which could not have been more mortifying to his self-esteem.

That woman, the most distinguished lady in the district, on whom he had bestowed so many gallant attentions for six years and, unfortunately, in plain sight of everyone; that proud woman, whose disdain had made him blush so many times, had taken as her lover a little workman disguised as a tutor. And, so that nothing might be lacking in the resentment of the superintendent of the workhouse, Madame de Rênal worshiped her lover.

"And," added the maid with a sigh, "Monsieur Julien went to no trouble to make his conquest: he was always as cold as ever with Madame."

Elisa had not become certain of the facts until after the household had gone to the country, but she believed that the intrigue had begun much earlier.

"That must have been why he refused to marry me," she added bitterly. "And I, poor fool that I was, I talked it over with Madame de Rênal and asked her to speak to him for me!"

That very evening, Monsieur de Rênal received from town, along with his newspaper, a long anonymous letter which informed him in great detail of what was going on in his house.

Julien saw him turn pale as he read this letter, written on bluish paper, and glance at him with eyes full of malice. The mayor did not recover from his agitation for the rest of the evening; it was in vain that Julien tried to win his favor by asking him for explanations regarding the genealogies of the best families in Burgundy.

CHAPTER 20

Anonymous Letters

> Do not give dalliance
> Too much the rein; the strongest oaths are straw
> To the fire i' the blood.
> —*The Tempest*

As THEY WERE leaving the drawing room at midnight, Julien had time to say to his mistress, "Let's not see each other tonight, your husband is suspicious; I could swear that was an anonymous letter that he was reading with such loud sighs."

Fortunately, Julien locked himself in his room. Madame de Rênal conceived the mad idea that his warning was nothing but a pretext for not seeing her. She lost her head completely and came to his door at the usual hour. Julien, hearing a sound in the hall, instantly blew out his lamp. Someone tried to open his door; was it Madame de Rênal, or was it her jealous husband?

Early the next morning the cook, who was sympathetic to Julien, brought him a book on the cover of which he read these words in Italian: "*Guardate alla pagina 130.*"

He shuddered at the rashness of the action, turned to page one hundred thirty and found pinned to it the following letter, written in haste, bathed in tears and full of misspelled words. Madame de Rênal's spelling was usually very good; he was touched by this detail and began to forget her alarming imprudence.

Tonight you refused to open your door to me. There are times when I think I have never seen into the depths of your soul. I am frightened by the way you look at me. I am afraid of you. Dear God! Could it be that you have never loved me? In that case, let my husband discover our affair, let him lock me up for the rest of my life, in the country, away from my children! Perhaps that is God's will also. I shall die soon. But you will be a monster.

Don't you love me? Are you tired of my frenzies and my remorse, impious man? Do you want to ruin me? I am giving you an easy way to do so: go and show this letter to everyone in Verrières, or, rather, show it only to Monsieur Valenod. Tell him I love you; but no, do not utter such a blasphemy: tell him I worship you, that my life began only on the day I first saw you; that even in the wildest moments of my youth I never had the slightest idea of the happiness I owe to you; that I have sacrificed my life to you, that I am sacrificing my soul to you. And you know that I am sacrificing even more than that to you.

But what does that man know of sacrifice? Tell him, to irritate him, that I defy all slanders and that there is no longer any misfortune in the world for me except that of seeing a change in the only man who attaches me to my life. What a blessing it would be for me to lose it, to offer it as a sacrifice, and to fear no longer for my children!

You may be sure, my dear friend, that if there is an anonymous letter it came from that odious man who pursued me for six years with his loud voice, his stories of the jumps he had made on horseback, his conceit and the endless enumeration of all his admirable qualities.

Is there an anonymous letter? That, cruel man, is what I would like to discuss with you; but no, you were right. Holding you in my arms, perhaps for the last time, I could never have reasoned coldly, as I do when I am alone. From now on, our happiness will be more difficult to obtain. Will that upset you? Yes, on days when you have not received some interesting book from Monsieur Fouqué. The sacrifice is made: tomorrow, whether or not there really is an anonymous letter, I will tell my husband that I have also received an anonymous letter and that he must give you an honorable excuse, find some decent pretext, and send you back to your family without delay.

Alas, dear friend, we are going to be separated for two weeks, perhaps a month! But I do you justice: I know you will suffer as much as I. However, there is no other way to counteract the effect of that anonymous letter; it is not the first one my husband has received, and some of them were about me in the past. Alas, how I laughed at them in the past.

The whole purpose of my scheme is to make my husband believe that the letter came from Monsieur Valenod; I do not doubt that he is the author of it. If you leave the house, be sure to go and stay in Verrières. I will find a way to make my husband have the idea of spending two weeks there in order to prove to the fools in town that we are not on bad terms with each other. Once you are in Verrières, make friends with everyone, even the Liberals. I know that all the ladies will pursue you.

Do not quarrel with Monsieur Valenod, do not cut off his ears, as you threatened to do one day; on the contrary, be as friendly with him as you can. The most important thing is for everyone in Verrières to believe that Valenod, or someone else, is going to employ you as a tutor for his children.

My husband will never stand for that. But even if he should resign himself to it, at least you will be living in Verrières and I will see you occasionally. My children, who are so fond of you, will go to see you. Dear God! I feel that I love my children more because they love you. What remorse! How will it all end? . . . My mind is wandering. . . . Well, you understand what you must do: be gentle and polite with those crude people, and hide your contempt for them, I beg you on my knees; it is they who will decide our fate. Do not doubt for a moment that my husband will deal with you in whatever way "public opinion" dictates to him.

It is you who will provide me with the anonymous letter; arm yourself with patience and a pair of scissors. Take a book and cut out the words you will see below, then paste them on the sheet of light blue paper I am sending to you; it came to me from Monsieur Valenod. Be prepared for a search of your room: burn the pages of the book you have mutilated. If you do not find the words ready made, be patient enough to form them letter by letter. To spare you as much trouble as possible, I have made the anonymous letter too short. Alas, if you no longer love me, as I fear, how long mine must seem to you!

ANONYMOUS LETTER

Madame:

All your wily tricks are known, but those who have an interest in putting an end to them have been warned. Because I still have some feeling of friendship for you, I advise you to detach yourself completely from the little peasant. If you are wise enough to do this, your husband will believe that the warning he received was false, and he will be allowed to remain in his error. Remember that I know your secret and tremble, wretched woman. From now on you must tread the straight and narrow path. I will be watching you.

As soon as you have finished pasting the words which compose this letter (did you recognize Monsieur Valenod's style in it?), leave your room. I will come to meet you.

I will go into the village and come back with a troubled look on my face; and I actually will be greatly troubled. Oh, what a risk I am running, and all because you think you have guessed the existence of an anonymous letter! Then, with a dazed expression, I'll give my husband the letter that was supposedly handed to me by a stranger. As for you, go for a walk with the children along the road leading to the forest and do not come back until dinnertime.

From the top of the rocks you can see the tower of the dovecote. If all goes well, I will place a white handkerchief there; if not, you will see nothing.

Ingrate, will not your heart find a way to tell me you love me before you set off for that walk? No matter what happens, you may be sure of one thing: I would not live a single day longer if we were to part forever. Oh, what an unworthy mother I am! Those are vain words I have just written, dear Julien. I do not feel them; I can think of nothing but you now; I wrote them so that you would not condemn me. Now that I am about to lose you, what is the use of pretending? Yes! Let my soul seem horrible to you, but let me not lie to the man I adore! I have already been too deceitful in my life. I forgive you if you no longer love me. I do not have time to reread this letter. I regard my life as a small price to pay for the happy days I have spent in your arms. You know that they will cost me more than that.

CHAPTER 21

Conversation with a Master

Alas, our frailty is the cause, not we,
For such as we are made of, such we be.
                              —*Twelfth Night*

JULIEN SPENT an hour pasting words together with childish plea-sure. As he was leaving his room he met his pupils and their mother; she took the letter with a simplicity and courage whose calmness frightened him.

"Is the paste dry enough?" she asked him.

"Can this be the woman whose remorse was driving her mad?" he thought. "What are her plans now?" He was too proud to ask her; but never, perhaps, had she been more attractive to him.

"If things go wrong," she continued with the same com-posure, "everything will be taken away from me. Take this and bury it somewhere in the mountains; it may be my last resource some day." She handed him a red morocco case filled with gold and a few diamonds. "Go now."

She kissed the children, the youngest one twice. Julien stood motionless. She walked away from him rapidly, without looking at him.

From the moment he opened the anonymous letter, Monsieur de Rênal's life had been horrible. He had not been so upset since the time he had nearly been forced to fight a duel in 1816, and to do him justice, the prospect of receiving a bullet in his body had made him less unhappy than he was now. He examined the letter from every angle. "Isn't it a woman's handwriting?" he asked himself. "And if so, what woman wrote it?" He thought over every woman he knew in Verrières without being able to fix his suspicion on any one of them. "Could a man have dictated the letter? What man?" Here again, the same uncertainty. Most of the men he knew were jealous of him and no doubt hated him. "I'll have to talk it over with my wife," he said to himself, from force of habit, as he stood up from the armchair in which he had been sitting limply.

As soon as he was on his feet he clapped his hand to his forehead and exclaimed, "Good God! She's the one person I have to mistrust more than anyone else—she's my enemy now." And tears of rage welled up in his eyes.

As a just reward for that barrenness of heart which is the basis of all the practical wisdom of the provinces, the two men whom Monsieur de Rênal dreaded most at that moment were his two closest friends.

"After those two, I have perhaps ten friends," he told himself, and he thought of them one by one, estimating the degree of consolation he would be able to draw from each. "Every one of them!" he cried angrily. "Every one of them will be overjoyed at my terrible misfortune!" Happily for him, he believed himself to be greatly envied, and not without reason. Apart from owning a superb house in town, on which the King of ——— had just bestowed everlasting honor by sleeping in it, he had admirably renovated his country house at Vergy. The façade was painted white, and the windows were adorned with handsome green shutters. For a moment he was comforted by the thought of that splendor. As a matter of fact, his house was visible from a distance of three or four leagues, to the great detriment of all the other country houses, or châteaux, as their owners called them, in the vicinity, which had been left with the humble grayish color that time had given them.

Monsieur de Rênal could count on the tears and pity of one of his friends: the churchwarden of the parish. But he was an imbecile who wept over everything. This man was nevertheless his sole resource.

"What unhappiness can be compared to mine?" he cried out angrily. "Or what isolation?"

"Is it possible," the truly pitiable man asked himself, "that in my distress I don't have a single friend I can turn to for advice? I need advice, because I'm losing my reason, I can feel it! Oh, Falcoz! Oh, Ducros!" he cried out bitterly. These were the names of two childhood friends he had alienated by his arrogance in 1814. They were not of noble birth, and he had decided to change the terms of equality on which they had been living since their childhood.

One of them, Falcoz, a man of intelligence and feeling who was a paper merchant in Verrières, had bought a printing press in the capital of the department and founded a newspaper. The *Congrégation* had resolved to ruin him: his newspaper had been condemned and his printer's license revoked. In these unfortunate circumstances, he wrote to Monsieur de Rênal for the first time in ten years. The Mayor of Verrières saw fit to reply in the tone of an ancient Roman: "If the king's minister were to do me the honor of consulting me, I would say to him, 'Ruin all provincial printers without mercy and make printing a state monopoly, like the sale of tobacco.' "

Monsieur de Rênal was now filled with horror when he recalled the terms of this letter to a close friend, which had aroused general admiration in Verrières at the time it was written. "Who would have thought that, with my rank, my fortune and my decorations, I'd regret it one day?"

Shaken by such fits of anger, sometimes against himself and sometimes against everyone around him, he spent a terrible night; but fortunately it did not occur to him to spy on his wife.

"I'm used to Louise," he said to himself. "She knows all my affairs; if I were free to marry again tomorrow, I couldn't find anyone to take her place." He tried to console himself with the idea that his wife was innocent. This way of looking at the matter made it unnecessary for him to take a firm stand and suited him much better—so many wives were unjustly slandered!

"But what!" he cried out suddenly, nervously pacing up and down. "Shall I allow her to make a fool of me with her lover as though I were a nobody, a barefooted pauper? Must I let everyone in Verrières sneer at my complacency? Just think of everything they've said about Charmier!" (Charmier was a notorious local cuckold.) "Doesn't everyone smile whenever his name is mentioned? He's a good lawyer, but who ever talks about his eloquence? 'Oh, Charmier,' they say, 'Bernard's Charmier.' They refer to him by the name of the man who's dishonored him."

At other times Monsieur de Rênal said to himself, "Thank God I have no daughter; at least the way I'm going to punish my wife won't harm my children's careers. I may surprise the little peasant with her and kill them both. In that case, the tragic outcome of the situation may keep it from appearing ridiculous." This idea appealed to him; he thought it out in great detail. "The Penal Code is on my side, and, no matter what happens, our *Congrégation* and my friends on the jury will save me." He examined his hunting knife, which was very sharp; but the thought of blood terrified him.

"I might give the insolent tutor a good beating and throw him out of my house, but what a sensation that would cause in Verrières, and all over the department! After Falcoz' newspaper was condemned, when his editor was released from prison, I was influential in making him lose a position that paid six hundred francs a year. They tell me the wretched scribbler has dared to show his face again in Besançon; he could slander me skillfully, in such a way that it would be impossible for me to take him to court. Take him to court! . . . The insolent scoundrel would insinuate in a thousand ways that he'd told the truth. A man of noble birth who maintains his rank as I do is hated by all commoners. I may see my name in those horrible Paris newspapers. Oh, my God! What a disgrace to see the ancient name of Rênal dragged in the mud of ridicule! . . . If I ever travel, I'll have to change my name. . . . What! Give up the name that's the source of my pride and my strength? What a crowning disaster!

"If I don't kill my wife, if I drive her from my house in disgrace, she'll still have her aunt in Besançon, who will un-officially hand over her entire fortune to her. Then she'll go to live in Paris with Julien; people in Verrières will find out about it and I'll still be regarded as a dupe."

At this point the unhappy man noticed, from the pallor of his lamp, that day was about to break. He went out into the garden for a breath of fresh air. By now he had almost decided not to cause a scandal, especially since it would delight his good friends in Verrières.

His stroll in the garden calmed him a little. "No!" he exclaimed. "I won't deprive myself of my wife: she's too useful to me." He imagined with horror what his house would be like without her; his sole female relative was the Marquise de R——, who was old, stupid and malicious.

A very sensible idea occurred to him, but putting it into practice would have required far greater strength of character than the poor man possessed. "If I keep my wife," he said to himself, "I know myself: some day, when I'm annoyed with her, I'll reproach her for her crime. She's proud, so we'll have a quarrel, and it will all happen before she's received her inheritance from her aunt. How they'll all laugh at me then! My wife loves her children and everything will eventually go to them. But I'll be the talk of Verrières. 'What!' they'll say, 'he wasn't even able to take vengeance on his wife!' Wouldn't it be better for me to go no further than my suspicions and make no effort to become sure of anything? In that way I'd be tying my own hands and I wouldn't be able to reproach her for anything later."

The next moment, however, he was again dominated by his wounded vanity, and he laboriously tried to recall all the stratagems he had heard described in the billiard room of the Casino or the Noblemen's Club in Verrières when some glib talker interrupted the game to make merry at the expense of some cuckolded husband. How cruel those jests now seemed to him!

"Oh, God! Why isn't my wife dead? Then I'd be immune to

ridicule. If only I were a widower! I'd go to Paris and spend six months in the best social circles." After this momentary happiness at the thought of being a widower, his imagination returned to the means of making it a reality. Should he, at midnight, after everyone in the house had gone to bed, sprinkle a thin layer of bran in front of the door of Julien's room? The next morning, at dawn, he would be able to see footprints in it.

"But that's a worthless idea!" he suddenly cried angrily. "That wench Elisa would notice it, and soon everyone in the house would know I'm jealous."

In another story told at the Casino, a husband had made sure of his unfortunate plight by attaching a hair with a bit of wax in such a way that it sealed his wife's door and that of her lover.

After so many hours of indecision, this means of throwing light on his situation seemed definitely superior to him, and he was thinking about using it when, at a bend in the path, he encountered that wife whom he would have liked to see dead.

She was returning from the village, having gone to mass in the church of Vergy. A tradition, which was regarded as extremely dubious by cold and critical minds, but in which she believed, held that the little church now in use had originally been the chapel of the Lord of Vergy's castle. This idea obsessed her during the whole time she spent in the church with the intention of praying. She constantly imagined her husband killing Julien while hunting, as though by accident, and then making her eat his heart that evening.

"My fate," she said to herself, "depends on what he thinks when he hears me. After these fateful few minutes, I may never again have a chance to speak to him. He's not a wise man, guided by reason; if he were, I could use my own feeble reason to predict what he'd say or do. He'll decide our fate, he has the power to do it, so our fate depends on my cunning, on my ability to direct the thoughts of that temperamental man whose anger blinds him and prevents him from seeing half the things before his eyes. Dear God! I need ingenuity and self-control; where can I find them?"

She recovered her calm as though by magic when she entered the garden and saw her husband in the distance. The disorder of his hair and clothes showed that he had not slept. She handed him a letter that had been folded, but whose seal was broken. Without opening it, he stared at her with madness in his eyes.

"Here's an abominable letter," she said to him, "which a disagreeable-looking man, who claimed to know you and owe you a debt of gratitude, gave me as I was walking past the back of the lawyer's garden. I demand one thing of you: that you send Monsieur Julien back to his family, and without delay.'' She hastened to say this last sentence, a little prematurely, perhaps, in order to be rid of the horrible prospect of having to say it.

She was overjoyed when she saw how happy she had made her husband. From the way he stared at her she realized that Julien had guessed correctly. Instead of grieving over that very real misfortune, she said to herself, ''What intelligence! What keen perception! And in a young man who still has no experience of life! There's no limit to what he may accomplish some day. Alas, his success will make him forget me then.''

This little tribute of admiration to the man she adored completely restored her composure. She congratulated herself on her maneuver. ''I haven't been unworthy of Julien,'' she said to herself with sweet and intimate delight.

Without saying a word, for fear of committing himself, Monsieur de Rênal examined this second anonymous letter, composed, as the reader may recall, of printed words pasted onto a sheet of light blue paper. ''I'm being made to look foolish in every way,'' he thought, overwhelmed with weariness. ''More insults to look into, and still because of my wife!''

He was on the point of hurling coarse insults at her, but he restrained himself, with great difficulty, when he thought of the inheritance awaiting her in Besançon. Devoured by the need to vent his anger on something, he crumpled the second anonymous letter and swiftly strode away; he needed to remove himself from his wife's presence. A few moments later he came back to her, feeling calmer.

''We must take action and dismiss Julien,'' she said to him immediately. ''After all, he's nothing but a workman's son. You can compensate him with a few francs, and besides, he's so learned that he'll easily find another place for himself, in Monsieur Valenod's house, for example, or Monsieur de Maugiron's—they both have children. So you won't be doing him any harm. . . .''

''You're talking like the fool you are!'' cried Monsieur de Rênal in a thunderous voice. ''How can anyone expect to hear common sense from a woman? You pay no attention to serious things, so how could you know anything? Your apathy and laziness leave you just enough energy to chase butterflies! You're nothing but poor, weak creatures, and it's unlucky for us that we have you in our families. . . .''

Madame de Rênal let him speak, and he spoke for a long time; he was "working off his anger," to use a local expression.

"Monsieur," she finally replied to him, " I speak as a woman whose honor, her most precious possession, has been outraged."

Her self-possession remained unshaken throughout that trying conversation, on which the possibility of continuing to live under the same roof with Julien depended. She tried to find the ideas she believed to be best suited to guide her husband's blind rage. She had been insensitive to all the insulting remarks he had addressed to her; she did not even listen to them: she was thinking of Julien. "Will he be pleased with me?" she wondered.

"That little peasant," she said at length, "whom we've showered with kindness and even presents, may be innocent, but he's still the cause of the first affront I've ever received in my life. . . . Monsieur, when I read that abominable letter I promised myself that either he or I would leave your house!"

"Do you want to stir up a scandal that would dishonor both of us? You'd be making many people in Verrières jump for joy."

"It's true that everyone envies the prosperity you've brought to yourself, your family and the whole town through your wise management. . . . Well, I'll tell Julien to ask you for a leave of absence so that he can go and spend a month with that timber merchant in the mountains—a fit companion for the little workman."

"Don't do anything," replied Monsieur de Rênal rather calmly. "I demand above all that you refrain from speaking to him. You'd show your anger and turn him against me; you know how touchy the little gentleman is."

"He has no tact," said Madame de Rênal. "He may be learned, you know more about that than I do, but at heart he's nothing but a peasant. As for me, I've never thought much of him since he refused to marry Elisa. It would have given him an assured income, but he refused on the pretext that she sometimes paid secret visits to Monsieur Valenod."

"Ah!" said Monsieur de Rênal, raising his eyebrows in an exaggerated manner. "What? Did Julien tell you that?"

"No, not exactly; he always spoke to me about his vocation for the priesthood; but believe me, the first vocation of people of his class is to make sure they have enough bread for themselves. He gave me to understand clearly enough that he wasn't unaware of those secret visits."

"And I knew nothing about them!" cried Monsieur de Rênal, recovering all his fury and emphasizing each word. "Things are going on in my own house that I know nothing about. . . . What! There was something between Elisa and Valenod?''

"Oh, it's an old story, my friend," said Madame de Rênal, laughing. "There may not have been anything sinful about it, though. It was in the days when your good friend Valenod wouldn't have been at all sorry to have people in Verrières think that there was a little platonic love affair between him and me."

"That occurred to me once!" cried Monsieur de Rênal, striking his forehead furiously as he went from one discovery to another. "Why didn't you say something to me about it?"

"Should I have turned two friends against each other because of a little outburst of vanity on the part of our dear superintendent of the workhouse? Is there one woman in our circle of friends to whom he hasn't written a few witty and even slightly amorous letters?"

"Has he written to you?"

"He writes a great deal."

"I order you to show me those letters immediately!" And Monsieur de Rênal added six feet to his height.

"I'll do nothing of the sort," she replied with a gentleness that bordered on indifference. "I'll show them to you some day, when you're feeling a little calmer."

"You'll show them to me right now, by God!" shouted Monsieur de Rênal, beside himself with rage, yet happier than he had been at any other time during the past twelve hours.

"Will you swear to me," said Madame de Rênal very gravely, "that you will never quarrel with him over those letters?"

"Quarrel or no quarrel, I can take the foundling home away from him! But," he went on furiously, "I want to see those letters this instant! Where are they?"

"In one of the drawers of my writing desk; but I certainly won't give you the key."

"I can break it open," he cried, running toward her room.

True to his word, he took an iron bar and broke open a valuable figured mahogany writing desk which had come from Paris and which he had often polished with his coattail when he thought he detected a spot on it.

Meanwhile Madame de Rênal had run up the hundred and twenty steps of the dovecote and fastened the corner of a white handkerchief to one of the iron bars of the little window. She was the happiest of women. With tears in her eyes, she looked out toward the wooded slopes of the mountain. "Julien is probably watching for this happy signal under one of those spreading beeches,'' she thought. She strained her ears for a long time, then cursed the monotonous chirping of the cicadas and the singing of the birds. If it had not been for those annoying sounds, she might have heard a shout of joy coming from the mountain. Her avid eyes devoured the immense slope of dark verdure, unbroken as the surface of a meadow, formed by the treetops. ''Why isn't he clever enough,'' she asked herself with deep emotion, ''to invent some sort of signal to let me know his happiness is as great as mine?'' She did not come down from the dovecote until she began to fear that her husband might go there in search of her.

She found him furious. He was reading over Monsieur Valenod's insipid letters, which were not accustomed to being read with so much emotion.

Seizing a moment when a lull in his exclamations gave her a chance to make herself heard, she said, ''I still think my idea is good: Julien ought to go away for a while. No matter how well he knows Latin, he's still nothing but a peasant who's often coarse and tactless; every day, thinking he's being polite, he pays me exaggerated compliments in bad taste, which he learns by heart from some novel. . . .''

''He never reads novels,'' said Monsieur de Rênal, ''I made sure of that. Do you think I'm a blind master who doesn't know what goes on in his own house?''

''Well then, if he doesn't read those ridiculous compliments anywhere he invents them, which is worse. He's probably spoken about me in the same tone in Verrières. . . . And, without going so far,'' continued Madame de Rênal, pretending to make a discovery, ''he must have spoken that way in front of Elisa, which is almost the same thing as speaking in front of Monsieur Valenod!''

''Aha!'' cried Monsieur de Rênal, making the table and the whole room shake with one of the most violent blows ever struck by a human fist. ''The printed anonymous letter is on the same kind of paper as Valenod's letters!''

''At last!'' thought Madame de Rênal. She pretended to be thunderstruck by this discovery and, lacking the courage to add a single word, she walked to the other end of the room and sat down on the sofa there.

The battle was now won. She had great difficulty in preventing her husband from going off to speak to the supposed author of the anonymous letter.

''Why can't you understand that it would be a terrible mistake to make a scene with Monsieur Valenod without sufficient proof?'' she asked. "You're envied, monsieur, and who's to blame? Your own ability. You've become the most distinguished man in Verrières through your wise administration, the buildings you've erected in such good taste, the dowry I brought you, and especially the considerable fortune we can expect to inherit from my good aunt, a fortune whose size is greatly exaggerated.''

"You're overlooking my noble birth," said Monsieur de Rênal with a faint smile.

"You're one of the most distinguished gentlemen in the province," Madame de Rênal quickly continued. "If the king were free and could do justice to birth, you'd no doubt have a place in the Chamber of Peers," etc., etc. "And when you're in such a magnificent position, do you want to give those who envy you something to gossip about? To speak to Monsieur Valenod about his anonymous letter would be to proclaim all over Verrières— and even in Besançon, throughout the whole province!—that an ordinary commoner, admitted, perhaps imprudently, to the friendship *of a Rênal,* has found a way to offend you. If these letters you've just discovered proved that I returned Monsieur Valenod's love, then you ought to kill me—I'd have deserved it a hundred times over—but you still shouldn't show any anger toward him. Remember that all your neighbors are waiting only for a pretext to take vengeance on you for your superiority; remember that in 1816 you helped to bring about certain arrests. That man who took refuge on his roof . . .''

"I remember that you have neither consideration nor friendship for me!" cried Monsieur de Rênal with all the bitterness awakened in him by such a memory. "And I haven't been made a peer!''

"I think, my friend," said Madame de Rênal with a smile, "that I'll be richer than you some day, that I've been your companion for twelve years, and that for these reasons I ought to be allowed to have some voice in your affairs, especially the one we're discussing now. If you prefer Monsieur Julien to me," she added with a show of ill-concealed rancor, "I'm prepared to go and spend the winter with my aunt.''

These words were well chosen; they expressed a firmness which apparently sought to cloak itself in courtesy. They caused Monsieur de Rênal to make up his mind, although, in accordance with provincial custom, he continued to speak for a long time and went over all the arguments again. His wife let him speak; there was still some anger in his tone. Finally two hours of useless verbiage exhausted the strength of a man who had just spent an entire night in a fit of rage. He decided on the course of action he was going to follow with regard to Monsieur Valenod, Julien and even Elisa.

Once or twice during that all-important scene, Madame de Rênal was on the verge of feeling a certain sympathy for the very real unhappiness of the man who had been her friend for twelve years. But true passions are selfish. Furthermore, she was expecting at any moment an avowal of the anonymous letter he had received the night before, but that avowal never came. In order to be completely sure of her ground, she needed to know what ideas had been suggested to the man on whom her fate depended, for, in the provinces, husbands control public opinion. A husband who denounces his wife covers himself with ridicule, which is becoming less and less dangerous in France, but his wife, if he does not give her any money, sinks to the position of a working woman earning fifteen sous a day, and even then virtuous people have misgivings about employing her.

A concubine in a harem may love the sultan in spite of everything; he is all-powerful and she has no hope of robbing him of his authority by a series of wily maneuvers. The master's vengeance is terrible and bloody, but martial and noble: a dagger thrust ends everything. In the nineteenth century, a husband kills his wife with public contempt, by shutting the doors of all drawing rooms in her face.

The sense of danger was keenly aroused in Madame de Rênal when she returned to her room; she was shocked by the disorder in which she found it. The locks of all her pretty little chests had been broken and several floorboards had been pried up. "He would have treated me without pity!" she said to herself. "Just look at the way he's torn up this colored wood floor he loves so much! He turns purple with rage whenever one of the children walks on it with wet shoes. Now it's ruined forever!" The sight of such violence quickly silenced the reproaches she had been addressing to herself over her too rapid victory.

Julien came back with the children a short time before the dinner bell rang. At dessert, after the servants had withdrawn, Madame de Rênal said to him very coldly, "You have expressed a desire to go and spend two weeks in Verrières; Monsieur de Rênal is willing to give you a leave of absence. You may leave whenever you like, but, so that the children won't be wasting their time, their lessons will be sent to you every day and you will correct them."

"I certainly won't allow you more than a week," added Monsieur de Rênal curtly.

Julien read in his features the uneasiness of a man who is deeply tormented.

"He hasn't come to a decision yet," he said to his mistress when they were alone for a moment in the drawing room.

She hurriedly told him everything she had done since that morning. "I'll give you the details tonight," she added, laughing.

"A woman's perversity!" thought Julien. "What pleasure, what instinct leads them to deceive us?"

"You seem both enlightened and blinded by our love," he said to her with a certain coolness. "Your conduct today has been admirable, but do you think it would be wise for us to try to see each other tonight? This house is full of enemies; remember Elisa's passionate hatred of me."

"That hatred is very much like the passionate indifference you must feel for me."

"Indifferent or not, I must save you from the danger I've exposed you to. If Monsieur de Rênal should happen to speak to Elisa, one word from her might tell him everything. What's to prevent him from hiding outside my room, well armed . . ."

"What! You don't even have courage?" said Madame de Rênal with the haughtiness of a woman of noble birth.

"I will never lower myself to discussing my courage," replied Julien coldly. "That's ignoble. Let the world judge by my actions. But," he added, taking her hand, "you can't imagine how devoted I am to you, and how glad I am to be able to tell you good-bye before our cruel separation."

CHAPTER 22
Manners and Customs in 1830

> Man was given the power of speech to enable him to conceal his thoughts.
>
> —Father Malagrida

AS SOON as he arrived in Verrières, Julien began to reproach himself for his unfairness to Madame de Rênal. "I'd have despised her as an empty-headed woman," he thought, "if, out of weakness, she'd failed in her scene with Monsieur de Rênal! She carried it off like a diplomat, and yet I sympathize with the loser, who's my enemy! There's a certain middle-class pettiness in my attitude; my vanity is offended because Monsieur de Rênal is a man, a member of the vast and illustrious guild to which I have the honor of belonging. I'm a fool."

Father Chélan had refused the lodgings which the most distinguished Liberals of the district had vied with one another in offering him when his dismissal drove him from the presbytery. The two rooms he had rented were littered with his books. Julien, wishing to show the people of Verrières what a priest ought to be like, went to his father's sawmill, selected a dozen fir planks and carried them on his back the whole length of the main street. He borrowed some tools from an old friend and quickly made a kind of bookcase in which he arranged Father Chélan's books.

"I thought you'd been corrupted by the vanities of this world," the old man said to him, weeping with joy, "but this more than makes up for your childishness in wearing that glittering honor guard uniform which made you so many enemies."

Monsieur de Rênal had ordered Julien to live in his house in Verrières. No one suspected what had happened. On the third day after his arrival, Julien saw no less a personage than the sub-prefect, Monsieur de Maugiron, come into his room. It was only after two hours of insipid chatter and great lamentations over the maliciousness of men, the lack of honesty among those entrusted with the administration of public funds, the dangers threatening poor France, etc., etc., that Julien at last began to get some inkling of the reason for his visit. They were already outside on the landing and the poor tutor, on the verge of dismissal, was ushering out with all due respect the future prefect of some fortunate province when it pleased the latter to show concern for Julien's career, to praise his moderation in financial matters, etc., etc. Finally Monsieur de Maugiron put his arm around him in the most paternal manner and asked him if he would like to leave Monsieur de Rênal and enter the household of a government official who had children to educate and who, like King Philip, would thank heaven, not so much for having given them to him as for having caused them to be born in the vicinity of Monsieur Julien. Their tutor would receive a salary of eight hundred francs a year, payable not month by month, "which isn't noble," he said, "but quarterly, and always in advance."

It was now Julien's turn to speak, after an hour and a half of waiting for a chance to do so. His reply was perfect, and as long-winded as a pastoral letter; it suggested everything and stated nothing. It expressed respect for Monsieur de Rênal, veneration for the population of Verrières and gratitude to the illustrious sub-prefect. This sub-prefect, astonished at finding a more skillful Jesuit than himself, tried in vain to obtain some definite answer from him. Julien, delighted, took the opportunity to practice and began his answer all over again in different terms. No eloquent minister, seeking to monopolize the end of a session, when the members of the Chamber seem inclined to wake up, ever said less in more words. As soon as Monsieur de Maugiron was gone, Julien began to laugh like a madman. Taking advantage of his Jesuitical mood, he wrote Monsieur de Rênal a nine-page letter reporting everything that had been said to him and humbly asking for advice. "The scoundrel never even told me the name of the man who's making the offer!" he thought. "It's no doubt Monsieur Valenod, who sees my exile to Verrières as the result of his anonymous letter."

When he had dispatched his letter, Julien, as happy as a hunter walking out onto a plain teeming with game at six o'clock in the morning on a beautiful autumn day, went to seek Father Chélan's advice. But before he reached the good priest's house, Providence, wishing to shower him with blessings, brought him face to face with Monsieur Valenod, from whom he did not conceal the fact that he was torn by indecision; a poor young man like himself ought to devote himself entirely to the vocation which heaven had placed in his heart, but a vocation was not everything in this base world. In order to be a worthy laborer in the Lord's vineyard and not be completely unworthy of so many learned fellow laborers, it was necessary to have an education, to spend two very expensive years in the seminary in Besançon. It was therefore indispensable, one could even say that in a sense it was a duty, to save money, which was much easier with a salary of eight hundred francs, paid quarterly, than with six hundred francs which one spent month by month. On the other hand, did not heaven, in placing him with the Rênal children, and especially in inspiring him with a special affection for them, seem to be indicating to him that it would not be advisable to abandon their education for someone else's?

Julien attained such a degree of perfection in this kind of eloquence, which has replaced the swiftness of action of the Empire, that he finally became bored with the sound of his own voice.

When he came home he found one of Monsieur Valenod's

servants, in full livery, who had been looking for him all over
town to give him a note inviting him to dinner that same day.

Julien had never been in Monsieur Valenod's house, and only
a few days before he had been trying to think of a way to beat
him thoroughly with a stick without becoming involved with the
police. Although dinner was not to begin until one o'clock,
Julien judged it more respectful to present himself to the superintendent of the workhouse in his study at half-past twelve. He
found him displaying his importance in the midst of a large
number of cardboard folders.

Julien was not impressed by his bushy side whiskers, his
enormous quantity of hair, his Greek cap placed askew on the
top of his head, his embroidered slippers, the heavy gold chains
crossing his chest in all directions, and all the other trappings of
a provincial financier who regards himself as a ladies' man; they
only made him think more seriously of the beating he owed him.

He requested the honor of being introduced to Madame Valenod;
she was in her dressing room and could not receive visitors for
the moment. As a compensation, he was given the privilege of
watching the superintendent of the workhouse groom himself.
They then went to Madame Valenod's room, where she introduced her children to him with tears in her eyes.

Madame Valenod, one of the most important ladies in Verrières,
had a big mannish face to which she had applied rouge for this
great ceremony, in which she displayed all the pathos of maternal love.

Julien thought of Madame de Rênal. His mistrust made him
susceptible almost exclusively to those memories which are called
forth by contrast, but they moved him deeply. This tendency was
strengthened by the appearance of Monsieur Valenod's house.
He was shown through it. Everything in it was magnificent and
new, and he was told the price of each piece of furniture. But he
felt that there was something ignoble about it, something that
smelled of stolen money. Everyone in it, including the servants,
seemed to be composing his expression to ward off contempt.

The tax collector, the excise officer, the chief of the local
gendarmery and two or three other public officials arrived with
their wives. They were followed by a few rich Liberals. Dinner
was announced. It occurred to Julien, who was already in a very
bad humor, that on the other side of the dining room wall there
were poor prisoners whose ration of meat had perhaps been
"chiseled" to pay for the tasteless luxury with which his hosts
expected to dazzle him.

"They may be hungry right now," he said to himself; his throat contracted and he found it impossible to eat and difficult to speak. It was much worse a quarter of an hour later, when they began to hear, at long intervals, a few snatches of a popular and, it must be admitted, slightly indecent song being sung by one of the inmates. Monsieur Valenod glanced at one of his servants in full livery; he left the room and the singing soon stopped. At that moment a servant offered Julien some Rhine wine in a green glass, and Madame Valenod was careful to point out to him that the wine cost nine francs a bottle, direct from the vineyard. Julien, holding his green glass, said to Monsieur Valenod, "I don't hear that horrible song any more."

"Of course not!" replied the superintendent triumphantly. "I had the rascal silenced."

This was too much for Julien; he had the manner, but not yet the heart he needed for his ecclesiastical career. Despite all his hypocrisy, which he had so often practiced, he felt a large tear run down his cheek. He tried to hide it with the green glass, but it was absolutely impossible for him to do honor to the Rhine wine. *"He stopped him from singing!"* he said to himself. "And you allow it, O God!"

Fortunately, no one noticed his ill-bred emotion. The tax collector had struck up a Royalist song. During the uproar of the refrain, sung in chorus, Julien's conscience said to him, "This is the sordid kind of wealth you'll acquire, and you'll enjoy it only in these conditions and in company such as this! You'll have a position worth perhaps twenty thousand francs a year, but, while you gorge yourself with meat, you'll have to stop the poor prisoner from singing; you'll serve your guests food bought with money you've stolen from his miserable rations, and during your dinner he'll be more wretched than ever! O Napoleon! How sweet it was in your time to climb to fortune through the dangers of battle! But to increase so ignobly the suffering of the unfortunate . . ."

I confess that the weakness Julien displayed in this soliloquy gives me a poor opinion of him. He would have been a worthy colleague of those conspirators in yellow gloves who aspire to change the entire way of life of a great country, but do not wish to have the slightest scratch on their conscience.

Julien was sharply recalled to his role. It was not to daydream and say nothing that he had been invited to dinner in such good company.

A retired textile manufacturer, a corresponding member of the Academies of Besançon and Uzès, addressed him from the other end of the table to ask him if what everyone said about his astonishing progress in the study of the New Testament was true.

Deep silence suddenly fell over the room and a New Testament in Latin appeared as though by magic in the hands of the learned member of two academies. In accordance with Julien's instructions, half a sentence was read to him at random. He recited; his memory did not fail him and the wondrous feat was admired with all the noisy exuberance of people who have just finished their dinner. He looked at the glowing faces of the ladies; several of them were not unattractive. He had already singled out the wife of the tax collector who sang so well.

"I'm really ashamed of speaking Latin for so long in front of these ladies," he said, looking at her. "If Monsieur Rubigneau" (this was the member of the two academies) "will be kind enough to read a Latin sentence at random, instead of going on with the Latin text, I'll try to improvise a translation."

This second test brought his glory to new heights.

There were in the room several rich men who had once been Liberals, but who were the happy fathers of children eligible for scholarships and had therefore suddenly become converted since the last mission. Despite this shrewd maneuver, Monsieur de Rênal had not been willing to receive them in his house. These worthy people, who knew Julien only by reputation and from having seen him on horseback the day the King of ———— came to Verrières, were his most vociferous admirers. "When will these fools tire of listening to this Biblical language, which means nothing to them?" he thought. On the contrary, however, that style amused them by its strangeness; they laughed at it. But Julien himself had grown tired.

He stood up gravely as the clock struck six and spoke of a chapter of Ligorio's new theology, which he had to study in order to be able to recite his lesson to Father Chélan the next day. "Because my business," he added pleasantly, "is to make others recite lessons and also recite them myself."

Everyone laughed heartily and admired him; this is the kind of wit that is appreciated in Verrières. He was already on his feet, and the others all stood up also, in defiance of etiquette; such is the power of genius. Madame Valenod retained him for another quarter of an hour: he simply had to hear the children recite their catechism. They made the most amusing mistakes, which he alone noticed; he made no attempt to correct them. "What

ignorance of the first principles of religion!'' he thought. At
length he bowed, thinking he was about to make his escape, but
he still had to listen to one of La Fontaine's fables.

''That author is quite immoral,'' he said to Madame Valenod.
''In one of his fables about Monsieur Jean Chouart he dared to
ridicule everything that's most respectable. The best commenta-
tors strongly disapprove of him.''

Julien received four or five invitations to dinner before leaving
the house. ''That young man is an honor to the district!'' cried
all the guests at once; they were in a very lively mood. They
went so far as to speak of a living allowance voted out of
municipal funds, to enable him to continue his studies in Paris.

While this rash proposal was echoing in the dining room,
Julien adroitly made his way to the front door. ''Oh, what swine!
What swine!'' he exclaimed three or four times in a low voice as
he enjoyed the pleasure of breathing in the fresh air.

He felt himself a thorough aristocrat at that moment, he who
had been offended for so long by the disdainful smile and
haughty sense of superiority he found lurking behind all the
politeness with which he was treated in Monsieur de Rênal's
house. He could not help feeling the extreme difference. ''Let's
even overlook the fact that his money was stolen from the poor
prisoners,'' he said to himself as he walked away, ''and that he
stops them from singing besides; would it ever occur to Monsieur de Rênal to tell his guests the price of each bottle of wine
he serves them? And when Monsieur Valenod enumerates his
possessions, which he does constantly, if his wife is present he
can't speak of his house, his land, and so on, without saying
your house, *your* land.''

During dinner this lady, apparently so sensitive to the joys of
ownership, had made an abominable scene with a servant who
had broken a wine glass and ''spoiled one of her sets''; and the
servant had answered her with the most outrageous insolence.

''What a household!'' exclaimed Julien. ''I wouldn't live with
them if they gave me half the money they steal. Sooner or later
I'd betray myself: I wouldn't be able to hide my contempt for
them.''

It was nevertheless necessary for him, in accordance with
Madame de Rênal's orders, to attend several dinners of the same
kind. He now stood in high favor; he was forgiven for his guard
of honor uniform, or, rather, that imprudence was the true cause
of his success. Soon everyone in Verrières was discussing the
question of who would be victorious in the struggle for the

learned young man's services, Monsieur de Rênal or the superintendent of the workhouse. These two gentlemen and Father Maslon formed a triumvirate which had been tyrannizing the town for a number of years. People were jealous of the mayor, and the Liberals had reason to complain of him, but, after all, he was a nobleman and therefore born for superiority, whereas Monsieur Valenod's father had left him an income of less than six hundred francs. The people of the town had been obliged to pass from pity for the shabby apple-green coat they had all seen him wear in his youth to envy of his Norman horses, his gold chains, the clothes he ordered from Paris—in short, all his present prosperity.

In the swirl of that society which was so new to Julien, he believed he had discovered one honorable man: a geometrician named Gros who was said to be a Jacobin. Julien, who had sworn never to say anything except what he himself believed to be false, was forced to content himself with suspicions with regard to Monsieur Gros. He received from Vergy large packets of lessons to be corrected. He was advised to see his father often, and he fulfilled that disagreeable obligation. In short, he was redeeming his reputation rather well when he was surprised one morning to feel himself awakened by two hands placed over his eyes.

It was Madame de Rênal, who had just come into town. Running up the stairs four at a time while leaving her children occupied with a pet rabbit they had brought with them, she had reached his room a short time before them. It was a sweet moment, but it was very short: Madame de Rênal disappeared when her children arrived with the rabbit, which they wanted to show to their friend. Julien gave a warm welcome to all of them, even the rabbit. It seemed to him that he had rejoined his family; he was aware that he loved those children, that he liked to chatter with them. He was surprised by the sweetness of their voices and the nobility of their manners; he needed to clear his mind of all the vulgar behavior and disagreeable thoughts amid which he had been living in Verrières. There was always the fear of want, always the struggle between luxury and poverty. In speaking of the roast on the table, the people in whose homes he dined revealed things that humiliated them and sickened their listeners.

"You aristocrats are right to be proud," he said to Madame de Rênal. And he told her about all the dinners he had endured.

"Why, you're the man of the hour!" she said. She laughed

heartily when she thought of the rouge which Madame Valenod felt obliged to put on her cheeks whenever she was expecting Julien. "I think she has designs on your heart," she added.

They had a delightful lunch together. The presence of the children, although apparently a hindrance, actually increased the common happiness. Those poor children did not know how to express their joy at seeing Julien again. The servants had not failed to tell them that he had been offered two hundred francs more to educate the little Valenods.

In the middle of lunch, Stanislas-Xavier, still pale from his grave illness, suddenly asked his mother the value of his silverware and the mug from which he was drinking.

"Why do you want to know?"

"I want to sell them and give the money to Monsieur Julien, so he won't be a dupe for staying with us."

Julien embraced him with tears in his eyes. Madame de Rênal wept outright while Julien, who had taken Stanislas on his lap, explained to him that he ought not to use the word "dupe" in that sense because, so employed, it was a servant's expression. Seeing the pleasure he was giving Madame de Rênal, he tried to explain, using picturesque examples which amused the children, what it meant to be a dupe.

"I understand," said Stanislas, "it's the crow who's foolish and drops his cheese, and it's picked up by the fox, who's a flatterer."

Madame de Rênal, in a transport of joy, covered her children with kisses, which she could hardly do without leaning slightly on Julien.

Suddenly the door opened; it was Monsieur de Rênal. His stern, dissatisfied countenance formed a strange contrast with the sweet joy driven away by his presence. Madame de Rênal turned pale; she felt herself incapable of denying anything. Julien loudly told the mayor the story of the silver mug which Stanislas had wanted to sell. He was sure the story would be badly received. First of all, he knew that Monsieur de Rênal frowned from force of habit at the mere mention of money. "The use of that word," he often said, "is always a preface to some demand on my purse."

But here there was more than money involved: his suspicions had been intensified. The air of happiness which animated his family in his absence was not designed to improve matters with a man dominated by such a sensitive vanity. When his wife praised the graceful and witty manner in which Julien explained new ideas to his pupils, he said, "Yes, yet I know he turns my children against me! It's very easy for him to be a hundred times more pleasant with them than I am, because, after all, I'm the master. Everything these days tends to make *lawful* authority odious. Poor France!"

Madame de Rênal did not take time to examine the shades of meaning in the way her husband had greeted her. She had just glimpsed a possibility of spending twelve hours with Julien. She had a great many purchases to make in town and she declared that she insisted on dining in a tavern; in spite of everything her husband said and did, she clung to her idea. The children were enraptured at the very mention of the word "tavern," which modern prudery takes such delight in pronouncing.

Monsieur de Rênal left his wife in the first draper's shop she entered and went off to pay a few calls. He came back more morose than ever; he was convinced that everyone in town was discussing him and Julien. Actually, no one had yet said anything to him that would give him reason to suspect the offensive aspects of the public's comments; those which had been repeated to him concerned only the question of whether Julien would remain with him at six hundred francs or accept the eight hundred francs offered by the superintendent of the workhouse.

Monsieur Valenod had encountered Monsieur de Rênal at a social gathering and given him the cold shoulder. His conduct was not without a certain adroitness. There are few thoughtless actions in the provinces: feelings are so rare there that they are plowed under.

Monsieur Valenod was what is called, a hundred leagues from Paris, a *faraud*: a species marked by a coarse, brazen character. His triumphant career, since 1815, had accentuated his admirable tendencies. He reigned, so to speak, in Verrières, under the orders of Monsieur de Rênal; but he was much more active and, blushing at nothing, putting his nose into everything, constantly visiting, writing and speaking; forgetting humiliations and lacking all personal pretensions, he had succeeded in counterbalancing the mayor's influence with the ecclesiastical authorities. Monsieur Valenod had in effect said to the grocers of the district, "Give me the two biggest fools among you"; to the lawyers, "Point out the two most ignorant"; to the unlicensed physicians, "Show me your two biggest charlatans." And when he had assembled the most brazen and shameless members of each profession, he had said to them, "Let us reign together."

The manners of these men were offensive to Monsieur de

Rênal. Valenod's coarse nature was offended by nothing, not even when young Father Maslon as much as called him a liar in public, which he did rather frequently.

But, in the midst of his prosperity, Monsieur Valenod needed to fortify himself, by insolent little actions concerning points of detail, against the harsh truths of which he was well aware that everyone had a right to remind him. His activities had doubled since the alarm which Monsieur Appert's visit had aroused in him. He had made three more journeys to Besançon, sent several letters by every post and had others delivered by strangers who came to his house after nightfall. He had been wrong, perhaps, to have old Father Chélan dismissed, for that vindictive action had caused him to be regarded, by several pious ladies of good birth, as a profoundly malicious man. Furthermore, this service rendered had placed him under a strong obligation to the vicar-general, Monsieur de Frilair, who gave him strange missions to carry out. His affairs had reached this point when he indulged in the pleasure of writing an anonymous letter. To climax his embarrassment, his wife had informed him that she wished to make Julien a member of her household; the idea appealed strongly to her vanity.

In this position, Monsieur Valenod foresaw a decisive scene with his former confederate Monsieur de Rênal. The latter would speak harshly to him; that would not disturb him, but the mayor might also write to Besançon, or even to Paris. A cousin of some minister or other might suddenly descend on Verrières and take charge of the workhouse. Monsieur Valenod decided to place himself on friendlier terms with the Liberals; it was for this reason that he had invited several of them to the dinner at which Julien had recited his Latin. They would give him powerful support against the mayor. But meanwhile there might be an election, and it was all too obvious that control of the workhouse and a vote for the wrong party were incompatible.

Madame de Rênal, who had clearly discerned these machinations, described them to Julien as he gave her his arm to escort her from one shop to another and eventually to the Cours de la Fidélité, where they spent several hours that were almost as peaceful as those they had spent together in Vergy.

During this time, Monsieur Valenod was seeking to avoid a decisive scene with his former superior by taking the initiative in adopting a bold attitude toward him. This method succeeded on that particular day, but it increased the mayor's ill humor.

Never has vanity, in conflict with the greediest and most

ignoble aspects of a petty love of money, placed a man in a more wretched state than that in which Monsieur de Rênal found himself as he entered the tavern. Never, on the other hand, had his children been gayer or happier. This contrast brought his irritation to its peak.

"As far as I can see, I'm unwelcome in my own family," he said as he entered, in a tone which he sought to make imposing.

His wife's only reply was to draw him aside and tell him how necessary it was to send Julien away. The hours of happiness she had just enjoyed had given her back the self-assurance and determination she needed in order to carry out the course of action she had been planning for the past two weeks.

The poor mayor's distress was made still greater by his knowledge of the fact that the people of Verrières often made public jests about his fondness for money. Monsieur Valenod had the generosity of a robber, whereas Monsieur de Rênal had contributed in a manner that was more prudent than magnanimous to the last five or six collections on behalf of the Brotherhood of Saint Joseph, the Congregation of the Virgin, the Congregation of the Blessed Sacrament, etc.

Among the country gentlemen in and around Verrières, skillfully classified in the records kept by the collecting brethren according to the amount of their contributions, Monsieur de Rênal's name had more than once appeared on the last line. It was useless for him to protest that he made no profits; the clergy are very touchy on this point.

CHAPTER 23
The Sorrows of a Government Official

Il piacere di alzar la testa tutto l'anno è ben pagato da certi quarti d'ora che bisogna passar.

—Casti

BUT LET us leave this little man to his little fears; why did he take a man of spirit into his house when what he needed was one with the soul of a lackey? Why did he not know how to choose his servants? The usual course of events in the nineteenth century is that when a powerful and noble personage encounters a man of spirit he kills him, banishes him, imprisons him or humiliates him so deeply that he is foolish enough to die of sorrow. In this instance it so happens that it is not yet the man of spirit who is suffering.

The great misfortune of the small towns of France, and of elected governments, like that of New York, is the impossibility of overlooking the fact that there are people like Monsieur de Rênal in the world. In a town of twenty thousand inhabitants, such men form public opinion, and public opinion has terrifying power in a country which has a constitution. A man endowed with a noble and generous heart, who would be your friend if he did not live a hundred leagues away from you, judges you in accordance with the public opinion of your town, which is formed by the fools whom chance has made noble, rich and mediocre. Woe to any man who stands out above the rest!

The Rênals left for Vergy immediately after dinner, but two days later Julien saw them all return to Verrières. Within less than an hour he discovered, to his great surprise, that Madame de Rênal was concealing something from him. She broke off her conversations with her husband as soon as he appeared, and she seemed almost to want him to go away. Julien did not wait to be told twice. He became cold and reserved; Madame de Rênal noticed this and did not seek an explanation. "Is she going to put someone else in my place?" he wondered. "She was so intimate with me only day before yesterday! But they say that's how great ladies act. They're like kings, who are never more gracious to anyone than to a minister who will find a letter of dismissal waiting for him when he comes home."

Julien noticed that in those conversations which ceased abruptly at his approach, there was frequent mention of a large house belonging to the town of Verrières; it was old, but spacious and comfortable, and it stood opposite the church in the most advantageous commercial location in town. "What connection can there be between that house and a new lover?" he wondered. In his chagrin he repeated to himself those charming little lines written by Francis I, which still seemed new to him, for Madame de Rênal had taught them to him less than a month before. At that time, by how many vows, by how many caresses had the truth of each line been denied!

> *Souvent femme varie,*
> *Bien fol est qui s'y fie.**

---

*A woman often changes,
  Quite mad is he who trusts her.

Monsieur de Rênal left for Besançon in a stagecoach. It had taken him two hours to decide to make this journey; he seemed deeply perturbed. When he returned, he dropped a large package wrapped in gray paper on the table.

"This will take care of that stupid matter," he said to his wife.

An hour later, Julien saw the billposter carry the large package away; he eagerly followed him. "I'll learn the secret at the first street corner," he thought.

He waited impatiently behind the billposter while he spread paste on the back of the bill with his heavy brush. As soon as it was stuck in place, Julien was able to satisfy his curiosity by reading a detailed announcement of the fact that there would be a sale by public auction of the lease of that large old house whose name had recurred so often in the conversations between Monsieur de Rênal and his wife. The sale was announced for the following day at two o'clock in the town hall, on the extinction of the third candle. Julien was strongly disappointed; he considered the sale to be on quite short notice: how could all the bidders learn about it in time? But, aside from this, the bill, which was dated two weeks earlier and which he read from beginning to end in three different places, told him nothing.

He went to examine the vacant house. The caretaker, unaware of his approach, was saying mysteriously to a friend, "Nothing but a waste of time! Father Maslon promised him he'd have it for three hundred francs, and when the mayor balked at that, he was called to the bishop's palace by the vicar-general."

Julien's arrival appeared to disturb the two friends; they said nothing more.

Julien did not fail to attend the auction. There was a large crowd in a dimly lighted room. Everyone seemed to be watching everyone else in a strange manner. All eyes were fixed on a table on which Julien saw three small lighted candles standing in a tin plate. The auctioneer was shouting, "Three hundred francs, gentlemen!"

"Three hundred francs! That's outrageous!" murmured one man to another. Julien was standing between them. "It's worth more than eight hundred! I'm going to raise the bid."

"You'll be cutting off your nose to spite your face," said his companion. "What are you going to gain by turning Father Maslon against you, along with Monsieur Valenod, the bishop, his terrible vicar-general and all the rest of the gang?"

"Three hundred twenty francs!" shouted the first man.

"Stupid idiot!" said the other. "And one of the mayor's spies is right here," he added, pointing to Julien.

Julien turned sharply to punish him for this remark, but the two natives of Franche-Comté had ceased paying any attention to him. The sight of their self-possession restored his own. Just then the last candle went out and the auctioneer's drawling voice awarded the house, for nine years, to Monsieur de Saint-Giraud, head clerk in the prefect's office at ———, for the sum of three hundred thirty francs.

As soon as the mayor had left the room, the comments began.

"Grogeot's rashness has earned thirty francs for the town," said one man.

"But Monsieur de Saint-Giraud will have his revenge," replied another. "He'll make him regret it!"

"What a disgusting trick!" said a fat man on Julien's left. "I'd have given eight hundred francs for that house, for my factory, and even then it would have been a bargain!"

"Well, what do you expect?" said a young Liberal manufacturer. "Isn't Monsieur de Saint-Giraud a member of the *Congrégation?* Don't his four children have scholarships? Poor man! The town of Verrières had to give him a bonus of five hundred francs, that's all."

"And to think the mayor couldn't stop it!" remarked a third man. "He's an Ultra, it's true, but he's not a thief."

"Not a thief! They're all a pack of thieves! Everything goes into a common fund and they divide it up at the end of the year. But there's young Sorel; let's leave."

Julien went home in a very bad humor. He found Madame de Rênal extremely sad.

"Were you at the auction?" she asked him.

"Yes, madame; I had the honor of being regarded as the mayor's spy there."

"If he'd listened to me, he'd have taken a trip somewhere."

Just then Monsieur de Rênal appeared, looking very somber. They all had dinner in silence. Monsieur de Rênal ordered Julien to go to Vergy with the children; the trip was gloomy. Madame de Rênal tried to comfort her husband: "You should be used to it by now, my dear."

That evening they sat around the fireplace in silence; the crackling of the blazing beech logs was their only distraction. It was one of those moments of dejection which occur in even the most closely united families. Then one of the children cried joyfully, "There's the doorbell! The doorbell!"

"By God, if that's Monsieur de Saint-Giraud coming to badger me again on the pretext of thanking me," cried the mayor, "I'll give him a piece of my mind! That's going too far! It's Valenod he ought to thank, and I'm the one who's been compromised. What am I going to say if those cursed Jacobin newspapers get hold of the story and make me into another Monsieur Nonante-Cinq?"**

Just then a very handsome man with long black side whiskers entered the room preceded by a servant.

"Mister Mayor, I am Signor Geronimo. Here is a letter which Monsieur le Chevalier de Beauvaisis, the French attaché in Naples, gave me for you when I left—which was only nine days ago," added Signor Geronimo gaily, looking at Madame de Rênal. "Signor de Beauvaisis, your cousin and my good friend, madame, tells me you speak Italian."

The Neapolitan's good humor changed that sad evening into a very gay one. Madame de Rênal insisted that he stay for supper. She set the entire household in motion, wishing at any cost to divert Julien's thoughts from the epithet of "spy," which had rung in his ears twice that day.

Signor Geronimo was a famous singer who was well-bred, yet also extremely gay, qualities which, in France, have almost ceased to be compatible. After supper he sang a little duet with Madame de Rênal and told delightful stories. At one o'clock in the morning the children cried out in protest when Julien suggested that they go to bed.

"Just one more story!" said the eldest.

"The next one will be about me, signorino," said Signor Geronimo. "Eight years ago I was, like you, a young student in the conservatory in Naples, by which I mean that I was your age, although I didn't have the honor of being the son of the illustrious mayor of the beautiful town of Verrières."

This remark made Monsieur de Rênal sigh and glance at his wife.

"Signor Zingarelli," continued the young singer, slightly exaggerating his accent, which made the children burst into laughter, "was an extremely stern master. He isn't liked in the conservatory, but he always wants people to act as though they

---

**In 1830, during the trial of a Liberal pamphleteer, the judge used the dialectical expression *nonante-cinq* ("ninety-five") instead of the standard French *quatre-vingt-quinze*. The Liberals thereafter jeeringly referred to him as "Monsieur Nonante-Cinq."
—L.B.

liked him. I went out as often as I could. I went to the little San Carlino theater, where I heard music worthy of the gods; but, good heavens, how was I to scrape together the eight soldi it cost for a seat in the orchestra? An enormous sum!" he said, looking at the children, who laughed again. "Signor Giovannone, the director of the San Carlino, heard me sing. I was sixteen. 'This boy is a treasure!' he said. He came to me and asked me, 'Would you like me to engage you, my friend?'

" 'How much will you give me?' I asked.

" 'Forty ducats a month,' he said. That, gentlemen, is a hundred sixty francs. I seemed to see paradise open up before my eyes.

" 'But how,' I asked Giovannone, 'can I persuade the stern Zingarelli to let me go?'

" '*Lascia fare a me,*' he replied."

"Leave it to me!" cried the eldest child.

"Precisely, my young noble lord. Signor Giovannone said to me, 'First of all, *caro,* a tiny little contract.' I signed and he gave me three ducats. I'd never seen so much money before. Then he told me what to do.

"The next day I asked for an interview with the terrible Signor Zingarelli. His old servant showed me into the room.

" 'What do you want from me, you scoundrel?' said Zingarelli.

" '*Maestro,*' I said to him, 'I'm sorry for all my misdeeds. Never again will I leave the conservatory by climbing over the iron fence. I'm going to work twice as hard as before.'

" 'If I weren't afraid of spoiling the finest bass voice I've ever heard,' he said, 'I'd lock you up on bread and water for two weeks, you rascal!'

" '*Maestro,*' I went on, 'I'm going to set an example for the whole school, *credete a me.* But I ask one favor of you: if anyone should come and ask you to let me sing outside the conservatory, refuse to let me go; say you can't do it.'

" 'And who the devil do you think will ask for a good-for-nothing like you?' he said. 'Do you think I'll ever let you leave the conservatory? Are you trying to make a fool of me? Get out of here! Get out,' he said, trying to give me a kick in the backside, 'or you'll be living on bread and water in a cell!'

"An hour later Signor Giovannone came to see him and said, 'I've come to ask you to make my fortune: let me have Geronimo. If he sings in my theater, my daughter can get married this winter.'

" 'What do you want with that rascal?' said Zingarelli. 'I

refuse: you won't have him. And besides, even if I gave my consent he wouldn't want to leave the conservatory; he just told me so himself.'

" 'If his willingness is all that matters,' said Giovannone gravely as he pulled my contract out of his pocket, *'carta canta!* Here's his signature!'

"Zingarelli immediately began to pull on the bell cord with all his might. 'Throw Geronimo out of the conservatory!' he shouted, boiling with rage. So they expelled me, and I split my sides laughing. That same evening I sang the *Aria del Moltiplico*. Polichinello wants to get married, he counts on his fingers all the things he'll need for his house, and he constantly gets tangled up in his calculations."

"Oh, please sing that aria for us, monsieur!" said Madame de Rênal.

Geronimo sang, and everyone wept with laughter. Signor Geronimo did not go to bed until two o'clock in the morning, leaving the entire family enchanted with his good manners, his obligingness and his gaiety.

The next day, Monsieur and Madame de Rênal gave him the letters he needed for the French court.

"So there's duplicity everywhere!" thought Julien. "There's Signor Geronimo on his way to London with a salary of sixty thousand francs, but if it hadn't been for the shrewdness of the director of the San Carlino, his divine voice might not have been heard and admired until ten years later. . . . I'd much rather be a Geronimo than a Rênal. He's not so highly honored by society, but he doesn't have the chagrin of holding auctions like the one that took place today, and his life is gay."

One thing astonished Julien: the weeks of solitude he had spent in Monsieur de Rênal's house in Verrières had been a period of happiness for him. He had encountered disgust and gloomy thoughts only at the dinners to which he had been invited; in that empty house, was he not free to read, write and reflect without being disturbed? He was not torn from his radiant dreams every few moments by the painful necessity to study the workings of a base mind in order, worse still, to deceive it by hypocritical words or actions.

"Can happiness be so close to me?" he thought. "The cost of such a life is practically nothing; I can either marry Mademoiselle Elisa or become Fouqué's partner, as I choose. . . ." But the traveler who has just scaled a steep mountain sits down on the summit and finds perfect pleasure in resting; would he be happy if he were forced to rest forever?

Alarming thoughts had begun to invade Madame de Rênal's mind. In spite of her resolutions, she had told Julien all about the auction. "He'll no doubt make me forget all my vows!" she thought.

She would have sacrificed her life without hesitation to save that of her husband, if she had seen him in danger. She had one of those noble and romantic hearts for which seeing the possibility of a generous action without performing it is the source of a remorse nearly equal to that of a crime. Nevertheless, there were oppressive days when she was unable to drive away the thought of the extreme happiness she would enjoy if, suddenly left a widow, she were free to marry Julien.

He loved her sons much more than their father did and, despite his stern justice, they adored him. She realized that if she married Julien she would have to leave Vergy, whose shade was so dear to her. She saw herself living in Paris, continuing to provide her sons with an education that aroused everyone's admiration. She, her children and Julien would all be perfectly happy.

A strange effect of marriage, such as the nineteenth century has made it! The boredom of married life invariably destroys love, when love has preceded marriage. And yet, as a philosopher might point out, this boredom soon causes, in people rich enough not to work, a profound distaste for all peaceful forms of enjoyment, and it creates in all women, except those with hearts of stone, an inclination to fall in love.

The philosopher's observation makes me excuse Madame de Rênal, but the people of Verrières were not so tolerant; unknown to her, her scandalous love affair was the talk of the town. Thanks to this great topic of conversation, there was less boredom than usual in Verrières that autumn.

Autumn and part of winter went by quickly. It was now time to leave the woods of Vergy. The members of good society in Verrières began to grow indignant because their disapproval was producing so little effect on Monsieur de Rênal. In less than a week a number of solemn individuals, who compensated themselves for their usual gravity by indulging in the pleasure of carrying out such missions, implanted the cruelest suspicions in his mind, although they used extremely moderate language in doing so.

Monsieur Valenod, playing his hand cautiously, had found

Elisa a place in a noble and highly respected household which included five other women. She was afraid, she said, that she might not be able to find employment during the winter, and she had asked this family for only about two thirds of what she had received from the mayor. Of her own accord, she had the excellent idea of going to confess to the retired parish priest, Father Chélan, as well as to the new one, so that she could give them both a detailed account of Julien's love affair.

Two days after his arrival in town, Father Chélan sent for Julien at six o'clock in the morning.

"I ask you nothing," he said to him. "In fact, I beg you and, if necessary, order you not to tell me anything. But I demand that you leave Verrières within three days, either for the seminary in Besançon or your friend Fouqué's house. He's still willing to give you an excellent position. I've planned everything; you must leave Verrières and not come back for a year."

Julien made no reply; he was trying to decide whether or not his honor ought to be offended by the arrangements which the priest, not being his father, had made for him.

"Tomorrow at this same time, I'll have the honor of seeing you again," he said to him at length.

Father Chélan, who expected to crush the resistance of such a young man, spoke a great deal. Julien, his face and posture expressing great humility, did not say a word.

He finally left and hurried off to warn Madame de Rênal, whom he found in despair. Her husband had just spoken to her with a certain frankness. The natural weakness of his character, drawing encouragement from the prospect of her inheritance from her aunt in Besançon, had made him decide to regard her as completely innocent. He had just confessed to her the strange condition in which he found public opinion in Verrières. The people were wrong, they were being misled by certain envious individuals, but what was there to do?

For a moment Madame de Rênal had the illusion that Julien might accept Monsieur Valenod's offer and remain in Verrières. But she was no longer the same artless and timid woman she had been the year before; her fateful passion and her remorse had enlightened her. She soon had the painful experience of proving to herself, as she listened to her husband, that at least a temporary separation from Julien had become essential. "If he's not with me," she thought, "he'll drift back into those ambitious plans that are so natural for a man who has no money. And I'm so rich! And my wealth is so useless to my happiness! He'll forget me. Charming as he is, he'll be loved, and he'll fall in love. Oh, what a wretched woman I am! . . . But what can I complain of? God is just. I can't take credit for putting an end to my sin; it's taken away my judgment. It was within my power to bribe Elisa; nothing could have been easier. I didn't take the trouble to reflect for a moment—all my time was taken up with fantastic dreams inspired by my love. And now I'm lost.''

Julien was struck by the fact that Madame de Rênal voiced no selfish objections when he gave her the terrible news of his departure. She was obviously making an effort to hold back her tears.

''We need to be strong, my friend,'' she said. She cut off a lock of her hair. ''I don't know what I'll do, but if I die, promise me you'll never forget my children. Near or far, try to make them grow up to be honorable men. If there should be another revolution, all noblemen will be massacred, and their father may emigrate, because of that peasant who was killed on a roof. Watch over the family. . . . Give me your hand. Good-bye, my love. These are our last moments together. After this great sacrifice, I hope I'll have the courage to consider my reputation.''

Julien had been expecting despair. He was touched by the simplicity of this farewell.

''No, I won't accept your farewell this way,'' he said. ''I'll leave—everyone wants me to, even you. But, three days after my departure, I'll come back to see you at night.''

Madame de Rênal's life was transformed. Julien really did love her, since he himself had had the idea of seeing her again! Her terrible grief gave way to one of the most powerful surges of joy she had ever experienced in her life. Everything became easy for her. The certainty of seeing her lover again took away all the heartbreaking pain of those last moments. From then on, both her conduct and her expression were noble, firm and perfectly decorous.

Monsieur de Rênal returned shortly afterward; he was beside himself with rage. He finally spoke to his wife of the anonymous letter he had received two months earlier.

''I'm going to take it to the Casino,'' he said, ''and show everybody that it came from that despicable Valenod, after I picked him up out of the gutter and made him into one of the richest commoners in Verrières! I'll disgrace him in public, and then I'll fight a duel with him. He's gone too far!''

''I might be left a widow!'' thought Madame de Rênal. But almost at the same moment she said to herself, ''If I don't prevent that duel, as I'm sure I can, I'll be guilty of murdering my husband.''

Never before had she handled his vanity with so much skill. In less than two hours, using arguments which he himself discovered, she made him see that he ought to show more friendship than ever toward Monsieur Valenod and even take Elisa into the house again. Madame de Rênal needed courage to make up her mind to see the girl who was the cause of all her misfortune. But this idea had come to her from Julien.

Finally, after having been placed on the right track three or four times, Monsieur de Rênal arrived of his own accord at the financially distressing idea that, for him, the most disagreeable possibility was that, with all the public agitation and gossip in Verrières, Julien might stay there as the tutor of Monsieur Valenod's children. It was clearly to Julien's advantage to accept the offer of the superintendent of the workhouse. It was essential for Monsieur de Rênal's reputation, however, that Julien should leave Verrières to enter the seminary in Besançon or Dijon. But could he be persuaded to do so? And, if so, how would he be able to live?

Monsieur de Rênal, seeing the imminence of financial sacrifice, was in greater despair than his wife. For her part, after this conversation she was in the condition of a sensitive man who, weary of life, has taken a dose of stramonium; he ceases to act except from inertia, so to speak, and he no longer takes an interest in anything. Thus Louis XIV, as he was dying, was led to say, ''When I was king . . .'' An admirable remark!

Early the next morning Monsieur de Rênal received an anonymous letter. This one was written in the most insulting style. The coarsest words applicable to his position appeared in every line. It was the work of some envious subordinate. This letter brought back the thought of fighting a duel with Monsieur Valenod. Soon his courage rose to ideas of immediate action. He left the house alone, went to the gunsmith's, bought a pair of pistols and had them loaded.

''After all,'' he said to himself, ''even if Emperor Napoleon's strict administration should return, I wouldn't have to worry about being accused of misappropriating one single sou. At the very most, I've sometimes shut my eyes to things, but I have some good letters in my desk authorizing me to do so.''

Madame de Rênal was alarmed by her husband's cold anger; it brought back the sinister thought of widowhood which she found so hard to put out of her mind. She shut herself up in private with him and spoke with him for several hours, but in vain: the new anonymous letter had decided him. She finally succeeded in transforming the courage to challenge Monsieur Valenod to a duel into the courage to offer Julien six hundred francs as a living allowance for a year in the seminary. Monsieur de Rênal, heaping a thousand curses on the day when he had conceived the baneful idea of taking a tutor into his house, forgot the anonymous letter.

He consoled himself a little with a thought which he did not reveal to his wife: with skill, and by taking advantage of the young man's romantic ideas, he hoped to make him agree to refuse Monsieur Valenod's offer for a smaller sum.

Madame de Rênal had much greater difficulty in convincing Julien that if he sacrificed, for the sake of her husband's reputation, the position worth eight hundred francs a year which the superintendent of the workhouse had publicly offered him, he had a perfect right to accept some compensation without shame.

"But I never considered accepting his offer," he said repeatedly, "not even for an instant. You've made me too accustomed to a life of refinement; the vulgarity of those people would kill me."

Cruel necessity, with its hand of iron, bent Julien's will. His pride offered him the illusion that he would accept the mayor's money only as a loan, signing a note agreeing to repay it in five years with interest.

Madame de Rênal still had several thousand francs hidden in a little cave in the mountains. She offered him this money, trembling and realizing all too clearly that it would be angrily refused.

"Do you want to make the memory of our love abominable?" he said.

Julien finally left Verrières. Monsieur de Rênal was overjoyed, for, when the fateful moment of accepting the money arrived, the sacrifice proved to be too great for Julien and he flatly refused. Monsieur de Rênal threw his arms around his neck with tears in his eyes, and when Julien asked him for a letter of recommendation his enthusiasm was so great that he could not find words magnificent enough to praise his conduct. Our hero had saved up five louis, and he intended to ask Fouqué for a similar amount.

He was deeply moved, but by the time he was one league away from Verrières, where he had left so much love behind, he was no longer thinking of anything except the joy of seeing a great capital and military center like Besançon.

During this short three-day separation, Madame de Rênal was deceived by one of love's cruelest illusions. Her life was bearable: between her and the depths of despair stood that final meeting she was to have with Julien. She counted the hours, the minutes that separated her from it. At last, during the night of the third day, she heard in the distance the signal they had agreed upon. After having exposed himself to a thousand dangers, Julien appeared before her.

From that moment on she had but a single thought: "I'm seeing him for the last time." Far from responding to her lover's eagerness, she was like a scarcely animated corpse. If she forced herself to tell him she loved him, it was with an awkward air that was almost a proof to the contrary. Nothing was able to divert her mind from the cruel idea of eternal separation. Julien, with his usual mistrust, thought for a moment that he had already been forgotten. His offended remarks to that effect were received only with large tears flowing in silence and an almost convulsive pressure on his hand.

"But how in God's name do you expect me to believe you?" he replied to his mistress's cold protestations. "You'd show a hundred times more sincere affection to Madame Derville, or to a mere acquaintance!"

Madame de Rênal, petrified, did not know what to say. "It's impossible to be unhappier than I am. . . . I hope I'm going to die. . . . I feel my heart freezing. . . ." Such were the longest answers he was able to obtain from her.

When the approach of dawn made it necessary for him to leave, her tears stopped completely. Without saying a word, without returning his kisses, she watched him tie a knotted rope to the window. It was in vain that Julien said to her, "Now we've reached the situation you've longed for so much. From now on you'll live without remorse; you'll no longer regard your children as already in the grave whenever they feel the slightest bit indisposed."

"I'm sorry you can't kiss Stanislas good-bye," she replied coldly.

The frigid embraces of that living corpse finally made a deep impression on Julien; for several leagues he was unable to think of anything else. His heart was broken and, before going over the mountain, he continued to look back often, until the steeple of the Verrières church was out of sight.

CHAPTER 24
A Capital

So much noise, so many busy people! So many plans for the future in a twenty-year-old head! What a distraction from love!

—Barnave

AT LENGTH he could discern black walls on a faraway mountain: it was the citadel of Besançon. "How different it would be for me," he said to himself with a sigh, "if I were coming to that noble fortified city to become a second lieutenant in one of the regiments assigned to its defense!"

Besançon is not only one of the most beautiful cities in France, it also abounds in refined and intelligent people. But Julien was only a young peasant and had no way of approaching the distinguished men there.

He had borrowed a suit of secular clothing from Fouqué, and it was in this attire that he crossed the drawbridges. With his mind full of the history of the siege of 1674, he was determined to see the ramparts and the citadel before shutting himself up in the seminary. He was nearly arrested by the sentries two or three times when he entered places from which the military engineers excluded the public in order to be able to sell twelve or fifteen francs' worth of hay each year.

After his attention had been occupied for several hours by the height of the walls, the depth of the moats and the awesome appearance of the cannons, he passed in front of a large café on the boulevard. He stood motionless in admiration; although he read the word "Café" painted in large letters above the two enormous doors, he could not believe his eyes. He made an effort to control his timidity; he ventured to step inside and found himself in a room thirty or forty feet long and at least twenty feet high. Everything was an enchantment for him that day.

Two games of billiards were in progress. The waiters were calling out the scores as the players moved busily around the tables in the midst of a crowd of onlookers. Clouds of tobacco smoke, pouring from their mouths, enveloped them all in a blue haze. The impressive height of these men, their rounded shoulders, their heavy gait, their enormous side whiskers, the long frock coats covering their bodies—everything attracted Julien's attention. These noble sons of ancient Bisontium spoke only in shouts, and each of them gave himself the air of a ferocious warrior. Julien stood still and admired everything, reflecting on the immensity and splendor of a great capital like Besançon. He felt that he would never have the courage to request a cup of coffee from one of those haughty-looking gentlemen who were calling out the scores of the billiard games.

But the young lady behind the counter had noticed the charming face of the country boy standing three paces from the stove with his little bundle under his arm and gazing at a gleaming white plaster bust of the king. This young lady, a tall native of Franche-Comté, extremely well made and dressed in the style necessary to give the proper tone to a café, had already said twice, in a low voice designed to be heard by Julien alone, "Monsieur! Monsieur!" He looked into a pair of large, tender blue eyes and realized that it was he who was being addressed.

He quickly stepped over to the counter and the pretty girl behind it, as though he were marching against the enemy. As he was carrying out this great maneuver, his bundle fell to the floor.

What pity our provincial will inspire in the young students of Paris, who, by the age of fifteen, already know how to enter a café with such a distinguished air! But those boys, so well trained at fifteen, have begun to turn "common" by the time they are eighteen. The passionate timidity which one finds in the provinces is sometimes overcome, and then it teaches its conqueror how to will. "I must tell her the truth," thought Julien, who was becoming courageous by struggling against his shyness, as he approached the pretty girl who had deigned to speak to him.

"Madame," he said to her, "I've just come to Besançon for the first time in my life. I'd like to have a cup of coffee and a roll, for which I'll pay you."

The girl smiled slightly and then blushed; she was afraid, for the sake of the handsome young man, of the ironic attention and witticisms of the billiard players. He might be frightened and never come back.

"Sit down here, near me," she said to him, pointing to a marble-topped table almost completely hidden by the enormous mahogany counter which jutted out into the middle of the room.

She leaned over the counter, thus giving herself a chance to display her superb figure. Julien noticed it and all his ideas changed. The beautiful young lady had just placed a cup, some sugar and a roll in front of him. She hesitated to call a waiter to bring some coffee, realizing that with his arrival her private conversation with Julien would come to an end.

Julien was thoughtfully comparing her blonde, vivacious beauty with certain memories which often troubled him. The thought of the passion of which he had been the object took away nearly all his shyness. The beautiful girl had only a moment; she looked searchingly into his eyes.

"This pipe smoke makes you cough," she said. "Come here for breakfast tomorrow morning before eight o'clock—I'm almost alone then."

"What's your name?" asked Julien with the engaging smile of happy shyness.

"Amanda Binet."

"Will you allow me to send you a little bundle the size of this one an hour from now?"

The fair Amanda reflected for a moment and said, "I'm watched, so what you ask might get me in trouble. But I'll write my address on a card—put it on your bundle and send it to me without fear."

"My name is Julien Sorel," said the young man. "I have neither friends nor relatives in Besançon."

"Oh, I see!" she exclaimed joyfully. "You've come to study law, haven't you?"

"No, alas!" replied Julien. "I'm being sent to the seminary."

Utter discouragement darkened Amanda's face and she called a waiter; she had courage now. The waiter poured out some coffee for Julien, without looking at him.

Amanda was taking in money at the counter. Julien was proud of having dared to speak. A quarrel had broken out at one of the billiard tables. The shouts and accusations of the players, echoing through the enormous room, made a din which astonished Julien. Amanda was pensive and kept her eyes lowered.

"If you like, mademoiselle," he said to her with sudden self-assurance, "I'll say I'm your cousin."

This slight air of authority pleased Amanda. "He's not just a little nobody," she thought. She said to him very quickly, without looking at him, for her eyes were occupied in seeing whether anyone was approaching the counter, "I'm from Genlis, near Dijon; say you're from Genlis, too, and that you're my mother's cousin."

"I will."

"Every Thursday, at five o'clock, in summer, the seminary students come past the café here."

"If you're thinking of me, have a bouquet of violets in your hand when I go past."

Amanda looked at him in astonishment. Her look changed Julien's courage into boldness; however, he blushed deeply as he said to her, "I've fallen madly in love with you, I feel it in my heart."

"Don't talk so loud!" she said in alarm.

Julien decided to quote some phrases from an odd volume of *La Nouvelle Héloïse* which he had found in Vergy. His memory served him well. He had been reciting *La Nouvelle Héloïse* to Mademoiselle Amanda, who was delighted, for ten minutes, and he was happy with his courage, when suddenly her face took on a frigid expression: one of her lovers had just come through the door of the café.

He walked up to the counter, whistling and rolling his shoulders, and looked at Julien. In an instant Julien's mind, which was always rushing to extremes, was filled with nothing but thoughts of a duel. He turned deathly pale, pushed back his cup, assumed an air of self-assurance and attentively examined his rival. While this rival's head was lowered as he casually poured himself a glass of brandy at the counter, Amanda ordered Julien with a glance to lower his eyes. He obeyed, and for two minutes he sat motionless in his chair, pale, resolute and thinking only of what was about to happen; he was truly superb at that moment. The rival had been surprised by Julien's eyes; after drinking his brandy in one gulp, he said a few words to Amanda, put his hands in the pockets of his loose frock coat and walked over to a billiard table, whistling and looking at Julien.

Julien leapt to his feet, boiling with rage; but he did not know how to go about being insolent. He set down his little bundle and went over to the billiard table, walking as arrogantly as he could.

In vain did prudence warn him, "But if you fight a duel as soon as you arrive in Besançon, your ecclesiastical career will be ruined."

"It doesn't matter—I won't have it said that I let myself be insulted with impunity."

Amanda saw his courage; it made a charming contrast with the simplicity of his manners. In an instant, she preferred him to the tall young man in the frock coat. She stood up and, pretending to keep her eye on someone who was passing in the street, quickly placed herself between Julien and the billiard table.

"Don't frown at that gentleman," she said, "he's my brother-in-law."

"What do I care about that?" replied Julien. "He stared at me."

"Do you want to get me in trouble? Of course he stared at you, and he may even come over and talk to you. I told him you were a relative of my mother and that you'd just come from Genlis. He's from Franche-Comté and he's never been past Dôle, on the Burgundy road, so say whatever you like to him and don't be afraid."

Julien was still hesitant; she added quickly, her barmaid's imagination supplying her with lies in abundance, "Of course he stared at you, but it was when he was asking me who you were. He's rude to everybody; he didn't mean to insult you."

Julien watched the alleged brother-in-law buy a number in the pool that was being formed at the farther of the two billiard tables, then he heard his loud voice call out threateningly, "Now it's my turn."

Julien abruptly pushed past Amanda and took a step toward the billiard table. She seized his arm and said, "Come and pay me first."

"She's right," he thought. "She's afraid I may leave without paying."

Amanda's agitation was as great as his own and her face had turned a bright red. She counted out his change as slowly as she could, repeating to him under her breath, "Leave the café immediately, or I won't like you any more, even though I like you very much now."

Julien left, but slowly. "Isn't it my duty," he thought, "to walk over to that rude oaf, whistling as I go, and stare back at him?" This uncertainty kept him on the boulevard in front of the café for an hour, watching to see whether his man would come outside. He did not appear and Julien finally walked away.

He had been in Besançon only a few hours and he already had a reason for remorse. The old army surgeon had once, in spite of his gout, given him a few fencing lessons; this was the only skill he could now place in the service of his anger. But this difficulty would have meant nothing to him if he had known how to express his anger by some means other than a slap; if they had come to blows, his rival, an enormous man, would have beaten him and left him lying on the floor.

"For a poor devil like me, with neither protectors nor money," thought Julien, "there won't be much difference between a seminary and a prison. I'll have to go to some inn, change into my black suit and leave my secular clothes there. I'll put them on again if I ever manage to leave the seminary for a few hours, and then I can easily go to see Mademoiselle Amanda.'' This reasoning was quite sound, but he walked past all the inns without daring to enter any of them.

Finally, as he was passing in front of the Hôtel des Ambassadeurs for the second time, his anxious eyes met those of a plump woman, still fairly young, with a ruddy complexion and an expression of cheerful happiness. He went up to her and told her his story.

"Of course, my handsome young abbé,'' said the landlady of the Hôtel des Ambassadeurs, "I'll keep your clothes for you and I'll even keep them dusted off for you. In this weather, broadcloth clothes shouldn't be left lying for too long." She took a key and personally showed him to a room, advising him to make out a list of the things he was going to leave behind.

"Oh, how nice you look like that, Abbé Sorel!" she said to him later when he came down to the kitchen. "I'm going to order a good dinner for you, and," she added in a low voice, "it will cost you only twenty sous, instead of the fifty everyone else pays, because you'll have to be careful with your little purse."

"I have ten louis," replied Julien with a certain pride.

"Good heavens!" exclaimed the good landlady in alarm. "Don't talk so loud! There are a lot of thieves in Besançon and they'll steal your ten louis in no time at all. Whatever you do, never go into the cafés; they're full of scoundrels."

"Really?" said Julien, to whom this remark gave food for thought.

"Never go anywhere except here; I'll make coffee for you. Remember that you'll always find a friend here, and a good dinner for twenty sous; I don't think you could ask for a better bargain than that. Go sit down at the table, I'll serve you myself."

"I couldn't eat," said Julien, "I'm too nervous: I'm going to the seminary as soon as I leave here."

The good woman would not let him go until she had stuffed his pockets with provisions. Finally he set out for his awesome destination as the landlady, standing on the steps of the inn, pointed out the way to him.

CHAPTER 25
The Seminary

> Three hundred thirty-six dinners at eighty-three centimes each, three hundred thirty-six suppers at thirty-eight centimes each, chocolate for everyone who's entitled to it—think of how much money can be made on that contract!
>
> —Valenod of Besançon

HE SAW the gilded iron cross on the door from a distance. He approached slowly; his legs seemed to be giving way beneath him. "So this is the hell on earth I won't be able to escape from!" he thought.

He finally made up his mind to ring. The sound of the bell echoed as though in a deserted place. Ten minutes later a pale man dressed in black came to open the door. This porter had a strange face: the bulging green pupils of his eyes were rounded like those of a cat, the motionless contours of his eyelids announced the impossibility of any warmth of feeling, and his thin lips were stretched in semicircles over his protruding teeth. This face did not suggest a criminal nature, but rather that total lack of sensitivity which is far more terrifying to young people. The only feeling which Julien's rapid glance could discern in that long, pious countenance was profound contempt for anything one might wish to speak to him about, if it did not concern the interests of heaven.

Julien raised his eyes with an effort and, in a voice made tremulous by the pounding of his heart, explained that he wished to speak to Father Pirard, the rector of the seminary. Without a word, the man in black motioned him to follow. They walked up two flights of a wide staircase with a wooden banister; the warped steps sloped downward from the wall and seemed on the point of collapse. A small door, surmounted by a wooden graveyard cross painted black, was opened after some difficulty, and the porter showed him into a gloomy, low-ceilinged room whose whitewashed walls were adorned with two large paintings which had been blackened by time. There Julien was left alone; he was panic-stricken, his heart was pounding violently and he would have been glad to weep if he had dared to do so. A deathly silence reigned throughout the building.

After a quarter of an hour, which seemed like a day to Julien, the porter with the sinister face reappeared on the threshold of a door at the other end of the room and, without deigning to speak, motioned him to come forward. He entered a room that was still larger than the first one and very badly lighted. Its walls were also whitewashed, but it contained almost no furniture. As he walked past, Julien noticed, in a corner near the door, a wooden bed, two straw-bottomed chairs and a small armchair made of fir planks, without a cushion. At the other end of the room, near a small window whose panes had turned yellow and which was decorated with neglected flowerpots, he saw a man in a shabby cassock sitting at a table. He appeared to be angry. He was engaged in picking up little slips of paper one after the other and arranging them on his table after writing a few words on them. He was not aware of Julien's presence. The latter stood motionless in the middle of the room, where he had been left by the porter, who had gone out, shutting the door behind him.

Ten minutes went by in this way; the shabbily dressed man was still writing. Julien's anxiety and terror were so great that he felt as though he were on the verge of fainting. A philosopher would have said, perhaps mistakenly, "Such is the violent impression made by ugliness on a soul created to love beauty."

The man writing at the table raised his head; Julien was not aware of this for a moment, and even after he had noticed it he continued to stand still, as though he had been struck dead by the terrible gaze that was fixed on him. His troubled eyes were barely able to distinguish a long face covered all over with red spots, except for the forehead, which was deathly pale. Between those red cheeks and that white forehead shone a pair of small black eyes well suited to strike terror into the bravest heart. The vast expanse of the forehead was outlined by thick, straight, jet-black hair.

"Well, are you going to come closer or not?" the man said at length, impatiently.

Julien advanced with faltering steps, and finally, ready to collapse and paler than he had ever been before in his life, he stopped three paces away from the small, unpainted softwood table covered with slips of paper.

"Closer," said the man.

Julien advanced still further, stretching out his hand as though seeking something on which to lean his weight.

"Your name?"

"Julien Sorel."

"You took a long time to get here," said the man, again fixing his terrible gaze on him.

Julien could not endure that gaze; putting out his hand as though to support himself, he fell full length on the floor.

The man rang. Julien had lost only the use of his eyes and the strength to move; he heard footsteps coming toward him.

Someone picked him up and placed him in the little wooden armchair. He heard the terrifying man say to the porter, "He's apparently an epileptic; that's all I needed!"

When Julien was able to open his eyes again, the red-faced man had resumed his writing; the porter was gone. "I must be brave," our hero said to himself, "and above all I must hide what I feel." (He felt violent nausea.) "If I should have an accident, God only knows what they'll think of me."

Finally the man stopped writing, cast a sidelong glance at Julien and said, "Are you in condition to answer me now?"

"Yes, monsieur," replied Julien in a feeble voice.

"Good."

The man in black had half risen and was impatiently trying to find a letter in one of the drawers of his softwood table, which creaked as he opened it. He found the letter, sat down again and said to Julien, looking at him with an expression that made him feel as though he were about to lose the little life he had left, "You've been recommended to me by Father Chélan, the best parish priest in the diocese, an upright man if ever there was one, and my friend for the last thirty years."

"Oh, then I have the honor of speaking to Father Pirard!" said Julien weakly.

"Apparently so," retorted the rector of the seminary, looking at him with irritation. His small eyes shone more brightly than ever, and then there was an involuntary movement of the muscles at the corners of his mouth. His face was like that of a tiger anticipating the pleasure of devouring its prey.

"Chélan's letter is short," he said, as though speaking to himself. "*Intelligenti pauca*. These days, one cannot write too little." He read the letter aloud:

I am sending you Julien Sorel, of this parish, whom I christened nearly twenty years ago. He is the son of a sawyer who is rich but gives him nothing. Julien will be an outstanding laborer in the Lord's vineyard. He is not lacking in either memory or intelligence, and he has a reflective mind. But will his vocation last? Is it sincere?

"*Sincere!*" repeated Father Pirard with an expression of surprise, looking at Julien; but by now his gaze had become less devoid of any trace of humanity. *"Sincere!"* he said once again, lowering his voice and returning to the letter:

I ask you to grant Julien a scholarship; he will qualify for it by taking the necessary examinations. I have taught him a little theology, the tried and true theology of men like Bossuet, Arnault and Fleury. If this young man does not suit you, send him back to me; the superintendent of the workhouse, whom you know well, has offered him eight hundred francs a year to be his children's tutor.

My mind is at rest, thanks be to God. I am recovering from the terrible blow. *Vale et me ama.*

Father Pirard, reading more slowly as he came to the signature, uttered with a sigh the name "Chélan."

"His mind is at rest," he said. "Yes, his virtue deserved that reward; may God also grant it to me if I should find myself in the same situation!"

He looked up and made the sign of the cross. At the sight of this sacred sign, Julien felt a lessening of the horror which had frozen him ever since he had entered the building.

"I have here three hundred twenty-one aspirants to the holiest of all callings," Father Pirard said at length in a tone that was stern but not malicious. "Only seven or eight of them have been recommended to me by men like Father Chélan, so, among the three hundred twenty-one, you will be the ninth. But my protection is neither favor nor weakness: it means increased attention and severity against vice. Go lock that door."

Julien made an effort to walk and managed not to fall. He noticed that a small window, beside the door through which he had entered, afforded a view of the countryside. He looked at the trees; the sight of them made him feel better, as though he had just seen some old friends.

"Loquerisme linguam latinam?" ("Do you speak Latin?"), Father Pirard asked him when he returned.

"Ita, pater optime" ("Yes, excellent father"), replied Julien, who was beginning to recover his senses. Certainly no one in the world had ever seemed less excellent to him than Father Pirard during the last half-hour.

The conversation continued in Latin. The expression of Father Pirard's eyes became gentler and Julien recovered a certain amount of self-assurance. "How weak I am," he thought, "to let myself be overawed by these appearances of virtue! This man is probably nothing but a scoundrel like Father Maslon.'' And he congratulated himself on having hidden nearly all his money in his boots.

Father Pirard examined Julien on theology and was surprised at the extent of his knowledge. His surprise increased when he questioned him on the Holy Scriptures in particular, but when he began to ask him about the doctrines of the Fathers, he saw that Julien scarcely knew even the names of Saint Jerome, Saint Augustine, Saint Bonaventura, Saint Basil, etc.

"Here's a fine example," thought Father Pirard, "of that fatal tendency toward Protestantism for which I've always reproached Chélan—a thorough, too thorough, acquaintance with the Holy Scriptures.'' (Julien had just spoken to him, without having been questioned on the subject, of the *true* dates of authorship of the Book of Genesis, the Pentateuch, etc.) "What does all this endless examination of the Holy Scriptures lead to if not *personal judgment,* in other words, the most horrible Protestantism? And, along with that rash learning, there's no knowledge of the Fathers to counterbalance the tendency.''

But the astonishment of the rector of the seminary knew no bounds when, questioning Julien on the authority of the pope and expecting him to cite the maxims of the ancient Gallican church, he heard the young man repeat everything in Monsieur de Maistre's book.

"A strange man, Chélan,'' thought Father Pirard. "Has he shown him that book only to teach him to laugh at it?'' It was in vain that he questioned Julien in an attempt to discover whether or not he seriously believed in Monsieur de Maistre's doctrine: the young man answered only with his memory.

From then on, Julien felt completely at ease; he was confident of his self-control. After prolonged consideration, he decided that Fathar Pirard's severity was no longer anything but an affectation. True enough, if it had not been for the principles of austere gravity which he had imposed on himself in dealing with his theology students for the past fifteen years, the rector of the seminary would have embraced Julien in the name of logic, so great were the clarity, precision and succinctness of his answers.

"Here's a bold and healthy mind," he said to himself, "but *corpus debile.*'' (''The body is weak.'')

"Do you often fall like that?'' he asked Julien in French, pointing to the floor.

"It was the first time in my life,'' replied Julien. "The porter's face chilled my blood,'' he added, blushing like a child.

Father Pirard almost smiled. "Such is the effect of the vanities of this world," he said. "You're apparently accustomed to smiling faces, veritable theaters of falsehood. The truth is austere, monsieur. But isn't our task in this world severe also? You'll have to keep watch over your conscience and make sure it guards you against this weakness: *excessive sensitivity to vain outward charms.*

"If you hadn't been recommended to me," he went on, returning to the Latin language with marked pleasure, "by a man like Father Chélan, I'd speak to you in the vain language of this world, to which you're apparently too well accustomed. 'The full scholarship for which you're applying,' I'd say to you, 'is the most difficult thing in the world to obtain.' But Father Chélan would have earned very little by his fifty-six years of apostolic labors if he couldn't dispose of a seminary scholarship."

After these remarks, Father Pirard advised Julien not to join any society or secret *congrégation* without his consent.

"I give you my word of honor," said Julien with the warm earnestness of an honorable man.

The rector of the seminary smiled for the first time. "That expression is out of place here," he said. "It's too suggestive of the vain honor of men of the world, which leads them into so many errors, and often into crime. You owe me holy obedience by virtue of paragraph seventeen of the Bull *Unam Ecclesiam* of Saint Pius V. I'm your ecclesiastical superior. In this house, my dear son, to hear is to obey. How much money do you have?"

"Now we're coming to the point," thought Julien. "That's the reason for the 'dear son.' "

"Thirty-five francs, father."

"Keep a careful record of how you spend that money; you'll have to give me an account of it."

This rigorous interview had lasted for three hours. Julien went to summon the porter.

"Show Julien Sorel to cell number 103," Father Pirard told the man. As a mark of special distinction, he was giving Julien a room to himself. "And carry his trunk there," he added.

Julien lowered his eyes and saw his trunk directly in front of him; he had been looking at it for three hours without recognizing it.

When he reached cell number 103—it was a small room, eight feet square, on the top floor of the building—he noticed that it overlooked the ramparts, and farther on he could see the beautiful plain which the Doubs separates from the city.

"What a charming view!" he exclaimed. As he said this to himself he was not conscious of the meaning of his words; the violent emotions he had experienced in the short time he had been in Besançon had completely exhausted his strength. He sat down by the window in the sole wooden chair that was in his cell and immediately fell fast asleep. He did not hear the supper bell, nor the bell for evening services; he had been forgotten.

When the first rays of the sun awakened him the following morning, he found himself lying on the floor.

CHAPTER 26

The World, or What the Rich Man Lacks

> I am alone in the world; no one deigns to think of me. All those whom I see making their fortunes have a hardness of heart which I do not feel in myself. They hate me because of my good-natured kindness. Ah! I shall die soon, either from hunger or from the sorrow of seeing men so hard-hearted.
>
> —Young*

HE QUICKLY brushed off his clothes and went downstairs. He was late and an assistant master sternly rebuked him for it. Instead of trying to excuse himself, Julien crossed his arms over his chest and said contritely, *"Peccavi, pater optime."* ("I have sinned, excellent father.")

This was a highly successful beginning. The shrewdest students saw that they would be dealing with a man who was not new to the game. During the recreation period, Julien found himself an object of general curiosity. But he manifested nothing but reserve and silence. Following the principles he had laid down for himself, he regarded his three hundred twenty-one fellow students as so many enemies; and the most dangerous enemy of all, in his eyes, was Father Pirard.

A few days later, he had to choose a confessor. A list was presented to him. "Good God! What do they think I am?" he said to himself. "Do they think I can't take a hint?" And he chose Father Pirard.

---

*Unable to trace the English source of this passage, I have translated the French in which Stendhal quotes it. It might be added that there is good evidence to suggest that Stendhal either invented or paraphrased from memory many of the quotations he places at the beginning of his chapters.—L.B.

Although he did not know it, this was a decisive step. A boyish little student, a native of Verrières who had declared himself to be Julien's friend the first day they met, told him he might have acted more wisely if he had chosen Father Castanède, the assistant rector. "He's Father Pirard's enemy," he added, leaning toward Julien's ear, "and Father Pirard is suspected of Jansenism."

All the first steps taken by our hero, who had such great confidence in his own shrewdness, were, like his choice of a confessor, foolish mistakes. Misled by all the presumption of a man of imagination, he took his intentions for facts and regarded himself as a consummate hypocrite. His folly went so far as to reproach himself for his success in that art of the weak. "Alas, it's my only weapon," he thought. "In another era, I'd have earned my bread by acting in the face of the enemy, and my actions would have spoken for themselves."

Satisfied with his conduct, he looked around him: everywhere he found the appearance of the purest virtue. Nine or ten of the students lived in the odor of sanctity and had visions like Saint Theresa or Saint Francis when he received the Stigmata on Mount Verna, in the Appenines. But this was a secret, concealed by their friends. These poor young visionaries were nearly always in the infirmary. A hundred or so of the others combined a robust faith with untiring industry. They worked to the point of making themselves ill, but without learning a great deal. Two or three of them distinguished themselves with genuine ability; one of these was a certain Chazel. But Julien felt an aversion to them, and they to him.

The remainder of the three hundred twenty-one students were only coarse creatures who were not too sure of the meaning of the Latin words they repeated all day long. They were nearly all sons of peasants, and they preferred to earn their living by reciting a few Latin words, rather than by tilling the soil.

It was after making this observation, in the first few days, that Julien promised himself he would succeed rapidly. "Intelligent men are needed in every calling," he thought, "because, after all, there's work to be done. Under Napoleon, I'd have been a sergeant; among these future parish priests, I'll be a vicar-general. Before they came here, all these poor devils had been manual laborers ever since their childhood, and they lived on curds and black bread. In their thatched-roof cottages, they ate meat only five or six times a year. Like the Roman soldiers who found war a time of rest, these crude peasants are enchanted the luxuries of the seminary."

Julien never read anything in their lackluster eyes except satisfied physical need after dinner and anticipated physical pleasure before. Such were the men among whom he would have to distinguish himself. But what he did not know, and what they had no intention of telling him, was that to take first honors in the various courses in dogma, ecclesiastical history, etc., which are studied in the seminary, was in their eyes nothing but a sin of vainglory. Ever since Voltaire and the establishment of bicameral government, which at bottom represents nothing but *suspicion* and *personal judgment* and instills the pernicious habit of *mistrusting* in the minds of the people, the Church of France seems to have realized that books are its real enemies. A submissive heart is everything in its eyes; success in studies, even sacred studies, is regarded as suspect, and rightly so. What is to prevent the superior man from going over to the other side, like Siéyè or Grégoire! The trembling Church clings to the pope as the sole chance of salvation. Only the pope can attempt to paralyze personal judgment and, by the pious pomp and ceremony of his court, make an impression on the bored and sick minds of worldly people.

Julien, having half realized these various truths, even though everything said in a seminary tends to deny them, fell into deep melancholy. He worked hard and quickly succeeded in learning things that are very useful to a priest, although he considered them utterly false and had no interest in them whatever. He believed there was nothing else for him to do.

"Have I been forgotten by everyone on earth?" he thought. He did not know that Father Pirard had received and thrown into the fire several letters postmarked Dijon in which, despite the perfectly decorous style in which they were written, the most intense passion was discernible. The love they expressed seemed to be opposed by great remorse. "So much the better," thought Father Pirard; "at least it wasn't an impious woman the young man was in love with."

One day Father Pirard opened a letter which seemed to be half obliterated by tears; it was an eternal farewell.

> At last *[the writer said to Julien]* heaven has granted me the grace of being able to hate, not the author of my sin, who will always be dearer to me than anything else in the world, but my sin itself. The sacrifice has been made, my has not been made without tears, as you can see. vation of those to whom I am bound, and whom you

have loved so much, has prevailed. A just but terrible God can no longer wreak vengeance on them for their mother's sins. Farewell, Julien; be just toward men.

The end of this letter was almost completely illegible. The writer gave an address in Dijon, yet hoped that Julien would never reply, or that at least he would use words which a woman who had returned to virtue could read without blushing.

Julien's melancholy, aided by the mediocre food supplied to the seminary by the contractor for dinners at eighty-three centimes a head, was beginning to affect his health when Fouqué suddenly appeared in his room one morning.

"At last I've managed to get in!" he said. "I know it's not your fault, but I came to Besançon five times without ever being able to see you. I even posted someone at the gate of the seminary; why the devil don't you ever go out?"

"I'm testing myself."

"You seem very different. But at last I've managed to see you again. Two good five-franc coins have just taught me I was a fool not to have offered them the first time I came."

The conversation between the two friends was endless. Julien changed color when Fouqué said to him, "By the way, did you know that the mother of your pupils has become a terribly pious woman?" And he spoke in that offhand manner which makes such a strange impression on the passionate soul whose most precious interests the speaker has just shaken without being aware of it. "Yes, my friend, she's full of the most exalted kind of piety. They say she makes pilgrimages. But, to the eternal shame of Father Maslon, who spied on poor Father Chélan for so long, Madame de Rênal won't have anything to do with him. She goes to confession in Dijon or Besançon."

"She comes to Besançon?" asked Julien, blushing.

"Rather often," replied Fouqué with a quizzical air.

"Do you have any copies of the *Constitutionnel* on you?"

"What?"

"I want to know if you have any copies of the *Constitutionnel*," replied Julien with perfect calm. "It's sold for thirty sous a copy here."

"What! Liberals even in the seminary?" cried Fouqué. "Poor France!" he added, imitating Father Maslon's hypocritical tone and honeyed manner.

This visit would have made a profound impression on our he if, the next day, a few words addressed to him by the l student from Verrières, who seemed so childish to him, had not led him to make an important discovery. Ever since his arrival at the seminary, Julien's conduct had been nothing but a series of mistakes. He bitterly laughed at himself.

Actually, the most important actions of his life were skillfully carried out, but he paid no attention to details, and the shrewdest students in a seminary are concerned with nothing else. He was therefore regarded by his fellow students as a freethinker. He had betrayed himself in all sorts of little ways.

In their eyes, he stood convicted of the appalling vice of *thinking and judging for himself,* instead of blindly following *authority* and example. Father Pirard had been of no help to him; not once had he spoken to him outside the confessional, and even there he listened much more than he spoke. Things would have been quite different for Julien if he had chosen Father Castanède as his confessor.

As soon as he became aware of his foolishness, he was no longer bored. He wanted to learn the full extent of the harm that had been done and, for that purpose, he emerged a little from the haughty and obstinate silence with which he had repulsed his fellow students. It was then that they took vengeance on him. His advances were received with a contempt that went to the point of derision. He realized that, ever since his arrival at the seminary, there had not been one hour, especially during the recreational periods, which had not borne consequences either for or against him, which had not either increased the number of his enemies or won him the good will of some student who was genuinely virtuous or seemed less coarse than the others. The damage to be repaired was enormous, and the task would be extremely difficult. From then on his attention was constantly on the alert; he had to assume an entirely different character.

The movements of his eyes, for example, gave him a great deal of difficulty. It is not without reason that they are kept lowered in such places. "How presumptuous I was in Verrières!" he said to himself. "I thought I was living, but I was only preparing myself for life; now at last I'm in the world such I'll find it until I've played out my part, surrounded by real ... es. What an enormous difficulty this everlasting hypocrisy ... ld put the labors of Hercules to shame! The Hercules of ... ies is Sixtus V, who, for fifteen years on end, de- ... his modesty forty cardinals who had seen him hot- ... nd arrogant all through his youth.

"So learning means nothing here!" he went on in irritation. "Learning dogma, sacred history, and so on, counts only in appearance. Everything they say about it is meant to make fools like me fall into the trap. Alas, my only merit was my rapid learning, my ability to grasp all that nonsense! Could it be that in their hearts they value it at its true worth? Do they judge it as I do? And I was foolish enough to be proud of myself! By always winning the first honors in my classes I've done nothing but make bitter enemies for myself. Chazel, who's more learned than I am, always puts into his compositions some stupid blunder that sends him back to the fiftieth place; if he gets first place, it's only because he wasn't thinking. Oh, how useful a word, one single word from Father Pirard would have been to me!"

As soon as Julien's eyes were opened, the long exercises in ascetic piety, such as saying the rosary five times a week, singing hymns to the Sacred Heart, etc., which had seemed so mortally boring to him before, now became his most interesting moments of action. Severely examining himself, and seeking above all not to overestimate his own abilities, he did not aspire at first, like the students who served as models for the others, to be constantly performing some *significant* action, i.e., one which manifests some form of Christian perfection. In a seminary, there is a way of eating a soft-boiled egg which reveals the progress one has made in the life of piety.

The reader, who is perhaps smiling, will please remember all the mistakes which Father Delille made while eating an egg when he had been invited to lunch by a great lady of the court of Louis XVI.

Julien sought at first to achieve the *non culpa*: the state of the young seminary student whose walk, way of moving his arms and eyes, etc., do not indicate anything truly worldly, but do not yet show the man absorbed in thoughts of the next world or the "utter nothingness" of this one.

Julien constantly saw, written with charcoal on the walls of the corridors, sentences such as the following: "What are sixty years of trial, compared to an eternity of bliss, or an eternity of boiling oil in hell?" He no longer despised them: he realized that he must have them continually before his eyes. "What will I be doing all my life?" he thought. "I'll be selling places in heaven to the faithful. And how will those places be made visible to them? By the difference between my outward appearance and that of a layman."

Even after several months of unremitting application, he still looked as though he *thought*. The set of his lips and the way he moved his eyes did not reveal an implicit faith ready to believe anything and uphold anything, even by martyrdom. It made him angry to see himself surpassed in this respect by the most boorish peasants. There were good reasons to explain why they never looked as though they were thinking.

What pains he took to achieve that sanctimonious, narrow face, that expression of blind, fervent faith, ready to believe anything and suffer anything, which one finds so frequently in the convents and monasteries of Italy, and of which Guercino has left us laymen such perfect examples in his church paintings.

On great holidays the students were given sausages and sauerkraut. Those sitting near Julien at table had observed that he was unmoved by these delicacies; this had been one of his first offenses. His fellow students regarded it as a sign of the most stupid hypocrisy, and nothing had made him more enemies. "Look at the fine gentleman, look at the conceited fool," they said, "who pretends to despise our best rations: sausages and sauerkraut! The scoundrel! The pompous ass! The sinner!" Julien ought to have refrained from eating part of it as an act of penance, making a sacrifice of it, and said to some friend, pointing to the sauerkraut, "What can a man offer to an all-powerful Being if not voluntary suffering?" He lacked the experience which makes it so easy to see such things.

"Alas, the ignorance of these young peasants, my fellow students, is a great advantage to them!" he thought in moments of discouragement. "When they first come to the seminary, the professor doesn't have to rid them of the appalling number of worldly ideas I brought with me and which they read on my face, no matter what I do."

Julien studied, with an attentiveness bordering on envy, the most boorish of the young peasants who came to the seminary. Up to the moment when they were told to take off their rateen jackets and don their black cassocks, their education was limited to a profound and boundless respect for "dry and liquid money," as they say in Franche-Comté. (This is the time-honored and eloquent term by which the natives of the province express the sublime concept of hard cash.)

Happiness, for those students, as for the heroes of Voltaire's stories, consisted above all in eating well. Julien discovered in nearly every one of them an innate respect for the man who wears a coat made of fine cloth. People with such sentiments value "distributive justice," such as is meted out by our courts, at its true worth, and even lower than its true worth. "What's to be gained," they often repeated among themselves, "by going to court against a big man?"

"Big" is the word used in the Jura valleys to denote a rich man. It is easy to imagine the respect of such people for the richest party of all: the government! Not to smile with respect at the very mention of the prefect's name is regarded by the peasants of Franche-Comté as a rash act; and rashness, among the poor, is swiftly punished by lack of bread.

After being almost suffocated at first by his feeling of contempt, Julien finally began to feel pity: the fathers of most of his fellow students had often come home to their thatched-roof huts on a winter evening and found neither bread, chestnuts nor potatoes there. "Is it surprising," he thought, "that for them a happy man is first of all one who has just had a good dinner and, after that, one who owns a good coat? My fellow students have a firm vocation: they see in the ecclesiastical calling a long continuation of the happiness of eating a good dinner and wearing a warm coat in winter."

Julien happened to hear a young student, gifted with imagination, say to his companion, "Why shouldn't I become pope some day, like Sixtus V, who was a swineherd?"

"Only Italians ever become pope," replied his friend, "but you can be sure they'll draw lots among us to fill posts as vicars-general, canons and maybe even bishops. Monsieur P——, the Bishop of Châlons, is the son of a cooper; that's my father's trade."

One day, in the middle of a lesson in dogma, Father Pirard sent for Julien. The poor young man was delighted to escape from the physical and moral atmosphere in which he was immersed.

The rector received him in the same manner that had frightened him so terribly on the day of his arrival at the seminary. "Explain to me what is written on this playing card," he said to him in a way that made him wish the earth would swallow him up.

Julien read: "Amanda Binet, Café de la Girafe, before eight o'clock. Say you are from Genlis, and my mother's cousin." He saw the immensity of the danger; Father Castanède's spies had stolen the address from him.

"The day I came here," he replied, looking at Father Pirard's forehead, for he could not endure his terrible gaze, "I was trembling: Father Chélan had already told me the seminary was full of informers and all sorts of maliciousness. Spying and the accusation of one's fellow students are encouraged here. Heaven wills it so, in order to show young priests life as it is, and inspire them with disgust for the world and its vanities.''

"So now you're making a speech to me, you young scoundrel!" said Father Pirard, furious.

"In Verrières," said Julien coldly, "my brothers used to beat me when they had some reason to be jealous of me. . . .''

"Come to the point!" cried Father Pirard, almost beside himself.

Without letting himself be the least bit intimidated, Julien resumed his narrative: "The day I arrived in Besançon, toward noon, I was hungry and I went into a café. My heart was filled with repugnance for such a profane place, but I thought my dinner would cost me less there than at an inn. A lady who seemed to be the mistress of the place took pity on me because I looked inexperienced. 'Besançon is full of dishonest people,' she said to me, 'and I'm afraid for you, monsieur. If you should have any trouble, ask me to help you. Send me a message before eight o'clock; if the porters of the seminary refuse to deliver it, say you're my cousin and that you come from Genlis. . . .' "

"Your long-winded story will be investigated!" cried Father Pirard, who, unable to sit still, was pacing up and down the room. "Go to your cell!"

He followed Julien and locked him in. Julien immediately began to examine his trunk, at the bottom of which the fatal card had been carefully hidden. Nothing was missing from the trunk, but several things had been disarranged; and yet he had always kept the key on him. "How lucky," he thought, "that during the time of my blindness I never accepted Father Castanède's offer to give me permission to leave the seminary; I understand his kindness now. I might have been weak enough to change clothes and go to see the fair Amanda; I'd have been lost. When they gave up hope of being able to use their information in that way, in order not to waste it they used it to denounce me."

The rector sent for him again two hours later.

"You weren't lying," he said to Julien, looking at him less sternly, "but you can't imagine how imprudent it was of you to keep that address. Poor boy! Ten years from now it may still do you harm."

CHAPTER 27

First Experience of Life

> Good God! The present age is like the Ark of the Lord: woe to anyone who touches it!
>
> —Diderot

THE READER will be kind enough to allow us to give very few clear and precise facts about this period of Julien's life. Not that we lack them, far from it; but what he saw in the seminary may be too black for the moderate coloring we have sought to maintain in these pages. Our contemporaries who suffer from certain things cannot recall them without a horror which destroys every other pleasure, even that of reading a story.

Julien had little success in his attempts to maintain a hypocritical demeanor. He sank into periods of disgust and even utter discouragement; he had failed, and in a base profession, too. The slightest outside help would have enabled him to sustain his determination; the difficulty to be overcome was not great, but he felt as lonely as a ship abandoned in the middle of the ocean. "And even if I succeed," he said to himself, "think of spending the rest of my life in such bad company! Gluttons who think of nothing but the bacon omelet they're going to devour at dinner, or men like Father Castanède, for whom no crime is too black! They'll rise to power, but at what a price, great God! Man's will is powerful, I read that everywhere; but is it strong enough to overcome such disgust? The task of great men used to be easy: no matter how terrible the danger, they found it beautiful. Who but myself can realize the ugliness of everything around me?"

This was the most trying moment of his life. It would be so easy for him to enlist in one of the fine regiments stationed in Besançon! He could become a Latin teacher; he needed so little to keep himself alive! But then he would no longer have a career, no longer a future to stir his imagination: it would be death. Here are the details of one of his wretched days.

One morning he said to himself, "My presumption has often led me to congratulate myself on being different from other young peasants. Well, I've lived long enough now to see that difference breeds hatred." This great truth had just been demonstrated to him by one of his most annoying failures. He had worked for a week to make himself agreeable to a student who lived in the odor of sanctity. He had been walking with him in the courtyard, submissively listening to idiotic nonsense that bored him to tears, when suddenly a storm arose. When the thunder rumbled, the saintly student rudely pushed him away and cried out, "Listen! It's every man for himself in this world and I don't want to be hit by lightning: God may strike you dead as an atheist, as a Voltaire."

With his teeth clenched in rage and his eyes raised toward the sky furrowed by streaks of lightning, Julien cried out to himself, "I'd deserve to be overwhelmed if I went to sleep during the storm! Let's try to win over some other stupid oaf."

The bell rang for Father Castanède's course in sacred history. On that particular day he was teaching the young peasants, who were still filled with such dread of their fathers' hard work and poverty, that the government, which was such an awesome entity in their eyes, had no real and legitimate power except that which was delegated to it by God's vicar on earth.

"Make yourselves worthy of the pope's loving kindness by the saintliness of your lives, and by your obedience," he added. "Be like 'a rod in his hands' and you will attain a magnificent position in which you will be in supreme command, away from all supervision, a secure position, of which the government pays a third of the stipend and the faithful, edified by your sermons, the other two thirds."

After leaving his classroom, Father Castanède stopped in the courtyard in the midst of his students, who were more attentive than usual that day.

"The saying that a man's position is as valuable as he makes it is especially true of a parish priest," he said to the students standing around him. "I myself have seen mountain parishes where the incidental fees amounted to more than those of many priests living in large towns. There was just as much money, and besides that there were fat capons, eggs, fresh butter and all sorts of other pleasant benefits. And in places like that, the parish priest takes first place without the shadow of a doubt: there's no good meal to which he isn't invited and during which he isn't treated with respect," etc., etc.

The students divided into groups as soon as Father Castanède left them and went up to his room. Julien was included in none of these groups: he was left alone like an outcast. In each one of them he saw a student toss a coin; if he guessed heads or tails correctly, his companions concluded that he would soon have one of those parishes with the fat fees.

Then came the anecdotes. One young priest, ordained for less than a year, had given a pet rabbit to the maid of an old parish priest and persuaded him to request him as his assistant; a few months later, for the old priest had died quite promptly, the young priest had taken his place in the wealthy parish. Another had succeeded in getting himself appointed as the successor of a parish priest in a large and prosperous country town by being present at all the meals of the paralytic old priest and gracefully carving his chickens for him.

Seminary students, like young men in every profession, exaggerate the effect of such little stratagems, which have an extraordinary quality about them and strike the imagination.

"I must get used to these conversations," thought Julien. When they were not talking about sausages and remunerative positions, they discussed the worldly side of ecclesiastical doctrines: the conflicts between bishops and prefects, mayors and parish priests. The idea of a second God gradually became apparent to Julien, but a God far more awesome and powerful than the first; this second God was the pope. The students said to each other, but in hushed tones and when they were sure they would not be overheard by Father Pirard, that if the pope did not take the trouble to appoint all the prefects and mayors in France, it was only because he had assigned this task to the King of France by naming him the eldest son of the Church.

It was at about this time that Julien decided he could improve his standing among his fellow students by making use of Monsieur de Maistre's book, *Du Pape*. He did, in fact, astonish them, but this was only one more misfortune for him. He displeased them by expressing their opinions better than they could themselves. Father Chélan had been rash with Julien, as he had been rash with himself. After giving him the habit of reasoning accurately and not allowing himself to be taken in by empty words, he had neglected to tell him that, in a person who is held in little esteem, this habit is a crime; for all sound reasoning gives offense.

Julien's eloquent speech was therefore regarded as another crime. After thinking about him a great deal, his fellow students succeeded in expressing in two words all the horror he aroused in them: they nicknamed him Martin Luther, "mainly," they said, "because of that infernal logic he's so proud of."

Several young students had fresher complexions and could be considered handsomer than Julien, but he had white hands and could not conceal certain habits of personal cleanliness. This advantage was a disadvantage in the sad institution into which fate had cast him. The dirty peasants among whom he lived declared that he had extremely lax morals. We are afraid that a full account of our hero's endless misfortunes would tire the reader. For example, his more robust fellow students tried to make a practice of beating him; he was obliged to arm himself with a metal compass and to announce, but only by gestures, that he would defend himself with it. Gestures cannot be used in a spy's report as advantageously as words.

CHAPTER 28

A Procession

> All hearts were moved. God's presence seemed to have descended into those narrow Gothic streets, adorned with draperies along both sides and covered with a thick layer of sand by the loving care of the faithful.
>
> —Young*

JULIEN TRIED in vain to make himself appear humble and stupid. He was unable to win favor: he was too different. "And yet," he said to himself, "all these professors are very perceptive men, chosen from among a thousand others; why aren't they pleased with my humility?" It seemed to him that only one of them took advantage of his readiness to believe anything and appear to be taken in by anything. This was Father Chas-Bernard, master of ceremonies of the cathedral, where, for the past fifteen years, he had been given the hope that he would be made a canon; meanwhile he taught sacred oratory in the seminary. During the time of his blindness, this course had been one of those in which Julien had most frequently taken first place. Father Chas had used this as a reason for showing friendship toward him and, on leaving his classroom, he would often take him by the arm for a stroll in the garden.

"What does he have in mind?" wondered Julien. He found with astonishment that Father Chas spoke to him for hours on end of the vestments which the cathedral possessed. Besides the mourning vestments, there were seventeen chasubles trimmed with braid. A great deal was expected from the aged Madame de Rubempré; for at least seventy years this lady, who was now

---

*Cf. note at beginning of Chapter 26.—L.B.

ninety, had been keeping her wedding gowns, made of superb Lyons silk embroidered in gold. "Just imagine, my friend," said Father Chas, coming to a standstill and opening his eyes wide, "there's so much gold in that cloth that it stands up by itself! Most people in Besançon believe that, through Madame de Rubempré's will, the treasury of the cathedral will be enriched with more than ten chasubles, not to mention four or five copes for important occasions. I'll go even further," he added, lowering his voice: "I have good reason to believe that she'll leave us eight magnificent silver-gilt candlesticks that are supposed to have been bought in Italy by the Duke of Burgundy, Charles the Bold, whose favorite minister was one of her ancestors."

"But what's he leading up to with all this nonsense?" wondered Julien. "This careful preparation has been going on for what seems like a century, and still nothing has come of it. He must really mistrust me! He's shrewder than all the others, because I can easily guess their secret motives within two weeks. It's understandable: his ambition has been suffering for fifteen years!"

One evening, in the middle of his fencing lesson, Julien was sent for by Father Pirard, who said to him, "Tomorrow is Corpus Christi. Father Chas-Bernard needs you to help him decorate the cathedral. Go there and be obedient."

Father Pirard called him back and added, with an air of sympathy, "It's for you to decide whether you want to take the opportunity to go somewhere else in town."

"Incedo per ignes" ("I have secret enemies"), replied Julien.

Early the next morning he walked to the cathedral with his eyes lowered. The sight of the streets, and of the activity that was beginning to reign in the city, did him good. On all sides, people were draping the fronts of their houses for the procession. All the time he had spent in the seminary now seemed to him no more than an instant. His thoughts were in Vergy, and with the pretty Amanda Binet, whom he might encounter, for her café was not far away. In the distance he caught sight of Father Chas-Bernard standing in front of his beloved cathedral; he was a fat man with a cheerful, candid face. That day he was exultant: "I was waiting for you, my dear son," he called out as soon as he saw Julien. "You're welcome here. This day's work will be long and hard, so let's fortify ourselves with a first breakfast; the second one will come at ten o'clock, during high mass."

"I do not wish to be alone for a single instant, monsieur,"

replied Julien gravely. "Please notice," he added, pointing to the clock above them, "that I've arrived at one minute to five."

"Oh, so you're afraid of those malicious young rascals at the seminary! It's very kind of you to pay any attention to them at all. Is a road any worse because there are thorns in the hedges on both sides of it? The travelers go their way and leave the wicked thorns to wither where they are. But we must go to work, my dear friend, to work!"

Father Chas had been right in saying that the work would be long and hard. There had been a great funeral service in the cathedral the day before and it had been impossible to make any preparations; it was therefore necessary, in a single morning, to cover each of the Gothic pillars which form the nave and the two aisles with a kind of red damask coat thirty feet high. The bishop had brought in four upholsterers from Paris by mail coach, but these gentlemen could not do everything themselves and, far from correcting the awkwardness of their Besançon colleagues, they increased it by laughing at them.

Julien saw that he would have to climb up the ladders himself; his agility stood him in good stead. He undertook to direct the local upholsterers. Father Chas, delighted, watched him bustling about from one ladder to another. When all the pillars had been covered with damask, the next task was to place five enormous bundles of feathers on the canopy above the high altar. Its magnificent gilded wooden top was supported by eight large twisted columns of Italian marble. But in order to reach the center of the canopy, above the tabernacle, it was necessary to walk along an old and possibly worm-eaten wooden cornice forty feet above the floor.

The sight of this perilous path had extinguished the gaiety, so effervescent until then, of the Parisian upholsterers; they looked at it from below, discussed it at length and did not go up. Julien seized the bundles of feathers and ran up the ladder. He arranged them admirably on the crown-shaped ornament at the center of the canopy. When he reached the bottom of the ladder, Father Chas-Bernard embraced him.

"*Optime!*" exclaimed the good priest. "I'll tell the bishop about this!"

The ten o'clock breakfast was very gay. Father Chas had never before seen his church looking so beautiful.

"My dear disciple," he said to Julien, "my mother used to rent chairs in this venerable basilica, so I was brought up in this mighty edifice. Robespierre's reign of terror ruined us. I was only eight years old at the time, but I was already serving at masses in private houses; I was given a meal on the day of the mass. No one knew how to fold a chasuble better than I did: the gold braid was never broken. Since the restoration of the Faith by Napoleon, I've had the good fortune to be in charge of everything in this venerable metropolitan church. Five times a year I see it decked out in these beautiful ornaments. But never before has it been so resplendent, never have the strips of damask been so well draped as they are today, never have they clung so tightly to the pillars."

"At last he's going to tell me his secret," thought Julien. "He's talking to me about himself now; he's becoming effusive." But nothing indiscreet was said by that obviously excited man. "And yet he's worked hard and he's happy," thought Julien. "And he's drunk plenty of good wine. What a man! What an example for me! He takes the cake!" (This was a slangy expression he had picked up from the old army surgeon.)

When the *Sanctus* of the high mass sounded, Julien expressed a desire to put on a surplice in order to follow the bishop in the superb procession.

"You're forgetting about the thieves, my dear friend!" cried Father Chas. "What an idea! The procession is about to go out and the church will soon be deserted; you and I will keep watch over it. We'll be lucky if we lose only a few yards of that beautiful gold braid around the bottoms of the pillars. That's another gift from Madame de Rubempré; it comes from her great-grandfather, the famous count. It's pure gold, my dear friend," he added, speaking in Julien's ear in a tone that clearly showed his excitement. "Nothing false about it! I'll assign you to inspect the north aisle; don't leave it. I'll take care of the south aisle and the nave. Keep an eye on the confessionals; it's from there that the women the thieves use as spies watch for a moment when our backs are turned."

As he finished speaking, the clock struck a quarter to twelve; the big bell immediately began to toll. It rang in full peal; Julien was moved by its rich, solemn tone. His imagination was no longer on earth. The odor of the incense and the rose petals which had been strewn in front of the Blessed Sacrament by children dressed as Saint John heightened his exaltation.

The deep sound of the bell ought to have made Julien think only about the work of twenty men earning fifty centimes each, assisted, perhaps, by fifteen or twenty of the faithful. He should have thought of the wear and tear on the ropes and the wooden framework, of the danger to the bell itself, which falls every two hundred years, and he should have tried to think of some way of diminishing the ringers' wages, or of paying them with some indulgence or other favor drawn from the treasures of the Church without strain on her purse.

Instead of being absorbed in these wise reflections, however, Julien's mind, exalted by the rich, virile sounds of the bell, was wandering in imaginary space. He would never make a good priest or a great administrator. Minds that are moved in this way are capable only, at the very most, of producing an artist. Here Julien's presumption stands out with crystal clarity. Fifty, perhaps, of his fellow seminary students, made attentive to the realities of life by the public hatred and Jacobinism they had been taught to see lurking behind every bush, would have thought of nothing except the ringers' wages while listening to the great bell of the cathedral. They would have estimated with the genius of a Barême whether the public's emotion was worth the money paid to the ringers. If Julien had chosen to consider the material interests of the cathedral, his mind, soaring beyond the goal, would have thought of saving forty francs from the income of the church and lost an opportunity to avoid an expenditure of twenty-five centimes.

While the procession was slowly making its way through Besançon in the most beautiful weather imaginable, halting at all the magnificent temporary altars which the local authorities had vied with one another in erecting, the church remained in deep silence. A dim light and a pleasant coolness reigned in it, and it was still scented with the perfume of the flowers and the incense.

The silence, the profound solitude and the coolness of the long aisle made Julien's reverie sweeter. He had no fear of being disturbed by Father Chas, who was occupied in another part of the edifice. His soul had almost left its mortal shell, which was slowly strolling up and down the north aisle entrusted to his surveillance. His mind was all the more at rest because he had ascertained that there were only a few pious women in the confessionals. His eyes stared without seeing.

However, he was half roused from his trance by the sight of two extremely well-dressed women who were kneeling, one in a confessional, the other beside her on a chair. He looked at them without paying any attention to them, but, whether from a vague sense of his duty or because of his unconscious admiration of the simple but noble manner in which they were dressed, he noticed that there was no priest in the confessional. "It's strange," he thought, "that those two beautiful ladies aren't kneeling before some temporary altar, if they're pious, or sitting in the best seats on some balcony, if they're worldly. How well cut that dress is! What grace!" He slackened his pace, trying to examine them more closely.

The one who was kneeling in the confessional turned her head slightly when she heard the sound of Julien's footsteps in the midst of the profound silence. Suddenly she uttered a little cry and fainted.

As her strength failed her, this lady, already kneeling, fell backward; her friend, who was near her, hurried to assist her. At the same time, Julien saw the shoulders of the lady who was falling. A twisted strand of large pearls, well known to him, caught his attention. What was his state when he recognized Madame de Rênal's hair! It was she. The lady trying to hold up her head and prevent her from falling all the way to the floor was Madame Derville. Julien, beside himself with emotion, rushed forward; Madame de Rênal's fall might also have brought down her friend if he had not supported both of them. He saw Madame de Rênal's head drooping on her shoulder; she was pale and completely unconscious. He knelt to help Madame Derville place that charming head on the support of a straw-bottomed chair.

Madame Derville turned around and recognized him. "Go away, monsieur, go away!" she said to him in a tone of violent anger. "Above all, she mustn't see you again. It's easy to understand why the sight of you fills her with horror: she was so happy before she met you! Your conduct is atrocious. Hurry, go away, if you have any shame left."

These words were spoken with such authority, and Julien was so weak at that moment, that he went away. "She's always hated me," he said to himself, thinking of Madame Derville.

Just then the nasal chant of the leading priests in the procession rang through the church; the procession was returning. Father Chas-Bernard repeatedly called to Julien, who did not hear him at first. He finally came to take him by the arm behind a pillar, where Julien had taken refuge, more dead than alive. He wanted to present him to the bishop.

"You're not feeling well, my son," said Father Chas when he saw him so pale and almost unable to walk. "You've worked too hard." He gave him his arm. "Come, sit down on the little bench for the man who gives out the holy water. You'll be behind me; I'll hide you." They were now beside the main door. "Don't worry, we still have at least twenty minutes before the bishop gets here. Try to pull yourself together. I'll hold you up when he passes, because I'm still strong and vigorous, in spite of my age.''

But when the bishop came by, Julien was trembling so violently that Father Chas abandoned the idea of presenting him.

''Don't be too upset about it,'' he said. ''I'll find another opportunity.''

That evening he sent to the chapel of the seminary ten pounds of candles which, he said, had been saved by Julien's efforts and the promptness with which he had had them extinguished. The poor boy felt as though he himself had been extinguished: he had not had a single thought in his head since seeing Madame de Rênal.

CHAPTER 29
The First Step Forward

> He knew the times in which he was living, he knew his
> district, and now he is rich.
>
> —*Le Précurseur*

JULIEN HAD not yet recovered from the state of dazed preoccupation into which he had been plunged by the event in the cathedral when, one morning, the stern Father Pirard sent for him.

''Father Chas-Bernard has just written me a favorable letter about you,'' he said. ''On the whole, I'm rather well pleased with your conduct. You're extremely imprudent, and even thoughtless, although you don't give that impression; so far, however, your heart has been sound and even generous, and you have a superior mind. All in all, I see in you a spark that mustn't be neglected.

''After fifteen years of labor, I'm about to leave this seminary. My crime is that of having allowed the students to exercise their free will, and of having neither protected nor opposed the secret society of which you've spoken to me during confession. Before leaving, I want to do something for you; I'd have acted two months sooner, because you deserve it, if it hadn't been for the denunciation based on the address of Amanda Binet which was found in your room. I'm appointing you as tutor in the Old and New Testaments.''

Julien, carried away with gratitude, thought seriously of falling to his knees and giving thanks to God, but he yielded to a more genuine impulse: he went up to Father Pirard, took his hand and raised it to his lips.

"What are you doing!" cried the rector angrily; but Julien's eyes were more eloquent than his action.

Father Pirard looked at him in astonishment, like a man who, in the course of long years, has become unaccustomed to encountering delicate emotions. This attention betrayed him; his voice faltered.

"Yes, my son," he said, "I'm fond of you! Heaven knows it's completely against my will. I ought to be just and have neither hatred nor love for anyone. Your career will be full of difficulties. I see something in you that offends the vulgar. Jealousy and slander will pursue you. No matter where Providence places you, your companions will never see you without hating you; and if they pretend to like you, it will be only in order to betray you more surely. There is only one remedy for that: seek help only from God, who has made the hatred of others unavoidable in order to punish you for your presumption. Keep your conduct pure; that's the only resource I can see for you. If you hold fast to the truth with unshakable tenacity, sooner or later your enemies will be confounded."

It had been so long since Julien had heard a friendly voice that we must forgive him a moment of weakness: he burst into tears. Father Pirard opened his arms to him; it was a very precious moment for both of them.

Julien was wild with joy; this promotion was the first he had ever obtained and its advantages were enormous. In order to understand them, one must have been condemned to spend whole months without an instant of solitude, and in close contact with companions who were irritating at best, and mostly unbearable. Their shouts alone would have been enough to derange a delicate constitution. Those well-fed and well-dressed peasants could express their boisterous joy and feel that it was complete only when they were shouting at the top of their lungs.

Julien would now have dinner alone, or nearly so, an hour later than the other students. He had a key to the garden and could take walks in it at times when it was deserted.

To his great astonishment, he noticed that the others hated him less than before; he had expected, on the contrary, an increase in their hatred. His secret desire to be left alone, which was all too obvious and which had earned him so much enmity, was no longer a sign of ridiculous arrogance. In the eyes of the coarse creatures around him, it was now a just awareness of his own dignity. Their hatred diminished perceptibly, especially among the youugest of his fellow students, who had now become his pupils, and whom he treated with great courtesy. Little by little he even gained supporters, and it became bad form to call him Martin Luther.

But what good would it do to name his enemies and his friends? That kind of thing is ugly, especially when the description is accurate. And yet these are the people's only teachers of morality, and what would become of the people without them? Will the newspaper ever be able to replace the parish priest?

Since Julien's promotion, the rector of the seminary had made it a point never to speak to him alone. This conduct was prudent for both the master and the disciple, but above all it was a *trial*. Father Pirard, stern Jansenist that he was, had an inflexible principle: "If you regard a man as having merit, then place obstacles in the way of everything he wants and everything he undertakes. If his merit is genuine, he will surely be able to surmount your obstacles or find a way around them."

It was the hunting season. Fouqué had the idea of sending a stag and a boar to the seminary in the name of Julien's family. The dead animals were left in the corridor between the kitchen and the refectory, where all the students saw them on their way to dinner. They were a great object of curiosity. The boar, dead though he was, frightened the youngest students; they touched his tusks. No one spoke of anything else for a week.

This gift, which placed Julien's family in that segment of society which one must respect, dealt a mortal blow to jealousy. It was a mark of superiority consecrated by fortune. Chazel and all the other outstanding students made overtures to Julien and almost reproached him for not having informed them of his family's wealth, thereby exposing them to the risk of failing to show proper respect for money.

There was a military draft, from which Julien was exempted in his capacity as a seminary student. This incident moved him deeply. "So now I've lost forever the moment when, twenty years ago, a heroic life would have begun for me!" he thought.

Strolling alone in the garden of the seminary, he overheard the conversation of some masons who were working on the wall.

"Well, we'll have to go—there's another draft."

"In the *other man's* time, that would have been all right! A mason could get to be an officer then, even a general; it really happened."

"But look what it's like now! Beggars are the only ones that go off to the army. If a man has money, he stays home."

"If you're born poor, you stay poor, and that's all there is to it."

"Is it true what they say, that the *other man* is dead?" put in a third mason.

"It's rich people that say that! They're afraid of him."

"What a difference! How things got done in his time! And to think he was betrayed by his own marshals! What traitors they were!"

This conversation consoled Julien a little. As he walked away he repeated with a sigh, *"The only king whose memory is still kept by the people."*

Examination time came. Julien answered the questions brilliantly. He saw that even Chazel was trying to show all his knowledge.

On the first day, the examiners appointed by the famous vicar-general, Monsieur de Frilair, were greatly annoyed at having to give first place, or at least second place, on their list to Julien Sorel, who had been pointed out to them as Father Pirard's favorite. Bets were made in the seminary that, on the list of the general examination, Julien would win first place, which carried with it the honor of having dinner with the bishop. But at the end of one session, during which the topic was the Fathers of the Church, a clever examiner, after questioning Julien on Saint Jerome and his passion for Cicero, went on to speak of Horace, Virgil and other profane authors. Unknown to his fellow students, Julien had learned a great many passages from these authors by heart. Carried away by his success, he forgot where he was and, at the repeated requests of the examiner, enthusiastically quoted and paraphrased several of Horace's odes. After drawing him in deeper and deeper for twenty minutes, the examiner abruptly changed his tone and bitterly reproached him for wasting his time on those profane studies and filling his head with useless or criminal ideas.

"You're right, monsieur, I'm a fool," said Julien humbly, realizing that he had been the victim of a clever stratagem.

This ruse on the part of the examiner was regarded as an underhanded trick, even in the seminary, but this did not prevent Monsieur de Frilair, the clever man who had so ably organized the framework of the Besançon *Congrégation* and whose dispatches to Paris made the judges, the prefect and even the generals of the garrison tremble, from writing, with his powerful hand, the number 198 beside Julien's name. He was delighted at thus being able to mortify his enemy, the Jansenist Pirard.

For the past ten years his main concern had been to remove him as rector of the seminary. Father Pirard, personally following the plan of conduct he had outlined to Julien, was sincere, devout, aloof from intrigue and devoted to his duty. But heaven, in its wrath, had given him that irascible temperament which is so sensitive to insults and hatred. Not one of the affronts that were inflicted on him was lost on that ardent soul. He had been ready to hand in his resignation a hundred times, but he believed himself to be useful in the post in which Providence had placed him. "I'm preventing the spread of Jesuitism and idolatry," he would say to himself.

At the time of the examinations, it had been perhaps two months since he had last spoken to Julien, and yet he was ill for a week when he received the official letter annnouncing the results of the competition and saw the number 198 beside the name of the student he regarded as the glory of the seminary. The only compensation for his severe character was to concentrate every means of vigilance on Julien. He was delighted to find in him neither anger, plans for revenge nor discouragement.

A few weeks later, Julien started when he received a letter: it was postmarked Paris. "At last," he thought, "Madame de Rênal has remembered her promises." A gentleman who signed himself Paul Sorel and professed to be related to him had sent him a bill of exchange for five hundred francs. The letter stated that if Julien continued his successful study of the best Latin authors, a similar sum would be sent to him each year.

"It's she, it's her kindness!" thought Julien with deep emotion. "She wants to console me; but why isn't there a single affectionate word in the letter?"

He was mistaken about this letter: Madame de Rênal, guided by her friend Madame Derville, was entirely absorbed in her profound remorse. Against her will, she often thought of the strange young man whose acquaintance had upset her entire life, but she had sternly forbidden herself to write to him.

If we spoke the language of the seminary, we might recognize a miracle in that bill of exchange for five hundred francs and say that it was Abbé de Frilair himself that heaven had employed to make this gift to Julien.

Twelve years earlier, Abbé de Frilair had arrived in Besançon with an extremely light valise which, according to the story, contained his entire fortune. He was now one of the wealthiest landowners in the department. In the course of his growing prosperity, he had bought half of a certain estate, the other half of which had passed by inheritance to Monsieur de La Mole. Hence a great lawsuit between these two gentlemen.

Despite the brilliant life he led in Paris and the posts he held at court, the Marquis de La Mole realized that it was dangerous to fight in Besançon against a powerful vicar-general who had the reputation of making and unmaking prefects. Instead of requesting a gratuity of fifty thousand francs, disguised under some heading that would be admitted into the budget, and allowing Abbé de Frilair to win that wretched lawsuit over fifty thousand francs, the marquis became stubbornly determined. He thought he was in the right: a fine reason!

Now, if we may be allowed to say so, where is the judge who does not have a son, or at least a relative, to help along in the world? To enlighten the most blind, a week after obtaining the first decision, Abbé de Frilair took the bishop's carriage and personally delivered the Cross of the Legion of Honor to his lawyer. Monsieur de La Mole, somewhat taken aback by his adversary's tactics and feeling that his own lawyers were weakening, asked the advice of Father Chélan, who referred him to Father Pirard.

At the time of our story, their correspondence had been continuing for several years. Father Pirard plunged into the affair with all the forcefulness of his passionate character. Constantly seeing the marquis' lawyers, he studied his case and, finding him to be in the right, began to support him openly against the all-powerful vicar-general. The latter was outraged at such insolence, and from an insignificant Jansenist, too!

"You can see what they're worth, those court noblemen who claim to have so much power!" he said to his intimate friends. "Monsieur de La Mole hasn't even sent a wretched cross to his agent in Besançon, and now he's going to let him be unceremoniously dismissed from his post. And yet I receive letters telling me that the noble peer never lets a week go by without going to display his cordon bleu in the drawing room of the Keeper of the Seals, whoever he may be."

Despite all of Father Pirard's activities and the fact that Monsieur de La Mole was always on excellent terms with the Minister of Justice, and even more so with his officials, all that he had been able to accomplish, after six years of effort, was to avoid losing his case entirely.

Constantly in correspondence with Father Pirard over an affair whose progress they both followed with passion, the marquis had finally come to appreciate his type of mind. Little by little, in spite of the enormous difference between their respective social positions, their correspondence had taken on a tone of friendship. Father Pirard told the marquis that his enemies were seeking, through their malicious intrigues against him, to force him to hand in his resignation. In the anger aroused in him by what he regarded as the infamous stratagem employed against Julien, he wrote about the young man in one of his letters to the marquis.

Although extremely rich, this great nobleman was not at all miserly. He had never once been able to make Father Pirard accept even a reimbursement of the money he had spent for postage as a result of the lawsuit. He seized on the idea of sending five hundred francs to his favorite student. He took the trouble to write the accompanying letter in his own hand. This made him think of Father Pirard.

One day the latter received a short note requesting him to go at once, for an urgent matter, to an inn on the outskirts of Besançon. When he arrived there he found Monsieur de La Mole's steward.

"The marquis has instructed me to bring you his carriage," the man said to him. "He hopes that, after reading this letter, you will choose to leave for Paris in four or five days. I'll spend the time inspecting the marquis' estates in Franche-Comté; please let me know how long you will need. Then, on whatever day suits you best, we'll leave for Paris."

The letter was short:

Rid yourself, my dear monsieur, of all the chicanery of the provinces, come to Paris and breathe a more peaceful atmosphere. I am sending you my carriage, with orders to await your decision for four days. I will wait for you myself, in Paris, until Tuesday. All I need is your consent, monsieur, to accept, in your name, one of the best ecclesiastical posts in the vicinity of Paris. The wealthiest of your parishioners has never seen you, but he is more strongly devoted to you than you can imagine; he is the Marquis de La Mole.

Without being aware of it, the stern Father Pirard loved his seminary, even though it was filled with enemies; he had devoted all his thoughts to it for the past fifteen years. Monsieur de La Mole's letter was for him like the sudden appearance of a surgeon under orders to perform a painful but necessary operation. His dismissal was certain. He agreed to meet the steward in three days.

For forty-eight hours he was in a fever of uncertainty. Finally he wrote to Monsieur de La Mole and composed, for the bishop, a letter that was a masterpiece of ecclesiastical style, although somewhat long. It would have been difficult to find language more irreproachable, or breathing more sincere respect. And yet this letter, designed to make Abbé de Frilair spend a trying hour with his superior, articulated all the serious grounds for complaint and even descended to the sordid little annoyances which, after having been endured with resignation for six years, were now forcing Father Pirard to leave the diocese.

Wood was stolen from his shed, his dog had been poisoned, etc., etc.

When he had finished writing this letter he sent someone to awaken Julien, who, at eight o'clock in the evening, was already asleep, as were all the other students.

"Do you know where the bishop's palace is?" he asked him in excellent Latin. "Take this letter to him. I won't try to hide the fact that I'm sending you among wolves. Be all eyes and ears. Don't tell any lies in your answers, but remember that the man who's questioning you might take real delight in being able to harm you. I'm glad, my son, that I can give you this experience before I leave you, because I won't conceal from you that the letter you're going to deliver contains my resignation."

Julien stood motionless; he was deeply attached to Father Pirard. In vain did prudence say to him, "After this honorable man's departure, the Sacred Heart faction will take away my position of tutor, and perhaps even expel me"; he was unable to think of himself. He was bothered by a sentence which he wanted to phrase in a polite manner, but he was utterly incapable of concentrating his attention on it.

"Well, my friend, aren't you going?"

"I was thinking, monsieur," said Julien timidly, "that they say you've never put anything aside during your long administration. I have six hundred francs . . ." Tears prevented him from continuing.

"That too will be noted," said the ex-rector of the seminary coldly. "Go to the bishop's palace, it's getting late."

As luck would have it, Abbé de Frilair was in attendance in the drawing room of the bishop's palace that evening; the bishop was dining at the prefecture. It was therefore to Abbé de Frilair himself that Julien delivered the letter, although he did not recognize him.

Julien was amazed to see this priest boldly open the letter addressed to the bishop. The vicar-general's handsome face soon expressed surprise mingled with intense pleasure, then it assumed an even more solemn expression than before. While he was reading, Julien, impressed with his good looks, had time to examine him. His face would have had more gravity if it had not been for the extreme shrewdness which appeared in some of its features, and which would even have given an impression of duplicity if the possessor of that handsome face had ceased for a moment to control it. The nose, which was extremely prominent, formed a single straight line and unfortunately gave to a profile that was otherwise quite distinguished an irremediable resemblance to the physiognomy of a fox. Furthermore, this priest who appeared to be so deeply concerned with Father Pirard's resignation was dressed with an elegance which pleased Julien greatly, and which he had never seen displayed by any other priest.

It was not until later that Julien learned about Abbé de Frilair's special talent: he knew how to amuse the bishop, a charming old man who was made to live in Paris and regarded Besançon as a place of exile. This bishop had very bad eyesight and he was passionately fond of fish; Abbé de Frilair removed the bones from the fish that were served to him.

Julien was silently watching the priest as he reread the letter of resignation when suddenly the door was noisily opened. A richly attired servant walked swiftly through the room. Julien scarcely had time to turn toward the door; he saw a little old man wearing a pectoral cross. He bowed deeply. The bishop gave him a kindly smile and went into the next room. The handsome priest followed him and Julien was left alone in the drawing room, whose pious splendor he was able to admire at leisure.

The Bishop of Besançon, an intelligent man whose spirit had been tried but not crushed by the long hardships of the Emigration, was more than seventy-five years old, and he cared infinitely little about what would happen in ten years.

"Who's that perceptive-looking seminary student I think I saw as I went through the drawing room?" he asked. "Aren't they supposed to be in bed at this hour, according to my regulations?"

"This one is wide awake, I can assure you, Monsignor, and he's brought some excellent news: the resignation of the only Jansenist left in your diocese. The terrible Father Pirard has finally taken a hint."

"Well," said the bishop with a malicious smile, "I defy you to replace him with a man who's worth as much as he is. And to show you how much he's worth, I'm going to invite him to dinner tomorrow."

The vicar-general tried to slip in a few words concerning the choice of a successor. The prelate, having little inclination to discuss business, said to him, "Before we install the next rector, let's try to find out something about this one's resignation. Send in that seminary student; truth comes from the mouths of babes."

Julien was summoned. "I'm going to find myself between two inquisitors," he thought. Never had he felt more courageous.

As he entered the room, two tall valets, better dressed than Monsieur Valenod himself, were undressing the bishop. The prelate, before coming to the subject of Father Pirard, saw fit to question Julien about his studies. He spoke a little about dogma and was amazed. Next he turned to the classics, to Virgil, Horace and Cicero. "Those names," thought Julien, "earned me my number 198. I have nothing to lose, so let's try to shine." He succeeded; the bishop, an excellent classicist himself, was delighted.

During dinner at the prefecture, a young lady, justly celebrated, had recited the poem "La Madeleine." He was in the mood for literary conversation; he quickly forgot Father Pirard, and all his other affairs, to discuss with the seminary student the question of whether Horace was rich or poor. He quoted several odes, but occasionally his memory failed him, and then Julien would immediately recite the entire ode, with an air of modesty. What struck the bishop was that Julien never departed from his conversational tone: he recited his twenty or thirty Latin verses as though he were speaking of what took place in the seminary. They spoke for a long time about Virgil and Cicero. Finally the prelate could not help complimenting the young student.

"It would be impossible to have made better progress in your studies," he said.

"Monsignor," replied Julien, "your seminary can offer you one hundred ninety-seven students much less unworthy of your praise."

"What do you mean?" asked the prelate, surprised by this figure.

"I can give you official proof in support of what I have the honor of saying to you, Monsignor. In the annual examination of the seminary, answering questions on precisely the subjects that have just won me your praise, I was given number 198."

"Ah! This is Father Pirard's favorite!" cried the bishop, laughing and looking at Abbé de Frilair. "We should have expected it; but it's fair play. Isn't it true, my friend," he added, turning to Julien, "that you were roused out of bed to be sent here?"

"Yes, Monsignor. I've left the seminary alone only once before in my life: to help Father Chas-Bernard decorate the cathedral on Corpus Christi."

"*Optime!*" said the bishop. "So it was you who showed such courage in placing the bundles of feathers on the canopy! They make me shudder each year; I'm always afraid they may cost me a man's life. You'll go far, my friend; but I don't want to put an end to your career, which will be brilliant, by letting you die of hunger."

In accordance with an order from the bishop, a servant brought in some biscuits and Malaga wine, to which Julien did justice. Abbé de Frilair gave evidence of an even greater appetite, for he knew that his bishop liked to see people eat gaily and heartily.

The prelate, becoming more and more pleased with the end of his evening, spoke of ecclesiastical history for a moment. He saw that Julien did not understand. He then went on to the moral condition of the Roman Empire under the emperors around the time of Constantine. The end of paganism was accompanied by that state of disquietude and doubt which now troubles the sad and weary minds of the nineteenth century. The bishop noticed that Julien scarcely even knew the name of Tacitus. To his surprise, Julien candidly replied that that author was not in the library of the seminary.

"I'm delighted to hear it," said the bishop gaily. "You've solved a problem for me: for the last ten minutes I've been trying to think of a way to thank you for the pleasant evening you've given me so unexpectedly: I didn't expect to find a Doctor of the Church in one of the students of my seminary. Although it isn't a very canonical present, I'm going to give you a set of Tacitus."

The prelate had eight superbly bound volumes brought in and, on the title page of the first, he personally wrote a Latin inscription to Julien Sorel. He took pride in his fine command of the Latin language. Finally he said to Julien, in a serious tone that contrasted sharply with the one in which he had carried on the rest of the conversation, "Young man, *if you behave sensibly,* you'll have the best parish in my diocese some day, and it won't be a hundred leagues away from my episcopal palace, either; but you must *behave sensibly.*"

Julien, laden with his volumes, left the bishop's palace in great astonishment just as the clock struck midnight.

The bishop had not said a word to him about Father Pirard. Julien was surprised above all by the prelate's extreme politeness. He had never imagined such urbanity of manner, combined with such an air of natural dignity. He was greatly impressed by the contrast when he returned to the somber Father Pirard, who was waiting for him impatiently.

"*Quid tibi dixerunt?*" ("What did they say to you?"), he called out to him loudly as soon as he saw him.

Julien found some difficulty in translating the bishop's conversation into Latin. "Speak French, and repeat his own words, without adding or omitting anything," said the ex-rector in his harsh voice and profoundly inelegant manner.

"What a strange present for a bishop to make to a young seminary student!" he said as he turned the pages of the superb set of Tacitus, whose gilded edges seemed to fill him with horror.

It was two o'clock in the morning when, after listening to an extremely detailed report, he allowed his favorite student to return to his room.

"Leave me the first volume of your Tacitus, the one containing the bishop's inscription," he said. "That line of Latin will be your lightning rod in this seminary after I'm gone. *Erit tibi, fili mi, successor meus tanquem leo quaerens quem devoret.*" ("My successor will be to you, my son, as a furious lion seeking someone to devour.")

The next morning Julien found something strange in the way his fellow students spoke to him. It made him all the more reserved. "It's the effect of Father Pirard's resignation," he thought. "Everyone in the seminary knows about it, and I'm regarded as his favorite. There must be something insulting behind this attitude." But he was unable to discern it. There was, on the contrary, an absence of hatred in the eyes of all those whom he encountered in the dormitories. "What can this mean?" he wondered. "It's no doubt a trap, so I'd better play my hand cautiously." Finally the little student from Verrières said to him, laughing, "*Cornelii Taciti Opera Omnia.*" ("The Complete Works of Tacitus.")

At these words, which were overheard, all the others began to vie with one another in complimenting Julien, not only on the magnificent gift he had received from the bishop, but also on the two-hour conversation with which he had been honored. They knew all about it, down to the smallest details. From then on there was no more envy; everyone basely curried favor with him. Father Castanède, who, only the day before, had treated him with the utmost insolence, now came to take him by the arm and invite him to lunch.

Due to a fateful trait of Julien's character, the insolence of those coarse creatures had greatly distressed him; their servility now disgusted him and gave him no pleasure.

Toward noon, Father Pirard took leave of his students, not without addressing a stern discourse to them. "Do you want the honors of this world," he said to them, "all social advantages, the pleasure of commanding, that of flouting the law and being insolent to everyone with impunity? Or do you want to win your eternal salvation? The least advanced among you have only to open your eyes to distinguish between the two paths."

No sooner had he left than the devout members of the *Sacred Heart of Jesus* went to chant a *Te Deum* in the chapel. No one in the seminary had taken the ex-rector's discourse seriously. "He's angry at having been dismissed" was the comment made on all sides; not one student was naïve enough to believe in a voluntary resignation from a position which provided so much contact with important contractors.

Father Pirard took a room at the best inn in Besançon, declaring, on the pretext of imaginary personal affairs, that he would remain there for two days.

The bishop invited him to dinner and, to amuse himself at his vicar-general's expense, he tried to make him shine. They had reached dessert when there came from Paris the strange news that Father Pirard had been appointed to the magnificent parish of N——, four leagues outside Paris. The good prelate congratulated him sincerely. He saw in the whole affair a well-played game which put him in a good humor and gave him the highest opinion of Father Pirard's abilities. He gave him a superb testimonial written in Latin and silenced Abbé de Frilair when he ventured to protest.

That evening, the bishop carried his admiration into the house of the Marquise de Rubempré. It was a great piece of news for the high society of Besançon. People made all sorts of conjectures about the extraordinary favor that had been bestowed on Father Pirard. They already saw him as a bishop. The shrewdest observers believed that Monsieur de La Mole had become a minister, and that evening they took the liberty of smiling at the imperious airs which Abbé de Frilair gave himself in society.

The next morning, people almost followed Father Pirard in the streets, and the tradesmen stood outside the doors of their shops when he went to see the marquis' judges. For the first time, he was given a polite reception. The stern Jansenist, indignant at everything he saw, spent a long time working with the lawyers he had chosen for the Marquis de La Mole, and then he left for Paris. He was weak enough to tell two or three friends he had known since his school days, who accompanied him to the carriage and admired the coat of arms it bore, that after fifteen years as rector of the seminary, he was leaving Besançon with only five hundred twenty francs in savings. These friends embraced him with tears in their eyes and later said to each other, "The good man could have spared himself that lie; it's too ridiculous."

The vulgar, blinded by the love of money, were not capable of understanding that it was in his sincerity that Father Pirard had found the strength to struggle alone for six years against Marie Alacoque, the *Sacred Heart of Jesus,* the Jesuits and his bishop.

CHAPTER 30
An Ambitious Man

> There is only one true title of nobility left: that of Duke. Marquis is ridiculous, but at the word "Duke," people turn their heads.
>
> —*The Edinburgh Review**

FATHER PIRARD was surprised by the Marquis de La Mole's noble air and almost gay tone. However, the future minister received him without any of those lordly little mannerisms which are outwardly so polite, but actually so impertinent to anyone who understands them. They would have been a waste of time, and the marquis was too deeply involved in important matters to have any time to waste. For the past six months he had been scheming to make both the king and the nation accept a certain ministry which, out of gratitude, would make him a duke.

For years he had been vainly asking his lawyer in Besançon for a clear and precise report on his lawsuits in Franche-Comté.

---

*Cf. note at beginning of Chapter 26.—L.B.

How was the eminent lawyer to explain them to him when he did not understand them himself? The small piece of paper which Father Pirard gave him explained everything.

"My dear Father Pirard," he said, after disposing of all polite formalities and personal inquiries in less than five minutes, "in the midst of my supposed prosperity, I lack the time to give serious attention to two little matters which are nevertheless rather important: my family and my own affairs. I devote great attention to the fortunes of my house, and I may carry them far; I look after my pleasures, and that's what ought to come before everything else, at least in my opinion," he added, noticing the astonishment in Father Pirard's eyes. Although he was a sensible man, Father Pirard was amazed to hear an old man speak so frankly of his pleasures.

"There are no doubt people in Paris who are willing to work," continued the great nobleman, "but they're all living in garrets. As soon as I become involved with a man, he takes an apartment on the third floor and his wife chooses a day of the week to entertain guests; as a result, no more work and no more effort, except to be, or appear to be, a man of the world. That's their only interest as soon as they have enough bread.

"For my lawsuits, strictly speaking, and also for each lawsuit in particular, I have lawyers who work themselves to death; one of them died of consumption only day before yesterday. But, for my affairs in general, would you believe, monsieur, that for the past three years I've given up all hope of finding a man who, while he's writing for me, will deign to give a little serious thought to what he's doing? But all this is only a preface.

"I respect you and, I venture to add, even though this is the first time I've ever seen you, I like you. Will you be my secretary, with a salary of eight thousand francs, or even twice that much? I'll still make a profit, believe me, and I'll make it my business to keep your fine parish open for you, for the day when we no longer suit each other."

Father Pirard refused; but, toward the end of the conversation, the genuine perplexity in which he saw the marquis suggested an idea to him. "In my seminary," he said, "I left behind a young man who, if I'm not mistaken, is going to be brutally persecuted. If he were a monk, he'd already be *in pace*. So far, he knows nothing but Latin and the Holy Scriptures, but it's not impossible that some day he will show great talent, either for preaching or the guidance of souls. I don't know what he'll do, but he has the sacred fire and he may go far. I'd counted on giving him to our bishop, if we'd ever had one with something of your way of looking at men and affairs.''

"What kind of background does your young man have?" asked the marquis.

"He's said to be the son of a sawyer who lives in our mountains, but I'm more inclined to think he's the illegitimate son of some rich man. I once saw him receive an anonymous, or pseudonymous, letter containing a bill of exchange for five hundred francs.''

"Ah! It's Julien Sorel," said the marquis.

"How do you know his name?" asked Father Pirard in astonishment.

As he was blushing at his own question, the marquis said to him, "I can't tell you that.''

"Well," said Father Pirard, "you might try making him your secretary. He's energetic and intelligent; in short, it's worth trying.''

"Why not?" said the marquis. "But would he be the kind of man to let his palm be greased by the prefect of police or someone else who wants to spy on me? That's my only objection.''

After Father Pirard's favorable assurances, the marquis took out a thousand-franc banknote and said, "Send this to Julien Sorel for his traveling expenses and tell him to come to me.''

"It's easy to see you live in Paris," said Father Pirard. "You know nothing of the tyranny that weighs down on us poor provincials, especially on priests who aren't on friendly terms with the Jesuits. They won't let Julien Sorel leave; they'll manage to cover themselves with clever excuses: they'll write to me that he's ill, my letters will have been lost in the mail, and so on.''

"I'll have the minister write a letter to the bishop some time in the next few days," said the marquis.

"I was forgetting one precaution," said Father Pirard. "Although the young man is of humble birth, he has a proud heart, and he won't be of any use to you if his pride is offended— you'd only make him stupid.''

"I like that," said the marquis. "I'll make him my son's companion: will that do?''

Some time later, Julien received a letter postmarked Châlons and written in a hand he did not recognize; in it he found a draft on a merchant in Besançon and instructions to go to Paris without delay. The letter was signed with a fictitious name, but Julien started when he opened it. A large blot of ink had fallen in the middle of the thirteenth word: this was the signal he had agreed upon with Father Pirard.

Less than an hour later, Julien was summoned to the bishop's palace, where he was welcomed with paternal warmth. Interspersed with quotations from Horace, the bishop paid him, on the exalted destiny awaiting him in Paris, a number of adroit compliments which required an explanation by way of thanks. Julien was unable to say anything, primarily because he knew nothing, and the bishop developed a great deal of respect for him. One of the minor priests of the palace wrote a note to the mayor, who hastened to come in person with a passport already signed, but with a blank space for the name of the traveler.

Before midnight, Julien was in the house of his friend Fouqué, whose sober mind was more astonished than delighted with the future that seemed to be awaiting Julien.

"Eventually," said the member of the Liberal party, "it will lead you to a government position, which will force you to take some action that will be pilloried in the newspapers. It will be through your disgrace that I'll have news of you. Remember that, even from a financial point of view, it's better to earn a hundred louis in a good timber business, where you're your own master, than to be paid four thousand francs by a government, even King Solomon's."

Julien saw in this nothing but the pettiness of a middle-class provincial mind. He was at last going to appear on the stage of great events. He preferred to have less security and greater opportunities. In his heart there was no longer the slightest fear of starvation. Everything else in his mind was eclipsed by the good fortune of going to Paris, which he imagined to be populated by intelligent people, extremely scheming and hypocritical, but as refined as the Bishop of Besançon and the Bishop of Agde. He humbly represented himself to his friend as having been deprived of his free will by Father Pirard's letter.

The next day, toward noon, he arrived in Verrières the happiest of men: he expected to see Madame de Rênal again. His first visit was to his first protector, the good Father Chélan. He was given a stern reception.

"Do you think you're under any obligation to me?" said Father Chélan, without answering his greeting. "You'll have lunch with me; during that time I'll send someone to rent another horse for you, and you'll leave Verrières *without seeing anyone*."

"To hear is to obey," replied Julien with the expression of a seminary student. From then on there was no discussion of anything except theology and Latin scholarship.

He mounted his horse, rode a league and then, having reached a forest and seeing no one who could observe him entering it, he plunged into it. At sundown he had a peasant take his horse to the nearest relay station. Later he entered the house of a wine-grower, who agreed to sell him a ladder and then accompany him, carrying it, to the small forest above the Cours de la Fidélité in Verrières.

"He must be some poor young man escaping from the draft," thought the peasant as he took leave of him, "or perhaps a smuggler. But what do I care? I got a good price for my ladder, and I myself have smuggled a few watch movements in my day."

It was a very dark night. Toward one o'clock in the morning, Julien entered Verrières, carrying his ladder. He descended as soon as he could to the bed of the stream which ran through Monsieur de Rênal's magnificent gardens at a depth of ten feet, closed in by walls along both sides. Using his ladder, he climbed up easily. "What kind of reception will the watchdogs give me?" he thought. "Everything depends on that." The dogs barked and ran toward him, but he whistled softly and they came up to rub themselves against him.

Then, climbing from terrace to terrace, although all the iron gates were locked, he easily arrived beneath the window of Madame de Rênal's bedroom, which, on the side facing the garden, was only eight or ten feet above the ground. In the shutters there was a small heart-shaped opening which he knew well. To his great chagrin, this little opening was not lighted by the glow of a night lamp inside.

"Good God!" he exclaimed. "Madame de Rênal isn't in that room tonight! Or could the night lamp have gone out? Where can she be sleeping? The family is in Verrières, because I found the dogs here; but in that room, without a night lamp, I may meet Monsieur de Rênal himself, or a stranger, and then what a scandal!"

The most prudent course of action was to withdraw, but this idea was repugnant to Julien. "If it's a stranger," he thought, "I'll run away as fast as I can, leaving my ladder behind me; but if it's she, what kind of reception will she give me? She's fallen into repentance and profound piety, I have no doubt of that; but she hasn't forgotten me completely, because she wrote to me not long ago." This consideration decided him.

With trembling heart, but determined nevertheless to see her or perish in the attempt, he threw some pebbles against the shutter. No response. He leaned his ladder against the wall beside the window and tapped on the shutter himself, softly at first, then more loudly. "No matter how dark it is," he thought, "a gun can still be fired at me." This thought reduced his mad undertaking to a question of bravery.

"Either there's no one in this bedroom tonight," he thought, "or whoever is in it is awake by now, so I no longer need to take any precautions for that person; all I have to do is try not to be heard by the people sleeping in the other bedrooms."

He climbed down his ladder, placed it against one of the shutters, climbed back up and, putting his hand through the heart-shaped opening, he had the good fortune to find rather quickly the wire attached to the hook which closed the shutter. He pulled on that wire; with unspeakable joy he felt that the shutter was no longer locked and was yielding to the pressure of his hand. "I must open it little by little and let her recognize my voice," he thought. He opened the shutter wide enough to allow him to put his head inside and repeated softly, "It's a friend."

He listened intently and ascertained that the deep silence inside the bedroom was unbroken by any sound. But there was definitely no night lamp on the hearth, not even a half-extinguished one. This was a very bad sign.

"Look out for a rifle shot!" he thought. He reflected for a moment, then ventured to tap the window pane with his finger. No response. He tapped more loudly. "Even if I break the glass, I must finish this one way or the other," he told himself. As he was tapping very loudly, he seemed to see a white form crossing the bedroom in the darkness. Finally he no longer had any doubt: he saw a form which seemed to be coming toward him with extreme slowness. Suddenly he saw a cheek pressed against the window pane in front of his eyes.

He started and drew back a little. But the night was so dark that, even at that distance, he could not tell whether or not it was Madame de Rênal. He feared a first cry of alarm; for the past few moments he had heard the dogs prowling around the foot of the ladder with low growls. "It's I," he repeated rather loudly, "a friend." No answer; the white phantom had disappeared. "Please let me in, I must speak to you, I'm too unhappy!" And he knocked almost hard enough to break the glass.

He heard a sharp little sound: the catch of the window had been lifted. He pushed it open and sprang lightly into the bedroom.

The white phantom was moving away from him. He seized it by the arm: it was a woman. All his ideas of courage vanished. "If it's she," he thought, "what will she say?" What was his emotion when a faint cry told him it was Madame de Rênal!

He pressed her in his arms; she was trembling, and she scarcely had the strength to push him away.

"Wretch! What are you doing here?"

Her quavering voice was scarcely able to articulate these words. Julien felt genuine indignation in them.

"I've come to see you after fourteen months of cruel separation."

"Go away, leave me immediately. Oh, Father Chélan, why did you stop me from writing to him? I could have prevented this horror." She pushed him away with truly extraordinary strength. "I repent my crime; God has been kind enough to enlighten me," she repeated in a choked voice. "Go away, hurry!"

"After fourteen months of unhappiness, I certainly won't leave you without speaking to you. I want to know everything you've done. Oh, I've loved you enough to deserve that confidence! . . . I want to know everything."

In spite of her will, Madame de Rênal's heart felt the power of this tone of authority.

Julien, who had been holding her in a passionate embrace and resisting her efforts to free herself, ceased to press her in his arms. This reassured her a little.

"I'm going to draw up the ladder," he said, "so that it won't give me away if some servant has been awakened by the noise and comes out to look around."

"Oh, leave! Leave instead!" she said to him with genuine anger. "What do I care about men? God sees the horrible scene you're making with me, and He'll punish me for it. You're taking a cowardly advantage of the feelings I once had for you, but which I no longer have. Do you hear me, Monsieur Julien?"

He was drawing up the ladder very slowly, in order not to make any noise.

"Is your husband in town?" he asked, not to defy her, but from force of habit.

"Please don't talk to me that way, or I'll call my husband. I'm already guilty because I didn't send you away immediately, no matter what might have happened. I feel sorry for you," she said to him, seeking to wound his pride, which she knew to be extremely sensitive.

Her refusal to speak to him familiarly, the abrupt manner in which she was severing ties which had once been so tender and on which he still counted, carried Julien's amorous rapture to the point of frenzy.

"What! Is it possible that you no longer love me?" he said to her in that heartfelt tone to which it is so difficult to listen coldly.

She did not answer. As for him, he was weeping bitterly; he completely lacked the strength to speak. "So I've been totally forgotten by the only person who ever loved me!" he thought. "What's the use of living any longer?" All his courage had left him as soon as he no longer had to fear the danger of encountering a man; everything had vanished from his heart, except love.

He wept for a long time in silence. She heard the sound of his sobbing. He took her hand; she tried to draw it back at first, but then, after a few almost convulsive movements, she let him hold it. It was extremely dark; they both found themselves sitting on her bed.

"How different things were fourteen months ago!" thought Julien, and his tears increased. "So absence always destroys human feelings! The best thing for me to do is to go away."

"Please tell me what's happened to you," he said at length, embarrassed by her silence, in a voice that was almost stifled by sorrow.

"I'm sure," she replied in a harsh tone which impressed him as hostile and reproachful, "that my failings were known in Verrières when you left. You'd acted so rashly! Some time later, when I was in despair, the worthy Father Chélan came to see me. For a long time he tried in vain to make me confess. One day he had the idea of taking me to the church in Dijon where I took my first communion. There he ventured to broach the subject . . ." She was interrupted by a flow of tears. "What a moment of shame! I confessed everything. The good man was kind enough not to overwhelm me with the weight of his indignation; he shared my sorrow. At that time I wrote letters to you every day, but I didn't dare to send them; I carefully hid them, and when I was too unhappy I would lock myself in my room and read them over.

"Finally Father Chélan persuaded me to give them to him. . . . Some of them, written with a little more prudence than the others, were sent to you; you never answered."

"Never, I swear to you, did I ever receive a letter from you while I was in the seminary!"

"Good heavens! Who could have intercepted them?"

"Imagine my anguish: until the day I saw you in the cathedral, I didn't even know if you were still alive."

"God gave me grace," said Madame de Rênal, "to understand how greatly I was sinning against Him, against my children and against my husband. He's never loved me the way I thought I loved you then. . . ."

Julien threw himself in her arms, without any conscious purpose and beside himself with emotion. But she pushed him away and continued rather firmly:

"My worthy friend Father Chélan made me understand that in marrying Monsieur de Rênal I had pledged all my affections to him, even those of which I was still ignorant, and which I'd never experienced before our fateful relationship. . . . Since the sacrifice of those letters, which were so dear to me, my life has gone on, if not happily, at least rather peacefully. Don't trouble it now; be my friend . . . my best friend." Julien covered her hands with kisses; she felt that he was still weeping. "Don't weep, you hurt me so! . . . Now tell me what you've been doing." He was unable to speak. "I want you to tell me what kind of life you led in the seminary," she repeated, "then I want you to leave me."

Without thinking of what he was saying, Julien told her of the constant intrigue and jealousy he had encountered in the seminary at first, then of his more peaceful life after he was appointed tutor.

"It was then," he added, "that, after a long silence which was no doubt intended to make me realize what I see all too clearly now—that you no longer love me and that you've become indifferent toward me . . ." Madame de Rênal pressed his hands. "It was then that you sent me five hundred francs."

"Never!" said Madame de Rênal.

"It was a letter postmarked Paris and signed 'Paul Sorel,' to avoid suspicion."

There was a short discussion about the possible origin of this letter. The emotional atmosphere changed. Without realizing it, they had both abandoned their solemn tone and returned to one of tender intimacy. The darkness was so intense that they could not see each other, but the sound of their voices said everything. Julien put his arm around her waist; this movement was fraught with danger. She tried to push his arm away, but he rather cleverly distracted her attention at that moment with an interesting point in his narrative. His arm was as though forgotten, and it remained in the position it had occupied.

er many conjectures as to the origin of the letter containing the five hundred francs, he resumed his narrative. He recovered some of his self-assurance as he spoke of his past life, which held so little interest for him in comparison to what was happening to him now. His attention was wholly concentrated on the way in which his visit would end. "You must leave," Madame de Rênal continued to say to him from time to time, in a curt tone.

"What a disgrace for me if I'm sent away!" he thought. "My remorse over it will poison the rest of my life. She'll never write to me, and God only knows when I'll be anywhere near Verrières again!" From that moment, all the heavenly bliss of his situation rapidly vanished from his heart. Sitting beside the woman he adored, nearly holding her in his arms, in that bedroom where he had once been so happy, in the midst of profound darkness, well aware that for the last few minutes she had been weeping, and feeling, from the movement of her bosom, that she was sobbing, he had the misfortune to become a cold strategist, almost as calculating and almost as cold as when, in the courtyard of the seminary, he had found himself the butt of some malicious joke on the part of one of his fellow students who was stronger than himself. He prolonged his narrative and spoke of the unhappy life he had led since his departure from Verrières.

"So," Madame de Rênal said to herself, "after a year's absence, with almost nothing to refresh his memory, while I was forgetting him, he was completely absorbed in the happy days he'd spent in Vergy." Her sobbing increased. Julien saw the success of his narrative. He realized that he must now use his final weapon: he abruptly came to the letter he had just received from Paris. "I've taken leave of the bishop," he said.

"What! You're not going back to Besançon? You're going to leave us forever?"

"Yes," replied Julien resolutely, "I'm leaving a district where I've been forgotten even by the woman I've loved more than anything else in the world, and I'm leaving it forever. I'm going to Paris. . . ."

"You're going to Paris!" cried Madame de Rênal rather loudly. Her voice was almost stifled by tears and showed the full intensity of her grief. Julien needed this encouragement: he was about to attempt a maneuver which might decide everything against him, and before her exclamation, not being able to see, he had been totally ignorant of the effect he was succeeding in producing. He hesitated no longer; the fear of remorse had given him complete control over himself.

"Yes, madame," he said coldly, standing up, "I'm leaving you forever, so be happy. Good-bye."

He took a few steps toward the window and began to open it. Madame de Rênal ran over to him and threw herself in his arms.

Thus, after three hours of conversation, Julien obtained what he had so passionately desired during the first two hours. The return of their tender intimacy and the eclipse of Madame de Rênal's remorse would have given him divine happiness if they had come a little sooner, but now, having been obtained by artifice, they were only a victory. Despite his mistress's entreaties, he insisted on lighting the night lamp.

"Don't you want me to have any memory of having seen you?" he said. "Do you want the love that's no doubt shining in those charming eyes to be lost for me? Shall the whiteness of this pretty hand be invisible to me? Remember that I'm soon going to leave you, and perhaps for a long time!"

"How shameful!" thought Madame de Rênal, but she could refuse nothing to that idea of lifelong separation, which made her burst into tears.

The fir trees on the mountain to the east of Verrières were now clearly outlined in the early light of dawn. Instead of leaving, Julien, intoxicated with pleasure, asked her to let him spend the whole day hidden in her bedroom and postpone his departure until the following night.

"Why not?" she replied. "This fatal relapse has destroyed all my self-respect, and it will make me unhappy forever." And she pressed him rapturously to her heart. "My husband has changed: he's suspicious now. He thinks I've deceived him in every way in this affair, and he's very angry with me. If he hears the slightest sound, I'm lost; he'll drive me out like the wretched woman I am."

"Ah, there's one of Father Chélan's expressions!" said Julien. "You wouldn't have spoken to me like that before my cruel departure for the seminary; you loved me then!"

He was rewarded for the coldness he put into these words: he saw his mistress instantly forget the danger in which her husband's presence placed her and begin to think of the far greater danger of seeing Julien doubt her love. The daylight was swiftly growing brighter and illuminating the room; once again Julien felt all the pleasure of pride when he was able to see in his arms, and almost at his feet, that charming woman, the only one he had ever loved, who, a few hours earlier, had been completely absorbed in the fear of a terrible God and in devotion to her duty. Resolutions fortified by a year of constancy had not been able to hold out against his courage.

Soon they heard sounds in the house, and Madame de Rênal's mind was troubled by a consideration to which she had hitherto given no thought. "That malicious Elisa is going to come into this room," she said to her lover. "What can we do with this long ladder? Where can we hide it? I'll carry it up to the attic!" she cried suddenly, in an almost playful tone.

"There, that's the face I remember!" said Julien, delighted. "But you'll have to go through the servant's room."

"I'll leave the ladder in the hall, call the servant and send him on an errand."

"Remember to prepare some explanation in case he should notice the ladder in the hall as he passes."

"Yes, my angel," said Madame de Rênal, kissing him. "And you, be sure to hide under the bed quickly if Elisa comes in here while I'm gone."

Julien was astonished by this sudden gaiety. "So," he thought, "the approach of physical danger, far from upsetting her, restores her gaiety, because she forgets her remorse! A really superior woman! Ah, there's a heart in which it's glorious to reign!" He was overjoyed.

Madame de Rênal took hold of the ladder; it was obviously too heavy for her. Julien came to her aid. He was admiring her graceful figure, which was so far from giving any evidence of strength, when suddenly, without help, she seized the ladder and picked it up as though it were a chair. She quickly carried it to the hall on the fourth floor, where she laid it down against the wall. She called the servant, then went up to the dovecote in order to give him time to dress.

Five minutes later, when she returned to the hall, she saw that the ladder was no longer there. What had become of it? If Julien had not been in the house, this danger would scarcely have affected her. But what if her husband saw the ladder at that moment! The consequences might be appalling. She frantically looked all over the house and finally discovered the ladder in the attic, where the servant had taken it and, in fact, hidden it. This circumstance was strange; at any other time it would have alarmed her.

"What do I care," she thought, "what may happen in twenty-four hours, after Julien is gone? Won't everything be horror and remorse for me then?''

She had a vague feeling that she ought to take her own life, but what did that matter? After a separation which she had believed to be eternal, he had come back to her, she was with him again, and what he had done in order to come to her showed so much love!

In relating the incident of the ladder to Julien she asked him, ''What shall I reply to my husband if the servant tells him he found that ladder?'' She was thoughtful for a moment. ''It will take them twenty-four hours to discover the peasant who sold it to you.'' She threw herself in his arms and pressed him convulsively. ''Oh, to die, to die like this!'' she cried out, covering him with kisses. ''But you mustn't die of hunger,'' she said, laughing. ''Come, first I'm going to hide you in Madame Derville's room, which is always kept locked.''

She stood watch at the end of the hall as Julien ran along it. ''Be sure not to open the door if anyone knocks,'' she said to him as she locked him in. ''Anyway, it would only be the children playing some joke among themselves.''

''Bring them into the garden, below the window,'' said Julien, ''so that I can have the pleasure of seeing them; and make them speak.''

''Yes, yes!'' cried Madame de Rênal as she walked away.

She came back soon with oranges, biscuits and a bottle of Malaga wine; it had been impossible for her to steal any bread.

''What's your husband doing?'' asked Julien.

''He's writing out sales contracts with some peasants.''

But it was past eight o'clock and there were many sounds of movement in the house. If Madame de Rênal were not seen, people would begin looking for her everywhere; she was obliged to leave him. Soon she came back again, against all caution, bringing him a cup of coffee; she was trembling that he might die of hunger.

After breakfast she managed to lead the children beneath the window of Madame Derville's room. Julien saw that they had grown a great deal, but they seemed to have taken on an air of coarseness, or else his ideas had changed. Madame de Rênal spoke to them about him. The eldest boy replied with expressions of friendship for his former tutor and regret for his absence, but it appeared that the two younger ones had nearly forgotten him.

Monsieur de Rênal did not go out that morning; he was constantly going up and down the stairs, occupied in concluding bargains with the peasants to whom he was selling his potato crop. Until dinnertime, Madame de Rênal did not have a single instant to give to her prisoner. After the dinner bell had sounded and the meal was on the table, she had the idea of smuggling a bowl of hot soup to him. As she was silently approaching the door of the bedroom in which he was hidden, carefully carrying the bowl, she suddenly found herself face to face with the same servant who had hidden the ladder that morning. He too was walking silently along the hall, as though listening. Julien had probaby been careless and let the sound of his footsteps be heard. The servant went away, somewhat embarrassed. Madame de Rênal boldly entered Julien's room; this encounter made him shudder.

"You're afraid," she said to him, "but I'd face all the dangers in the world without a qualm. I'm afraid of only one thing: the moment when I'll be alone again after you've gone." And she ran from the room.

"Ah!" thought Julien, in a state of exaltation. "Remorse is the only danger that sublime soul dreads!"

Night finally came. Monsieur de Rênal went off to the Casino.

His wife had complained of a severe headache; she withdrew to her room, hastened to send Elisa away and then quickly got out of bed to unlock Julien's door.

It turned out that he actually was starving. She went to the pantry for some bread. He heard a loud shriek. She came back and told him that as she was entering the pantry without a light, walking toward the cupboard in which the bread was kept, she had put out her hand and touched a woman's arm. It was Elisa who had uttered the loud shriek he had heard.

"What was she doing there?" he asked.

"She was either stealing a few sweetmeats or spying on us," said Madame de Rênal with utter indifference. "But fortunately I found some pâté and a big loaf of bread."

"What's in there?" asked Julien, pointing to the pockets of her apron. She had forgotten that they had been filled with bread ever since dinner.

He pressed her in his arms with intense passion; never before had she seemed so beautiful to him. "Even in Paris," he thought confusedly, "I'll never find a nobler heart." She had all the awkwardness of a woman unaccustomed to details of this kind, and at the same time she had the true courage of one who fears only dangers of a different and far more terrible order.

While Julien was eating his supper with a hearty appetite, and his mistress was joking with him about the simplicity of his meal, for she had a horror of speaking seriously, the door of the room was suddenly shaken violently. It was Monsieur de Rênal.

"Why have you locked yourself in?" he shouted to her.

Julien scarcely had time to slip under the sofa.

"What!" said Monsieur de Rênal as he entered. "You're fully dressed, you're having supper, and you've locked your door?"

At any other time this question, asked with full conjugal hostility, would have upset Madame de Rênal, but she realized that her husband had only to bend down a little to see Julien, for he had angrily sat down in the chair Julien had been occupying a moment before, opposite the sofa.

Her headache served as an excuse for everything. While her husband was lengthily relating to her the details of the pool he had won in the billiard room of the Casino—"A pool of nineteen francs, by God!" he added—she noticed Julien's hat lying on a chair three paces in front of them. Her presence of mind redoubled; she began to undress herself and, at a certain moment, quickly passing behind her husband, she threw a dress over the chair with the hat on it.

Monsieur de Rênal finally left. She asked Julien to repeat the story of his life in the seminary. "Last night," she said, "I wasn't listening to you; while you were talking I was thinking only of how I could give myself the courage to send you away."

She was imprudence personified. They were speaking quite loudly, and it was somewhere around two o'clock in the morning, when they were interrupted by a violent knock on the door. It was Monsieur de Rênal again.

"Open the door, hurry!" he said. "There are burglars in the house! Saint-Jean found their ladder this morning."

"This is the end of everything!" cried Madame de Rênal, throwing herself in Julien's arms. "He's going to kill us both—he doesn't believe there are any burglars. I'm going to die in your arms, happier in my death than I've been in my life." She made no reply to her husband, who was becoming angry; she clung to Julien in a passionate embrace.

"Save Stanislas' mother," he said to her, looking at her imperiously. "I'm going to jump down into the courtyard from the window of the dressing room and escape through the garden; the dogs have recognized me. Make a bundle of my clothes and throw it down into the garden as soon as you can. Meanwhile, let him break open the door. Above all, confess nothing. I forbid you to say anything: it's better for him to have suspicions than certainty.''

"You'll kill yourself when you jump down!" was her only reply and her only anxiety.

She went with him to the window of her dressing room, then she took time to hide his clothes. She finally opened the door to her husband, who was boiling with rage. He searched the bedroom and the dressing room without a word, then left. Julien's clothes were thrown down to him, he picked them up and ran swiftly toward the lower end of the garden, in the direction of the Doubs.

As he was running, he heard a bullet whistle past him, then the sound of a rifle shot.

"That wasn't Monsieur de Rênal," he thought. "He's not that good a shot." The dogs were running silently beside him; a second shot apparently broke the leg of one of them, for it began to yelp pitifully. Julien leapt over the wall of a terrace, ran for fifty yards under cover, then began to flee in another direction. He heard voices calling to one another and distinctly saw the servant, his enemy, fire a rifle. A farmer also came to shoot at him from the other side of the garden, but Julien had already reached the bank of the Doubs, where he put on his clothes.

An hour later, he was a league away from Verrières, on the road to Geneva. "If there's any suspicion," he thought, "they'll look for me on the road to Paris."

BOOK II

◐

*She is not pretty
—she wears no rouge.*
—Sainte-Beuve

CHAPTER 1
The Pleasures of Country Life

O rus quando ego te aspiciam!
—Horace

"HAVE YOU come to wait for the mail coach to Paris, monsieur?" asked the keeper of an inn at which he had stopped for breakfast.

"I can take the one leaving today or wait till tomorrow, it makes no difference," replied Julien.

The mail coach arrived as he was making this show of indifference. There were two seats vacant.

"What! It's you, my poor Falcoz!" said a traveler who had come from the direction of Geneva to a man who entered the coach with Julien.

"I thought you'd settled down somewhere near Lyons," said Falcoz, "in a charming valley beside the Rhône."

"I settled down all right—I'm running away."

"Running away! What do you mean? You, Saint-Giraud, with that honest face of yours, have you committed some crime?" said Falcoz, laughing.

"I might as well have! I'm running away from the abominable life one leads in the provinces. I love cool forests and rustic tranquillity, as you well know: you've often accused me of being a romantic. I never wanted to hear politics mentioned again, and I've been driven away by politics."

"What party do you belong to?"

"None, and that's the cause of all my trouble. These are my only politics: I love music and painting, a good book is a major event in my life, and I'll soon be forty-four years old. How much longer do I have to live? Fifteen, twenty, thirty years at the most. Well, I say that thirty years from now ministers will be a little more astute, but exactly as honorable as they are today. The history of England serves as a mirror to show me our future. There will always be a king who wants to extend his prerogatives; the rich men of the provinces will always be kept awake at night by the ambition to become a member of the Chamber of Deputies, and by the glory and the hundreds of thousands of francs amassed by Mirabeau—they'll call it being a Liberal and loving the people. The Royalists will always be obsessed by the desire to be a peer of France or a Gentleman of the Privy Chamber. On board the Ship of State, everyone will always want to be at the helm, because the post is well paid. Won't there ever be a poor little place for the man who merely wants to be a passenger?''

''Come to the point of your story—it must be a very amusing one, considering your peaceful disposition. Is it the last election that's driving you from the provinces?''

''My trouble dates from further back. Four years ago I was forty, and I had five hundred thousand francs; I'm four years older now, and I probably have fifty thousand francs less. I'll no doubt lose that much on the sale of my château at Monfleury, near the Rhône—a magnificent location.

''In Paris, I was tired of the constant play-acting that's forced on one by what you call nineteenth-century civilization. I longed for good-naturedness and simplicity. I bought an estate in the mountains near the Rhône, the most beautiful place in the world. The curate of the village and the country squires of the vicinity were very friendly to me for the first six months, and I often invited them to dinner. 'I left Paris,' I told them, 'because I never wanted to talk or hear talk of politics again for the rest of my life. As you know, I haven't subscribed to any newspaper. The fewer letters the postman brings me, the happier I am.'

''That didn't suit the curate; soon I was besieged with all sorts of indiscreet requests, annoyances and so on. I wanted to give two or three hundred francs a year to the poor; instead, I was asked to give the money to the Society of Saint Joseph, of the Virgin, and so on. I refused, and then I was insulted in a hundred different ways. I was foolish enough to take offense. I could no longer go out in the morning to enjoy the beauty of the mountains without encountering some annoyance or other that interrupted my thoughts and unpleasantly reminded me of men and their maliciousness. For example, during the Rogation processions, whose chant I like (it's probably a Greek melody), my fields were no longer blessed, because the curate said they belonged to an unbeliever. A pious old peasant woman's cow died; she said it was because of the nearness of a pond belonging to me, an unbeliever, a free-thinker from Paris, and a week later I found my fish floating on the surface with their bellies in the air—they'd been poisoned with lime. I was surrounded by chicanery in every form. The justice of the peace, an honest man but afraid of losing his position, always decided against me. The peaceful countryside became a hell on earth for me.

"As soon as they saw me abandoned by the curate, who was head of the village *Congrégation*, and not supported by the retired captain who was the leader of the Liberals, they all attacked me, even the mason who'd been living for the past year on the money I paid him, even the wheelwright who tried to cheat me with impunity when he repaired my plows. In order to have some support and win at least a few of my lawsuits, I became a Liberal; but, as you mentioned, those devilish elections came and I was asked to vote . . ."

"For a stranger?"

"Not at all: for a man I knew only too well. I refused, a terribly rash action! From then on I had the Liberals to contend with too, and my position became intolerable. I think that if the curate had taken it into his head to accuse me of murdering my maid, there would have been twenty witnesses from both parties who would have sworn they saw me commit the crime."

"You want to live in the country without serving your neighbors' passions, without even listening to their gossip—what a mistake!"

"Well, I've corrected it now. Monfleury is for sale. I'll lose fifty thousand francs if I must, but I'm overjoyed: I'm leaving that inferno of hypocrisy and chicanery. I'm going to seek solitude and rustic peace in the only place where they exist in France: in a fifth-floor apartment overlooking the Champs-Elysées. And even so I'm wondering if I shouldn't begin my political career in the Roule quarter by distributing consecrated bread to the parishioners."

"None of that would have happened to you under Bonaparte," said Falcoz, his eyes shining with anger and regret.

"That's true, but why wasn't he able to keep himself in power, your Bonaparte? He's the cause of everything I'm suffering from today."

At this point Julien's attention doubled. He had realized from the first word that the Bonapartist Falcoz was Monsieur de Rênal's former boyhood friend, repudiated by him in 1816, and that the philosopher Saint-Giraud must be a brother of that head clerk of the prefecture of —— who knew how to have houses belonging to the municipality auctioned off to him at a low price.

"And your Bonaparte was the cause of all that," continued Saint-Giraud. "An honest, perfectly harmless forty-year-old man with five hundred thousand francs can't settle down in the provinces and find peace there: he's driven out by Bonaparte's priests and noblemen."

"Oh! Don't say anything against him!" cried Falcoz. "France has never been so highly respected by other countries as during the thirteen years of his reign. In those days, there was greatness in everything that was done."

"Your emperor, may the devil take him," said the forty-four-year-old man, "was great only on the battlefield and when he reorganized the financial system in 1802. What did everything he did after that amount to? With his chamberlains, his pomp and his receptions in the Tuileries, he brought out a new edition of all the silly nonsense of the monarchy. It was a revised edition and it might have been good for another century or two. The priests and the nobility have tried to go back to the old edition, but they don't have the iron hand necessary to make the public buy it."

"Now there's the language of a former printer!"

"Who's driving me off my estate?" the printer went on angrily. "The priests, whom Napoleon brought back with his Concordat, instead of treating them the way the State treats doctors, lawyers and astronomers, regarding them merely as citizens, without worrying about the trade by which they earn their living. Would there be insolent noblemen today if your Bonaparte hadn't created barons and counts? No, they were out of fashion. Next to the priests, it was the minor country noblemen who irritated me most, and who forced me to become a Liberal."

The discussion was endless; this theme will occupy the minds of Frenchmen for the next half-century. As Saint-Giraud continued to repeat that it was impossible to live in the provinces, Julien timidly suggested the example of Monsieur de Rênal.

"That's a good one, young man!" cried Falcoz. "He's made himself into a hammer so that he won't have to be an anvil, and a terrible hammer at that. But I see him outflanked by Valenod. Do you know that scoundrel? He's the real thing. What will your Monsieur de Rênal say when he sees himself put out of office one fine day, with Valenod taking his place?"

"He'll be left alone with his crimes," said Saint-Giraud. "So you know Verrières, do you, young man? Well, Bonaparte—may heaven confound him—and his monarchist nonsense made possible the reign of the Rênals and the Chélans, which has brought on the reign of the Valenods and the Maslons."

This gloomy political conversation astonished Julien and distracted him from his voluptuous daydreams.

His first sight of Paris, seen in the distance, made little

impression on him. His dreams of the future had to struggle against the still vivid memory of the twenty-four hours he had just spent in Verrières. He swore to himself that he would never abandon his mistress's children and that he would give up everything to protect them if the impertinences of the priests should ever lead to a republican government and persecution of the nobility.

What would have happened on the night he returned to Verrières if, when he leaned his ladder against the window of Madame de Rênal's bedroom, he had found that bedroom occupied by a stranger, or by Monsieur de Rênal? But also what bliss he had experienced during those first two hours, when his mistress sincerely wanted to send him away and he had pleaded his cause as he sat beside her in the darkness! A heart like Julien's is pursued by such memories for a whole lifetime. The rest of their meeting was already merging into the first period of their love, fourteen months earlier.

Julien was roused from his deep meditation when the carriage stopped. They had just entered the courtyard of the post office on the rue Jean-Jacques Rousseau.

"I want to go to Malmaison," he said to the driver of a cabriolet who approached him.

"At this hour, monsieur? What for?"

"What does it matter to you? Take me there."

True passion thinks only of itself. That, it seems to me, is why passions are so ridiculous in Paris, where your neighbor always insists that you give a great deal of thought to him. I shall refrain from describing Julien's raptures at Malmaison. He wept. What? In spite of the ugly white walls, erected that year, which cut the park into pieces? Yes, sir: for Julien, as for posterity, there was nothing between Arcole, Saint Helena and Malmaison.

That evening, Julien hesitated a long time before entering the theater; he had strange ideas about that place of perdition.

A profound mistrust prevented him from admiring present-day Paris; he was moved only by the monuments left behind by his hero.

"So here I am in the center of intrigue and hypocrisy!" he thought. "This is where Abbé de Frilair's protectors reign."

On the evening of the third day, his curiosity won out over his intention to see everything before presenting himself to Father Pirard. The latter coldly explained to him the kind of life awaiting him in Monsieur de La Mole's house.

"If, after a few months, you haven't proved to be useful," he said, "you'll return to the seminary, but under good conditions. You'll live in the house of the marquis, one of the greatest noblemen in France. You'll dress in black, but like a man who's in mourning, not like an ecclesiastic. I demand that you pursue your theological studies three times a week in a seminary in which I'll introduce you. Each day at noon you'll go to the marquis' library, where he'll give you letters to write concerning his lawsuits and other matters. In the margin of each letter he receives, he writes a short summary of the answer it requires. I've claimed that within three months you'll be able to compose those answers in such a way that he'll be able to sign eight or nine of them out of every twelve you give him for his signature. At eight o'clock in the evening you'll put his desk in order, and at ten o'clock you'll be free.

"It's possible that some old lady or some soft-voiced man may hint at enormous advantages, or, to put it more plainly, may offer you money to show the letters received by the marquis. . . ."

"Oh, monsieur!" exclaimed Julien, blushing.

"It's strange," said Father Pirard with a bitter smile, "that, poor as you are, and after a year in the seminary, you still have those outbursts of righteous indignation. You must have been quite blind!

"Could it be the result of his blood?" he murmured, as though to himself. "The strange thing," he added, looking at Julien, "is that the marquis knows you . . . I don't know how. He'll give you a salary of a hundred louis to begin with. He's a man who acts only from caprice, that's his weakness; he'll vie with you in childish actions. If he's satisfied with you, your salary may later go as high as eight thousand francs.

"But you must realize," Father Pirard went on sternly, "that he won't give you all that money for your handsome face. You must be useful to him. If I were in your place, I'd speak very little, and above all I'd never speak of things I knew nothing about.

"Oh, yes—I've made some inquiries for you: I was forgetting Monsieur de La Mole's family. He has two children: a daughter and a nineteen-year-old son who's the last word in elegance and a madman who never knows at noon what he'll be doing at two o'clock. He's intelligent and brave; he fought in the Spanish campaign. The marquis hopes, I don't know why, that you'll become young Count Norbert's friend. I've told him you're an excellent Latin scholar; perhaps he expects you to teach his son a few ready-made comments on Cicero and Virgil.

"If I were in your place, I wouldn't let that handsome young man joke with me; and before responding to his friendly advances, which will be perfectly polite but somewhat spoiled by irony, I'd make him repeat them to me more than once.

"I won't conceal from you that the young Comte de La Mole will no doubt despise you at first because you're only a commoner. One of his ancestors was at court and had the honor of being decapitated on the Place de Grève on April 26, 1574, for a political intrigue. As for you, you're the son of a Verrières sawyer, and furthermore you're employed by his father. Weigh these differences carefully, and study the history of his family in Moreri; the flatterers who come to dinner in their house occasionally make what they call delicate allusions to it.

"Be careful how you respond to the pleasantries of Count Norbert de La Mole, Squadron Commander of Hussars and a future peer of France, and don't come to me to complain later."

"It seems to me," said Julien, blushing deeply, "that I shouldn't even answer a man who has contempt for me."

"You have no idea of what that kind of contempt is like: it will manifest itself only in exaggerated compliments. If you were a fool, you might let yourself be taken in by them; if you want to succeed you *must* let yourself be taken in by them."

"If I become tired of all that some day," said Julien, "will I be regarded as an ingrate if I return to my little cell number 103?"

"All the sycophants of the household will no doubt slander you," replied Father Pirard, "but I'll intervene. *Adsum qui feci.* I'll say the decision came from me."

Julien was distressed by the bitter and almost malicious tone he detected in Father Pirard's voice; this tone completely spoiled his last reply.

The fact is that his liking for Julien troubled his conscience, and it was with a kind of religious terror that he took such a direct part in shaping another person's destiny.

"You'll also see," he added in the same ungracious tone, and as though performing a painful duty, "the Marquise de La Mole. She's a tall blonde woman, pious, proud, extremely polite and still more insignificant. She's the daughter of the old Duc de Chaulnes, so famous for his aristocratic prejudices. That great lady is a kind of summary, in high relief, of everything that makes up the basic character of women of her rank. She makes no secret of the fact that having ancestors who fought in the Crusades is the only advantage she respects. Money comes only a long way behind. That surprises you? We're no longer in the provinces, my friend.

"In her drawing room you will hear several great noblemen speak of our princes in a strangely flippant manner. As for Madame de La Mole, she respectfully lowers her voice whenever she mentions a prince, and especially a princess. I don't advise you to say in her presence that Philip II or Henry VIII was a monster. They were *kings*, and that gives them an inalienable right to everyone's respect, especially the respect of people of humble birth, like you and me. However, we're priests—for she'll regard you as one—and, in that capacity, she considers us to be lackeys necessary to her salvation."

"Monsieur," said Julien, "it seems to me that I won't be in Paris for long."

"As you like; but remember that a man of our calling has no hope of success except through the great noblemen. With that indefinable element in your character—at least it's indefinable for me—if you don't succeed you'll be persecuted; there's no middle way for you. Don't deceive yourself. Other people can see that you're not pleased to have them speak to you; in a sociable country like this, you're doomed to disaster if you don't reach a position that commands respect.

"What would have become of you in Besançon if it hadn't been for this caprice on the part of the Marquis de La Mole? Some day you'll understand what an extraordinary thing he's doing for you and, if you're not a monster, you'll be eternally grateful to him and his family. How many poor priests, more learned than you, have lived for years in Paris on the fifteen sous they receive for their masses and the ten sous they're paid for their lectures in the Sorbonne! . . . Remember what I told you last winter about the early years of that scoundrel Cardinal Dubois. Are you by any chance so proud as to think you have more ability than he?

"I, for example, a peaceful and mediocre man, I expected to die in my seminary; I was childish enough to become attached to it. Well, I was about to be dismissed when I handed in my resignation! Do you know what my fortune consisted of? I'd saved up five hundred twenty francs, no more, no less; I didn't have a single friend, and I had two or three acquaintances at most. Monsieur de La Mole, whom I'd never seen, rescued me from my predicament; he had only to say a word and I was given a parish whose residents are all well-to-do people, above the more vulgar vices, and whose stipend is so far out of proportion to my work that it makes me ashamed. I've spoken to you for so long only in order to put a little ballast in your head.

"One more thing: I have the misfortune to be hot-tempered; it's possible that you and I may stop speaking to each other.

"If the marquise's arrogance, or her son's irritating pranks, makes the house definitely intolerable for you, I advise you to finish your studies in some seminary thirty leagues from Paris, and in the north rather than in the south. There's more civilization in the north, and less injustice; and," he added, lowering his voice, "I must admit that the proximity of the Paris newspapers frightens the petty tyrants.

"If we continue to enjoy each other's company, and if the marquis' household doesn't suit you, I'll offer you a post as my curate, and I'll give you half of my income from the parish. I owe you that and still more," he added, cutting short Julien's expressions of gratitude, "for the extraordinary offer you made me in Besançon. If, instead of five hundred twenty francs, I'd had nothing, you'd have saved me."

The harshness had vanished from Father Pirard's voice. To his great shame, Julien felt tears in his eyes; he longed to throw himself in his friend's arms. He could not help saying to him, with the manliest air he was capable of assuming, "I've been hated by my father from the time I was born, it was one of my greatest misfortunes; but I'll no longer complain about my fate: I've found another father in you, monsieur."

"Good, good," said Father Pirard in embarrassment; then, appropriately recalling a phrase befitting the rector of a seminary, he said, "You must never say 'fate,' my son: always say 'Providence.' "

The cabriolet came to a stop. The driver raised the bronze knocker on an enormous door: they had arrived at the Hôtel de La Mole: and, so that the passers-by would have no doubt about the identity of the building, these words could be read on a slab of black marble above the door.

This affectation displeased Julien. "They tremble with fear of the Jacobins," he thought, "they see a Robespierre with his tumbril behind every bush, they're so obsessed that they're often hilariously funny, and yet they advertise their house that way, so that the mob will recognize it and pillage it if there's a riot!" He communicated his thoughts to Father Pirard.

"Ah, poor boy, you'll soon be my curate. What an appalling idea for you to have!"

"I can't think of anything more obvious," said Julien.

The gravity of the porter, and especially the cleanliness of the courtyard, had filled him with admiration. It was a beautiful sunny day. "What magnificent architecture!" he said to his friend.

It was one of those town houses with abominably commonplace façades that were built in the Faubourg Saint-Germain toward the end of Voltaire's life. Never have the fashionable and the beautiful been so far apart.

CHAPTER 2

Entry into Society

> Ridiculous and touching memory: the first drawing room in which one appeared at the age of eighteen, alone and unsupported! A woman's glance was enough to intimidate me. The more I tried to please, the more awkward I became. I formed the most inaccurate ideas of everything; I either surrendered myself for no reason or regarded a man as my enemy because he had given me a serious look. But then, amid the terrible sufferings of my shyness, how beautiful a beautiful day was!
> —Kant

JULIEN STOPPED in the middle of the courtyard, gaping in amazement.

"Try to look sensible!" said Father Pirard. "First horrible ideas come into your mind, then you act like a child! Have you forgotten Horace's *nil mirari* [no enthusiasm]? You must realize that when this tribe of lackeys see you established here, they'll try to make a fool of you; they'll regard you as an equal who has been unjustly placed above them. Beneath a show of friendliness, good advice and a desire to guide you, they'll try to make you fall into some stupid blunder or other."

"I defy them to do that," said Julien, biting his lip; and he resumed all his mistrust.

The drawing rooms on the second floor through which the two men passed on their way to the marquis' study would have seemed to you, dear reader, as depressing as they were sumptuous. If they had been given to you exactly as they were, you would have refused to live in them; they were the home of boredom and dreary conversation. They doubled Julien's enchantment. "How could anyone be unhappy living in such a magnificent house?" he thought.

Finally they came to the ugliest room of that superb suite; scarcely any daylight penetrated into it. There they found a thin little man with lively eyes and a blond wig. Father Pirard turned to Julien and introduced him. This was the marquis. Julien found him so polite that he had difficulty in recognizing him. This was no longer the great nobleman with the haughty face whom he had seen in the abbey at Bray-le-Haut. It seemed to Julien that his wig was much too thick. Thanks to this observation, he was not at all intimidated. His first impression of the descendant of Henri III's friend was that he cut a rather sorry figure. He was very thin and fidgeted a great deal. But he soon recognized that the marquis had a politeness that was even more agreeable to the person he was addressing than that of the Bishop of Besançon himself. The interview lasted for less than three minutes. As they were leaving, Father Pirard said to Julien, "You looked at the marquis the way you would have looked at a painting. I'm not an expert in what these people call politeness, and you'll soon know more about it than I do, but the boldness of your stare didn't seem very polite to me."

They had climbed back into their cabriolet. The driver stopped near the boulevard and Father Pirard led Julien into a suite of large drawing rooms. Julien noticed that there was no furniture in them. He was looking at a magnificent gilded clock representing a subject which, in his opinion, was highly indecent, when an extremely elegant gentleman approached him with an affable expression on his face. Julien bowed slightly.

The gentleman smiled and put his hand on his shoulder. Julien started and leapt backward. His face was flushed with anger. Father Pirard, in spite of his gravity, laughed until tears came into his eyes. The gentleman was a tailor.

"I leave you at liberty for two days," Father Pirard said to him as they were leaving; "you can't be introduced to Madame de La Mole until then. Anyone else in my place would shelter you like a young girl during these first few hours of your stay in this modern Babylon. Ruin yourself immediately, if you must ruin yourself, and I'll be delivered from my weakness of thinking about you. Day after tomorrow, in the morning, the tailor will bring you two suits; give five francs to the boy who tries them on you. Otherwise, don't let these Parisians hear the sound of your voice. If you say a word, they'll find a way to make you look foolish. That's their special talent. Day after tomorrow, come to see me at noon. . . . All right, go, ruin yourself. . . . I was forgetting: go and order some boots, some shirts and a hat at these addresses.''

Julien looked at the handwriting of the addresses.

"It's the marquis' writing," said Father Pirard. "He's an active man who foresees everything, and he prefers to do things himself rather than order someone else to do them. He's taking you into his household so that you'll spare him the trouble of attending to such details. Will you be intelligent enough to do all the things that quick-witted man will suggest to you in a few words? Time will tell: be on your guard!''

Without a word, Julien went to the shops whose addresses he had been given. He noticed that he was received with respect and that the bootmaker, in entering his name in his register, wrote, "M. Julien de Sorel.''

In the Père-Lachaise cemetery, a gentleman who appeared to be extremely obliging, and still more Liberal in his speech, offered to show Julien the tomb of Marshal Ney, which a shrewd administration has deprived of the honor of an epitaph. But after parting with this Liberal, who, with tears in his eyes, almost threw his arms around him, Julien no longer had a watch. Two days later, enriched by this experience, he presented himself at noon to Father Pirard, who studied him attentively.

"It may be that you're going to become a fop," said Father Pirard sternly. Julien looked like a young man in deep mourning; he was actually quite presentable, but the good priest was too provincial himself to see that Julien still had that swing of the shoulders which, in the provinces, indicates both elegance and importance. When the marquis saw Julien he judged his graces in a manner so different from that of Father Pirard that he said to him, "Would you have any objection to Monsieur Sorel's taking dancing lessons?''

Father Pirard was dumbfounded. "No," he replied at length, "Julien isn't a priest.''

The marquis, climbing a little hidden staircase two steps at a time, personally installed our hero in an attractive attic room overlooking the immense garden of the house. He asked him how many shirts he had ordered from the shirtmaker.

"Two," replied Julien, embarrassed at seeing such a great nobleman descend to such details.

"Very well," said the marquis with a serious expression and in a somewhat curt and imperative tone which set Julien's mind to work, "order twenty-two more. Here's your first quarter's salary.''

On the way down from the attic, the marquis summoned an elderly man. "Arsène," he said to him, "you will serve Monsieur Sorel." A few minutes later, Julien found himself alone in a magnificent library; it was a thrilling moment. In order not to be taken by surprise in his emotion, he walked over and hid himself in a dark little corner, and from there he rapturously contemplated the gleaming backs of the books.

"I'll be able to read all that!" he said to himself. "How could I be unhappy here? Monsieur de Rênal would have considered himself dishonored forever if he'd done one hundredth of what the Marquis de La Mole has just done for me. . . . But let's see the letters I have to copy."

When this task was finished, he ventured to approach the books. He nearly went mad with joy when he found an edition of Voltaire's works. He ran to open the door of the library to avoid being taken by surprise. He then gave himself the pleasure of opening each of the eighty volumes. They were magnificently bound, a masterpiece of the best craftsman in London. This was more than was needed to bring Julien's admiration to its peak.

An hour later the marquis came in, looked over the copies and noticed with astonishment that Julien had written *cela* with a double *l*: *cella*. "Could everything Father Pirard told me about his learning be nothing but a story?" thought the marquis. Greatly discouraged, he said to him gently, "You're not sure of your spelling?"

"No, I'm not," replied Julien, without the slightest thought of the harm he was doing himself; he was moved by the marquis' kindness, which made him think of Monsieur de Rênal's arrogance.

"It's all a waste of time, this experiment with a little priest from Franche-Comté," thought the marquis. "But I had such great need of a trustworthy man!"

"*Cela* has only one *l*," he said to Julien. "When you've finished copying your letters, take the dictionary and look up all the words whose spelling you're not sure of."

At six o'clock the marquis sent for him. Looking at Julien's boots with obvious dismay, he said to him, "I'm to blame for overlooking something: I didn't tell you that every day at half-past five you must dress."

Julien looked at him without understanding him.

"I mean put on stockings. Arsène will remind you; today I'll make your excuses for you."

As he said these words, Monsieur de La Mole showed Julien into a drawing room resplendent with gilding. On similar occa-

sions, Monsieur de Rênal had never failed to quicken his step in
order to have the honor of being the first to go through the door.
As a result of his former employer's petty vanity, Julien stepped
on the marquis' feet and caused him great pain because of his
gout. "Oh! Besides everything else, he's awkward!" thought the
marquis.

He introduced Julien to a tall and impressive-looking woman.
It was the marquise. Julien found that she had an impertinent air,
somewhat like Madame de Maugiron, the wife of the sub-prefect
of the district of Verrières, when she attended the Saint Charles
Day dinner. A little bewildered by the extreme splendor of the
drawing room, he did not hear what Monsieur de La Mole was
saying. The marquise scarcely deigned to look at him. There
were a few men present, among whom Julien recognized, with
unspeakable delight, the young Bishop of Agde, who had been
kind enough to speak to him a few months earlier at the ceremony at Bray-le-Haut. The prelate was no doubt alarmed by the
affectionate glances Julien shyly cast at him, and he had no
desire to recognize the young provincial.

The men gathered in the drawing room struck Julien as having
something melancholy and restrained about them; people speak
softly in Paris, and they do not exaggerate trifles.

A handsome, slender and extremely pale young man with a
mustache came in toward half-past six; he had a very small head.

"You'll always keep us waiting," said the marquise as he
kissed her hand.

Julien realized that this was the Comte de La Mole. He found
him charming at first sight. "Is it possible," he wondered, "that
this is the man whose offensive jokes are supposed to drive me
out of this house?"

As he examined Count Norbert, Julien noticed that he was
wearing boots and spurs. "And I'm expected to wear low shoes,
apparently as an inferior," he thought. They sat down to table.
Julien heard the marquise speak sternly, raising her voice a little.
Almost at the same moment he saw a young lady, with light
blonde hair and a very good figure, who came in and sat down
opposite him. He did not find her at all attractive; on looking at
her attentively, however, he thought that he had never seen such
beautiful eyes; but they gave evidence of an extremely cold
heart. Later he decided that they were the eyes of a person who
was bored and scrutinized other people, yet never forgot the
obligation to be imposing.

"Madame de Rênal had very beautiful eyes, too," he thought.

"Everyone complimented her on them; but they had nothing in common with these." He did not have enough experience to discern that it was the flame of wit that shone from time to time in the eyes of Mademoiselle Mathilde, as he heard her called. When Madame de Rênal's eyes became animated, it was with the flame of passion, or of noble indignation on hearing a report of some malicious action. Toward the end of the meal, Julien found a word to describe the kind of beauty possessed by Mademoiselle Mathilde's eyes: "They're scintillating," he said to himself. Aside from that, she bore a painful resemblance to her mother, for whom his dislike was growing steadily stronger, and he ceased looking at her. Count Norbert, on the other hand, impressed him as admirable in every way. Julien was so captivated by him that it never entered his head to be jealous of him and hate him because he was richer and nobler than himself.

Julien thought that the marquis looked bored. During the second course he said to his son, "Norbert, I want to ask you to take a friendly interest in Monsieur Julien Sorel, whom I've just made a member of my staff, and of whom I intend to make a man, if that [cella] can be done. . . . He's my secretary," he added to the man sitting beside him, "and he spells *cela* with a double *l*."

Everyone looked at Julien, who gave Norbert a slightly exaggerated bow; but, on the whole, they were all satisfied with his expression.

The marquis had apparently spoken of the kind of education Julien had received, for one of the guests attacked him on the subject of Horace. "It was precisely in discussing Horace," thought Julien, "that I was successful with the Bishop of Besançon; evidently he's the only author these people know." From then on his self-assurance did not falter. This transition was made easy for him by the fact that he had just decided that Mademoiselle de La Mole would never be a woman in his eyes. Since his experience in the seminary, he expected nothing but the worst from people, and he did not allow himself to be intimidated by them easily. He would have been completely at ease if the dining room had been furnished with less splendor. Specifically, he was still overawed by a pair of eight-foot mirrors in which he occasionally looked at his conversational partner while discussing Horace.

His sentences were not too long for a provincial. He had beautiful eyes whose sparkle was enhanced by his trembling, or, when he had made a good answer, his happy shyness. He was found to be pleasant. This kind of examination injected a little interest into a solemn dinner party. The marquis motioned the man speaking to Julien to press him hard. "Can it be possible that he does know something after all?" he thought.

Julien discovered ideas as he answered, and he lost enough of his shyness, not to display wit, which is impossible for anyone who does not know the language used in Paris, but to express original ideas, although he did so with neither grace nor aptness. And it could be seen that he had a thorough knowledge of Latin.

His adversary was a member of the Académie des Inscriptions et Belles-Lettres who, by chance, knew Latin; he found Julien to be an excellent classicist, lost all fear of embarrassing him and began to try in earnest to get the better of him. In the heat of combat, Julien finally forgot the magnificent furnishings of the dining room and began to express ideas about the Latin poets which the other man had never read in any book. As an honorable man, he gave the young secretary credit for them. Fortunately, a discussion arose over the question of whether Horace had been rich or poor: a charming, sensual and carefree man who wrote verses for his own amusement, like Chapelle, the friend of Molière and La Fontaine; or a poor devil of a poet laureate attached to the court and composing odes for the king's birthday, like Southey, Lord Byron's accuser. They spoke of the state of society under Augustus and under George IV; in both periods the aristocracy was all-powerful, but in Rome it saw its power wrested from it by Maecenas, who was only a knight, and in England it had reduced George IV to nearly the same position as the Doge of Venice. This discussion seemed to draw the marquis from the state of torpor into which boredom had plunged him at the beginning of dinner.

Julien knew nothing about all those modern names, such as Southey, Lord Byron and George IV, which he now heard for the first time. But no one failed to notice that whenever there was any mention of events which had taken place in Rome and with which it was possible to become acquainted through reading the works of Horace, Martial, Tacitus, etc., he had an incontestable superiority. He boldly appropriated several ideas he had learned from the Bishop of Besançon during the famous discussion he had had with that prelate; they were not among those which were the least appreciated.

When they grew tired of discussing poets, the marquise, who made it a rule to admire everything that amused her husband, deigned to look at Julien. "The awkward manners of this young ecclesiastic may be hiding a learned man,'' the academician, who was sitting beside her, said to her; and Julien heard something of what he was saying. Ready-made phrases were congenial to his hostess's mind; she adopted this one concerning Julien, and was glad she had invited the academician to dinner. ''He amuses Monsieur de La Mole,'' she thought.

CHAPTER 3
First Steps

> That immense valley, filled with bright lights and so many thousands of people, dazzles my eyes. Not one of them knows me, all are superior to me. My head reels.
> —*Poemi dell'av. Reina*

EARLY THE NEXT morning, Julien was making copies of letters in the library when Mademoiselle Mathilde came in through a little private door, thoroughly concealed by the backs of books. While he was admiring this contrivance, she seemed greatly surprised and almost annoyed at encountering him there. With her hair in curlpapers, she impressed him as hard, haughty and almost masculine.

Mademoiselle de La Mole had a secret habit of stealing books from her father's library without leaving any evidence. Julien's presence made her expedition useless that morning, which annoyed her particularly because she had come for the second volume of Voltaire's *La Princesse de Babylone*—a worthy complement to an eminently monarchistic and religious education that was a masterpiece of the Sacred Heart! That poor girl, at nineteen, already needed the spice of wit to make her interested in a novel.

Count Norbert appeared in the library toward three o'clock; he had come to study a newspaper in order to be able to talk politics that evening, and he was glad to see Julien, whose existence he had forgotten. He treated him with perfect graciousness and suggested that they go riding together. ''My father has given us leave of absence till dinner,'' he said.

Julien understood this ''us'' and found it charming. ''Good heavens, Count,'' he replied, ''if it were a question of chopping down an eighty-foot tree, squaring it and sawing it into planks, I venture to say I'd make a good showing; but riding a horse is something I haven't done more than six times in my life.''

"Well, then, this will be the seventh," said Norbert.

Remembering the time the King of ———— came to Verrières, Julien secretly believed himself to be a superior horseman. But, on the way back from the Bois de Boulogne, in the very middle of the rue du Bac, he fell from his horse when he abruptly tried to avoid a cabriolet, and covered himself with mud. It was fortunate for him that he had two suits. At dinner the marquis, for the sake of conversation, asked him about his ride; Norbert quickly replied for him without going into any details.

"The count is very kind to me," said Julien. "I thank him for it and fully appreciate it. He was good enough to give me the gentlest and handsomest horse, but, after all, he couldn't tie me to the saddle and, for lack of that precaution, I fell off right in the middle of that long street near the bridge."

Mademoiselle Mathilde tried in vain to dissimulate a burst of laughter, then she indiscreetly asked for details. Julien satisfied her curiosity with great simplicity and a certain unconscious grace.

"This young priest shows great promise," said the marquis to the academician. "Imagine a provincial being candid in a situation like that! Such a thing has never been seen before and will never be seen again! And then he tells about his misfortune in front of *ladies!*"

Julien set his listeners so thoroughly at ease over his mishap that, at the end of dinner, when the general conversation had taken another turn, Mademoiselle Mathilde asked her brother questions concerning the details of the unfortunate incident. As she continued, and as Julien's eyes met hers several times, he ventured to reply directly, even though he was not questioned, and all three of them finally began to laugh like three young inhabitants of some village in the heart of a forest.

The next day Julien attended two lectures on theology, then returned to transcribe a score of letters. He found sitting near him in the library a young man who was quite carefully dressed, but whose general appearance was ignoble and whose expression was one of envy.

The marquis entered.

"What are you doing here, Monsieur Tanbeau?" he said to the newcomer sternly.

"I thought—" began the young man with a servile smile.

"No, monsieur, you *didn't think*. This is an attempt, but an unfortunate one."

Young Tanbeau stood up, furious, and walked out. He was a

nephew of the academician, Madame de La Mole's friend, and he intended to take up a literary career. The academician had persuaded the marquis to take him as a secretary. Tanbeau, who worked in a separate room, having learned of the favor being bestowed on Julien, wanted to share it, and that morning he had come in and set up his writing desk in the library.

At four o'clock Julien ventured, after some hesitation, to go to see Count Norbert. He was about to go riding and was embarrassed, for he was perfectly polite.

"I think," he said to Julien, "that you'll go to riding school soon; and after a few weeks I'll be delighted to go riding with you."

"I wanted to have the honor of thanking you for your kindness to me. Believe me, monsieur," added Julien with a very serious air, "when I say that, I'm aware of everything I owe to you. If your horse wasn't injured as a result of my awkwardness yesterday, and if he's free, I'd like to ride him today."

"At your own risk and peril, my dear Sorel. Assume that I've already made all the objections required by caution; the fact is that it's four o'clock and we have no time to lose."

When he was in the saddle, Julien asked the young count, "What should I do to keep from falling off?"

"All sorts of things," replied Norbert, laughing heartily. "For example, sit back in the saddle."

Julien broke into a rapid trot. They were crossing the Place Louis XVI.

"There are too many carriages here, you young daredevil!" said Norbert. "And with careless drivers, too! Once you're on the ground, their tilburies will run over you; they won't risk injuring their horses' mouths by pulling up short."

At least twenty times he saw Julien on the point of falling; but finally their ride ended without mishap.

When they returned to the house, the young count said to his sister, "Allow me to introduce a bold daredevil."

At dinner, speaking to his father from one end of the table to the other, he paid tribute to Julien's courage; it was the only thing one could praise in his way of riding. That morning the young count had heard the servants who were grooming the horses in the courtyard use Julien's fall as a pretext for mocking him outrageously.

In spite of all this kindness, Julien soon felt himself completely isolated in the midst of the family. All their manners and customs were strange to him, and he made mistakes in all of them. His blunders were the delight of the servants.

Father Pirard had left for his parish. "If Julien is a frail reed," he thought, "let him perish; if he's a man of spirit, let him make his way alone."

CHAPTER 4

The Hôtel de La Mole

> What is he doing here? Does he like it here? Does he think
> people will like him?
>
> —Ronsard

IF EVERYTHING seemed strange to Julien in the noble drawing room of the Hôtel de La Mole, this young man, pale and dressed in black, seemed in turn highly singular to those who deigned to notice him. Madame de La Mole suggested that her husband send him away on some mission or other on days when certain important people had been invited to dinner.

"I want to carry the experiment through to the end," replied the marquis. "Father Pirard maintains that we're wrong to crush the self-esteem of the people we take into our houses. 'One can lean only on something that resists,' and so on. There's nothing wrong with the young man except his unknown face; he might as well be deaf and dumb."

"In order to keep my bearings," Julien said to himself, "I must write down the names of the people I see come into the drawing room, and a few words about their characters."

At the head of his list he placed five or six friends of the family who sought to win his favor as a measure of precaution, believing him to be protected by a caprice on the part of the marquis. They were insignificant and more or less obsequious men; but it must be said in praise of this class of people, such as are found today in the drawing rooms of the aristocracy, that they were not equally obsequious with everyone. Some of them would have let themselves be abused by the marquis, but would have revolted against a harsh word addressed to them by Madame de La Mole.

There was too much pride and too much boredom underlying the characters of the master and mistress of the household; they were so accustomed to relieving their boredom by insulting others that they could not expect to have any true friends. But, except on rainy days, and in moments of furious boredom, which were rare, they were always found to be perfectly polite.

If the five or six sycophants who showed such paternal friendship for Julien had deserted the Hôtel de La Mole, the marquise would have been exposed to long intervals of solitude, and, in the eyes of women of her rank, solitude is a terrible thing: it is the mark of *disgrace*.

The marquis treated his wife with great consideration. He saw to it that her drawing room was sufficiently filled, but not with peers, however: he found his new colleagues not noble enough to come to his house as friends, and not entertaining enough to be admitted as subordinates.

It was not until much later that Julien discovered these secrets. The policies of the government in power, which form the chief topic of conversation in middle-class houses, are never mentioned in houses like that of the marquis, except in times of distress.

The need to amuse oneself is still so pressing, even in this age of boredom, that even on evenings when there was a dinner party, as soon as the marquis had left the drawing room, everyone else fled. As long as one did not speak lightly of God, the clergy, the king, the men in power, the artists patronized by the court, or anything established; as long as one said nothing good about Béranger, the opposition press, Voltaire, Rousseau, or anyone who took the liberty of speaking with a little candor; and, above all, as long as one never talked politics, one could freely discuss anything.

No income of three hundred thousand francs, no cordon bleu can prevail against such a drawing-room code. The slightest living idea was regarded as uncouth. In spite of good breeding, perfect manners and the desire to be agreeable, boredom was written on every face. The young men who came to pay their respects, afraid of saying something which might arouse the suspicion that they had been thinking, or reading some forbidden book, lapsed into silence after making a few elegant comments about Rossini and the weather.

Julien observed that the conversation was usually kept going by two viscounts and five barons whom Monsieur de La Mole had known during the Emigration. These gentlemen enjoyed incomes of from six to eight thousand francs; four of them supported the *Quotidienne* and three the *Gazette de France*. There was one of them who, every day, related some new court anecdote in which he made lavish use of the word "admirable." Julien noticed that he had five decorations, while most of the others had only three.

On the other hand, there were ten liveried footmen to be seen in the anteroom, ices or tea were served every quarter of an hour throughout the evening, and at midnight there was a kind of supper with champagne. It was for these reasons that Julien sometimes remained to the end; otherwise, it was difficult for him to understand how anyone could listen seriously to the kind of conversation that usually took place in that magnificently gilded drawing room. Occasionally he would look at the speakers to see whether they themselves regarded what they were saying as ridiculous. "My Monsieur de Maistre, whose works I know by heart," he thought, "expresses himself a hundred times better, and yet I find him terribly boring."

Julien was not the only one who was aware of this mental stagnation. Some consoled themselves by eating a great many ices, others with the pleasure of saying for the rest of the evening, "I just left the Hôtel de La Mole, where I heard that Russia . . ."

Julien learned from one of the sycophants that, less than six months earlier, Madame de La Mole had rewarded twenty years of diligent attentions by securing a prefecture for the poor Baron le Bourguignon, who had been a sub-prefect ever since the Restoration. This great event had rekindled the zeal of all the other sycophants; it would not have taken a great deal to offend them before, but now they no longer took offense at anything.

There was seldom any outright discourtesy, but on two or three different occasions Julien had already overheard the marquis and his wife exchange brief remarks that were painful for those sitting next to them at table. These two noble personages did not conceal their sincere contempt for everyone who was not descended from ancestors who *"rode in the royal coaches."* Julien noticed that the word "Crusades" was the only one which gave to their faces an expression of deep seriousness, mingled with respect. Their usual respect always had a shade of condescension in it.

In the midst of this magnificence and boredom, Julien was interested in nothing but Monsieur de La Mole; he was pleased to hear him protest one day that he had had nothing to do with poor Le Bourguignon's promotion. This was out of consideration for the marquise; Julien had learned the truth from Father Pirard.

One morning Father Pirard was working with Julien in the

marquis' library on the endless lawsuit with Abbé de Frilair. "Monsieur," said Julien, "is dining every day with the marquise one of my duties, or is it a special favor that's being shown to me?"

"It's a signal honor!" replied the priest, shocked. "Monsieur N——, the academician, who's been diligently paying court to them for the past fifteen years, has never been able to obtain such an honor for his nephew, Monsieur Tanbeau."

"For me, monsieur, it's the most painful part of my position. I was less bored in the seminary. I sometimes see even Mademoiselle de La Mole yawn, and yet she ought to be used to the amiability of the friends of the family. I'm afraid I'll fall asleep. Please get permission for me to go and have dinner for forty sous in some obscure inn."

Father Pirard, a true *parvenu*, was very sensitive to the honor of dining with a great nobleman. While he was trying to make Julien understand this feeling, a slight sound made them look around. Julien saw Mademoiselle de La Mole listening to them. He blushed. She had come to get a book and had overheard everything; it made her feel a certain respect for Julien. "There's a man who wasn't born on his knees," she thought, "like that old priest. Good heavens, how ugly he is!"

At dinner, Julien did not dare to look at her, but she was kind enough to speak to him. A great many people were expected that evening, and she urged him to remain after dinner. The young women of Paris are not very fond of middle-aged people, especially when they are not well dressed. Julien had not required much shrewdness to perceive that the members of Monsieur le Bourguignon's circle, when they remained in the drawing room, had the honor of being the usual target of Mademoiselle de La Mole's witticisms. That evening, whether or not there was a certain affectation on her part, she was cruel to the bores who were present.

Mademoiselle de La Mole was the center of a little group that gathered nearly every evening behind the marquise's enormous easy chair. Among them were the Marquis de Croisenois, the Comte de Caylus, the Vicomte de Luz and two or three other young officers, friends of Norbert or his sister. These gentlemen sat on a big blue sofa. At one end of this sofa, the end opposite the one occupied by the sparkling Mathilde, Julien sat silently on a rather low straw-bottomed chair. This modest position was envied by all the sycophants; Norbert decently maintained his father's young secretary there by either speaking to him directly or mentioning his name once or twice in the course of the evening.

That evening, Mademoiselle de La Mole asked him if he knew the height of the hill on which the citadel of Besançon stands. Julien found it impossible to say whether or not it was higher than Montmartre. He often laughed heartily at what was said in that little group, but he felt incapable of inventing anything similar. It was like a foreign language which he understood and admired, but which he could not speak.

That evening, Mathilde's friends waged constant warfare against the people who entered the magnificent drawing room. The friends of the family were given first preference, being better known. One may easily judge whether Julien was attentive; everything interested him, both the substance of things and the way in which they were ridiculed.

"Ah, there's Monsieur Descoulis!" said Mathilde. "He's not wearing his wig. Does he expect to earn a prefecture with his genius? He's displaying his bald forehead—he claims it's full of lofty ideas."

"He's a man who knows everyone in the world," said the Marquis de Croisenois. "He also visits my uncle, the cardinal. He's capable of maintaining a lie with each one of his friends for years on end, and he has two or three hundred friends. He knows how to nourish friendship, that's his special talent. On a winter morning at seven o'clock you can see him, just as you see him now, already spattered with mud, standing at the door of some friend's house.

"From time to time he quarrels with someone and writes seven or eight letters about the quarrel. Then he patches it up and turns out seven or eight letters overflowing with friendship. But he's at his best in the frank and sincere effusiveness of an honest man who keeps nothing hidden in his heart. He uses that maneuver whenever he has some favor to ask. One of my uncle's vicars-general is wonderful when he tells the story of Monsieur Descoulis' life since the Restoration. I'll bring him with me some time."

"Well, I wouldn't believe his stories," said the Comte de Caylus. "It's only professional jealousy between insignificant people."

"Monsieur Descoulis will be mentioned in history," said the marquis. "He brought about the Restoration in company with the Abbé de Pradt, Monsieur de Talleyrand and Monsieur Pozzo di Borgo."

"That man has handled millions," said Norbert, "and I can't understand why he comes here to swallow my father's sarcastic quips, which are often abominable. 'How many times have you betrayed your friends, my dear Descoulis?' he called out to him the other day, from one end of the table to the other."

"But is it true that he's betrayed people?" asked Mademoiselle de La Mole. "Who hasn't betrayed someone at one time or another?"

"What!" said the Comte de Caylus to Norbert. "You have Monsieur Sainclair, the famous Liberal, in your house! What the devil is he doing here? I must go over to him and speak to him, and make him speak to me; they say he's very intelligent."

"But what kind of a welcome will your mother give him?" asked Monsieur de Croisenois. "His ideas are so extravagant, so generous, so independent. . . ."

"Look," said Mademoiselle de La Mole, "there's your independent man bowing almost to the floor in front of Monsieur Descoulis and taking his hand. I almost thought he was going to raise it to his lips."

"Descoulis must be on better terms with the government than we thought," said Monsieur de Croisenois.

"Sainclair comes here to get elected to the Academy," said Norbert. "Look how he's bowing to Baron L——, Croisenois."

"He's lower than if he fell to his knees," said Monsieur de Luz.

"My dear Sorel," said Norbert, "you're intelligent, but you're still fresh from your mountains; make sure you never bow the way that great poet does, not even to God the Father Almighty."

"Ah! There's the intelligent man *par excellence*: Baron Bâton," said Mademoiselle de La Mole, faintly imitating the voice of the servant who had just announced him.

"I think even your servants laugh at him," said Monsieur de Caylus. "Baron Bâton—what a name!"

" 'What's in a name?' as he said to us the other day," said Mathilde. "Imagine the Duc de Bouillon being announced for the first time! I think the public only has to get used to it. . . ."

Julien walked away from the sofa. Still unappreciative of the subtle charms of delicate mockery, he felt that a witticism had to be founded on reason before he could laugh at it. He saw nothing in those young people's remarks except a tone of indiscriminate derision, and he was shocked by it. His provincial, or English, prudishness went so far as to see envy in it, although he was certainly mistaken in this.

"Count Norbert," he said to himself, "whom I've seen make three drafts of a twenty-line letter to his colonel, would be very happy if he'd ever written one single page like those of Monsieur Sainclair."

Passing unnoticed because of his lack of importance, Julien successively approached several groups of people; he followed Baron Bâton from a distance and tried to hear him speak. The remarkably intelligent man looked ill at ease, and Julien did not see him recover something of his poise until after he had hit upon three or four pungent phrases. It seemed to Julien that his kind of intelligence required space. The baron did not make remarks: in order to shine, he needed three or four sentences of six lines each.

"He doesn't talk, he lectures," said someone behind Julien. He turned around and blushed with joy on hearing Count Chalvet addressed by name. He was the most perspicacious man of his time. Julien had often seen his name in the *Mémorial de Sainte-Hélène*, and in the fragments of history dictated by Napoleon. Count Chalvet was concise in his speech; his epigrams were flashes of lightning, well aimed, vigorous and sometimes profound. When he spoke on any question, the discussion immediately took a step forward. He brought facts to bear on it; it was a pleasure to listen to him. In politics, however, he was a shameless cynic.

"I'm independent," he was saying to a gentleman wearing three decorations, whom he was apparently ridiculing. "Why should I have the same opinion today that I had six weeks ago? In that case, my opinion would be my tyrant."

Four serious-looking young men who were standing around him frowned at this remark; such gentlemen do not care for facetiousness. The count saw that he had gone too far. Fortunately he caught sight of the outwardly honest and inwardly devious Monsieur Balland. The count engaged him in conversation; people began to gather around them, realizing that poor Balland was about to be placed on the rack. Although horribly ugly, Monsieur Balland, by dint of moralizing and morality, and after some first steps in society which are difficult to relate, had married a very rich woman, who later died; he then married another very rich woman, who was never seen in society. He enjoyed, in all humility, an income of sixty thousand francs, and had self-seeking flatterers of his own. Count Chalvet spoke to him about all this, without pity. There was soon a group of thirty people around them. Everyone smiled, even the serious-looking young men, the hope of the future.

"Why does he come to Monsieur de La Mole's house, where he's obviously a laughingstock?" wondered Julien. He went over to Father Pirard to ask him the reason.

Monsieur Balland slipped away.

"Good!" said Norbert. "That's one of my father's spies gone; only that little cripple Napier is left."

"Could that be the answer to the riddle?" thought Julien. "But in that case, why does the marquis receive Monsieur Balland?"

The stern Father Pirard was scowling in a corner of the drawing room as he listened to the footmen announcing the guests. "So this is nothing but a den of thieves!" he said, like Basile. "I see no one come here except people of ill repute."

The fact was that the stern priest was not acquainted with the distinguishing marks of high society. But, from his friends the Jansenists, he had acquired some very precise notions of the men who make their way into drawing rooms either by their extreme adroitness in serving all parties, or by their shamefully acquired fortunes. For a few minutes that evening he spontaneously answered Julien's eager questions, then he stopped short, deeply afflicted at having always to speak ill of everyone; he imputed it to himself as a sin. Hot-tempered, a Jansenist and believing in the duty of Christian charity, his life in society was a constant conflict.

"What a face that Father Pirard has!" Mademoiselle de La Mole was saying as Julien returned to the sofa.

Julien felt irritated, and yet she was right. Father Pirard was unquestionably the most honorable man in the room, but his blotched face, contorted by the pangs of his conscience, made him look hideous at that moment. "Let's see you judge people by their faces after this!" thought Julien. "It's precisely when Father Pirard's sensitive conscience is reproaching him for some minor shortcoming that he looks horrible, while on the face of that Napier, a notorious spy, there's nothing but pure and tranquil happiness." Nevertheless, Father Pirard had made great concessions to his party: he had engaged a servant and was very well dressed.

Julien noticed something strange happening in the drawing room: all eyes turned toward the door and there was a sudden lull in the conversation. A footman was announcing the famous Baron de Tolly, to whom the elections had just drawn everyone's attention. Julien stepped forward and saw him quite clearly. The baron was the head of an electoral college, and he had had the brilliant idea of causing the little slips of paper bearing the votes of one of the parties to disappear. By way of compensation, however, he had replaced them with an equal number of other little slips of paper bearing a name that pleased him. This decisive maneuver had been noted by one of the electors, who had hastened to congratulate him on it. The good man was still pale from the incident. Certain evil-minded persons had uttered the word "prison." Monsieur de La Mole gave him a cold reception. The poor baron made a hasty withdrawal.

"He must be leaving us so quickly because he has an appointment with Monsieur Comte,"* said Count Chalvet; everyone laughed.

In the midst of a few taciturn great noblemen and a group of schemers, most of them disreputable but all quite intelligent, who successively arrived in Monsieur de La Mole's drawing room that evening (it was rumored that he was about to become a minister), young Tanbeau was having his first taste of battle. If he had not yet acquired much fineness of perception, he made up for it, as will be seen, by the vigor of his remarks.

"Why don't they sentence that man to ten years in prison?" he was saying as Julien approached his group. "Reptiles ought to be kept at the bottom of a pit; they must be left to die in darkness, otherwise their venom becomes deadlier and more dangerous. What's the use of fining him three thousand francs? He's poor, it's true, and so much the better, but his party will pay his fine for him. He should have been fined five hundred francs and sentenced to ten years in a dungeon."

"Good God! Who's the monster they're talking about?" thought Julien, admiring his colleague's vehement tone and abrupt gestures. The thin, drawn little face of the academician's favorite nephew was hideous at that moment. Julien learned that he was referring to the greatest poet of the day. "Monster!" he cried, half aloud, and tears of noble indignation welled up in his eyes. "Oh, you little wretch!" he thought. "I'll make you pay for those words! . . . And yet he's typical of the men who carry out dangerous missions for the party of which the marquis is one of the leaders! And that illustrious man he's slandering—how many decorations, how many sinecures could he have accumulated if he'd sold himself, I won't say to Monsieur de Nerval's abject

---

*A famous sleight-of-hand artist of the time.—L.B.

ministry, but to one of those passably honest ministers we've seen succeeding one another?''

Father Pirard beckoned to Julien from across the room; Monsieur de Le Mole had just said something to him. But when Julien, who at that moment was listening with downcast eyes to the lamentations of a bishop, was finally free to join his friend, he found him cornered by the abominable Tanbeau. The little wretch detested him as the source of the favor shown to Julien, and had come to pay court to him.

"When will death deliver us from that rotten old carcass?" It was in such terms of biblical vigor that the little man of letters was now speaking of the estimable Lord Holland. His special distinction was a thorough knowledge of the biographies of living men, and he had just made a rapid survey of all those who might aspire to a position of some influence under the new king of England.

Father Pirard walked into an adjoining room and Julien followed him. "The marquis doesn't like scribblers, I warn you," he said to Julien. "It's his one antipathy. Know Latin and Greek, if possible, and the history of the Egyptians, the Persians and so on, and he'll honor you and protect you as a scholar. But don't write a single page in French, especially on serious matters that are above your station in life: he'd call you a scribbler and turn against you. Can it be that, living in a great nobleman's house, you don't know the remark the Duc de Castries made about d'Alembert and Rousseau? 'They want to reason about everything, yet they have less than three thousand francs a year.' ''

"Everything becomes known," thought Julien, "here as in the seminary!" He had written nine or ten rather grandiloquent pages, a kind of historic eulogy of the old army surgeon, who, he said, had made a man of him. "And I always kept that little notebook under lock and key!" he said to himself. He went up to his room, burned the manuscript and returned to the drawing room. The brilliant scoundrels had left; only the men with decorations remained.

Around the table, which the servants had just brought in fully laid, were seven or eight ladies, all extremely noble, pious and affected, between thirty and thirty-five years of age. The distinguished Madame de Fervaques, a marshal's widow, entered with apologies for the lateness of the hour: it was after midnight. She sat down beside the marquise. Julien was deeply moved: her eyes and expression were like those of Madame de Rênal.

There were still a number of people in Mademoiselle de La Mole's group. She and her friends were engaged in deriding the poor Comte de Thaler. He was the only son of the famous Jew, renowned for the wealth he had acquired by lending kings money with which to wage war on other nations. The Jew had just died, leaving his son an income of three hundred thousand francs a month and a name that was, alas, only too well known. This singular position called for either simplicity of character or great strength of will. Unfortunately, however, the count was only a placid man filled with pretensions aroused in him by his flatterers.

Monsieur de Caylus maintained that he had been given the will to ask for the hand of Mademoiselle de La Mole (who was being courted by the Marquis de Croisenois, who would eventually become a duke with an income of a hundred thousand francs).

"Oh, don't accuse him of having any will!" said Norbert in a tone of pity.

What this poor Comte de Thaler lacked most of all was, perhaps, a will of his own. From that point of view, he was worthy of being a king. Constantly taking advice from everyone, he did not have the courage to follow any suggestion through to the end.

Mademoiselle de La Mole said that his face alone would be enough to fill her with unending delight. It was a strange mixture of uneasiness and disappointment, but from time to time it clearly displayed surges of self-importance and that air of authority which the richest man in France ought to possess, especially when he is rather handsome and not yet thirty-six years old.

"He's timidly insolent," said Monsieur de Croisenois. The Comte de Caylus, Norbert and two or three young men with mustaches jeered at him to their hearts' content without his suspecting it. They finally sent him on his way at one o'clock.

"Are those your famous Arabian horses waiting for you at the door in this weather?" Norbert asked him.

"No, it's a new team that cost me much less," replied Monsieur de Thaler. "I paid only five thousand francs for the left-hand horse, and the one on the right is worth only a hundred louis; but I assure you he's harnessed only at night, and that's because his trot is exactly like the other's."

Norbert's remark made the count reflect that it was proper for a man like him to be interested in horses, and that he must not let his get wet. He went home, and the other young gentlemen left a few moments later, deriding him as they went.

"So," thought Julien as he heard them laughing on the stairs, "I've been allowed to see the extreme opposite of my position! My income is less than twenty louis and I've found myself beside a man with an income of twenty louis an hour, and yet they laughed at him. . . . A sight like that is a cure for envy."

CHAPTER 5

Sensitivity and a Pious Lady

> They are so accustomed to insipid conversation that any idea with the slightest bit of life in it seems vulgar to them. Woe to anyone who says something original!
>
> —Faublas

AFTER SEVERAL months of trial, here is the stage which Julien had reached by the time the family steward gave him his third quarter's salary. Monsieur de La Mole had entrusted him with the task of supervising the administration of his estates in Brittany and Normandy. He had been placed in charge of the correspondence relating to the famous lawsuit with Abbé de Frilair. Father Pirard had given him instructions.

From the short notes which the marquis scrawled in the margins of the letters and documents of all kinds that were sent to him, Julien composed letters that were nearly always signed.

In the school of theology, his teachers complained of his lack of diligence, but they nevertheless regarded him as one of their outstanding students. These various tasks, attacked with all the fervor of thwarted ambition, had quickly robbed him of the fresh complexion he had brought with him from the provinces. His pallor was a merit in the eyes of his young companions at the seminary. He found them much less malicious, much less inclined to fall to their knees before a franc than those of Besançon; for their part, they believed him to be consumptive.

The marquis had given him a horse. Fearing that one of the seminary students might see him when he was out riding, Julien had told them that the doctors had prescribed this exercise for him. Father Pirard had taken him to several Jansenist houses. Julien was astonished; the idea of religion was firmly bound up in his mind with those of hypocrisy and the hope of making money. He admired those stern, pious men who were not preoccupied with income and expenditures. Several of them had come to regard him as a friend and sometimes gave him advice. A new world opened up before him. In one Jansenist house he met a certain Count Altamira, who was nearly six feet tall, a Liberal under sentence of death in his own country, and very pious. He was struck by this strange contrast between piety and love of freedom.

Julien was no longer on good terms with the young count. Norbert felt that he had answered some of his friends too sharply when they joked with him. Having once or twice been guilty of a breach of decorum, Julien had made it a rule never to speak to Mademoiselle Mathilde unless she spoke to him first. Everyone in the Hôtel de La Mole was perfectly polite to him, but he felt that he had fallen from favor. His provincial common sense explained this change by the common proverb, "Familiarity breeds contempt."

Perhaps he saw things a little more clearly than in the beginning, or perhaps the first spell cast on him by Parisian urbanity had faded away.

As soon as he stopped working he was seized with deadly boredom; such is the withering effect of the politeness, so admirable but also so carefully measured and finely graduated according to position, which distinguishes high society. A heart with a little sensitivity is aware of the artifice.

One can no doubt reproach the provinces for their vulgarity and lack of manners; but people there show a little emotion in their conversation. In the Hôtel de La Mole, Julien's self-esteem was never wounded, but often, at the end of the day, as he took his candle in the anteroom, he felt as though he were going to weep. In the provinces, if you have an accident on entering a café, the waiter will take an interest in you; but if that accident involves something offensive to your pride, as he sympathizes with you he will repeat ten times the word that makes you wince. In Paris, people are considerate enough to conceal their laughter, but you always remain a stranger.

We shall pass over in silence a host of little incidents which would have made Julien appear ridiculous if he had not been, in a sense, beneath ridicule. His absurd sensitivity led him into countless blunders. All his amusements were precautionary measures: he practiced pistol shooting every day, and he was a promising pupil of the most famous fencing masters. As soon as he had a little free time, instead of employing it in reading, as he had done in the past, he hurried to the riding school and asked for the most vicious horses. When he went out with the riding master, he was almost invariably thrown off.

The marquis found him useful because of his unremitting application to his work, his silence and his intelligence, and he gradually placed him in charge of all his business affairs that were somewhat difficult to disentangle. At times when his lofty ambitions gave him some respite, the marquis did business with a certain shrewdness; being in a position to receive useful information, he made some good speculations. He bought houses and woodlands. But he easily lost his temper: he would give away hundreds of louis, then go to court over a few hundred francs. A high-spirited rich man seeks amusement, not results, in his business transactions. The marquis needed a chief of staff who could arrange his financial matters in such a way that they would be clear and easy to comprehend.

Madame de La Mole, despite her great circumspection, occasionally ridiculed Julien. Great ladies have a horror of the unexpected reactions produced by sensitivity; such things are the very antithesis of decorum. The marquis defended him two or three times: "He may be ridiculous in your drawing room, but he triumphs in his office." For his part, Julien believed he had discovered the marquise's secret. She deigned to take an interest in everything as soon as the Baron de La Joumate's arrival was announced. He was a cold man with an impassive face. He was short, thin, ugly, and very well dressed; he spent his days at court and, as a rule, said nothing about anything. Such was his way of thinking. Madame de La Mole would have been intensely happy, for the first time in her life, if she had been able to make him her daughter's husband.

CHAPTER 6

Intonation

> Their lofty mission is to judge calmly the minor events of the everyday life of the various peoples. Their wisdom must forestall great anger over little things, or over events which the voice of renown transfigures by withdrawing them to a distance.
> —Gratius

FOR A NEWCOMER whose pride always prevented him from asking questions, Julien did not stumble into too many serious blunders. One day when he had been driven into a café on the rue Saint-Honoré by a sudden shower, a tall man wearing a beaver frock coat, taken aback by his somber gaze, returned his stare, precisely as Mademoiselle Amanda's lover had done in Besançon.

Julien had too often reproached himself for overlooking that first insult to tolerate this man's stare. He asked for an explanation of it. The man in the frock coat immediately replied with a stream of foul abuse. Everyone in the café gathered around them and passers-by stopped in front of the door. As a provincial precaution, Julien always carried two small pistols; his hand convulsively gripped them in his pocket. He kept his self-control, however, and confined himself to repeating to his man at short intervals, "Give me your address, monsieur. I despise you."

The persistence with which he clung to these eight words finally impressed the onlookers. "What's the matter with the one who's doing all the talking?" said one of them. "He ought to give the other man his address." The man in the frock coat, hearing this opinion reiterated, flung five or six calling cards at Julien's face. Fortunately none of them hit him; he had promised himself not to use his pistols unless he was touched. The man walked away, not without turning back from time to time to shake his fist at him and insult him.

Julien found himself dripping with sweat. "So it's within the power of the vilest of men to arouse me to such a pitch!" he said to himself angrily. "How can I stifle this humiliating sensitivity?"

He would have liked to fight the duel immediately, but he was stopped by one difficulty. Where, in that great city of Paris, could he find a second? He did not have a single friend. He had made several acquaintances, but all of them, without exception, had dropped him after seeing him for six weeks or so. "I'm unsociable, and now I'm being cruelly punished for it," he thought. Finally it occurred to him to seek out a former lieutenant of the 96th regiment, a poor devil named Liévin with whom he had frequently practiced fencing. Julien was sincere with him.

"I'm willing to be your second," said Liévin, "but on one condition: if you don't wound your man, you must fight with me, on the spot."

"It's a bargain," said Julien, shaking his hand with enthusiasm.

They went to see Monsieur C. de Beauvoisis at the address given on his calling cards, in the heart of the Faubourg Saint-Germain.

It was seven o'clock in the morning. Not until he had himself announced did it occur to Julien that the man might be that young relative of Madame de Rênal, formerly employed in the embassy at Rome or Naples, who had given the singer Geronimo a letter of introduction.

He had handed the tall footman one of the cards which had been thrown at him the day before, along with one of his own. He and his second were kept waiting for a good three-quarters of an hour; finally they were shown into an admirably elegant apartment, where they found a tall young man dressed like a fashion plate. His features embodied all the perfection and insipidity of classic Greek beauty. His remarkably narrow head was crowned with a mass of beautiful and meticulously curled blond hair; not a single strand was out of place. "It was to have his hair curled that way," thought the lieutenant of the 96th, "that the stupid fop kept us waiting." His multicolored dressing gown, his morning trousers—everything, down to his embroidered slippers, was correct and marvelously neat. His face, aristocratic and vacuous, proclaimed that his ideas were few and conventional: the ideal of the polished gentleman, a horror of jesting and the unexpected, and a great deal of gravity.

Julien, to whom the lieutenant had explained that to keep a man waiting for so long, after having rudely thrown calling cards in his face, was an additional insult, strode boldly into Monsieur de Beauvoisis' apartment. He intended to be insolent, but at the same time he wanted to appear well-bred.

He was so astonished by the gentleness of Monsieur de Beauvoisis' manner, by his air of mingled stiffness, self-importance and smugness, and by the admirable elegance of everything around him, that he instantly lost all thought of being insolent. This was not the same man he had seen the day before. His surprise at finding such a distinguished gentleman instead of the rude individual he had met in the café was so great that he was unable to think of anything to say. He held out one of the cards that had been thrown at him.

"That's my name," said the fashionable gentleman, in whom Julien's black coat, at seven o'clock in the morning, inspired little respect. "But I really don't understand . . ."

His intonation made some of Julien's anger return. "I've come to fight a duel with you, monsieur," he said. And he rapidly explained the situation to him.

Monsieur Charles de Beauvoisis, after careful consideration, was rather pleased with the cut of Julien's black coat. "It's obviously one of Staub's," he said to himelf as he listened to Julien. "His vest is in good taste, and his boots are well made; but, on the other hand, that black coat so early in the morning! . . . He must be wearing it to help him escape a bullet."

As soon as he had given himself this explanation, he again

began to treat Julien with perfect politeness, almost the same politeness he would have shown to an equal. The discussion was rather long, for the situation was delicate; but finally Julien was forced to yield to the evidence. The aristocratic young man before him bore no resemblance to the coarse individual who had insulted him the day before.

Julien, feeling strongly disinclined to leave, dragged out the discussion. He observed the self-satisfaction of the Chevalier de Beauvoisis (it was thus that he referred to himself), who was offended by the fact that Julien addressed him simply as "monsieur."

Julien admired his gravity, which, though mingled with a certain modest fatuity, never left him for a moment. He was astonished by the singular way he moved his tongue when he pronounced his words. . . . But, after all, there was in none of this any reason to pick a quarrel with him.

The young diplomat graciously offered to fight a duel, but the ex-lieutenant of the 96th, who for the past hour had been sitting with his legs apart, his hands on his thighs and his elbows turned outward, decided that his friend Monsieur Sorel was not the kind of man to pick a useless quarrel with another man simply because someone had stolen his calling cards.

Julien left the house in a very bad temper. The Chevalier de Beauvoisis' carriage was waiting for him in the courtyard, in front of the steps. Julien happened to look at it and recognized the coachman as the man he had met the day before.

It took him only a few moments to see the man, grab his long coat, pull him down from the seat and beat him with his riding crop. Two footmen tried to defend their fellow servant. They struck Julien with their fists. He instantly cocked one of his small pistols and fired at them; they fled. It was all over in a minute.

The Chevalier de Beauvoisis came down the steps with the most comical gravity, repeating in his aristocratic accent, "What's this? What's this?" He was obviously consumed with curiosity, but his diplomatic dignity did not allow him to show any greater interest. When he learned the details of the incident, his expression was still divided between haughtiness and that slightly facetious composure which should never be absent from a diplomat's face.

The lieutenant of the 96th realized that Monsieur de Beauvoisis wanted to fight a duel; he diplomatically tried to keep the advantages of the initiative for his friend. "Now there's a good reason to fight a duel!" he exclaimed.

"I should think so," replied the diplomat. "I'm dismissing this scoundrel," he said to his footmen. "Someone else will have to take his place." The carriage door was opened; the chevalier insisted that Julien and his second get in before him. They went to find one of Monsieur de Beauvoisis' friends, who suggested a quiet spot for the duel. The conversation on the way was quite correct. The only thing out of the ordinary was the diplomat in his dressing gown.

"These gentlemen are true noblemen," thought Julien, "but they're not boring like the people who come to dinner at Monsieur de La Mole's house. . . . And I see why," he added a moment later. "It's because they're not afraid to be indecent." They were speaking of the dancers who had been singled out by the audience during the performance of a ballet the previous evening. The two gentlemen alluded to spicy anecdotes of which Julien and his second, the lieutenant of the 96th, were totally ignorant. Julien was not foolish enough to pretend to know about them; he confessed his ignorance with good grace. This frankness pleased the chevalier's friend; he related the anecdotes to him in great detail, and very skillfully.

Julien was astounded by one incident. The carriage was held up for a moment by a temporary altar that was being constructed in the middle of the street for the Corpus Christi procession. The two gentlemen ventured to make several jests; the parish priest, according to them, was the son of an archbishop. Never would anyone have dared to make such a remark in the house of the Marquis de La Mole, who wanted to become a duke.

The duel was over in an instant. Julien received a bullet in the arm; his wound was bandaged with handkerchiefs, which were then soaked with brandy, and the Chevalier de Beauvoisis politely asked him to let him take him home in the same carriage that had brought him to the scene of the duel. When Julien gave the Hôtel de La Mole as his address, the young diplomat and his friend exchanged a glance. Julien's cabriolet was there, but he found the two gentlemen's conversation infinitely more entertaining than that of the worthy lieutenant of the 96th.

"Good God!" thought Julien. "Is this all there is to a duel? How lucky I was to find that coachman again! How unhappy I'd be if I hadn't been able to avenge the insult I received in a café!" The entertaining conversation had been almost uninterrupted. Julien realized then that diplomatic affectation was good for something.

"So boredom isn't inherent in conversation among highborn

aristocrats!'' he thought. ''These two joked about the Corpus
Christi procession, and they're not afraid to tell very indecent
stories in graphic detail. The only thing their conversation really
lacks is intelligent political discussion, but they more than make
up for that lack by their gracious manners and the perfect aptness
of their expressions.'' Julien felt strongly drawn toward them.
''How glad I'd be to see them often!'' he thought.

They had scarcely taken leave of each other when the Chevalier
de Beauvoisis hurried off to make inquiries. The answers he
received were not impressive. He was extremely curious to
become better acquainted with his erstwhile adversary. Would it
be proper to pay him a visit? The little information he was able
to obtain was not very encouraging.

''This is terrible!'' he said to his second. ''I can't admit that I
fought a duel with a man who's nothing but Monsieur de La Mole's
secretary, and only because my coachman stole my calling cards!''

''There's certainly a possibility of ridicule in the incident.''

That same evening, the Chevalier de Beauvoisis and his friend
told everyone they saw that Monsieur Sorel, a perfectly well-
bred young man, incidentally, was the illegitimate son of one of
the Marquis de La Mole's closest friends. This assertion was
accepted without difficulty. Once it was established, the young
diplomat and his friend deigned to pay several visits to Julien
during the two weeks he spent in his room.

He confessed to them that he had gone to the opera only once
in his life. ''That's dreadful!'' he was told. ''No one ever goes
anywhere else. As soon as you're able to leave the house, you
must go to hear *Le Comte Ory*.''

At the opera, the Chevalier de Beauvoisis introduced him to
the famous singer Geronimo, who was enjoying enormous success at the time.

Julien nearly paid court to the chevalier; he was enchanted by
his mixture of self-respect, mysterious self-importance and youthful fatuity. For example, the chevalier stammered a little because
he often had the honor of seeing a great nobleman who had that
defect. Never before had Julien met anyone who combined
entertaining ridiculousness with the perfect manners that a poor
provincial should try to imitate.

He was seen at the opera with the Chevalier de Beauvoisis;
this association made people talk about him.

''Well,'' Monsieur de La Mole said to him one day, ''so now
you're the illegitimate son of a rich gentleman from Franche-
Comté, a close friend of mine!''

He cut Julien short when he tried to protest that he had had nothing to do with spreading the rumor.

"Monsieur de Beauvoisis didn't like the idea of having fought a duel with a sawyer's son."

"I know, I know," said Monsieur de La Mole. "And now it's up to me to give some consistency to the story, which suits my purposes. But I want to ask you a favor that will cost you no more than half an hour of your time: every night when there's a performance at the opera house, go to the lobby at half-past eleven and watch the members of high society as they come out. I still notice provincial mannerisms in you at times; you must get rid of them. And besides, it won't be a bad idea for you to know, at least by sight, certain important people to whom I may some day send you on an errand. Go to the box office and make yourself known; your admission has been arranged."

CHAPTER 7
An Attack of Gout

> And I was promoted, not because of my merit, but because my master had the gout.
>
> —Bertolotti

THE READER may be surprised by this free and almost friendly tone; we have forgotten to mention that for the past six weeks the marquis had been kept at home by an attack of gout.

Mademoiselle de La Mole and her mother were at Hyères, with the marquise's mother. Count Norbert saw his father only a few moments at a time; they were on very good terms, but they had nothing to say to each other. Monsieur de La Mole, reduced to Julien's company, was amazed to find that he had ideas. He had him read the newspapers to him. The young secretary was soon able to pick out the interesting passages. There was a new paper which the marquis abhorred; he had sworn never to read it, and each day he spoke of it. Julien laughed and was pleased to see the poverty of the resistance opposed to an idea by those in power. This pettiness on the part of the marquis gave him back all the self-assurance he was in danger of losing while spending evenings alone with such a great nobleman. The marquis, annoyed with the present, had Julien read Livy to him; he was amused by his improvised translation of the Latin text.

One day the marquis said, in that tone of exaggerated politeness which often made Julien impatient, "Allow me, my dear Sorel, to make you a present of a blue coat. When it's convenient for you to put it on and come to see me in it, you'll be, in my eyes, the younger brother of the Comte de Retz, in other words, the son of my friend the old duke."

Julien did not understand very clearly what was in the marquis' mind. That very evening he tried out a visit in the blue coat; the marquis treated him as an equal. Julien had a heart worthy of appreciating true politeness, but he had no conception of its delicate nuances. Before this whim on the part of the marquis, he would have sworn that it was impossible to be treated by him with more courteous consideration. "What an admirable talent!" he thought. When he stood up to leave, the marquis apologized for not being able to see him to the door because of his gout.

Julien was preoccupied with a singular thought: "Can he be mocking me?" he wondered. He went to seek the advice of Father Pirard, who, less polite than the marquis, answered him only by whistling and changing the subject. The next morning, Julien presented himself to the marquis in his black coat with his portfolio and the letters that were ready to be signed. He was received in the old manner. That evening he wore his blue coat; the marquis' attitude toward him was entirely different, and just as polite as the evening before.

"Since you're not too bored by the visits you're kind enough to pay to a poor, sick old man," the marquis said to him, "you ought to speak to him about the minor incidents of your life, but frankly and without thinking of anything except relating them clearly and amusingly. Because we must have amusement; that's the only real thing there is in life. A man can't save my life on the battlefield every day, or make me a present of a million francs; but if I had Rivarol here beside my chaise longue, he'd relieve me of an hour's suffering and boredom every day. I knew him well in Hamburg, during the Emigration."

And the marquis told Julien anecdotes about Rivarol and the people of Hamburg, who had to strain their minds to the breaking point to understand a witty remark.

Monsieur de La Mole, reduced to the company of the young ecclesiastic, made an effort to rouse him into greater animation. He goaded Julien's pride. Since he had been asked for the truth, Julien resolved to tell him everything, except for two things: his fanatical admiration for a name that irritated the marquis, and his complete unbelief, which was rather unbecoming in a future priest. His little affair of honor with the Chevalier de Beauvoisis had come at a very opportune moment. The marquis laughed until tears came into his eyes at the scene in the café on the rue Saint-Honoré, with the coachman hurling foul abuse at Julien. This was a period of perfect frankness in the relationship between master and protégé.

Monsieur de La Mole was interested in that strange personality. At first he encouraged Julien's absurdities in order to be entertained by them, but soon he found more interest in gently correcting the young man's false conceptions. "Other provincials who come to Paris," thought the marquis, "admire everything, but this one hates everything. They have too much affectation, he doesn't have enough; and fools take him for a fool."

The attack of gout was prolonged by the intense cold of winter; it lasted for several months.

"People become fond of a pretty spaniel," thought the marquis; "why am I so ashamed of my fondness for this young ecclesiastic? He has an original character. I treat him like a son—well, what's wrong with that? This whim, if it lasts, will cost me a diamond worth five hundred louis in my will."

Once the marquis had realized the firmness of his protégé's character, he began to entrust him with some new business matter every day.

Julien had noted with alarm that the great nobleman sometimes gave him contradictory instructions about certain matters. This might make serious trouble for him. He no longer worked with the marquis without bringing in a notebook in which he wrote down the instructions and had the marquis initial them. He engaged a clerk who recorded the instructions relating to each affair in a special notebook, in which copies of all letters concerning it were also kept.

At first this system seemed to be the most ridiculous and tedious thing imaginable, but in less than two months the marquis became aware of its advantages. Julien suggested that he be allowed to engage a clerk with banking experience to keep double-entry accounts of all receipts and expenditures on properties whose management was entrusted to him.

These measures made the marquis' own financial affairs so clear to him that he was able to indulge in the pleasure of making two or three new speculations without the aid of his broker, who had been robbing him.

"Take three thousand francs for yourself," he told his young assistant one day.

"My conduct might be slandered, monsieur."

"What do you want, then?" asked the marquis crossly.

"I'd like you to be kind enough to make out a formal order to pay me three thousand francs and enter it in the books in your own handwriting. All this bookkeeping was Father Pirard's idea, incidentally." With an expression as bored as that of the Marquis de Moncade listening to his steward, Monsieur Poisson, rendering his accounts, the marquis wrote out the order.

In the evening, when Julien appeared in his blue coat, there was never any mention of business. The marquis' kindness was so flattering to our hero's constantly suffering self-esteem that soon, in spite of himself, he felt a certain fondness for the charming old man. It was not that Julien had any sensibility, as the word is understood in Paris; but he was not a monster, and no one, since the death of the old army surgeon, had spoken to him with such kindness. He noticed with surprise that the marquis showed a polite consideration for his self-esteem which he had never found in the old surgeon. He finally realized that the surgeon had been prouder of his cross than the marquis was of his cordon bleu. The marquis' father had been a great nobleman.

One day, at the end of a morning session, to which Julien had come in his black coat for the purpose of discussing business, the marquis found him so entertaining that he kept him for two hours and insisted on giving him some banknotes which his broker had just brought him from the Bourse.

"I hope, monsieur," said Julien, "that I won't be failing to show the profound respect I owe to you if I beg you to let me say a few words."

"Speak, my friend."

"I must ask you, monsieur, to allow me to decline your gift. It's not addressed to the man in black, and it would completely destroy the relationship you've been kind enough to tolerate with the man in blue." He bowed respectfully and left the room without looking at the marquis.

This incident amused the marquis. That evening he told Father Pirard about it. "The time has come when I must confess something to you, my dear Father Pirard," he said. "I know about Julien's birth, and I authorize you not to keep this confidence secret."

"His action this morning was noble," he thought, "and I'm making him a nobleman."

Some time later, the marquis was at last able to leave the house.

"Go and spend a month or two in London," he said to Julien. "Special couriers and other messengers will bring you the letters I receive, along with my notes. You'll write the replies and send them to me, enclosing each letter with its reply. I've calculated that there will be only five days' delay."

As he traveled post along the road to Calais, Julien was puzzled as he thought of the futility of the alleged business on which he was being sent.

We shall not describe his feeling of hatred, almost of horror, when he set foot on English soil. His mad passion for Bonaparte is well known by now. In every officer he saw a Sir Hudson Lowe, in every great nobleman a Lord Bathurst, ordering the infamies of Saint Helena and being rewarded for it with ten years in office.

In London he finally became acquainted with the mysteries of elegant fatuity. He made friends with some young Russian noblemen who initiated him.

"You're predestined, my dear Sorel," they said to him. "Nature has given you that cold expression of being 'a thousand leagues away from the sensations of the present,' which we try so hard to acquire."

"You don't understand the age you're living in," Prince Korasov said to him. "*Always do the opposite of what people expect of you.* That, I assure you, is the only religion of our time. Don't be eccentric or affected, because then people will expect eccentricity and affectation of you, and you won't be obeying the precept."

Julien covered himself with glory one day in the drawing room of the Duke of Fitz-Folke, who had invited him and Prince Korasov to dinner. They were kept waiting for an hour. The way Julien behaved in the midst of the twenty people who were waiting is still cited by young embassy secretaries in London. His expression was pricelessly amusing.

In spite of the pleasantries of his friends the dandies, he was determined to meet Philip Vane, the only philosopher England has produced since Locke. He found him finishing his seventh year in prison. "The aristocracy is in deadly earnest in this country," thought Julien. "And furthermore, Vane is dishonored, insulted," etc.

Julien found him in good spirits; his boredom was relieved by the rage of the aristocracy. "He's the only lighthearted man I've met in England," thought Julien as he left the prison.

"The most useful idea for tyrants is that of God," Vane had said to him. . . . We shall suppress the rest of his philosophy as being cynical.

When he returned to Paris, Monsieur de La Mole asked him, "What amusing ideas have you brought me from England?" Julien was silent. "Well, what ideas have you brought back, amusing or otherwise?" said the marquis sharply.

"First of all," said Julien, "the sanest Englishman is mad for an hour a day; he's haunted by the demon of suicide, who is the national deity.

"Secondly, wit and genius lose twenty-five percent of their value when they land in England.

"Thirdly, nothing in the world is as beautiful, admirable and appealing as the English landscape."

"Now it's my turn," said the marquis. "First of all, why did you go to the ball at the Russian Embassy and say that in France there are three hundred thousand young men of twenty-five who are passionately eager for war? Do you think that was being very kind to kings?"

"I don't know what to say when I speak to our great diplomats," said Julien. "They have a mania for opening serious discussions. If you confine yourself to the commonplace ideas of the newspapers, you're regarded as a fool. If you allow yourself to say something true and original, they're taken aback and don't know what to answer, and at seven o'clock the next morning they send the first secretary of the embassy to tell you that you've behaved improperly."

"Well said!" exclaimed the marquis, laughing. "Just the same, my profound young man, I'll wager you haven't guessed why you were sent to England."

"I beg to differ with you," said Julien. "I went there to have dinner once a week in the house of the king's ambassador, who's the most courteous of men."

"You went there to get this cross," said the marquis. "I don't want you to discard your black coat, and I've become accustomed to the more amusing tone I've adopted with the man in the blue coat. Until further notice, keep this in mind: when I see you wearing this cross, you'll be the son of my friend the Duc de Retz, who's been engaged in diplomatic work for the past six months without knowing it. Please note," added the marquis with a very serious expression, cutting short Julien's expressions of gratitude, "that I have no desire to change your calling. That's always a mistake and a misfortune for both the protector and the protégé. When you become bored with my lawsuits, or when you no longer suit me, I'll ask for a good parish for you, like Father Pirard's, *and nothing more,*" added the marquis very drily.

Julien's decoration set his pride at ease; he spoke much more freely. He less frequently felt himself insulted or made the target of those remarks to which it is possible to give a discourteous interpretation, and which anyone may let slip in the course of an animated conversation.

His decoration earned him a singular visit: it was from the Baron de Valenod, who had come to Paris to thank the minister for his baronage and establish good relations with him. He was about to be made Mayor of Verrières in place of Monsieur de Rênal, who had lost his position.

Julien laughed inwardly when Monsieur de Valenod gave him to understand that it had just been discovered that Monsieur de Rênal was a Jacobin. The fact was that the newly made baron was the candidate supported by the ministry in the election that was about to take place, and that in the principal electoral college of the department, which was in truth strongly Ultra-Royalist, it was Monsieur de Rênal who was being put forward by the Liberals.

Julien unsuccessfully tried to learn something about Madame de Rênal; the baron, apparently remembering their former rivalry, remained inscrutable. He finally asked Julien for his father's vote in the forthcoming election. Julien promised to write to him.

"You ought to introduce me to the Marquis de La Mole, my dear chevalier."

"I ought to, that's true," thought Julien, "but a scoundrel like him! . . ." Then he said aloud, "My position in the Hôtel de La Mole is really too humble to allow me to take it upon myself to introduce anyone."

Julien told the marquis everything: that evening he informed him of Valenod's pretensions and related his actions and behavior since 1814.

"Not only will you introduce the new baron to me tomorrow," said Monsieur de La Mole seriously, "but I'm going to invite him to dinner day after tomorrow. He'll be one of our new prefects."

"In that case," said Julien coldly, "I request that my father be given the position of superintendent of the workhouse."

"Excellent!" said the marquis, recovering his gaiety. "Your request is granted. I was expecting to hear some moralizing; you're developing."

Julien learned from Monsieur de Valenod that the man in charge of the office of the national lottery in Verrières had just died. He found it amusing to give this position to Monsieur de Cholin, the old idiot whose petition he had once found in Monsieur de La Mole's bedroom. The marquis laughed heartily over the petition, which Julien recited to him as he presented for his signature the letter asking the Minister of Finance for the position.

Monsieur de Cholin had scarcely been appointed when Julien learned that the position had been requested by the deputies of the department for Monsieur Gros, the celebrated geometrician. That noble-hearted man had an income of only fourteen hundred francs, and every year he had lent six hundred francs to the late holder of the position, to help him support his family.

Julien was amazed by what he had done. "And how are the dead man's family living now?" he wondered. This thought wrung his heart. "But this is nothing," he said to himself. "If I want to succeed, I'll have to commit many more acts of injustice, and know how to conceal them beneath resounding sentimental phrases. Poor Monsieur Gros! He's the one who deserved this cross, and I'm the one who has it; and I must conform to the policy of the government that gave it to me."

CHAPTER 8

Which Decoration Distinguishes Its Wearer?

"Your water doesn't refresh me," said the thirsty genie.
"Yet it's the coolest well in all of Diar Bekir."

—Pellico

ONE DAY Julien returned from the charming estate at Villequier, on the banks of the Seine, in which Monsieur de La Mole took a special interest because, of all his estates, it was the only one that had belonged to the celebrated Boniface de La Mole. When he entered the house he found the marquise and her daughter, who had just returned from Hyères.

Julien was now a dandy, and he understood the art of living in Paris. He treated Mademoiselle de La Mole with perfect coolness. He seemed to have lost all memory of the time when she had asked him so gaily for details of his way of gracefully falling off a horse.

Mademoiselle de La Mole found him taller and paler. There was no longer anything provincial about his bearing and appearance; this was not true of his conversation: there was still something noticeably too serious, too earthy about it. Despite these rational qualities, however, it gave no evidence of inferiority, thanks to his pride; others simply felt that he still regarded too many things as important. But they saw that he was a man who would back up what he said.

"He lacks lightness, but not intelligence," said Mademoiselle de La Mole to her father as she joked with him about the decoration he had given Julien. "My brother has been asking you for it for the past eighteen months, and he's a La Mole!"

"Yes, but Julien does unexpected things, which has never been true of the La Mole you've mentioned."

The Duc de Retz was announced. Mathilde felt an irresistible impulse to yawn; each time she saw him she was reminded of her father's drawing room with its ancient gildings and old familiar faces. She formed a dismally boring image of the life she was going to resume in Paris. But when she was in Hyères she longed for Paris.

"And yet I'm nineteen!" she thought. "That's the age of happiness, according to those gilt-edged fools." She was looking at nine or ten volumes of recent poetry which had accumulated on the console table of the drawing room during her stay in Provence. It was her misfortune to be more intelligent than Messieurs de Croisenois, de Caylus, de Luz and the rest of her friends. She imagined everything they would say to her about the beautiful skies of Provence, poetry, the South, etc., etc.

Her beautiful eyes, in which could be seen profound boredom and, worse still, despair of ever finding pleasure, rested on Julien. At least he was not exactly like everyone else.

"Monsieur Sorel," she said in that piercing, curt and completely unfeminine tone employed by upper-class women, "are you going to Monsieur de Retz's ball tonight?"

"Mademoiselle, I haven't had the honor of being introduced to the duke." (The proud provincial gave the impression that these words and this title burned his mouth.)

"He's asked my brother to bring you to his house. And if you come, you can tell me about the Villequier estate: we may go there in the spring. I'd like to know if the house is habitable, and if the countryside is as pretty as people say. There are so many unjustly acquired reputations!" Julien made no reply. "Come to the ball with my brother," she added, very curtly.

Julien bowed respectfully. "So, even during a ball," he thought, "I'm accountable to every member of the family. Don't I receive a salary to deal with business matters?" His irritation made him add, "God only knows whether what I say to the daughter will upset the plans of the father, brother or mother! This house is like the court of a reigning monarch. You're expected to be a complete nonentity, yet never give anyone cause for complaint.

"How I dislike that highborn girl," he thought as he watched Mademoiselle de La Mole walking toward her mother, who had called her over to present her to some of her women friends. "She exaggerates every fashion—her dress is nearly falling off her shoulders. . . . She's even paler than before she went away. . . . Her hair is so blonde that it's completely colorless! The light seems to shine right through it. What arrogance in the way she bows and looks at people! What queenly gestures!"

Mademoiselle de La Mole had just called to her brother as he was leaving the drawing room. Count Norbert came up to Julien. "My dear Sorel," he said, "where would you like me to meet you at midnight to take you to Monsieur de Retz's ball? He expressly instructed me to bring you."

"I know very well to whom I owe such kindness," replied Julien with a deep bow.

His irritation, unable to find anything objectionable in the polite and even friendly tone in which Norbert had spoken to him, began to vent itself on the reply he had made to the count's civil invitation. He found a touch of servility in it.

When he arrived at the ball that night, he was struck by the magnificence of the Hôtel de Retz. The front courtyard was covered with an enormous awning of crimson twill studded with golden stars; nothing could have been more elegant. Beneath this awning, the courtyard had been transformed into a grove of blooming orange trees and oleanders. Since care had been taken to bury the tubs sufficiently deep, the oleanders and orange trees appeared to be growing in the ground. Sand had been spread over the path of the carriages.

All this made a great impression on our provincial. He had never conceived of such magnificence. In an instant, his excited imagination was a thousand leagues away from his bad humor. In the carriage, on their way to the ball, Norbert had been happy, while everything looked black to Julien; as soon as they entered the courtyard, their moods were reversed.

Norbert was conscious only of a few details to which, in the midst of all that splendor, it had not been possible to devote careful attention. He estimated the cost of each item, and Julien noticed that, as the total grew larger and larger, he began to show increasing signs of jealousy and rancor.

As for Julien, he was spellbound, filled with admiration and almost intimidated by the strength of his emotion as he entered the first of the rooms in which there was dancing. People were pressing through the door of the second room, and the crowd was so dense that it was impossible for him to advance. The décor of this second room represented the Alhambra in Granada.

"She's the queen of the ball, you can't deny it," said a young man with a mustache, whose shoulder was digging into Julien's chest.

"Mademoiselle Fourmont was considered the prettiest all winter," replied the man beside him, "but now she realizes that she's slipped down to second place. Look at her strange expression."

"She's certainly spreading every sail to win admiration. Look at her gracious smile as soon as she's dancing alone in the quadrille. It's really priceless!"

"Mademoiselle de La Mole seems to have complete control of the pleasure she's getting from her triumph, which she's fully aware of. She acts as though she were afraid of pleasing anyone who speaks to her."

"Well said! That's the whole art of being attractive."

Julien unsuccessfully tried to catch a glimpse of this attractive woman; seven or eight men taller than himself prevented him from seeing her.

"There's a great deal of coquettishness in that noble reserve," said the young man with the mustache.

"And those big blue eyes that she lowers so slowly just when they look as though they're about to give her away!" said the man beside him. "Really, nothing could be cleverer!"

"Notice how common the fair Fourmont looks beside her," said a third man.

"That air of reserve seems to say, 'How charming I'd be to you if you were the man worthy of me!'"

"And who could be worthy of the sublime Mathilde?" said the first young man. "Some reigning monarch, handsome, witty, well built, a hero in battle and no more than twenty years old."

"A natural son of the Emperor of Russia . . . who'd be given a domain to rule over in honor of the marriage; or simply the Comte de Thaler, who looks like a dressed-up peasant."

The crowd in the doorway thinned out and Julien was able to enter.

"Since she seems so remarkable to these fops," he thought, "she's worth studying. I'll understand what perfection means to these people."

Just as he caught sight of her, Mathilde looked at him. "Duty calls," he said to himself; but there was annoyance only in his expression. Curiosity made him walk toward her with a pleasure which her extremely low-cut gown increased in a way that was really not very flattering to his self-esteem. "There's youth in her beauty," he thought. Five or six young men, among whom he recognized those he had heard talking at the door, stood between him and her.

"You, monsieur," she said to him, "you've been here all winter: isn't it true that this is the finest ball of the season?" He made no reply. "I think the Coulon quadrille is wonderful, and those ladies dance it beautifully."

The young men turned around to see who was the lucky man from whom she was determined to get an answer. It was not an encouraging one:

"I'm not a good judge, mademoiselle. I spend all my time writing; this is the first time I've ever seen such a magnificent ball."

The young men with mustaches were scandalized.

"You're a wise man, Monsieur Sorel," said Mathilde with more marked interest. "You look on all these balls, all these festivities, with the eye of a philosopher, like Rousseau. These follies surprise you without enchanting you."

One word had just extinguished Julien's imagination and driven all illusion from his heart. His lips took on an expression of disdain which was, perhaps, a little exaggerated.

"In my opinion," he replied, "Jean-Jacques Rousseau was a fool when he set himself up as a judge of high society; he didn't understand it, and he judged it with the heart of a lackey risen above his station."

"He wrote *The Social Contract*," said Mathilde in a tone of veneration.

"While he preached the establishment of a republic and the abolition of royal prerogatives, the *parvenu* was overjoyed if a duke altered the course of his after-dinner promenade to accompany one of his friends."

"Ah, yes! At Montmorency the Duc de Luxembourg accompanied a Monsieur Coindet part of the way to Paris," said Mademoiselle de La Mole, filled with exuberant delight by her first taste of the joys of pedantry. She was intoxicated with her own erudition, somewhat like the academician who discovered the existence of King Feretrius. Julien's eyes remained piercing and stern. Mathilde had had a moment of enthusiasm; she was now profoundly disconcerted by the coldness of her conversational partner. She was all the more taken aback because it was usually she who produced that effect on others.

Just then the Marquis de Croisenois eagerly moved toward her. For a time he stood three paces away from her, unable to make his way through the crowd. He looked at her, smiling at the obstacle. The young Marquise de Rouvray, Mathilde's cousin, was beside him. She was leaning on the arm of her husband, to whom she had been married for only two weeks. The Marquis de Rouvray, also quite young, had all that fatuous love which overcomes a man when, having made a marriage of convenience arranged solely by the family lawyers, he finds that he has an exquisitely beautiful wife. Monsieur de Rouvray was going to become a duke on the death of a very aged uncle.

While the Marquis de Croisenois, unable to move through the crowd, was looking at Mathilde with a smile, she turned her large sky-blue eyes on him and the men standing beside him. "What could be more insipid than this whole group?" she thought. "There's Croisenois, who hopes to marry me; he's gentle, polite and has perfect manners, like Monsieur de Rouvray. If it weren't for the boredom they cause, these gentlemen would be very likable. He, too, will take me to balls with that same look of smug satisfaction. A year after we're married, my carriage, my horses, my clothes, my country house twenty leagues from Paris, will all be as impressive as possible, exactly what it takes to make a social climber die of envy—someone like the Comtesse de Roiville, for example. And then? . . ."

Mathilde became bored in anticipation. The Marquis de Croisenois had succeeded in reaching her and speaking to her, but she let her mind wander without listening to him. The sound of his voice mingled with the confused clamor of the ball. Her eyes mechanically followed Julien, who had moved away with a respectful, but proud and dissatisfied expression. Over in a corner, apart from the swirling crowd, she caught sight of Count

Altamira, who was under sentence of death in his own country, and with whom the reader has already become acquainted. During the reign of Louis XIV, one of his ancestors had married a Prince de Conti; the memory of this fact gave him some protection against the agents of the *Congrégation*.

"I can't think of anything that distinguishes a man except a death sentence," thought Mathilde. "It's the only thing that can't be bought. . . . Ah! I just made a witty remark to myself! What a shame it didn't occur to me at a time when I'd have been given credit for it!"

Mathilde had too much good taste to drag into her conversation a witticism prepared in advance; but she also had too much vanity not to be delighted with herself. A look of happiness replaced the boredom that had been apparent in her features. The Marquis de Croisenois, who was still speaking to her, thought he saw a sign of success and redoubled his eloquence.

"What could a malicious critic object to in my witty remark?" thought Mathilde. "I'd answer him, 'The title of baron or viscount can be bought; decorations are given away: my brother just received one, and what has he ever done? An officer's rank can be obtained: ten years of garrison duty, or a relative who's the Minister of War, and you become a major, like Norbert. A large fortune? That's still the most difficult thing to acquire, and therefore the most meritorious. That's odd! It's just the opposite of what the books say. . . . Well, 'to acquire a fortune, you marry Monsieur Rothschild's daughter.'

"That remark of mine really has something to it. A death sentence is still the only thing no one's tried to solicit."

"Do you know Count Altamira?" she asked Monsieur de Croisenois.

She seemed to have returned from such a distance, and this question had so little connection with anything the poor marquis had been saying to her for the past five minutes, that his amiability was disconcerted. Yet he was a quick-witted man, and widely known as such.

"Mathilde is a little strange at times," he thought. "It's a drawback, but she'll give her husband such a fine social position! I don't know how the Marquis de La Mole does it: he's on good terms with the best people in every faction; he's a man who can't go under. And besides, Mathilde's strangeness could pass for genius. Combined with noble birth and a large fortune, genius isn't ridiculous, and then what a distinction it is! Also, when she wants to, she can show that mixture of wit, character and aptness of thought that makes for perfect charm. . . .''

Since it is difficult to do two things at once, the marquis replied to Mathilde absent-mindedly as though reciting a lesson: ''Who doesn't know poor Count Altamira?'' And he told her the story of his ridiculous, absurd and unsuccessful conspiracy.

''Very absurd!'' exclaimed Mathilde, as though speaking to herself. ''But he acted. I want to see a man; bring him to me,'' she said to the marquis, who was deeply shocked.

Count Altamira was one of the most open admirers of Mademoiselle de La Mole's proud and almost arrogant manner; she was, according to him, one of the most beautiful women in Paris.

''How beautiful she'd be on a throne!'' he said to Monsieur de Croisenois; and he let himself be led to her without difficulty.

There are many people in society who would like to establish the principle that nothing is such bad form as a conspiracy; it reeks of Jacobinism. And what could be more unattractive than an unsuccessful Jacobin?

Mathilde's eyes gave the impression that she joined Monsieur de Croisenois in regarding Altamira's Liberalism as ridiculous, but she listened to him with pleasure.

''A conspirator at a ball—what a delightful contrast!'' she thought. In this conspirator, with his black mustache, she seemed to see a lion in repose; but she soon realized that his whole mind was filled with a single viewpoint: utility, admiration for the useful. The count considered nothing worthy of his attention except that which might give his country bicameral government. He was glad to leave Mathilde, the prettiest woman at the ball, because he saw a Peruvian general enter the room.

Despairing of Europe, poor Altamira was reduced to thinking that when the South American countries became strong and powerful, they would give Europe back the freedom which Mirabeau had sent to them.

A swirling mass of young men with mustaches had surrounded Mathilde. She saw clearly that Altamira had not fallen under her spell and she felt piqued by his departure; she saw his black eyes sparkle as he spoke to the Peruvian general. She looked at the young Frenchmen around her with that deep seriousness which none of her rivals could imitate. ''Which of these men,'' she thought, ''could get himself sentenced to death, even if the chances were all on his side?''

Her strange gaze flattered the least intelligent, but it worried the others. They dreaded the outburst of some sharp remark that would be difficult to answer.

"Good birth," she thought, "gives a man a hundred qualities whose absence would offend me—I know that from the example of Julien—but it also atrophies those qualities of heart that make a man get himself sentenced to death."

Just then someone standing near her said, "That Count Altamira is the second son of the Prince of San Nazaro-Pimentel. It was a Pimentel who tried to save Conradin, who was beheaded in 1268. They're one of the noblest families in Naples."

"There's a fine proof of my maxim that good birth robs a man of the strength of character needed to incur a death sentence!" thought Mathilde. "I'm apparently doomed to talk nonsense tonight. Well, since I'm only a woman like all the rest, I'd better dance." She yielded to the entreaties of the Marquis de Croisenois, who had been asking her to dance a galop with him for the past hour. In order to take her mind off her misadventure in philosophy, she did her best to make herself utterly enchanting; Monsieur de Croisenois was enraptured.

But neither dancing, the desire to please one of the handsomest men at court, nor anything else could distract Mathilde. Her triumph could not have been more complete: She was the queen of the ball. She was aware of this, but it left her cold.

"What a colorless life I'll lead with a creature like Croisenois!" she thought as he escorted her back to her seat an hour later. "Where does pleasure exist for me," she added sadly, "if, after an absence of six months, I don't find it in the midst of a ball that arouses the envy of every woman in Paris? And I'm surrounded by the admiration of a group of people who couldn't possibly be more distinguished. None of them are middle-class, except for a few peers and a Julien or two. And yet," she continued with increasing sadness, "what advantages I've been given by fate! Celebrity, wealth, youth—everything, alas, except happiness!

"The most doubtful of my advantages are those that people have been talking to me about all evening. I believe them when they say I'm intelligent, because they're obviously all afraid of me. If they dare to broach a serious subject, after five minutes of conversation they arrive all out of breath, and as though making a great discovery, at something I've been repeating to them for an hour. I'm beautiful: I have that advantage for which Madame de Staël would have sacrificed everything, but the fact remains that I'm bored to tears. Is there any reason why I should be less bored after I've changed my name to that of the Marquis de Croisenois?

"But, dear God!" she added, feeling almost as though she were going to cry, "isn't he a perfect man? He's a masterpiece of modern education; you can't look at him without his finding something charming, and even witty, to say to you; he's brave. . . . But that Sorel is so strange," she said to herself, and the expression of her eyes changed from melancholy to anger. "I told him I had something to say to him, and he hasn't condescended to come back!"

CHAPTER 9
The Ball

> Elegant clothing, a blaze of candlelight, perfumes; so many
> pretty arms and lovely shoulders; bouquets, the captivating
> strains of Rossini's music, paintings by Ciceri! I am carried
> away!
>
> —*The Travels of Uzeri*

"YOU'RE IN A bad humor," the Marquise de La Mole said to her. "That's bad form at a ball, I warn you."

"It's only a headache," replied Mathilde disdainfully. "It's too hot in here."

Just then, as though to justify her, the aged Baron de Tolly fainted and fell to the floor; he had to be carried out. There was talk of apoplexy; it was an unpleasant incident.

Mathilde paid no attention to it. She had made it a rule never to look at old men or anyone known to be in the habit of saying sad things.

She danced in order to avoid conversation about the stroke of apoplexy, which was not apoplexy at all, for the baron was up and about two days later.

"But Monsieur Sorel still hasn't come," she said to herself after she had danced. She was almost looking around for him when she caught sight of him in another room. She was surprised to note that he seemed to have lost that expression of impassive coldness that was so natural to him; he no longer had the air of an Englishman.

"He's talking with my condemned man, Count Altamira!" she thought. "His eyes are full of somber passion, and he looks like a prince in disguise; his glance is prouder than ever."

Julien was approaching the place where she was standing, still talking with Altamira. She stared at him, studying his features, trying to find in them those noble qualities which earn a man the honor of being sentenced to death. As he passed by her, she heard him say to Count Altamira, "Yes, Danton was a man!"

"Good heavens!" she thought. "Can he be another Danton? But he has such a noble face, and Danton was so horribly ugly, a butcher, I believe." Julien was still fairly close to her; she did not hesitate to call out to him. She was aware and proud of asking a question that was extraordinary for a young lady: "Wasn't Danton a butcher?"

"Yes, in the eyes of certain people," replied Julien with an expression of ill-disguised contempt, his eyes still ablaze from his conversation with Altamira, "but, unfortunately for people of good birth, he was actually a lawyer in Méry-sur-Seine. In other words, mademoiselle," he added maliciously, "he began his career like a number of peers I see here tonight. It's true that, from the point of view of beautiful women, Danton had one enormous disadvantage: he was extremely ugly."

These last words were spoken rapidly, in an extraordinary tone that was certainly not very polite. Julien waited for a moment, the upper part of his body slightly inclined, with an air of proud humility. He seemed to say, "I'm paid to answer you, and I live on my salary." He did not deign to look up at Mathilde. With her beautiful eyes extraordinarily wide open and fixed on him, she seemed to be his slave. Finally, since the silence remained unbroken, he looked at her the way a servant looks at his master when awaiting his orders. Although his eyes squarely met hers, which were still fixed on him with a strange expression, he walked away from her with noticeable haste.

"To think that he, who's really so handsome," thought Mathilde at length, coming out of her reverie, "should speak such praise of ugliness! His conduct is never studied! He's not like Caylus or Croisenois. He has something of the air my father adopts when he gives such a good imitation of Napoleon at a ball." She had completely forgotten about Danton. "I'm certainly feeling bored tonight." She seized her brother's arm and, to his great chagrin, forced him to take her for a stroll around the ballroom. She had conceived the idea of following the condemned man's conversation with Julien.

The crowd was enormous. She nevertheless managed to catch up with them just as Altamira was approaching a tray to take an ice, two paces in front of her. He was speaking to Julien with his body turned halfway around. He saw an arm in an embroidered sleeve taking an ice from the same tray. The embroidery seemed to attract his attention; he turned all the way around to see the person to whom the arm belonged. His black eyes, so noble and candid, instantly took on a slight expression of disdain.

"Look at that man," he said rather softly to Julien. "He's Prince d'Arceli, the Ambassador of ———. This morning he asked your French Foreign Minister, Monsieur de Nervel, to extradite me. There he is, over there, playing whist. Monsieur de Nerval is rather inclined to hand me over, because we gave you back two or three conspirators in 1816. If they turn me over to my king, I'll be hanged within twenty-four hours. And it will be one of these handsome gentlemen with mustaches who'll arrest me."

"The infamous wretches!" exclaimed Julien, half aloud.

Mathilde did not lose a single syllable of their conversation. Her boredom had vanished.

"They're not so infamous," said Count Altamira. "I spoke of myself in order to give you a vivid impression. Look at Prince d'Arceli: he glances at his Golden Fleece every five minutes; he can't get over the pleasure of seeing that trinket on his chest. The poor man is really nothing but an anachronism. A hundred years ago the Golden Fleece was an outstanding honor, but then it would have been far beyond his reach. Today, among people of good birth, only men like Arceli are delighted with it. He was willing to have a whole town hanged in order to get it."

"Is that the price he paid for it?" asked Julien with anxiety.

"No, not exactly," replied Altamira coldly. "He may have had thirty or so rich landowners of his district, who were said to be Liberals, thrown into the river."

"What a monster!" exclaimed Julien again.

Mademoiselle de La Mole, leaning her head forward with the keenest interest, was so close to him that her beautiful hair was nearly touching his shoulder.

"You're very young!" replied Altamira. "I told you I had a married sister in Provence; she's kind, gentle and still pretty; she's an excellent mother, faithful to all her duties, and religious without being sanctimonious."

"What's he leading up to?" wondered Mademoiselle de La Mole.

"She's happy," went on Count Altamira, "and she was happy in 1815. At that time I was in hiding in her house, on her estate near Antibes. Well, the moment she heard of Marshal Ney's execution, she began to dance!"

"I can't believe it!" said Julien, horror-stricken.

"That's party spirit," said Altamira. "There are no true passions left in the nineteenth century; that's why people are so bored in France. The cruelest acts are committed, but without cruelty."

"So much the worse!" said Julien. "When people commit crimes they should at least take pleasure in committing them; that's the only good thing about them, the only thing that makes it possible to find any justification for them."

Mademoiselle de La Mole, completely forgetting what she owed to herself, had moved in so close that she was almost between Julien and Altamira. Her brother, whose arm she was holding, accustomed to obeying her wishes, was looking elsewhere in the room and, in order to maintain his dignity, he pretended to have been stopped by the crowd.

"You're right," said Altamira. "People do everything without pleasure and without remembering what they've done—even when they've committed a crime. I could point out ten men, perhaps, in this ballroom who will be damned as murderers. They've forgotten about it, and so has the world. Some of them are moved to tears if their dog breaks his leg. At the Père-Lachaise cemetery when, as you so charmingly say in Paris, flowers are cast on their graves, we're informed that they combined all the virtues of the knights of old, and told of the mighty deeds of their ancestors during the reign of Henri IV. If, despite the good offices of Prince d'Arceli, I'm not hanged, and if I'm ever able to regain possession of my fortune in Paris, I'll invite you to have dinner with nine or ten murderers who are honored and feel no remorse. At that dinner, you and I will be the only men whose hands aren't stained with blood, but I'll be despised, and almost hated, as a bloodthirsty Jacobin monster, and you'll be despised simply as a commoner intruding in good society."

"That's perfectly true," said Mademoiselle de La Mole.

Altamira looked at her in astonishment; Julien did not deign even to glance at her.

"I'd like to point out," continued Count Altamira, "that the revolution I happened to lead was unsuccessful only because I wasn't willing to cut off three heads and distribute among our supporters seven or eight millions that were in a coffer to which I had the key. My king, who's now eager to have me hanged, and who was on intimate terms with me before the revolt, would have given me the Grand Cordon of his Order if I'd had those three heads cut off and distributed the money in that coffer, because I'd have been at least partially successful, and my country would have had some sort of Charter. . . . That's the way this world goes—it's a game of chess."

"At that time," said Julien, his eyes blazing, "you didn't know the rules of the game; now . . ."

"I'd have heads cut off, is that what you mean to say? And I wouldn't be a Girondist, as you implied I was only the other day? . . . I'll answer you," said Altamira sadly, "after you've killed a man in a duel, and even that is much less hideous than to have a man put to death by an executioner."

"But the end justifies the means!" said Julien. "If, instead of being a nonentity, I had a certain amount of power, I'd be willing to have three men hanged in order to save the lives of four."

His eyes expressed both passion for justice and contempt for the vain judgments of men; they met those of Mademoiselle de La Mole, who was standing close beside him, and his contempt, far from changing into a civil and gracious expression, seemed to increase.

She was deeply offended, but it was no longer in her power to forget him. She walked away angrily, drawing her brother with her. "I must drink some punch, and dance a long time," she said to herself. "I'm going to choose the best possible men to dance with, and I'm going to attract attention at any cost. . . . Good, here's the notoriously impertinent Comte de Fervaques."

She accepted his invitation and they danced together. "We'll see which of us is more impertinent," she thought. "But if I'm going to make him look thoroughly ridiculous, I'll have to make him talk."

Soon everyone else in the quadrille was merely going through the motions of dancing. No one wanted to miss a single one of Mathilde's cutting sallies. Monsieur de Fervaques became disconcerted and, finding only elegant words instead of ideas, began to simper. Mathilde, who was in a bad mood, was cruel to him and made him her enemy.

She danced until dawn and left the ballroom horribly tired. But in the carriage the little strength she had left was still employed in making herself sad and unhappy. She had been scorned by Julien, and she was unable to scorn him.

Julien's happiness was at its peak. Without being aware of it, he was carried away by the music, the flowers, the beautiful women, the general elegance and, above all, by his own imagination, which was lost in dreams of glory for himself and freedom for all mankind.

"What a magnificent ball!" he said to the count. "There's nothing lacking."

"Thought is lacking," replied Altamira. And his face betrayed that contempt which is all the more caustic because one realizes that politeness imposes the duty of concealing it.

"You're here, count—doesn't that make thought present also, and conspiring thought at that?"

"I'm here because of my name. But thought is hated in your drawing rooms. It must never rise above the level of a music-hall verse; then it's rewarded. But if a man thinks, and if there's any vigor or originality in his remarks, you call him a cynic. Isn't that the name one of your judges gave to Courier? You put him in prison, along with Béranger. In France, anyone whose mind is worth anything is thrown to the police by the *Congrégation*; and the 'best people' applaud.

"That's because your time-worn society values decorum above everything else. . . . You'll never rise higher than military valor; you'll have Murats, but never a Washington. I see nothing in France except vanity. A man who speaks spontaneously may easily make some rash remark, and then his host considers himself dishonored."

As the count said these words his carriage, which was taking Julien home, stopped in front of the Hôtel de La Mole. Julien was completely captivated by his conspirator. Altamira had paid him this fine compliment, obviously springing from deep conviction: "You don't have the frivolity of a Frenchman, and you understand the principle of *utility*."

It so happened that, only two evenings before, Julien had seen *Marino Faliero*, a tragedy by Monsieur Casimir Delavigne. "Doesn't Israel Bertuccio, a lowly dockyard carpenter, have more character than all those Venetian noblemen?" thought our rebellious plebeian. "And yet they're people whose proven nobility goes back to the year 700, a century before Charlemagne, while the noblest people who were at Monsieur de Retz's ball tonight can trace their ancestry only as far as the thirteenth century, and even then there are plenty of gaps. Well, among those Venetian noblemen, so great by birth, but so atrophied, so feeble in character, Israel Bertuccio is the man who's remembered.

"A conspiracy wipes out all titles given by social caprice. In a conspiracy, a man immediately assumes the rank assigned to him by his attitude toward death. Even intelligence loses some of its supremacy. . . .

"What would Danton be today, in this age of Valenods and Rênals? Not even a deputy public prosecutor. . . . What am I saying? He'd sell himself to the *Congrégation*; he'd be a minister, because, after all, the great Danton was known to steal. Mirabeau also sold himself. Napoleon stole millions in Italy: otherwise he'd have been stopped short by poverty, like Pichegru. Only Lafayette has never stolen. Is it necessary to steal, and to sell oneself?" This question baffled Julien. He spent the rest of the night reading the history of the Revolution.

The next day, as he wrote his letters in the library, he was still unable to think of anything except his conversation with Count Altamira. "As a matter of fact," he said to himself after a long reverie, "if those Spanish Liberals had compromised the people with a few crimes, they wouldn't have been swept away so easily. They were only presumptuous, chattering children. . . . Like me!" he cried out suddenly, as though waking up with a start. "What difficult thing have I ever done to give myself the right to judge those poor devils who, after all, dared to attempt something once in their lives, and began to act? I'm like a man who stands up from table and cries out, 'I won't have dinner tomorrow, but that won't prevent me from being as strong and cheerful as I am today.' Who knows what a man feels halfway through a great action? After all, such things aren't done as easily as firing a pistol. . . ."

These lofty thoughts were interrupted by the unexpected arrival of Mademoiselle de La Mole, who had just entered the library. He was so carried away by his admiration for Danton, Mirabeau and Carnot, who had been able to avoid being vanquished, that he looked at her without thinking about her, without greeting her, almost without seeing her. When his large, wide-open eyes finally became aware of her presence, the light in them died out. She noticed this with bitterness.

It was in vain that she asked him for a volume of Vély's *Histoire de France*, which was on the top shelf, making it necessary for him to bring the longer of the two ladders. He put the ladder in place, brought down the volume and handed it to her, still without being able to give her a thought. As he was absent-mindedly taking the ladder back, he bumped his elbow against the glass of one of the bookcases; the splinters, clattering on the floor, awakened him at last. He hastened to apologize to Mademoiselle de La Mole; he tried to be civil, but he was nothing more. She saw clearly that she had disturbed him and that, rather than talk to her, he would have preferred to go on thinking of whatever had been occupying his mind before her arrival. After looking at him for a long time, she slowly left him.

He watched her walk away, enjoying the contrast between the simplicity of her present attire and her elegant splendor of the night before. The difference in her expression was almost equally striking. Mathilde, who had been so haughty at the Duc de Retz's ball, now had an almost supplicating look in her eyes. "That black dress really shows the beauty of her figure even better," thought Julien. "But why is she in mourning? If I ask someone the reason, it will turn out that I've made another blunder."

He had by now descended from the heights of his rapturous meditation. "I'll have to reread all the letters I've written this morning," he thought. "God only knows how many omissions and stupid mistakes I'll find in them!" As he was reading the first of these letters with forced attention, he heard the rustle of a silk dress close by. He quickly turned around: Mademoiselle de La Mole was standing two paces away from his table, laughing. This second interruption angered Julien.

As for Mathilde, she had just become acutely aware that she meant nothing to him. Her laughter was intended to cover her embarrassment; it succeeded in doing so.

"You're obviously thinking of something very interesting, Monsieur Sorel," she said. "Can it be some curious anecdote concerning the conspiracy that sent Count Altamira here to us in Paris? Tell me what you're thinking about, I'm dying to know; I'll be discreet, I give you my word!" She was astonished by these words as she heard herself saying them. What! Pleading with an inferior! Her embarrassment became more intense; she added lightly, "What can have made you abandon your usual coldness and become an inspired creature, like one of Michelangelo's prophets?"

This eager and indiscreet questioning wounded Julien deeply and brought back all his madness.

"Was Danton right to steal?" he asked her brusquely, and with an expression that became increasingly ferocious. "And what about the revolutionaries of Piedmont and Spain—should they have compromised the people with crimes? Should they have given away all the posts in the army, all the decorations, even to men without merit? Wouldn't the people who wore those decorations have dreaded the return of the king? Should the treasury in Turin have been pillaged? In short, mademoiselle," he said, moving toward her with a terrifying expression, "should a man who wants to drive ignorance and crime from the face of the earth pass over it like a whirlwind and do evil almost indiscriminately?"

Mathilde was frightened; unable to meet his gaze, she recoiled a few steps. She looked at him for a moment, then, ashamed of her fear, walked gracefully out of the library.

CHAPTER 10

Queen Marguerite

Love! In what madness do you not contrive to make us find pleasure?

—*Letters of a Portuguese Nun*

JULIEN REREAD his letters. As he heard the dinner bell he said to himself, "How ridiculous I must have seemed to that Parisian doll! How foolish of me to tell her what I was really thinking about! But maybe it wasn't so foolish after all. On that occasion, the truth was worthy of me. But why did she come to question me about personal matters? Such questions from her are indiscreet. It was bad manners. My thoughts on Danton aren't part of the work her father pays me for. . . ."

As he entered the dining room, he was distracted from his irritation by the sight of Mademoiselle de La Mole's deep mourning, which impressed him all the more forcibly because no one else in the family was dressed in black.

After dinner he found himself completely free of the feverish exaltation that had possessed him all through the day. Fortunately the academician who knew Latin was one of the dinner guests. "There's the man who'll ridicule me the least," thought Julien, "if my question about Mademoiselle de La Mole's mourning is an awkward blunder, as I assume it will be."

Mathilde was looking at him with a singular expression. "There's a good example of the coquetry of Parisian women, the way Madame de Rênal described it to me," he thought. "I wasn't nice to her this morning: she wanted to talk to me and I didn't give in to her whim, so now she has more respect for me. There will no doubt be the devil to pay later: her haughty pride will find a good way to take vengeance. I defy her to do her worst. How different from the woman I've lost! What natural charm she had! What simplicity! I knew her thoughts before she did. I saw them taking form. My only rival in her heart was the fear of her children's death; it was a reasonable, natural emotion, and I found it lovable even though it made me suffer. I was a fool. The ideas I'd formed of Paris prevented me from appreciating that sublime woman. Good God, what a difference! And what do I find here? Cold, arrogant vanity, every shade of self-esteem, and nothing more.''

Everyone was leaving the table. "I mustn't let anyone get hold of my academician," thought Julien. He approached him as they were walking out into the garden, assumed a meek, submissive attitude and sympathized with his rage over the success of *Ernani*.

"If we were still in the days of the *lettres de cachet!* . . ." he said.

"Then he wouldn't have dared!" exclaimed the academician with a gesture in the style of Talma.

With regard to a flower, Julien quoted several words from Virgil's *Georgics* and declared that nothing could equal Father Delille's poetry. In short, he flattered the academician in every way. Then he said, with an air of utter indifference, "I imagine Mademoiselle de La Mole has received a legacy from some uncle, for whom she's in mourning."

"What!" said the academician, stopping short. "You live in this house and you don't know about her mania? As a matter of fact, it's strange that her mother lets her do such things; but, between you and me, people in this house aren't exactly distinguished for their strength of character. Mademoiselle Mathilde has enough for all of them, and she leads them by the nose. Today is the thirtieth of April!" He stopped talking and looked at Julien significantly. Julien smiled as intelligently as he could.

"What connection can there be between leading a whole household by the nose, wearing a black dress and the thirtieth of April?" he wondered. "I must be even more foolish than I thought."

"I must confess . . ." he said to the academician, and his eyes continued to question him.

"Let's take a stroll around the garden," said the academician, delighted to see an opportunity to tell a long and elegant story. "What! Is it possible that you don't know what happened on the thirtieth of April, 1574?"

"Where?" asked Julien, astonished.

"On the Place de Grève."

Julien was so bewildered that this name did not enlighten him. Curiosity and the expectation of hearing something tragic, so much in keeping with his character, gave his eyes that expression of eager interest which a storyteller loves to see in his audience. The academician, delighted to find a virgin ear, told Julien at great length how, on April 30, 1574, the handsomest man of his time, Boniface de La Mole, and his friend Annibal de Coconasso, a Piedmontese gentleman, were beheaded on the Place de Grève. La Mole was the idolized lover of Queen Marguerite of Navarre. "And note," remarked the academician, "that Mademoiselle de La Mole's name is *Mathilde-Marguerite*." La Mole was also the favorite of the Duc d'Alençon and a close friend of his mistress's husband, the King of Navarre, later Henri IV. On Shrove Tuesday of the year 1574, the court was at Saint-Germain, with poor King Charles IX, who was slowly dying. La Mole tried to rescue the princes, his friends, who were being held captive at court by Queen Catherine de Medici. He brought two hundred horsemen to the walls of Saint-Germain, the Duc d'Alençon became frightened and La Mole was quickly handed over to the executioner.

"But what impresses Mademoiselle Mathilde," said the academician, "as she herself told me seven or eight years ago, when she was twelve, because she has a head on her shoulders, what a head! . . ." And he raised his eyes to the sky. "The thing that strikes her in that political catastrophe is the fact that Queen Marguerite of Navarre, hidden in a house facing the Place de Grève, dared to ask the executioner for her lover's head. And the following night, at midnight, she took that head with her in her carriage and went to bury it with her own hands in a chapel at the foot of the hill of Montmartre."

"Incredible!" exclaimed Julien, deeply moved.

"Mademoiselle Mathilde despises her brother because, as you can see, he has no interest in all that ancient history and doesn't wear mourning on the thirtieth of April. Ever since that famous execution, in memory of the close friendship between La Mole and Coconasso, who, being an Italian, was named Annibal, all the men of the family have borne that name. And," added the academician, lowering his voice, "according to Charles IX himself, Coconasso was one of the most brutal murderers on August 24, 1572. But how is it possible, my dear Sorel, that you, a member of the household, are ignorant of these things?"

"Then that's why Mademoiselle de La Mole called her brother 'Annibal' twice during dinner," said Julien. "I thought I hadn't heard correctly."

as a reproach. It's strange that the marquise allows such
ness. . . . That girl's husband will have a lot to put up
with."

These words were followed by five or six satirical remarks.
Julien was shocked by the spiteful joy that shone in the academician's eyes. "Here we are, two servants talking against their
masters!" he thought. "But I shouldn't be surprised by anything
this academician does."

One day Julien had caught him on his knees in front of the
marquise, begging her to make sure that one of his nephews in
the provinces was granted a license to sell tobacco.

That evening one of Mademoiselle de La Mole's maids, who
pursued Julien as Elisa had once done, gave him to understand
that her mistress's mourning was not worn to attract attention.
That strange idiosyncrasy was rooted in the depths of her character. She really loved that La Mole, the lover of the most intelligent queen of her age, who died because he tried to save his
friends. And what friends! The first prince of the blood and
Henri IV.

Accustomed to the perfect naturalness that shone in all of
Madame de Rênal's behavior, Julien saw nothing but affectation
in all the women of Paris, and whenever he felt the slightest
inclination to melancholy he could find nothing to say to them.
Mademoiselle de La Mole was an exception.

He was beginning to cease regarding as hardness of heart the
kind of beauty that is based on nobility of demeanor. He had
long conversations with Mademoiselle de La Mole, who, on
pleasant spring days, sometimes took a walk with him in the
garden, before the open windows of the drawing room. One day
she told him she was reading d'Aubigné's history, and Brantôme.
"What strange books for her to read!" thought Julien. "And the
marquise won't let her read the novels of Sir Walter Scott!"

One day, her eyes sparkling with that pleasure which is proof
of sincere admiration, she related to him the action of a young
woman during the reign of Henri III, about which she had just
read in l'Etoile's memoirs: discovering that her husband was
unfaithful to her, she had stabbed him.

Julien's self-esteem was flattered. A person surrounded by
great deference and who, according to the academician, held
sway over the entire household, had deigned to speak to him in a
manner that could almost be taken for something like friendship.

"I was mistaken," he thought a short time later "It isn't
familiarity; I'm only like the confidant in a tragedy: she needs to

talk to someone. I'm regarded as a learned man in this house. I'm going to read Brantôme, d'Aubigné and l'Etoile, then I'll be able to challenge some of the stories she talks to me about. I want to stop playing the part of a passive confidant.''

Little by little his conversations with Mathilde, whose manner was at once so imposing and so casual, became more interesting. He forgot to play the sad part of a plebeian in revolt. He found her well read and even intelligent. Her opinions in the garden were quite different from those she professed in the drawing room. Sometimes with him she showed an enthusiasm and a frankness which contrasted sharply with her usual cold, haughty manner.

"The Wars of the League were the heroic age of France," she said to him one day, her eyes shining with intelligence and fervor. "In those days, men fought to achieve some specific aim, to bring about the triumph of their party, not just to win some trivial medal, the way they did in the time of your emperor. You must agree that there was less selfishness and pettiness. I love that age."

"And Boniface de La Mole was the hero of it," he said to her.

"At least he was loved as it's perhaps sweet to be loved. What woman alive today wouldn't be horrified at the thought of touching her lover's severed head?"

Madame de La Mole called her daughter. In order to be useful, hypocrisy must be concealed, and Julien, as we have seen, had half confided his admiration for Napoleon to Mademoiselle de La Mole.

"That's the enormous advantage they have over us," thought Julien, left alone in the garden. "The history of their ancestors raises them above vulgar feelings, and they don't have to worry constantly about making a living! What a misfortune!" he added bitterly. "I'm unworthy of reasoning about such lofty matters; I probably can't see them clearly. My life is a series of hypocrisies, because I don't have an income of a thousand francs to buy my daily bread with."

"What are you daydreaming about there, monsieur?" asked Mathilde as she ran up to him, out of breath. There was a touch of intimacy in her question.

Julien was tired of despising himself. Out of pride, he told her frankly what he was thinking. He blushed deeply on mentioning his poverty to someone who was so rich. He sought to make it plain from his dignified tone that he was not asking for anything.

He had never before seemed so handsome to Mathilde; she now found in his features an expression of sensitivity and frankness which he often lacked.

Less than a month later, Julien was strolling thoughtfully in the garden of the Hôtel de La Mole, but his face no longer had that look of hardness and philosophical arrogance which had been given to it by constant awareness of his own inferiority. He had just escorted Mademoiselle de La Mole to the door of the drawing room; she claimed to have hurt her foot while running with her brother.

"She leaned on my arm in a very strange way!" thought Julien. "Am I a conceited fool, or is it true that she's taken a liking to me? She listens to me with such a sweet expression, even when I confess all the sufferings of my pride to her! And she's so haughty with everyone else! Those people in the drawing room would be amazed if they saw the look on her face. I'm sure she doesn't have that kind, gentle expression with anyone else."

He tried not to form an exaggerated idea of that singular friendship. He compared it to an armed truce. Each day when they met, before resuming the almost intimate tone of the day before, they almost asked each other, "Are we going to be friends or enemies today?" In the first few remarks they exchanged, what was actually said had no importance. Neither of them was concerned with anything except form. Julien had realized that he would be lost if he tolerated one single insult from that haughty girl. "If I must quarrel with her," he thought, "wouldn't it be better to do it right from the start, by standing up for the lawful rights of my pride, rather than by repelling the marks of contempt that would soon follow the slightest neglect of what I owe to my personal dignity?"

Several times, on days when she was in a bad temper, Mathilde tried to adopt the manner of a great lady with him; she made these attempts with extraordinarily subtle skill, but he vigorously repulsed them.

One day he interrupted her abruptly: "Does Mademoiselle de La Mole have any orders to give her father's secretary? He must listen to her orders and obey them with respect, but, aside from that, he has nothing to say to her. He isn't paid to tell her his thoughts."

This aspect of their relationship, and the singular suspicions in his mind, drove away the boredom he had found in the magnificent drawing room, where everyone was afraid of everything and it was considered improper to speak lightly about anything.

"It would be amusing if she were in love with me," he thought. "But whether she loves me or not, I'm on intimate terms with an intelligent girl before whom I see everyone in the house tremble, especially the Marquis de Croisenois, that polished young gentleman, so gentle and brave, who combines all the advantages of birth and fortune, a single one of which would fill my heart with joy! He's madly in love with her, or at least he's as much in love as a Parisian can be, and he plans to marry her. How many letters Monsieur de La Mole has had me write to the two lawyers who are drawing up the marriage contract! In the morning I'm in a subordinate position, pen in hand, but two hours later, here in the garden, I triumph over that charming young man, because, after all, her preference for me is obvious and undisguised. Also, she may hate him as her future husband; she's proud enough for that. In that case, the favors she shows me are granted to me only as an inferior in whom she can confide.

"But no, either I'm going mad or she's trying to make me fall in love with her; the more I treat her with coldness and respect, the more she seeks me out. That might be part of a plan, or an affectation. Are Parisian women that good at pretending? What do I care! Appearances are in my favor, so I'll make the most of them. My God, but she's beautiful! How attractive those big blue eyes are when I see them close to me, looking at me the way they often do! What a difference between this spring and last spring, when I was living in misery, sustaining myself only by strength of character, in the midst of those three hundred dirty, malicious hypocrites! I was almost as malicious as they were. . . ."

In moments of mistrust he thought, "That girl is trying to make a fool of me. She and her brother are working together to play some joke on me. But she seems to have such contempt for his irresolute character. 'He's brave,' she said to me one day, 'but that's all; and even so he was brave only when he was facing the swords of the Spaniards. In Paris, everything frightens him: he sees the danger of ridicule everywhere.' He never dares to have a thought that departs from what's fashionable. I'm always the one who has to come to his defense. A girl of nineteen! Is it possible at that age to be faithful to a self-prescribed code of hypocrisy every minute of the day?

"On the other hand, when she turns those big blue eyes on me with a certain strange expression, Count Norbert always goes away. That seems suspicious to me; shouldn't he be indignant with his sister for paying special attention to a *servant* in their house? That's how I've heard the Duc de Chaulnes refer to me.'' At this recollection, anger replaced all other feelings. ''Is it only because the crotchety old duke likes to cling to old-fashioned ways of speaking?

''Anyway, she's pretty!'' he went on, glaring like a tiger. ''I'll seduce her and then go away, and woe to anyone who tries to stop my escape!''

This idea became his sole concern; he was no longer able to think of anything else. His days went by like hours. Whenever he tried to fix his attention on some serious matter, he would invariably sink into a profound reverie from which he would awaken a quarter of an hour later, his heart palpitating with ambition and his head in a whirl as he repeated this question to himself: ''Does she love me?''

CHAPTER 11

A Girl's Power

I love her beauty, but I fear her mind.
                              —Mérimée

IF JULIEN had employed in studying what went on in the drawing room the time he spent in forming an exaggerated idea of Mathilde's beauty, or in working himself into a rage over her arrogance, which was natural in her family, but which she was forgetting for him, he would have realized how she exercised such power over everyone around her. As soon as anyone displeased her, she knew how to punish him with a witty remark that was so carefully phrased, so well chosen, so outwardly inoffensive and so skillfully timed that the wound grew deeper the more one reflected on it, until eventually the victim's offended vanity was suffering horribly.

Since she attached no value to many things that were of serious concern to the rest of the family, she always seemed to be coolly self-possessed to them. The drawing rooms of the aristocracy are pleasant to mention after one has left them, but that is all. The utter insignificance of the conversation, and above all the banal remarks which go even beyond the demands of hypocrisy, finally exhaust one's patience with their nauseating sweetness. Politeness in itself is nothing, except when one first becomes acquainted with it. Julien learned this from experience after his first enchantment, his first amazement. "Politeness," he said to himself, "is only the absence of the anger that would be aroused by bad manners." Mathilde was often bored; perhaps she would have been bored anywhere. At such times, sharpening a cutting remark became an amusement and a genuine pleasure to her.

It was perhaps in order to have victims a little more entertaining than her distinguished relatives, or the academician and the five or six other persons of inferior rank who paid court to them, that she had given hope to the Marquis de Croisenois, the Comte de Caylus and two or three other young men of the highest distinction. They were nothing to her except new subjects for epigrams.

We shall confess with regret, for we like Mathilde, that she had received letters from several of them, and had occasionally answered them. We hasten to add that she was not a typical young lady of our time. In general, the pupils of the noble Convent of the Sacred Heart cannot be reproached for lack of prudence.

One day the Marquis de Croisenois gave her back a rather compromising letter which she had written to him the day before. He expected to further his own cause to a great degree by this outstanding mark of prudence. But imprudence was precisely what Mathilde liked in her correspondence. She took pleasure in gambling with her fate. She did not speak to him for six weeks.

She was amused by these young men's letters, but, according to her, they were all alike. They were always full of the most profound, the most melancholy passion.

"Every one of them is the same perfect gentleman, ready to set out for the Holy Land," she said to her cousin. "Have you ever seen anything more insipid? So these are the letters I'm going to receive all my life! They must change only every twenty years, according to the kind of occupation that's in vogue. They must have been less colorless during the Empire. In those days, fashionable young men had either seen or performed actions that *really* had something of greatness about them. The Duc de N——, my uncle, fought at Wagram."

"How much intelligence does it take to slash someone with a

saber?'' said Mademoiselle de Sainte-Héridité, Mathilde's cousin. ''And when they've done it, how often they talk about it!''

''Well, I like to listen to those stories. Having been in a *real* battle, one of Napoleon's battles, in which ten thousand soldiers were killed, is a proof of courage. Exposing oneself to danger elevates the soul and saves it from the boredom in which all my poor admirers seem to be plunged; and their boredom is contagious. Which of them has any idea of doing something out of the ordinary? They're trying to win my hand in marriage—a magnificent exploit! I'm rich and my father will help his son-in-law to succeed. Oh, if only he could find one who'd be a little entertaining!''

Mathilde's energetic, direct and picturesque way of looking at things had a bad effect on her speech, as one can see. Her remarks often seemed in bad taste to her refined friends. If she had been less sought-after, they would almost have admitted that her language was something a little too colorful to be in keeping with feminine delicacy.

For her part, she was extremely unjust to the handsome horsemen who fill the Bois de Boulogne. She envisaged the future, not with terror—that would have been a vivid emotion—but with a disgust that is quite rare at her age.

What could she desire? Fortune, high birth, intelligence and beauty, according to what people said, and she herself believed—all those things had been heaped upon her by the hand of fate.

Such were the thoughts of the most envied heiress in the Faubourg Saint-Germain when she began to find pleasure in taking long walks with Julien. She was amazed by his pride; she admired the adroitness of that humble commoner. ''He'll find a way to make himself a bishop, like Father Maury,'' she said to herself.

She soon became preoccupied with the sincere, unfeigned resistance which our hero opposed to a number of her ideas. She thought about it, gave her cousin detailed reports of their conversations and found that she never succeeded in depicting their full character.

A sudden thought enlightened her: ''I've had the good fortune to fall in love!'' she told herself one day with an incredible surge of joy. ''I'm in love, I'm in love, it's obvious! At my age, what else but love could arouse strong emotions in a young, beautiful and intelligent girl? No matter what I do, I'll never feel any love for Croisenois, Caylus or anyone like them. They're perfect, too perfect, perhaps; in any case, they bore me.''

She ran over in her mind all the descriptions of passion she had read in *Manon Lescaut, La Nouvelle Héloïse, Letters of a Portuguese Nun,* etc. Anything except a great passion was, of course, out of the question: a trivial love affair would have been unworthy of a girl of her age and birth. She gave the name of love only to that heroic sentiment which occurred in France in the days of Henri III and Bassompierre. That kind of love never yielded basely to obstacles. Its purpose was not to inject amusement into life; rather, it changed life. ''What a misfortune for me,'' she thought, ''that there's no real court now, like that of Catherine de Medici or Louis XIII! I feel myself equal to the boldest and greatest actions. What wouldn't I do with a great-hearted king, like Louis XIII, sighing at my feet! I'd lead him to Vendée, as the Baron de Tolly says so often, and from there he'd reconquer his kingdom; then there'd be no more Charter. . . . And Julien would help me. What does he lack? A name and a fortune. He'd make a name for himself and acquire a fortune.

''Croisenois lacks nothing, and yet all his life he'll never be anything but a duke who's half Ultra-Royalist and half Liberal, an irresolute man, talking when he should be acting, always avoiding extremes, *and therefore always in the second rank*.

''Where is the great action that isn't an *extreme* when it's first undertaken? It's only after it's been accomplished that it seems possible to ordinary people. Yes, it's love with all its miracles that's going to reign in my heart; I feel it from the fire that's inside me. Heaven owed me this favor—now it won't have heaped all its advantages on one person in vain. My happiness will be worthy of me. None of my days will coldly resemble the day before. I've already shown boldness and greatness of heart by daring to fall in love with a man so far below me in social position. I wonder if he'll continue to be worthy of me. At the first sign of weakness I see in him, I'll abandon him. A girl of my birth, and with the knightly character that's so kindly imputed to me [this was one of her father's expressions], shouldn't act like a fool.

''Isn't that what I'd be doing if I were in love with the Marquis de Croisenois? I'd have a new edition of the happiness of my cousins, whom I despise so thoroughly. I know in advance everything the poor marquis would say to me, and everything I'd have to reply to him. What good is a love that makes you yawn? You might as well become pious. I'd have a contract-signing ceremony, like that of my youngest cousin, during which the elderly relatives would be overcome with tender emotion, unless they were angry because of some final clause inserted in the contract the day before by the other party's lawyer.''

CHAPTER 12

Is He Another Danton?

> *A need of excitement,* such was the character of my aunt, the beautiful Marguerite de Valois, who shortly afterward married the King of Navarre, whom we now see reigning in France under the name of Henri IV. A need to gamble was the whole secret of that charming princess's character; it was the source of her quarrels and reconciliations with her brothers, from the age of sixteen onward. Now with what can a young lady gamble? With her most precious possession: her reputation, the honor of her entire life.
>
> —Memoirs of the Duc d'Angoulême, natural son of Charles IX

''BETWEEN JULIEN and me there's no contract to be signed, no lawyer to arrange the middle-class ceremony; everything is heroic, everything will arise from chance. Except for his lack of noble rank, it's like the love of Marguerite de Valois for young La Mole, the most distinguished man of his day. Is it my fault that the young men of the court are such strong supporters of convention and turn pale at the mere idea of any adventure that goes beyond the commonplace? A little journey to Greece or Africa is the height of daring for them, and even then they can move only in a troop. As soon as they find themselves alone, they're afraid, not of Bedouin lances, but of ridicule, and that fear drives them mad.

''My little Julien, on the other hand, likes to act only alone. He's a superior man who never thinks of seeking the support and help of others! He despises others, and that's why I don't despise him.

''If, with his poverty, he were of noble birth, my love would be vulgar and silly, a commonplace misalliance. I wouldn't want such a love; it wouldn't have anything of what characterizes a great passion: the enormous difficulties to be overcome and the dark uncertainty of the outcome.''

Mademoiselle de La Mole was so absorbed in these lofty thoughts that the next day, without realizing what she was doing, she praised Julien while speaking with the Marquis de Croisenois and her brother. Her eloquence rose to such heights that it irritated them.

"Be on your guard with that determined young man!" cried her brother. "If there's another revolution, he'll have us all guillotined!"

She refrained from answering, and hastened to joke with the two of them about their fear of determination, which was actually a fear of the unexpected, of finding themselves at a loss in the face of it. "Always, gentlemen," she said, "there's always that fear of ridicule, a monster which, unfortunately, died in 1816."

"There's no more ridicule," Monsieur de La Mole would occasionally remark, "in a country where there are two parties." His daughter had understood his meaning.

"So, gentlemen," she said to Julien's enemies, "you'll have been afraid all your lives, and then you'll be told, 'It wasn't a wolf, it was only its shadow.' "

She left them a short time later. She had found her brother's remark horrible; it worried her a great deal, but by the next day she had come to regard it as the highest possible praise.

"In this age, when all determination is dead," she thought, "his determination frightens them. I'll tell him what my brother said: I want to see what reply he'll make. But I'll choose one of those moments when his eyes are shining. Then he can't lie to me.

"He'll be another Danton!" she added, after a long and vague reverie. "Suppose there were another revolution; what part would Croisenois and my brother play? It's written in advance: sublime resignation. They'd be heroic sheep, letting themselves be slaughtered without a word. Their only fear when dying would still be the fear of showing bad form. My little Julien would shoot the Jacobin who came to arrest him if he had the slightest hope of escaping. *He's* not afraid of showing bad form."

This last thought made her pensive; it awakened painful memories and took away all her boldness. It reminded her of the sarcastic remarks of Messieurs de Caylus, de Croisenois, de Luz and her brother. These gentlemen were unanimous in accusing Julien of having a "priestly" air, i.e., humble and hypocritical.

"But," she thought suddenly, her eyes shining with joy, "by the bitterness and frequency of their sarcastic remarks they prove, in spite of themselves, that he's the most distinguished man we've seen this winter. What do his faults matter, or his ridiculous qualities? He has greatness, and they're offended by it, they who are otherwise so good-natured and indulgent. Of course he's poor, and he studied for the priesthood; they're officers and they have no need to study: it's easier that way.

"In spite of all the disadvantages of his eternal black coat and his priestly expression, which he must maintain, poor boy, if he doesn't want to starve, it's obvious that his merit frightens them. And he discards that priestly expression as soon as we've been alone together for a few moments. Whenever they say something they regard as clever and original, isn't their first glance always at Julien? I've seen that very clearly. And yet they know very well that he never speaks to them unless they ask him a question. I'm the only one he speaks to voluntarily; he considers me high-minded. He answers their objections only just enough to be polite, then he immediately resumes his respectful silence. With me, he discusses things for hours on end, and he isn't sure of his ideas as long as I make the slightest objection. Well, there hasn't been any shooting this winter; only words have attracted attention. And my father, a superior man who will greatly advance the fortune of our family, respects Julien. Everyone else hates him, but no one despises him, except my mother's pious friends."

The Comte de Caylus had, or pretended to have, a great passion for horses; he spent most of his time in his stable and frequently had lunch there. This great passion, combined with his habit of never laughing, gave him a position of great respect among his friends. He was the leader of their little circle.

The next day, as soon as they had gathered behind Madame de La Mole's easy chair, Julien being absent, Monsieur de Caylus, supported by Croisenois and Norbert, sharply attacked Mathilde's high opinion of Julien, without any plausible pretext and almost as soon as he saw her. She instantly understood this maneuver, and she was delighted by it.

"They've all banded together against a man of genius," she thought, "who doesn't have an income of ten louis and who can answer them only when they question him. They're afraid of him in his black coat—what would they feel if he were wearing epaulettes?"

She had never been more brilliant. From the very first onslaught she overwhelmed Caylus and his allies with caustic wit. When she had silenced the distinguished officers' sarcastic verbal fire she said to Monsieur de Caylus, "If tomorrow some country squire from the mountains of Franche-Comté were to discover that Julien was his illegitimate son and give him a name and a few thousand francs, in six weeks he'd have a mustache like yours, gentlemen, and in six months he'd be a cavalry officer like you, gentlemen. And then the greatness of his character wouldn't be ridiculed. I can see you, my duke-to-be, forced to fall back on that ancient specious argument: the superiority of the court nobility to the provincial nobility. But what would be left for you if I chose to drive you into a corner, if I were malicious enough to make Julien's father a Spanish duke who'd been a prisoner of war in Besançon in the time of Napoleon and who, to soothe his conscience, acknowledged Julien on his death-bed?''

These suppositions of illegitimate birth were regarded by Messieurs de Caylus and de Croisenois as being in rather bad taste. That was all they saw in Mathilde's reasoning.

Despite Norbert's submission to his sister, the meaning of her words was so clear that he took on a solemn expression which, it must be admitted, was rather ill-suited to his smiling, good-natured face. He ventured to say a few words.

"Are you ill, my friend?" replied Mathilde with mock seriousness. "You must be very ill to answer joking with moralizing. Moralizing from you! Are you trying to become a prefect?"

Mathilde quickly forgot the Comte de Caylus' look of rancor, Norbert's irritation and Monsieur de Croisenois' silent despair. She had to come to a decision with regard to a frightful idea which had just taken possession of her.

"Julien is quite sincere with me," she thought. "A young man his age, in an inferior position, and made unhappy by an extraordinary ambition, needs a woman to love him. I may be that woman, but I see no sign of love in him. With his fearless character, he would have spoken to me of his love."

This uncertainty, this inner debate, which occupied her constantly from then on and for which she found new arguments each time Julien spoke to her, completely banished those moments of boredom to which she was so strongly inclined.

As the daughter of an intelligent man who might become a minister and give the clergy back their woodlands, Mademoiselle de La Mole had been the object of the most extravagant flattery in the Convent of the Sacred Heart. There is nothing which can counterbalance such a misfortune. She had been convinced that, because of her advantages of birth, fortune, etc., she ought to be happier than other girls. This is the source of the boredom of princes, and of all their follies.

Mathilde had not escaped from the baneful influence of this idea. No matter how intelligent a girl may be, at the age of ten she is not on her guard against the flattery of an entire convent, especially when it appears to be so well grounded.

From the moment she concluded that she was in love with Julien, she ceased to be bored. Every day she congratulated herself on her decision to indulge in a great passion. "That kind of amusement has many dangers," she thought. "So much the better! A thousand times better! Without a great passion I was languishing in boredom during the best period of a woman's life from sixteen to twenty. I've already wasted my best years, forced, as my only pleasure, to listen to the senseless chatter of my mother's friends, who, I'm told, weren't quite so severe in Coblentz in 1792 as their conversation is today."

While Mathilde was troubled by these grave doubts, Julien could not understand the long looks she gave him. He did, however, notice an increase in the coldness of Count Norbert's manner, and a greater degree of haughtiness in that of Messieurs de Caylus, de Luz and de Croisenois. He was accustomed to this. It was a misfortune that sometimes befell him as the result of an evening during which he had shone more brightly than befitted his position. If it had not been for the special favor shown him by Mathilde, and the curiosity which the entire circle aroused in him, he would have avoided following those distinguished young men with mustaches into the garden when they accompanied Mademoiselle de La Mole there after dinner.

"Yes, Mademoiselle de La Mole looks at me in a very special way, I can't deny it," thought Julien. "But even when she looks at me with her beautiful blue eyes in the most unrestrained way, I can still see something critical, self-possessed and malicious in them. Can it possibly be love? How differently Madame de Rênal looked at me!"

Once when Julien had followed Monsieur de La Mole into his study after dinner, he quickly returned to the garden. As he boldly approached Mathilde's group he overheard a few words spoken in a loud voice. She was tormenting her brother. Julien distinctly heard his own name mentioned twice. He greeted them; there was suddenly a deep silence, and unsuccessful attempts were made to break it. Mademoiselle de La Mole and her brother were too agitated to find another topic of conversation. Messieurs de Caylus, de Croisenois, de Luz and one of their friends treated Julien with icy coldness. He walked away.

CHAPTER 13

A Conspiracy

Disconnected remarks and chance meetings are transformed into undeniable proofs in the eyes of a man of imagination if there is some flame burning in his heart.

—Schiller

THE NEXT DAY he again surprised Norbert and his sister as they were talking about him. A deathly silence fell when he arrived, as had happened the day before. His suspicions knew no bounds. "Have these charming young people decided to make a fool of me?" he wondered. "That's much more likely, I must admit, much more natural than Mademoiselle de La Mole's supposed passion for a poor devil of a secretary. First of all, do people like that really have passions? Ridiculing others is their strong point. They're jealous of my poor little superiority in conversation. Jealousy is another one of their weaknesses. These facts may explain everything. Mademoiselle de La Mole wants to convince me that she's attracted to me, simply to make a fool of me in the eyes of her future husband."

This cruel suspicion completely changed Julien's attitude. It found in his heart a nascent love which it had no difficulty in destroying. This love was founded only on Mathilde's rare beauty, or rather on her queenly manner and admirable way of dressing. In this respect, Julien was still a _parvenu_. A pretty woman of the world is said to be what most amazes an intelligent peasant when he makes his way into the highest ranks of society. It was not Mathilde's character that had caused Julien to dream during the preceding days; he was sensible enough to realize that he knew nothing about it. What he saw of it might be nothing but pretense.

For example, Mathilde would not have missed Sunday mass for anything in the world, and she went to church with her mother nearly every day. If, in the drawing room of the Hôtel de La Mole, some incautious individual forgot where he was and allowed himself to make the remotest allusion to some jest against the real or supposed interests of the Church or the Crown, Mathilde instantly became frigidly serious. Her face, which was usually so full of provocative animation, would take on all the impassive haughtiness of an old family portrait.

But Julien had ascertained that she always had one or two of Voltaire's most philosophical works in her bedroom. He himself often secretly borrowed a few volumes of the handsome, magnificently bound edition; by moving all the volumes a short distance apart from each other, he concealed the absence of the one he had taken out. But he soon discovered that someone else was also reading Voltaire. He resorted to a seminary stratagem: he placed a few strands of horsehair over the volumes he considered likely to interest Mademoiselle de La Mole. They disappeared for weeks at a time.

Monsieur de La Mole, annoyed with his bookseller, who kept sending him all the "false memoirs," instructed Julien to buy all new books that were somewhat sensational. But, to prevent the poison from spreading through the household, Julien was ordered to place these books in a small bookcase in the marquis' own bedroom. He soon noticed that if one of these new books was in any way hostile to the interests of the Church or the Crown, it promptly disappeared. It was certainly not Norbert who was reading them.

Julien, exaggerating the importance of this discovery, believed Mademoiselle de La Mole to have the duplicity of a Machiavelli. He regarded this supposed villainy as an attraction, almost the only mental attraction she possessed. He was driven to this extreme by his boredom with hypocrisy and virtuous conversation. He excited his own imagination, rather than letting himself be carried away by his love.

It was after losing himself in dreams of the elegance of Mademoiselle de La Mole's figure, her excellent taste in dress, the whiteness of her hands, the beauty of her arms, and the nonchalance of all her movements, that he found himself in love with her. Then, to complete the spell, he imagined her to be a Catherine de Medici. Nothing was too profound or too criminal for the character he ascribed to her. It was the ideal of the Maslons, the Frilairs and the Castanèdes whom he had admired in his younger days; it was for him, in a word, the ideal of Paris.

Could there be anything more comical than to impute profundity or criminality to the Parisian character?

"It's possible that this trio may be trying to make a fool of me," thought Julien. The reader knows little of his character if he has not already seen the cold, somber expression his face assumed in response to Mathilde's glances. She was astonished by the bitter irony with which her assurances of friendship were repulsed on the two or three occasions when she ventured to express them.

Stung by this odd behavior, her heart, normally cold, bored and responsive only to things of the mind, became as passionate as its nature allowed it to be. But there was also a great deal of pride in her nature, and the first stirrings of a feeling which made all her happiness depend on another person were accompanied by somber melancholy.

Julien had already learned enough since his arrival in Paris to discern that this was not the barren melancholy of boredom. Instead of being eager, as she had once been, for soirées, plays and amusements of all kinds, she now avoided them.

Music sung by Frenchmen bored her to tears, and yet Julien, who made it his duty to be in the opera house at the end of each performance, noticed that she let herself be taken there as often as she could. It seemed to him that she had lost a little of the perfect poise which shone in all her actions. She sometimes replied to her friends with witticisms that were so forceful as to be insulting. She seemed to have taken a dislike to the Marquis de Croisenois. "That young man must be madly in love with money," thought Julien, "not to have left her flat, no matter how rich she is!" As for himself, indignant at such outrages to masculine dignity, he treated her more coldly than ever. He often went so far as to answer her rather discourteously.

Despite his determination not to be taken in by her marks of interest, they were so obvious on some days, and Julien, whose eyes were beginning to be opened, found her so pretty, that he was sometimes embarrassed by them.

"The cleverness and self-control of these young nobles will eventually triumph over my lack of experience," he thought. "I must go away and put an end to all this." The marquis had just entrusted him with the management of a number of small estates and houses which he owned in lower Languedoc. A journey was necessary; Monsieur de La Mole reluctantly consented to it. Except in matters of high ambition, Julien had become his right-hand man.

"Actually, they haven't taken me in," thought Julien as he prepared for his departure. "Whether the sarcastic remarks she

makes to those gentlemen are real or only intended to give me
confidence, they've amused me. If there's no conspiracy against
the sawyer's son, her conduct is inexplicable, but it's at least as
inexplicable for the Marquis de Croisenois as it is for me.
Yesterday, for example, her irritation was quite genuine, and I
had the pleasure of seeing my favored position put to rout a
young man who's as noble and rich as I am plebeian and
penniless. That's my finest victory; it will cheer me up as I roll
across the plains of Languedoc in my post chaise.''

He had told no one of his departure, but Mathilde knew better
than he that he was going to leave Paris the next day, and for a
long time. She complained of a splitting headache which was
made worse by the stuffy air of the drawing room. She walked in
the garden for a long time and used her caustic wit so vigorously
against Norbert, the Marquis de Croisenois, Caylus, Luz, and
several other young men who had come to dinner at the Hôtel de
La Mole, that she forced them to leave her. She looked at Julien
in a strange way.

''That look may be nothing but a piece of play-acting,'' he
thought. ''But what about her hurried breathing, and all her
agitation? Well, who am I to judge these things? It's a question
of the subtlest and most sublime art of Parisian women. She
must have learned that hurried breathing, which nearly moved
me, from Léontine Fay, whom she's so fond of.''

They had been left alone together; their conversation was
obviously languishing. ''No! He feels nothing for me,'' Mathilde
said to herself with genuine unhappiness.

As he was taking leave of her, she squeezed his arm tightly.
''You'll receive a letter from me tonight,'' she said to him in a
voice that was so choked as to be unrecognizable; Julien was
immediately touched by it. ''My father,'' she went on, ''has a
just appreciation of the services you render him. You must not
leave tomorrow; find some excuse.'' And she ran away.

Her figure was enchanting. It would have been impossible to
have prettier feet; she ran with a grace which delighted Julien.
But could anyone have guessed what his second thought was,
after she was completely out of sight? He was offended by the
imperious tone in which she had uttered the words ''you must.''
Louis XV, when he was about to die, was also deeply angered
by the words ''you must,'' clumsily used by his chief physician,
and Louis XV was no *parvenu*.

An hour later a servant handed Julien a letter; it was quite
simply a declaration of love.

"The style isn't too affected," he thought, seeking by his literary comments to restrain the joy that contracted his cheeks and forced him to laugh in spite of himself. "So," he suddenly exclaimed, his emotion being too strong to be restrained, "I, a poor peasant, have received a declaration of love from a great lady! As for me," he added, suppressing his joy as much as possible, "I haven't done at all badly. I've managed to preserve the dignity of my character. I've never said I was in love with her."

He began to study her handwriting; it was small, graceful and slanted. He needed some physical occupation to distract himself from a joy that bordered on delirium.

"Your departure forces me to speak. . . . It would be beyond my strength to stop seeing you."

A sudden thought struck him as a great discovery, interrupting his examination of Mathilde's letter and doubling his joy. "I've won out over the Marquis de Croisenois!" he exclaimed. "I, who say only serious things! And he's so handsome! He has a mustache and an attractive uniform, and he always finds some clever, witty remark to make, just at the right time."

It was a wonderful moment for Julien; he wandered aimlessly around the garden, wild with joy.

Some time later he went upstairs to his office and had himself announced to the Marquis de La Mole, who had fortunately not gone out. He easily proved to him, by showing him a few stamped documents which had arrived from Normandy, that his pursuit of the Norman lawsuits forced him to postpone his departure for Languedoc.

"I'm glad you're not leaving," said the marquis when they had finished talking business. "I like to see you." Julien walked out; this last remark embarrassed him.

"And I'm going to seduce his daughter!" he thought. "I may make it impossible for her to marry the Marquis de Croisenois, on whom his hopes for the future depend; if he isn't made a duke, at least his daughter will have a duchess's stool at court." He considered leaving for Languedoc in spite of Mathilde's letter, in spite of the explanation he had given to the marquis. This flash of virtue quickly faded away.

"What a good-natured fool I am to take pity on a family of that rank when I'm a humble plebeian!" he thought. "I, whom the Duc de Chaulnes refers to as a servant! How does the marquis increase his enormous fortune? By selling some of his securities when he learns at court that a *coup d'état* is going to appear likely the next day. And I, cast down to the lowest rank by a stepmotherly Providence who's endowed me with a noble heart and refused to give me a private income of even a thousand francs a year, which means that I have nothing to live on, *literally nothing to live on*—why should I refuse a pleasure that's offered to me, a clear spring welling up to quench my thirst in the burning desert of mediocrity that I'm crossing with such pain? Oh no, I'm not that stupid! It's every man for himself in this desert of selfishness known as life." And he recalled some of the disdainful glances cast at him by Mademoiselle de La Mole, and especially by the *ladies* among her friends.

The defeat of his recall to virtue was completed by the thought of the pleasure of triumphing over the Marquis de Croisenois. "How I'd like him to challenge me to a duel!" he said to himself. "How confidently I'd thrust my sword into him now!" And he pantomimed a thrust in *seconde*. "Before this, I was nothing but a lowly pedant, basely taking advantage of a little courage. Now that I've received this letter, I'm his equal. Yes," he went on with infinite delight, speaking slowly, "our merits have been weighed in the balance, and the poor sawyer from the Juras has won out over the marquis.

"Good!" he cried out. "Now I know how to sign my answer. Don't imagine, Mademoiselle de La Mole, that I've forgotten my rank. I'll make you realize clearly and vividly that it's for a sawyer's son that you're betraying a descendant of the famous Guy de Croisenois, who went off to the Crusades with Saint Louis."

Julien could not contain his joy. He was obliged to go down into the garden. His room, in which he had locked himself, seemed so narrow to him that he felt unable to breathe.

"I, a poor peasant from the Juras!" he repeated again and again. "I, condemned to wear this gloomy black coat forever! Alas, twenty years ago I'd have worn a uniform as they do! In those days, a man like me was either killed or became a general by the age of thirty-six." His letter, which he held tightly clutched in his hand, gave him the stature and bearing of a hero. "Nowadays, it's true, in this black coat it's possible to have an income of a hundred thousand francs a year and a cordon bleu by the age of forty, like the Bishop of Beauvais.

"Well," he went on, laughing like Mephistopheles, "I'm more intelligent than they are; I know how to choose the uniform of my time." His ambition rose higher than ever, and he felt an increased attachment to his ecclesiastical attire. "How many cardinals have won positions of authority, even though they were of humbler birth than myself! My fellow countryman Granville, for example.''

Julien's exaltation gradually subsided and prudence rose to the surface. He said to himself, like his master Tartuffe, whose role he knew by heart:

> "I might believe those words an honest trick . . .
> I will not trust such sweet and gentle speech
> Unless her favors, after which I sigh,
> Assure me that she has not told a lie.''*

"Tartuffe was also ruined by a woman," he thought, "and he was as good a man as any. . . . My answer may be shown to others. . . . But there's a remedy for that," he added, speaking slowly and in a tone of controlled ferocity. "I'll begin it with the most emotional phrases in the sublime Mathilde's letter.

"Yes, but four of Monsieur de Croisenois' lackeys will rush at me and snatch the original away from me.

"No, because I'll be well armed, and it's known that I'm accustomed to firing at lackeys.

"Well, one of them may be courageous; he'll attack me. He'll have been promised a hundred napoleons. I'll either kill him or wound him; good, that will be exactly what they want. I'll be thrown into jail quite legally; I'll appear in police court and, with complete justice and equity on the part of the judges, I'll be sent to Poissy to keep company with Messieurs Fontan and Magalon. There I'll sleep all jumbled up with four hundred dirty scoundrels. . . . And yet I'm supposed to feel pity for these people!'' he cried, impetuously leaping to his feet. "Do they have any pity for the people of the Third Estate when they have them in their clutches?'' These words were the dying sigh of his gratitude to Monsieur de La Mole, which, until then, had been tormenting him against his will.

"Not so fast, noble gentlemen, I understand that Machiavellian maneuver; Father Maslon or Father Castanède in the seminary couldn't have done any better. You'll take away the letter that 'incited' me and I'll be a second edition of Colonel Caron at Colmar.

"Just a moment, gentlemen; I'm going to send the fatal letter to Father Pirard in a well-sealed packet. He's an honest man, a

---

*Tartuffe, Act IV, Scene 5.

Jansenist, and therefore immune to all financial temptation. Yes, but he opens letters . . . I'll send this one to Fouqué."

It must be admitted that the look in Julien's eyes was frightful, and that the expression of his face was hideous: it was filled with unalloyed criminality. He was the very type of the unhappy man at war with the whole of society.

"To arms!" he cried. And he descended the front steps of the house in one bound. He went into the stall of the public scribe down the street; he frightened the man. "Copy this," he said, handing him Mademoiselle de La Mole's letter.

While the scribe was working, Julien wrote a letter to Fouqué asking him to keep a precious trust for him. "But," he thought, ceasing to write, "the censors in the post office will open my letter and give you the one you're seeking, gentlemen. . . . No, that won't do." He went out and bought an enormous Bible from a Protestant bookseller, skillfully concealed Mathilde's letter in its binding, had it packed and sent it off on the mail coach, addressed to one of Fouqué's workmen whose name was not known to anyone in Paris.

This done, he briskly and joyfully walked back to the Hôtel de La Mole. "Now I begin my attack!" he cried, locking himself in his room and throwing off his coat.

"What, mademoiselle!" he wrote to Mathilde. *"Can it be true that Mademoiselle de La Mole has sent, through her father's servant Arsène, a seductive letter to a poor sawyer from the Juras, no doubt in order to ridicule his simplicity. . . ."* And he transcribed the clearest sentences of the letter he had just received.

His own letter would have done credit to the diplomatic circumspection of the Chevalier de Beauvoisis. It was only ten o'clock; Julien, intoxicated with happiness and a sense of his own power, so new to a poor devil like himself, went off to the Italian Opera. He heard his friend Geronimo sing. Never before had music filled him with such exaltation. He was a god.

CHAPTER 14
A Girl's Thoughts

> What perplexity! What sleepless nights! Good heavens! Am
> I going to make myself contemptible? He himself will despise
> me. But he's leaving, he's going away.
> —Alfred de Musset

MATHILDE HAD NOT written her letter without inner struggle. Whatever the beginning of her interest in Julien may have been, it soon came to dominate the pride which had been the sole ruler of her heart ever since she had begun to know herself. It was the first time her cold, haughty soul had ever been carried away by a passionate feeling. But if her passion dominated her pride, it still remained faithful to the habits of that pride. Two months of inner struggle and new sensations had renovated, so to speak, her entire moral being.

Mathilde thought she saw happiness before her. This vision, which wields supreme power over a courageous heart when it is allied with superior intelligence, had to struggle for a long time against dignity and all ordinary notions of duty. She went into her mother's room at seven o'clock one morning and begged her to let her go off to Villequier. The marquise did not even deign to answer her and advised her to go back to bed. This was the last effort made by everyday wisdom and deference to accepted ideas.

The fear of behaving badly, and of running counter to the ideas held as sacred by such people as Caylus, Luz and Croisenois, had little power over her; she did not regard such creatures as capable of understanding her, and she would have consulted them only if it had been a question of buying a carriage or an estate. Her real terror was that Julien might be dissatisfied with her. "Perhaps he, too, has only the appearance of a superior man," she thought.

She abhorred a lack of character; it was her sole objection to the handsome young men who surrounded her. The more they deftly ridiculed everything that departed from fashion, or unsuccessfully tried to imitate it, the more they lost favor in her eyes.

They were brave, and that was all. "And even so," she thought, "what kind of bravery do they have? Bravery in a duel; but a duel is only a ceremony. Everything is known beforehand, even what a man ought to say as he falls. Lying on the ground with his hand over his heart, he must generously forgive his adversary and say a few words to be conveyed to some fair lady, who is often imaginary, or who will go to a ball on the day of his death, to avoid arousing suspicion.

"They'll face danger at the head of a cavalry squadron gleaming with steel, but what about a danger that's solitary, strange, unforeseen and truly hideous?

"Alas, it was at the court of Henri III that one found men who were great in character as well as by birth! Oh, if Julien had fought at Jarnac or Moncontour, I'd no longer have any doubts! In those days of vigor and strength, Frenchmen weren't mere puppets. The day of battle was almost the day of least perplexity.

Their lives weren't shut in like Egyptian mummies, under wrappings that are always common to everyone, always the same.

"Yes, there was more real courage in going home alone at eleven o'clock at night, after leaving the Hôtel de Soissons, occupied by Catherine de Medici, than in running off to Algiers today. A man's life was a series of hazards. Nowadays, civilization and the prefect of police have eliminated hazard. The unexpected has vanished; if it crops up in someone's ideas, it's overwhelmed with epigrams; if it crops up in events, our fear is so great that no cowardice is beneath us. No matter what madness our fear drives us to, it's always excused. What a degenerate and boring age! What would Boniface de La Mole have said if, raising his severed head from the tomb in 1793, he'd seen seventeen of his descendants let themselves be taken like sheep, to be guillotined two days later? Death was certain, but it would have been bad form to put up any resistance and at least kill a Jacobin or two. Ah, in the heroic age of France, Julien would have been the cavalry officer and my brother the young priest, a model of decorum, with virtue in his eyes and reason on his lips."

A few months earlier, Mathilde had despaired of ever meeting anyone who differed a little from the common pattern. She had found a certain happiness in taking the liberty of writing to a few young men of high society. This unseemly boldness, so imprudent for a young lady, might have dishonored her in the eyes of Monsieur de Croisenois, his father, the Duc de Chaulnes, and his entire household, who, seeing the projected marriage broken off, would have wanted to know why. In those days, she was unable to sleep at night after she had written one of her letters. But they were only replies.

And now she dared to say that she was in love. She had written to a young man in the lowest rank of society, and she had been *the first to write* (a terrible phrase!). This fact, if it were discovered, would ensure her eternal dishonor. Which of the women who came to visit her mother would dare to defend her? What remark could be found for them to repeat in order to soften the blow of the horrible contempt of the drawing rooms?

Speaking was bad enough, but *writing*! . . . "There are some things one doesn't write!" exclaimed Napoleon when he learned of the surrender of Baylen. And it was Julien who had quoted that remark to her, as though giving her a lesson in advance!

But all this was still nothing: Mathilde's anguish had other causes. Ignoring the terrible effect on society and the ineradicable stain that would make her an object of scorn, for it was an outrage to her caste, she was about to write to a man who was very different from Croisenois, Luz and Caylus. The depth and mystery of Julien's character would have been frightening even in a commonplace relationship, but she was about to make him her lover, perhaps her master!

"What claims he'll make on me if he ever has me completely in his power!" she thought. "In that case, I'll say to myself, like Medea, *'Amid all these perils, I still have myself.'* "

Julien, she believed, had no veneration for noble birth. Worse still, perhaps he had no love for her!

In these last moments of terrible doubt, her ideas of feminine pride came to the fore. "Everything must be out of the ordinary in the life of a girl like me!" she cried impatiently. Then the pride that had been instilled in her from the cradle onward began to struggle against her virtue. It was at this point that the news of Julien's forthcoming departure precipitated everything. (Such characters are fortunately quite rare.)

Late that night, Julien was malicious enough to order a footman who was courting Mathilde's maid to carry a heavy trunk down to the porter's lodge for him. "This maneuver may have no result," he thought, "but if it succeeds she'll think I've left." He went to sleep delighted with his trick. Mathilde was awake all night.

Early the next morning, he left the house unnoticed, but he returned before eight o'clock. He had scarcely entered the library when Mademoiselle de La Mole appeared in the doorway. He handed her his reply. He felt that it was his duty to speak to her; he certainly could not have found a better opportunity, but she refused to listen to him and went away. He was delighted, for he had not known what to say to her.

"If all this isn't a game arranged in advance with Count Norbert," he thought, "it was obviously my cold glances that kindled the odd kind of love that highborn girl has decided to feel for me. I'd be a little more foolish than I ought to be if I ever let myself be drawn into any kind of liking for that big blonde doll." This reasoning left him colder and more calculating than he had ever been before.

"In the battle that's about to begin," he added, "her pride in her birth will be like a high hill forming a military position between us. It's there that we'll have to maneuver. I made a serious mistake by staying in Paris; postponing my trip will degrade me and expose me to danger if all this is nothing but a game. What risk would there have been in leaving? I'd have been mocking them, if they were mocking me. And if her interest in me is at all real, I'd have made it a hundred times stronger.''

Mademoiselle de La Mole's letter had given his vanity such keen pleasure that, while laughing at what had happened to him, he had forgotten to give serious thought to the advisability of his departure. It was a fatal trait of his character to be extremely sensitive to his mistakes. He was highly annoyed by this one, and he had almost ceased thinking about the incredible victory that had preceded his minor setback when, toward nine o'clock, Mademoiselle de La Mole reappeared in the doorway of the library, flung a letter at him and fled.

''This is apparently going to be a novel in letter form,'' he said as he picked this one up. ''The enemy has made a false move; now I'm going to bring coldness and virtue into action.''

The letter requested a definite answer with a haughtiness that increased his inner gaiety. He indulged in the pleasure of writing a two-page letter in which he mocked those who were attempting to ridicule him and, as a final jest, toward the end of it he announced that he was going to leave Paris the following morning.

''The garden will be a convenient place to give it to her,'' he thought when he had finished his letter, and he went there. He looked up at the window of her room. It was on the second floor, beside her mother's apartment, but there was a large mezzanine beneath it; the second floor was therefore so high that he could not be seen from her room as he strolled, holding his letter in his hand, along the lane bordered with linden trees. The arch formed by the neatly trimmed trees hid him from sight. ''What's the matter with me?'' he said to himself angrily. ''I've been careless again! If they're trying to make a fool of me, letting myself be seen with a letter in my hand will be serving my enemies' cause.''

Norbert's room was directly above his sister's, and if Julien were to come out from under the arch formed by the trimmed branches of the linden trees, the count and his friends would be able to follow all his movements.

Mademoiselle de La Mole appeared at her window. He furtively showed her his letter; she bowed her head. He immediately began to run up to his room; on the great staircase he happened to meet the fair Mathilde, who seized the letter with easy grace and laughing eyes.

''What passion there was in poor Madame de Rênal's eyes,'' he thought, ''when, even after six months of intimate relations, she dared to receive a letter from me! I don't think she ever once looked at me with laughter in her eyes.''

He did not express the rest of his reaction so clearly to himself; was he ashamed of the frivolity of his motives? ''But also what a difference,'' his mind added, ''in the elegance of her morning gown and everything else about her appearance! Any man of good taste who sees Mademoiselle de La Mole from thirty yards away can guess the rank she holds in society. That's what can be called obvious merit.''

As he was jesting with himself, he still did not admit to himself everything that was in his mind; Madame de Rênal had had no Marquis de Croisenois to sacrifice to him. His only rival had been that ignoble sub-prefect, Monsieur Charcot, who called himself ''Charcot de Maugiron'' because there were no more Maugirons.

At five o'clock Julien received a third letter, also flung to him from the doorway of the library. Mademoiselle de La Mole fled once again. ''What a mania for writing,'' he said to himself, laughing, ''when it's so easy for us to speak to each other! The enemy wants to have letters from me, that's clear—and quite a few of them, too!'' He did not hasten to open this letter. ''More elegant phrases,'' he thought; but he turned pale when he read it. There were only eight lines:

> I need to speak to you, I must speak to you, tonight. Be in the garden at exactly one o'clock. Take the gardener's long ladder, which is near the wall, place it against my window and climb up to my bedroom. The moon will be shining, but that does not matter.

CHAPTER 15

Is It a Conspiracy?

> Oh, how cruel is the interval between the conception of a great enterprise and its execution! What vain terrors! What irresolution! Life is at stake—much more is at stake: honor!
> —Schiller

''THIS IS becoming serious,'' thought Julien. ''And a little too clear,'' he added after a moment of reflection. ''What! That beautiful young lady can speak to me in the library with a freedom which, thank God, is unconditional; the marquis never comes in while I'm here, for fear I might show him my accounts;

he and Count Norbert, the only people who ever come here, are absent all day long and it's easy for me to watch for their return—and yet the sublime Mathilde, for whom a ruling monarch wouldn't be too noble, wants me to commit an act of appalling recklessness!

"It's clear that they want to ruin me, or make a fool of me at the very least. At first they tried to ruin me through letters, but it turned out that I wrote nothing rash, so now they must have some action that's as clear as daylight. Those pretty little gentlemen think I'm either too stupid or too conceited. What an idea! They expect me to go out in the brightest moonlight in the world and climb up a ladder to a second floor that's twenty-five feet above the ground! There would be plenty of time to see me, even from the neighboring houses! I'd cut a fine figure on my ladder!" He went up to his room and began to pack his trunk, whistling as he did so. He had made up his mind to leave without even answering.

But this wise decision did not give him much peace of mind. "What if Mathilde happens to be sincere?" he said to himself suddenly, after he had locked his trunk. "In that case, she'll regard me as a craven coward. I'm a man of humble birth, so I need to show noble qualities, ready on demand, without need of obliging suppositions, and clearly proven by actions that speak for themselves. . . ."

He paced up and down his room for a quarter of an hour. "What's the use of denying it?" he said finally. "I'll be a coward in her eyes. I'll lose not only the most dazzling girl in high society, as everyone said at the Duc de Retz's ball, but also the divine pleasure of seeing the Marquis de Croisenois, the son of a duke and a future duke himself, sacrificed to me. He's a charming young man who has everything I lack: the knack of always saying the right thing, noble birth, fortune. . . .

"For the rest of my life I'll be pursued by regret, not for her—there are plenty of mistresses, but, as old Don Diego says, 'there is only one honor!' And now, there's no denying it, I'm retreating from the first danger that's presented itself, because that duel with Monsieur de Beauvoisis was almost nothing but a joke. This is completely different. I may be shot by a servant, but that's the least important danger: I may be dishonored.

"This is becoming serious, my boy," he added, speaking with a Gascon gaiety and accent. "Honor is at stake. A poor devil like me, cast into such a low rank by fate, will never find such an opportunity again; I'll have other adventures with women, but they'll be minor affairs. . . ."

He reflected for a long time, pacing swiftly up and down the floor and stopping abruptly from time to time. A magnificent marble bust of Cardinal Richelieu had been placed in his room; his eyes were involuntarily drawn to it. Illuminated by the light of his lamp, the bust seemed to be looking at him sternly and reproaching him for lacking that daring which ought to come so naturally to a Frenchman. "In your time, great man, would I have hesitated?" he thought.

"At the very worst," he said to himself at length, "let's suppose that this is a trap; then it's a disgraceful one and very compromising for a young lady. They know I'm not the kind of man to remain silent, so I'll have to be killed. That was all very well in 1574, in the days of Boniface de La Mole, but the La Mole of today would never dare to do such a thing. These people are no longer the same. Mademoiselle de La Mole is so envied! Four hundred drawing rooms would echo with her shame tomorrow, and with what pleasure!

"The servants gossip among themselves about the marked preference she shows for me; I know that, I've heard them myself. . . .

"But then there are her letters! They may believe I have them on me. I'll be taken by surprise in her room and they'll snatch them away from me. I'll be dealing with two, three, four men, how do I know? But where will they find those men? Where in Paris can anyone find hirelings who'll be discreet? They're afraid of the law. . . . Of course! It will be Caylus, Croisenois and Luz themselves! They'll have been tempted by the circumstances and the foolish figure I'll cut in the midst of them. Beware of Abelard's fate, my young secretary!

"All right, then, gentlemen, you'll bear my marks! I'll strike at your faces, like Caesar's soldiers at Pharsalia. . . . As for the letters, I can put them in a safe place."

He made copies of the last two letters, hid them in a volume of the fine edition of Voltaire in the library and took the originals to the post office himself.

On his return he exclaimed in surprise and terror, "What madness I'm about to rush into!" He had spent a quarter of an hour without thinking clearly about what he was going to do during the approaching night. "But if I don't go through with it, I'll despise myself later! I'll have doubts about my action for the rest of my life, and for me such doubts will mean bitter unhappiness. Haven't I already felt it over Amanda's lover? I think it would be easier for me to forgive myself for a straightforward crime; as soon as I confessed it, I'd stop thinking about it.

"What! After an incredible stroke of good fortune has raised me above the crowd and placed me in rivalry with a man who bears one of the noblest names in France, shall I lightheartedly declare myself his inferior? When all is said and done, it would be cowardly of me not to go. That word decides everything!" he cried, standing up. "And besides, she's very pretty. If this isn't a trap, what mad risks she's taking for me! . . . If it's a practical joke, well then, gentlemen, it's within my power to turn it into a serious matter, and that's just what I'll do.

"But what if they tie my arms as soon as I enter her bedroom? They may have set some ingenious trap!

"It's like a duel," he said to himself, laughing. "There's a parry for every thrust, as my fencing master says; but God, who wants the duel to come to an end, makes one of the opponents forget to parry. Besides, here's something to answer them with." He took his pistols from his pocket and, although the priming was in good condition, he renewed it.

There were still long hours to wait; to give himself something to do, he wrote to Fouqué:

> My friend, open the enclosed letter only in case of accident, if you hear that something strange has happened to me. Then, cross out the names in the manuscript I'm sending you, make eight copies of it and send them to the newspapers in Marseilles, Bordeaux, Lyons, Brussels, etc. Ten days later, have the manuscript printed and send the first copy to the Marquis de La Mole, then, two weeks later, scatter the other copies in the streets of Verrières at night.

The short justificatory report, written in narrative form, which Fouqué was to open only in case of accident, was as little compromising as possible to Mademoiselle de La Mole, but it nevertheless contained a precise description of Julien's situation.

He was just sealing his little packet when the dinner bell rang; it made his heart beat faster. His imagination, preoccupied with the narrative he had just written, was filled with tragic presentiments. He had seen himself seized by a group of servants, bound hand and foot and carried into a cellar with a gag in his mouth. There one of the servants would keep watch over him, and if the honor of the noble family required that the incident have a tragic ending, it would be easy to finish everything with one of those poisons which leave no trace; they would then say that he had died of some illness and take his dead body back to his room.

Carried away by his own story, like a playwright, Julien was genuinely afraid when he entered the dining room. He looked at all the liveried servants. He studied their faces, "Which are the ones that have been chosen for tonight's undertaking?" he wondered. "In this family, memories of the court of Henri III are so present, so often called to mind, that, believing themselves to be outraged, they'll be more resolute than other people of their rank." He looked at Mademoiselle de La Mole, seeking to read in her eyes the plans of her family; she was pale, and her face struck him as having a certain medieval quality about it. Never before had she given him such an impression of grandeur; she was truly beautiful and imposing. He nearly fell in love with her. *"Pallida morte futura,"* he said to himself. ("Her pallor announces her great designs.")

After dinner he went to the garden, pretending to take a casual stroll, but in vain: Mademoiselle de La Mole did not appear. Speaking to her at that time would have lifted a great weight from his heart.

Why not admit it? He was afraid. Since he had already resolved to act, he abandoned himself to this feeling without shame. "If only I find the courage I need when it's time to act," he said to himself, "what does it matter what I'm feeling now?" He went off to reconnoiter the scene of action and try the weight of the ladder.

"This is an instrument I seem fated to use, here as in Verrières!" he said to himself, laughing. "But what a difference! Before," he added with a sigh, "I wasn't forced to mistrust the woman for whom I was exposing myself to danger. And also, what a difference in the danger! If I'd been killed in Monsieur de Rênal's gardens, there would have been no dishonor for me. My death could easily have been made to seem inexplicable. Here, what abominable tales will be told about me in the drawing rooms of the Hôtel de Chaulnes, the Hôtel de Caylus, the Hôtel de Retz, and so on—everywhere, in short! Posterity will regard me as a monster.

"For two or three years," he continued, laughing at himself. But this thought overwhelmed him. "And where will I find justification? If Fouqué has my pamphlet printed, it will be only one more infamy. What! I'm received into a house and, to show my gratitude for the hospitality that's shown me, for the kindness that's showered on me, I print a pamphlet about what takes place there! I attack the women's honor! Ah, it's a thousand times better to be a dupe!''

That evening was horrible.

CHAPTER 16
One O'clock in the Morning

> This garden was very large and had been laid out with perfect taste only a few years before. But the trees had once stood in the famous Pré-aux-Clercs, so celebrated in the days of Henri III; they were more than a century old. The garden had a certain rustic air.
>
> —Massinger

HE WAS about to write a letter to Fouqué countermanding his previous instructions when the clock struck eleven. He noisily turned the key in the lock of his door, as though he were locking himself in. Then he stealthily crept out to see what was happening all over the house, especially on the fifth floor, where the servants lived. He saw nothing unusual. One of Mademoiselle de La Mole's maids was giving a party; the servants were gaily drinking punch. "Those who are laughing like that," thought Julien, "must not be taking part in tonight's enterprise; they'd be more serious."

Finally he went down into the garden and stood in a dark corner. "If they intend to conceal everything from the servants in the house, they'll have the men who are supposed to take me by surprise come in over the garden wall. If Monsieur de Croisenois is planning this with any level-headedness, he must have realized that it would be less compromising for the young lady he wants to marry if I'm captured before I enter her bedroom."

He carried out a thorough military reconnaissance. "My honor is at stake," he thought. "If I make a blunder, it won't be an excuse in my own eyes to say to myself, 'I didn't think of that.' "

The weather was dishearteningly clear. By eleven o'clock the moon had risen, and by half-past twelve it was shining brightly on the side of the house facing the garden.

"She's mad," thought Julien. As the clock struck one, there was still a light in Count Norbert's windows. Julien had never been so afraid in all his life; he saw only the dangers of the undertaking and had no enthusiasm.

He went to get the enormous ladder, waited five minutes to leave time for a countermanding order, and then, at five minutes past one, he leaned the ladder against Mathilde's window. He climbed up quietly with his pistol in his hand, astonished at not being attacked. As he neared the window it opened noiselessly.

"You've come, monsieur," Mathilde said to him with deep emotion. "I've been watching you for the last hour."

Julien was greatly embarrassed. He did not know how to act; he felt no love at all. In his embarrassment he remembered that he must be daring: he tried to kiss her.

"No, don't!" she said, pushing him away.

Overjoyed at being repulsed, he hastened to look around; the moonlight was so bright that the shadows it cast in her room were black. "There may very well be men hidden in here without my seeing them," he thought.

"What do you have in the side pocket of your coat?" asked Mathilde, delighted to find a topic of conversation. She was suffering intensely; the sentiments of reserve and timidity that are so natural in a well-bred young lady had reasserted their power over her and were now tormenting her.

"I have all sorts of daggers and pistols," replied Julien, equally delighted to have something to say.

"You must lower the ladder," said Mathilde.

"It's enormous, and it may break the windows of the drawing room below, or the windows of the mezzanine."

"You mustn't break any windows," said Mathilde, unsuccessfully trying to adopt a tone of ordinary conversation. "It seems to me you could lower the ladder with a rope tied to the top rung. I always have a supply of rope in my room."

"And this is a woman in love!" thought Julien. "She dares to say she loves me! All this self-assurance and rationality in her precautions tells me rather plainly that I'm not triumphing over Monsieur de Croisenois as I stupidly believed: I'm merely succeeding him. But then what do I care? Am I in love with her? I'm triumphing over the marquis in the sense that he'll be greatly annoyed to have a successor, and still more annoyed that the successor should be me. How arrogantly he looked at me last night in the Café Tortoni, pretending not to recognize me! How rudely he greeted me later, when he could no longer avoid it!"

Julien had tied the rope to the top rung of the ladder and was gently lowering it, leaning far out over the balcony to make sure it would not touch the windows. "This is a fine chance to kill me," he thought, "if anyone is hiding in her room." But deep silence continued to reign everywhere.

The ladder touched the ground. He succeeded in laying it down flat in the bed of exotic flowers that extended along the wall.

"What will my mother say when she sees her beautiful plants crushed?" said Mathilde. "You must throw down the rope," she added with perfect calm. "If it were seen hanging from the balcony, it would be a rather difficult thing to explain."

"But how me go away?" said Julien playfully, imitating the Creole dialect. (One of the maids in the house was from Santo Domingo.)

"You go away through door," said Mathilde, delighted with this idea. Then she thought, "Ah, how worthy of my love this man is!"

Julien had just dropped the rope into the garden; Mathilde squeezed his arm. He thought he had been seized by an enemy; he spun around, drawing his dagger. She had thought she heard someone opening a window. They stood still without moving or breathing. The moon shone full on them. The sound was not repeated and their alarm subsided.

Then embarrassment returned; it was intense on both sides. Julien made sure that the door was fastened with all its bolts. He seriously thought of looking under the bed, but he did not dare; one or two lackeys might be hidden beneath it. Finally, fearing a future reproach from his prudence, he looked.

Mathilde had fallen into all the anguish of extreme shyness. She was horrified by her position.

"What have you done with my letters?" she asked at length.

"What a fine chance," thought Julien, "to disconcert those gentlemen, if they're listening, and avoid a battle!" Then he said to Mathilde, "The first one is hidden in a large Protestant Bible which last night's mail coach is now taking far away from here." He spoke very distinctly as he entered into these details, and in such a way as to be overheard by anyone who might be hiding in the two large mahogany wardrobes which he had not dared to examine. "The other two are also in the mail, following the same route as the first one."

"Good heavens! Why all those precautions?" said Mathilde in amazement.

"Why should I lie?" thought Julien, and he confessed all his suspicions to her.

"So that's why you made your letters so cold!" exclaimed Mathilde in a tone which contained more consternation than tenderness.

Julien was not aware of this nuance. She had just addressed him as *tu*,* and this made him lose his head, or at least his suspicions vanished; his stature grew in his own eyes. He dared to put his arms around that girl who was so beautiful and who filled him with such respect. He was only half repulsed.

He resorted to his memory, as he had done in Besançon with Amanda Binet, and recited several of the finest phrases from *La Nouvelle Héloïse*.

"You have a manly heart," she replied, without paying too much attention to his fine phrases. "I wanted to test your courage, I admit it. Your first suspicions and your determination prove that you're even more intrepid than I thought." She was forcing herself to address him as *tu*, and she was obviously more attentive to this strange way of speaking than she was to the meaning of what she was saying. After a few moments, this intimate form of address, employed in a manner that was utterly bare of tender feelings, no longer gave Julien any pleasure. He was amazed at his lack of happiness; finally, in order not to feel it, he resorted to his reason. He saw himself esteemed by that proud young lady who never bestowed praise without restriction; with this line of thought he achieved a happiness based on self-esteem.

It was not, it is true, that ecstasy of the soul which he had sometimes experienced with Madame de Rênal; far from it! There was nothing tender in his feelings during these first moments. What he felt was a keen happiness arising from his ambition, and he was ambitious above everything else. He spoke once again of the people he had suspected, and of the precautions he had devised. As he spoke, he was thinking of how to take advantage of his victory.

Mathilde, still deeply embarrassed and apparently appalled at her own action, seemed delighted to have found a topic of conversation. They discussed means of seeing each other again. Julien took exquisite pleasure in being able to give new proofs of his intelligence and courage during this discussion. They were dealing with extremely shrewd people, and young Tanbeau was

---

*The second person singular pronoun, usually used only between people on familiar or intimate terms with each other.—L.B.

undoubtedly a spy, but he and Mathilde were not without cunning either.

What could be easier for them than to meet in the library and make arrangements for everything?

"I can appear in any part of the house without arousing suspicion," added Julien, "almost even in Madame de La Mole's room." It was absolutely necessary to go through her room in order to reach her daughter's. If Mathilde thought it better for him always to come by means of a ladder, he would expose himself to that slight danger with a heart overflowing with joy.

As she listened to him speak, Mathilde was shocked by his air of triumph. "So now he's my master!" she thought. She was already in the grip of remorse. Her reason was horrified by the arrant folly of what she had done. If she had been able to, she would have annihilated herself and Julien. When, from time to time, the strength of her will silenced her remorse, she was tormented by feelings of shyness and wounded modesty. The horrible state in which she now found herself had come as a complete surprise to her.

"But I must speak to him," she said to herself at length. "It's an accepted convention: one speaks to one's lover." Then, in order to perform her duty, and with a tenderness that appeared much more in the words she used than in her tone of voice, she told him of the various decisions she had made with regard to him during the past few days.

She had decided that if he had the courage to come to her room with the aid of the gardener's ladder, as she had instructed him to do, she would give herself to him without reserve. But never were such tender things expressed in a colder or more formal tone. So far, their rendezvous had been frigid. It was enough to make one hate the thought of love. What a lesson in morality for a rash young woman! Is it worth while to ruin one's future for such a moment?

After a long period of indecision, which, to a superficial observer, might have appeared to be the effect of the most resolute hatred, so difficult was it for even a will as firm as hers to overcome the feelings which a woman owes to herself, Mathilde finally became Julien's mistress.

To tell the truth, their ecstasy was somewhat forced. Passionate love was still not so much a reality as a model which they were imitating.

Mademoiselle de La Mole believed that she was fulfilling a duty to herself and to her lover. "The poor boy has shown supreme courage,'' she said to herself. ''I must make him happy, or else I'll be the one who shows lack of character.'' But she would have been willing to endure an eternity of unhappiness in order to avoid the cruel necessity that was now imposed on her.

Despite the terrible violence of her inner struggle, she remained in perfect control of her speech.

No regret, no reproach came to mar that night which seemed strange rather than happy to Julien. How different it was from his last twenty-four-hour stay in Verrières! ''These fine Parisian ways have managed to spoil everything, even love!'' he said to himself in his extreme injustice.

He abandoned himself to these reflections while standing inside one of the large mahogany wardrobes, where Mathilde had told him to hide at the first sound from the adjoining room, which was that of Madame de La Mole. Mathilde accompanied her mother to mass, the maids soon left the room and Julien easily made his escape before they came back to finish their work.

He mounted a horse and rode into the most solitary recesses of the Bois de Meudon. He was much more astonished than happy. The happiness which took possession of his heart from time to time was like that of a young second lieutenant who, as a result of some amazing exploit, has just been made a colonel on the field by the commanding general. He felt himself transported to a lofty height; everything that had been above him the day before was now either beside him or far below him. His happiness gradually increased as he rode farther away.

If there was no tenderness in his heart, it was because, strange as the word may seem, Mathilde, in all her conduct toward him, had been performing a *duty*. There was nothing unexpected for her in all the events of that night except the unhappiness and shame she had found in place of the divine ecstasy spoken of in novels.

''Can I have been mistaken?'' she wondered. ''Is it possible that I don't love him?''

CHAPTER 17

An Old Sword

I now mean to be serious—it is time,
Since laughter now-a-days is deem'd too serious,
A jest at vice by virtue's called a crime.
                                        —*Don Juan*

SHE DID not appear at dinner. That evening she came into the drawing room for a few moments, but she did not look at Julien. This behavior seemed strange to him. "But," he thought, "I must admit that I know the ways of high society only by the everyday actions I've seen a hundred times; she'll no doubt give me some good reason for all this." Nevertheless, driven by the most intense curiosity, he studied all the expressions of Mathilde's face; he could not deny that she looked cold and malicious. This was clearly not the same woman who, the night before, had felt, or pretended to feel, transports of joy that were too extreme to be genuine.

The next day, and the day after, there was the same coldness on her part; she did not look at him, she seemed unaware of his existence. Julien, consumed with intense anxiety, was a thousand leagues away from the feelings of triumph which had completely filled his heart the first day. "Could it by any chance be a return to virtue?" he wondered. But this word was too middle-class for the haughty Mathilde.

"In the ordinary situations of life," he thought, "she has hardly any belief in religion. She values it as useful to the interests of her caste. But isn't it possible that ordinary feminine delicacy has made her deeply regret what she's done?" He believed himself to be her first lover.

At other times he said to himself, "But I must admit that there's nothing artless, simple or tender in her behavior; I've never seen her act more like a queen who's just stepped down from her throne. Can it be that she despises me? It would be like her to reproach herself for what she's done for me, solely because of my humble birth."

While Julien, filled with prejudices derived from books and his memories of Verrières, was pursuing the vain dream of a tender mistress who ceases to give any thought to her own existence as soon as she had made her lover happy, Mathilde's vanity was furious with him. Since she had ceased to be bored for the past two months, she no longer dreaded boredom; thus, without in the least suspecting it, Julien had lost his greatest advantage.

"I've given myself a master!" she said to herself as she nervously paced the floor of her room. "He's full of honor, it's true, but if I push his vanity too far he'll take vengeance by revealing the nature of our relationship."

It is one of the misfortunes of our age that even the strangest deviations of conduct do not cure boredom. Julien was Mathilde's first lover, and in that situation in life which gives a few tender illusions to even the hardest of hearts, she was tormented by bitter reflections.

"He has enormous power over me," she thought, "because he rules by terror and can punish me horribly if I push him too far." This idea alone was enough to make her inclined to insult him, for courage was the prime quality of her character. Nothing could give her any excitement, or relieve her underlying, constantly recurring boredom, except the idea that she was placing her whole existence at stake.

On the third day, since she obstinately refused to look at him, Julien followed her, obviously against her will, into the billiard room after dinner.

"So, monsieur, you apparently think you've acquired some very strong rights over me," she said to him with scarcely controlled anger, "because, in opposition to my clearly expressed wishes, you insist on speaking to me. How can you be so cruel and treacherous as to talk to me like this? Do you realize that no one else in the world has ever dared so much?"

Nothing could have been more amusing than the conversation between these two young lovers; without realizing it, they were animated by intense hatred for each other. Since neither of them had a patient disposition, and since, moreover, they were both accustomed to the ways of polite society, they soon reached the point of telling each other unequivocally that they had broken off their relationship forever.

"I swear I'll never reveal your secret," said Julien, "and I'd even add that I'd never speak to you again if it weren't for the fact that your reputation would suffer from such a noticeable change." He bowed respectfully and walked away.

He had performed without difficulty what he regarded as a duty; he was far from believing himself to be deeply in love with Mademoiselle de La Mole. He had no doubt been in love with her three days before, when she had hidden him in the large mahogany wardrobe, but everything swiftly changed in his heart as soon as he realized that he had broken off with her forever. His cruel memory began to retrace every detail of that night which had left him so cold during his actual experience of it.

On the second night after their declaration of eternal estrangement, Julien nearly lost his reason when he was forced to admit to himself that he was in love with Mademoiselle de La Mole.

This discovery was followed by terrible inner struggles; all his feelings had been thrown into confusion.

Two days later, instead of being haughty with Monsieur de Croisenois, he could almost have embraced him and burst into tears.

His constant unhappiness gave him a glimmer of common sense; he made up his mind to leave for Languedoc, packed his trunk and went to the post house. His heart sank when, at the stagecoach office, he was told that, by a rare chance, there was a seat vacant in the coach for Toulouse the next day. He reserved it and returned to the Hôtel de La Mole to inform the marquis of his departure.

Monsieur de La Mole had gone out. More dead than alive, Julien went to the library to wait for him. What was his emotion when he found Mademoiselle de La Mole there!

When she saw him she took on an expression of hostility that was impossible for him to misunderstand. Carried away by his unhappiness, bewildered by his surprise, he had the weakness to say to her, in a tender tone that came straight from his heart, "Don't you love me any more?"

"I'm horrified at having given myself to the first man who came along," said Mathilde, weeping with rage against herself.

"The first man who came along!" cried Julien, and he rushed toward an old medieval sword that was kept in the library as a curiosity.

His anguish, which he had believed extreme when he spoke to her, had just been increased a hundredfold by the tears of shame he now saw her shedding. He would have been the happiest of men if he could have killed her.

Just as he drew the sword, not without difficulty, from its ancient scabbard, Mathilde, happy to be experiencing such a new sensation, proudly walked toward him; her tears had ceased to flow.

The thought of the Marquis de La Mole, his benefactor, presented itself vividly to his mind. "I was about to kill his daughter!'' he said to himself. ''How horrible!'' He started to throw down the sword. ''She's sure to burst out laughing at such a melodramatic action,'' he thought; this idea brought back all his self-possession. He looked at the blade of the old sword curiously, as though examining it to see if it had any rust spots, then he put it back into its scabbard and, with great tranquillity, hung it up again on the gilded bronze nail which supported it.

This whole action, which was very slow toward the end, lasted for at least a minute; Mademoiselle de La Mole looked at him in astonishment. ''So I was just on the verge of being killed by my lover!'' she said to herself. This thought took her back to the finest days of the age of Charles IX and Henri III.

She stood motionless, and seemingly taller than usual, in front of Julien, who had just put the sword back in place; she looked at him with eyes from which all hatred had vanished. It must be admitted that she was enchanting at that moment; certainly no woman had ever less resembled a ''Parisian doll'' (this expression summed up Julien's greatest objection to the women of that city).

''I'm about to fall back into my weakness for him,'' thought Mathilde. ''He'll certainly think he's my lord and master if I have a relapse just after I've spoken to him so firmly.'' She turned and fled.

''My God, but she's beautiful!'' thought Julien as he watched her run away. ''There's the girl who threw herself into my arms less than a week ago! . . . And those moments will never return! And it's my fault! What she did was extraordinary, and a great honor to me, but at the time I didn't appreciate it! . . . I must admit that I was born with a very unimaginative and unfortunate character.''

The marquis entered; Julien hastened to inform him of his departure.

''Where are you going?'' asked Monsieur de La Mole.

''To Languedoc.''

''I'm afraid you'll have to change your plans: you're reserved for a higher destiny. If you leave at all, it will be for the north. . . . In fact, to use a military expression, I'm confining you to your quarters. You will please not leave the house for more than two or three hours at a time: I may need you at any moment.''

Julien bowed and walked away without a word, leaving the marquis greatly astonished; he was unable to speak, and he locked himself in his room. There he was free to exaggerate the cruelty of his fate.

"So I can't even go away!" he thought. "God only knows how many days the marquis will keep me in Paris! Good God, what will become of me! And I don't have a single friend I can go to for advice: Father Pirard wouldn't let me finish my first sentence, and Count Altamira would suggest that I become involved in some conspiracy to distract myself. Meanwhile I'm going mad, I feel it, I'm mad! Who can guide me, what will become of me?"

CHAPTER 18
Painful Moments

> And she admits it to me! She goes into all the details! Her lovely eyes, gazing into mine, portray the love she feels for another!
>
> —Schiller

MADEMOISELLE DE LA MOLE, delighted, could think of nothing but the joy of having been on the verge of being killed. She went so far as to say to herself, "He's worthy of being my master, because he was about to kill me. How many handsome young society gentlemen would have to be melted together to produce one such surge of passion? And I must confess that he looked very handsome when he climbed up on the chair to put the sword back, in exactly the same picturesque position the interior decorator had hung it in before! After all, it wasn't so foolish of me to love him." If some honorable means of reconciliation had presented itself to her at that moment, she would have seized it gladly.

Julien, securely locked in his room, was in the grip of black despair. In his madness he thought of throwing himself at her feet. If, instead of hiding himself in an inaccessible place, he had wandered through the house and garden in order to be on hand for any opportunity, he might have changed his horrible misery into blissful happiness in a single instant.

But the finesse for whose absence we are reproaching him would have excluded his sublime gesture of seizing the sword, which now gave him such distinction in the eyes of Mademoiselle de La Mole. Her caprice, which was to Julien's advantage, lasted for the rest of the day; she formed a charming image of the short moments during which she had loved him, and she regretted that they were past.

"Actually," she said to herself, "my passion for the poor boy lasted, as far as he's concerned, only from one o'clock in the morning, when I saw him come up the ladder with his pistols in the side pocket of his coat, until eight o'clock. It was a quarter of an hour later, while I was at mass in Saint-Valère's, that I began to think he was going to regard himself as my master, and that he might very well try to make me obey him out of fear."

After dinner, far from avoiding Julien, she spoke to him and almost compelled him to follow her into the garden; he obeyed. This was an important test. Almost without realizing it, she was yielding to the love she was beginning to feel for him again. She found extreme pleasure in walking beside him; she cast curious glances at the hands which, that morning, had seized a sword to kill her.

After such an action, after everything that had happened, it was out of the question for them to talk with each other in the same way as they had done before. She gradually began to speak to him intimately and confidentially about the state of her heart. She found a strange, exquisite pleasure in this kind of conversation; she went so far as to tell him of the momentary attraction she had once felt toward Monsieur de Croisenois, and then later toward Monsieur de Caylus. . . .

"What! Monsieur de Caylus too!" cried Julien; and all the bitter jealousy of a forsaken lover burst forth in these words. Mathilde correctly judged what was behind them and was not offended. She continued to torture him by giving him detailed and vivid descriptions of her past feelings, speaking in a tone of intimate truthfulness. He saw that she was depicting things that were present before her eyes. He noted painfully that she was making discoveries in her heart as she spoke. The misery of jealousy can go no further. To suspect that a rival is loved is painful enough, but to hear the love he inspires described in detail by the woman one adores is certainly the height of suffering.

Oh, how terribly Julien was punished at that moment for the pride which had led him to set himself above men like Caylus and Croisenois! With what intense and heartfelt chagrin he now exaggerated their slightest advantages! With what ardent sincerity he now despised himself!

Mathilde now seemed to him more than divine; there are no words strong enough to depict the intensity of his admiration. As he walked beside her he furtively glanced at her hands, her arms and her queenly figure. He was on the verge of falling at her feet, overcome with love and despair, and crying out to her, "Have pity on me!"

"And this beautiful girl," he thought, "so superior to everyone else in the world, who once loved me, will probably love Monsieur de Caylus before long!"

He could not doubt her sincerity; the accent of truth was too obvious in everything she said. And, to bring his suffering to its peak, there were moments when she became so engrossed in describing the feelings she had once had for Monsieur de Caylus that she spoke of him as though she still loved him. There was certainly love in the tone of her voice, he was clearly aware of that.

He would have suffered less if his chest had been flooded with molten lead. Having reached such a climax of unhappiness, how could the poor boy have guessed that it was because she was speaking to him that she found such pleasure in recalling the faint stirrings of love she had once felt for Monsieur de Caylus or Monsieur de Croisenois?

No words could describe Julien's anguish. He was listening to those detailed confessions of love felt for others in the same linden-bordered lane in which, only a few days before, he had been waiting for the clock to strike one so that he could enter her bedroom. A human being cannot endure more intense suffering.

This cruel kind of intimacy lasted for a full week. Mathilde sometimes seemed to seek, and sometimes not to avoid, opportunities of speaking to him; and the subject of their conversation, to which they both seemed to return with a kind of cruel pleasure, was always the feelings she had experienced for other men. She told him of the letters she had written; she even recalled the words she had used in them and quoted whole sentences to him. Toward the end of that week she seemed to contemplate Julien with a kind of malicious joy. She saw the weakness of her tyrant, which meant that she could allow herself to love him, and his suffering gave her keen pleasure.

It was easy to see that Julien had no experience of life; he had not even read any novels. If he had been a little less shy and awkward, and if he had calmly said to Mathilde, whom he so deeply adored and who was making such strange confessions to him, "Admit that, even though those other gentlemen are superior to me, I'm still the one you love," perhaps she would have been happy to have him guess what was in her heart; at least his success would have depended entirely on the grace with which he expressed this idea, and on the moment he chose to do so. In any case, he would have extricated himself advantageously from a situation that was about to become monotonous to Mathilde.

"So you no longer love me, and I adore you!" he said to her one day, beside himself with love and sorrow. This foolish blunder was almost the worst he could have made. These words destroyed in the twinkling of an eye all the pleasure she had found in speaking to him about the state of her heart. She was beginning to feel astonished that, after what had happened, he was not offended by the things she told him; just before he made this stupid remark, she had come to believe that perhaps he no longer loved her. "Pride has no doubt extinguished his love," she had thought. "He's not the kind of man to see creatures like Caylus, Luz and Croisenois, who he says are so superior to him, preferred to him with impunity. No, I'll never see him at my feet again!"

On the preceding days, in the artlessness of his sorrow, Julien had often sincerely praised the distinguished qualities of these gentlemen, even going so far as to exaggerate them. This nuance had not escaped Mademoiselle de La Mole; it surprised her, but she did not guess the reason for it. Julien's frenzied heart, in praising a rival whom he believed to be loved, shared his happiness.

His frank but foolish remark changed everything in an instant: sure that he loved her, Mathilde utterly despised him.

She was walking in the garden with him when he made his awkward blunder; she left him, and her last glance expressed the most frightful contempt. When she returned to the drawing room, she spent the entire evening without looking at him. By the next day, her contempt had completely filled her heart; there was no longer any question of the feeling which, for a whole week, had made her find so much pleasure in treating him as her most intimate friend: the sight of him was now disagreeable to her. Soon her feelings developed into outright disgust; no words could describe the extreme contempt she felt whenever she happened to see him.

Julien had understood nothing of what had been taking place in her heart for the past week, but his clear-sighted vanity discerned her scorn. He had the good sense to appear before her as seldom as possible, and he never looked at her.

But it was not without mortal anguish that he deprived himself of her presence to a certain extent. This seemed to make his misery still more intense. "The courage of a man's heart can't go any further,'' he said to himself. He spent most of his time sitting in front of a small window in the attic of the house; he kept the shutters carefully closed, and from there, at least, he could see her whenever she came into the garden. Imagine his feelings when he saw her walking there after dinner with Monsieur de Caylus, Monsieur de Luz or some other man for whom she had confessed a slight stirring of love in the past!

He had previously had no conception of such intense unhappiness. Sometimes he almost cried aloud in his pain; that resolute heart was at last thrown into complete and utter turmoil. Any thought not connected with Mademoiselle de La Mole had become odious to him; he was incapable of writing even the simplest letters.

"You're mad," the marquis said to him one morning.

Julien, trembling lest he be found out, spoke of an illness and succeeded in making the marquis believe him. Fortunately for him, Monsieur de La Mole joked with him at dinner about his forthcoming journey; Mathilde gathered that he might be absent for a long time. Julien had been avoiding her for several days now, and the distinguished young men who had everything that was lacking in that pale, somber creature, whom she had once loved, no longer had the power to distract her from her reverie.

"An ordinary girl," she said to herself, "would have sought out the man of her choice among the young men who attract the most attention in a drawing room, but one of the characteristics of genius is that it doesn't drag its thoughts in the rut traced out by the common herd. If I become the companion of a man like Julien, who lacks only the fortune I possess, I'll continually attract attention—I won't pass unnoticed in life. Far from living in constant dread of a revolution, like my cousins, who are so afraid of the common people that they don't dare to scold a postilion who drives their carriage badly, I'll be sure to play a part in it, and a great part, because the man I've chosen has character and boundless ambition. What does he lack? Friends and money? I'll give them to him."

But in her thoughts she was treating Julien as an inferior man whose career she could determine whenever and however she chose, and whose love she did not even allow herself to doubt.

CHAPTER 19
The Comic Opera

O how this spring of love resembleth
The uncertain glory of an April day;
Which now shows all the beauty of the sun,
And by and by a cloud takes all away!
—Shakespeare

ABSORBED IN THOUGHTS of the future and of the extraordinary part she hoped to play in it, Mathilde soon came to miss even the dry, metaphysical discussions she had often had with Julien. Tired of such lofty thoughts, she sometimes also missed the moments of happiness she had once known with him; these last memories did not come back to her without remorse, which overwhelmed her at certain moments.

"But if a girl like me forgets her duties," she said to herself, "it ought to be only for a man of merit; it won't be said that it was his handsome mustache or the graceful way he rides his horse that seduced me, but rather his profound discussions of the future awaiting France, his ideas about the possible resemblance between the events that are going to swoop down on us and the Revolution of 1688 in England.

"I was seduced," she replied to her remorse; "I'm a weak woman, but at least I wasn't led astray by outward charms, like an empty-headed schoolgirl.

"If there's a revolution, why shouldn't Julien Sorel play the part of Roland, and I that of Madame Roland? I like that part better than Madame de Staël's; immoral conduct will be an obstacle in our time. Certainly no one will reproach me for a second act of weakness; I'd die of shame."

Mathilde's thoughts were not all so serious, it must be admitted, as the meditations we have just transcribed.

She cast furtive glances at Julien; she found a charming grace in even his most insignificant actions.

"I've no doubt succeeded in destroying the slightest idea in his mind that he has any rights over me," she thought. "The expression of unhappiness and deep passion with which the poor boy made that naïve declaration of love to me in the garden a week ago proves it; I must admit that it was very strange of me to turn against him because of a remark that was so full of respect and passion. Am I not his wife? His remark was quite natural and, I must confess, it was sweet of him to say it. He was still in love with me after those endless conversations in which I spoke to him, with a great deal of cruelty, I admit, of nothing but the faint stirrings of love which the boredom of the life I led once made me feel for those young society gentlemen of whom he's so jealous. Oh, if he only knew how little danger they represent! Compared to him, how insipid they are to me, how they all seem to be exact copies of each other!''

As she was making these reflections, Mathilde idly drew pencil sketches on a page of her album, in order not to appear too distracted to her mother, who was looking at her. One of the profiles she had just drawn amazed and delighted her: it was a striking likeness of Julien. "It's the voice of heaven!" she thought, enraptured. 'Here's one of the miracles of love: I've drawn his portrait without knowing what I was doing!''

She rushed off to her room, locked herself in and made a concentrated, serious effort to draw a portrait of Julien, but she was unsuccessful: the profile drawn by accident was still the best likeness. She was enchanted by it; she regarded it as undeniable evidence of her great passion.

She did not lay aside her album until quite late, when the marquise sent for her to go to the Italian Opera. She had only one thought: to stare at Julien in such a way as to make her mother invite him to accompany them.

He did not appear; the ladies had only commonplace people in their box. During the first act of the opera, Mathilde dreamed of the man she loved with passionate emotion; but in the second act a maxim of love, sung, it must be admitted, to a melody worthy of Cimarosa, penetrated her heart. The heroine of the opera sang, "I must be punished for the excessive adoration I feel for him, I love him too much!"

As soon as she heard this sublime aria, everything else in the world vanished for her. She was spoken to, she did not answer; her mother scolded her, she could scarcely bring herself to look at her. Her ecstasy reached a state of exaltation and passion comparable to the most violent emotions that Julien had felt for her during the past few days. The melody, full of divine grace, accompanied by the words which seemed so strikingly appropriate to her own situation, occupied every moment in which she was not thinking directly of Julien. Thanks to her love of music, that evening she felt the way Madame de Rênal always felt when she thought of him. Intellectual love is no doubt more self-aware than true love, but it has only isolated moments of ardor; it knows itself too well, it constantly criticizes itself; far from leading the mind astray, it is only a creation of the mind.

When they returned to the house, in spite of everything Madame de La Mole said, Mathilde claimed to have a fever and spent part of the night practicing the aria on her piano. She sang the words to the famous melody which had enchanted her:

> Devo punirmi, devo punirmi,
> Se troppo amai . . .

The result of this night of madness was that she believed she had succeeded in triumphing over her love.

(This page will harm its unfortunate author in more ways than one. Frigid hearts will accuse him of indecency. He does not insult the young women who shine in the drawing rooms of Paris by assuming a single one of them to be subject to the mad impulses which degraded Mathilde's nature. This character is totally imaginary, and even imagined as being far outside those social habits which will assure the civilization of the nineteenth century such a distinguished place among that of all other centuries. There is certainly no lack of prudence in the young ladies who have adorned the ballrooms this winter.

I do not think, either, that they can be accused of despising a great fortune, horses, fine estates and everything else that assures an agreeable position in society. Far from seeing only boredom in all these advantages, they usually make them the object of their most constant desires, and if there is any passion in their hearts it is for these things alone.

And neither is it true that love takes it upon itself to further the careers of young men who, like Julien, are endowed with a certain amount of talent; rather, they attach themselves with unshakable tenacity to some particular clique, and when that clique triumphs, all the blessings of society are showered upon them. Woe to the studious man who does not belong to any clique! He will be reproached for even his minor, doubtful successes, and lofty virtue will triumph by robbing him. A novel, gentlemen, is a mirror carried along a highway. Sometimes it reflects to your view the azure of the sky, sometimes the mire of the puddles in the road. And the man who carries the mirror on his back will be accused by you of immorality! His mirror shows the mire and you blame the mirror! Blame, rather, the road in which the puddle lies, and still more the road inspector who lets the water stagnate and the puddle form.

Now that it is well established that a character like Mathilde's is impossible in our virtuous and equally prudent age, I am less afraid of arousing indignation by continuing my account of the charming girl's follies.)

She spent the next day watching for opportunities of proving to herself that she had vanquished her mad passion. Her chief aim was to displease Julien in every way; but none of his movements escaped her notice.

Julien was too unhappy and, above all, too deeply agitated to guess the meaning of such a complicated maneuver of passion; still less was he able to see the aspects of it that were favorable to him. He fell a victim to it; never, perhaps, had his misery been so intense. His mind had so little control over his actions that if a gloomy philosopher had said to him, "Try to take swift advantage of the conditions that are about to become favorable to you; in the kind of intellectual love that flourishes in Paris, one mood can't last for more than two days," he would not have understood him. But, however overwrought he might be, he still had his honor. His first duty was discretion; he realized that. To ask for advice, to describe his torment to the first person he met would have given him a happiness comparable to that of the poor wretch who, crossing the desert, receives a drop of cold water from the sky. He recognized the danger and was afraid he might answer indiscreet questions with a flood of tears; he locked himself in his room.

He saw Mathilde take a long walk in the garden; when she finally left it he went down into it. He walked over to a rose bush from which she had plucked a flower.

The night was dark; he was able to abandon himself to his misery without fear of being seen. It was obvious to him that Mademoiselle de La Mole was in love with one of the young officers with whom she had just been speaking so gaily. He himself had once been loved by her, but she had realized how little merit he possessed.

"And it's true, I have so little!" he said to himself with deep conviction. "When all is said and done, I'm extremely insignificant, vulgar, boring to others and unbearable to myself." He was utterly disgusted with all his good qualities, with all the things he had once ardently loved; and in that state of "inverted imagination" he attempted to judge his life with his imagination. This is the error of a superior man.

The idea of suicide occurred to him several times; this image was full of charm, like a vision of blissful rest; it was like a glass of cold water given to a poor wretch dying of thirst and heat in the desert.

"My death will increase her contempt for me!" he cried out. "What a memory I'll leave behind!"

Plunged into this last abyss of misery, a human being has no resource but courage. Julien did not have enough genius to say to himself, "I must dare to act," but as he was looking up at the window of Mathilde's room he saw through the shutters that she was putting out her light; he imagined that charming bedroom which he had seen, alas, only once in his life. His imagination went no further.

The clock struck one; as soon as he heard it he said to himself, "I'm going to climb up the ladder."

This was a flash of genius; sound reasons then thronged into his mind. "How could I be any worse off than I am now?" he thought. He ran over to the ladder; the gardener had attached it with a chain. He broke the hammer off one of his pistols and, animated at that moment by superhuman strength, used it to twist one of the links of the chain holding the ladder; a few minutes later he tore it loose and leaned the top of it against Mathilde's window.

"She'll be angry, she'll overwhelm me with contempt," he thought, "but what do I care? I'll give her a kiss, one last kiss, then I'll go to my room and kill myself. . . . My lips will have touched her cheek again before I die!"

He flew up the ladder and tapped on the shutter. After a few moments Mathilde heard him; she tried to open the shutters, but the ladder was in the way. He clung to one of the iron hooks used to keep the shutters open and, gravely risking a fall, shook the ladder violently, shifting it a little to one side. Mathilde was able to open the shutter.

He rushed into the room more dead than alive.

"It's really you!" she said, throwing herself into his arms.

Who could describe the intensity of Julien's happiness? Mathilde's was almost as great.

She spoke to him against herself, she accused herself to him. "Punish me for my horrible pride," she said, pressing him so tightly in her arms that she nearly suffocated him. "You're my master, I'm your slave: I must beg you on my knees to forgive me for trying to rebel." She slipped from his arms to fall at his feet. "Yes, you're my master," she went on, still intoxicated with love and happiness. "Rule me forever, punish your slave severely whenever she tries to rebel."

At another moment she tore herself from his arms and lit a candle, and it was only with enormous difficulty that Julien prevented her from cutting off one side of her hair.

"I want to remind myself that I'm your servant," she said. "If I'm ever led astray by my detestable pride, point to my hair and say, 'It's no longer a question of love, or whatever emotion your heart may be feeling; you've sworn to obey: obey in the name of honor.' "

But it is better not to describe such madness and ecstasy.

Julien's virtue was equal to his happiness. "I must climb down the ladder," he said to Mathilde when he saw dawn appearing above the faraway chimneys to the east, beyond the garden. "The sacrifice I'm imposing on myself is worthy of you; I'm depriving myself of several hours of the most amazing happiness a human soul can experience. It's a sacrifice I'm making to your reputation; if you know my heart, you realize what violence I'm doing to myself. Will you always be to me what you are now? But honor speaks, and that's enough. I must tell you that, after our first meeting, suspicion was not directed entirely against thieves. Monsieur de La Mole has posted a watchman in the garden. Monsieur de Croisenois is surrounded by spies; what he does every night is known. . . ."

"Poor man!" exclaimed Mathilde, and she burst out laughing. Her mother and one of the maids were awake; suddenly questions were addressed to her through the door. Julien looked at her; she turned pale, scolded the maid and did not deign to answer her mother.

"But if it occurs to them to open the window they'll see the ladder!" said Julien.

He embraced her once again, leapt out onto the ladder and slid rather than climbed down it; in a moment he was on the ground.

Three seconds later the ladder was back in its place beneath the linden trees and Mathilde's honor was safe. When Julien recovered his senses he found himself covered with blood and half naked; he had injured himself while precipitously sliding down the ladder.

The intensity of his happiness had restored all the resoluteness of his character: if twenty men had confronted him at that moment, attacking them singlehanded would have been only one more pleasure for him. Fortunately, his martial valor was not put to the test. He put the ladder back in its usual place, fastened the chain again and did not forget to go back and obliterate the marks left by the ladder in the bed of exotic flowers beneath Mathilde's window.

As he was running his hand over the soft earth in the darkness to make sure that the marks were entirely obliterated, he felt something fall on his hands: it was one whole side of Mathilde's hair, which she had cut off and thrown down to him.

She was at her window. "That was sent to you by your servant," she said rather loudly. "It's a token of my eternal obedience. I renounce the use of my reason; be my master."

Julien, overcome, was on the verge of bringing back the ladder and climbing back up to her room. Finally reason prevailed.

Coming back into the house from the garden was not an easy matter. He managed to force open the door of a cellar; once inside the house, he was obliged to break open the door of his room as silently as possible. In his agitation he had left everything behind in the little bedroom he had just abandoned so hastily, even the key that was in the pocket of his coat. "If only she thinks to hide all those mortal remains!" he thought.

Fatigue finally prevailed over happiness, and as the sun rose he sank into a deep sleep.

The luncheon bell had great difficulty in awakening him; he took his place in the dining room. Mathilde entered shortly afterward. For a moment his pride was enraptured when he saw the love shining from the eyes of that beautiful girl who was surrounded by so much homage; but soon his prudence had reason to be alarmed. On the pretext that she had had little time to arrange her hair, Mathilde had combed it in such a way that he could see at first glance the extent of the sacrifice she had made for him by cutting off part of it the night before. If anything could have spoiled such a beautiful face, Mathilde would have succeeded in doing so: one whole side of her lovely ash-blonde hair was cut unevenly to within half an inch of her head.

Her entire conduct during lunch was in keeping with this first rash action. She acted as though she were determined to make everyone aware of her mad passion for Julien. Fortunately, that day Monsieur de La Mole and the marquise were preoccupied with a forthcoming ceremony in which the cordon bleu was to be bestowed on several gentlemen, in whose number Monsieur de Chaulnes was not included. Toward the end of the meal, Mathilde, in speaking to Julien, addressed him as "my master." He blushed to the whites of his eyes.

Whether by chance or by express design on the part of Madame de La Mole, Mathilde was not alone for an instant that day. In the evening, however, as she was going from the dining room into the drawing room, she found an opportunity to say to Julien, "All my plans have been destroyed; I hope you won't think I had anything to do with it. Mother has just decided that one of her maids will sleep in my room every night."

The day went by with the speed of lightning. Julien's happiness was at its peak. By seven o'clock the next morning he was already in the library, hoping that Mademoiselle de La Mole would deign to come there; he had written her an endless letter.

He did not see her until long hours later, at lunch. Her hair was now arranged with the greatest care; the place where it was cut off had been concealed with consummate skill. She looked at him once or twice, but politely and calmly; there was no longer any question of calling him "my master."

Julien's astonishment left him breathless. . . . Mathilde was reproaching herself for nearly everything she had done for him. On sober reflection, she had decided that he was, if not a truly commonplace man, at least one who did not stand out far enough above the common run of humanity to deserve all the strange acts of madness she had dared to commit for him. On the whole, she gave little thought to love; that day she was tired of loving.

As for Julien, the emotions that filled his heart were those of a boy of sixteen. Horrible doubt, bewilderment and despair successively took possession of him during that meal which seemed to last forever.

As soon as he could decently leave the table, he rushed headlong rather than ran to the stable, personally saddled his horse and set off at a gallop; he was afraid he might dishonor himself by some act of weakness. "I must kill the feelings in my heart with physical fatigue," he thought as he galloped through the Bois de Meudon. "What have I done, what could I have said to deserve such disfavor?"

When he came back to the house he said to himself, "I mustn't do or say anything today, I must be as dead physically as I am emotionally. Julien is no longer alive; it's only his corpse that's still moving."

CHAPTER 20
The Japanese Vase

At first his heart does not realize the full intensity of his misery; he is more disconcerted than grieved. But as he gradually recovers the use of his reason, he feels the depth of his misfortune. All the pleasures of life have been destroyed for him, he can feel nothing but the sharp claws of despair tearing at his breast. But why speak of physical pain? What pain felt by the body alone can be compared to this?

—Jean Paul

THE DINNER BELL was ringing; Julien had time only to dress. In the drawing room he found Mathilde, who was pleading with her brother and Monsieur de Croisenois not to go to Suresnes and spend the evening in the house of Madame de Fervaques. It would have been difficult to behave more winsomely and charmingly toward them.

After dinner Messieurs de Luz and de Caylus came in with several of their friends. Along with the cult of sisterly affection, Mademoiselle de La Mole seemed to have resumed that of strict decorum as well. Although the weather was delightful that evening, she refused to go out into the garden; she insisted that everyone stay in the vicinity of the easy chair in which Madame de La Mole was seated. The blue sofa was the center of the group, as in winter.

Mathilde had taken a dislike to the garden, or at least it seemed utterly boring to her: it reminded her of Julien.

Unhappiness dulls the mind. Our hero was foolish enough to stop beside that little straw-bottomed chair which had once witnessed such brilliant triumphs. No one said a word to him that evening; his presence seemed to be unnoticed, or even worse. Those of Mademoiselle de La Mole's friends who were sitting near him, on the end of the sofa, acted almost as though they were deliberately turning their backs on him, or at least so it seemed to him.

"I've lost favor at court," he thought. He decided to study for a moment the people who were attempting to crush him with their disdain.

Monsieur de Luz's uncle held an important post in the king's household; as a result, the handsome officer mentioned the following interesting piece of information at the beginning of his conversation with everyone who came his way: his uncle had set out for Saint-Cloud at seven o'clock and expected to spend the night there. This fact was brought into the conversation in an extremely casual manner, but it never failed to appear.

As he observed Monsieur de Croisenois with the stern eye of unhappiness, Julien noted the enormous influence which that pleasant good-natured young man attributed to occult causes. He went so far as to become gloomy and irritated whenever he saw an event of any importance ascribed to some simple and quite natural cause. "There's a beginning of madness there," thought Julien. "His character is strikingly similar to that of Emperor Alexander, as Prince Korasov described him to me." During his first year in Paris, poor Julien, fresh from the seminary and dazzled by the graces, so new to him, of all those charming young men, had been unable to do anything but admire them. Their true characters were only now beginning to take shape before his eyes.

"I'm playing an unworthy part here," he thought suddenly. He would have to leave his little straw-bottomed chair in a way that would not be too awkward. He tried to think of one, asking an imagination that was totally occupied with other matters to supply him with something new. He had to resort to his memory, which, it must be admitted, was not very rich in resources of that kind. The poor boy still had very little experience of the ways of the world; he was therefore thoroughly and obviously awkward when he stood up to leave the drawing room. His unhappiness was too apparent in his whole manner. For the past three quarters of an hour he had been treated as an importunate inferior from whom one does not take the trouble to hide what one thinks of him.

However, the critical observations he had just been making about his rivals prevented him from taking his misfortune too tragically; and, to bolster his pride, he had the memory of what had happened two nights before. "Whatever their countless advantages over me may be," he thought as he walked out into the garden alone, "Mathilde has never been to any of them what, twice in my life, she's deigned to be to me."

His wisdom went no further. He had no understanding of the character of the singular woman whom chance had made absolute mistress of all his happiness.

The next day he did nothing except tire himself and his horse to death. That evening he made no further attempt to approach the blue sofa, to which Mathilde remained faithful. He noticed that Count Norbert did not deign even to look at him when he met him in the house. "He must be doing terrible violence to himself—he's so polite by nature," thought Julien.

Sleep would have been a boon to him. Despite his physical fatigue, however, seductive memories had begun to invade his imagination. He did not have enough sagacity to see that by taking long horseback rides in the woods around Paris, which affected only himself and not at all Mathilde's heart or mind, he was leaving his fate in the hands of chance.

It seemed to him that only one thing would bring infinite relief to his sorrow: to speak to Mathilde. And yet what would he dare to say to her?

He was deeply pondering this question at seven o'clock one morning when he saw her walk into the library.

"I know, monsieur, that you want to speak to me."

"Good God! Who told you that?"

"I know it, what does it matter to you how I learned it? If you have no honor, you can ruin me, or at least try to; but that danger, which I don't regard as real, won't prevent me from being sincere. I no longer love you, monsieur; I was deceived by my foolish imagination. . . ."

At this terrible blow, Julien, mad with love and pain, tried to vindicate himself. Nothing could have been more absurd. Can one vindicate oneself for failing to please? But reason no longer had any control over his actions. A blind instinct impelled him to delay the deciding of his fate. It seemed to him that as long as he was speaking, everything was not yet finished. Mathilde was not listening to his words, the sound of them irritated her; she could not conceive how he could have the audacity to interrupt her.

The remorse of her virtue and of her pride made her equally unhappy that morning. She was overwhelmed by the horrible thought that she had given certain rights over herself to a little ecclesiastic, a peasant's son. "It's almost," she said to herself at moments when she exaggerated her misfortune, "as if, after dreaming of the strength, the noble qualities and the distinction of the man I'd love, I had to reproach myself for having let myself be led astray by one of the footmen."

For a bold, proud character, it is only one step from anger against oneself to rage against others; in such cases, transports of fury give one keen pleasure. In an instant Mademoiselle de La Mole's feelings rose so high that she overwhelmed Julien with the most vehement expressions of contempt. She had a great deal of intelligence, and this intelligence excelled in the art of torturing the self-esteem of others and wounding it cruelly.

For the first time in his life, Julien found himself under attack by a superior mind animated by the most violent hatred against him. Far from giving any thought to defending himself at that moment, he came to share Mathilde's contempt for him. As he heard her shower him with cruel expressions of scorn, skillfully designed to destroy any good opinion he might have of himself, it seemed to him that she was right and that she was not saying enough.

As for her, her pride took exquisite pleasure in thus punishing him and herself for the adoration she had felt a few days earlier.

She had no need to invent or think for the first time of the cruel things she was saying to him with such satisfaction. She was merely repeating what the advocate of the party opposed to love had been saying to her in her heart for the past week.

Each word increased Julien's horrible misery a hundredfold. He tried to flee, but she gripped his arm with authority.

"Please notice," he said to her, "that you're speaking very loudly; you'll be heard in the next room."

"What does that matter?" she replied proudly. "Who will dare to tell me I've been overheard? I want to cure your petty self-esteem forever of any ideas it may have conceived about me."

When Julien was able to leave the library, he was so amazed that he felt his unhappiness less keenly. "She doesn't love me anymore!" he repeated to himself, speaking aloud as though to teach himself his position. "She apparently loved me for nine or ten days, and I'll love her the rest of my life. Is it possible that only a few days ago she meant nothing, nothing at all to my heart?"

Mathilde's heart was flooded with the joy of victorious pride: she had been able to break with him forever! Such a complete triumph over such a strong inclination made her perfectly happy. "Now that little gentleman will realize, once and for all," she thought, "that he doesn't have any power over me and never will." She was so happy that, at that moment, she really felt no love for him.

After such a terrible, such a humiliating scene, love would have become impossible for a person less passionate than Julien. Without departing for an instant from what she owed to herself, Mademoiselle de La Mole had said to him some of those unpleasant things that are so well calculated that they appear true even when one looks back on them calmly.

The conclusion which Julien drew at the beginning of that amazing scene was that Mathilde's pride was boundless. He was firmly convinced that everything between them was over forever, and yet the next day, at lunch, he was awkward and shy in her presence. This was a fault of which no one could have accused him until then. In little things as well as in great ones, he was clearly aware of both his duties and his desires, and he acted accordingly.

That day, after lunch, Madame de La Mole asked him for a seditious but rather rare pamphlet which her parish priest had secretly brought to her that morning; as Julien was taking it from a console table he overturned an old blue porcelain vase, the ugliest thing imaginable.

Madame de La Mole stood up with a cry of distress and came over to examine the fragments of her cherished vase. "It was old Japanese porcelain," she said; "it came to me from my great-aunt, the Abbess of Chelles; it was a present from the Dutch to the Duke of Orléans during his regency, and he gave it to his daughter. . . ."

Mathilde had followed her mother, delighted to see the end of the blue vase she had considered so hideous. Julien was silent and not too greatly upset; he saw Mademoiselle de La Mole standing close beside him.

"This vase," he said to her, "has been destroyed forever, and the same is true of a feeling that was once master of my heart. Please accept my apologies for all the foolish acts it has made me commit." And he walked out of the rcom.

"One would really think," said Madame de La Mole as he was leaving, "that Monsieur Sorel is proud and happy over what he just did."

This remark went straight to Mathilde's heart. "It's true," she thought. "My mother has guessed rightly: that's really how he feels." Only then did she lose the joy that had been given to her by her scene with him the day before. "Very well, then, it's all over," she said to herself with apparent calm. "I've been left with a great example; my mistake was horrible and humiliating. It will make me wiser for the rest of my life."

"If only I'd been telling the truth!" thought Julien. "Why am I still tormented by the love I feel for that mad girl?"

This love, far from dying down as he hoped, made rapid progress. "She's mad, it's true," he said to himself, "but is she any less adorable for that? Could any girl be prettier than she is?'' Were not all the keen delights that can be offered by the most elegant civilization abundantly united in Mademoiselle de La Mole? These memories of past happiness took possession of Julien and swiftly destroyed all the work of his reason. Reason struggles in vain against memories of this kind; its grim efforts only increase their charm.

Twenty-four hours after breaking the old Japanese vase, Julien was decidedly one of the unhappiest of men.

CHAPTER 21

The Secret Note

For I have seen everything I am relating; and while I may
have been deceived when I saw it, I will certainly not deceive
you in telling you about it.
                              —From a letter to the author

THE MARQUIS sent for him. Monsieur de La Mole seemed younger; his eyes were glowing.

"Let's talk about your memory for a moment," he said to Julien. "I'm told it's phenomenal! Could you learn four pages by heart, then go and repeat them in London, without changing a single word?"

The marquis was irritably crumpling that day's edition of the *Quotidienne* and vainly trying to dissimulate an extremely serious expression which Julien had never seen on his face before, not even when he was concerned with the Frilair lawsuit.

Julien already had enough worldly wisdom to realize that he ought to appear to be completely taken in by the nonchalant tone the marquis had assumed. "This edition of the *Quotidienne* may not be very entertaining," he said, "but, with your permission, monsieur, tomorrow morning I'll have the honor of reciting it to you from beginning to end."

"What! Even the advertisements?"

"With complete accuracy, and without leaving out a single word."

"Will you give me your word on that?" asked the marquis with sudden gravity.

"Yes, monsieur; only the fear of failing to keep it could disturb my memory."

"It's just that I forgot to ask you the question yesterday. I won't ask you to swear never to repeat what you're about to hear; I know you too well to insult you in that way. I've answered for you, and I'm going to take you to a drawing room in which twelve peple will be gathered; you will take notes on what each of them says.

"Don't be alarmed, it won't be a confused conversation; everyone will speak in his turn, although I won't say in an orderly manner," added the marquis, resuming that light, witty tone which was so natural to him. "While we're speaking, you'll write twenty pages or so, then you'll come back here with me and we'll reduce those twenty pages to four. Those four pages will be the ones you'll recite to me tomorrow morning, instead of the entire *Quotidienne*. You'll leave immediately afterward. You must travel post like a young man making a journey for his own amusement. Your aim will be to pass unnoticed by everyone. You'll go to see a very important person. There you'll need more skill. You'll have to deceive everyone around him, because among his secretaries and servants are men who are in the pay of our enemies and who watch for our agents in order to intercept them.

"You'll have an insignificant letter of introduction. When His Excellency looks at you, take out this watch of mine, which I'm lending you for the journey. You may as well take it now, and give me yours.

"The duke himself will write down at your dictation the four pages you'll have learned by heart. When that's been done, but not before, mind you, you may, if His Excellency questions you, tell him about the meeting you're going to attend.

"There's one thing that will keep you from being bored during the journey: between Paris and the minister's residence, there are people who would like nothing better than to fire a shot at Abbé Sorel. In that case, his mission would come to an end and I'd see a long delay, because, my friend, how could we learn of your death? Your zeal couldn't go so far as to send us an announcement of it.

"Hurry off right now and buy yourself a complete suit of clothes," the marquis continued with a serious expression. "Dress yourself in the style of two years ago. You must look rather carelessly dressed this evening. During the journey, however, you will dress as usual. Does that surprise you? Has your suspicious mind guessed the reason? Yes, my friend, one of the venerable personages whom you're going to hear expressing his opinions this evening is quite capable of sending ahead information by means of which it may be possible for someone to give you at least a dose of opium in some good inn where you'll have ordered supper.''

"It would be better,'' said Julien, "to travel thirty leagues farther and avoid the direct route. It's a question of Rome, I imagine. . . .''

The marquis assumed an expression of haughty dissatisfaction which Julien had not seen him wear so noticeably since Bray-le-Haut. "You'll learn about that, monsieur, when I see fit to tell you,'' he said. "I don't like questions.''

"That wasn't a question,'' said Julien effusively, "I swear it wasn't, monsieur; I was thinking aloud, trying to decide in my own mind what the safest route would be.''

"Yes, it seems that your mind was very far away. Never forget that an emissary, especially one your age, must never appear to force the confidence that's shown in him.''

Julien felt deeply mortified; he was in the wrong. His self-esteem sought an excuse and could not find one.

"You must realize,'' added Monsieur de La Mole, "that a man always appeals to his heart when he's done something foolish.''

An hour later Julien was in the marquis' antechamber wearing a shabby outfit: his suit was ancient, his tie was doubtfully white and there was something boorish about his entire appearance.

When he saw him, the marquis burst out laughing, and it was only then that Julien was completely vindicated.

"If this young man betrays me,'' thought Monsieur de La Mole, "whom can I trust? And yet when one acts, one must trust someone. My son and his distinguished friends of the same stamp have enough courage and loyalty for a hundred thousand others. If it came to fighting, they'd perish on the steps of the throne; they know how to do everything—except what's needed right now. May the devil take me if I can think of a single one of them who's capable of learning four pages by heart and traveling a hundred leagues without being tracked down. Norbert could get himself killed like his ancestors, but that's also the merit of a conscript. . . .''

The marquis sank into a deep reverie. "And even getting himself killed—perhaps Sorel could do that as well as Norbert,'' he thought.

"Let's get into the carriage,'' he said, as though to drive away an unwelcome thought.

"Monsieur,'' said Julien, "while this coat was being altered for me I learned the first page of today's *Quotidienne* by heart.''

The marquis took the newspaper. Julien recited without missing a single word. ''Good,'' thought the marquis, who was feeling very diplomatic that evening; ''in the meantime the young man isn't noticing what streets we're traveling along.''

They arrived in a large and rather gloomy-looking drawing room, partly paneled and partly hung with green velvet. In the middle of the room, a sullen footman was setting up a large dinner table, which he later converted into a conference table by means of an immense green cloth covered with inkstains, a relic of some ministry office.

The master of the house was an enormous man whose name was not mentioned; he impressed Julien as having the expression and the eloquence of a man who is digesting a good meal.

At a sign from the marquis, Julien had remained at the lower end of the table. In order not to appear awkward, he began to sharpen some quills. Out of the corner of his eye he counted seven men, but he could see only their backs. Two of them seemed to be speaking to Monsieur de La Mole on terms of equality; the others seemed more or less deferential.

Another man came in without being announced. ''That's strange,'' thought Julien; ''no one is announced in this drawing room. Can that precaution have been taken in my honor?'' Everyone stood up to greet the newcomer. He wore the same extremely distinguished decoration as three of the other men who were already in the room. They spoke rather softly. In judging the newcomer, Julien had to be content with what he could deduce from his features and his general appearance. He was short and stocky, with a ruddy complexion and glowing eyes which reavealed nothing except the viciousness of a wild boar.

Julien's attention was abruptly distracted by the almost immediate arrival of a very different kind of man. He was tall and very thin, and he was wearing three or four vests. His eyes were kind, his gestures polished. ''He looks exactly like the Bishop of Besançon,'' thought Julien. The man was obviously an ecclesiastic; he did not appear to be more than fifty or fifty-five. No one could have looked more fatherly.

The young Bishop of Agde appeared; he seemed to be greatly surprised when, looking around at those present in the room, his eyes fell on Julien. He had not spoken to him since the ceremony at Bray-le-Haut. His look of surprise embarrassed and irritated Julien. ''What!'' he thought. ''Will knowing a man always turn out to be a misfortune for me? I'm not the least bit intimidated by all these great noblemen whom I've never seen before, but this young bishop's glance chills my heart! No one can deny that I'm a very strange and unfortunate man."

An extremely dark little man made a noisy entrance and began to speak from the moment he appeared in the doorway; he had a sallow complexion and looked somewhat mad. As soon as this relentless talker arrived, the others began to form into groups, apparently to avoid the boredom of listening to him.

As they moved farther away from the fireplace, they came nearer to the lower end of the table, where Julien was sitting. His expression became more and more embarrassed, for, after all, no matter how hard he tried, he could not avoid hearing them and, however limited his experience might be, he realized all the importance of the things they were discussing without any attempt at concealment, and how anxious the apparently great personages standing before him must be to have such things remain secret!

Already, working as slowly as possible, Julien had sharpened at least twenty quills; this resource was now about to fail him. He looked in vain for an order in Monsieur de La Mole's eyes; the marquis had forgotten him.

"What I'm doing is ridiculous," thought Julien as he sharpened his quills, "but such mediocre-looking men who have been entrusted with such important matters, either by others or by themselves, must be very sensitive. There's something inquisitive and not very respectful in my unfortunate way of looking at people, and they'd no doubt be offended by it; but if I definitely lower my eyes, I'll look as though I'm trying not to miss anything they say."

His embarrassment was intense; he was hearing extraordinary things.

CHAPTER 22
The Discussion

> The Republic—today, for every man who would sacrifice everything for the common welfare, there are thousands, millions of others who acknowledge nothing except their pleasures and their vanity. In Paris, a man is respected for his carriage, not for his virtue.
>
> —Napoleon: *Mémorial*

THE FOOTMAN hurried into the room, announcing: "His Grace, the Duke of ———."

"Hold your tongue, you fool!" said the duke as he entered. He spoke these words so well and with such majesty that Julien thought that knowing how to express anger with a footman must be the sum total of this great personage's knowledge. Julien raised his eyes and lowered them immediately. He had so fully guessed the newcomer's importance that he was afraid his glance might be an indiscretion.

The duke was a man of fifty who dressed like a dandy and walked with a springy step. He had a narrow head, a large nose and a face that jutted forward in downward curves. It would have been difficult for anyone to look either nobler or more insignificant. His arrival was a signal for the meeting to begin.

Julien's physiognomical observations were abruptly interrupted by the voice of Monsieur de La Mole. "Allow me to present Abbé Sorel," he said. "He's gifted with an amazing memory; it was only an hour ago that I spoke to him about the mission with which he might be honored, and, in order to give me proof of his memory, he learned the entire first page of the *Quotidienne* by heart."

"Ah! The reports from abroad by that poor N———," said the master of the house. He eagerly took the newspaper, looked at Julien with an expression that was comical in its attempt to appear important and said to him, "Go ahead, monsieur."

The silence was unbroken and all eyes were fixed on Julien; he recited so well that after twenty lines the duke said, "That's enough." The little man with the look of a wild boar sat down. He was the chairman, for as soon as he was seated he pointed out a card table to Julien and motioned him to place it beside him. Julien sat down at it with all his writing materials. He counted twelve men seated around the green cloth.

"Monsieur Sorel," said the duke, "go into the next room; we'll send for you later."

The master of the house took on a worried expression. "The shutters aren't closed," he said to the man beside him. Then he stupidly called out to Julien, "There's no need to look out the window."

"I've been dragged into a conspiracy, at the very least," thought Julien. "Fortunately it's not the kind that leads to the Place de Grève. Even if there were danger in it, I owe that much to the marquis, and more. I'd be glad to have a chance to make up for all the sorrow my folly may cause him some day!"

As he was thinking of his folly and of his unhappiness, he looked at his surroundings in such a way that he would never forget them. Only then did he recall that he had not heard the marquis tell the footman the name of the street, and that the marquis had sent for a cabriolet, something he had never done before.

Julien was left to his reflections for a long time. He was in a room hung with red velvet decorated with wide gold braid. There was a large ivory crucifix on the console table, and on the mantelpiece a copy of Monsieur de Maistre's book, *Du Pape*, gilt-edged and magnificently bound. He opened it in order not to appear to be listening. From time to time the voices became loud in the next room. Finally the door opened and he was summoned.

"Remember, gentlemen," said the chairman, "that from now on we are speaking before the Duke of ————. This gentleman," he said, pointing to Julien, "is a young ecclesiastic who is devoted to our sacred cause and who, with the aid of his astonishing memory, will easily repeat every word we say.

"I yield the floor to this gentleman," he said, indicating the man with the fatherly expression, who was wearing three or four vests. Julien felt that it would have been more natural to name the gentleman with the vests. He took some paper and wrote at great length.

(At this point the author would have liked to insert a page of asterisks. "That would be in bad taste," says the publisher, "and for such a frivolous book a lack of good taste means death."

"Politics," replies the author, "is a stone tied to the neck of literature which will submerge it in less than six months. Politics in the middle of things of the imagination is like a pistol shot in the middle of a concert. The noise is loud without being forceful. It isn't in harmony with the sound of any instrument. This political discussion will mortally offend half my readers and bore the others, who have found a much more precise and vigorous account of such matters in their morning newspapers. . . ."

"If your characters don't talk politics," says the publisher, "they'll no longer be Frenchmen of 1830, and your book will no longer be a mirror, as you claim it to be. . . .")

Julien's written report covered twenty-six pages. Here is a very colorless condensation of it, for, as always, I have had to eliminate the absurdities, whose abundance would have seemed either offensive or scarcely plausible. (See the *Gazette des Tribunaux*.)

The man with the vests and the fatherly expression (he may have been a bishop) smiled often, and when he did so, his eyes, encircled by fluttering eyelids, took on a strange gleam and an expression that was less irresolute than usual. This personage, who was asked to speak first in the presence of the duke ("But what duke?" wondered Julien), apparently in order to state the various opinions and perform the functions of a solicitor general, seemed to Julien to fall into the uncertainty and lack of clear conclusions for which these magistrates are so often reproached. In the course of the discussion, the duke actually did reproach him for it.

After several sentences of moralizing and indulgent philosophy, the man with the vests said, "Noble England, guided by a great man, the immortal Pitt, spent forty billion francs to defeat the Revolution. If this assembly will allow me to broach a melancholy subject with a certain frankness, England did not sufficiently understand that, with a man like Bonaparte, especially when there was nothing with which to oppose him except a set of good intentions, personal means were the only decisive ones that could be employed. . . ."

"Ah! More praise of assassination!" said the master of the house with a worried expression.

"Spare us your sentimental homilies!" exclaimed the chairman angrily, his wild boar's eyes gleaming ferociously. "Go on," he said to the man with the vests. The chairman's cheeks and forehead turned purple.

"Noble England," continued the speaker, "is crushed today because every Englishman, before paying for his daily bread, is obliged to pay the interest on the forty billion francs that were used against the Jacobins. They no longer have a Pitt. . . ."

"They have the Duke of Wellington," said a military personage, assuming an air of great self-importance.

"Please, gentlemen, silence!" cried the chairman. "If we go on quarreling it will have been useless to bring in Monsieur Sorel."

"We all know the gentleman is full of ideas," said the duke irritably, looking at the interrupter, a former general under Napoleon. Julien saw that this remark was an allusion to something personal and highly offensive. Everyone smiled; the turncoat general appeared to be beside himself with rage.

"There is no longer a Pitt, gentlemen," continued the speaker with the discouraged air of a man who despairs of making his hearers listen to reason. "And even if there were a new Pitt in

England, a nation cannot be deceived twice by the same means. . . ."

"That's why a conquering general, a Bonaparte, is impossible in France from now on!" cried the military interrupter.

This time neither the chairman nor the duke dared to show anger, although Julien thought he could see in their eyes a strong desire to do so. They lowered their eyes, and the duke contented himself with sighing in such a way that he could be heard by everyone.

But the speaker had lost his temper. "Some of you are impatient for me to finish," he said heatedly, completely discarding the smiling courtesy and measured speech which Julien had believed to be the natural expression of his character. "Some of you are impatient for me to finish; you give me no credit for the efforts I'm making not to offend anyone's ears, no matter how long they may be. Well, gentlemen, I'll be brief.

"And I'll tell you in very plain words: England no longer has one single penny to use for the good cause. If Pitt himself were to come back, even with his genius he wouldn't be able to deceive the small landowners of England, because they know that the short campaign of Waterloo alone cost them a billion francs. Since you want blunt statements," added the speaker, growing more and more animated, "I'll say to you, *Help yourselves*, because England doesn't have one guinea to help you with, and when England doesn't pay, Austria, Russia and Prussia, who have only courage and no money, can carry out only one or two campaigns against France.

"One can hope that the young soldiers brought together by Jacobinism will be beaten in the first campaign, and in the second, perhaps; but in the third—even if I must pass for a revolutionary in your prejudiced eyes—in the third, you'll have the soldiers of 1794, who were no longer the regimented peasants of 1792."

At this point there were interruptions from several different directions at once.

"Monsieur," said the chairman to Julien, "go into the next room and make a neat copy of the beginning of the report you've written." Julien left with great regret. The speaker had just begun to discuss possibilities that were the usual subject of his meditations. "They're afraid I'll laugh at them," he thought.

When he was called back into the room, Monsieur de La Mole was saying, with a seriousness which, to Julien, who knew him, seemed quite comical:

" . . . Yes, gentlemen, it is especially of this unfortunate people that one may ask, 'Will it be a god, a table or a basin?'

" 'It will be a god!' cries the fabulist. It is to you, gentlemen, that this profound and noble sentence seems to apply. Act for yourselves, and noble France will once again appear nearly the same as our ancestors made her, and as we ourselves still saw her before the death of Louis XVI.

"England, or her noble lords at least, abhors our ignoble Jacobinism as much as we do; without English gold, Austria, Russia and Prussia can fight only two or three battles. Will that be enough to bring about a beneficent occupation, like the one Monsieur de Richelieu so stupidly threw away in 1817? I do not think so."

Here there was an interruption, but it was drowned in hisses from all sides. It had come once again from the former imperial general, who wanted a cordon bleu and wished to have an outstanding position among those who were drawing up the secret note.

"I do not think so," repeated Monsieur de La Mole after the tumult had died down. He emphasized the "I" with an insolence that delighted Julien. "That was a good stroke," thought the latter as he made his pen fly almost as fast as the marquis' words. "With one well-said word, Monsieur de La Mole has wiped out that turncoat's twenty campaigns."

"It is not on foreigners alone," went on the marquis in the most measured tones, "that we may depend for a new military occupation. All those young men who write incendiary articles in the *Globe* will provide you with three or four thousand young captains, among whom there may be a Kléber, a Hoche, a Jourdan or a Pichegru, though not so well-intentioned."

"We failed to honor him," said the chairman. "We should have kept his memory immortal."

"There must be two parties in France," continued Monsieur de La Mole, "but not in name only: we must have two parties clearly defined and sharply divided. Let us know whom we have to crush. On the one hand, the journalists, the electors, public opinion—in a word, youth and all those who admire it. While they stupefy themselves with the sound of their empty words, we have the undeniable advantage of consuming the budget."

Here there was another interruption.

"You, monsieur," said Monsieur de La Mole to the interrupter with admirable haughtiness and ease, "you don't consume, if the word offends you, you devour forty thousand francs set aside for you in the state budget and eighty thousand which you receive from the civil list.

"Very well, monsieur, since you force me into it, I'll boldly take you as an example. Like your noble ancestors who went off to the Crusades with Saint Louis, you ought, for those hundred twenty thousand francs, to show us at least a regiment, a company, or let's say half a company, even if it were made up of only fifty men ready to fight and so strongly devoted to the good cause that they're willing to die for it. You have only servants of whom you yourself would be afraid if there were an uprising.

"The throne, the altar and the nobility may perish any day, gentlemen, as long as you haven't created in each department a force of five hundred *devoted* men; but I mean devoted, not only with all the valor of the French, but also with the constancy of the Spanish.

"Half of this force must be composed of our children, our nephews; of true noblemen, in short. Each of them will have at his side, not some chattering little townsman ready to raise aloft the tricolor cockade if 1815 should return, but a good, simple, straightforward peasant, like Cathelineau. Our nobleman will have indoctrinated him; if possible, they should have been suckled by the same wet nurse. Let each of us sacrifice *one fifth* of his income to form that devoted little troop of five hundred men in each department; then you may count on a foreign occupation. Foreign soldiers will never penetrate even as far as Dijon unless they're sure of finding five hundred comrades-in-arms in each department.

"Foreign kings will listen to you only when you inform them that there are twenty thousand noblemen ready to take up arms to open the gates of France to them. This service, you say, is painful; gentlemen, it is the price we must pay for our lives. Between freedom of the press and our existence as noblemen, there is a war to the death. Either become manufacturers and peasants, or take up your guns. Be timorous if you will, but not stupid; open your eyes.

"*Form your batallions,* I say to you, in the words of the Jacobin song; then there will arise some noble Gustavus Adolphus who, moved by the imminent danger to the monarchical principle, will swiftly advance three hundred leagues beyond his own country and do for you what Gustavus did for the Protestant princes. Will you go on talking without acting? In fifty years there will be nothing in Europe but presidents and republics, and not a single king. And along with those four letters, K-I-N-G, the priests and the noblemen will also disappear. I see only *candidates* currying favor with unwashed *majorities*.

"It is useless for you to say that at this moment France does not have one general of good standing, known and loved by all, that the army is organized only to serve the interests of the throne and the altar, that all its seasoned veterans have been discharged, while each Prussian and Austrian regiment has fifty noncommissioned officers who have been under fire. Two hundred thousand young men of the lower middle classes are passionately eager for war. . . ."

"We've heard enough unpleasant truths," said, in a tone of self-importance, a grave personage who apparently occupied a high position in the ecclesiastical hierarchy, for Monsieur de La Mole smiled pleasantly instead of showing irritation, which was a clear sign to Julien. "We've heard enough unpleasant truths, gentlemen; let's sum up: the man who has to have his gangrenous leg amputated would be foolish to say to his surgeon, 'This diseased leg is perfectly sound.' Forgive me the expression, gentlemen: the noble Duke of ——— is our surgeon."

"There, it's been said at last!" thought Julien. "It's toward ——— that I'll be galloping tonight."

CHAPTER 23

The Clergy, Woodlands and Freedom

> The first law of every creature is that of self-preservation, of staying alive. You sow hemlock and expect to see ripening ears of grain!
>
> —Machiavelli

THE GRAVE personage continued to speak; it was easy to see that he knew his subject. With gentle, measured eloquence, which pleased Julien immensely, he put forward the following great truths:

"First of all, England does not have one guinea to spend for us; economy and Hume are the fashion there. Not even the *Saints* will give us any money, and Mr. Brougham will only laugh at us.

"Secondly, without English gold it is impossible to obtain more than two campaigns from the kings of Europe; and two campaigns will not be enough against the lower middle classes.

"Thirdly, it is necessary to form an armed party in France, because otherwise the monarchical principle in Europe will not risk even those two campaigns.

"The fourth point which I venture to set before you as self-evident is this: *It is impossible to form an armed party in France without the clergy.* I say it to you boldly, gentlemen, because I am going to prove it to you. We must give the clergy everything. First, because, pursuing their own affairs day and night, and guided by men of great ability who are established far beyond the storms, three hundred leagues from your frontiers . . ."

"Ah! Rome! Rome!" cried the master of the house.

"That's right, monsieur: *Rome*!" retorted the cardinal proudly. "Whatever more or less ingenious jests may have been current in your youth, I say boldly, in 1830, that the clergy, guided by Rome, are the only people to whom the lower classes listen.

"Fifty thousand priests repeat the same words on the day designated by their leaders, and the common people, who, after all, provide the soldiers, will be more deeply moved by the voices of their priests than by all the little poems in the world." (This personal thrust provoked some murmurs.)

"The clergy are more clear-sighted than you," continued the cardinal, raising his voice. "We have been responsible for every step you've taken toward that all-important goal: *to have an armed party in France.*" At this point he brought forward facts: "Who was it that sent eighty thousand rifles to Vendée," etc., etc.

"As long as the clergy are deprived of their woodlands, they possess nothing. As soon as a war breaks out, the minister of finance writes to his agents that no one has any money except the priests. At heart, France is irreligious and loves war. Whoever gives it to her will be doubly popular, because waging war means starving the Jesuits, to speak like the vulgar herd; waging war means delivering those monsters of pride, the French, from the threat of foreign intervention."

The cardinal's audience listened with approval. . . . "Monsieur de Nerval ought to leave the ministry," he said. "His name is a source of needless irritation."

At these words, everyone stood up and began to speak at once. "They're going to send me out again," thought Julien; but even the wise chairman had forgotten his presence and his existence.

All eyes turned toward a man whom Julien recognized. It was Monsieur de Nerval, the chief minister, whom he had seen at the Duc de Retz's ball.

"The tumult was at its height," as the newspapers say when speaking of the Chamber. At the end of a good quarter of an hour there was comparative silence again.

Then Monsieur de Nerval stood up, assuming the air of an apostle. "I will not declare to you," he said in a strange voice, "that my office means nothing to me. It has been pointed out to me, gentlemen, that my name doubles the strength of the Jacobins by turning moderates against us. I would therefore willingly resign; but the ways of the Lord are visible only to a few. Also," he added, looking directly at the cardinal, "I have a mission. Heaven has said to me, 'You shall either bring your head to the scaffold or re-establish absolute monarchy in France and reduce the Chambers to what Parliament was under Louis XIV.' And that, gentlemen, *I will do.*"

He stopped speaking and sat down. There was deep silence.

"There's a good actor," thought Julien. As usual, he made the mistake of attributing too much intelligence to other people. Animated by the debates of such a lively evening, and especially by the sincerity of the discussion, at that moment Monsieur de Nerval believed in his mission. He had great courage, but no common sense.

Midnight struck during the silence that followed the noble words, "That, gentlemen, *I will do.*" Julien found that there was something impressive and funereal about the sound of the clock. He was deeply moved.

The discussion soon began again with increasing energy and, above all, incredible naïveté. "These men will have me poisoned," thought Julien at certain moments. "How can they say such things before a plebian?"

Two o'clock struck, and they were still talking. The master of the house had long since gone to sleep; Monsieur de La Mole was obliged to ring to have fresh candles brought in. Monsieur de Nerval, the minister, had left at a quarter to two, not without having frequently studied Julien's face in a mirror that was beside him. His departure seemed to put everyone at ease.

"God only knows what that man will say to the king!" whispered the man with the vests to his neighbors while the candles were being changed. "He can make us look ridiculous and ruin our future. You must admit he showed rare conceit, and even impudence, in coming here tonight. He used to come here before he became a minister, but a portfolio changes everything; it overshadows all a man's other interests. He should have realized that."

As soon as the minister was gone, Bonaparte's general had shut his eyes. He now spoke for a time of his health and his wounds, then looked at his watch and left.

"I'll wager," said the man with the vests, "that the general is running after the minister; he'll apologize for having been here and claim he has us under his thumb."

When the servants, who were half asleep, had finished changing the candles, the chairman said, "Let us now begin to deliberate, gentlemen; let us stop trying to convince one another. Let us consider the terms of the note that will be before the eyes of our friends abroad in forty-eight hours. We have spoken of ministers; now that Monsieur de Nerval has left us, we can say: What do we care about ministers? We shall impose our will on them."

The cardinal approved with a subtle smile.

"Nothing could be easier, it seems to me, than to sum up our position," said the young Bishop of Agde with the concentrated and controlled passion of the most ardent fanaticism. He had remained silent until then. His eyes, which Julien had been observing, were gentle and calm at first but they had begun to blaze after the first hour of discussion. Now his heart overflowed like lava from Vesuvius.

"Between 1806 and 1814," he said, "England made only one mistake: that of not dealing directly and personally with Napoleon. As soon as that man had created dukes and chamberlains, as soon as he had restored the throne, the mission with which God had entrusted him was accomplished; he was ready to be destroyed. The Holy Scriptures teach us in more than one passage how to put an end to tyrants." (Here followed a number of Latin quotations.)

"Today, gentlemen, it is not a man who must be destroyed: it is Paris. All France copies Paris. What would be the use of arming your five hundred men in each department? It would be a hazardous and endless task. Why involve France in something that concerns only Paris? Paris alone, with her newspapers and her drawing rooms, has done the damage. This modern Babylon must perish.

"There must be decisive action to put an end to the conflict between Paris and the Church. This drastic solution will even further the worldly interests of the monarchy. Why did Paris scarcely dare to breathe under Bonaparte? Ask the canon of Saint-Roche. . . ."

*   *   *

It was not until three o'clock in the morning that Julien left with Monsieur de La Mole.

The marquis was weary and ashamed. For the first time, there was a note of pleading in his voice as he spoke to Julien. He asked him to swear never to reveal the excesses of zeal (these were his own words) which he had happened to witness. "Don't mention them to our friend abroad," he said, "unless he seriously insists on knowing something about our young lunatics. What do they care if the government is overthrown? They'll become cardinals and take refuge in Rome. As for us, in our châteaux, we'll be massacred by the peasants."

The secret note which the marquis drew up from Julien's long twenty-four-page report was not ready until a quarter to five.

"I'm tired to death," said the marquis, "and this note shows it; it's not very clear toward the end. I'm more dissatisfied with it than with anything else I've ever done in my life. All right, my friend," he added, "go get a few hours' rest, and, in case there should be an attempt to kidnap you, I'll lock you in your room."

The next day, the marquis took Julien to an isolated château outside Paris, where they found a group of singular individuals whom Julien judged to be priests. He was given a passport which bore an assumed name but indicated at last the true destination of his journey, which he had so far pretended not to know. He climbed into a carriage alone.

The marquis had no misgivings about his memory: Julien had recited the secret note for him several times; but he was greatly afraid he might be intercepted.

"Be sure to give the impression that you're only a young fop traveling to kill time," he said to him in a friendly tone as he was leaving the drawing room. "There may have been more than one traitor at our meeting last night."

The journey was swift and rather sad. Almost by the time he was out of sight of the marquis, Julien had forgotten all about the secret note and his mission and was thinking only of Mathilde's contempt.

In a village a few leagues beyond Metz, the postmaster came out to tell him that there were no more horses. It was ten o'clock at night; Julien, highly annoyed, ordered supper. He strolled back and forth in front of the door, then gradually passed unnoticed into the stableyard. He saw no horses there. "Just the same, that man was acting strangely," he thought. "His boorish eyes were examining me."

He was beginning, as one can see, not to believe everything

that was said to him. He was thinking of slipping away after supper and, in order to learn something about the countryside at any rate, he left his room and went to warm himself at the kitchen fire. What was his joy when he saw Signor Geronimo, the famous singer!

Ensconced in an armchair which he had had placed near the fire, the Neapolitan was groaning loudly and talking more, all by himself, than the twenty gaping German peasants around him.

"These people are ruining me!" he cried out to Julien. "I've promised to sing in Mainz tomorrow. Seven sovereign princes have gathered there to hear me. But let's go outside for a breath of air," he added, with a significant look.

When he had gone a hundred paces down the road and was well out of earshot he said to Julien, "Do you know what's going on? The postmaster here is a scoundrel. As I was strolling around I gave a franc to a little rascal and he told me everything. There are more than a dozen horses in a stable at the other end of the village. Somebody wants to delay a certain courier."

"Really?" said Julien with an innocent expression.

Discovering the trick was not everything: they still had to leave; but Geronimo and his friend could not manage to do so. "Let's wait till daylight," the singer said finally; "they're suspicious of us. It may be you or me they're after. Tomorrow morning we'll order a good breakfast; while it's being prepared, we'll go out for a walk, make our escape, hire some horses and go on to the next post house."

"But what about your baggage?" asked Julien, thinking that perhaps Geronimo himself had been sent to intercept him. It was time to have supper and go to bed. Julien was still in his first sleep when he was awakened with a start by the voices of two people who were talking in his room without taking any great pains to keep from being heard.

He recognized the postmaster, who was holding a shaded lantern. The light was directed toward the carriage trunk, which Julien had had brought up to his room. Beside the postmaster stood a man who was calmly rummaging in the open trunk. Julien could see only the sleeves of his coat, which were black and very tight.

"It's a cassock," he thought, and he quietly gripped the two small pistols he had placed under his pillow.

"Don't worry about waking him up, father," said the postmaster. "They were given some of that wine you prepared yourself."

"I can't find any trace of papers," replied the priest. "A great deal of linen, oils, pomades and other trifles; he's a young man of the world, occupied with his pleasures. The messenger must be the other one, the one who pretends to have an Italian accent."

The two men came closer to Julien to search the pockets of his traveling coat. He was strongly tempted to kill them as thieves. There would certainly be no dangerous consequences. He longed to do it. "I'd be a fool," he said to himself. "I'd be endangering my mission."

"He's no diplomat," said the priest after the coat had been searched. He moved away, fortunately for him.

"If he touches me in my bed, it will be too bad for him," thought Julien. "He may very well come over and try to stab me; I certainly won't let him do that."

The priest turned his head; Julien half opened his eyes. He was astounded: it was Father Castanède! As a matter of fact, although the two men tried to speak rather softly, he had thought from the beginning that he recognized one of the voices. He was seized with an overwhelming desire to rid the world of one of its vilest scoundrels. . . . "But I must remember my mission!" he said to himself.

The priest and his acolyte left the room. A quarter of an hour later, Julien pretended to wake up. He called out and woke up the whole house.

"I've been poisoned!" he cried. "I'm in horrible pain!" He wanted a pretext for going to Geronimo's aid. He found him unconscious from the laudanum that had been put into his wine.

At supper, fearing some trick of this kind, Julien had drunk only some chocolate he had brought with him from Paris. He could not manage to awaken Geronimo enough to make him decide to leave.

"If I were offered the whole kingdom of Naples," said the singer, "I wouldn't give up the exquisite pleasure of sleeping now."

"But what about the seven sovereign princes?"

"Let them wait."

Julien set off alone and reached the house of the great personage without further incident. He wasted an entire morning in unsuccessfully soliciting an interview. Fortunately, toward four o'clock, the duke decided to go out for some fresh air. Julien saw him leave the house on foot, and he did not hesitate to approach him and ask him for alms. When he was a few feet away from the great personage, he took out the Marquis de La Mole's watch and pointedly showed it to him. "Follow me at a distance," said the duke, without looking at him.

After they had walked a quarter of a league, the duke abruptly entered a small coffeehouse. It was in a bedroom of this sordid inn that Julien had the honor of reciting his four pages to the duke. "Begin again, and go more slowly," he was told when he had finished.

The duke took notes. "Go to the next post house on foot," he told Julien. "Leave your baggage and your carriage here. Go to Strasbourg as best you can, and on the twenty-second of this month" (it was then the tenth) "be in this same coffeehouse at half-past twelve. Stay here for half an hour. Keep silence!"

These were the only words that Julien heard. They were enough to fill him with the deepest admiration. "That's how affairs ought to be handled," he thought. "What would this great statesman say if he'd heard those frenzied chatterboxes three days ago?"

Julien took two days to reach Strasbourg. It seemed to him that there was nothing for him to do there. He took a long detour. "If that devilish Father Castanède recognized me," he thought, "he's not the kind of man who'll be easily thrown off the track. . . . And what pleasure it would give him to make a fool of me and defeat my mission!"

Father Castanède, head of the secret agents of the *Congré-gation* along the entire northern frontier, had fortunately not recognized him. And the Jesuits of Strasbourg, although extremely zealous, had no thought of keeping an eye on Julien, who, with his decoration and his blue frock coat, looked like a young soldier deeply concerned with his personal appearance.

CHAPTER 24
Strasbourg

Infatuation! You have all the intensity of love, all its capacity for feeling sorrow. Only its enchanting pleasures and sweet delights are beyond your sphere. I could not say, as I watched her sleeping, "She is all mine, with her angelic beauty and her sweet frailties! There she lies, delivered into my power just as heaven made her, in its mercy, to enchant a man's heart."

—Schiller

FORCED TO spend a week in Strasbourg, Julien sought to distract himself with thoughts of military glory and devotion to his country. Was he therefore in love? He had no idea; he knew only in his tormented heart that Mathilde was the absolute mistress of his happiness as well as his imagination. He needed all the strength of his character to keep himself from sinking into despair. It was beyond his power to think of anything that had no connection with Mademoiselle de La Mole. Ambition and petty triumphs of vanity had once distracted him from the feelings Madame de Rênal had aroused in him. Mathilde had absorbed everything: he found her everywhere in his future.

He foresaw failure on all sides in this future. The same young man whom we saw so presumptuous and proud in Verrières had now fallen into an excess of ridiculous modesty.

Three days earlier, he could have killed Father Castanède with pleasure; now, in Strasbourg, if a child had picked a quarrel with him, he would have felt that the child was in the right. In thinking back on the adversaries and enemies he had encountered in his life, he found that he had always been in the wrong.

This was because he now had as an implacable enemy that powerful imagination which had formerly been constantly employed in depicting brilliant successes for him in the future.

The utter solitude of a traveler's life strengthened the domination of that dark imagination. What a treasure a friend would have been! "But," thought Julien, "is there a single heart that beats for me? And even if I had a friend, wouldn't honor command me to keep eternal silence?"

He was sadly riding through the countryside around Kehl, a small market town on the banks of the Rhine, immortalized by Desaix and Gouvion Saint-Cyr. A German peasant was pointing out to him the narrow streams, the roads and the little islands in the Rhine which the courage of these great generals had made famous. Guiding his horse with his left hand, Julien held spread out in his right the magnificent map which adorns the first edition of Marshal Saint-Cyr's memoirs. A merry shout made him raise his head.

It was Prince Korasov, his London friend who, several months earlier, had revealed to him the first principles of elegant fatuity. Faithful to this great art, Korasov, who, having arrived in Strasbourg the day before, had spent only the past hour in Kehl and had never in his life read a single line about the siege of 1796, began to explain it all to Julien. The German peasant looked at him in amazement, for he knew enough French to understand the gross misstatements the prince was making. Julien's mind was a thousand leagues away from what the peasant was thinking; he looked at the handsome young man in astonishment, admiring the graceful way he rode his horse.

"What a fortunate character he has!" he thought. "How well his trousers fit, how elegantly his hair is cut! Alas, if I'd been like that, she might not have taken a dislike to me after loving me for three days!"

When the prince had finished his siege of Kehl he said to Julien, "You look like a Trappist monk; you're exaggerating the principle of gravity I taught you in London. A gloomy expression is never in good taste: it's a bored expression that's needed. If you're sad, then there must be something you lack, something in which you've failed. *That's an admission of inferiority.* If you're bored, on the other hand, it's whatever or whoever has vainly tried to please you that's inferior. You must realize, my friend, what a serious mistake you're making."

Julien threw a coin to the peasant, who was listening to them open-mouthed.

"Good!" said the prince. "You did that with grace, with noble disdain! Very good!" And he spurred his horse to a gallop. Julien followed him in dazed admiration.

"Ah!" he thought, "if I'd been like that, she wouldn't have preferred Croisenois to me!" The more his reason was shocked by the prince's absurdities, the more he despised himself for not admiring them and regarded himself as unfortunate in not having them. "That's the way I ought to be," he thought. Self-contempt can go no further.

The prince found him decidedly melancholy. "Look here, my friend," he said to him as they returned to Strasbourg, "you're positively ill-mannered. Have you lost all your money, or can it be that you're in love with some little actress?"

The Russians imitate French ways, but they are always fifty years behind. They have now reached the time of Louis XV.

This jest about love brought tears to Julien's eyes. "Why shouldn't I consult this amiable man?" he said to himself suddenly.

"Yes, you're right, my friend," he said to the prince. "You've found me in Strasbourg very much in love—a forsaken lover, in fact. A charming woman, who lives in a town near here, has jilted me after three days of passion, and the change is killing me." Using fictitious names, he described Mathilde's actions and character.

"You needn't go on," said Korasov. "In order to give you confidence in your doctor, I'll finish the story for you. Either this woman's husband has an enormous fortune, or, and this is more likely, she herself belongs to one of the noblest families in the district. She must have something to be proud of."

Julien nodded; he no longer had the heart to speak.

"Very well," said the prince, "here are three rather bitter pills which you must swallow immediately: First, every day you must see Madame. . . . What's her name?"

"Madame de Dubois."

"What a name!" said the prince with a burst of laughter. "But forgive me: to you it's sublime. You must see Madame de Dubois every day, but be sure not to seem cold and offended to her; remember the great principle of our time: be the opposite of what people expect. Show yourself to her exactly as you were a week before she honored you with her favors."

"Oh, I was calm then!" exclaimed Julien in despair. "I thought I felt sorry for her. . . ."

"The candle burns the moth," continued the prince, "a comparison as old as the world.

"First, see her every day; second, pay court to a woman who's a member of her social circle, but without showing any passion—do you understand? It's a difficult part to play, I won't conceal it from you; you'll be pretending, and if anyone sees through you, you'll be lost."

"She has so much intelligence and I have so little! I'm lost," said Julien sadly.

"No, it's just that you're more in love than I thought. Madame de Dubois is profoundly self-centered, like all women to whom heaven has given either too high a rank or too much money. She looks at herself instead of looking at you, so she doesn't know you. During the two or three outbursts of passion for you that she's allowed herself to indulge in, with great efforts of imagination, she saw in you the hero of her dreams, not what you actually are. But what the devil, these things are elementary, my dear Sorel! Are you really nothing but a schoolboy?

"Aha! Let's go into this shop: I see a charming black cravat that looks as though it were made by John Anderson of Burlington Street. As a favor to me, please buy it and throw away that ignoble black rope you have around your neck.

"And now," the prince went on as they left the shop of the best haberdasher in Strasbourg, "what kind of people does Madame de Dubois see? Good God, what a name! Don't be angry, my dear Sorel, I can't help it. . . . To whom will you pay court?''

"To a consummate prude, the daughter of an immensely rich stocking merchant. She has the most beautiful eyes in the world and I find them infinitely attractive. She certainly occupies the highest position in the society of the district, but, amid all her grandeur, she blushes and becomes completely disconcerted if anyone happens to mention business or shops. And unfortunately her father was one of the best-known merchants in Strasbourg.''

"So if someone mentions business," said the prince, laughing, "you can be sure your fair lady will be thinking of herself and not of you. That absurdity is divine and very useful: it will prevent you from ever losing your head in the presence of her beautiful eyes. Your success is certain.''

Julien was thinking of Madame de Fervaques, the marshal's widow, who often came to the Hôtel de La Mole. She was a beautiful foreigner who had married the marshal a year before his death. Her whole life seemed to have no other object than to make people forget that she was the daughter of a manufacturer, and, in order to amount to something in Paris, she had become the leading champion of virtue.

Julien sincerely admired the prince; what would he not have given to have his ridiculous traits! The conversation between the two friends was endless; Korasov was delighted: never before had a Frenchman listened to him for so long. "So," thought the enraptured prince, "at last I've succeeded in being listened to by giving lessons to my teachers!''

"We thoroughly agree," he repeated to Julien for the tenth time: "not the faintest shadow of passion when you're speaking to the young beauty, the daughter of the Strasbourg stocking merchant, in front of Madame de Dubois. On the other hand, burning passion when you write to her. Reading a well-written love letter is the supreme pleasure for a prude; it's a moment of unrestraint. She's not playing a part, she dares to listen to her own heart; therefore, two letters a day.''

"Never! Never!" said Julien, disheartened. "I'd rather be pounded to pieces in a mortar than compose three sentences! I'm a corpse, my friend, don't expect anything more from me. Let me die by the roadside.''

"Who said anything about composing sentences? In my valise I have ten volumes of love letters in manuscript. There are letters for every type of feminine character; some are designed for the loftiest virtue. Didn't Kalisky pursue the prettiest Quakeress in all England at Richmond Terrace—you know, about three leagues outside London?''

Julien was less unhappy when he left his friend at two o'clock in the morning.

The next day the prince called in a copyist, and two days later Julien had fifty-three precisely numbered love letters designed to overcome the dreariest and most sublime virtue.

''There aren't fifty-four,'' said the prince, ''because Kalisky was finally sent packing; but what does it matter if you're mistreated by the stocking merchant's daughter, since you only want to affect Madame de Dubois' heart?''

They went riding together every day; the prince was enthusiastically fond of Julien. Not knowing how to give him proof of his sudden affection, he finally offered him the hand of one of his cousins, a wealthy heiress in Moscow. ''And once you're married,'' he added, ''my influence and the decoration you're wearing will make you a colonel within two years.''

''But this decoration wasn't given to me by Napoleon—far from it.''

''What's the difference?'' said the prince. ''Didn't he invent it? It's still by far the highest decoration in Europe.''

Julien was on the point of accepting, but his duty called him back to the great personage. On leaving Korasov he promised to write to him. He received the reply to the secret note he had delivered and quickly set out for Paris. But he had scarcely been alone for two consecutive days when leaving France and Mathilde seemed to him an ordeal worse than death. ''I won't marry the millions Korasov has offered me,'' he said to himself, ''but I will follow his advice. After all, the art of seduction is his profession; he's been thinking about that alone for fifteen years, since he's thirty now. He can't be accused of lacking intelligence; he's shrewd and wary; ardor and poetry are impossible in such a character. He's a procurer—all the more reason why he shouldn't make mistakes.

''I must and I will pursue Madame de Fervaques. She may bore me a little, but I'll look at her beautiful eyes, which are so much like the ones that once loved me more than any others in the world. And she's a foreigner—a new type of character to observe.

''I've lost my reason, I'm foundering; I must follow a friend's advice and not trust my own judgment.''

CHAPTER 25
The Ministry of Virtue

> But if I indulge in this pleasure with so much prudence and
> circumspection, it will no longer be a pleasure for me.
> —Lope de Vega

ALMOST AS SOON as he returned to Paris, and on leaving the study
of the Marquis de La Mole, who appeared to be extremely
disconcerted by the dispatches presented to him, our hero hurried
off to see Count Altamira. In addition to the distinction of being
under sentence of death, this handsome foreigner had a great
deal of gravity and the good fortune to be deeply religious.
These two merits and, more than anything else, his high birth,
were very much to the liking of Madame de Fervaques, who saw
him often.

Julien solemnly confessed to him that he was in love with her.

"She's a woman of the purest and highest virtue," replied
Altamira, "although it's a little Jesuitical and pompous. There
are days when I understand every word she uses, but not the
meaning of the sentence as a whole. She often makes me think I
don't really know French as well as people say I do. Becoming
acquainted with her will make people talk about you and give
you a certain weight in society. But let's go to see Bustos," said
Count Altamira, who had an orderly mind; "he once paid court
to her."

Don Diego Bustos demanded a lengthy explanation of the
matter without saying a word himself, like a lawyer in his office.
He had a fat, monkish face with a black mustache, and his
gravity was unequaled; in short, he was a good *Carbonaro*.

"I understand," he said at length to Julien. "Has Madame de
Fervaques had lovers or not? Have you therefore any chance of
success? That is the question. In other words, for my part, I
failed. Now that I'm no longer resentful, I reason as follows:
she's often in a bad temper and, as I'll prove to you in a
moment, she's quite vindictive. I don't see in her that irascible
temperament which is the mark of genius and which covers
every action with a veneer of passion. On the contrary, she owes
her rare beauty and fresh complexion to the calm, phlegmatic
temperament of the Dutch."

Julien was growing impatient with the Spaniard's slowness and imperturbable placidity; from time to time, in spite of himself, he let slip a few monosyllables.

"Are you going to listen to me?" asked Don Diego Bustos gravely.

"Forgive my *furia francese*," said Julien. "I'm all ears."

"Madame de Fervaques, then, is strongly inclined to hatred. She mercilessly persecutes people she's never seen—lawyers, or poor devils of literary men who have written songs like Collé's; you know:

> *J'ai la marotte*
> *D'aimer Marote . . ."*

And Julien had to endure the song from beginning to end. The Spaniard took delight in singing in French. This divine song was never listened to with greater impatience. When it was over, Don Diego Bustos said, "Madame de Fervaques had the author of this song dismissed from his post: *'Un jour l'amant au cabaret . . .'"*

Julien shuddered for fear he might decide to sing it. He contented himself with analyzing it. It was truly blasphemous and hardly decent.

"When she became angry at that song," said Don Diego, "I pointed out to her that a woman of her rank shouldn't read all the nonsense that's published. No matter how much progress piety and decorum make, there will always be a literature of the cabaret in France. When Madame de Fervaques had had the author, a poor devil on half pay, dismissed from a post worth eighteen hundred francs a year, I said to her, 'Be on your guard: you've attacked that rhymester with your weapons; he may answer you with his rhymes. He'll write a song about virtue. The gilded drawing rooms will be on your side, but people who like to laugh will repeat his epigrams.' Do you know what she replied to me, monsieur? 'To serve the interests of the Lord,' she said, 'I'd be glad to have everyone in Paris see me walk to my martyrdom. It would be a new sight in France; the common people would learn to respect nobility. It would be the happiest day of my life.' I'd never seen her eyes look more beautiful."

"And they're so magnificent!" exclaimed Julien.

"I see you're in love. . . . So," continued Don Diego Bustos gravely, "she doesn't have that irascible temperament that makes one inclined to take vengeance. If she likes to harm people

nevertheless, it's because she's unhappy; I suspect an *inner
unhappiness*. Isn't it possible that she's a prude who's grown
tired of her trade?''

The Spaniard looked at him in silence for at least a minute.

"That's the whole question," he added solemnly, "and it's
from that direction that you can draw a certain amount of hope. I
did a great deal of thinking during the two years I offered myself
as her humble servant. Your entire future, my amorous young
man, hinges on this great problem: Is she a prude who's tired of
her trade, and cruel because she's unhappy?"

"Or else," said Altamira, finally emerging from his profound
silence, "could it be what I've already told you twenty times:
simply a question of French vanity? It's the memory of her
father, the famous cloth merchant, that causes the unhappiness of
her naturally cold and gloomy heart. There can be only one kind
of happiness for her: to live in Toledo and be tormented every day
by a confessor who shows her the gaping jaws of hell."

As Julien was leaving, Don Diego said to him, more gravely
than ever, "Altamira tells me you're one of us. Some day you'll
help us reconquer our freedom, so I'll be glad to help you in this
little diversion. It will be good for you to become acquainted
with Madame de Fervaques' style: here are four letters in her
own hand."

"I'll copy them," said Julien, "and bring them back to you."

"And you'll never tell anyone a word of what we've been
saying?"

"Never, I swear it on my honor!" cried Julien.

"Then may God come to your aid," said the Spaniard; and he
silently accompanied Altamira and Julien to the head of the
stairs.

This scene made our hero feel a little more cheerful; he nearly
smiled. "And here's the pious Altamira," he thought, "who's
helping me succeed in an adulterous adventure."

All during Don Diego Bustos' solemn conversation, Julien had
been attentive to the clock of the Hôtel d'Aligre as it struck the
hours. It was now nearly dinnertime; he was going to see Mathilde
again! He returned to the house and dressed with great care.

"That's my first blunder," he said to himself as he walked
down the stairs. "I must follow the prince's prescription to the
letter."

He went back up to his room and put on the simplest possible
traveling clothes. "Now," he thought, "I'll have to be careful
how I look at her." It was only half-past five, and dinner was at

six. He decided to go into the drawing room, which he found empty. When he saw the blue sofa he fell to his knees and kissed the place where Mathilde rested her arm; he shed tears and his cheeks began to burn. "I must get rid of this stupid sensitivity," he said to himself angrily, "or it will betray me." He picked up a newspaper for the sake of appearance and walked back and forth between the drawing room and the garden three or four times.

It was only when he was standing trembling and well hidden beneath a large oak tree that he dared to look up at Mademoiselle de La Mole's window. It was tightly closed. He nearly fell to the ground, and he stood for a long time leaning against the tree; then, with faltering steps, he went over to look at the gardener's ladder again.

The link of the chain which he had once forced open in circumstances that were, alas, so very different from his present ones, had not been repaired. Carried away by a mad impulse, he pressed it to his lips.

After wandering for a long time back and forth between the drawing room and the garden, Julien found himself terribly tired; this was his first success and he was keenly aware of it. "My eyes will be dull and won't betray me!" he thought. Little by little, the guests were arriving in the drawing room; the door never opened without filling Julien's heart with mortal anguish.

They sat down to table. Finally Mademoiselle de La Mole appeared, still faithful to her habit of keeping others waiting. She blushed deeply when she saw Julien; she had not been told of his arrival. Following Prince Korasov's recommendations, Julien looked at his hands; they were trembling Agitated beyond all expression by this discovery, he was fortunate enough to appear only tired.

Monsieur de La Mole praised him. The marquise spoke to him a few moments later and addressed a kind remark to him with regard to his fatigue. Julien kept repeating to himself, "I mustn't look at Mademoiselle de La Mole too much, but my eyes mustn't avoid her, either. I must appear to be as I really was a week before my misfortune. . . ." He had reason to be satisfied with his success and remained in the drawing room. Attentive for the first time to the mistress of the house, he made every effort to get the men of her circle to talk and keep the conversation alive.

His politeness was rewarded: at eight o'clock Madame de Fervaques was announced. Julien slipped away and reappeared shortly afterward, dressed with the greatest care. Madame de La

Mole was infinitely grateful to him for this mark of respect and, wishing to show her satisfaction, spoke to Madame de Fervaques of his journey. He sat down beside Madame de Fervaques in such a way that Mathilde could not see his eyes. From this position, following all the rules of the art, he made Madame de Fervaques the object of his rapt admiration. The first of the fifty-three letters which Prince Korasov had given him began with an eloquent discourse on this sentiment.

Madame de Fervaques announced that she was going to the comic opera. Julien hurried there; he met the Chevalier de Beauvoisis, who took him into a box reserved for the Gentlemen of the Chamber, right beside that of Madame de Fervaques. Julien looked at her constantly. "I must keep a diary of the siege," he said to himself on the way home; "otherwise I'll forget my strategy." He forced himself to write two or three pages on this boring subject, and thereby succeeded—a wonderful achievement!—in giving scarcely any thought to Mademoiselle de La Mole.

Mathilde had nearly forgotten him during his absence. "After all, he's only a commonplace man," she thought. "His name will always remind me of the greatest mistake of my life. I must sincerely return to conventional standards of virtue and honor; a woman has everything to lose if she disregards them." She showed herself willing at last to allow the conclusion of the arrangements for her marriage to the Marquis de Croisenois, which had been prepared so long before. He was wild with joy. He would have been greatly astonished if someone had told him that there was resignation at the bottom of Mathilde's attitude which made him so proud.

All her ideas changed when she saw Julien again. "He's my real husband," she said to herself. "If I sincerely return to virtue, he's the man I ought to marry."

She expected urgent entreaties and expressions of unhappiness on his part. She prepared her replies, for he would no doubt try to say a few words to her after dinner. Far from it, however: he firmly remained in the drawing room and did not even look in the direction of the garden (God knows with what difficulty he refrained from doing so!). "It will be better to have our discussion right away," thought Mademoiselle de La Mole. She went into the garden alone; Julien did not appear. She strolled past the glass doors of the drawing room and saw him busily engaged in describing to Madame de Fervaques the old ruined castles which crown the hillsides on the banks of the Rhine and give them so much character. He was becoming fairly proficient in composing the sentimental and picturesque phrases which are known as *wit* in some drawing rooms.

Prince Korasov would have been extremely proud if he had been in Paris: that evening was exactly what he had predicted. And he would have approved of Julien's conduct on the following days.

An intrigue among the members of the government behind the throne was about to bestow the cordon bleu on a number of people. Madame de Fervaques demanded that her great-uncle be made a knight of the order. The Marquis de La Mole was making the same claim for his father-in-law; they united their efforts and Madame de Fervaques came to the Hôtel de La Mole nearly every day. It was from her that Julien learned that the marquis was about to become a minister: he was proposing to the court clique a very ingenious plan for abolishing the Charter, without commotion, within three years.

Julien could expect to be made a bishop if Monsieur de La Mole became a minister; but, to his eyes, these great possibilities were as though covered by a veil. His imagination saw them only vaguely and, so to speak, in the distance. The wretched unhappiness with which he was obsessed made him see all the interests of his life centered in his relationship with Mademoiselle de La Mole. He calculated that after five or six years of careful effort, he would succeed in making her love him again.

It is easy to see that his cool head had been reduced to a state of complete irrationality. Of all the qualities that had previously distinguished him, only a little constancy of purpose remained. Physically faithful to the plan of conduct laid down for him by Prince Korasov, he took up a position rather close to Madame de Fervaques' chair every evening, but he was unable to think of a single word to say.

The effort he imposed on himself to appear cured of his love in Mathilde's eyes absorbed all the strength of his soul; he remained beside Madame de Fervaques like a creature scarcely alive; even his eyes, as happens in extreme physical suffering, had completely lost their luster.

Since Madame de La Mole's views were never anything but a reflection of the opinions of the husband who might some day make her a duchess, for the past few days she had been praising Julien's merits to the skies.

CHAPTER 26
Platonic Love

There also was of course in Adeline
    That calm patrician polish in the address,
Which ne'er can pass the equinoctial line
    Of anything which Nature could express:
Just as a Mandarin finds nothing fine,
    At least his manner suffers not to guess
That anything he views can greatly please.
            —*Don Juan*, XIII. 84

"THERE'S A TOUCH of madness in the way this whole family looks at things," thought Madame de Fervaques. "They're all infatuated with their young ecclesiastic, who can't do anything except listen, although with rather attractive eyes, it's true."

Julien, for his part, found in her manner a nearly perfect example of that "patrician calm" which denotes punctilious courtesy and, still more, the inability to feel any keen emotion. Any unexpected action, any lack of self-control, would have shocked her almost as much as the absence of majestic dignity toward one's inferiors. The slightest sign of spontaneous feeling would have seemed to her a kind of "emotional intoxication" for which one ought to blush, and which was extremely detrimental to what a person of exalted rank owed to himself. Her greatest pleasure was to discuss the king's latest hunting party, and her favorite book was the *Mémoires du Duc de Saint-Simon*, especially the genealogical part.

Julien knew the place which, due to the way the lights were arranged, was most favorable to Madame de Fervaques' type of beauty. He always went there in advance, but he was careful to turn his chair in such a way that he would not see Mathilde. Astonished at this determination to hide himself from her, one evening she left the blue sofa and came over to work at a little table near Madame de Fervaques' chair. Julien could see her at rather close range by looking below Madame de Fervaques' hat. Her eyes, which held absolute sway over him, frightened him at first, then they violently shook him out of his usual apathy; he spoke, and spoke well.

He addressed his words to Madame de Fervaques, but his sole aim was to act on Mathilde's heart. He became so animated that

Madame de Fervaques was finally unable to understand what he was saying.

This was a first point in his favor. If it had occurred to him to follow it up with a few words of German mysticism, exalted piety and Jesuitism, Madame de Fervaques would have instantly classified him in her mind among the superior men who have been called upon to regenerate our age.

"Since he has the bad taste to talk so long and so heatedly to Madame de Fervaques," thought Mademoiselle de La Mole, "I won't listen to him any more." She kept her word for the rest of the evening, though with difficulty.

At midnight, when she took her mother's candlestick to accompany her to her room, her mother stopped on the stairs to praise Julien in glowing terms. This climaxed Mathilde's irritation; she was unable to go to sleep. One thought soothed her: "A man I despise can still pass for a man of merit in Madame de Fervaques' eyes."

As for Julien, he had acted and therefore felt less unhappy. His eyes happened to fall on the Russian leather portfolio in which Prince Korasov had placed the fifty-three love letters he had given him. He saw a note at the bottom of the first letter: *"Send no. 1 a week after the first meeting."*

"I'm late!" exclaimed Julien. "It's been a long time since I first met Madame de Fervaques!" He immediately began to copy this first love letter; it was a homily filled with remarks about virtue, and horribly dull. He was fortunate enough to fall asleep over the second page.

A few hours later the bright sunlight surprised him with his head resting on the table. He usually experienced one of the most painful moments of his life when, on awakening in the morning, he realized his unhappiness anew. On that particular morning, he was almost laughing as he finished copying his letter. "Is it possible," he asked himself, "that there really was a young man who wrote like this?" He counted several sentences nine lines long. At the end of the original he saw a note in pencil: *"Deliver these letters in person, on horseback, black cravat, blue frock coat. Hand the letter to the porter with a contrite expression and deep melancholy in your eyes. If you see a maid, wipe your eyes furtively. Speak to the maid."*

All these instructions were faithfully carried out.

"What I'm doing is very bold," thought Julien as he left the Hôtel de Fervaques, "but so much the worse for Korasov. Daring to write to a woman so famous for her virtue! She's going to treat me with the utmost contempt, and nothing could amuse me more. It's actually the only kind of comedy I can appreciate. Yes, it will amuse me to cover with ridicule that odious creature I call *myself*. If I listened to myself, I'd commit some crime to distract myself.''

For the past month, the moment when he brought his horse back to the stable had been the high point of his day. Korasov had expressly forbidden him to look, on any pretext whatever, at the mistress who had rejected him. But the sound of his horse's hooves, which she knew so well, and the way he knocked on the stable door with his riding crop to summon one of the men, sometimes drew Mathilde to her window. She stood behind the curtain, but it was so thin that Julien could see through it. By looking up in a certain way from under the brim of his hat, he could see her form without seeing her eyes. ''Therefore,'' he said to himself, ''she can't see mine, so I'm not really looking at her.''

That evening, Madame de Fervaques treated him exactly as though she had not received the philosophical, metaphysical and religious dissertation which he had handed to the porter that morning with such great melancholy. The evening before, chance had revealed to Julien a means of being eloquent: he placed himself in such a way that he could see Mathilde's eyes. For her part, she left the blue sofa a moment after Madame de Fervaques arrived; this meant deserting her usual circle. Monsieur de Croisenois seemed appalled by this new caprice; his obvious chagrin dulled the sharpest pangs of Julien's anguish.

This unexpected development in his life made him speak with inspired eloquence; and, since vanity steals into even those hearts which serve as temples of the most august virtue, Madame de Fervaques said to herself as she stepped into her carriage, ''Mademoiselle de La Mole is right: that young priest has distinction. My presence must have intimidated him during the first few days. As a matter of fact, everybody one meets in this house is quite frivolous; the only virtue I see here is aided by old age, and has great need of the chilling hand of time. That young man must have been able to see the difference. He writes well; but I'm very much afraid that his request to be enlightened by my advice, which he makes in his letter, may actually be only a feeling unaware of its own nature.

''Still, though, how many conversions have begun that way! What makes me optimistic about this one is the difference betwen his style and that of the other young men whose letters I've had occasion to see. It's impossible not to recognize a certain fervent eloquence, a profound earnestness and a great deal of conviction in the prose of that young ecclesiastic; he must have Massillon's gentle virtue.''

CHAPTER 27

The Best Positions in the Church

Services! Talents! Merit! What of that? Join a clique.
—*Télémaque*

THUS THE thought of a bishopric was for the first time mingled with that of Julien in the mind of a woman who, sooner or later, would probably be distributing the best positions in the Church of France. This advantage would scarcely have interested him; his thoughts did not rise to anything beyond his present unhappiness. Everything increased it: for example, the sight of his own room had become unbearable to him. At night, when he came back to it with his candle, each piece of furniture, each little ornament seemed to take on a voice to inform him bitterly of some new detail of his misery.

That night, as he walked into his room with a buoyancy he had not felt for a long time, he said to himself, ''I've got some forced labor ahead of me; let's hope the second letter will be as boring as the first.''

It was more so. What he was copying seemed so absurd to him that he eventually began to transcribe it line by line, without thinking of the meaning. ''It's even more pompous,'' he thought, ''than the official documents of the Treaty of Münster, which my diplomacy teacher made me copy in London.''

Only then did he remember Madame de Fervaques' letters, the originals of which he had forgotten to return to the solemn Spaniard, Don Diego Bustos. He took them out; they were almost as full of turgid nonsense as those of the young Russian nobleman. They were completely vague. They could mean anything or nothing. ''That's the Aeolian harp of style,'' thought Julien. ''In the midst of the loftiest reflections on the vanity of this world, on death, infinity, and so on, I see nothing real except an abject fear of ridicule.''

The monologue we have just abridged was repeated every night for two weeks. Falling asleep while transcribing a kind of commentary on the Apocalypse, going to deliver a letter the next day with a melancholy air, bringing his horse back to the stable in the hope of seeing Mathilde's dress, working, putting in an appearance at the opera on evenings when Madame de Fervaques did not come to the Hôtel de La Mole—such were the monotonous events of Julien's life. There was more interest in it when Madame de Fervaques came to see the marquise, because then he could catch a glimpse of Mathilde's eyes from under the brim of Madame de Fervaques' hat, and he became eloquent. His picturesque and sentimental phrases were beginning to take on a form that was both more striking and more elegant.

He was fully aware that what he said was absurd in Mathilde's eyes, but he wanted to impress her with the elegance of his conversational style. "The falser the things I say to her," he thought, "the more I ought to please her." Then, with deplorable boldness, he began to exaggerate certain aspects of nature. He quickly realized that, in order not to appear vulgar to Madame de Fervaques, he must above all avoid simple and rational ideas. He either continued in this direction or cut short his amplification of the subject at hand, according to whether he saw success or indifference in the eyes of the two noble ladies he was trying to please.

On the whole, his life was less wretched than it had been in the days when he spent his time doing nothing.

"But here I am," he said to himself one night, "copying the fifteenth of these abominable dissertations; the first fourteen have been faithfully delivered to Madame de Fervaques' porter. I'll soon have the honor of having filled all the pigeonholes of her desk. And yet she treats me exactly as though I hadn't written to her! What will be the end of all this? Can it be that my constancy bores her as much as it does me? I must admit that Korasov's Russian friend, the one who was in love with the beautiful Quakeress of Richmond, was a terrible man in his day; no one could be more tiresome."

Like all mediocre men who happen to observe the strategy of a great general, Julien completely failed to understand the attack which the young Russian had launched against the heart of the virtuous English woman. The first forty letters were designed only to make her forgive him for being so bold as to write to her. He had to make that sweet young lady, who may have been bored to tears, acquire the habit of receiving letters that were perhaps a little less insipid than her everyday life.

One morning a letter was delivered to Julien. He recognized

Madame de Fervaques' coat of arms and broke the seal with an eagerness that would have seemed quite impossible to him a few days earlier: it was only an invitation to dinner.

He hastened to read over Prince Korasov's instructions. Unfortunately, the young Russian had tried to be as frivolous as Dorat just when he should have been simple and intelligible; Julien was unable to guess what attitude he ought to adopt during dinner at Madame de Fervaques' house.

The drawing room was extremely magnificent, gilded like the Gallery of Diana in the Tuileries, with oil paintings on the wooden paneling. There were patches of light paint on these pictures. Julien later learned that the subjects had seemed rather indecent to the mistress of the house and that she had had them altered. "What a moral age we live in!" he thought.

In this drawing room he noticed three of the men who had been present at the drafting of the secret note. One of them, the Bishop of ———, Madame de Fervaques' uncle, controlled the distribution of benefices, and it was said that he could refuse nothing to his niece. "What an enormous advance I've made, yet how indifferent it leaves me!" thought Julien with a melancholy smile. "Here I am, dining with the famous Bishop of ———."

The dinner was mediocre, the conversation exasperating. "It's like the table of contents of a bad book," thought Julien. "All the greatest subjects of human thought are proudly broached. After listening for three minutes you wonder which is greater, the pompousness of the speaker or his abominable ignorance."

The reader has no doubt forgotten that little man of letters named Tanbeau, the nephew of the academician and a future professor, who seemed to have undertaken to poison the drawing room of the Hôtel de La Mole with his vile slander. It was due to this little man that Julien had first conceived the idea that, while Madame de Fervaques did not answer his letters, it was quite possible that she felt a certain indulgence for the feeling that dictated them. Monsieur Tanbeau's black heart was tormented when he thought of Julien's successes; but, on the other hand, a man of merit cannot, any more than a fool, be in two places at once. "If Sorel becomes the sublime widow's lover," thought the future professor, "she'll give him some advantageous position in the Church, and I'll be rid of him in the Hôtel de La Mole."

Father Pirard also gave Julien long sermons on his success in the Hôtel de Fervaques. There was *sectarian jealousy* between the austere Jansenist and the Jesuitical, reformatory and monarchial drawing room of the virtuous widow.

CHAPTER 28
Manon Lescaut

> Now once he was firmly convinced of the prior's asinine stupidity, he nearly always succeeded by calling white black and black white.
>
> —Lichtemberg

THE RUSSIAN'S instructions stated emphatically that one must never contradict in conversation the woman to whom one was writing. One must never, under any circumstances, depart from the role of an ecstatic admirer; the letters were all based on that supposition.

One evening at the opera, in Madame de Fervaques' box, Julien enthusiastically praised the ballet of *Manon Lescaut*. His only reason for doing so was that he found it dull. Madame de Fervaques declared that this ballet was greatly inferior to Abbé Prévost's novel.

"What!" thought Julien, astonished and amused. "A person of such lofty virtue praising a novel!" Two or three times a week, Madame de Fervaques professed utter contempt for the novelists who, with their vulgar works, sought to corrupt a generation of young people who were, alas, all too prone to errors of the senses.

"In that immoral and dangerous kind of literature," continued Madame de Fervaques, "*Manon Lescaut* is said to occupy one of the highest places. The frailties and deserved sufferings of a sinful heart are depicted in it, I'm told, with rather profound truthfulness; but that didn't prevent your Bonaparte from declaring on Saint Helena that it was a novel written for lackeys."

This remark made Julien's mind recover all its alertness. "Someone has tried to turn her against me by telling her of my enthusiasm for Napoleon," he thought. "It's affected her so deeply that she's given in to the temptation to make me aware of her disapproval." This discovery amused him and made him amusing for the rest of the evening.

As he was taking leave of Madame de Fervaques in the lobby of the opera house, she said to him, "Remember, monsieur, that one mustn't love Bonaparte when one loves me; one may at most accept him as a necessity imposed by Providence. Besides, he had too rigid a mind to appreciate great works of art."

"When one loves me!" Julien repeated to himself. "That means either nothing or everything. There are secrets of language that we poor provincials don't possess." And he thought a great deal about Madame de Rênal as he copied an immense letter to be delivered to Madame de Fervaques.

"Why is it," she said to him the next day with an air of indifference which he regarded as badly feigned, "that you speak to me of London and Richmond in a letter which you apparently wrote to me last night after leaving the opera?"

Julien was extremely embarrassed: he had copied the letter line by line without thinking of what he was writing, and he had apparently forgotten to replace the words "London" and "Richmond," which were in the original, with "Paris" and "Saint-Cloud." He began two or three sentences, but was unable to finish them; he felt himself on the verge of breaking into uncontrollable laughter. Finally, searching for words, he managed to express this thought: "Exalted by a discussion of the greatest, the most sublime interests of the human mind, my own may have become distracted as I wrote to you."

"I'm making a good impression," he thought, "so I can spare myself the boredom of spending the rest of the evening here." He hurried out of the Hôtel de Fervaques. That night, taking another look at the original of the letter he had copied the night before, he quickly found the fatal passage in which the young Russian spoke of London and Richmond. He was quite surprised to find this letter almost tender.

It was the contrast between the apparent frivolity of his speech and the sublime, almost apocalyptic profundity of his letters that had made Madame de Fervaques take a special interest in him. She was especially pleased by the length of his sentences; this was not that choppy style made fashionable by the shockingly immoral Voltaire! Although our hero did everything he could to banish all trace of common sense from his conversation, it still had a certain impious and anti-Royalist tinge to it which did not escape Madame de Fervaques. Surrounded by people who were eminently moral, but who often did not have one idea in the course of an entire evening, she was deeply impressed by anything resembling originality; but at the same time she felt it her duty to be offended by it. She called this shortcoming "bearing the imprint of this frivolous age."

But drawing rooms such as hers are worth visiting only when

one has something to solicit. The reader no doubt shares all the boredom of that life devoid of interest which Julien was leading. These are the barren wastes of our journey.

During all the time taken up in Julien's life by the Fervaques episode, Mademoiselle de La Mole had to make great efforts to keep from thinking about him. Her heart was torn by violent conflicts; sometimes she flattered herself that she despised that gloomy young man, but, against her will, she was captivated by his conversation. What astonished her above all was his utter insincerity: everything he said to Madame de Fervaques was a lie, or at least a scandalous dissimulation of his true point of view, which Mathilde knew so well on nearly all subjects. She was impressed by this Machiavellianism. "What cunning!" she thought. "How different he is from those pompous fools or vulgar scoundrels, like Monsieur Tanbeau, who use the same language!"

Nevertheless, some days were horrible for Julien. It was in order to carry out the most painful of duties that he appeared in Madame de Fervaques' drawing room every day. His efforts to play a part were robbing his soul of the little strength it had left. Often, at night, as he was crossing the enormous courtyard of the Hôtel de Fervaques, it was only by reasoning and force of character that he managed to keep himself from sinking into utter despair.

"I overcame despair in the seminary," he would say to himself, "and yet what appalling prospects I had before me then! Whether I succeeded or failed, I saw myself forced in either case to spend the rest of my life in close company with the most despicable and disgusting creatures under the sun. The following spring, only eleven short months later, I was perhaps the happiest of all young men my age."

But quite often all these fine arguments were powerless in the face of horrible reality. He saw Mathilde at lunch and dinner every day. From the numerous letters which Monsieur de La Mole dictated to him, he knew that she was about to marry Monsieur de Croisenois. This amiable young man was already coming to the house twice a day; the jealous eyes of a forsaken lover did not miss a single one of his actions.

Whenever he thought he had seen Mademoiselle de La Mole treating her suitor affectionately, Julien could not help looking lovingly at his pistols when he returned to his room. "Oh, how much wiser I'd be," he said to himself, "to cut the marks off my linen, go to some lonely forest twenty leagues from Paris and put an end to this hateful life there! I'd be a stranger in the district, so my death would remain hidden for two weeks, and who would give a thought to me after two weeks had gone by!"

This reasoning was quite sensible. But the next day a glimpse of Mathilde's arm between her sleeve and her glove was enough to plunge our young philosopher into memories that were cruelly painful, but which nevertheless made him cling to life. "All right!" he would say to himself then, "I'll follow this Russian policy through to the end. But what will come of it? As for Madame de Fervaques, after I've copied those fifty-three letters I certainly won't write any more. As for Mathilde, these six weeks of painful pretending will either have no effect on her anger or win me a moment of reconciliation. My God! I'd die of joy!" And he was unable to pursue his thoughts any further.

When, after a long reverie, he succeeded in picking up the thread of his reasoning again, he said to himself, "So I'd gain one day of happiness, after which she'd begin to treat me harshly again, because, alas, I have so little power to please her! And then I'd have used up my last resource, I'd be ruined, lost forever. . . .

"What guarantee can she give me, with her character? Alas, my lack of merit is the answer to everything. My manners will be unrefined, my way of speaking will be heavy and monotonous. My God! Why am I myself?"

CHAPTER 29
Boredom

> Sacrificing oneself to one's passions, well and good. But to passions one does not have! . . . O sad nineteenth century!
> —Girodet

AFTER HAVING read Julien's long letters without pleasure at first, Madame de Fervaques was now beginning to take great interest in them; but one thing grieved her: "What a shame Monsieur Sorel isn't really a priest!" she thought. "One could admit him to a kind of intimacy then, but with that decoration and those almost secular clothes, one is exposed to unkind questions, and how can one answer them?" She did not finish the rest of her thought: "Some malicious friend may imagine, and even tell others, that he's a lowly cousin of mine on my father's side, some tradesman decorated by the National Guard."

Until she met Julien, her greatest pleasure had been to write the word *Maréchale** before her name. Then the vanity of a *parvenue*, morbid and quick to take offense, began to struggle against a budding attraction. "It would be so easy for me," she said to herself, "to make him a vicar-general in some diocese near Paris! But his name is simply Monsieur Sorel, and besides that he's a mere secretary to Monsieur de La Mole! It's disheartening!"

Her heart, which was afraid of everything, was now, for the first time, moved by an interest alien to her pretensions to rank and social superiority. Her old porter noticed that whenever he brought her a letter from that handsome young man who looked so sad, he was sure to see her face lose the distracted and dissatisfied air that she was always careful to assume at the approach of one of her servants.

Ever since she had begun to think about Julien, the boredom of leading a life whose prime object was to impress others, while at the bottom of her heart she took no real pleasure in this kind of success, had become so intolerable to her that an hour spent with the singular young man in the evening was enough to insure that her maids would not be mistreated at any time during the following day. His growing influence withstood a number of skillfully written anonymous letters. It was in vain that young Tanbeau supplied Messieurs de Luz, de Croisenois and de Caylus with two or three clever calumnies which they took pleasure in spreading abroad, without caring too much about the truth of the accusations. Madame de Fervaques, whose mind was not made to resist such vulgar methods, confided her doubts to Mathilde and was always comforted.

One day, after having asked three times if there were any letters, Madame de Fervaques suddenly made up her mind to reply to Julien. This was a victory won by boredom. At the second letter she was almost stopped by the impropriety of writing such a vulgar address in her own hand: *M. Sorel, c/o M. le Marquis de La Mole.*

That evening she said to him curtly, "You must bring me some envelopes with your address on them."

"So now I've been appointed as a kind of footman-lover," thought Julien; he bowed, taking pleasure in wrinkling up his face to look like Arsène, the marquis' old valet.

He brought her the envelopes that same evening, and early the

---

*A title assumed by the wife of a marshal.—L.B.

next morning he received a third letter. He read five or six lines of it at the beginning, and two or three toward the end. It consisted of four pages of small, cramped handwriting.

She gradually acquired the pleasant habit of writing to him nearly every day. He replied with faithful copies of the Russian letters and, such is the advantage of a pompous style, she was not at all surprised at how little relation there was between her letters and his replies.

How it would have irritated her pride if young Tanbeau, who had appointed himself to spy on Julien's activities, had been able to inform her that all her letters were carelessly tossed, unopened, into Julien's drawer!

One morning the porter, without respect for Madame de Fervaques' seal and coat of arms, was on his way to the library to deliver one of her letters when Mathilde encountered him and saw the envelope with the address in Julien's handwriting. She went into the library as the porter was coming out. The letter was still on the edge of the table; Julien, who was very busy writing, had not put it into his drawer.

"This is something I can't tolerate!" cried Mathilde, seizing the letter. "You're forgetting me completely, me, your wife! Your conduct is horrible, monsieur."

At these words, her pride, amazed at the frightful impropriety of her action, choked her; she burst into tears, and it soon seemed to Julien that she was unable to breathe.

Surprised and bewildered, he was not clearly aware of all the glory and happiness this scene held for him. He helped her to sit down; she nearly abandoned herself to his arms. The first moment after he perceived this movement was one of extreme joy. The second brought thoughts of Korasov: "I can ruin everything with a single word."

His arms stiffened, so painful was the effort imposed on him by his strategy. "I mustn't even allow myself to press this lovely, yielding body to my heart, or she'll despise me and treat me harshly," he thought. "What a terrible character!"

As he cursed Mathilde's character he loved her a hundred times more for it; it seemed to him that he was holding a queen in his arms.

The pangs of wounded pride that were rending Mademoiselle de La Mole's heart were redoubled by Julien's impassive coldness. She was far from having enough self-possession to seek to read in his eyes what he was feeling for her at that moment. She could not bring herself to look at him; she trembled that she might meet an expression of scorn.

Sitting motionless on the couch in the library with her head turned away from him, she was in the grip of the keenest anguish which pride and love can inflict on the human heart. What a shameful act she had just unthinkingly committed!

"It was reserved for me, wretched creature that I am," she thought, "to see my most indecent advances repulsed! And repulsed by whom?" added her pride, maddened by suffering. "By one of my father's servants!"

Then she said aloud, "I will not tolerate it!" Furiously leaping to her feet, she opened the drawer of Julien's desk, a few feet in front of her. She stood as though frozen in horror when she saw nine of ten unopened letters, all exactly like the one the porter had just brought in. On all the envelopes she recognized Julien's handwriting, more or less disguised.

"So!" she cried, beside herself with rage. "Not only are you on close terms with her, but you despise her! You, a little nobody, you despise Madame de Fervaques!

"Oh, forgive me, my darling!" she said a moment later, throwing herself at his feet. "Despise me if you will, but love me: I can't go on living without your love." And she fell into a dead faint.

"There she is, the proud creature—at my feet," thought Julien.

CHAPTER 30

A Box at the Opera

As the blackest sky
Foretells the heaviest tempest.
—*Don Juan*, I. 73

IN THE MIDST of all these tempestuous emotions, Julien was more astonished than happy. Mathilde's insults showed him how wise the Russian policy was. "*Say little, do little*, that's my only salvation," he thought.

He picked up Mathilde and set her down on the couch without a word. She was gradually overcome by tears. To give herself some appearance of composure, she took Madame de Fervaques' letters in her hands and slowly broke the seals. She started nervously when she recognized Madame de Fervaques' handwriting. She leafed through the letters without reading them; most of them were six pages long.

"Answer me at least," she said at length in a supplicating tone of voice, but without daring to look at him. "You know very well that I'm proud; it's the misfortune of my position, and even of my character, I admit it. So Madame de Fervaques has stolen your heart from me. . . . Has she made for you all the sacrifices to which my fatal love led me?"

A gloomy silence was Julien's only answer. "By what right," he thought, "does she ask me for a betrayal of confidence unworthy of an honorable man?"

Mathilde tried to read the letters, but her tear-filled eyes made it impossible for her.

She had been unhappy for the past month, but her proud heart had been far from acknowledging its own feelings. Chance alone had brought on this explosion. For a moment, jealousy and love had prevailed over pride. She was seated on the couch, close beside him. He saw her hair and her alabaster neck; for an instant he completely forgot his duty to himself: he put his arm around her waist and almost pressed her to his chest.

She slowly turned her head toward him. He was astonished by the sorrow in her eyes; it was so intense that he scarcely recognized them. He felt his strength abandoning him, so mortally painful was the act of courage he was imposing on himself. "Those eyes will soon express nothing but cold disdain," he thought, "if I give in to the joy of loving her." At that moment, however, in a faint voice and in words that she scarcely had the strength to utter, she was repeating her assurances of how much she regretted certain actions which had been prompted by excessive pride.

"I'm proud, too," said Julien almost inarticulately, and his features showed the ultimate degree of physical exhaustion.

Mathilde quickly turned toward him again. Hearing his voice was a joy she had almost ceased to hope for. She now recalled her pride only to curse it; she wished she could discover new, strange and incredible acts that would prove to him how much she adored him and detested herself.

"It was probably because of my pride," continued Julien "that you were once attracted to me for a moment; and it's certainly because of my courageous strength of will, which is fitting in a man, that you respect me now. I may be in love with Madame de Fervaques. . . ."

Mathilde started, and her eyes took on a strange expression. She was about to hear her sentence pronounced. This movement did not escape Julien; he felt his courage weaken.

"Ah!" he thought, listening to the sound of the empty words his lips were pronouncing, as he would have listened to a sound alien to himself, "if only I could cover your pale cheeks with kisses, without your feeling it!"

"I may be in love with Madame de Fervaques," he went on, his voice growing still weaker, "but I certainly have no positive proof of her interest in me. . . ."

Mathilde looked at him; he bore up under her gaze, or at least he hoped his face had not betrayed him. He felt himself filled with love to the innermost recesses of his heart. Never before had he adored her so intensely; he was almost as feverish as she was. If she had had enough courage and presence of mind to maneuver, he would have fallen at her feet, renouncing all vain pretense. He had strength enough to go on speaking. "Ah, Korasov!" he exclaimed inwardly. "Why aren't you here? How I need a word from you to guide my conduct!" Meanwhile his voice was saying:

"Lacking any other feeling, gratitude alone would be enough to attach me to Madame de Fervaques; she has shown me indulgence, she has consoled me when I was despised. . . . I may not, perhaps, place unbounded faith in certain manifestations which are no doubt extremely flattering, but which may also be of very short duration."

"Oh!" exclaimed Mathilde.

"Very well, then, what guarantee will you give me?" asked Julien in a sharp, vigorous tone which seemed to abandon for a moment the circumspect forms of diplomacy. "What guarantee, what god will assure me that the position to which you now seem willing to restore me will last for more than two days?"

"The intensity of my love, and of my unhappiness if you no longer love me," she said, taking his hands and turning toward him. This abrupt movement displaced her cape a little: Julien saw her lovely shoulders. The slight disorder of her hair brought back sweet memories. . . .

He was about to yield. "One rash word," he told himself, "and I'll make that long series of days spent in despair begin all over again. Madame de Rênal used to find reasons for doing what her heart demanded; this girl of high society lets her heart be moved only after she's given herself good reasons to prove that it ought to be moved.'' He saw this truth in the twinkling of an eye, and in the twinkling of an eye he regained his courage.

He drew back his hands, which Mathilde had clasped in hers, and stepped back from her with marked respect. Human courage can go no further. He then busied himself in gathering up all of Madame de Fervaques' letters, which were scattered over the couch, and said to her with extreme and, under the circumstances, cruel politeness, ''Mademoiselle de La Mole will please allow me to reflect on all this.'' He swiftly walked away and left the library; she heard him close all the doors in succession.

''The monster isn't at all perturbed! . . .'' she thought. ''But what am I saying? He's not a monster! He's wise, discreet, kind—I'm the one who has all the faults imaginable.''

This attitude persisted. She was almost happy that day, for she had surrendered herself completely to love; one would have thought that her heart had never been troubled by pride—and what pride!

She started with horror when, that evening in the drawing room, a footman announced Madame de Fervaques; his voice sounded sinister to her. She could not stand the sight of Madame de Fervaques, and she hurriedly walked away. Julien, who took little pride in his painful victory, had been afraid of what his eyes might reveal, and had not dined at the Hôtel de La Mole.

His love and his happiness increased rapidly as the battle receded further into the past; he had already reached the point of reproaching himself: ''How could I have resisted her!'' he thought. ''What if she stops loving me? One moment can change that proud heart, and I must admit I treated her abominably.''

That evening he felt that it was absolutely necessary for him to appear at the Italian Opera in Madame de Fervaques' box. She had expressly invited him; Mathilde would not fail to learn of his presence there, or of his discourteous absence. Despite the undeniable soundness of this argument, he did not have the strength, at the beginning of the evening, to plunge into society. If he talked, he would lose half his happiness.

Ten o'clock struck: it was absolutely necessary for him to put in an appearance.

Fortunately he found Madame de Fervaques' box filled with women, and he was relegated to a seat by the door, completely hidden by their hats. This position saved him from appearing ridiculous: the divine tones of Carolina's despair in *Il Matrimonio Segreto* made him burst into tears. Madame de Fervaques saw these tears; they formed such a sharp contrast with the usual manly firmness of his face that the great lady's soul, which had been saturated for so long with everything that is most corrosive in the pride of a *parvenue*, was touched by them. The little that was left of a woman's heart in her moved her to speak. She wanted to enjoy the sound of his voice at that moment.

"Have you seen the La Mole ladies?" she asked him. "They're in the third tier." Julien instantly thrust his head out of the box, leaning rather impolitely on the balustrade. He saw Mathilde; her eyes were glistening with tears.

"And yet it's not their day for the opera," he thought. "What zeal!"

Mathilde had persuaded her mother to go to the Italian Opera, despite the unsuitable position of the box which had been eagerly offered to them by one of the sycophants who frequented the house. She wanted to see whether Julien would spend that evening with Madame de Fervaques.

CHAPTER 31
Frighten Her

So this is the glorious miracle of your civilization! You have made love into an everyday affair.

—Barnave

JULIEN HURRIED to Mademoiselle de La Mole's box. Her eyes, wet with tears, were the first thing he saw; she was weeping without reserve. There were only insignificant people in the box: the friend who had lent it and a few men of her acquaintance. Mathilde placed her hand on Julien's; she seemed to have forgotten all fear of her mother. Almost choked by her tears, she said only this word to him: *"Guarantees!"*

"At least I mustn't speak to her," thought Julien, deeply moved himself, and hiding his eyes with his hand as best he could, on the pretext of shielding them from the light of the chandelier which dazzles the occupants of the third tier of boxes. "If I speak, she can no longer doubt the depth of my emotion, the sound of my voice will betray me; everything can still be lost."

His inner struggles were much more painful than they had been that morning; his heart had had time to become moved. He was afraid he might give Mathilde's vanity a chance to feel triumphant. Intoxicated with love and desire, he forced himself not to speak to her.

This, in my opinion, is one of the finest traits of his character; a man capable of such self-control may go far, *si fata sinant*.

Mademoiselle de La Mole insisted on taking Julien home. Fortunately it was raining heavily. But the marquise seated him opposite her, spoke to him constantly and made it impossible for him to say a word to her daughter. One would have thought the marquise was looking after his happiness. No longer afraid of losing everything because of the intensity of his emotion, he now abandoned himself to it without restraint.

Dare I tell you that when Julien returned to his room he covered with kisses the love letters Prince Korasov had given him?

"O great man!" he cried out in his frenzy. "How much I owe to you!"

He gradually recovered a little self-possession. He compared himself to a general who has just won the first phase of a great battle. "My advantage is certain, and enormous," he thought, "but what will happen tomorrow? One moment may ruin everything."

He impulsively opened the memoirs dictated by Napoleon on Saint Helena and forced himself to read them for two long hours; his eyes alone were reading, but he forced himself to go on nonetheless. As he was engaged in this singular occupation, his head and his heart, which had risen to the loftiest heights, were busily at work without his being aware of it. "Her heart is very different from Madame de Rênal's," he said to himself, but he went no further.

"Frighten her!" he suddenly cried out, throwing his book aside. "My enemy will obey me only as long as she's afraid of me, then she won't dare to despise me."

He paced up and down his little room, drunk with joy. To tell the truth, his happiness was due more to pride than to love.

"Frighten her!" he repeated to himself proudly, and he had reason to be proud. "Even in her happiest moments, Madame de Rênal always doubted that my love was equal to hers. Here, it's a demon that I'm subjugating, so I must really *subjugate*!"

He knew very well that the next morning, by eight o'clock, Mathilde would be in the library; he did not go there until nine o'clock, burning with love, but with his head dominating his heart. Not one minute went by, perhaps, without his repeating to himself, "I must keep her constantly occupied with this great doubt: 'Does he love me?' Her brilliant position, and the flattery of everyone who speaks to her, make her a little too sure of herself.''

He found her seated on the couch, pale and calm, but apparently incapable of making a single movement. She held out her hand to him and said, ''I've offended you, my darling, it's true; can you be angry with me?''

He had not been expecting this extremely simple tone. He was on the point of betraying himself.

''You want guarantees, my darling,'' she went on, after a silence which she had hoped to hear broken. ''That's only fair. Elope with me, let's go to London. . . . I'll be ruined forever, dishonored. . . .'' She had the courage to withdraw her hand from his so that she could cover her eyes with it. All her feelings of modesty and feminine virtue had returned to her heart. ''All right, dishonor me!'' she said at length with a sigh. ''That's a *guarantee*.''

''Yesterday I was happy because I had the courage to be severe with myself,'' thought Julien. After a short moment of silence he managed to control his heart enough to say in an icy tone, ''Once we're on our way to London, once you're dishonored, to use your expression, how do I know you'll love me? That my presence in the post chaise won't be unwelcome to you? I'm not a monster: having ruined your reputation would be only one more sorrow to me. It's not your position in society that's the obstacle: unfortunately it's your character. Can you yourself be sure that you'll love me for a week?''

(''Oh, if she'll love me for a week, only a week,'' he murmured to himself, ''I'll die of happiness! What do I care about the future, what do I care about life? And that divine happiness can begin again at this very moment if I will it—it depends entirely on me!'')

Mathilde saw that he was thoughtful.

''So I'm completely unworthy of you,'' she said, taking his hand.

He kissed her, but the iron hand of duty immediately gripped his heart. ''If she sees how much I adore her,'' he thought, ''I'll lose her.'' And, before leaving her arms, he resumed all the dignity that befits a man.

On that day, and the days that followed, he was able to conceal the intensity of his bliss; there were times when he even refused himself the pleasure of holding her in his arms. At other times, the delirium of his happiness prevailed over the counsels of prudence.

It was beside a bower of honeysuckle in the garden, arranged so as to conceal the ladder, that he had once been accustomed to stand and look at the shutters of Mathilde's window from afar, weeping over her inconstancy. There was a very large oak close by, and its trunk had sheltered him from prying eyes. As he walked with her past this same spot, which reminded him so vividly of his intense unhappiness, the contrast between his past despair and his present bliss was too strong for his character; tears flooded his eyes and, pressing his mistress's hand to his lips, he said to her, "Here I lived entirely in thoughts of you; here I used to watch those shutters, waiting for hours on end for the happy moment when I'd see this hand open them. . . ."

His weakness was complete. He portrayed to her, in true colors which one does not invent, the depth of his despair at that time. Brief interjections bore witness to his present happiness, which had put an end to that terrible pain. . . .

"Good God, what am I doing!" he thought, suddenly recovering his reason. "I'm ruining everything!"

Panic-stricken, he thought he could already see less love in Mademoiselle de La Mole's eyes. This was an illusion; but his face abruptly took on a new expression and turned deathly pale. His eyes became blank for an instant, and an expression of haughtiness not devoid of malice soon replaced that of the most sincere and unrestrained love.

"What's the matter, my darling?" asked Mathilde with tenderness and anxiety.

"I'm lying," said Julien angrily, "and I'm lying to *you*. I reproach myself for it, and yet God knows I respect you enough not to lie to you. You love me, you're devoted to me, and I have no need to make pretty speeches to please you."

"Good heavens! All those wonderful things you've been telling me for the last few minutes—they were nothing but pretty speeches?"

"Yes, and I bitterly reproach myself for them, my dearest. I once invented them for a woman who loved me and bored me. . . . That's the worst defect of my character; I'm denouncing myself to you. Forgive me."

Bitter tears streamed down Mathilde's cheeks.

"As soon as a reminder of something that's offended me sets me to thinking for a moment," continued Julien, "my detestable memory, which I now curse, offers me its resources and I misuse them.''

''Then I've unwittingly done something that's displeased you?'' asked Mathilde with charming simplicity.

''One day, I remember, as you were passing by these honeysuckles, you picked a flower; Monsieur de Luz took it from you and you let him keep it. I was only a few feet away.''

''Monsieur de Luz? That's impossible,'' said Mathilde, with the haughtiness that was so natural to her. ''I don't do things like that.''

''I'm certain you did,'' said Julien curtly.

''Well then, it's true, my darling,'' said Mathilde, sadly lowering her eyes. She was positive that for many months she had not allowed Monsieur de Luz to do such a thing.

Julien looked at her with inexpressible tenderness. ''No,'' he said to himself, ''she doesn't love me *less*.''

That evening she laughingly reproached him for his attraction to Madame de Fervaques; a commoner in love with a *parvenue*! ''Hearts of that kind are perhaps the only ones my Julien can't inflame; she'd already made you into a real dandy,'' she said, toying with his hair.

During the period in which he had believed himself to be despised by Mathilde, Julien had become one of the best-dressed men in Paris. But he still had one advantage over other men of that type: once he had finished dressing, he gave no further thought to his appearance.

One thing annoyed Mathilde: Julien went on copying the Russian letters and sending them to Madame de Fervaques.

CHAPTER 32
The Tiger

Alas! why these things and not others?
                    —Beaumarchais

AN ENGLISH TRAVELER relates how he lived on friendly terms with a tiger he had raised; he caressed it, but he always kept a loaded pistol on the table.

Julien abandoned himself to his great happiness only at times when Mathilde could not read it in his eyes. He scrupulously performed the duty of addressing a few harsh words to her from time to time. Whenever her sweetness, which he observed with astonishment, and her unquestioning devotion to him were about to rob him of all his self-control, he had the courage to leave her abruptly.

For the first time, Mathilde was in love. Life, which had always dragged along at a snail's pace for her, now took wings.

However, since her pride had to have some outlet, she sought to expose herself boldly to all the risks that her love could make her run. It was Julien who was cautious; and it was only when there was a question of danger that she did not yield to his will. But, submissive and humble with him, she was all the more arrogant toward everyone else in the house who approached her, relatives and servants alike.

In the evening, amid sixty people in the drawing room, she would call Julien over to speak with him in private and for a long time.

Once when young Tanbeau sat down beside her she asked him to go to the library and bring her the volume of Smollett containing the Revolution of 1688. He hesitated. "There's no hurry," she added, with an expression of insulting disdain that was a balm to Julien's heart.

"Have you noticed the look in that little monster's eyes?" he asked her.

"His uncle has put in ten or twelve years of service in this drawing room—if it weren't for that, I'd have had him dismissed immediately."

Her conduct toward Messieurs de Croisenois, de Luz, etc., while outwardly quite polite, was actually no less insulting. She bitterly reproached herself for all the confessions she had made to Julien in the past, especially since she did not dare to admit to him that she had exaggerated the almost completely innocent marks of interest she had given these gentlemen.

In spite of her finest resolutions, her feminine pride prevented her every day from saying to Julien, "It was because I was speaking to you that I took pleasure in describing my weakness in not taking my hand away when Monsieur de Croisenois happened to touch it lightly as he laid his hand on a marble table."

Now, whenever one of these gentlemen spoke to her for a few moments, she would almost immediately find some question to ask Julien, and this was a pretext for keeping him at her side.

*   *   *

She became pregnant and joyfully told Julien the news.

"Do you doubt me now? Isn't this a guarantee? I'm your wife forever."

Julien was profoundly disconcerted by this announcement. He nearly forgot the guiding principle of his conduct. "How can I be willfully cold and insulting to this poor girl who's ruining herself for me?" he thought. Whenever she looked the slightest bit indisposed, even on those days when the awesome voice of wisdom made itself heard, he no longer had the courage to address to her one of those cruel remarks which were so indispensable, according to his experience, to the continuance of their love.

"I'm going to write to my father," she said to him one day. "He's more than a father to me: he's a friend; and as such I think it would be unworthy of both of us to try to deceive him, even for a moment."

"Good God! What are you going to do?" said Julien in alarm.

"My duty," she replied, her eyes gleaming with joy. She felt that her attitude was nobler than her lover's.

"But he'll drive me out of his house in disgrace!"

"That's his right, and we must respect it. I'll give you my arm and we'll walk out the front door together in broad daylight."

Julien, amazed, asked her to delay action for a week.

"I can't," she replied. "Honor speaks, and my duty is clear; I must carry it out, and immediately."

"Then I order you to wait!" said Julien at length. "Your honor is safe, I'm your husband. That momentous step will change both our positions. I'm also within my rights. Today is Tuesday; the Duc de Retz is having a reception next Tuesday: when Monsieur de La Mole comes home that evening, the porter will give him the fateful letter. . . . His only thought is to make you a duchess, I'm sure of it, so think what his grief will be!"

"Do you mean to say 'think of his vengeance'?"

"I may feel pity for my benefactor, I may be heartbroken at the thought of doing him harm, but I fear no one, and I never will."

Mathilde gave in to him. This was the first time he had spoken to her with authority since she had announced her condition to him. He had never loved her so much before. The tender side of his nature was glad to use her condition as an excuse for ceasing to make cruel remarks to her. He was deeply perturbed by the thought of a confession to Monsieur de La Mole. Was he going to be separated from Mathilde? And, no matter how great her sorrow at seeing him go, would she still be thinking of him a month after his departure?

He felt an almost equal horror of the just reproaches the marquis might address to him.

That evening he confessed to Mathilde this second source of chagrin, and then, carried away by his love, he also confessed the first.

She changed color. "Would it really make you unhappy to spend six months away from me?" she asked.

"Terribly unhappy; it's the only misfortune in the world that I view with terror."

Mathilde was overjoyed. Julien had played his part so conscientiously that he had succeeded in making her think that she was more in love with him than he with her.

The fateful Tuesday soon arrived. When he came home at midnight, the marquis found a letter whose envelope bore instructions to open it personally and only when there were no witnesses present:

Dear Father,

All social bonds between us are broken; only those of nature remain. After my husband, you are and always will be the dearest person in the world to me. My eyes fill with tears as I think of the pain I am going to cause you, but, so that my shame will not become public, and to give you time to deliberate and act, I have been unable to postpone any longer the confession that I owe you. If your affection for me, which I know to be very great, will grant me a small allowance, I will go to live anywhere you say, in Switzerland, for example, with my husband. His name is so obscure that no one will recognize your daughter in Madame Sorel, daughter-in-law of a sawyer of Verrières. That is the name which it has been so painful for me to write.

I dread, for Julien's sake, your anger, which will be so just in appearance. I shall not be a duchess, father, but I knew that when I fell in love with him, for it was I who loved him first, and it was I who seduced him. I have inherited too noble a heart from you and our ancestors to let my attention be arrested by anything that is or seems to me to be vulgar. It was in vain that, in order to please you, I considered Monsieur de Croisenois. Why did you place true merit before me? You yourself told me when I returned from

Hyères, "That young Sorel is the only person I find entertaining." The poor boy is as deeply afflicted as I am, if that
is possible, by the pain this letter will cause you. I cannot
prevent you from being angry with me as my father; but
continue to love me as a friend.

Julien respected me. If he spoke to me occasionally, it
was only because of his profound gratitude to you, for the
natural pride of his character inclines him to reply only
officially to people of superior rank. He has a keen, innate
sense of social differences. It was I—I blush to confess it to
my best friend, and such a confession will never be made to
anyone else—who pressed his arm one day in the garden.

Twenty-four hours from now, why should you be angry
with him? My fault is irreparable. If you demand it, I will
be the one to convey to you the assurance of his profound
respect and of his despair at having displeased you. You
will never see him, but I will go to rejoin him anywhere he
wishes. It is his right and my duty; he is the father of my
child. If your kindness will grant us six thousand francs a
year to live on, I will accept it with gratitude; if not, Julien
intends to settle in Besançon and take up the profession of
teacher of Latin and literature.

No matter how low the position from which he starts, I
am certain that he will rise. With him, I have no fear of
obscurity. If there should be a revolution, I am sure that he
will play a leading part. Could you say the same of any of
those who have asked for my hand? They have fine estates—I
cannot see in this fact alone any reason for admiration.
My Julien would attain a high position even under the
present regime if he had a million francs and my father's
protection. . . .

Mathilde, who knew the marquis to be a man who acted
entirely on first impulses, had written eight pages.

"What should I do?" thought Julien while the marquis was
reading this letter. "Where does, first, my duty lie and, second,
my interest? My debt to him is enormous: if it hadn't been for
him, I'd have been nothing but an insignificant scoundrel, and
not enough of a scoundrel to avoid being hated and persecuted
by all the others. He's made me a man of the world. The times
when it's *necessary* to be a scoundrel will be less frequent and my
actions will be less ignoble. That's more than if he'd given me a
million. I owe this decoration to him; and the appearance of

having performed diplomatic services, which has raised me above
the crowd.

"If he picked up his pen to prescribe my conduct, what would
he write? . . ."

Julien was suddenly interrupted by Monsieur de La Mole's old
valet: "The marquis wants to see you immediately, whether
you're dressed or not."

As he walked along with Julien, the valet added softly, "He's
beside himself; be careful."

CHAPTER 33

The Hell of the Weak

> In cutting this diamond, a clumsy workman robbed it of
> some of its most brilliant facets. In the Middle Ages, nay,
> even in the days of Richelieu, Frenchmen had the *strength to
> will*.
>
> —Mirabeau

JULIEN FOUND the marquis furious. For the first time in his life,
perhaps, the great nobleman was guilty of bad form: he overwhelmed Julien with all the insults that came to his lips. Our
hero was taken aback and his patience was tried, but his gratitude remained unshaken. "How many fine plans, cherished for
so long in the back of his mind, the poor man is now seeing
destroyed in an instant!" he thought. "But I owe him an answer;
my silence would increase his anger." This answer was supplied
by the role of Tartuffe:

"I'm not an angel. . . . I've served you well, and you've paid
me generously . . . I was grateful, but I'm only twenty-two. . . .
In this house my thoughts were understood only by you, and by
that charming young lady."

"Monster!" cried the marquis. "Charming! Charming! The
day you found her charming, you should have left!"

"I tried to; I asked you at the time to let me go to Languedoc."

Tired of furiously pacing up and down, the marquis, crushed
by his sorrow, sank into a chair. Julien heard him murmur,
"He's not a malicious man."

"No, I'm not to you!" cried Julien, falling to his knees. But
he felt deeply ashamed of this impulse and stood up again very
quickly.

The marquis was utterly distraught. When he saw Julien's action he again began to overwhelm him with atrocious insults worthy of a hackney driver. The novelty of these oaths was perhaps a distraction.

"What! My daughter's name will be Madame Sorel! She won't be a duchess!" Each time these two ideas presented themselves to his mind in such clear terms, Monsieur de La Mole was tortured, and his emotions were no longer under his control. Julien was afraid the marquis might beat him.

During his lucid intervals, and when he began to grow accustomed to his misfortune, the marquis' reproaches became quite rational. "You should have gone away, monsieur," he said. "It was your duty to go away. . . . You're the lowest of men. . . ."

Julien stepped over to the table and wrote:

For a long time my life has been unbearable to me; I am putting an end to it. I beg the marquis to accept, along with the assurance of my boundless gratitude, my apologies for the embarrassment which may result from my death in his house.

"Please read what I've written on this piece of paper, monsieur," he said. "Either kill me or have me killed by your valet. It's one o'clock in the morning; I'm going to walk in the garden near the wall at the far end."

"Go to the devil!" the marquis shouted after him as he walked out.

"I understand," thought Julien; "he wouldn't be sorry to have me spare his valet the task of bringing about my death. . . . Let him kill me, that's a satisfaction I'm offering him. . . . But I love life, by God! . . . I owe myself to my son."

This idea, which had just clearly occurred to him for the first time, completely absorbed his mind after the first few minutes of his walk had been taken up with the awareness of danger.

This entirely new interest made him prudent. "I need advice on how to deal with that fiery man," he thought. "He's completely irrational, he's capable of anything. Fouqué is too far away, and besides, he wouldn't understand the feelings of a heart like the marquis'.

"Count Altamira . . . Could I be sure of eternal silence? My request for advice mustn't be a definite action that would complicate my situation. Alas, only the somber Father Pirard is left. . . .

His mind has been narrowed by Jansenism. Some scoundrel of a Jesuit would know more about the world, and be more what I need. . . . Father Pirard is capable of beating me as soon as I tell him about my sin.''

The spirit of Tartuffe came to Julien's aid: "All right," he thought, "I'll go and make my confession to him." This was his final decision after having walked in the garden for at least two hours. He had abandoned the idea that he might be surprised by a rifle shot, and he was growing sleepy.

Very early the next morning, he was several leagues outside Paris, knocking on the stern Jansenist's door. He found, to his great astonishment, that Father Pirard was not terribly surprised by his confession.

"Perhaps I ought to reproach myself," said the priest, more worried than angry. "I thought I'd guessed your love. My friendship for you, you little wretch, prevented me from warning her father. . . .''

"What's he going to do?" asked Julien anxiously. (He loved Father Pirard at that moment, and it would have been extremely painful for him to have a scene with him.) "I see three possibilities," he went on. "First, Monsieur de La Mole can have me killed." And he told about the suicide note he had given the marquis. "Second, he can have Count Norbert challenge me to a duel and shoot me."

"Would you accept the challenge?" asked Father Pirard furiously, standing up.

"You didn't let me finish. I would certainly never shoot at the son of my benefactor.

"Third, he can send me away. If he says to me, 'Go to Edinburgh, go to New York,' I'll obey. Then Mademoiselle de La Mole's condition can be concealed; but I'll never allow him to have my son done away with."

"That, you may be sure, will be the first idea that occurs to that corrupt man. . . .''

In Paris, Mathilde was in despair. She had seen her father toward seven o'clock. He had shown her Julien's note; she trembled with the fear that he might have thought it noble to put an end to his own life. "And without my permission!" she said to herself with a grief that was mingled with anger.

"If he's dead, I'll die too," she said to her father. "It's you who'll be the cause of his death. . . . You'll rejoice over it, perhaps. . . . But I swear to his departed spirit that first I'll go into mourning and make myself known publicly as his *widow*,

Madame Sorel; I'll send out funeral cards, you can count on
it. . . . You'll find me neither irresolute nor cowardly.''

Her love went to the point of madness. For his part, Monsieur
de La Mole was left speechless.

He began to take a fairly rational view of what had happened.
Mathilde did not appear at lunch. The marquis felt that an
immense weight had been lifted from him, and above all he felt
flattered when he discovered that she had said nothing to her
mother.

Julien arrived toward noon. The sound of his horse's hooves
rang out in the courtyard. He dismounted. Mathilde sent for him
and threw herself in his arms almost under the eyes of her maid.
He was not very grateful for this outburst; he was still feeling
circumspect and calculating as a result of his long conference
with Father Pirard. His imagination had been dulled by the
careful examination of possibilities. Mathilde told him with tears
in her eyes that she had seen his suicide note.

"My father may change his mind," she said. "Do me the
favor of leaving for Villequier immediately. Get back on your
horse and ride away from the house before they leave the table.''

Since Julien's expression of coldness and surprise remained
unchanged, she burst into tears. "Let me look after our affairs!"
she cried excitedly, clasping him in her arms. "You know very
well that I'm not separating myself from you of my own free
will. Write to me, but send your letters to my maid and have the
address written in a strange hand; as for me, I'll write you
volumes. Good-bye; hurry, go away.''

These last words wounded Julien, but he obeyed nevertheless.
"It's fated," he thought, "that even in their best moments these
people will always find a way to offend me.''

Monsieur de La Mole did not have the courage to act as a
father usually does in such circumstances. Mathilde firmly resisted all his *prudent* plans. She steadfastly refused to negotiate
on any basis other than this: She would be Madame Sorel and
live in poverty with her husband in Switzerland, or in her father's
house in Paris. She vehemently rejected the suggestion that she
give birth to her child in secret. "Then the possibility of slander
and dishonor would begin for me," she said. "Two months after
the wedding, I'll go on a journey with my husband, and it will
be easy for us to claim that my son was born at a suitable time.''

Received at first with outbursts of rage, her determination
finally made the marquis feel uncertain.

In a moment of tenderness he said to his daughter, "Look, here's a certificate for shares worth ten thousand francs a year: send it to your Julien, and tell him to act quickly to make it impossible for me to take it back."

In order to *obey* Mathilde, whose love of giving orders he knew well, Julien had made an unnecessary journey of forty leagues; he was at Villequier, putting the farmers' accounts in order. The marquis' gift brought about his return. He went to ask sanctuary of Father Pirard, who, during his absence, had become Mathilde's most useful ally. Each time he was questioned by the marquis, he proved to him that any course of action other than a public marriage would be a crime in the eyes of God.

"And fortunately," added the priest, "worldly wisdom is in accord with religion in this case. With Mademoiselle de La Mole's fiery character, could you count on her for one moment to keep a secret she hadn't imposed on herself? If you don't allow the straightforward course of a public marriage, society will concern itself much longer with this strange misalliance. Everything must be said once and for all, without any mystery, or even the appearance of it."

"That's true," said the marquis thoughtfully. "If we follow that line of action, any talk of the marriage three days after it happens will be nothing but the repetitious chatter of people who have no ideas of their own. We must take advantage of some important government measure against the Jacobins and slip past unnoticed in its wake."

Two or three of Monsieur de La Mole's friends were of Father Pirard's opinion. The great obstacle, in their eyes, was Mathilde's resolute character. But, after all these fine arguments, the marquis' heart was still unable to accept the idea of giving up all hope of a duchess's stool for his daughter.

His memory and his imagination were filled with all sorts of tricks and underhanded stratagems which had still been possible in his youth. To yield to necessity, to be afraid of the law seemed to him absurd and dishonoring for a man of his rank. He was now paying dearly for those enchanting dreams about his cherished daughter's future in which he had been indulging for the past ten years.

"Who could have foreseen it?" he said to himself. "A girl with such a haughty character, such a lofty mind, prouder than I am of the name she bears! A girl whose hand had been asked of me in advance by all the most illustrious names in France!

"We must give up all thought of prudence. This is an age in which everything is thrown into disorder! We are marching toward chaos."

CHAPTER 34

An Intelligent Man

> As he rode along on his horse, the prefect said to himself, "Why shouldn't I become a minister, president of the council, a duke? This is how I would make war. . . . By this means I would put all innovators in irons."
>
> —*Le Globe*

No ARGUMENT is strong enough to destroy the power of ten years of pleasant daydreams. The marquis found it unreasonable to be angry, but he could not bring himself to forgive. "If only Julien could die by accident . . ." he occasionally said to himself. It was thus that his saddened imagination found some solace in pursuing the most absurd fantasies. They paralyzed the influence of Father Pirard's wise reasoning. A month went by in this way, without a single step forward in the negotiations.

In this family affair, as in political affairs, the marquis had sudden brilliant ideas which would fire his enthusiasm for three days. During this time, no plan of action could please him because it was supported by sound arguments; an argument found favor in his eyes only insofar as it supported his pet scheme. For three days he would work with all the ardor and enthusiasm of a poet to arrange things in a certain way; by the following day he had ceased to think about it.

At first Julien was disconcerted by the marquis' dilatory behavior, but after several weeks had gone by he began to conclude that Monsieur de La Mole had not decided on any specific course of action in the matter.

Madame de La Mole and the rest of the household believed that Julien was traveling in the provinces to look after the administration of the estates; he was actually in hiding in Father Pirard's house and saw Mathilde nearly every day. She went to spend an hour with her father every morning, but sometimes they went for weeks on end without mentioning the matter that occupied all their thoughts.

"I don't want to know where that man is," the marquis said to her one morning. "Send him this letter." Mathilde read:

My estates in Languedoc bring in 20,600 francs a year. I am giving 10,600 francs to my daughter and 10,000 francs to Monsieur Julien Sorel. I am transferring ownership of the property itself, of course. Tell the notary to draw up two separate deeds of gift and bring them to me tomorrow; after that, there will be no further relations between us. Ah, monsieur, ought I to have expected all this?

The Marquis de La Mole

"Thank you very much," said Mathilde gaily. "We'll move into the Château d'Aiguillon, between Agen and Mermande. They say the scenery there is as beautiful as in Italy."

Julien was greatly surprised by this gift. He was no longer the stern, cold man we have known. The destiny of his son absorbed all his thoughts in advance. This unexpected fortune, rather sizable for such a poor man, made him ambitious. He saw himself and his wife with an income of 30,000 francs. As for Mathilde, all her feelings were absorbed in adoration of her husband, for this was what her pride always called Julien. Her great, her only ambition was to have her marriage recognized. She spent her time exaggerating the lofty wisdom she had shown in binding her destiny to that of a superior man. Personal merit was fashionable in her mind.

Their almost constant separation, the multiplicity of affairs and the little time they had for talking of love completed the good effect of the sensible policy Julien had devised some time before. Mathilde finally began to lose patience at having to see so little of the man she had succeeded in really loving. In a fit of anger she wrote to her father, beginning her letter like Othello:

My choice proves quite clearly that I have preferred Julien to the pleasures which society offered to the daughter of the Marquis de La Mole. Those pleasures of prestige and petty vanity mean nothing to me. I have been living apart from my husband for nearly six weeks now. That is long enough to show my respect for you. I will leave my father's house before next Thursday. Your kind gifts have made us rich. No one knows my secret except the worthy Father Pirard. I will go to his house, he will marry us, and an hour after the ceremony we will be on our way to Languedoc; we will never return to Paris unless you order us to.

But what pierces my heart is that all this will be a piquant

subject of gossip against me and against you. May not the
epigrams of a foolish public force our excellent Norbert to
challenge Julien to a duel? In that case, I know him, I
would have no power over him. We would find in his heart
something of a plebeian in revolt. I beg you on my knees,
father, to come to my wedding in Father Pirard's church
next Thursday. Some of the sting will be taken out of the
gossip, the life of your only son and that of my husband
will be made safe, etc., etc.

The marquis felt strangely disconcerted by this letter. He now
had to *make up his mind*. All his little habits, all his unrefined
friends had lost their influence.

In these strange circumstances, the strongest traits of his character, formed by the events of his youth, regained all their
power. The misfortunes of the Emigration had made him a man
of imagination. After having enjoyed for two years an immense
fortune and every distinction at court, in 1790 he had been cast
into the frightful miseries of the Emigration. This harsh school
had altered his twenty-two-year-old soul. Basically, he was
encamped among his present riches more than he was dominated
by them. But this same imagination which had preserved his soul
from the gangrene of gold had also made him the victim of a
frantic desire to see his daughter adorned with a distinguished
title.

At one point during the six weeks which had just passed, the
marquis, impelled by a caprice, had decided to make Julien rich;
he regarded poverty as ignoble and dishonoring for himself and
as impossible for his daughter's husband; he handed out his
money freely. The next day, his imagination having taken another course, it seemed to him that Julien would understand the
mute language of this generosity with money, change his name,
exile himself to America and write to Mathilde that he was dead
to her. Monsieur de La Mole imagined this letter already written
and followed out its effect on his daughter's character. . . .

On the day when he was roused from these youthful dreams
by Mathilde's *real* letter, after thinking for a long time about
either killing Julien or making him disappear, he began to dream
of building a brilliant career for him. He would have him take
the name of one of his estates; and why should he not have his
own peerage passed on to him? The Duc de Chaulnes, his
father-in-law, had spoken to him several times, after his only son

had been killed in Spain, of his desire to transmit his title to Norbert. . . .

"It cannot be denied," thought the marquis, "that Julien has a singular aptitude for business matters, boldness and, perhaps, even brilliance. . . . But at the bottom of his character I see something alarming. That's the impression he makes on everyone, so there must be something real in it." (The more difficult this reality was to grasp, the more it alarmed the imaginative old marquis.)

"My daughter put it very aptly the other day" (in a letter which we have not recorded): " 'Julien has not affiliated himself with any drawing room or any clique.' He hasn't provided himself with any support against me, not the slightest resource in case I should abandon him. . . . But does that show ignorance of the present state of society? . . . Two or three times I've said to him, 'The only real and profitable candidacy is for acceptance in a drawing room.'

"No, he doesn't have the cunning, wary mind of a lawyer who never loses a minute or an opportunity. . . . He's not at all a character in the style of Louis XI. On the other hand, he seems to accept the most ungenerous maxims. . . . I'm completely baffled. . . . Could it be that he repeats those maxims to himself to serve as a dam against his passions?

"One thing is clear at least: he can't tolerate contempt; that gives me some hold over him.

"He doesn't worship noble birth, it's true; he doesn't respect us instinctively. . . . That's a defect; but, after all, the heart of a seminary student shouldn't find anything intolerable except lack of pleasures and money. He's very different: he can't put up with contempt at any price."

Urged on by his daughter's letter, Monsieur de La Mole realized the necessity of making up his mind. "In any case," he thought, "here's the great question: Has Julien's audacity gone so far as to make him try to seduce my daughter because he knows I love her above all else in the world and that I have an income of three hundred thousand francs? Mathilde claims it's not true. . . . No, Julien my boy, this is one point on which I don't want to have any illusions.

"Did he fall in love with her sincerely and unexpectedly? Or was it only a vulgar desire to raise himself to a high position? Mathilde is shrewd: she realized from the start that any such suspicion could turn me violently against him, hence her confession that she was the first to fall in love. . . .

"Imagine a girl with her haughty character forgetting herself to the point of making physical advances! Pressing his arm in the garden one night—how disgusting! As though she didn't have a hundred less indecent ways of making him aware of her attraction to him! 'He who excuses himself accuses himself.' I don't trust Mathilde. . . ."

The marquis' reflections were more conclusive than usual that day. Habit prevailed nonetheless: he decided to gain time and write to his daughter; for they wrote to each other from one end of the house to the other: he did not dare to discuss matters with her and oppose her will. He was afraid he might conclude everything with a sudden concession. He wrote the following letter:

Refrain from committing any further acts of madness; here is a commission as Lieutenant of Hussars for Monsieur le Chevalier Julien Sorel de La Vernaye. You can see what I am doing for him. Do not oppose my wishes, do not question me. See that he leaves within twenty-four hours to report to Strasbourg, where his regiment is stationed. I am enclosing a draft on my banker. I expect to be obeyed.

Mathilde's love and joy knew no bounds. Wishing to take advantage of her victory, she replied immediately:

Monsieur de La Vernaye would be at your feet, overcome with gratitude, if he knew everything you have deigned to do for him. But, in the midst of this generosity, my father has forgotten me; your daughter's honor is in danger. One indiscretion may leave an eternal stain which an income of sixty thousand francs could not efface. I will send the commission to Monsieur de La Vernaye only if you give me your word that in the course of next month my marriage will be celebrated in public, at Villequier. Shortly after that period of time, which I beg you not to exceed, your daughter will be unable to appear in public except under the name of Madame de La Vernaye. How grateful I am to you, dear papa, for saving me from the name of Sorel, etc., etc.

The reply was unexpected:

Obey, or I will take everything back. Tremble, rash girl. I do not know what kind of man your Julien is, and you know less than I. He must leave for Strasbourg and watch his conduct carefully. I will let you know my wishes two weeks from now.

This extremely firm reply astonished Mathilde. "I don't know Julien"—this thought plunged her into a reverie which soon ended in the most enchanting suppositions; but she believed them to be the truth. "My Julien's mind hasn't put on the shoddy little *uniform* of the drawing rooms, and my father doesn't believe in his superiority, precisely because of what proves it. . . .

"Still, though, if I don't obey this slight stirring of character on his part, I see the possibility of a public scene; a scandal would lower my standing in society, and it might make me less attractive to Julien. After the scandal . . . ten years of poverty; and the folly of choosing a husband for his merit can be saved from ridicule only by the most dazzling opulence. If I live apart from my father, at his age he may forget me. . . . Norbert will marry some charming, wily woman: Louis XIV was bewitched in his old age by the Duchesse de Bourgogne. . . ."

She decided to obey, but she was careful not to let Julien know about her father's letter; his fiery temperament might have led him to commit some foolish act.

That evening, when she told him that he was a Lieutenant of Hussars, his joy was unbounded. It can easily be imagined in view of the ambition of his entire life, and the passion he now felt for his son. The change of name filled him with astonishment.

"At last," he thought, "my story has reached its climax, and the credit is all mine. I've succeeded in making myself loved by this monster of pride," he added, looking at Mathilde. "Her father can't live without her, nor she without me."

CHAPTER 35

A Storm

O God, give me mediocrity!
—Mirabeau

His MIND was preoccupied; he responded only halfheartedly to her expressions of ardent tenderness. He remained taciturn and somber. Never before had he appeared so great, so adorable to her. She dreaded some subtle impulse of his pride which might upset the entire situation.

She saw Father Pirard come to the house early next morning. Was it not possible that, through him, Julien had fathomed something of her father's intentions? Might not the marquis himself have written to him in a moment of caprice? After such great good fortune, what explanation could there be for Julien's air of severity? She did not dare to question him.

She *did not dare*! She, Mathilde! From then on, there was something vague, mysterious, almost terrifying in her feeling for Julien. Her barren heart felt all the passion that is possible in a person brought up in the midst of that overabundance of civilization which Paris admires.

Early the next morning, Julien was in Father Pirard's house. A team of post horses arrived in the courtyard drawing a dilapidated chaise rented from the neighboring post house.

"Such a carriage is no longer in keeping with your position," said the stern priest gruffly. "Here's twenty thousand francs which Monsieur de La Mole is giving you as a present; he expects you to spend it within the year, but he wants you to try to make yourself as little ridiculous as possible." (In such a large sum lavished on a young man, the priest saw nothing but an opportunity for sin.)

"The marquis adds: 'Monsieur Julien de La Vernaye will have received this money from his father, whom there is no need to describe more fully. Monsieur de La Vernaye may see fit to give a gift to Monsieur Sorel, a sawyer in Verrières, who took care of him in his childhood.' I can carry out that part of his instructions," added Father Pirard. "I've at last persuaded Monsieur de La Mole to come to terms with Abbé de Frilair, who's such a Jesuit. His influence is decidedly too strong for us. The tacit

recognition of your noble birth by that man who rules over
Besançon will be one of the implicit terms of our agreement.''

Julien could no longer control his emotion; he embraced Father Pirard; he saw himself recognized.

"Come now! What's the meaning of this worldly vanity?"
said the priest, pushing him away. "As for Sorel and his sons, I
will offer them, in my name, a pension of five hundred francs a
year for each of them as long as I'm satisfied with them.''

Julien had already grown cold and distant. He thanked Father
Pirard, but in very vague terms which committed him to nothing.
"Is it really possible," he wondered, "that I'm the illegitimate
son of some great nobleman exiled to our mountains by the
terrible Napoleon?" This idea seemed less improbable to him at
every moment. "My hatred for my father would be a proof . . .
I'd no longer be a monster!"

A few days after this monologue, the Fifteenth Regiment of
Hussars, one of the most distinguished in the army, was drawn
up in battle array on the parade ground in Strasbourg. The
Chevalier de La Vernaye was seated on the finest horse in
Alsace, which had cost him six thousand francs. He had been
commissioned a lieutenant without ever having been a second
lieutenant, except on the muster roll of a regiment of which he
had never heard.

His impassive air, his stern, almost hostile eyes, his pallor and
his imperturbable self-possession had begun to make his reputation from the first day. Shortly afterward, his perfect, measured
politeness and his skill with the pistol and the sword, which he
made known without too much affectation, made his companions
lose all thought of joking audibly at his expense. After five or six
days of hesitation, the general opinion of the regiment declared
itself in his favor. "That young man has everything," said the
facetious old officers, "except youth."

From Strasbourg Julien wrote to Father Chélan, the former
parish priest of Verrières, who was now approaching the extreme
limits of old age:

You have probably learned, with a joy of which I have
no doubt, of the events which have led my family to make
me rich. I am sending you five hundred francs, which I beg
you to distribute quietly, without mentioning my name, to
the unfortunate people who are now poor as I was in the
past, and whom you are no doubt helping as you once
helped me.

Julien was intoxicated with ambition, not with vanity; never-theless he devoted a great deal of his attention to his outward appearance. His horses, his uniforms and the liveries of his servants were all kept in a state of impeccability that would have done honor to the punctiliousness of a great English nobleman. Although only a lieutenant who had received his commission by special favor, after the second day he began to calculate that, in order to be commander-in-chief of an army by the age of thirty at the latest, like all great generals, he would have to be something more than a lieutenant by the age of twenty-three. He thought of nothing but glory and his son.

It was in the midst of transports of the most unbridled ambi-tion that he was surprised by a young footman of the Hôtel de La Mole who came to deliver a letter from Mathilde:

> All is lost. Come back as quickly as possible: sacrifice everything, desert if necessary. As soon as you arrive, wait for me in a hackney beside the little door to the garden of the house at no. —, rue ———. I will come to speak to you; I may be able to let you into the garden. All is lost, and, I fear, irretrievably. Count on me; you will find me devoted and steadfast in the face of adversity. I love you.

Within a few minutes, Julien obtained leave from his colonel and rode out of Strasbourg at full speed; but the terrible anxiety with which he was consumed did not allow him to continue this mode of travel any further than Metz. He leapt into a post chaise, and it was with nearly incredible speed that he reached the appointed place, beside the little door to the garden of the Hôtel de La Mole. This door opened and Mathilde, forgetting all concern for the opinions of others, threw herself in his arms. Fortunately it was only five o'clock in the morning and the streets were still deserted.

"All is lost," she said. "My father, dreading my tears, went away Thursday night. Where did he go? No one knows. Here's his letter, read it." And she climbed into the carriage with Julien.

> I could forgive anything except the plan of seducing you because you are rich. That, wretched girl, is the horrible truth. I give you my word of honor that I will never consent to your marrying that man. I promise him an income of ten thousand francs a year if he will live far away, beyond the

French frontier, or, better still, in America. Read the letter I have received in reply to my request for information. It was the impudent young man himself who urged me to write to Madame de Rênal. I will never read one line from you about him. Both you and Paris have become abominable to me. I urge you to keep the strictest secrecy about what is going to happen. Give up that vile man *completely* and you will regain a father.

"Where is Madame de Rênal's letter?" asked Julien coldly.
"Here it is; I didn't want to show it to you until you were prepared for it."

What I owe to the sacred cause of religion and morality forces me, monsieur, to the painful step I take in writing to you. An inflexible principle now commands me to harm my neighbor, but it is in order to avoid a greater evil. The sorrow I feel must be overcome by a sense of duty. It is only too true, monsieur, that the conduct of the person about whom you have asked me to tell the truth may have seemed inexplicable or even honorable. It was no doubt deemed advisable to conceal or disguise part of the truth; discretion required it, as well as religion. But that conduct, about which you wish to be informed, has been in fact extremely reprehensible, more so than I can say. Poor and self-seeking, it was with the aid of the most consummate hypocrisy, and by seducing a weak and unhappy woman, that the man in question sought to make a career for himself and win a respected position in society. It is part of my painful duty to add that I am forced to believe that Monsieur J. has no religious principles. I have no choice but to believe that one of his methods of succeeding in a house is to try to seduce the woman who has the most influence. Under cover of apparent disinterestedness and phrases taken from novels, his great and only object is to succeed in gaining control over the master of the house and his fortune. He leaves behind him unhappiness and eternal regret, etc., etc., etc.

This letter, extremely long and half effaced by tears, was undeniably in Madame de Rênal's handwriting; it was even written with greater care than usual.

*   *   *

"I can't blame Monsieur de La Mole," said Julien when he had finished reading it. "He's just and wise. What father would want to give his beloved daughter to such a man! Good-bye."

He leapt out of the hackney and ran to his post chaise, which was waiting for him at the end of the street. Mathilde, whom he seemed to have forgotten, took a few steps to follow him; but the stares of the tradesmen who were coming to the doors of their shops, and to whom she was known, forced her to hurry back into the garden.

Julien had set off for Verrières. During this rapid journey he was unable to write to Mathilde as he had intended; his hand made nothing but illegible scrawls on the paper.

He arrived in Verrières on a Sunday morning. He went to see the local gunsmith, who overwhelmed him with congratulations on his recent good fortune. It was the talk of the district. Julien had great difficulty in making him understand that he wanted a pair of pistols. At his request, the gunsmith loaded them.

The "three bells" were sounding. This is a well-known signal in French villages; after the various peals of the morning, it announces that mass is about to begin.

Julien entered the newly built church of Verrières. All the tall windows of the edifice were veiled with crimson curtains. He found himself a few paces behind Madame de Rênal's pew. It seemed to him that she was praying fervently. The sight of that woman who had loved him so deeply made his arm tremble so violently that at first he was unable to carry out his plan. "I can't do it," he said to himself, "it's physically impossible for me."

Just then the young cleric who was serving at mass rang the bell for the Elevation of the Host. Madame de Rênal bowed her head, which for an instant was almost entirely covered by the folds of her shawl. Julien no longer recognized her so clearly; he fired one of his pistols at her and missed. He fired a second shot; she fell.

CHAPTER 36
Painful Details

Do not expect any weakness on my part. I have avenged myself. I have deserved death and here I am. Pray for my soul.
—Schiller

JULIEN STOOD motionless; he no longer saw anything. When he recovered his senses a little, he saw the whole congregation fleeing from the church; the priest had left the altar. Julien began to walk rather slowly behind some women who were screaming as they went out. One woman, trying to flee more quickly than the others, pushed him violently; he fell. His feet became entangled in a chair that had been overturned by the crowd; as he got up, he felt something grip his neck: it was a gendarme in full uniform who was arresting him. Mechanically, Julien tried to use his small pistols, but a second gendarme seized his arms.

He was taken to prison. They entered a room, his hands were manacled and he was left alone after being locked in with a double turn of the key. All this was done very quickly, and he was unconscious of it.

"Well, it's all over," he said aloud when he recovered his senses. "Yes, in two weeks the guillotine . . . unless I kill myself before then."

His reasoning went no further; his head felt as though it were being violently squeezed. He looked to see if someone were holding it. A few moments later he fell into a deep sleep.

Madame de Rênal was not mortally wounded. The first bullet had gone through her hat; as she turned around, the second shot had been fired. The bullet had struck her in the shoulder and, surprisingly, had been deflected by the shoulder blade, which it nevertheless shattered, onto a Gothic pillar, from which it broke off an enormous splinter of stone.

When, after a long and painful dressing, the surgeon, a solemn man, said to Madame de Rênal, "I answer for your life as for my own," she was deeply afflicted. For a long time she had been sincerely yearning for death. Her letter to Monsieur de La Mole, which her present confessor had ordered her to write, had dealt the final blow to that woman who had been weakened by

too much sorrow. This sorrow came from Julien's absence; she
called it remorse. Her confessor, a virtuous and fervent young
ecclesiastic who had recently arrived from Dijon, clearly saw the
truth of the matter.

"To die this way, but not by my own hand, isn't a sin," she
thought. "God will forgive me, perhaps, for rejoicing over my
death." She did not dare to add, "And to die by Julien's hand is
the height of bliss for me."

As soon as she was rid of the presence of the surgeon and all
the friends who had flocked to see her, she summoned Elisa, her
maid.

"The jailer," she said to her, blushing deeply, "is a cruel
man. He will no doubt treat him harshly, thinking it will please
me. . . . That idea is unbearable to me. Couldn't you go to the
jailer, as though of your own accord, and give him this little
packet containing several louis? Tell him that religion doesn't
allow him to mistreat him. . . . But it's absolutely essential that
he speak to no one about this gift of money."

It was to the circumstances we have just described that Julien
owed the humane treatment he received from the jailer of Verrières.
This jailer was still Monsieur Noiroud, the perfect law official, whom
we have seen so frightened by the presence of Monsieur Appert.

A judge appeared in Julien's cell. He wore a pompous expression. Julien knew that he was soliciting a tobacco license for one
of his nephews. The sight of this man was painful to him and
diminished his courage.

"I've committed premeditated murder," Julien said to him.
"I bought the pistols from Monsieur ————, the gunsmith, and
had him load them for me. Article 1342 of the Penal Code is
quite clear; I deserve death and I expect it."

The judge's petty mind did not understand this frankness; he
multiplied his questions, hoping to make the accused contradict
himself in his replies.

"But can't you see," said Julien, smiling, "that I'm making
myself as guilty as you could wish? Leave me, monsieur; you
won't fail to get the prey you're after. You'll have the pleasure
of passing sentence on me. Spare me your presence."

"I still have one tiresome duty to perform," thought Julien.
"I must write to Mademoiselle de La Mole."

I have taken my revenge [he told her]. Unfortunately my
name will appear in the newspapers, and I cannot escape

from this world incognito; please forgive me for that. I will die within two months. My vengeance was terrible, like the pain of being separated from you. From now on I forbid myself either to write or to speak your name. Never speak of me, even to my son; silence is the only way to honor me. To ordinary men I will be a common murderer. Allow me to speak the truth in this supreme moment: you will forget me. This great catastrophe, which I advise you never to mention to a living soul, will have exhausted for several years all the romantic and adventurous strains which I saw in your character. You were made to live with the heroes of the Middle Ages; show their firmness of character. Let what must happen take place in secret and without compromising yourself. Take an assumed name and confide in no one. If it is absolutely necessary for you to have the help of a friend, I bequeath you Father Bernard. Speak to no one else; above all, you must not speak to anyone of your social class, such as Luz or Caylus.

A year after my death, marry Monsieur de Croisenois, I beg you, I order you as your husband. Do not write to me; I would not answer. Although much less wicked than Iago, it seems to me, I will say as he did, "From this time forth I never will speak word."

No one will hear me speak or see me write; my last words, as well as my last adoring thoughts, will have been for you.

J. S.

It was after sending off this letter that Julien, having slightly recovered his senses, was extremely unhappy for the first time. All the hopes of his ambition had to be torn from his heart one after the other by the awesome words, "I'm going to die." Death in itself did not seem horrible to him. His whole life had been nothing but a long preparation for misfortune, and he had been careful not to overlook that misfortune which is regarded as the greatest of all.

"What!" he said to himself. "If in sixty days I had to fight a duel with a man who's an extremely good swordsman, would I be so weak as to think about it constantly, and with terror in my soul?"

He spent over an hour trying to see into the depths of his own heart with regard to this matter. After he had seen clearly what was there, after the truth had appeared to him as distinctly as one of the pillars of his prison, he began to think of remorse.

"Why should I feel any? I was wronged atrociously; I've killed, I deserve death, but that's all. I'll die after having settled my account with humanity. I'll leave no unfulfilled obligations behind me, I owe nothing to anyone. There will be nothing shameful about my death except the instrument of it; that alone, it's true, will be more than enough to shame me in the eyes of the townspeople of Verrières; but, from an intellectual point of view, what could be more contemptible! There's still one way I could make them respect me: I could scatter gold coins to the crowd as I go to my death. Linked with the idea of gold, my memory would be glorious to them."

After these reflections, which seemed self-evident to him a minute later, he said to himself, "I have nothing more to do on this earth." He then fell fast asleep.

Toward nine o'clock in the evening he was awakened by the jailer, who was bringing him his supper.

"What are people saying in Verrières?"

"Monsieur Julien, the oath I took before the crucifix in the royal court, on the day I was installed in my post, obliges me to keep silence."

He said nothing more, but he remained in the cell. The sight of this vulgar hypocrisy amused Julien. "I must make him wait a long time," he thought, "for the five francs for which he wants to sell me his conscience."

When the jailer saw the meal being finished without any attempt at bribery, he said, with a sly, ingratiating expression, "My friendship for you, Monsieur Julien, forces me to speak, even though they say it's against the interests of justice, since it may help you to draw up your defense. . . . You're a kind young man, Monsieur Julien; you'll be glad to hear that Madame de Rênal is getting better."

"What! She's not dead?" cried Julien, thunderstruck.

"What! You didn't know?" said the jailer with an expression of bewilderment which soon changed to one of joyful greed. "It would be only fair, monsieur, for you to give something to the surgeon, who, according to law and justice, shouldn't have said anything. But, as a favor to you, monsieur, I went to see him, and he told me everything. . . ."

"In short, the wound isn't fatal," said Julien impatiently, stepping toward him. "Will you answer for that with your life?"

The jailer, a six-foot giant, became frightened and retreated toward the door. Julien saw that he was going the wrong way to arrive at the truth; he sat down again and threw a napoleon to Monsieur Noiroud.

As the jailer's story proved to him that Madame de Rênal's wound was not fatal, Julien began to feel himself overcome by tears.

"Get out!" he said abruptly.

The jailer obeyed. As soon as the door was closed Julien cried out, "My God! She's not dead!" And he fell to his knees, weeping hot tears.

At that supreme moment he believed in God. What matter the hypocrisies of the priests? Can they take away any of the truth and sublimity of the idea of God?

Only then did he begin to repent of the crime he had committed. By a coincidence that saved him from despair, it was only then that he came out of the state of physical irritation and semi-insanity in which he had been plunged since leaving Paris for Verrières.

His tears sprang from a noble source; he had no doubt about the sentence that was awaiting him. "So she'll live!" he said to himself. "She'll live to forgive me and love me. . . ."

The jailer awakened him very late the next morning. "You must have a wonderful heart, Monsieur Julien," he said. "I came in twice and decided not to wake you. Here are two bottles of very good wine sent to you by Father Maslon, our parish priest."

"What? Is that scoundrel still here?" said Julien.

"Yes, monsieur," replied the jailer, lowering his voice, "but don't talk so loud, it might do you harm."

Julien laughed heartily. "At the point I've reached, my friend, only you could do me any harm, if you stopped being gentle and humane. . . . You'll be well paid," he said, stopping short and resuming his imperious air, which he justified immediately by the gift of a coin.

Monsieur Noiroud told him again, and in great detail, everything he had learned about Madame de Rênal, but he said nothing about Mademoiselle Elisa's visit.

The jailer was as base and compliant as it is possible to be. An idea crossed Julien's mind: "This misshapen giant probably earns no more than three or four hundred francs, because his prison is hardly crowded; I can guarantee him ten thousand francs if he'll escape to Switzerland with me. . . . The difficulty will be to convince him of my good faith.'' The idea of the long discussion he would have to have with such a vile creature filled him with disgust; he began to think of something else.

That evening it was too late. A post chaise came to take him away at midnight. He was quite pleased with the gendarmes who were his traveling companions. In the morning, when he reached the prison of Besançon, they were kind enough to lodge him on the upper story of a Gothic tower. He judged that the architecture was of the early fourteenth century; he admired its grace and pleasing delicacy. Through a narrow gap between two walls on the far side of a wide courtyard, there was a magnificent view.

The next day he was formally questioned; after this he was left in peace for several days. His mind was calm. He could see nothing complicated in his case: ''I tried to kill, I must be killed.''

He pursued the matter no further. The trial, the annoyance of appearing in public, his defense—he regarded these things as slight difficulties, tedious ceremonies which he would not have to think about until the day actually arrived. The moment of death scarcely absorbed any more of his attention: ''I'll think about it after the sentence.'' Life was not boring for him; he began to consider all things in a new light. He no longer had any ambition. He seldom thought of Mademoiselle de La Mole. His remorse occupied his mind a great deal and often brought the image of Madame de Rênal before his eyes, especially in the silence of the night, which, in that lofty tower, was broken only by the cries of the ospreys.

He thanked heaven that he had not wounded her fatally. ''It's amazing!'' he thought. ''I thought she'd forever destroyed my future happiness with her letter to Monsieur de La Mole, and yet, less than two weeks after the date of that letter, I no longer give any thought to the things that occupied my mind then. . . . Two or three thousand francs a year to live quietly in a mountain village like Vergy . . . I was happy then . . . I didn't realize how happy I was!''

At other times he would leap up from his chair with a start. ''If I'd wounded Madame de Rênal fatally, I'd have killed myself. . . . I need to be certain of that in order not to regard myself with horror.

''Shall I kill myself? That's the great question. Those judges, who are such sticklers for formalities, who are so eager to convict the poor man on trial, and who'd hang the finest citizen in order to get a decoration to put on their chests—I'd escape from their power, from their insults in bad French, which the local newspapers will call eloquence. . . ."

A few days later he said to himself, "I can still live for five or six weeks, more or less. . . . Kill myself? No, by God! Napoleon went on living. . . .

"Besides, I find life pleasant now; my room is quiet, and there are no bores here," he added, laughing. And he began to make a list of the books he wanted to have sent from Paris.

CHAPTER 37

A Prison Tower

The tomb of a friend.
—Sterne

HE HEARD a loud noise in the corridor; it was not an hour when anyone usually came up to his cell. An osprey flew away screaming, the door opened and the venerable Father Chélan, trembling all over and holding a cane in his hand, threw himself in his arms.

"Oh, dear God, is it possible, my son! . . . Monster, I should say!" And the worthy old man was unable to say another word. Julien was afraid he might fall. He had to lead him to a chair. The hand of time had weighed heavily on that man who had once been so energetic. It seemed to Julien that he was no longer anything but the shadow of himself.

When he had caught his breath he said, "Only day before yesterday I received your letter from Strasbourg with the five hundred francs for the poor of Verrières. It was brought to me in the mountains at Liveru, where I've gone to live with my nephew Jean. Yesterday I learned of the catastrophe. . . . O God, is it possible?" The old man was no longer weeping; he looked as though his mind were blank, and he added mechanically, "You'll need your five hundred francs, so I've brought it back to you."

"I need to see you, father!" cried Julien, deeply moved. "I have more than enough money."

But he could no longer get a coherent answer. From time to time Father Chélan would shed a few tears which rolled silently down his cheeks, then he would look at Julien and appear to be dazed at seeing him take his hands and raise them to his lips. His face, which had once been so full of life, and which had formerly expressed the noblest sentiments with such vigor, now wore a constant air of apathy. A man who looked like a peasant soon came to take the old priest away. "You mustn't tire him and make him speak too much," he said to Julien, who realized that he was the nephew. This visit left Julien plunged in bitter sorrow which held back his tears. Everything seemed to him sad and void of consolation; he felt his heart turned to ice in his chest.

This moment was the most painful he had experienced since his crime. He had just seen death in all its ugliness. All his illusions of lofty courage and nobility had been scattered like clouds before a storm.

This terrible condition lasted for several hours. After mental poisoning, one needs physical remedies and champagne. Julien would have considered himself cowardly if he had resorted to such things. Toward the end of a horrible day, spent entirely in pacing up and down his narrow cell, he cried out, "I'm mad! The sight of that poor old man should have plunged me into this black melancholy only if I were fated to die an ordinary death; but a swift death in the flower of youth is precisely what will save me from that sad decay."

Despite all his reasoning, he found himself deeply moved, like an ordinary weak-willed man, and therefore made unhappy by Father Chélan's visit. No longer was there anything stalwart or grandiose about him, no longer any Roman virtue; death now seemed higher to him, and less easy.

"That will be my thermometer," he said to himself. "This evening I'm ten degrees below the courage needed to raise me to the level of the guillotine. This morning I had that courage. But then what's the difference, as long as it comes back to me when I need it?" This idea of a thermometer amused him, and finally succeeded in distracting him.

When he woke up the next morning he was ashamed of the day before. "My happiness, my peace of mind are at stake," he thought. He almost decided to write to the attorney general to ask that no one be allowed to visit him. "And what about Fouqué?" he thought. "If he has the courage to come to Besançon, how great his grief will be!"

It had been two months, perhaps, since he had last given a thought to Fouqué. "I was an utter fool in Strasbourg," he said to himself. "My thoughts never went beyond my coat collar." Memories of Fouqué occupied his mind for a long time and filled him with tender emotion. He paced up and down his cell in agitation. "I'm at least twenty degrees below the level of death now. . . . If this weakness increases, it will be better to kill myself. What a joy it will be to the Maslons and the Valenods if I die like a contemptible wretch!"

Fouqué arrived; the simple, kindly man was distraught with sorrow. His sole idea, if he had one at all, was to sell everything he owned so that he could bribe the jailer to let Julien escape. He spoke at great length about Monsieur de Lavalette's escape.

"You're causing me pain," said Julien. "Monsieur de Lavalette was innocent. Without meaning to, you're making me think about the difference. . . . But is it true? What! You'd sell everything you own?" he added, suddenly becoming wary and mistrustful again.

Fouqué, delighted to see his friend at last responsive to his dominant idea, gave him a long and detailed account, calculated to within a hundred francs, of how much he would get for each one of his possessions.

"What a sublime effort for a provincial landowner to make!" thought Julien. "How much thrift, how many petty acts of stinginess, which made me blush when I saw them, he's sacrificing for me! None of those handsome young men I saw in the Hôtel de La Mole, and who read *René,* would do any of those ridiculous things, but, except for those who are very young and have inherited fortunes, and don't know the value of money, which one of those elegant Parisians would be capable of such a sacrifice?"

All of Fouqué's grammatical mistakes, all his crude mannerisms disappeared, and Julien threw himself in his arms. Never have the provinces, compared with Paris, received a finer tribute. Fouqué, delighted with the enthusiasm he read in his friend's eyes, took it as a sign that he had consented to escape.

This vision of the sublime restored to Julien all the strength which Father Chélan's visit had taken away from him. He was still very young, but, in my opinion, he was a healthy plant. Instead of going from tenderness to craftiness, as most men do, with age he would have acquired kindness and a sensitivity to tender emotions, he would have been cured of his insane mistrustfulness. . . . But what is the use of these vain predictions?

Interrogations were becoming more frequent, despite Julien's efforts; his answers were all designed to shorten the legal processes: "I've killed, or at least I tried to, and with premeditation," he repeated every day. But the judge placed formalities above all else. Julien's declaration did not shorten his interrogations at all; the judge's self-esteem was offended. Julien did not know that at one point it had been decided to transfer him to a horrible dungeon, and that it was thanks to Fouqué's efforts that he had been left in his attractive room a hundred and eighty steps above the ground.

Abbé de Frilair was one of the important men who bought their firewood from Fouqué. The worthy merchant succeeded in obtaining an interview with the all-powerful vicar-general. To his inexpressible delight, Monsieur de Frilair informed him that, appreciating Julien's good qualities and the services he had once rendered to the seminary, he intended to speak to the judges in his favor. Fouqué glimpsed a hope of saving his friend, and as he left, bowing all the way to the floor, he asked the vicar-general to distribute the sum of ten louis for masses imploring the acquittal of the accused.

Fouqué was radically mistaken. Monsieur de Frilair was not a Valenod. He refused and even tried to make the good peasant understand that he would do better to keep his money. Seeing that it was impossible to express himself clearly without imprudence, he advised him to give the ten louis as alms for the poor prisoners, who, as a matter of fact, were in need of everything.

"That Julien is a strange creature," thought Monsieur de Frilair. "His action is inexplicable, and nothing ought to be inexplicable to me. . . . Perhaps it will be possible to make a martyr of him. . . . In any case, I'll find out what's behind this affair, and I may find an opportunity of frightening Madame de Rênal, who has no respect for us and detests me in her heart. . . . Perhaps I may be able to find in all this some way to bring about an impressive reconciliation with Monsieur de La Mole, who has a weakness for that little seminary student."

The agreement terminating his lawsuit had been signed a few weeks earlier, and Father Pirard had left Besançon, not without speaking of Julien's mysterious birth, on the very day when the unfortunate young man had tried to kill Madame de Rênal in the church of Verrières.

Julien now saw only one more disagreeable event between him and death: a visit from his father. He consulted Fouqué about his idea of writing to the attorney general to ask to be excused from having any visitors. This horror of seeing his father, and in such circumstances, profoundly shocked the timber merchant's honest bourgeois heart. He now thought he understood why so many people passionately hated his friend. Out of respect for his sorrow, he concealed what he felt.

"In any case," he replied coldly, "that order of solitary confinement wouldn't apply to your father."

CHAPTER 38

A Powerful Man

But her actions are so mysterious, her figure so elegant! Who can she be?

—Schiller

THE DOORS of the prison were opened at a very early hour the next morning. Julien awoke with a start. "Oh, my God!" he thought. "Here comes my father! What an unpleasant scene!"

At the same moment, a woman dressed as a peasant threw herself in his arms and hugged him convulsively. He had difficulty in recognizing her: it was Mademoiselle de La Mole.

"You're so cruel!" she said. "I didn't know where you were until I received your letter. And it wasn't until I came to Verrières that I found out about what you call your crime, but which was nothing but a noble vengeance that shows me all the grandeur of the heart that beats in your breast."

Despite his prejudices against Mademoiselle de La Mole, which he did not clearly admit to himself, Julien found her extremely attractive. How could he fail to see in her whole way of acting and speaking a noble, disinterested sentiment that was far above anything a petty and commonplace heart would have dared to feel? It seemed to him that he was still in love with a queen; he yielded to her enchantment, and a few moments later he said to her with rare nobility of thought and speech:

"The image of the future was clearly outlined before my eyes. After my death, I would bring about your marriage to Monsieur de Croisenois, who would be marrying a widow. The noble but somewhat romantic heart of that charming widow, astonished and converted to the worship of ordinary prudence by an event that was singular, tragic and great for her, would deign to recognize the young marquis' very real merit. You would resign yourself to commonplace happiness: prestige, wealth, high rank. . . . But, dear Mathilde, your arrival in Besançon, if it's suspected, will be a mortal blow to Monsieur de La Mole, and I'll never forgive myself for that. I've already caused him so much sorrow! The academician will say that he has warmed a serpent in his bosom.''

"I must confess I wasn't expecting so much cold reason, so much concern for the future," said Mademoiselle de La Mole half angrily. "My maid, who's almost as prudent as you are, took out a passport for herself, and it was under the name of Madame Michelet that I came here by stagecoach.''

"And was it just as easy for Madame Michelet to come here to see me?''

"Ah, you're still the same superior man, the one I singled out above all others! First of all, I offered a hundred francs to a judge's secretary, who claimed it was impossible for me to enter this prison. But after he took my money, the honest man made me wait and raised objections; I thought he was thinking of robbing me. . . .'' She stopped.

"Well?'' said Julien.

"Don't be angry, my darling," she said, kissing him. "I had to give my name to the secretary, who took me for a young Paris seamstress in love with the handsome Julien. . . . Those are his own words, in fact. I swore to him I was your wife, and I'll have permission to see you every day.''

"Her foolish action is complete," thought Julien. "I wasn't able to prevent it. After all, Monsieur de La Mole is such a great nobleman that public opinion will easily find an excuse for the young colonel who will marry this charming widow. My death will cover everything.'' And he abandoned himself with ecstasy to Mathilde's love; there was madness in it, greatness of soul and all sorts of strange things. She seriously proposed that they kill themselves together.

After these first surges of emotion, and when she was sated with the happiness of seeing Julien, a keen curiosity suddenly took possession of her. She studied her lover and found him to be far superior to anything she had imagined. He seemed to be the reincarnation of Boniface de La Mole, but more heroic.

Mathilde went to see the leading lawyers of the district and offended them by offering them money too crudely; but they finally accepted it.

She soon concluded that, in questionable matters of far-reaching importance, in Besançon everything depended on Abbé de Frilair. At first, under the obscure name of Madame Michelet, she encountered insurmountable difficulties in her efforts to secure an interview with the all-powerful leader of the *Congrégation*. But rumors began to spread through the city about the beauty of a young seamstress who was madly in love with the young Abbé Julien Sorel and had come to Besançon from Paris to comfort him.

Mathilde hurried through the streets of Besançon on foot, hoping she would not be recognized. In any case, she felt that it would not be entirely useless to her cause to make a strong impression on the common people. In her folly she dreamed of rousing them to revolt to save Julien's life as he was walking to his death. She believed that she was dressed simply and in a way befitting a woman in sorrow; she was actually dressed in a way that attracted everyone's gaze.

She had become an object of general attention in Besançon when, after a week of solicitations, she obtained an audience with Monsieur de Frilair.

Despite all her courage, the idea of an influential member of the *Congrégation* and that of profound and crafty villainy were so intimately connected in her mind that she trembled as she rang the doorbell of the bishop's palace. Scarcely able to walk, she had to climb the stairs leading to the vicar-general's apartment. The loneliness of the episcopal palace chilled her heart. "I may sit down in a chair," she thought, "the chair may seize my arms and I'll have vanished. Whom could my maid ask about me? The captain of the gendarmerie will be sure not to do anything. . . . I'm isolated in this great city!"

Her first glance at the apartment reassured her. To begin with, a footman in extremely elegant livery had opened the door for her. The drawing room in which she was asked to wait displayed that refined and delicate luxury, so different from vulgar ostentation, which one finds in Paris only in the best houses. As soon as she saw Monsieur de Frilair coming toward her with a paternal expression, all thought of a horrible crime vanished from her mind. She did not even find on his handsome face the mark of that forceful and somewhat savage virtue which is so distasteful to Parisian society. The faint smile which animated the features of the priest who controlled everything in Besançon denoted a man of good breeding, a cultured prelate and a skillful administrator. Mathilde felt as though she were back in Paris.

It took him only a few moments to lead her to admit that she was the daughter of his powerful adversary, the Marquis de La Mole.

"I'm not Madame Michelet, it's true," she said, resuming all her haughtiness of manner, "and that admission costs me little, because I've come to consult you, monsieur, about the possibility of Monsieur de La Vernaye's escape. In the first place, he's guilty only of having lost his head for a moment; the woman he shot is in good condition. In the second place, in order to bribe the minor officials, I can supply fifty thousand francs here and now, and guarantee to pay twice that amount. And finally, my gratitude and that of my family will find nothing impossible for the man who has saved Monsieur de La Vernaye."

Monsieur de Frilair seemed surprised by this name. Mathilde showed him several letters from the Minister of War addressed to Monsieur Julien Sorel de La Vernaye.

"You can see, monsieur," she said, "that my father had set out to make a career for him. I married him in secret; my father wanted him to be a field officer before publicly announcing a marriage that's a little unusual for a La Mole."

Mathilde noticed that Monsieur de Frilair's expression of kindness and gentle gaiety swiftly vanished as he began to make important discoveries. His features displayed shrewdness mingled with profound duplicity.

He was beginning to have doubts; he slowly read over the official documents again. "What advantage can I gain from these strange confessions?" he thought. "Here I am, suddenly on close terms with a friend of the famous Madame de Fervaques, the all-powerful niece of the Bishop of ——, who controls the appointment of bishops in France. What I regarded as far off in the future has just presented itself unexpectedly. This may lead me to the goal of all my hopes."

At first Mathilde was frightened by the sudden change in the features of the powerful man with whom she was alone in a remote apartment. "Come now!" she said to herself a short time later. "Wouldn't the worst thing have been not to make any impression on the cold selfishness of a priest who's sated with power and pleasure?"

Dazzled by this rapid and unforeseen path to the episcopacy that was opening up before his eyes, and astonished by Mathilde's intelligence, Monsieur de Frilair was off guard for a moment. Mademoiselle de La Mole saw him almost at her feet, so overcome with ambition and excitement that he trembled nervously.

"Everything's becoming clear," she thought. "Nothing will be impossible here for a friend of Madame de Fervaques." Despite a feeling of jealousy that was still quite painful, she had the courage to explain that Julien was a close friend of Madame de Fervaques and that he had seen the Bishop of —— in her house nearly every day.

"Even if a list of thirty-six jurymen were drawn by lot four or five times in succession from among the outstanding residents of this department," said the vicar-general with the harsh gaze of ambition, and stressing each word, "I would regard myself as quite unfortunate if nine or ten of the men on each list were not friends of mine, and the most intelligent of the lot. I would almost invariably have a majority, even more than necessary for a conviction; you can see, mademoiselle, how easy it is for me to bring about an acquittal." He stopped short, as though astonished by the sound of his own words; he was admitting things that are never said to the profane.

But Mathilde in her turn was dumbfounded when he told her that what most astonished and interested Besançon society in Julien's strange adventure was the fact that he had once inspired a great passion in Madame de Rênal and had shared it for a long time. Monsieur de Frilair easily perceived the extreme agitation caused by his remarks.

"I have my revenge!" he thought. "At last I've found a way to control this very determined young lady; I was afraid I'd never find one." Her distinguished and headstrong air redoubled in his eyes the charm of the rare beauty he now saw almost suppliant before him. He recovered all his self-possession and did not hesitate to twist the dagger in her heart.

"After all," he said nonchalantly, "I wouldn't be surprised if we learned that it was out of jealousy that Monsieur Sorel fired twice at the woman he had once loved so much. She's far from unattractive, and for a short time she'd been seeing a great deal of a certain Father Marquinot of Dijon, a kind of Jansenist, without any morals at all, the way they all are."

Monsieur de Frilair leisurely and voluptuously tortured the heart of the pretty girl whose secret he had discovered. "Why," he asked, staring at her with burning eyes, "should Monsieur Sorel have chosen the church if not because, at that very moment, his rival was celebrating mass there? Everyone agrees in attributing great intelligence and even greater prudence to the fortunate man you're protecting. What could have been simpler for him than to hide in Monsieur de Rênal's garden, which he knows so well? There, almost certain of not being seen, captured or suspected, he could have killed the woman of whom he was jealous."

This reasoning, so sound in appearance, made Mathilde lose her head completely. Her heart, so proud yet so steeped in all that barren prudence which high society regards as a faithful representation of human nature, was not made to understand in an instant the joy of flouting all prudence, a joy which can be so intense for an ardent soul. In the upper ranks of Parisian society, in which Mathilde had lived, passion can very rarely divest itself of prudence, and it is from the sixth floor that one jumps out of a window.

Finally Monsieur de Frilair became sure of his power. He gave Mathilde to understand (he was no doubt lying) that he could do whatever he liked with the public prosecutor who would conduct the case against Julien. After chance had designated the thirty-six jurors for the session, he would appeal directly and personally to at least thirty of them.

If Mathilde had not seemed so pretty to him, he would not have spoken so clearly to her until the fifth or sixth interview.

CHAPTER 39
Intrigue

> March 31, 1676. He that endeavoured to kill his sister in
> our house, had before killed a man, and it had cost his father
> five hundred écus to get him off; by their secret distribution,
> gaining the favour of the counsellors.
>
> —Locke

ON LEAVING the bishop's palace, Mathilde did not hesitate to send a courier to Madame de Fervaques; the fear of compromising herself did not stop her for a second. She begged her rival to obtain a letter for Monsieur de Frilair written entirely in the hand of the Bishop of ———. She even went so far as to implore her to hurry to Besançon herself. This was a heroic deed for a proud and jealous heart.

Following Fouqué's advice, she had wisely refrained from telling Julien what she was doing. Her presence troubled him enough without that. More virtuous at the approach of death than he had been during the rest of his life, he felt remorse not only over what he had done to Monsieur de La Mole but to Mathilde as well.

"Why is it," he thought, "that when I'm with her I find only moments of distraction and even of boredom? She's ruining herself for me and that's how I reward her! Am I really heartless?" He would have given very little thought to this question when he was ambitious; not to succeed had then been the only cause for shame in his eyes.

The uneasiness he felt in Mathilde's presence was all the more intense because he now inspired in her the wildest, most extraordinary passion. She spoke of nothing but the incredible sacrifices she wanted to make in order to save him.

Carried away by a feeling in which she gloried and which was stronger than all her pride, she would have liked to let no moment of her life go by without filling it with some extraordinary action. Her long conversations with Julien were taken up with the strangest plans, full of danger for her. The jailers, well paid, let her do as she pleased in the prison. Her ideas were not limited to sacrificing her reputation; she cared little whether or not she let all of society know of her condition. Falling to her knees in front of the king's carriage as it approached at a gallop in order to request Julien's pardon, attracting His Majesty's attention at the risk of being crushed beneath his carriage—this was one of the least fantastic schemes devised by her frenzied and courageous imagination. Through her friends in the royal household, she was sure to gain admission to the restricted areas of the Parc de Saint-Cloud.

Julien felt that he was scarcely worthy of so much devotion; to tell the truth, he was tired of heroism. It was to simple, artless and almost timid affection that he would have responded, whereas Mathilde's proud spirit, on the contrary, always needed the idea of an audience, of "other people." Amid all her anguish, all her fears for the life of her lover, whom she did not want to survive, Julien felt that she had a secret need to astonish the world with the depth of her love and the sublimity of her actions.

He was annoyed to find himself unmoved by all this heroism. How would he have felt if he had known of all the mad schemes with which Mathilde was overwhelming the good Fouqué's devoted but eminently sensible and limited mind?

Fouqué did not quite know what to disapprove of in her devotion; for he too would have sacrificed his whole fortune and exposed his life to the greatest dangers in order to save Julien. He was astounded by the amount of money Mathilde handed out. At first the sums spent in this way made a profound impression on him; he had all the provincial veneration for money.

Finally he discovered that Mademoiselle de La Mole's plans often changed and, to his great relief, he found a word to express his disapproval of a character that was so tiring for him: she was *unsteady*. It is only one step from this epithet to that of *unconventional*, the greatest anathema in the provinces.

"It's strange," thought Julien one day as Mathilde was leaving his cell, "that being the object of such a violent passion should leave me so indifferent! And I worshiped her two months ago! I've read that the approach of death makes a man lose interest in everything, but it's terrible to feel ungrateful and be unable to change. Am I an egotist?" He addressed the most humiliating reproaches to himself on this subject.

Ambition was dead in his heart; another passion had risen from its ashes: he called it remorse over having tried to kill Madame de Rênal. The fact was that he was hopelessly in love with her. He found a singular kind of happiness when, left absolutely alone and without fear of being interrupted, he could abandon himself completely to memories of the happy days he had spent long ago in Verrières or Vergy. The slightest incident of that time, which had all too quickly flown past, had an irresistible freshness and charm for him. He never thought of his successes in Paris; he was bored with them.

Mathilde's jealousy made her partially aware of this rapidly growing inclination. She saw clearly that she had to struggle against a love of solitude. Sometimes she would utter Madame de Rênal's name in terror, and she would see Julien start. From then on her passion knew neither bounds nor measure.

"If he dies, I'll die after him," she said to herself with all possible sincerity. "What would the people in the drawing rooms of Paris say if they saw a girl of my rank so strongly devoted to a lover who's doomed to die? We must go back to the age of heroes to find such sentiments; it was love of this kind that made hearts beat in the days of Charles IX and Henri III."

In the midst of her keenest raptures, as she pressed Julien's head to her heart, she would say to herself in terror, "What! This charming head is doomed to fall? Well then," she would add, with a heroism that was not without happiness, "my lips, which are now pressed against his beautiful hair, will be cold less than twenty-four hours later."

Memories of these moments of heroism and terrible pleasure held her in an iron grip. The idea of suicide, so absorbing in itself, and until then so far removed from her proud heart, entered it and soon established absolute dominion over it. "No, the blood of my ancestors hasn't grown lukewarm in coming down to me," she said to herself proudly.

"I have a favor to ask of you," her lover said to her one day. "Put your child in the care of a wet nurse in Verrières; Madame de Rênal will keep an eye on her."

"That's a harsh thing to say to me. . . ." And Mathilde turned pale.

"That's true, forgive me!" cried Julien, starting from his reverie and pressing her in his arms.

After drying her tears, he returned to his idea, but with more tact. He had given the conversation a melancholy philosophical turn. He spoke of the future that would so soon come to a close for him. "You must agree, my darling," he said, "that passion is an accident in life, but it's an accident that happens only to superior natures. . . . The death of my son would really be a stroke of good luck for your family's pride, and their subordinates will guess it. Neglect will be the lot of that child of sorrow and shame. . . . I hope that, at a time which I won't specify, but which my courage foresees, you will obey my last wish and marry the Marquis de Croisenois."

"What! After I've been dishonored?"

"Dishonor can't stain a name like yours. You'll be a widow, and the widow of a madman, that's all. I'll say even more: since money wasn't the motive of my crime, it won't be a dishonor. Perhaps by that time some philosophical legislator will have obtained, from the prejudices of his contemporaries, the suppression of capital punishment. Then some friendly voice will say, citing me as an example, 'And then there was Mademoiselle de La Mole's first husband. He was mad, but not malicious, not a criminal; it was absurd to cut off his head. . . .' Then my memory won't be infamous; at least after a certain time. . . . Your position in society, your fortune and, allow me to say it, your genius, will enable Monsieur de Croisenois, once he's your husband, to occupy a position which he could never have attained by himself. He has nothing but good birth and valor, and those qualities by themselves, which were enough to make a perfect gentleman in 1729, are an anachronism a century later, and do nothing but make a man pretentious. One must have other things besides to become a leader of French youth.

"You'll bring a resolute and enterprising character to the support of the political party in which you'll place your husband. You may be the successor of the Chevreuses and the Longuevilles of the Fronde. . . . But by then, my darling, the divine fire that now animates you will have grown a little cooler. . . .

"Allow me to tell you," he added, after many preparatory remarks, "that fifteen years from now you'll regard the love you once felt for me as an excusable folly, but a folly all the same. . . ."

He broke off suddenly and became pensive again. He found himself confronted once more by that idea which was so shocking to Mathilde: "Fifteen years from now Madame de Rênal will adore my son, and you'll have forgotten him."

CHAPTER 40

Peace of Mind

> It is because I was mad then that I am now sane. O philosopher, you who see only things of the moment, how short-sighted you are! Your eyes are not made to follow the underground workings of the passions.
>
> —Goethe

THIS CONVERSATION was cut short by an official interrogation, followed by a conference with the lawyer who was to conduct the defense. These were the only truly disagreeable moments in a life full of apathy and tender dreams.

"It was murder, premeditated murder," said Julien to both the judge and the lawyer. "I'm sorry, gentlemen," he added, smiling, "but that reduces your work to very little."

"After all," he thought, when he had managed to get rid of the two men, "I must be brave, and apparently braver than those two. They regard that duel with an unhappy ending as the worst of all misfortunes, as the 'king of terrors,' but I won't seriously concern myself with it until the day it happens.

"That's because I've known greater misfortune," he went on, philosophizing to himself. "I suffered much more during my first trip to Strasbourg, when I thought Mathilde had forsaken me. . . . And to think how passionately I yearned for that perfect intimacy which now leaves me so cold! . . . I'm actually happier alone than I am when that beautiful girl shares my solitude. . . ."

The lawyer, a man of rules and formalities, thought him mad and agreed with the public in believing that it was jealousy that had put the pistol into his hand. One day he ventured to suggest to Julien that this allegation, whether true or false, would make an excellent line of defense. But in the twinkling of an eye the accused again became a man of vehement passion. "On your life, monsieur," he cried, beside himself, "remember never to utter that abominable lie again!" For a moment the cautious lawyer was afraid of being murdered.

He was preparing his defense, for the decisive moment was

rapidly approaching. All over Besançon and the entire department, people talked of nothing but the famous case. Julien was ignorant of this detail, for he had requested that no one speak to him of such things.

That day, when Fouqué and Mathilde had tried to tell him of certain widespread rumors which, according to them, gave reason to hope, Julien had stopped them as soon as they began: "Let me go on living in my dreams," he said. "Your petty worries, your details of real life, all more or less wounding to my feelings, would drag me down from heaven. A man dies as best he can; as for me, I want to think about death only in my own way. What do I care about *other people*? My relations with *other people* will soon be cut short. Please don't talk to me about them anymore; it's enough that I have to be degraded in the eyes of the judge and the lawyer.

"It really seems that my destiny is to die while dreaming," he said to himself. "An obscure man like me, sure of being forgotten within two weeks, would be very foolish, I must admit, if he tried to act out a part. . . . And yet it's strange that I've learned the art of enjoying life only now that I see its end so near."

He spent these last days strolling back and forth along the narrow platform at the top of the tower, smoking excellent cigars which a courier sent by Mathilde had brought back from Holland, and without suspecting that his appearance was awaited every day by all the telescopes in town. His thoughts were in Vergy. He never spoke to Fouqué of Madame de Rênal, but on two or three occasions his friend told him that she was rapidly recovering, and the words reverberated in his heart.

While Julien's mind was nearly always in the realm of ideas, Mathilde, occupied with reality, as befits an aristocratic heart, had managed to bring the direct correspondence between Madame de Fervaques and Monsieur de Frilair to such a point of intimacy that the great word *bishopric* had been used openly.

The venerable prelate who controlled the distribution of benefices added a note in the margin of a letter to his niece: "Poor Sorel is only a young hothead; I hope he will be restored to us."

When he saw these words, Monsieur de Frilair's joy knew no bounds. He was certain that he would save Julien. "If it weren't for that Jacobin law which requires an endless list of jurors, and whose only real purpose is to deprive wellborn people of all their influence," he said to Mathilde on the day before the thirty-six jurors for the session were to be chosen by lot, "I could have guaranteed the verdict. I certainly got Father N—— acquitted."

The next day he was pleased to find, among the names drawn from the urn, five members of the *Congrégation* of Besançon, and, among those from outside the town, the names of Messieurs Valenod, de Moirod and de Cholin. "I can answer for those eight jurors without hesitation," he said to Mathilde. "The first five are nothing but machines, Valenod is my agent, Moirod owes me everything and Cholin is an imbecile who's afraid of everything."

The newspaper spread the names of the jurors all over the department and Madame de Rênal, to her husband's inexpressible terror, decided to go to Besançon. All that he was able to obtain from her was a promise not to leave her bed, in order to avoid the unpleasantness of being called to testify. "You don't understand my position," said the former Mayor of Verrières. "I'm now a 'Liberal renegade,' as they call me; I'm sure that scoundrel Valenod and Monsieur de Frilair will have no trouble in persuading the attorney general and the judges to make things as unpleasant as possible for me."

Madame de Rênal yielded to her husband's orders without difficulty. "If I appeared in court," she thought, "I'd seem to be asking for vengeance."

Despite all the promises of prudence she had made to her confessor and her husband, as soon as she arrived in Besançon she personally wrote to each of the thirty-six jurors:

I shall not appear at the trial, monsieur, because my presence might prejudice Monsieur Sorel's case. I desire only one thing in the world, and I desire it passionately: his acquittal. You may be sure that the horrible idea that an innocent man had been led to his death because of me would poison the rest of my life and no doubt shorten it. How could you condemn him to death while I am still alive? No, there can be no doubt: society does not have the right to take away life, especially the life of a man like Julien Sorel. Everyone in Verrières has seen him have moments of misguided passion. The poor young man has powerful enemies, but even among his enemies (and they are so numerous!), is there one man who questions his admirable talents and his profound learning? It is no ordinary man that you are about to judge, monsieur. For nearly eighteen months we knew him to be pious, virtuous and industrious; but two or three times a year he was seized with fits of melancholy which nearly made him lose his reason.

Everyone in Verrières, all our neighbors in Vergy, where we spent the summer, my entire family and the sub-prefect himself will acknowledge his exemplary piety; he knows the Holy Bible by heart from beginning to end. Would an impious man have studied for years to learn the Holy Scriptures? My sons will have the honor of presenting this letter to you. They are children; please question them, monsieur, and they will give you all the details about this young man which may still be necessary to convince you how barbarous it would be to condemn him to death. Far from avenging me, you would be bringing on my own death.

What can his enemies bring forward against this fact? The wound that resulted from one of those temporary losses of reason which even my children used to notice in their tutor is so far from dangerous that after less than two months it has not prevented me from coming to Besançon from Verrières by stagecoach. If I learn, monsieur, that you have the slightest hesitation about saving from the barbarity of the law a man whose guilt is so insignificant, I will leave my bed, where I remain only in obedience to my husband's orders, and come to throw myself at your feet.

Declare, monsieur, that premeditation has not been established, and you will not have to reproach yourself for the death of an innocent man, etc., etc.

CHAPTER 41
The Trial

> The district will long remember that famous trial. Interest in the accused was carried to the point of agitation, for his crime was striking, yet not atrocious. And even if it had been, the young man was so handsome! His brilliant career, so soon finished, aroused even greater sympathy. "Will he be sentenced to death?" the women asked all the men they knew, and they turned pale as they awaited the answer.
>
> —Sainte-Beuve

FINALLY THE day arrived, the day so dreaded by Madame de Rênal and Mathilde.

The strange appearance of the town increased their terror, and even Fouqué's stout heart was not unmoved. People from all over the province had flocked to Besançon to witness the outcome of the romantic case. For several days the inns had had no vacant rooms. The presiding magistrate had been overwhelmed with requests for admission; all the ladies in town wanted to attend the trial; portraits of Julien were being peddled in the streets, etc., etc.

Mathilde had been holding in reserve for this supreme moment a letter written entirely in the hand of the Bishop of ———. This prelate, who controlled the Church of France and appointed bishops as he saw fit, had deigned to request that Julien be acquitted. On the day before the trial, Mathilde took this letter to the all-powerful vicar-general.

At the end of the interview, just as she was leaving, she burst into tears. ''I can guarantee the jury's verdict,'' said Monsieur de Frilair, finally casting aside diplomatic reserve and almost moved himself. ''Among the twelve people appointed to determine whether your protégé's crime is clearly established, and especially whether or not it was premeditated, I can count on six friends who have a personal interest in my career, and I've made it clear to them that it's within their power to make me a bishop. Baron Valenod, whom I made Mayor of Verrières, has complete control over two of his subordinates, Monsieur de Moirod and Monsieur de Cholin. It's true that chance has given us two unsound jurors, but, even though they're confirmed Liberals, they faithfully obey my orders on important occasions, and I've asked them to follow Monsieur Valenod's lead in voting. I've learned that a sixth juror, an immensely wealthy manufacturer and a vociferous Liberal, is secretly hoping for a contract from the Ministry of War, and I'm sure he wouldn't want to displease me. I've had him notified that Monsieur Valenod has my final instructions.''

''And who is this Monsieur de Valenod?'' asked Mathilde anxiously.

''If you knew him, you'd have no doubt about the outcome of the trial. He's a bold talker, a coarse, impudent man who was born to lead fools. The year 1814 raised him from poverty and I'm going to make him a prefect. He's quite capable of beating the other jurors if they refuse to vote the way he wants them to.''

Mathilde felt somewhat reassured.

Another discussion was awaiting her that evening. In order to avoid prolonging a disagreeable scene whose outcome he regarded as certain, Julien was determined not to speak in his own defense. ''My lawyer will speak, that will be enough,'' he said to Mathilde. ''I'll be displayed as a spectacle to all my enemies for all too long a time anyway. Those provincials were offended by the rapid successes which I owe to you, and, believe me, there's not one of them who doesn't want me to be convicted, which won't prevent them from weeping like fools when I'm led to my death.''

"They want to see you humiliated, it's all too true," said Mathilde, "but I don't think they're cruel. My presence in Besançon and the sight of my sorrow have interested all the women; your handsome face will do the rest. If you say only a few words in front of your judges, everyone in the courtroom will be on your side. . . ."

At nine o'clock the next morning, when Julien left his cell to go into the courtroom, the gendarmes had great difficulty in forcing a passage through the enormous crowd packed into the courtyard. Julien had slept well, he was quite calm and he had no feeling except philosophic pity for that crowd of envious people who, without cruelty, were going to applaud his death sentence. He was greatly surprised when, having been detained for more than a quarter of an hour in the midst of them, he was forced to recognize that his presence inspired them with tender pity. He did not hear a single unpleasant remark. "These provincials are less malicious than I thought," he said to himself.

When he entered the courtroom he was struck by the elegance of the architecture. It was pure Gothic, with a great many charming little pillars delicately carved into the stone. He felt as though he were in England.

But soon his attention was absorbed by twelve to fifteen pretty women who, seated opposite the dock, filled the three galleries above the judges and the jury. When he turned toward the spectators, he saw that the circular gallery overhanging the amphitheater was filled with women. Most of them were young and seemed extremely pretty to him; their eyes were sparkling and full of interest. In the rest of the courtroom the crowd was enormous; people were pressing in through the doors and the guards were unable to obtain silence.

When all the eyes that had been seeking Julien perceived his presence as he sat down on the slightly raised seat reserved for him, he was greeted with a murmur of astonishment and tender sympathy.

He seemed to be less than twenty that day. He was dressed very simply, but with perfect grace; his hair and his forehead were charming; Mathilde had insisted on personally supervising his toilet. He was extremely pale. As soon as he took his seat he heard people saying on all sides, "Oh, how young he is! . . .

Why, he's only a boy! . . . He's much handsomer than his portrait."

"Prisoner," said the gendarme seated on his right, "do you see those six ladies up there in that gallery?" He pointed to a small gallery projecting above the jury. "There's the prefect's wife, and beside her is the Marquise de ———. She's very fond of you: I heard her talking to the examining magistrate. Then there's Madame Derville. . . ."

"Madame Derville!" exclaimed Julien, and he blushed deeply. "She'll write to Madame de Rênal when she leaves here," he thought. He had heard nothing about Madame de Rênal's arrival in Besançon.

The witnesses were examined; this took several hours. As soon as the public prosecutor began his speech, two of the ladies seated in the little gallery facing Julien burst into tears. "Madame Derville doesn't share their emotion," thought Julien. He noticed, however, that her face was flushed.

The public prosecutor spoke grandiloquently in ungrammatical French about the barbarity of the crime that had been committed; Julien noticed that the ladies sitting beside Madame Derville showed signs of violent disapproval. Several of the jurors, who were apparently acquainted with these ladies, spoke to them and seemed to reassure them. "That must be a good omen," thought Julien.

Until then he had been filled with unmixed contempt for all the men who were present at the trial. The public prosecutor's vapid eloquence had heightened this feeling of disgust. But gradually Julien's hard heart was softened by the undeniable evidence of the sympathy that others felt for him.

He was pleased with his lawyer's firm expression. "No flowery eloquence," he said to him as he was about to address the court.

"All that bombastic rhetoric pilfered from Bossuet and deployed against you has helped your case," said the lawyer. He was right: he had not spoken for five minutes before nearly all the women had their handkerchiefs in their hands. Encouraged, he addressed some extremely strong remarks to the jury. Julien trembled and felt himself on the verge of tears. "Good God!" he thought. "What will my enemies say?"

He was about to give in to the emotion that was taking possession of him when, fortunately for him, he saw the Baron de Valenod give him an insolent look. "The scoundrel's eyes are sparkling," he thought. "What a triumph for his petty soul! If my crime had no other consequence but that, I'd still curse it. God only knows what he'll tell Madame de Rênal about me!''

This thought wiped away all others. A short time later he was called back from his reflections by sounds of approval from the spectators. The lawyer had just finished his speech. Julien remembered that convention required him to shake his hand. The time had passed quickly.

Refreshments were brought to the accused and his lawyer. It was only then that Julien was struck by the fact that not a single woman had left the courtroom to have dinner.

"I'm starving," said the lawyer. "What about you?"

"So am I," replied Julien.

"Look," said the lawyer, pointing to the little gallery, "the prefect's wife is having her dinner brought up to her too. Keep up your courage, everything's going well."

The trial was resumed. Midnight struck as the presiding magistrate was making his summation. He was obliged to stop speaking. Amid the silence of the general anxiety, the reverberating strokes of the clock filled the room.

"My last day on earth has just begun," thought Julien. Soon he felt inflamed by the idea of duty. Until then he had controlled his emotion and kept his resolution not to speak, but when the presiding magistrate asked him if he had anything to say, he stood up. Before him he saw Madame Derville's eyes, which seemed to sparkle in the lamplight. "Could she by any chance be crying?" he wondered.

"Gentlemen of the jury," he said, "a horror of the contempt which I thought I could defy at the hour of my death forces me to speak. Gentlemen, I do not have the honor of belonging to your class; you see in me a peasant who has revolted against the lowliness of his position.

"I ask no mercy of you," he went on, his voice growing firmer. "I have no illusions: death is awaiting me, and it will be just. I am guilty of having attempted to kill a woman worthy of the highest respect and admiration. Madame de Rênal had been like a mother to me. My crime was atrocious, and it was *premeditated*. I therefore deserve death, gentlemen of the jury. But even if I were less guilty, I see men who, regardless of any pity my youth might deserve, would want to punish in me and discourage forever that class of young men who, born in an inferior rank of society, have the good fortune to secure a good education for themselves and the boldness to mingle with what the pride of rich men calls good society.

"That is my crime, gentlemen, and it will be punished with all the more severity because I am actually not being judged by my peers. In this jury I do not see a single peasant who has grown rich by his own efforts; I see only members of the middle class whom I have outraged. . . ."

Julien spoke in this vein for twenty minutes; he said everything that was in his heart. The public prosecutor, who aspired to the favors of the aristocracy, leapt from his seat several times, but, in spite of the somewhat abstract tone which Julien had given to the discussion, all the women burst into tears. Even Madame Derville held a handkerchief to her eyes. Before concluding, Julien returned to the premeditation of his crime, to his repentance, to the respect and unbounded filial adoration which, in happier times, he had felt for Madame de Rênal. . . . Madame Derville uttered a cry and fainted.

One o'clock struck as the jurors withdrew to their room. Not one woman had left her seat; several men had tears in their eyes. At first there was animated conversation, but then, as time went by and the jury did not return with their verdict, the general fatigue gradually began to calm the crowd of spectators. It was a solemn moment; the light in the courtroom had grown dimmer. Julien, extremely weary, heard people around him discussing whether this delay was a good or a bad sign. He saw with pleasure that everyone was on his side; the jury had not returned, and still not a single woman had left the room.

Just after two o'clock a great stir was heard. The little door of the jury room was opened and the Baron de Valenod stepped forward with a solemn, theatrical tread, followed by all the other jurors. He coughed, then declared that on his soul and conscience the unanimous verdict of the jury was that Julien Sorel was guilty of murder, and premeditated murder. This verdict entailed the death sentence; it was pronounced a moment later. Julien looked at his watch and thought of Monsieur de Lavalette; it was a quarter past two.

"Today is Friday," he thought. "Yes, but it's a lucky day for Valenod: he's condemned me to death. . . . I'm too closely guarded for Mathilde to be able to save me, like Madame de Lavalette. . . . So, three days from now, at this same hour, I'll know the truth about the 'Great Unknown.' "

Just then he heard a cry and was recalled to the things of this world. The women around him were sobbing; he saw that all eyes were turned toward a small gallery perched above the capital of a Gothic pilaster. He later learned that Mathilde had hidden herself there. Since the cry was not repeated, everyone turned back to look at Julien, for whom the gendarmes were trying to clear a passage through the crowd.

"Let's try not to give that ignoble Valenod a chance to laugh," thought Julien. "What hypocritical sorrow he showed when he gave the verdict that necessarily brings a death sentence with it, while the poor presiding magistrate, even though he's been a judge for many years, had tears in his eyes as he pronounced my sentence! What a joy for Valenod to have his revenge for our old rivalry over Madame de Rênal! . . . I'll never see her again! It's all over . . . I'm afraid a last farewell is impossible for us. . . . How happy I'd have been to tell her all the horror I feel for my crime!"

He spoke only these words to the court: "I consider myself rightly condemned to death."

CHAPTER 42*

WHEN JULIEN was taken back to prison he was placed in a cell reserved for prisoners under sentence of death. He, who usually noticed the smallest details, was at first unaware that he had not been taken back to his cell in the tower. He was thinking of what he would say to Madame de Rênal if, before the last moment, he should have the happiness of seeing her. He was sure she would interrupt him, and he tried to think of how he could express all his repentance in his first few words. "After such an action, how could I convince her that I love only her?" he thought. "After all, I tried to kill her out of ambition, or for love of Mathilde."

When he got into bed he found sheets made of coarse cloth. His eyes were opened. "Oh! I'm in a dungeon, because I've been condemned to death," he thought. "It's only right. Count Altamira once told me that, on the day before his death, Danton said in his booming voice, 'It's strange, but the verb "to guillotine" can't be conjugated in all tenses. One can say "I shall be guillotined" or "You will be guillotined," but you can't say "I have been guillotined." '

"Yet why not," Julien went on, "if there's another life? . . . But if I meet the God of the Christians I'm lost: he's a despot

---

*Stendhal himself, in his original version, deliberately refrained from giving titles to the last four chapters.

and, as such, he's filled with ideas of vengeance; his Bible speaks of nothing but horrible punishments. I've never loved him, and I've never been able to believe that anyone else could love him sincerely. He's without pity." (And Julien recalled several passages from the Bible.) "He'll punish me in an abominable way.

"But what if I meet Fénelon's God? Perhaps he'll say to me, 'Much shall be forgiven thee, for thou hast loved much. . . .'

"Have I loved much? Oh, I've loved Madame de Rênal! But my conduct was atrocious. There, as in so many other cases, simple, modest worth was abandoned in favor of surface glitter. . . .

"But what prospects I had! A Colonel of Hussars if we went to war, the secretary of a legation in time of peace, and later an ambassador, because I'd have soon acquired a good knowledge of diplomacy. . . . And even if I were a fool, would the Marquis de La Mole's son-in-law have had to fear any rivalry? All my stupid blunders would have been forgiven, or rather counted as merits. A man of merit, enjoying the most elegant kind of life in Vienna or London . . . Not exactly, monsieur: guillotined in three days."

Julien laughed heartily at his own sally. "A man really has two beings inside himself," he thought. "Who the devil thought of that malicious remark?

"Yes, that's right, my friend: guillotined in three days," he replied to his inner interrupter. "Monsieur de Cholin will rent a window and share the cost with Father Maslon. I wonder which of them will cheat the other."

He suddenly recalled this passage from Rotrou's *Venceslas:*

Ladislas: *My soul is ready.*

The king (his father): *So is the scaffold; lay your head on it.*

"A fine reply!" he thought as he fell asleep. Someone woke him the next morning by gripping him tightly.

"What, already!" said Julien, opening his haggard eyes. He thought the executioner had seized him.

It was Mathilde. "Fortunately she didn't understand what I meant," he thought. This reflection restored all his self-control. He found that Mathilde had changed profoundly, as though she had been ill for six months; she was truly unrecognizable.

"That infamous Frilair betrayed me," she said, wringing her hands; her fury kept her from weeping.

"Wasn't I admirable yesterday when I stood up to speak?" replied Julien. "I was improvising, for the first time in my life! I'm afraid it may be the last, too." At that moment he was playing on her character with all the self-possession of a skillful pianist fingering the keyboard of a piano. "I lack the advantage of noble birth, it's true," he added, "but Mathilde's lofty soul has raised her lover to her own level. Do you think Boniface de La Mole behaved any better in front of his judges?"

Mathilde was tender without affectation that day, like a poor girl living in an attic room, but she was unable to make him speak more clearly. Without knowing it, he was giving her back the torment she had often inflicted on him.

"No one knows the source of the Nile," he thought. "Man's eyes haven't been allowed to see the king of rivers in the form of an ordinary brook; and no human eye will ever see Julien weak, first of all because he isn't weak. But my heart is easily moved; the most commonplace words, if they're spoken in a tone of sincerity, can make my voice quaver and even bring tears to my eyes. How often people with arid hearts have despised me for that fault! They thought I was asking for mercy, and that's intolerable.

"They say Danton was moved by the memory of his wife when he was at the foot of the scaffold; but Danton had given strength to a nation of frivolous weaklings and prevented the enemy from reaching Paris. . . . I alone know what I might have done. . . . To everyone else I'm at best a 'might have been.'

"If Madame de Rênal had come here to my cell instead of Mathilde, would I have been able to control myself? The intensity of my despair and repentance would have been regarded by Valenod and all the patricians of the district as an ignoble fear of death. They're so proud, those weak-hearted creatures whose financial position places them beyond the reach of temptation! Monsieur de Moirod and Monsieur de Cholin, who've just condemned me to death, would have said, 'That's what it means to be born a sawyer's son! One can become learned and clever, but what about the heart? A noble heart isn't something that can be learned.' Even with poor Mathilde, who's crying now, or rather who can no longer cry . . ." he thought, looking at her reddened eyes. And he took her in his arms; the sight of genuine suffering made him forget his reasoning.

"She may have cried all night," he thought, "but some day how ashamed she'll be to remember this! She'll regard herself as having been led astray in her youth by a plebeian's base way of thinking. . . . Croisenois is weak enough to marry her, and it will be a good thing for him if he does. She'll give him a successful career,

> By virtue of the right
> That a steadfast mind imbued with vast designs
> Has o'er the cruder minds of common men.

"That's amusing! Since I've been doomed to die, all the poetry I ever learned in my life has been coming back to my mind. It must be a sign of decay. . . ."

Mathilde was repeating to him in a faint voice, "He's waiting in the next room." He finally paid attention to what she was saying. "Her voice is weak," he thought, "but its tone still shows her imperious character. She's lowering her voice to restrain her anger."

"Who's waiting?" he asked gently.

"The lawyer, to have you sign your appeal."

"I won't appeal."

"What! You won't appeal?" she said, her eyes sparkling with anger. "Would you please tell me why not?"

"Because I now feel that I have the courage to die without giving others too much cause for laughter. Who knows whether I'd be in such good condition two months from now, after a long confinement in this damp cell? I foresee visits from priests, from my father . . . Nothing in the world could be more unpleasant to me. I prefer to die as soon as possible."

This unexpected resistance awakened all the haughtiness of Mathilde's character. She had not been able to see Monsieur de Frilair before the hour when the cells of the Besançon prison are opened; her fury fell on Julien's head. She adored him, and yet, for a quarter of an hour, he again found in her imprecations against his character, and in her regrets over having fallen in love with him, all that arrogance which had once overwhelmed him with such cutting insults in the library of the Hôtel de La Mole.

"Heaven owed it to the glory of your lineage to let you be born a man," he said.

"But, for my part," he thought, "I'd be foolish to go on living for two more months in this disgusting cell, exposed to all the infamous and humiliating slander that the patrician faction

could invent against me, with this mad girl's curses as my only
consolation. . . . Well, day after tomorrow, I'll fight a duel with
a man who's noted for his coolness and remarkable skill."
("Very remarkable," said his Mephistophelian inner voice, "he's
never missed once.")

"All right, then, it's settled, and so much the better," he said
to himself as Mathilde's eloquence continued to flow. "No, by
God, I won't appeal!"

Having made this decision, he sank back into his reverie. . . .
"The postman will bring the newspaper at six o'clock, as
usual," he thought. "At eight o'clock, after Monsieur de Rênal
has read it, Elisa will tiptoe in and lay it on her bed. Later
she'll wake up and begin to read it; suddenly she'll become
agitated and her pretty hands will tremble. She'll go on reading till she comes to the words, '*At five minutes past ten he
had ceased to live. . . .*' She'll weep bitterly, I know her; it
won't matter that I tried to murder her: she'll have forgotten
all about it. And the woman whose life I tried to take will be
the only person who will sincerely weep over my death. What
a paradox!" And for a quarter of an hour, while Mathilde
continued to make a scene, he thought only of Madame de
Rênal.

In spite of himself, and even though he frequently replied to
what Mathilde was saying, he could not take his mind off the
memory of the bedroom in Verrières. He saw the Besançon
newspaper lying on the orange taffeta bedspread. He saw a white
hand clutching it convulsively; he saw Madame de Rênal weeping. . . . He followed the course of each tear down her charming
face.

Mademoiselle de La Mole, unable to obtain anything from
Julien, called in the lawyer. He was fortunately a former army
captain, a veteran of the Italian campaign of 1796, in which he
had fought with Manuel. For the sake of form, he opposed the
condemned man's decision. Julien, wishing to treat him with
respect, explained all his reasons to him.

"Well, that's one way to look at it," Monsieur Félix Vaneau
(this was the lawyer's name) finally said to him. "But you
have three full days in which to appeal, and it's my duty
to come back every day. If a volcano were to open up under
the prison some time within the next two months, you'd be
saved. Or you might die of some disease," he said, looking
at Julien.

Julien shook his head and said, "Thanks, you're an honorable man. I'll think it over."

And when at length Mathilde went away with the lawyer, he felt much greater friendship for the lawyer than for her.

CHAPTER 43

AN HOUR later, when he was sound asleep, he was awakened by tears which he felt dropping on his hand.

"Ah, it's Mathilde again," he thought, still half asleep. "It's just as I expected: she's come to attack my decision with tender sentiments." Bored by the prospect of another melodramatic scene, he did not open his eyes. The lines of Belphegor fleeing from his wife came back to his mind.

He heard a strange sigh; he opened his eyes: it was Madame de Rênal.

"Ah! I'm seeing you again before I die!" he cried, throwing himself at her feet. "Is this an illusion?

"But forgive me, madame," he added immediately, coming to his senses. "In your eyes I'm nothing but a murderer."

"Monsieur . . . I've come to beg you to appeal. I know you don't want to . . ." Her sobs choked her and she was unable to speak.

"Please forgive me."

"If you want me to forgive you," she said, standing up and throwing herself in his arms, "appeal against your death sentence immediately."

Julien covered her with kisses.

"Will you come to see me every day during those two months?"

"I swear I will. Every day, unless my husband forbids it."

"I'll sign the appeal!" cried Julien. "What! You forgive me? Is it possible?" He clasped her in his arms; he was wild with joy. She uttered a faint cry.

"It's nothing," she said. "You hurt me."

"I hurt your shoulder!" he exclaimed, bursting into tears. He stepped back a little and covered her hand with burning kisses. "Who could have foreseen all this the last time I saw you, in your bedroom in Verrières?"

"Who could have foreseen that I'd write that infamous letter to Monsieur de La Mole?"

"I want you to know that I've always loved you, that I've never loved anyone but you."

"Is it really possible?" cried Madame de Rênal, overjoyed in her turn. She leaned on Julien, who was kneeling before her, and for a long time they wept together in silence.

Julien had never known such a moment at any other time in his life.

Much later, when they were able to speak, Madame de Rênal said, "And what about that young Madame Michelet? Or rather Mademoiselle de La Mole, because I'm really beginning to believe that strange story!"

"It's true only in appearance," said Julien. "She's my wife, but she's not the mistress of my heart."

Interrupting each other a hundred times, they succeeded with difficulty in telling each other what they did not know. The letter to Monsieur de La Mole had been written by the young priest who was Madame de Rênal's confessor and then copied by her.

"What a horrible thing religion made me do!" she said. "And even so, I softened the worst passages in that letter. . . ."

Julien's outbursts of joy proved to her how completely he forgave her. Never before had he been so madly in love.

"And yet I consider myself religious," she said later in the course of their conversation. "I sincerely believe in God; I also believe, and it's been proven to me, in fact, that I'm committing a terrible crime, but as soon as I saw you, even after you shot me twice . . ." At this point Julien covered her with kisses despite her efforts to stop him.

"Stop," she said, "I want to reason with you, before I forget. . . . As soon as I saw you, all thought of duty vanished, and I now feel nothing but love for you. But love is too weak a word; I feel for you what I ought to feel only for God: a mixture of respect, love and obedience. . . . To tell the truth, I don't know exactly what you inspire in me. If you told me to stab your jailer, I'd commit the crime before I even took time to think about it. Explain that to me precisely before I leave you; I want to see clearly into my heart, because in two months we'll be separated. . . . By the way," she added, smiling, "will we really be separated?"

"I take back my word!" cried Julien, leaping to his feet. "I won't appeal against my death sentence if, by poison, knife, pistol, burning coals or any other means, you try to put an end to your life or harm yourself in any way."

Madame de Rênal's expression changed abruptly; deep tenderness gave way to profound thoughtfulness.

"What if we died immediately?" she said to him at length.

"Who knows what we'll find in the next world?" replied Julien. "Torment, perhaps; perhaps nothing at all. Can't we have two months of happiness together? There are many days in two months. I'll be happier than I've ever been before."

"You'll never have been so happy before?"

"Never," repeated Julien, enraptured. "I'm speaking to you as I speak to myself. God preserve me from exaggerating."

"To speak to me in that way is to command me," she said with a timid, melancholy smile.

"Then will you swear, by the love you bear for me, not to try to take your own life by any means, direct or indirect? Remember that you must live for my son, whom Mathilde will abandon to the care of servants as soon as she becomes the Marquise de Croisenois."

"I swear it," she said coldly, "but I want to take with me your appeal written and signed in your own hand. I'll go to see the attorney general personally."

"Be careful—you'll compromise yourself."

"After coming to see you in prison I'll be a subject of gossip in Besançon and all over Franche-Comté for the rest of my life," she said sorrowfully. "I've overstepped the bounds of strict propriety . . . I'm a dishonored woman; it's true that it's for your sake. . . ."

Her tone was so sad that Julien kissed her with a happiness that was completely new to him. It was no longer the intoxication of love: it was extreme gratitude. He had just realized, for the first time, the full extent of the sacrifice she had made for him.

Some charitable soul no doubt informed Monsieur de Rênal of the long visits his wife was paying to Julien's prison, for he sent his carriage to her three days later with orders to return to Verrières immediately.

This cruel separation had begun Julien's day badly; then two or three hours later he was informed that a certain priest who was known for his scheming character, but who had nevertheless been unable to make any progress among the Jesuits of Besançon, had posted himself in the street, just outside the prison gate. It was raining heavily and he was still there, playing the part of a martyr. Julien was in a bad mood and this ridiculous action annoyed him deeply.

He had already refused to see the priest that morning, but the man was determined to hear his confession and make a name for himself among all the young women of Besançon with the confidences he would pretend to have received from him.

He proclaimed loudly that he was going to remain at the prison gate all day and all night. "God has sent me to touch the heart of that apostate," he said, and the lowest elements of the population, always eager for a dramatic scene, had begun to gather around him.

"Yes, my brethren," he said to them, "I shall spend the day here, and the night, and every other day and night that follows. The Holy Ghost has spoken to me, I have a mission from on high: it is I who must save young Sorel's soul. Join your prayers to mine," etc., etc.

Julien had a horror of scandal and anything that might attract attention to him. He considered taking the opportunity to escape from this world unnoticed, but he still had some hope of seeing Madame de Rênal again and he was madly in love.

The prison gate faced one of the busiest streets in Besançon. His soul was tormented by the thought of that slovenly priest attracting a crowd and causing a scandal. "And I'm sure he's constantly repeating my name!" he thought. This moment was more painful to him than death.

Two or three times, at intervals of an hour, he called one of the jailers who was devoted to him and sent him to see if the priest was still at the prison gate.

"Monsieur, he's kneeling in the mud," the jailer said to him each time. "He's praying aloud and saying litanies for your soul."

"The impertinent scoundrel!" thought Julien. Just then he heard a dull murmur: it was the people uttering the responses to the litany. To climax his impatience, he saw even the jailer moving his lips as he repeated the Latin words.

"People are beginning to say," added the jailer, "that you must have a very hard heart to refuse that holy man's help."

"O my country, how barbarous you still are!" exclaimed Julien, carried away with rage. And he continued his reasoning aloud, giving no thought to the jailer's presence. "That man wants an article in the newspaper, and now he's sure of getting it. Oh, these wretched provincials! In Paris I wouldn't have been subjected to all these annoyances. People are more skillful in charlatanism there."

Finally he said to the jailer, "Bring in that saintly priest," and sweat streamed down his forehead. The jailer crossed himself and went out joyfully.

The saintly priest turned out to be horribly ugly, and he was even dirtier than he was ugly. The cold rain that was falling increased the darkness and dampness of the cell. The priest tried to embrace Julien and grew emotional as he spoke to him. His base hypocrisy was perfectly obvious; Julien was angrier than he had ever been before in his life.

A quarter of an hour after the priest's entrance, Julien found himself an utter coward. For the first time, death seemed horrible to him. He thought of the state of putrefaction in which his body would be two days after his execution, etc., etc.

He was about to betray himself with some sign of weakness, or throw himself at the priest and strangle him with his chain, when he hit upon the idea of asking the holy man to go off and say a good forty-franc mass for him that very day. Since it was nearly noon, the priest hurried away.

CHAPTER 44

As soon as he was gone, Julien began to weep bitterly, and he was weeping over his own death. It gradually occurred to him that if Madame de Rênal had been in Besançon he would have confessed his weakness to her. . . .

Just as he was most strongly regretting the absence of the woman he adored, he heard Mathilde's footsteps. "The worst thing about being in prison," he thought, "is that you can never refuse to receive visitors."

Everything Mathilde said to him served only to irritate him. She told him that, on the day of the trial, Monsieur de Valenod, having his appointment as prefect in his pocket, had dared to defy Monsieur de Frilair by giving himself the pleasure of condemning Julien to death.

"Just now Monsieur de Frilair said to me, 'Whatever made your friend arouse and attack the petty vanity of that "middle-class aristocracy"? Why did he talk about "caste"? He pointed out to them what they ought to do to defend their own political interests; the idiots hadn't given it a thought till then, and they were ready to weep. Then the interests of their class blinded them to the horror of condemning a man to death. You must admit that Monsieur Sorel is extremely inexperienced. If we don't succeed in saving him by requesting a reprieve, his death will be a kind of suicide. . . .' "

Mathilde naturally did not tell Julien something which she herself did not yet suspect: that Monsieur de Frilair, seeing Julien lost, had decided that it would be useful to his ambitions if he aspired to become his successor.

Almost beside himself with helpless rage and annoyance, Julien said to Mathilde, "Go listen to a mass for me, and leave me in peace for a few moments!" Mathilde, already extremely jealous of Madame de Rênal's visits and having just learned of her departure, realized the cause of his irritation and burst into tears.

Her grief was genuine; Julien saw this and it only increased his irritation. He felt an urgent need of solitude, and how was he to secure it?

Finally, after trying by every possible argument to make him soften his attitude, Mathilde left him alone; but Fouqué appeared at almost the same instant.

"I need to be alone," Julien said to his faithful friend; then, when he saw him hesitate, he added, "I'm making some notes for my request for a reprieve . . . and also . . . Do me a favor: never talk to me about death. If I need any special services on that day, let me be the first to mention them."

When Julien had at last managed to be alone, he found himself more depressed and cowardly than ever. The little strength remaining in his weakened heart had been exhausted in concealing his feelings from Mademoiselle de La Mole and Fouqué.

Toward evening he was comforted by this thought: "If I'd been told to prepare for my execution this morning, when death seemed so hideous to me, 'the eyes of the public would have goaded my pride.' My bearing might have been rather stiff, like that of a timid fool entering a drawing room, and a few perceptive people, if there are any among these provincials, might have guessed my weakness, but *no one would have seen it*."

And he felt himself relieved of part of his unhappiness. "I'm a coward right now," he repeated to himself in a singsong manner, "but no one will ever know it."

An even more disagreeable event lay in store for him the next day. For a long time his father had been announcing his intention to visit him; that morning, before Julien was awake, the white-haired old sawyer appeared in his cell.

Julien felt weak and he expected the most unpleasant reproaches. To climax his painful emotions, he now felt keen remorse over the fact that he did not love his father. "Chance placed us close together on this earth," he thought while the jailer was tidying up the cell a little, "and we've done just about as much harm to each other as we possibly could. He's come to give me the final blow as I'm about to die."

The old man's severe reproaches began as soon as they were left alone together. Julien could not hold back his tears. "What shameful weakness!" he said to himself angrily. "He'll talk to everyone about my lack of courage, and he'll exaggerate it; what a triumph for men like Valenod and all the other vile hypocrites who reign in Verrières! They have great power in France, they have all the social advantages. Until now I was able to say to myself, 'They make money, it's true, and all sorts of honors are showered on them, but I have a noble heart.' And now here's a witness whom everyone will believe and who will go all over Verrières spreading exaggerated reports of my weakness in the face of death! I'll have shown myself to be a coward in an ordeal that they can all understand!"

Julien was close to utter despair. He did not know how to get rid of his father; at that moment it was beyond his strength to carry off a pretense that would deceive the shrewd old man. He quickly turned over every possibility in his mind.

"I've saved up some money!" he suddenly cried out.

This stroke of genius instantly altered the old man's expression and Julien's position.

"How could I dispose of it?" he continued more calmly; the effect he had produced had obliterated all his feelings of inferiority.

The old sawyer was burning with a desire not to let that money slip away from him; he had the impression that Julien wanted to leave part of it to his brothers. He spoke heatedly for a long time. Julien felt able to be sarcastic: "Well," he said, "the Lord has given me an inspiration about my will. I'll give a thousand francs to each of my brothers and the rest to you."

"Good," said the old man, "it's only fair that I should have the rest; but, since God has been kind enough to touch your heart, if you want to die as a good Christian you ought to pay your debts. There's still the cost of your food, lodging and education, which I advanced to you, and which you're not considering. . . ."

"So this is a father's love!" Julien repeated to himself, heartbroken, when he was finally alone. Soon the jailer appeared.

"Monsieur," he said, "after a visit from the family I always

bring my guests a bottle of good champagne. It's a little
pensive, six francs a bottle, but it cheers the heart.''

"Bring me three glasses," said Julien with childish eagerness,
"and bring in two of the prisoners I hear walking up and down
the hall.''

The jailer brought in two former convicts who had just been
sentenced for new crimes and were now waiting to be sent back
to their prison. They were cheerful scoundrels and really quite
remarkable for their shrewdness, courage and self-possession.

"If you give me twenty francs," one of them said to Julien,
"I'll tell you the story of my life in detail. It makes good
listening!''

"But you'll probably lie to me," said Julien.

"Not at all! My friend here is jealous of my twenty francs and
he'll let you know about it if I don't tell you the truth.''

His story was abominable. It revealed a brave heart in which
there was only one passion: greed for money.

After they had gone, Julien was no longer the same man. All
his anger against himself had vanished. The terrible grief, aggra-
vated by cowardice, which had been gnawing at his heart since
Madame de Rênal's departure, had now been transformed into
melancholy.

"As I became less and less deceived by appearances," he
thought, "I'd have seen that the people who fill the drawing
rooms of Paris are either honest men like my father or clever
scoundrels like those convicts. They're right: the people in the
drawing rooms never get up in the morning with this urgent
question in mind: 'How will I get my dinner today?' And they
boast of their honesty! And when they're called to sit on a jury,
they proudly condemn a man who's stolen a few pieces of
silverware because he felt faint from hunger. But when there's a
court, when it's a question of winning or losing a ministerial
portfolio, my honest drawing room people fall into crimes exactly like those which the need to eat made those two convicts
commit. . . .

"There's no such thing as 'natural law': that expression is
nothing but an ancient piece of nonsense quite worthy of the
public prosecutor who was hunting me down the other day, and
whose ancestor was made rich by property confiscated by Louis
XIV. An action becomes unlawful only when there's some particular law forbidding it under pain of punishment. Before laws
are established, there's nothing *natural* except the strength of the
lion, or the needs of a creature suffering from hunger or cold—in

short, *necessity*. . . . No, the people who are honored by others are only scoundrels who have been lucky enough not to be caught red-handed. The prosecutor sent against me by society owes his wealth to an infamous act. . . . I committed a murder, and I've been justly sentenced, but, except for that single act, Valenod, who condemned me, is a hundred times more harmful to society.

"Well," added Julien sadly, but without anger, "in spite of his avarice, my father is worth more than all those men. He's never loved me. I'm about to climax everything by dishonoring him with my shameful death. That fear of lacking money, that exaggerated view of the wickedness of mankind which is known as avarice, makes him see a prodigious source of consolation and security in the three or four hundred louis I may leave him. Some Sunday, after dinner, he'll show his gold to his envious acquaintances in Verrières. 'At this price,' his glance will say to them, 'which of you wouldn't be delighted to have a son guillotined?' "

This philosophy may have been true, but it was of a nature to make one wish for death. Five long days went by in this manner. He was polite and gentle to Mathilde, whom he saw agitated by the most violent jealousy. One night he thought seriously of taking his own life. He was thoroughly unnerved by the black despair into which he had been plunged by Madame de Rênal's departure. He no longer found pleasure in anything, whether in reality or in imagination. Lack of exercise had begun to affect his health and give him the weak, excitable character of a young German student. He was losing that manly pride which rejects with a forceful oath certain ignominious ideas that assail the hearts of those in distress.

"I have loved truth," he thought. "Where is it? . . . Hypocrisy is everywhere, or at least charlatanism, even among the greatest and most virtuous of men." And his lips took on an expression of disgust. "No, man cannot trust man. . . . When Madame de ——— was taking up a collection for her poor orphans she told me that a certain prince had just given ten louis; it was a lie. But why use that example when there's Napoleon on Saint Helena! Pure charlatanism, a proclamation in favor of the King of Rome. My God! If a man like that, especially at a time when misfortune should have reminded him sharply of his duty, can stoop to charlatanism, what can one expect of the rest of the human race?

"Where is truth? In religion . . . Yes," he added, with a

bitter smile of extreme contempt, "in the mouths of men like
Maslon, Frilair and Castanède. . . . Perhaps in true Christianity,
whose priests would be paid no more than the Apostles were. . . .
But Saint Paul was paid with the pleasure of commanding, of
talking and making others talk about him. . . .

"Oh, if only there were a true religion! . . . What a fool I am!
I see a Gothic cathedral with ancient stained-glass windows, and
my weak heart imagines the priest who goes with those windows. . . . My soul would understand him, my soul needs
him. . . . But I find only a conceited fool with dirty hair, a man
like the Chevalier de Beauvoisis, minus his charm.

"But a real priest, a Massillon, a Fénelon . . . Massillon
made Dubois a bishop. Saint-Simon's memoirs have spoiled
Fénelon for me. But a real priest . . . Then loving hearts would
have a meeting place on earth. . . . We wouldn't be isolated. . . .
That good priest would speak to us of God. But which God? Not
the God of the Bible, a cruel, petty despot with a thirst for
vengeance . . . but Voltaire's God, just, good, infinite. . . ."

He was troubled by all the memories of that Bible which he
knew by heart. "But how is it possible, as soon as 'three are
gathered together,' to believe in the great name of God after the
terrible abuse our priests make of it?

"To live in isolation . . . What torment!

"I'm becoming insane and unjust," thought Julien, striking
his forehead. "I'm isolated here in this cell, but I haven't *lived
in isolation* on this earth; I had the powerful idea of *duty*. The
duty I laid down for myself, rightly or wrongly, was like the
sturdy trunk of a tree against which I leaned during the storm; I
rocked back and forth, I was shaken—after all, I was only
human—but I wasn't carried away.

"It's the damp air of this cell that's making me think of
isolation. . . .

"And why should I go on being hypocritical as I curse
hypocrisy? It's not death, this cell or the damp air that's depressing me: it's Madame de Rênal's absence. If I had to live
hidden in the cellar of her house in Verrières for weeks on end in
order to see her, would I complain?

"The influence of my contemporaries still prevails," he said
aloud, with a bitter laugh. "Talking to myself, all alone, with
death staring me in the face, I'm still a hypocrite. . . . O
nineteenth century!

"A hunter fires his gun in the forest, his quarry falls and he
rushes forward to seize it. His boot crashes into an anthill two

feet high, destroys the ants' dwelling, scatters the ants and their
eggs. . . . Even the most philosophical of the ants will never be
able to understand that terrifying, enormous black object, the
hunter's boot, which suddenly burst into their dwelling with
incredible speed, preceded by a frightful noise and accompanied
by a flash of reddish flame. . . .

"And so it is with death, life and eternity, things that would
be quite simple for anyone with organs vast enough to comprehend them. . . .

"A mayfly is born at nine o'clock in the morning of a long
summer day and dies at five o'clock in the afternoon: how could
it understand the word 'night'? But give it five more hours of life
and it will see and understand what night means.

"And so I'll die at the age of twenty-three; give me five more
years to live with Madame de Rênal."

And he began to laugh like Mephistopheles. "What madness
to discuss these great problems! First of all, I'm hypocritical, as
though there were someone here to listen to me. Secondly, I'm
forgetting to live and to love, when I have so few days left. . . .
Alas! Madame de Rênal is absent; perhaps her husband won't let
her come back to Besançon and go on dishonoring herself.
That's what makes me isolated, and not the absence of a just,
good and all-powerful God who would be neither malicious nor
eager for vengeance.

"Ah, if only He existed! . . . Alas, I'd fall at His feet and say
to Him, 'I deserve death, but, great God, good God, indulgent
God, give me back the woman I love!' "

The night was by now far advanced. After an hour or two of
peaceful sleep, Fouqué arrived.

Julien felt strong and resolute, like a man who sees clearly
into his own heart.

CHAPTER 45

"I DON'T want to send for poor Father Chas-Bernard," he said to
Fouqué. "It would be unfair to him: it would make him lose his
appetite for three days. But try to find me some Jansenist,
friend of Father Pirard who can't be corrupted by intrigue."

Fouqué had been waiting impatiently for this opening. Julien
properly discharged all his obligations to provincial public opinion. Thanks to Monsieur de Frilair, and in spite of his unfortunate choice of a confessor, Julien, in his cell, was under the

protection of the *Congrégation;* if he had behaved more shrewdly he might have been able to escape. But the bad air of the cell produced its effect; his reason grew weaker. This only made him all the happier when Madame de Rênal returned.

"My first duty is to you," she said as she embraced him. "I've run away from Verrières."

Julien showed no petty vanity when he was with her; he told her of all his weaknesses. She was kind and charming to him.

As soon as she left the prison that evening she summoned to her aunt's house the priest who had attached himself to Julien as though he were his prey; since he wanted only to win the good graces of the young women belonging to the high society of Besançon, she easily persuaded him to go and perform a novena in the abbey at Bray-le-Haut.

No words could express the depth and extravagance of Julien's love.

By being generous with money, and by using and abusing the influence of her aunt, a lady who was well known for her wealth and her piety, Madame de Rênal obtained permission to see him twice a day.

When Mathilde learned of this, her jealousy increased to the point of frenzy. Monsieur de Frilair had admitted to her that, great though his influence was, it was not great enough to allow him to flout all propriety to the point of obtaining permission for her to visit her lover more than once a day. She had Madame de Rênal followed to keep herself informed of her every move. Monsieur de Frilair exhausted all the resources of his extremely cunning mind in an effort to convince her that Julien was unworthy of her.

In the midst of all these torments she only loved him all the more, and nearly every day she made a terrible scene with him.

Julien was determined to remain an honorable man to the end in his conduct toward the poor girl he had so gravely compromised, but his unbridled passion for Madame de Rênal constantly won out over his intentions. When his implausible arguments failed to convince Mathilde of the innocence of her rival's visits he said to himself, "The end of the drama must be very close now; that's an excuse for me if I can't hide my feelings better."

Mademoiselle de La Mole learned of the death of the Marquis de Croisenois. The rich Monsieur de Thaler had ventured to make some unpleasant remarks about her disappearance and Monsieur de Croisenois had gone to ask him to retract them.

Monsieur de Thaler showed him some anonymous letters addressed to him; they were filled with details linked together so cleverly that it was impossible for the poor marquis not to guess the truth.

Monsieur de Thaler took the liberty of making some rather crude jests. Beside himself with anger and sorrow, Monsieur de Croisenois demanded such drastic apologies that the millionaire preferred a duel. Folly triumphed, and one of the most likable men in Paris met death before he had reached the age of twenty-four.

This death made a strange, unhealthy impression on Julien's weakened mind. "Poor Croisenois' conduct toward us was really very reasonable and honorable," he said to Mathilde. "He might very well have hated me and challenged me to a duel when you behaved so imprudently in your mother's drawing room, because the hatred that follows contempt is usually ferocious. . . ."

The death of Monsieur de Croisenois changed all of Julien's ideas about Mathilde's future; he spent several days trying to convince her that she ought to marry Monsieur de Luz. "He's a timid man, not too much of a Jesuit," he said to her, "and he'll no doubt put himself forward as one of your suitors. He's more modest and steadfast in his ambition than poor Croisenois was, and there's no dukedom in his family, so he won't hesitate to marry Julien Sorel's widow."

"She'll be a widow who despises great passions," Mathilde replied coldly, "because she's lived long enough to see her lover prefer another woman to her after six months, and a woman who's the cause of all their misfortune."

"You're unjust: Madame de Rênal's visits will provide the lawyer from Paris who's handling my appeal with some striking arguments: he'll paint a picture of the murderer honored by the attentions of his victim. It may make a good impression, and perhaps some day you'll see me the hero of some melodrama," etc., etc.

Furious jealousy without the possibility of vengeance, the prospect of constant hopeless sorrow (for even supposing Julien were saved, how could she win back his heart?), the shame and anguish of loving her faithless lover more than ever—these things had plunged Mademoiselle de La Mole into a gloomy silence from which neither Monsieur de Frilair's assiduous attentions nor Fouqué's blunt frankness could rouse her.

As for Julien, except for the time usurped by Mathilde's presence, he lived on love and with scarcely a thought of the future. As a curious result of this passion, absolute and without the slightest pretense, Madame de Rênal almost shared his gentle, unconcerned gaiety.

"In the past," he said to her, "when I could have been so happy during our walks through the woods of Vergy, my fiery ambition carried my mind off into imaginary realms. Instead of pressing against my heart the charming arm that was so close to my lips, I let the future take me away from you; I was absorbed in the countless battles I would have to fight in order to build a magnificent career for myself. . . . No, I'd have died without ever having known true happiness if you hadn't come to see me in this prison."

Two incidents came to trouble this peaceful life. Julien's confessor, Jansenist though he was, was not beyond the reach of a Jesuit intrigue, and he unwittingly became their instrument. One day he came in to tell Julien that, unless he wished to fall into the frightful sin of suicide, he must do everything possible to obtain his pardon. And since the clergy had a great deal of influence with the Ministry of Justice in Paris, there was one way in which he could try to achieve this purpose: he must make a spectacular announcement of his conversion.

"A spectacular announcement!" repeated Julien. "Ah, Father, I've caught you, too, play-acting like a missionary!"

"Your youth," the Jansenist went on gravely, "the attractive face given to you by Providence, the very motive of your crime, which remains inexplicable, the untiring and heroic efforts which Mademoiselle de La Mole has made to save you—everything, in short, including the amazing friendship your victim shows for you, has combined to make you the hero of the young women of Besançon. They've forgotten everything for you, even politics. Your conversion would echo in their hearts and make a deep impression on them. You can be of great service to religion—do you think I'd hesitate for the frivolous reason that the Jesuits would follow the same course in similar circumstances? If I did, they'd still be doing harm, even in this particular case which escapes their rapacity! That mustn't happen. . . . The tears your conversion will cause to flow will nullify the corrosive effect of ten editions of Voltaire's impious works."

"And what will I have left if I despise myself?" replied Julien coldly. "I was ambitious, but I won't reproach myself for it—I was acting in accordance with the standards of our time. Now I'm living from day to day. But, with everyone in the district watching me, I'd make myself miserable if I let myself fall into some act of cowardice. . . ."

The other incident, which affected Julien much more deeply, came from Madame de Rênal. Some scheming friend had succeeded in persuading the timid, guileless woman that it was her duty to go to Saint-Cloud and throw herself at the feet of King Charles X. She had already made the sacrifice of parting from Julien and, after such an effort, the unpleasantness of making a spectacle of herself, which at any other time she would have regarded as worse than death, now seemed to be nothing at all to her.

"I'll go to the king and admit openly that you're my lover," she said to Julien. "The life of a man like you must take precedence over all other considerations. I'll say you tried to kill me out of jealousy. There have been many examples of unfortunate young men saved in such cases by the humanity of the jury or the king. . . ."

"I'll stop seeing you, I'll have you kept out of my cell," cried Julien, "and I'll certainly kill myself in despair the next day, if you don't promise me you won't do anything that would make a public spectacle of both of us. The idea of going to Paris isn't your own. Tell me the name of the scheming woman who suggested it to you. . . .

"Let's be happy during the few days of this short life we have left. Let's hide our existence; my crime is all too conspicuous. Mademoiselle de La Mole has enormous influence in Paris, you can be sure she's doing everything that's humanly possible. Here in the provinces I have all the rich and influential people against me. Your action would embitter them still more, those rich, sober men for whom life is such an easy matter. . . . Let's not give any cause for laughter to the Maslons, the Valenods and countless other people worth more than they are."

The bad air of the cell was becoming unbearable to Julien. Fortunately, on the day when he was told he had to die, bright sunlight was gladdening all of nature and he felt full of courage. Walking in the open air was a delightful experience for him, like treading on land for a sailor who has been long at sea. "I'm ready," he said to himself, "everything is going well: my courage hasn't failed me."

Never had his head been so poetic as at the instant when it was about to fall. The sweetest moments he had known in the woods of Vergy thronged back into his mind with extreme vividness.

Everything took place simply and properly, without the slightest affectation on his part.

Two days earlier he had said to Fouqué, "I can't answer for my emotions; this damp, ugly cell gives me moments of fever during which I don't recognize myself. But as for fear, no; they won't see me turn pale."

He had arranged in advance for Fouqué to take Mathilde and Madame de Rênal away on the morning of his last day. "Take them in the same carriage," he had said to him, "and make sure the post horses are constantly galloping. They'll either fall into each other's arms or express deadly hatred for each other; in either case the poor women will be distracted a little from their terrible grief."

Julien had demanded that Madame de Rênal swear that she would live in order to watch over Mathilde's son.

"Who knows?" he had said to Fouqué one day. "Perhaps we still have sensations after death. I'd rather like to rest, since rest is the right word, in that little cave in the side of the high mountain that towers over Verrières. Several times, as I've already told you, when I'd gone up to that cave at night, and as I looked down over the richest provinces of France in the distance, ambition inflamed my heart: it was my only passion then. . . . In short, that cave is dear to me, and no one can deny that it's situated in a way that would make a philosopher's soul envious. . . . Well, the worthy members of the Besançon *Congrégation* turn everything into money; if you go about it in the right way, they'll sell you my mortal remains. . . ."

Fouqué was successful in this sad bargain. He was spending the night in his room alone, beside the body of his friend, when, to his great surprise, he saw Mathilde come in. A few hours earlier he had left her ten leagues from Besançon. Her face and eyes were distraught.

"I want to see him," she said.

Fouqué was too overcome to speak or leave his chair. He pointed to a large blue cloak on the floor; in it was wrapped all that remained of Julien.

She fell to her knees; the memory of Boniface de La Mole and Marguerite of Navarre no doubt gave her superhuman courage. Her trembling hands pulled back the cloak. Fouqué turned his eyes away.

He heard Mathilde walking swiftly around the room. She was lighting several candles. When he had the strength to look at her, he saw that she had placed Julien's head before her on a small marble-topped table and was kissing his forehead. . . .

Mathilde followed her lover to the tomb he had chosen for himself. A large number of priests escorted the bier and, alone in her carriage draped in mourning, she bore on her knees, unknown to everyone, the head of the man she had loved so deeply.

Having arrived in this way near the top of one of the towering mountains of the Juras, in the middle of the night, in that little cave magnificently illuminated by countless candles, twenty priests celebrated the Office of the Dead. All the inhabitants of the little mountain villages through which the procession had passed had followed it, drawn by the extraordinary nature of the strange ceremony.

Mathilde appeared in their midst in long mourning garments, and at the end of the service she had several thousand five-franc coins scattered among them.

Left alone with Fouqué, she insisted on burying her lover's head with her own hands. Fouqué nearly went mad with grief.

Under Mathilde's care, the crude cave was adorned with marbles sculptured in Italy at great cost.

Madame de Rênal was faithful to her promise. She did not attempt to take her own life in any way; but, with her children in her arms, she died three days after Julien.

Bantam Classics bring you the world's greatest literature—books that have stood the test of time—at specially low prices. These beautifully designed books will be proud additions to your bookshelf. You'll want all these time-tested classics for your own reading pleasure.

Titles by Fyodor Dostoevsky:

☐ 21216	THE BROTHERS KARAMAZOV	$3.95
☐ 21175	CRIME AND PUNISHMENT	$2.95
☐ 21352	THE IDIOT	$3.95
☐ 21144	NOTES FROM UNDERGROUND	$2.50

Titles by Leo Tolstoy:

☐ 21346	ANNA KARENINA	$3.50
☐ 21035	DEATH OF IVAN ILYICH	$1.95

Titles by Joseph Conrad:

☐ 21214	HEART OF DARKNESS & THE SECRET SHARER	$1.95
☐ 21361	LORD JIM	$2.25

Titles by George Eliot:

☐ 21180	MIDDLEMARCH	$4.95
☐ 21229	SILAS MARNER	$1.95

Titles by Ivan Turgenev:

☐ 21259	FATHERS AND SONS	$2.25

Look for them at your bookstore or use this page to order.
